MAXIM: THE COMPLETE TRILOGY

CLUB XXX NOVELS: SUBMIT, OBEY, & SURRENDER

LANA SKY

ACKNOWLEDGMENTS

Thanks so much to everyone who supported this draft along the way! Please keep in mind that this story includes dark, graphic and explicit content matter that is not suitable for readers under the age of 18—or for readers who are uncomfortable with the following subject matter: explicit sex, mentions of sexual abuse, mentions of child abuse, graphic depictions of violence, and mentions of self-harm.

SUBMIT

Maxim: Submit

Maxim: Submit By Lana Sky

Cover Design and Interior Formatting by Charity Chimni
Editing by Mickey Reed Editing
Proofreading by Charity Chimni

$3 75. That number is the only thing on my mind as Fuckface #3 rails me from behind.

That's what he calls it: *railing*.

If only he were actually good at it.

Damn near bored out of its skull, my brain takes his stupid term and spins it around, making a game out of it. *Rail. Railroad.* There are train tracks not too far from here, actually. I can hear the distant howl of the siren riding the still night air—the de facto theme song of a small fucking town like Mayer. The lonely whistle drowns out Fuckface's final groan as he thrusts deep, pinning me flat against an icy brick wall.

Thank fucking god. My palms are rubbed raw and sting as I let them fall to my side. Then I wait. The bastard knows the drill: in and out. But, instead of going for his wallet, he runs a meaty hand over the back of my head, gathering my hair in his fist.

"That was so fucking good, baby. I've never come so hard."

"Likewise," I choke out. I even sound nice. Ish. Kinda. After all, I still have to keep the act up until I get paid. The truth is, I don't orgasm. Ever.

Especially not with a man who smells worse than the overflowing dumpster a few blocks down.

When he doesn't move, I brace my hands flat against the wall and try to shimmy out from under him—but Fuckface must have drunk more liquid courage than usual tonight. His breath fans my neck, reeking like the toilets at Barney's after happy hour.

"You want to show me how good it felt?" He grinds his hips against my ass, showing off his flaccid, not-much-to-brag-about-even-when-hard dick. "How about a kiss?"

"How about an extra fifty?" I shrug him off and wrench the hem of my dress down while he staggers against the opposite wall. No more Miss Nice.

"Pay up." I stick my hand out.

He spits at it. "Bitch."

Ugh. Considering how many "frequent flier miles" this douche-wipe has racked up over the past six months alone, one might think he'd have learned some manners by now. Or at least the common fucking decency to pay upfront.

"You know the drill," I tell him, making my voice hard, the way Benny taught me to. I bet no one else's johns ever gave them this kind of shit. "Pay up."

Fuckface runs a hand over his gray stained t-shirt before fingering the pocket of his still open jeans. Considering what he did with those fingers only minutes ago—sloppily, I might add—it's disgusting fucking imagery. I hope the electric company doesn't mind the extra germs on their blood money.

"I don't know, baby," Fuckface says as he reaches for his wallet and thumbs through a stack of bills. "Have you really earned this?"

I crane my neck before I can help myself and catch a peek: fifties, fifties, fifties... He fishes out two and offers them to me.

Fucking asshole.

I snatch the money before he can pull it out of reach and snap my fingers impatiently. "*Baby*, you're a little short."

Fuckface chuckles. "Why don't you come and get it, you little bitch?"

Well, he did ask for it. I turn and take a few steps toward the mouth of the alley. The extra distance gives me enough time to reach along my hip and draw the knife strapped to my right outer thigh.

The dumb bastard didn't even notice it.

"Come back, you bitch," he tells me, laughing. I sense him behind me, his footsteps heavy and slow. "You know you need the money."

He's right. I do.

So I stop, letting him come up behind me. I wait until he palms my ass and tries to push up against me again. After tucking the handle of the knife into my palm, I turn and jam the butt of it into the fucker's beer gut with one hand while grabbing the wallet with the other.

"Nice doing business with ya," I tell him, snatching out the full amount he owes—along with a little extra for "service fees."

I drop the wallet while he groans behind me and leave the alley. Even on heels, I make it to the bus stop in ten minutes flat. I'm already on my way back to the city before the bastard can get his pants back up.

The money in my hand isn't anywhere near enough. But I'll make it last.

I don't have a fucking choice.

CHAPTER TWO

Everyone likes to think that their soul doesn't carry a price tag—and sure, some lucky sons of bitches never become desperate enough to find it. The first step is having to look at yourself in the mirror and no longer seeing a person, just an object with pretty eyes. She's worth about fifty a lay, you tell yourself—a hundred dollars tops.

Cha-ching.

When Benny first "scouted" me for a place in his business, the only question to leave my mouth was, "Will I get the money upfront?"

That's the way the cookie crumbles in this world. You'd sell your ass for a dime the moment the rent is due. Just as long as you could smell it first, feel the telltale promise of money in your hand. Hopefully it's enough so that the rabbit-eyed kids shackled to you don't have to eat their

Cheerios on the street corner tonight. Let's say that the kids aren't even yours.

That's my life.

There's no use crying about it. To be fucking honest, I don't think I have any tears left. So, when Benny calls me into his office for a "special" assignment the moment I get back from Mayer, I don't let myself think through the potential cons. I just accept.

"What's the job?"

Good old Benny wrings his fingers together. Though it doesn't take much to make a man like him nervous. Why the hell he chose pimp as a career, I will never know. At least he doesn't beat his girls. Sometimes, a few of us *don't* try to take advantage of him—like me.

"It's…a little fucked up," he says, staring down at the peeling tile floor of his office. It's really just a spare room in a laundromat on Fifth, but he put a desk in here and even has a secretary, Grace, who answers his burner phones and sometimes keeps the police off his tail with on-the-house blow jobs. "It's not exactly legal…"

I raise an eyebrow. "Benny, my outfit isn't legal." I gesture to the black, skintight dress I "borrowed" from JC Penney's the other night. As long as I keep the tag intact, I can have the bastard smuggled back into the store before the next inventory.

Any other night, the joke would have drawn a chuckle out of him. But Benny just sighs and drags on the lit cigarette perched at the corner of his mouth. "Not like that. This is some freaky shit, Frankie."

I roll my eyes. "Freaky shit? Getting fucked in an alley butt-ass naked because you can't afford to get a drop of some loser's cum on your dumbass dress is freaky shit." My elbows still sting from the friction of being pressed against the brick wall while FuckFace #3 did his business. "How much does it pay?"

Benny Ireland never shies away from talking about money. His entire profession is built upon it, for chrissakes. But, rather than lay out any solid figures, he sighs again. "There's this guy I want you to meet. Tomorrow. Noon. It's at a café downtown on the south side. Don't you fucking dare be late." He reaches into the pocket of his faded gray suit and pulls out a business card, which he places within my reach on the desk. "He can tell you more than I can."

"He the John?" I pick the card up between two fingers, eyeing the front of it. It's plain. There is no wording on either side: just a single silver letter X and a phone number.

"Don't know," Benny says, drawing another hit of his cig. "Don't think so. He's kinda old. Bald. Though it's not like you have a type."

"That's right. My *type* comes out of a cash register. Bills and quarters," I say, "You know me, Ben."

"Damn right I do." He puts his cigarette out in the ashtray, but his hands shake and he winds up getting more ash on the table than anywhere else. "Ever heard of the name Koslov?"

"Is that like a country or something?"

"I'll take that as a no," Benny says, rolling his eyes, but I think I hear him sigh. "Good. Trust me, you don't want to have heard of it."

"Why?"

"No reason." He shrugs and darts his gaze to the opposite end of the room. Any other night, I'd press harder. Make him squirm.

A night when my arms weren't scratched to shit.

"So what's this guy into for you to pick me?" I demand, tucking the business card beneath my bra strap. "Brunettes? Baby faces?" It's not like I have low self-esteem, but I do have two perfectly working eyes. Eyes that reveal a girl who is not too bad to look at, but nothing special either.

"You want the truth?" Benny leans back against his ratty armchair and cracks his knuckles one by one. "The bastard just came in and asked me to give him the most desperate, money-hungry girl I've got." He glances me over, frowning at what he sees, the prick. "You, baby, fit the bill in every fucking way."

"Thanks for the vote of confidence, Ben." I turn on my heel and kick the door to his office. There's no latch on it, so it flies open against the adjacent wall. The thud startles Grace, who's perched on the edge of a washing machine, painting her nails pink.

"Yikes, Frankie," she chirps in the high-pitched drawl she uses to lure in customers. Her shtick is that creepy Lolita shit, pink baby doll dress and all. "Benny do something to piss you off?"

I just look at her sideways and shrug. "Everybody pisses me off."

Grace nods slowly like I've just given her the answer to some million-dollar question. "Oh. Well, see you around, Frankie."

Well, isn't that the truth in a nutshell: I have no choice but to come around.

After working for a week straight, I'm still five hundred dollars short. Daisy will have to miss that fucking field trip she's been talking about—*again*. All because I'm too damn tired to tack on an extra blow job or waste an extra five minutes of my goddamn life for a few more bills.

I'm too tired.

Too hungry—once I eat, I can think. I can plan a way to score more cash in time.

I'll make it up to her.

I wonder if there's anything left over in the fridge. Some bread to make a goddamn sandwich. A piece of toast.

I'll make it up to her.

I don't even realize I'm already home until I stagger through the front door and catch the tail end of what seems to be World War III.

"You touch my doll again and I'll put my fist through your damn mouth—"

"Hey!" I slam the door behind me, marshaling all six rug rats to attention.

The threat came from the youngest, Ainsley, who stands barely taller than my knee. It's not too hard to see what pissed her off this time: a decapitated Barbie doll at her feet.

The culprit appears to be Eric, the second youngest, who keeps flashing Ains his middle finger when he thinks I'm not looking. *Great.* Standing between them are the four oldest. Mikie's been smoking again—I can smell him from here. Daisy has her shirt on backward, while Ollie and Ray are in the middle of a silent shoving match.

Sighing, I throw my head back, stare up at the ceiling, and count to ten out loud. Meanwhile, the bickering dies down. Without looking, I dig into my bra and fish out the wad of cash tucked inside. Then I snap my fingers and gesture in my general direction.

"Line up." I look down and find Mikie, the oldest at sixteen, standing in front of me with his hand outstretched and I quickly rip off a few fifty-dollar bills. "Electric," I tell him, pressing the money into his hands. "Drop it off on your way to school tomorrow. There's a ten in there for lunch. Don't forget to turn in your homework from last week too, and if I get a call from the principal tomorrow, I swear to God—"

"Got it," Mikie huffs, snatching for the money. "Damn it, Frankie. Chill." Then he steps aside.

I wave up the next two: they come as a packaged deal. "Heat," I tell Ray and Ollie. "Don't forget to pick up the neighbor's recycling on the way home, either. Whoever gets the most cans gets the extra slice the next time we order pizza."

"Oh holy shit!" Ray exclaims before shoving Ollie out of his way.

I have to sidestep them both in order to continue with the dispensing of the household chores. "This is for the rent stash," I tell Daisy, shoving some of the last few bills into her hands. "Take the ten for lunch."

"Um, Frankie?" She looks at me, her brown upturned eyes shining and hopeful. "About the field trip…"

Something in my chest feels tight. Fuck. I tug at the strap of my dress, but the damn sensation doesn't go away. "Hold on." I pry the money from her hands and count it. One hundred and fifty—every bit of the extra I stole from

Fuckface # 3. To make up for it, I'll have to work my ass off—literally—tomorrow night in order to have enough left over for the bills due at the end of the week. But what the fuck. It's not like having *almost* enough matters. "Take it," I say, tucking the money into her hands.

She frowns. "Are you sure we can—"

"I'll work something out." I wave her off and dig out my final few ones. "Milk money," I explain while the two youngest look up and nod. The moment I hand the cash over, they immediately start shrieking over who owes who what.

Ah, the rat race of life. It never ends. Not even here.

"Bed. Everyone," I command, jabbing my finger at the stairs.

They hustle off after ten minutes of whining, and I savor the silence composed of wailing sirens and the shouts from the neighbors next door. The place is a fucking wreck. Daisy must have made dinner tonight because there's a pan with something burned onto it soaking in the sink. The living room is a sea of book bags and loose pages of homework. Without any money to spare on bug spray, I find the roaches out in full force.

It feels like I wear out the bottom of my heels attempting to stomp on as many as I can while I tear through the house, picking shit up. Shoving shit somewhere else. Scraping shit off more shit.

When I'm elbow-deep in the middle of washing the dishes, my fingers slip on a knife and I cut myself on my wrist. Accidentally. Twice. As the blood-colored water circles the drain, only then can I finally fucking think. I hear shouting. Someone's threatening to blind someone else with toothpaste. Someone's crying. Someone's slamming doors.

The peeling walls around me form a prison. A hellhole.

It's all I've got.

So I just keep scrubbing until the dishes are clean and the water runs down the drain. Then I take the couch for the night, facing the door just in case that bitch decides to come walking through. I consider taking the dress off, but it's safer on me than it would be in the morning rush once the kids get up for school.

Besides, a little blood never hurt anyone.

CHAPTER THREE

I wake up after everyone's already gone—something I don't do too often. The house is silent when I finally crawl out from beneath the open sleeping bag someone draped over me. I find a lukewarm Pop-Tart beside a shitty cup of coffee on the end table near my head.

Daisy.

With a sigh, I haul myself upright and strip the dress off. Then I climb upstairs and wander through the maze of clothing spread across two bedrooms in search of a clean pair of jeans and a tee shirt. The jeans might be mine or Daisy's. The shirt is probably Mikie's.

When I start to brush my teeth, I notice that it's already wet courtesy of Ainsley, who doesn't seem to like using her smaller, pink toothbrush. I make do anyway, and I almost feel semi-normal after a belly full of sugary pastry and one of the beers I keep hidden at the back of the fridge in a bag marked *veggies*.

The buzz has only just kicked in when I finally glance down at my watch and then bust my ass racing across town to reach Penney's before my shift starts. I sneak in through the main entrance and drop the dress off at the fitting room rack. By eleven, I'm already three hours into a measly eight-hour shift that, when all is said and done, won't even net me half of what I need to make rent. Tomorrow, it's a night shift at the diner. My only prayer of getting by is scoring enough tips from the truckers who might stop in—any way I can.

"Hey, Francesca!"

I glance over my shoulder and find Meryl, the manager, shuffling across the store, her hands shoved into the pockets of her pants where she keeps her "totally prescription" pain meds.

"I'll take over the register," she tells me, coming around to my side of the counter. "You go home for the day. Terra needs the extra overtime. Her damn husband's in jail again. The poor girl's gotta put up bail."

It doesn't seem to faze her that a line of customers hears this little exchange. Dumbass Terra, her cousin twice removed, needs to steal the money out of *my* mouth in order to get her ass beaten for a few more nights before her husband winds up in a cell again.

Go figure.

My fingers shake, but I curl them into fists. Deep breaths and shit. "I was supposed to get thirty hours this week—"

"I'll give you priority on the schedule next month," Meryl assures me as her meaty fingers dart for the register.

Fuck this shit. I leave through the back entrance, nicking a sweater on my way out. This time, I don't justify it as being "borrowed." Instead, I pull it on in place of Mikie's shirt and rip the tags off.

Then I head south, digging my nails into my palms. *Good job, Frankie girl.* I'm on a goddamn roll—at least five hundred dollars in the hole already with no real way to make up for it. I could always head to Benny and see if he has any extra work, but…

Wait. I bite my lip and fish through my pockets, finding the crumpled-up business card stuffed inside one of them. I don't even remember grabbing it. Benny told me a time too, I think. Noon. For a meeting. Shit, where was it? I'm moving before I even really remember.

I don't show up at the address until close to one: a little café on the south side. Even at this time of day, it's not exactly hopping with activity. There's just one man inside, seated at a corner booth. He's oldish and bald like Benny said. He must be the client.

I plaster a fake smile on my face and run a hand through my hair. My fingers get stuck halfway and I have to tug them loose. Shit. I look down and find that the sweater I stole has deodorant stains on the side. My jeans have a hole in them. I have Pop-Tart breath.

And this man is wearing a tailored suit. He smells fancy. A silver pen rests between two of his fingers, and the leather notebook open in front of him is probably worth at least six shifts at JC Penney's. When he sees me, his eyes narrow and he runs a hand down the front of his black suit jacket. "Are you Francesca Marconi?"

I shrug. "Frankie."

The man nods once to himself and jots something down with his pen. "Have a seat."

I join him at the table, already weirded out by the place. It's quiet. Something tells me that it shouldn't be empty, even during a weekday. Then I happen to glance out the window and find another man in a black suit standing just beyond the main doors. When a smiling couple approaches the entrance, he shakes his head and points toward another café just down the street.

Alarm bells go off in my head.

"Did you rent the place out or something?" I ask the bald guy.

I'm not given an answer right away. He takes his time to rip open exactly four packets of those diet sugars and pours them all into a steaming cup of coffee beside him. Carefully, he stirs it up with a spoon. When he takes a sip, I notice the silver ring on his right hand. It looks real. It looks expensive. I can't take my eyes off it as he sets his mug to the side.

"My name is Lucius," he says, extending his hand toward me.

I take it and shake it once. His ring feels cold—*super* expensive.

"How old are you, Francesca?"

I look up and find him observing me, but it's not the kind of stare I'm used to. It's the way my mother's parole officer looked whenever he came by the house and I spun whatever lie I could to explain why she hadn't shown up that morning. He's searching for something.

"Nineteen," I say.

He nods again and scribbles something else down into his book. "Do you have HIV, hepatitis, syphilis, or any other STD?"

I cough to smother my shock. "Not that I know of."

"We'll do a blood test, to be sure." He glances over at the man standing outside and scribbles something else. "Now, allow me to ask the most pressing question."

I'm holding my breath. So, what will it be? Maybe he wants me to wear a little girl costume to get him off. Spank me. Do anal? Thinking about it creeps me out to the point that I shudder. But money makes the world go 'round and my universe is already about a million spins behind the starting line.

"Okay?" I prod when he doesn't spit the proposition out fast enough. "What's the deal?"

"My client is an unusual man, Francesca."

"*Your* client? I thought—"

"Let me just cut to the chase," Lucius says, folding his hands in front of him. "My client is an unusual man, Ms. Marconi. A man with very unusual tastes."

"Like what?" I ask. Benny said that this guy wanted someone desperate. Luckily for him, my goddamn picture was probably in the dictionary under that word by now.

"I won't mince words," Lucius says. "A lot more involvement than the usual tryst. You would be his *exclusive* companion."

Now, I have an idea of what this guy must want: some bitch to wear a collar and crawl around while he pretends to be Christian Grey.

Sounds weird, but I'll bite. "How much?"

It's funny how a year can change people. I used to tell myself I'd never give in to that sort of shit. And that I'd only give blow jobs just once a month if that bitch Meryl cut my hours short. I used to tell myself a lot of dumb lies.

"It's a compensatory payment system, to be sure," Lucius admits. He flips through the pages of his notebook and pulls a slip of paper out. It has wording printed on it. A list, I find as he slides it over to me.

Make that a contract.

Well, fuck me. I don't know whether to laugh or sigh. This guy really does think he's Christian Grey.

"The sixteen thousand is just the base salary," Lucius says as I drag the paper closer.

Then I stop thinking after that. My brain fucking short-circuits at the sight of a few zeros. Way too many. Enough for rent. Enough for food. Enough for a million fucking field trips.

But it's funny. The words that follow kill any excited butterflies that came alive in my stomach: *The aforementioned party will hereby agree to a base salary consisting of $16,000 per monthly quarter, barring any injury.*

My eyes skip down to read the rest and those cold, dead butterflies turn into stabbing scorpions.

Clause 1: *In the event of a burn, wound, cut, or any similar injury greater than ten inches in length or diameter, the aforementioned party will receive $1,000 per inch.*

Clause 2: *In the event that the aforementioned party is rendered unconscious and unresponsive—no pulse and/or pupil reaction—for a period of documented time extending more than one minute in duration, the party will receive $5,000 for each additional minute and $500 for each remaining second of.*

Clause 3: *In the event of accidental death…*

"What the hell is this?" I lunge away from the table, nearly knocking myself over in the process. My fingers shake. I have to curl them into fists to hide how badly.

Lucius takes another sip of his coffee. "I understand that this might seem overwhelming."

"You're not serious." I don't know what seems more insane or what disgusts me more. That a man might actually write a contract with seriously *maiming* a woman in mind or the fact that I'm already fucking considering it.

"If you are not interested, Ms. Marconi, then I thank you for your time and—"

"Would I get paid upfront?" The question is out of my mouth before I can stop it. My sweater itches. The taste of dried Pop-Tart lingers in my throat. I swallow it down.

"Well, of course." Lucius cocks his head and runs a hand over the pages in his notebook. "There is a one-thousand-dollar signing bonus. After you meet my client, of course. He will decide if you fit his requirements."

I nearly fall out of my chair. One thousand dollars—just for *meeting* someone. I've considered doing a frat party for less.

"But I'd get the money when?"

"After your first encounter. In cash," he adds.

Cash. I brace both hands flat against the table and drag myself forward until the rim of it digs into my chest. "S-so I just sign here?"

I jerk my chin to the paper, already reaching for the silver pen. I can think about the consequences later. I can *think* later.

"No." Lucius reaches into the breast pocket of his suit jacket and pulls out a different sheet of folded paper. It's crisper. Official. "You sign here. Please keep in mind that it includes a confidentiality agreement. You breathe a word as to the identity of my client and I can assure you that no expense, legal or otherwise, will be spared in ensuring that you sorely regret that decision."

His soft, professional tone takes on a hard edge as a hint of darkness peeks out from behind the blue in his eyes.

I don't say a damn thing in response. I just hold my hand out and he places the contract onto my palm, followed by the silver pen. The smart thing to do would be to read the damn thing over. Check for any fine print. Blah, blah, fucking bullshit.

I don't. I just sign on the first line I see without reading a damn word. The only thing I hear—the only thing I can fucking focus on—is the promise of a grand.

"So, when do I meet him?"

Lucius takes the contract and folds it up without doing any of the shit I feel like someone in his position should: make sure that this is what I *really* want. That I know exactly what I'm getting into. Instead, he tucks it between the pages of his notebook.

"Now," he says, rising to his feet. "Follow me, Ms. Marconi."

Follow me. He sounds like the bailiffs in the court when they lead my so-called mother away in handcuffs after one of her frequent convictions. That final.

A creeping sensation crawls down my spine when I stand and follow Lucius out to a black car near the curb. The figure I saw lurking outside the door is gone, but a glance at the driver's seat of the car reveals him behind the wheel.

"Ms. Marconi?" Lucius opens the door to the back seat, waiting for me to climb inside.

I do. No thinking. No regrets. To make sure, my nails dig into my wrist. Hard. Harder. Deeper. I don't stop until the pain cuts through the chaos in my mind. It's clear for five precious seconds, and I savor every last fucking one. Because once Lucius climbs in beside me and the car glides into traffic, I can't smother the fear anymore, and pinching doesn't help one damn bit.

I'm so stupid. I'm a goddamn idiot. Or, like Benny said, *I'm desperate.*

I let a list of everything I need money for by next week run through my mind. *Money. Money. Money.* The chant almost drowns everything else out. Almost.

"Ms. Marconi?"

The car's stopped. I glance over and find Lucius standing on the curb, his hand extended toward me.

"Have you changed your mind?"

I shake my head and scramble out after him. We're in front of a hotel. Or maybe a high-rise—all the rich-people places look the fucking same. This one's pretty big, gleaming in the overcast daylight. The name formed out of silver letters over the entrance reads *The Vermillion Building*.

A doorman is standing out front, watching me. The moment we make eye contact, he quickly turns away.

"Ms. Marconi?" Lucius comes up beside me and nods toward the building's entrance. "I'll take you to meet him now."

"Okay." I run my hands down the front of my sweater. It feels colder out than it did earlier. I can't stop shivering. Though, maybe it's all the hostility thrown my way by the rich bitches who sneer at me as they skip from their posh high rise.

This man, whoever he is, lives large. He'd have to if he's willing to cough up a few hundred dollars per centimeter of injury…

Don't go there. I shake the thought off and pour all of my effort into trailing Lucius across a big-ass lobby decorated in shades of black and silver. The luxury doesn't faze me too much; I've had a few rich clients before, men so cheap and horny that they'd toss a few hundred bucks at a hooker on my end of town.

They were all assholes who never tipped well—and they definitely wouldn't shell out a grand for signing a goddamn piece of paper.

"This way." Lucius enters an elevator with ebony walls, shifting over to leave me enough room.

It's a long way up. This client must live on the top floor. I can only watch the numbers above the closed doors illuminate one by one, marking our ascent. 30…31…40.

As the doors finally open, Lucius steps out into a long hallway with only one exit: a closed door at the very end. Once we reach it, he swipes a keycard into the fancy-looking console attached to the wall beside it and it opens.

"Come in," Lucius says.

I don't know how long I stare before I finally force myself to step forward. This guy must keep the AC blasting, even in the middle of winter. Goosebumps rise over my arms as I let myself take in the sleek entryway. The walls are black. The floors are gray marble. Everything sparkles.

Like a knife.

An odd noise disrupts the flawless impression: pounding. Violent. Brutal.

My heart is in my throat even before I follow Lucius toward that noise, down a short hallway and into a room that looks like it was ripped out of those creepy-ass horror movies Mikie likes to watch. Knives hang from the wall.

Hammers. All sorts of tools, some of them rusted from use. The floors are gray with dust, and in the center of the space is a metal pedestal that has a block of what looks like stone on top of it.

Two men are standing before it. While one attempts to beat the hell out of the stone with a sharp metal stick, the other speaks. He's the shorter of the two, wearing a black leather jacket and scruffy jeans. "We lost the shipment," he says, his voice shaking. "Got ambushed by those fucking chink bastards. But all we have to do is—"

"We?" The taller man laughs, shrugging. In an almost casual motion, the stick of metal in his hand leaves the hunk of marble and strikes the other man in the head with its next blow. Groaning, the shorter guy falls to his knees, clutching the back of his skull while blood spurts, coating his fingers and speckling the floor.

"Maxim," Lucius says softly, taking a step forward.

The bigger man turns, still swinging the bar of metal through the air. He's built like a bodybuilder: all muscle, very little fat. He's handsome too—or at least some women might call him that when there isn't brain matter on his chin. I wouldn't, even then. His dark eyes reveal nothing but shadow, nearly hidden by the blond hair framing a stern face that looks like it was carved directly from that block of stone behind him.

"You found a new one so soon?" His voice is deep. Gruff. I think I catch the hint of an accent, though I'm not sure.

Lucius nods while Maxim sets the metal bar on the pedestal and wipes his hands on the front of an already dusty pair of black pants.

"Is this her?" Maxim looks me over once and jerks his chin toward a stool beside a window without waiting for an answer. "Sit." The man on the floor whimpers, and Maxim sighs, turning to Lucius. "Can you clean up this mess?"

"Right away, sir." Without a care given for his expensive suit, Lucius marches over and hauls the bleeding man to his feet by the collar of his jacket. "I'll be in touch, Ms. Marconi," he tells me before leaving the room, the dazed —but alive—man in tow.

A minute later, I hear the main door open and close.

"I told you to sit."

I flinch; with no one else around, that order was meant for me. I swallow hard and approach the stool, turning around so that I face him directly.

Maxim returns his attention to his hunk of stone despite the pool of blood at his feet. His fingers flex, picking up the metal tool again—a chisel, I realize. Then he goes to fucking town. The muscles in his arm coil and pop as he rams the blunt end against the stone block with one hand and grabs a hammer on the table with the other. He strikes hard and the resulting thud echoes throughout the room.

Again. Faster. Harder.

Bang.

Bang!

BANG!

He's lost to the brutality. It feels like hours that I watch him pummel life into the stone until a figure begins to take shape: a woman, tall and slender, her arms reaching toward the ceiling.

She's flawless—until his next blow lands so hard that it sends a crack shooting through her perfectly crafted abdomen. Without warning, he throws the chisel and the hammer aside and they both go flying. The hammer strikes the wall and the chisel decapitates a potted plant in a nearby corner.

With a sigh, Maxim wipes his hands on the edge of his gray tee shirt and turns to face me again. "Did Lucius explain it to you?"

I force myself to nod. "Yeah…"

"*Yes*," he corrects, his eyes narrowing. "How so?"

"I-I um—"

"Do not stammer." He lopes away from the pedestal and approaches a table placed along a wall at the other end of the room. There's a water bottle on top of it, and he snatches for it before ripping the lid off. "Speak in complete sentences," he tells me. He definitely has an accent. Something European. Russian? "Did he show you the contract?"

"Y-yes. I mean, yes, he did."

Maxim nods. "And you read it? You agree to the terms?" He takes another sip of water, throwing his head back so far that I can't see his eyes.

My heart skips a beat while he's not watching. "Yes."

"And you agree to *all* of them?" His gaze cuts through me as he lowers his head again and wipes his mouth with the back of his hand.

I nod twice this time, but my stupid fingers twitch as if betraying the lie. I lace them together and dig my nails into the webs between the ones on my left hand. The pain bites deep—but not deep enough.

"Come here." He sets the water bottle aside and waves his hand, each finger flexing at the joint.

I stand and cross over to him. About a foot away, I stop—not consciously. It's the way his expression changes that makes my heels dig into the floor.

"Turn around."

I do. Hot fingers trace the back of my neck in return, sliding beneath the collar of my sweater to follow the line of my spine underneath. I jerk on the tips of my toes. I can't help it. Each of his nails brushes my skin. Caresses. *Pinches.* The pain shoots through me like the shock I got when I played with the electrical sockets as a kid. Hot and punishing.

"You agree to the terms?" As he speaks, another hand runs along the back of my head before gripping my ponytail. He tugs the elastic loose and stray pieces of hair get caught in each yank.

"Y-yes—" A sharper tug on my scalp turns the word into a gasp. My eyes water at the burning sting. I can't stop myself from reaching up, trying to brush the pain away.

"Don't." He spits the word out, grinding it into my skin. My hand falls. My body sways. Then he tugs harder, forcing me to step back into him. Against me, he feels like a brick wall, built unlike any other man I've ever been with. Solid.

"I will make this time quick," he tells me. "Afterward, we will decide whether or not to continue." His accent hardens, revealing what he really means. *I will decide.* "Do you understand, *kotyonok*?" Two of his fingers twist a piece of my hair, drawing on my scalp as I register that strange word. A nickname? "No. I think you don't," Maxim says before I can complete my train of thought.

All of a sudden, I'm let go. Without his support, I stagger forward and nearly trip over my own feet.

"Leave," he commands behind me. "Lucius will take you home. You can keep the money, but I will not have you waste my time."

He marches toward the pedestal, moving with so much tension that it sounds like a goddamn thunderstorm just broke out in the middle of the room. I can only stare as he fishes the chisel from the potted plant, spraying dirt through the air in an arc. Like blood.

I don't know how long I stand here. It feels like seconds. I'm trying to move—I *am.* Just as my toes twitch a fraction of an inch, he whirls around. When his eyes find mine, I don't see anything else. Just them: black. Dark. Deep. The moment my breathing hitches, it's like a switch being flipped. He shakes his head and the shadows disappear as he beckons me closer with a crooked finger. When I don't react, the finger becomes his entire hand, his voice like a roll of thunder.

"Come."

I rush over to him, my heart pounding, my hands trembling. Once again, something makes me stop just beyond his reach.

"You didn't read the contract, *kotyonok*," he tells me, his voice catching on the edge of an unstable sound I only have one word for: a growl. He takes a step toward me.

I jump. Frowning, he takes two more. My nerves kick into overdrive and I stagger back three as sweat runs down the back of my neck. I'll never be able to return this damn sweater now. As if knowing that, he grabs me by the wrist before I can go any farther. His fingers bite down over the edge of the sleeve. I hear a ripping sound.

"Look at me."

I can't disobey. Maybe because I never stopped looking. His eyes glow again and I swear I can see myself in them: a dumb little bitch too scared to run.

"I will give you five minutes," he tells me. One of his hands comes to cup my chin and my lungs heave to breathe him in. He smells like musk. Like anger. Like sweat. The rough pad of his thumb grazes my cheek, sliding to the corner of my mouth. He presses, dragging my lower lip down as his eyes stare dead into mine. "Five minutes to change your mind. That is long enough for most."

He turns away again, letting me go, and it's like for those five minutes I don't fucking exist. I just stand. Stare. Maxim goes at the stone block again, chiseling out the woman's shape. Despite her flaws, he beats her body into form, carving at the line of her hips, her eyes, her hair.

Thwack!

I swear that sparks fly with every blow.

Abruptly, he sets the hammer down again. "You've made your choice."

I don't even see his hand move before his fingers snag my collar, dragging me closer. Step by step. When I'm close enough, he moves so that I stagger against the table rather than into his chest.

"On your knees, *kotyonok*." His voice sounds normal again, still deep but less bitter. His fingers rake through my hair once before gathering it roughly into a ponytail. "Now."

He turns away again, letting me go while the command hangs in the air, a terrifying challenge.

This is the part where I earn that little signing bonus.

A thousand dollars is all I need. I tell myself that as I drop to my knees, bracing my hands on either side of me. My nails scrape the marble, slightly bending away from their beds. From the corner of my eye, I spot a swath of dark red. I'm only inches from that puddle of blood.

Disgust can't even fully set in before I feel him behind me, his massive palm running over the top of my head. "Turn around."

He's staring down at me, still holding the chisel, when I finally do. And I know the truth, here and now: No amount of money in the world is worth this.

Black eyes follow the line of my gaze and he smiles. "Not tonight, *kotyonok*," he tells me, setting the weapon down again. "No toys. Tonight will be quick." The smile fades as he cups my jaw and tilts my head back while manipulating the clasp of his jeans. "Open wide. At least pretend that you have what it takes before you run."

Run. His thumb pries my mouth open before the thought finishes. He sighs at the sight, flexing his hips to help loosen his jeans. He's wearing black boxers underneath, but even they don't disguise the shape of him. Big. Too big.

"Don't," he warns, the tip of his nail scraping my cheek before I even realize that my mouth is starting to close.

My lips freeze, half open, drool drying on my tongue. With none of the fanfare I'm used to, he peels his boxers down. His cock springs free.

My lips flutter together. Apart. Together. He's hard already. Thick veins circle the shaft, flexing in time with his pulse. It's not the length of him that makes me gulp— it's his sheer size. There is no way in hell I can take him.

"I told you to *open.*"

I don't catch the look that crosses his face until it's too late. His hand leaves my chin and moves to my throat, squeezing. I open my mouth so wide that I hear my jaw pop, but the pressure doesn't loosen. It gets tighter as he shifts in closer, jerking my head back. My brain goes away to that cold, quiet place where I can just ignore my body. My nails cut into my palms and I *feel* again. The pain is like a fence.

But it breaks the moment his hand slides around to the back of my neck and takes control over how much I can turn my head. I smell him: musk, raw, animal. His shirt covers most of his abdomen—I can only make out the definition of his hips. They seem carved into his skin. I remember the weapon resting inches away from my head and come up with another word. *Chiseled.*

"We will make this quick," he promises, his voice gritty.

I'm not trying to feel, not trying to see—but I can't miss the moment his hips jerk forward as he pries my jaws apart and then slams in. My teeth keep him out on the first thrust—my mouth just isn't wide enough. He has to force it open, using his fingers while yanking me forward.

That's all I know before my throat closes up. It's ripped open. My gag reflex goes haywire; I'm choking as he thrusts again, rocking on his heels, his mouth clenched in determination. The next second, he's just a blur. My lungs are exploding.

He's too big. Too deep. Too rough.

I can't breathe!

I try to push away, my hands clawing at his hips.

"Let me in," he commands as his cock slides over my tongue for a jagged second. The moment I try to suck in air, he slams back in, almost as if savoring the exact second I start to panic.

Everything goes black. White. My only coherent thought is to breathe in through my nose. *Breathe. Breathe. Breathe!* But it's impossible considering that my stomach is trying to crawl out of my throat. Something blocks its way hard, fast, ramming it back down.

"There." His fingers move through my hair, manipulating my head back farther. "Take *all* of it…like this."

My vision clears; I see his face: cold eyes and a blank expression. Black spots cover him up; they're everywhere. One. Ten. Fifty.

Then, all at once, he lets me go. I'm on my hands and knees. Air floods in down my ruined throat, and I'm running on pure instinct. *Breathe!* Even taking in oxygen hurts so damn much. Almost as bad as what comes up.

My wet fingers trace my mouth when I'm done gagging. They come away warm. Slippery. A coppery taste lingers over my tongue. But he didn't come. I know that, even before he grabs at my hair again, yanking me upright. The world spins and then I'm staring down at dust and wood. The table?

"Here."

Something is shoved into my hand. Something small, firm and cold. My fingers scramble to identify it as a sharp pain bites into my thumb.

"Look at it," Maxim commands, though he raises my hand himself when I'm too slow. "Feel it."

My eyes blink, fighting to adjust—but once they do, I only want to squeeze them shut. I'm holding a knife, one of those spring-loaded ones made of silver with a black leather handle. He makes sure I see the blade. That I notice my blood already painting the edge of it.

Then he forces me to guide it down to my inner thigh. I'm too damn stunned to pull away, and with a tiny bit of pressure, the blade slices through my skin: a burning, fiery line that extends down, down, down.

"A taste," he says while pulling the knife out of my grip. "Should you stay after this."

The wound burns, spanning the length of my thigh, all the way down to my knee. It was a warning—one I don't even get the chance to heed before his weight settles over me. One of his hands palms the back of my neck while the other slides around my hip and undoes the fastenings of my jeans. He pulls them down halfway and doesn't even bother with my panties. He just yanks the panel over with the pad of his thumb.

Make no noise—that's my one rule. No fake moaning. No whimpers. People always interpret them the wrong way. Usually, it's not hard to stay quiet, considering that most of my clients are fat fucks who get winded from fishing my money out of their goddamn wallets. At worst, I'd have to bite my tongue to hold a hiss of disgust back.

A finger. That's all he uses the first time, but it feels like so much more. Chisel, hammer. He tests me with one touch and then drives it home the next. Deep. Too deep.

My knees knock together, my body jerking against the surface of the table, held in place by him. *A finger.* I tell myself that over and over. It's just his finger that's sliding in, stretching me apart, tearing me open. *Another.*

"Relax," he warns as his palm flexes, pinning my skull flat against the table.

His hand withdraws as he muscles in closer, his hips against my bare ass. A crinkling sound cuts the air. Foil. It must take him only a second to get the condom out because, the next, he's in my stomach. He feels *that* deep, and my world narrows down to one purpose: keep *breathing.*

But it's impossible when my throat is on fire. Burning. Searing. Maybe it's out of sympathy for my pussy. How is it possible to feel *this* damn full? This sore.

This goddamn *open.*

When he moves, I see stars. I cry out, but the sound seems to egg him on. He grinds himself into me so hard the table rocks with every thrust, squealing at the joints.

I know pain: all of those "accidental" cuts. I know what it's like when a john gets too rough or tries to gain backdoor access. This is something else. It takes me far past silence. I'm just a body, a hole, used up.

I'm not sure at which point I realize he isn't even all the way inside me. He doesn't fit. Not even by half. Not right away. The resistance doesn't seem to surprise him. He just keeps ramming until my body has no choice but to relent and let him in, inch…by inch…

As he promised, he makes it quick.

One last battering thrust and he groans, his shudders racking through his body and into mine. I feel each jolt even with the condom, and then he slides out. In the hazy moments after, he says something else. Something raspy and gruff smothered into my hair that I barely comprehend.

"Good enough."

I can't respond. I just breathe. Loudly. Erratic. My body is one aching, used strip of flesh, but I just stay here, leaning against the table. Still shaking.

I try counting to ten, but it doesn't work. So I settle for counting to a thousand and picturing green.

I DON'T WAKE UP. I just come to, but I can't stand. I know that much. My stomach is cramping. My legs feel like mush, but I suffer through it all and blink up at the ceiling.

It's semi-dark, but there's just enough gray daylight to let me know that it's after dawn. The little shits have school. Mikie might try to skip without me there, if Daisy didn't burn the damn house down trying to make breakfast.

Rent's still due.

We need groceries. Laundry has to be done. If we don't get some goddamn bug spray, I might have more mouths to feed once the roaches demand a seat at the table.

I have too much damn shit to worry about to lie here on the floor. *Get up.* I flex my toes and flinch. They hurt too. So does my fucking head.

But I've been through worse. That's what I tell myself as I crawl onto my stomach and try to breathe. In and out. Out and in. Out. Out. Out.

I make one stupid noise when I try to stand up. Then I cut the pain off. He left my pants on. I slowly drag them back up and redo the clasp. My sweater feels too loose around the collar. I reach up and feel why: It's ripped.

So much for my job at Penney's.

The first few steps are the hardest. It takes me ten before I can cling to the wall beside the door and follow it out into the main room. The lights are off. The place seems empty. Maxim isn't waiting there when I fumble with the front door and pull it open.

Keep moving. I brace one hand against the wall of the hallway as I head for the elevator, riding it down to the lobby. When the doors open, someone is already standing there.

"Ms. Marconi." Lucius takes one look at me and steps aside, shrugging his suit jacket—a gray one this time—from his shoulders. He drapes it over me the moment I haul myself out of the elevator. I don't even have the strength to argue. He smells like coffee and rich cologne. Somehow on him, the scent isn't as offensive as it was on the Fuckfaces I screwed.

The next ten minutes pass in a blur as he steers me into that infamous black car, and it feels like I simply blink and find myself seated across from him in another café.

"Your payment," he says, reaching into a briefcase on the table in front of him. He fishes out a stack of bills while the waitress lurking around the edges of the room pretends not to stare. Once again, we're the only people inside, and I can make out the shadow of a man near the door, silently keeping watch. "One thousand, in full. If you would like to discuss continuing the contract, then we can—"

"No." I have to press my hands flat against the table to keep them from fucking shaking. "I've got to go home. I've got stuff to do."

"Of course." He nods and sets the money on the table between us. "As with any finalization of a contract, you have twenty-four hours to reconsider."

"So I can go?" I'm already reaching for the money. Grabbing it. Squeezing it. Whatever happened, it was worth it.

It was.

"Yes." Lucius nods again, and I jump to my feet.

Without a jacket, I don't have any way of hiding the money. I fold it up as much as I can and try to shove it into my pocket. The added fullness just makes the front of my pants feel tighter, which draws a groan from my lips before I can bite it back.

"I can see you to your home," Lucius suggests.

I should just leave and take my chances. But getting stabbed would be a rather ironic way to end the past twenty-four hours after having my brains fucked out.

"Okay."

I make him drop me off a block down from my place, and I don't miss the way he eyes the piece-of-shit houses. It's nothing like the posh high-rise he's used to.

"Have a nice day, Ms. Marconi," he says as I scramble out onto the curb.

I don't say anything back. Maybe I'm just too damn tired. My knees knock together with every step I take. A million deep, heavy breaths don't seem to fill my lungs up enough. I'm panting when I stagger up the front stoop and shove the door open.

It's still too early for the kids to be home from school. That means the person rummaging through my kitchen is either a burglar or a shitty-ass mother.

Frankly, I'd take the burglar.

"Frankie-girl!" Melanie stands in front of the sink, holding a frying pan in one hand and a dishcloth in the other. Someone must have let her in, considering that I changed the locks after the last time she'd blown through. Maybe they did it last night while I was lying unconscious on some stranger's creepy workshop floor. That's how Melanie rolls. She sneaks back into our lives when least expected, the biggest goddamn roach in this place.

"What the fuck are you doing here?"

"Honestly, Francesca." She sighs and starts to dry the pan with the rag. "Should you be talking to me like that?"

Her hair's red today. Her clothes look stolen: a pink, frilly shirt and jeans. Though, hell, it's not like I can judge. When your mommy runs off with your rent money, a twenty-dollar sweater from Penney's is the last fucking thing on the list of priorities.

"You're right," I tell her. "I shouldn't be talking to you at all. But you know who I *should* call right now? Your parole officer." I head for the end table, where Daisy keeps the TracFones that still have minutes left on them. I wrench open a drawer and grab the first one I see.

"Sweetie." Melanie sets the pan down and holds her hands out. "I'm not here to hurt you. I just wanted to talk. I've missed ya."

She's wearing makeup: blue eye shadow and fancy liner. I can't even afford ChapStick. Whatever mascara still clings to my lashes, I stole from a drug store two months ago.

She missed me.

I never wanted to see her.

"Just tell me what the hell you want."

"Baby…" She shakes her head and runs a hand full of fake nails through her equally fake hair. "Look. I just wanted to see you. All y'all. I've missed you guys. And… I'm getting married!" Her voice rises like she's fucking excited. Like she thinks I'll be too.

"How did you even get in here?" The kids are gone, but the house looks cleaner than usual. Too clean. Melanie was always a polite thief.

Fuck.

I head for the fridge and throw it open. The beer is missing from the veggies bag. So is all of the saved rent money. My stomach gets that awful sinking feeling, but I swallow it down. That's the funny thing about Melanie. I can't accuse her outright. Maybe Daisy did the smart thing and hid the stash somewhere else?

"I came around last night," Melanie says in one of her smug fucking tones. "You weren't home. Seems like you had a fun night."

I glance over and find her looking down her nose at me. I'm leaning against the fridge more than I should be, biting my lip so hard that I taste blood. My hair is a mess clinging to my scalp. My throat still hurts. I sound like Meryl after she comes back from a smoke break. My sweater is torn to shit.

But, even like this, I feel more responsible than she ever fucking did.

"Yeah, I did." I slam the fridge door shut. "That's what supporting six kids by yourself is, Melanie. Good fucking fun. Not that you would know anything about that."

"Is this what you're going to do whenever you see me from now on?" She crosses her arms over her chest and sighs. "Try to throw me on a guilt trip?"

Ah, but that's the butt of the joke. No one could ever make Melanie Ryder give a damn about someone other than herself.

"Just get the fuck out." I head for the table, swiping at the stacks of old junk mail piled on top of it.

"Ainsley had a bad dream last night," Melanie tells me while I stoop to snatch up the old flyers. "It's lucky that someone was here to comfort her—"

"Don't you fucking do that." The pile of newspapers slips through my grip and lands on the floor.

That's another thing about Melanie. She is a whore. A bitch. A skank. Just like me.

The only difference? I scraped up every ounce of what I had and used it to pack money into a bag of frozen peas every month just to get by. Not Melanie. She was perfectly fine with being a worthless, stupid slut.

"Don't you act like you coming around here for five minutes makes you some kind of fucking mother." I point to the door. Then I jerk my chin at the knife drawer—I know she knows what's in it. The moment the kids left, the bitch probably tore the entire place apart looking for more money. "Now get the fuck out."

"I just wanted to tell you the good news in person," she says, wringing her hands together.

At first, I assume she means her fourth straight marriage. But no. Her eyes are far too fucking shifty for that. I glance at the fridge again. If this stupid bitch so much as touched a dime of my money…

"My new guy, Burt. He's got his own business, baby. Well, he's starting one, anyway."

Oh, fuck. My lungs start to tighten up. I get that sick feeling again. My taste buds are too raw to taste much of anything, but I can still sense the puke rising at the back of my throat. Money. Money. Money. A parade of bills marches through my head. I dig the nail of my thumb into the finger beside it. Harder. Harder.

"All he needs is just a few bucks. Maybe a couple hundred, and by the end of the week, baby, we'll have it turned into a thousand."

"You took the money." I don't even have to see her face. I just know. The same way I know that Daisy was the one to give it to her. "You took *our* money."

"For us, baby," she insists. "Why don't you believe that?"

For us. That was the last thing about Melanie Ryder: She could sell the moon to an astronaut, as one of her last patsies used to say. She could make any idea seem like a good one. She dished out hope like heroin and got her suckers hooked. Daisy was always the weak link, but so was I until I turned sixteen and saw the true face of my so-called-mother.

"Get the fuck out." I'm too damn tired to scream. Or shout. I need to sleep. I need to shower. I need to investigate why the inside of my legs feel sticky. Warm.

"Baby, I know you don't believe me now, but in a few days, I'll be back and you can bet that—"

"Get out!" The kitchen blurs into one colorless blob, but I still manage to feel my way to the knife drawer and pull it open. I grab one at random and point it in her general direction. "Get out. And if you come near me or one of the kids again, I swear to god I will fucking kill you."

"You're tired, Frankie," Melanie says. "I know you don't mean that."

Either way, the bitch starts walking toward the front door. She already has it open when I get the urge to torture myself just a little further. For old time's sake and all.

"How much?"

"Hmm, baby?" Melanie pauses, her head tilted back to reveal the bone structure everyone swears up and down we share. I used to be proud of that, when people called us twins. In some ways, she still is my other half, I guess: everything I never want to be.

"How much money did you con out of Daisy?"

"Baby, I wasn't lying. I—"

"Enough!" I wave the knife to shut her up. "How. Much?"

She sighs. "Two fifty."

I can tell from the way she says it that she wanted more. That she thought I might have it. That she was desperate enough to stick around and beg me for it.

"Frankie, this really is the chance of a lifetime," she says, giving it one last shot.

My vision clears enough for me to make out the streaks of black stuff around her eyes. The smudges to her lipstick. The slightly uncombed quality of her hair. She worked hard to put on a good show, but some shit you just can't hide.

I don't even waste my breath on giving her another fuck off. I just turn around and flip the faucet of the sink on, drowning out the rest of whatever she says. My knife is still in my hand and my thumb keeps catching the edge of it. Over and over.

I don't know how long I have to ignore her before the door finally slams shut. I sink to my knees, using the counter for balance. My forehead is against the counter, the knife still slicing at my fingers until the pain swallows everything else. Then I reach into my pocket with my good hand and draw the money out.

The lower half of my jaw starts to throb as I fan the bills out beside me. There's so much of it. So little of it. Even with the rent covered, I'll still be in the hole. There are more bills to pay. Winter coats. Food. All of that stuff I never gave a damn about consuming when I was a snot-nosed kid clinging to Melanie's skirts—but even back then, she had never been just a mom. A cheese sandwich made with stale bread or an expired Pop-Tart was never what she was supposed to provide as my mother. Those were always extra payments from a loan I'll never fucking pay off. One I never asked to take out in the first place.

It feels like I sit here for days, bleeding over a thousand dollars. When I finally glance over at the spare cell phone lying beside me, I see that it's only been a minute. It doesn't take much of my pride to dial the number, in the end. It's answered on the second ring.

"Name," a gruff voice demands.

A part of me wants to hang up, but my thumb won't strike the right button. "It's Frankie—Francesca Marconi," I rasp once I remember how to speak.

"Oh." A heavy sigh blows from the speaker. "Ms. Marconi. How can I help you?"

"I changed my mind." While I talk, I pick up a loose fifty and hold it up to the light. The dead man printed on it sneers back at me, the prick. "I want to talk about extending the contract, or whatever."

"Excellent," Lucius says. He doesn't bother to ask any questions, and a part of me wonders why. Though, apparently, he made a habit out of fishing for women so hungry for a few bucks that they'd do anything to see the green. "You can meet me at this address in an hour." He rattles off a street I don't recognize. I have to use up what little bit of battery life the cell phone has left to connect to an unsecured Wi-Fi hotspot and search for it on the internet.

For some reason, I don't take the money when I finally stagger out of the house. I leave it there, a thousand dollars covered in blood. If Melanie comes back while I'm gone, she can fucking have it all.

Lucius picked another café. I guess he has a thing for coffee. Though, when I finally reach the place, I don't find the car out front or his little friend lurking beside the door. The moment I step inside, I realize why.

Another man dominates the center of the room. Dominates—that's the only way to put it. His massive body seems out of place seated on a wooden chair before a round table draped in a fancy white cloth. In sharp contrast, he's wearing black from head to toe. The color makes his blond hair glow almost. Like his eyes. They flicker in my direction the moment I creep toward the hostess podium, where a smiling waitress is standing to greet me.

"This way," she says without bothering to ask my name. She instinctively knows which table to stop beside, her eyes expectantly focused on Maxim, who sends her away with a wave of his hand.

To me, he just nods at the chair across from him. "Sit, *kotyonok*."

My knees bend on command, plopping me down onto a burgundy cushion. The table is already set. The silverware is legit silver, laid out in a line.

But there is only one place setting: his.

"I thought I should meet with you myself," Maxim says. "So that there can be no mistake as to what I expect from you."

His eyes flash, demanding a response.

"O-okay—"

"You should know that this isn't about companionship," he tells me. "In fact, this isn't even about sex."

One of his hands reaches across the table, the thumb of it coming to brush my lower lip. It's bitten: a wound I only remember as his touch stirs up the pain. My eyes start to blink, watering. He presses down harder.

When he finally draws his hand away, the thumb is red with blood. He stares at the drop for a second and then rubs it carefully into the tablecloth.

"I only want to hurt you," he tells me as his stare reconnects with mine. "However I want. Whenever I want. In any way that I can. Do you understand what I mean by that?"

"H-hurt me?" My voice is a fucking rasp as my belly clenches up at the reminder of the damage he's already dished out.

He folds his hands, watching me for what feels like hours as the café bustles with traffic around us. I swear our waitress has passed us at least five times, serving as many tables, before he speaks again.

"Come here." He pushes back from the table but remains seated. When I stand, he nods at his lap. "Sit."

I nervously dart my gaze around the rest of the café.

"Don't." The warning trickles from him, so softly that only I can hear it. "Sit."

It hurts to straddle him. With his size, it's like attempting to do a split. Pinpricks of pain shoot behind my eyelids the farther I spread my legs, so I focus on sucking in air, one breath after the other. The moment I'm on top of him, he easily shifts his weight, sliding his chair closer to the table. Too close. The rim of it digs into my lower back, but Maxim doesn't stop. I look down and find him flicking his fingers toward the ceiling.

"Up, *kotyonok*."

It isn't until he attempts to push into the table completely that I understand what he means. *Up.* I have to brace both hands on the table behind me and haul myself up before his weight traps me between it and his chest. The tines of a fork dig into my thigh as all of the silverware clings together when I scoot backward. My face is on fire, but no one seems to notice the scene unfolding.

"Look at me." His hand captures my chin to make me. "These people?" He shrugs one shoulder toward the rest of the café. "They mean nothing. If you are to be with me, that is the first thing you will need to learn. Their reactions, their judgment mean nothing."

He slides his other hand beneath my ass, lifting me from the table's surface altogether. I can only watch. I can only breathe. In and out. My sore pussy throbs as if it already knows just what he's planning.

"Strip." He tells me, even as his fingers leave my jaw and go directly to the front of my jeans before I can do it myself. With one yank, he undoes the zipper—undressing me on a table inside a public place.

I can't process it. I just find myself staring at a balding old man at the table directly across from us. He's steadily sipping his soup without a care in the world or a glance in my direction.

"Look at me."

Pain sears between my legs. I look down and find Maxim's hand there, rubbing against my open fly. A warning.

"Only me, *kotyonok*." His fingers rub again, while the ones beneath me hook within one of the belt loops of my jeans.

One hard yank nearly drags me off the table and onto his lap again. I know without him even having to say it not to move an inch, so I brace my weight back against my palms, arching my hips in the process.

Another tug later and my pants are down my thighs. He inhales when he sees what lurks underneath. I can't look, so I stare up at the ceiling as my jeans are pulled the rest of the way off and tossed aside. He doesn't bother with the same method for my panties.

A metallic clink proceeds the icy scrape tickling my inner thigh a second later, centered in a single point that grazes a path over to my hip. I can hear people laughing. Talking. No one gasps but me when the tip of the knife slides beneath the waistband of my panties. I feel a hard jerk and then the fabric is slowly peeled away by his hands. They're rough. Like sandpaper. Cold. Warm. I can't fucking explain just what he feels like. Maybe it's because pain mingles with every deliberate touch. His nails lead the charge, sharper than the knife.

"Look at me, *kotyonok.*"

His voice turns my body into a slave. I see what he's done. What's he's doing. While I watch, he slices through the other side of the thong. Then he gathers up the black fabric and pitches it onto the floor.

I can't help the sound that tears out of me when I look between my legs. Two purple bruises in the shape of handprints make twin marks on my inner thighs. Just beyond my pussy is a slight scarlet smear.

"You have a delicate little cunt. I hurt you. *Without* intending to." The pad of his thumb drifts down, running between my legs, coming away red. He doesn't look pleased about that. His eyes darken to the shade of his shirt as he raises his fingers to my mouth, pressing his thumb against my bottom lip.

I know what he wants. It's sick, but I fucking know. My tongue drifts out, flicking the bloody smears away, and I swallow hard without tasting.

Chuckling, Maxim lowers his hand—and rams it between my legs. His thumb circles my entrance. Once. Again. Harder. When he raises it again, his eyes contain a dare.

"Taste, *kotyonok*."

I lick my lips first, tasting bitter, dry flesh. I try to focus on that flavor as I lean forward, sticking my tongue out on cue. I'm about an inch away from his hand when I realize what he wants.

When my tongue finally touches him, it's like licking a frozen pole in the middle of winter. The icy, numbing jolt feels the same. Disgust makes me gag. *Just swallow.* All I have to do is swallow and I won't taste.

But he's watching me, waiting as my taste buds slowly register the substance they've picked up. Salt. Musk. Me. Drool floods my mouth, urging me to spit.

"Swallow," Maxim commands.

I do, and somehow, it all goes down without a fuss.

"Good." He pushes back from the table just enough so that he can take me in without having to crane his neck. His eyes flicker up and down the length of me before settling between my legs. His nostrils flare, inhaling my scent as my flesh is bared to him.

It takes everything I have in me not to slam my thighs together. *Focus on him.* I don't take my eyes off his face, trying to decipher any hint of what he might be thinking. Insanity most likely. He has to be insane. And, any minute, the manager of this place will storm over and order us out.

I tell myself that. I comfort myself with what a part of me knows is just a lie.

"Why do you want this?" Maxim wonders. His fingers fan out along his jaw, smearing blood onto his gold stubble. "You're young. You can find other clients. You don't seem familiar with sadism."

Sadism. My brain blanks at how dangerous he makes that word sound. The scary part? I don't even know what it means—I don't want to.

"I asked you a question." His eyes flash, and he sits straighter.

"I need the money," I blurt out.

Rather than seem insulted, he nods in response, still rubbing his chin. When his hand shoots out in an arch, I flinch, thinking I missed something, but a waitress appears at his shoulder seconds later.

Her eyes skim over me, her pretty smile perfectly in place. "How may I serve you, Mr. Koslov?"

Maxim waves his hand toward the table, and the woman nods before taking off.

"Did you really read the contract?" he wonders after she's gone. His eyes flick up to mine and narrow a dangerous fraction of an inch. "Be honest with me."

"Yes?" It's the Melanie in me that wants me to lie—but the man intimidates even my fucking genetics. "No."

"You didn't," Maxim says, deciding for himself which answer of the two is correct. "I suggest you educate yourself, *kotyonok*." He bends forward, rummaging through something at his feet. A bag? He withdraws a folder from whatever it is. "Read."

He tosses the stack between my legs.

It's black, containing a pile of pages that flutter as I flip it open and smear blood over them. It's the same list Lucius showed me, but this time, I inhale every fucking word. It's more than just a catalog of injuries and their corresponding prices.

So much more.

To start with, my eyes pick up where they left off: *In the event of accidental death, the designated relatives of the aforementioned party will receive a lump sum amount of $500,000.*

I wheeze, sucking in air. The room spins for a second, but I keep reading.

Clause 4: *The aforementioned party will remain with the undersigned for a duration of specified time, not to exceed forty hours per week.*

Clause 5: *The aforementioned party will submit fully to all terms stated by the undersigned. To void the contract at any time, the aforementioned party must invoke the use of the designated "safe word," nullifying the contract and forfeiting the entirety of the remaining payment.*

I tear my eyes away from the page and find Maxim watching me.

"I'd have to stay with you?"

"Read silently," he warns. "When you finish, we will discuss it all."

My throat jerks to swallow as I keep reading. It's all I can fucking do.

When I finally finish, my palms are slick. I can't seem to breathe in deeply enough. The light in the room is blinding. At the same time, it's too dark. Maxim's face is covered in shadow. I can only make out his smile: pure-white teeth in a beautiful, lethal row.

"I'm finished." I set the folder aside, letting it slip through my fingers and onto the edge of the table. It slides off, but Maxim doesn't reach for it and something warns me not to even try.

His eyes cut over my shoulder, just as the waitress appears beside me. On one of her hands is a steaming plate of food: steak, potatoes, and roasted vegetables. In the other is a mug of dark liquid. Coffee, I guess.

Maxim nods toward the table, and I start to climb down.

"No." His hand grabs my thigh, pinning me in place while the waitress sets his plate down right between my legs.

The hot rim sears whatever bits of my thighs come into contact with it. I fling my legs apart as far as I can, only to graze the mug of steaming coffee with the left one as the waitress sets it down too.

"Thank you," Maxim says, sending her off.

He turns his attention to his food, sizing up every item on his plate before reaching for a fork. I'm partially sitting on the one his fingers settle over, but he doesn't prompt me to move my thigh. He clenches the handle instead and pulls. Sharp, harsh pain bites so deep that I can taste it. My eyes flutter shut.

"Open, *kotyonok.*"

My vision snaps back into focus as he stabs at a roasted carrot and raises it close to my chin, allowing the smell to tickle my nose. A frown tugs at his mouth before I realize what he meant. *Open.*

I pry my lips apart far enough for him to slip the piece of carrot between them. *Shit.* It's too hot. I have to choke it down, my eyes watering.

"Good," Maxim growls, and I instinctively know what action satisfied him: not my obedience, but the pain.

He reaches for a steak knife and I shift my weight to lift my right thigh slightly in case he grabs it the same way he did the fork. His fingers close over the handle of the sharpest one. He pulls and then flips the blade at the last minute so that the edge bites into my skin regardless. Not hard enough to draw blood, just enough to sting.

"I didn't say you could move," he warns before cutting into his steak. Pink liquid pours out from the first cut. It's cooked rarer than most people I know would dare to eat. Without batting an eyelash, Maxim slices off a piece and spears it with the fork. "Open."

I obey. As the minutes pass, he winds up feeding me more of his food than himself. I quickly pick up on the method to his madness: He takes his time, giving me every morsel that wafts the most steam. After each bite, he watches me chew and I wait for his silent cue to swallow. He nods afterward. I breathe.

"Good, *kotyonok*," he tells me before taking a bite of steak for himself. "Very good."

My heart skips a beat, riding a merry-go-round of pain and fear. I think it's over. He doesn't seem interested in the final slice of steak and lets it linger on the edge of his plate while he samples the veggies. It's the very last thing left when he finally stabs it with the fork and raises it.

He sighs, his eyes between my legs. My skin is on fire, but I don't dare look away. I just wait.

Slowly, he lowers the steak. Too low. I can't fight the noise that breaks from my throat when he drags the meat along my inner thigh.

"I wish I could taste you myself." He sounds curious. Hungry. He wishes he could taste me, but I know why he can't.

I'm bleeding. I could be dirty. Lucius mentioned something about a blood test I have yet to take.

"Soon," Maxim says, shattering any coherent thought into a million pieces. "As for now, open, *kotyonok.*"

I obey, turning my brain off as he places the blood-stained meat on my tongue. I don't think about it. Not the taste. Not the flavor. I simply swallow, but a sharp pinch on my hip stops the food from going down.

"Not yet."

I have no choice but to let the food sit there, at the back of my throat. His eyes stare into mine, pinning me in place. Daring me to make a move without his say so. It feels like hours before he lowers the fork and nods.

I choke the meat down.

He smiles—or at least his lips lift higher than their usual stern line. It's the most terrifying thing I've ever seen.

"And *now*—" He sits back in his chair, tilting his head up to meet mine. "You may now ask your questions."

The folder is still on the floor. I glance at it and Maxim smiles again.

"Start with the one I know you can't stop thinking about."

I have to suck in a breath to get the words out. "I gotta—"

"Sentences." My punishment is a pinch on my hip, sharp and demanding.

"I mean, I would have to stay with you?"

He's right. That damn clause keeps circling my brain. Only the look in his eyes keeps me from dwelling on it. That dangerous promise. *I only want to hurt you.*

"Yes," he says while my heart shrivels up. "Three nights a week for the first week. To acclimate. Five nights after that."

"But I have kids."

His face doesn't change, and I can't tell if he thinks it's a lie or not. Slowly, his gaze returns to my pussy.

Oh. "T-they're not—"

"You may have a few days to make arrangements," Maxim says over me. "If you need additional funds, contact Lucius."

"But I—"

His eyes flash in warning. "Anything else, *kotyonok*?"

"Kotee..." I give up trying to parrot the term. "What does that mean—"

"Next question."

My brain changes tactics automatically. "T-the safe word?"

According to the contract, it was the only way out of this agreement. One word that could end it all. A kill switch.

"Yes?"

"What is it?"

He brushes his jaw with the tip of his thumb. "The women typically decide that for themselves."

The women. More than one. More than me. Desperate enough—pathetic enough—to do anything for cash.

"What do they usually pick?"

He cocks his head and seems to think for a minute. "The usual tropes. Red light. Stop now. Enough please. However, I suggest you select something you would never typically say. Once you utter the safe word, our contract is null and void. You only need to say it once."

Pick something that I would never say? Melanie herself, showing up once again out of the blue to fuck up everything, made one choice pretty fucking tempting.

"What will it be?" His tone demands an answer.

"Happy."

That creepy almost-smile shapes his mouth again. He sits forward, his hair framing his face. "It is typically a phrase. Something you would never say."

"Then *I'm* happy. I am happy."

I can't tell what he thinks of it. He just nods. "As you wish, *kotyonok*."

"So…" I lick my lips, flexing my fingers against the table. "M-may I ask another question?"

"Ask away."

"When would I start?" My voice catches, sticking the words at the back of my throat. It feels like asking about my execution date. "And get paid?"

Maxim flexes his arms at both wrists, straining the muscle coiled beneath his shirt. "You can contact Lucius within forty-eight hours once you've made your arrangements," he says. "As for payment."

He lunges forward and I flinch, but his hands reach between my outstretched legs, toward his feet. He snatches something else from what's there: a briefcase I see when I crane my neck. Whatever he lifts from it is black. Thick. An envelope.

He slides it onto the sliver of space in front of his plate. "Take this in advance. A taste."

He stands, flicking the edge of his collar between a forefinger and thumb. "Wait ten minutes before you leave," he tells me. "Don't move. I don't even think you should blink—not for as long as you can stand it. You leave so much as a second too early?" His thumb grazes my chin again, still red with my blood. "You will be punished when I see you again. Do you understand?"

I nod and he turns away from me. I watch him go, and he draws attention with every step he takes. It's only after he leaves that the other diners finally seem to notice me. Sitting here, half naked. Shameless. Motionless.

In the end, I don't wait ten minutes before leaving.

I wait fifteen.

CHAPTER SIX

I always used to fantasize about what I'd do if I won the lottery or something and had enough cash to kiss my jobs goodbye. I'd stroll into Penney's and bitch-slap fucking Meryl before telling her that she could fuck off forever. At the diner, I'd buy a round of pie for everyone and make it rain dollar bills over old Mr. and Mrs. Johansen, the owners.

But it's funny. With more money than God tucked into my pocket, it seems like all I can do is just scuttle from one place to the next and fill out the necessary paperwork without doing much else. When I'm asked for the reason *why* I'm quitting, I shrug and mutter, "Something came up."

To be more specific, Maxim Koslov came up— presumably while cutting me. Hurting me.

"I only want to hurt you, kotyonok."

Once I'm completely unemployed, I take the bus out to

the nearest mall. Without even touching the envelope, I buy Daisy a coat for her goddamn trip. Mikie gets a game system. Ainsley gets a doll. The twins get some toy set that looks violent and loud. At the register, I pull out the stack of Maxim's money and withdraw the first few bills while the cashier watches me in confusion. It's more than enough to cover it all.

Then I keep moving. I buy a new cell phone and put minutes on it. I also buy myself a new pair of shoes. Nothing fancy. Just something black. To hide dirt. Scuff marks. Blood…

After that, I head home, my arms bruised and sore as the weight of the bags bites into my skin. The kids aren't home when I stagger through the front door. The money is still there, lying in a row by the sink. I pick up each bill one by one and shove them into the veggie bag at the back of the fridge.

Then I haul myself up the stairs, climb into the tub, and run the faucet, lying here while the water slowly fills it. I've made it too hot though. Sweat drips down the back of my neck, my skin burning and turning an angry pink. By accident, I did it. Accident.

But at least I can think clearly for five damn minutes, and as always, only one thing matters: money.

And, after today, I only have one route to getting more.

I'll have to leave Mikie in charge, considering that Daisy just fucked up her last chance. I can't risk Melanie coming back and taking even more than she already has. I can't.

That's the only damn thing I'm sure of when I leave the tub and get dressed in someone's jeans and someone else's tank top. I snatch the black envelope from my other pants and shove it into the pocket of a pink sweatshirt I grabbed off Daisy's bed.

When I leave the house again, I head straight for downtown and don't stop until I reach the rental office. I pay three months in advance—that's how much the money in the envelope will cover. There's still enough left over for the gas and electric.

I used to think it would be fun having this kind of cash. In reality, I just feel numb. My body remembers what it had to do to earn it. What I had to suffer.

It's not worth it.

No, it *is* worth it.

It's worth it.

I tell myself that over and over until I'm back inside the house and the sounds of shouting drown the thoughts out.

"I SAID GIVE IT BACK!"

"Shut up." I don't even have to yell—not that I could. It's only as my voice rings out over Ainsley's that I realize just how fucking awful I sound.

"Are you sick, Frankie?" Daisy wonders while I slam the front door behind me. "You sound awful."

Her concern is easy to shrug off once I make out the chaos unfolding in the living room. They found the stuff. A graveyard of cardboard and plastic bags litters the floor. Ainsley got to my suitcase and stands in the middle of it, still wearing her muddy, tattered shoes.

"Frankie!" She observes me, her hands on her hips, lips pursed. "You want to hear what happened today? Bobby R. sat with Amy at recess and gave her his cookies! Then you know what he did?" Her eyes widen. "*Then* he poked her in the forehead and ran off with his friends. Amy says it's because he likes her. He *likes* her, so he hits her? Ugh boys are so weird. I told her she should punch him back—"

"Shut up," Eric calls from across the room. "No one cares! Hey Frankie, look at what I got." He brandishes one of his new toys.

Seeing them like this makes it all sink in. Maxim gave me two days to "make arrangements." I should take that time to find a way out. Steal his money. Ride off into the sunset. What memories does this piece-of-shit house hold that I couldn't find somewhere else? After all, Melanie taught me that nothing in this world is worth tethering yourself to. Not even your own damn kids.

"I have to go away for a few days," I say.

"Why?" They all try to speak at once.

"Can I come?"

"Where?"

"I don't want to go to fucking school—"

"Mikie's in charge," I say and they all shut up again.

Daisy watches me, her eyes wide with fear. Or maybe it's guilt.

Mikie steps forward, blocking her from view, and I shove every last dime I have into his hands. "If anything happens, call me." I give him my new number, and then the questions start all up again.

Though they aren't questions, really…

"Did Mom get that for you, too?"

"Did you see what she got me?"

"I can't believe the bitch actually came back."

Breathe. I squeeze my eyes shut and suck in air. In. Out. In. My hands clasp together, the nails of each finger digging into whatever skin they can reach. Pulling. Raking.

"Frankie?"

"I've got to leave…" I stumble toward the suitcase and snatch it by the handle with Ainsley still inside. She falls out and starts to cry. Daisy's the one to comfort her while I race up the stairs.

They're watching me. Whispering. Talking about me.

But that's not the fun part. *Melanie.* They think Melanie would really give a shit about them long enough to drop off a dollar, let alone hundreds worth of shit. That Melanie would sell her body and soul for rent.

That Melanie actually gave a fuck.

I'm not angry. Not even as I break into the one corner where Daisy still keeps her shit. It's at the very back of the room she shares with Ainsley in a cardboard box marked *Mom.* I dump it all onto the floor and find myself laughing out loud. Ainsley's shoes have holes in them. Daisy went without a winter coat all of last year, and so did I because the two youngest grew out of theirs too fast and needed new ones.

But, of course, even when she's not fucking here, Melanie has the nicest shit in the house. I think some of it is even designer. Shirts. Pants. Stuff she never came back for. She could always con some horny fuckface into buying her more, after all. A fancy handbag was her price tag.

Would she let a guy like Maxim do whatever the fuck he wanted to her? Maybe. But not for me, or any of the others. She'd probably up her rate and do it for *two* fancy handbags.

"Frankie?"

I flinch and find Daisy creeping near the doorway. The floor creaks so badly that I should have heard her. I can't think. My thumb pecks at my forefinger. Hard. Harder. Harder.

"Frankie…I… Mom came back, and I gave her—"

"I have to go." I snatch up the rest of Melanie's shit and shove it all into the suitcase. Daisy's still talking when I push past her and take the stairs two at a time. I should say goodbye or something. Kiss them all goodnight. Probably.

But I don't. I just push the door open and shove the suitcase out onto the stoop. "If anyone skips school, I will hunt you down and kick your ass." With that, I slam the door behind me.

Now, I can think. Three months with Maxim would give me enough money to survive for a year. I can't comprehend that. I can't dwell on it. I just latch onto the reality: a year of not worrying. Not hiding. Not fucking scraping and crawling to get by.

It sounds too damn good to be true.

It probably is.

I WALK ten blocks before I finally fish his business card from my pocket and dial the number Lucius gave me. I don't expect him to answer, but he does on the first ring. The only words to leave his mouth are, "If you have made your decision, Ms. Marconi, please supply the address where we might meet."

I give him the next block I reach, and not even ten minutes later, a fancy black car pulls up to the curb in front of me. The weirdo driver climbs out and circles around to take my suitcase and toss it into the trunk. Lucius is already waiting for me in the back seat.

"Good evening," he says. His hands are folded on his lap. He's not wearing a suit tonight, but dark pants, a gray coat, a sweater and a matching scarf wrapped neatly around his throat. "Mr. Koslov most likely won't be expecting you so soon. I can book a hotel room for you, in the meantime."

I don't know how to tell him that I already spent all the money he gave me. Instead, I dig the nails of one hand into the back of the other and wait while he pulls a cell phone from his pocket. He barely touches it before it starts to buzz.

"Lucius," he says, bringing the phone to his ear. His eyes cut over to me. "Yes, sir. Right away, sir." He hangs up and tucks the phone back into his pocket, a frown tugging at his mouth. "He said to bring you to him now."

Lucius doesn't explain how the hell Maxim could have known where I was. I don't have the balls to ask. Roughly ten minutes later, the driver pulls up before the black high-rise and there isn't time for fucking questions anyway.

"I will take you up." Lucius steps out onto the curb and extends his hand for mine.

Everything passes by in a blur. One minute, I'm outside, staring up at a building I could never dream to live in. The next, I'm dragging a brand-new suitcase into the entryway of a penthouse suite.

Maxim isn't here waiting, and I don't hear any sound coming from the room with the stone and tools.

"It is customary that I give the women a small tour of the layout," Lucius explains while adjusting the ends of his scarf. "This room is the main receiving area for guests."

He starts down a hallway that leads into what looks like a living room—the disgustingly rich variety. There isn't much furniture, but what little there is looks like it's made of real black leather accented with red silk pillows. The glass end tables might be crystal. Exotic plants sit in the corners within huge marble pots.

Classy.

"Over here is the dining room." He points a short distance down the hall.

It's bigger than the living room, dominated by a long, ebony table and polished chairs. By the time he shows me to a kitchen and a study, I have a general gist of the color scheme and style Maxim prefers. Dark colors: blacks, reds, grays. There are no family photos hung on the walls or personal touches like the decapitated Barbies or Kool-Aid stains in my house.

Just quiet, clean perfection.

"And this will be your room," Lucius explains as he opens one of the doors at the very end of the hall.

I can only stare as I follow him inside it. My room.

I've never had one. Not in all of those years living out of trailers with Melanie. She had already been working on her fourth kid when we moved into the house, and she took one of the only two bedrooms for herself.

My new room is large. There's a bed in the center of it, draped in a black canopy. Beneath it, the sheets are white and the marble flooring of the rest of the house becomes ivory carpeting. In the corner of the room is one of those fancy vanities with a mirror framed in white. Two French doors on the opposite end open up to the closet, I guess.

"There is a schedule," Lucius says while I brace my suitcase against the wall, "for how Maxim prefers his days to run. Since he doesn't seem to be here, you may dress for dinner and wait for him."

"D-dress?"

Lucius nods toward the closet. "The clothing is organized into three sections," he says. "Day clothing is in the first section. Then evening wear. Last is night clothing. If you can't find anything in your size, just make do with what you can and I'll send for the tailor in the morning."

He turns to leave, and I watch him go, too uneasy to voice the questions crawling up my throat. There are rooms he never showed me. I think it was on purpose. Maxim's rooms.

I wind up creeping back into mine and closing the door. Inside the closet, I find it divided up just like Lucius said. It's like three mini wardrobes shoved into one. In the first section, the clothing is lighter: pinks, whites, grays. Everything looks like a dress, made of lace. In the next one, the clothes are all black: longer dresses and a few crisp blouses and skirts. The last one just has flimsy nightgowns.

Rather than pick something for dinner, I grab a clean sweater out of my suitcase and a different pair of jeans. I sit on the bed for a while before I start pacing the middle of the room.

My room.

I can almost see the other women who've lived in it before me. Just imprints. Shadows. Someone who wore a medium. Another who wore an extra small. Someone who preferred heels. Another who liked flats.

It's like a hotel for the desperate and pathetic. I find myself staring at the bed next, wondering how many people have slept in it. Fucked on it.

Without deciding on a number, I wander out into the hallway, retracing the path Lucius took. My footsteps echo—it's that damn quiet in here. It's that damn large. My house could fit in the living room alone with plenty of room left over for Maxim to entertain.

It's nice, even on my second trip through, but I keep going until I reach the entryway, and then I continue past it until I'm surrounded by rows of sharp tools.

He finished the statue of the woman. She stares down at me, her arms reaching toward the ceiling, her hips flexed like she's dancing. A few details are missing, like the curls in her hair or the lines of her stomach, but it already seems perfect. Even with the jagged crack slicing through it all.

I think it takes minutes before I gather up the nerve to step closer to it. It would be taller than me even if it weren't on the pedestal. The dusky glow streaming in from the windows casts a bluish sheen over the stone. She almost looks alive. And if she were, I can imagine what she'd say: *What the fuck are you doing?*

"You were not given permission to enter this room, *kotyonok*."

I shiver at the sound of his voice: equal parts rage and something that could be amusement. I hear him laugh, but the step he takes toward me sounds heavy. Deliberate.

"Come here."

I turn around. He's near the doorway, leaning against it, his arms crossed over his chest. He's wearing the same clothing he wore at the café: the black shirt and pants. Here, with very little lighting, the shadow makes his eyes seem darker. His body looms over mine, even taller than I remember.

"I must break you in." It's a promise as his hand cups my chin, tilting my head back to meet his gaze directly. His eyes narrow, scanning my face. "Did Lucius give you the tour?" he wonders before pulling away.

"Y-yes," I choke out, digging my nails into my wrist. Sharp. Deep. "Yes, he did."

Maxim's eyes narrow further. "Then I assume that nothing in the wardrobe was in your size?"

Shit. I swallow hard, trying to keep the truth from showing. Learning from Melanie, I've turned lying into an art form. "I didn't think so—"

"Come." He turns on his heel and leads me to the room designated as mine.

I watch him approach the closet and throw both doors open. His fingers skim the clothing in the evening section and he pulls out a dress. Then another. Several more.

"Strip," he tells me without turning around.

My teeth sink into my bottom lip as my hands start for the clasp of my pants.

"The sweater first," Maxim says, and I change tack.

It's cold in the room. I'm shaking as I wind the fabric of my shirt up and over my head. Something tells me to take my bra off before he can even issue the command himself. Then I wait…

After another minute of searching through the clothes, he looks at me over his shoulder. His eyes perform a lazy sweep down my naked torso. He nods. "Continue."

This time, he watches as I work on the stubborn zipper of my jeans. It takes me five tries to get the damn thing undone. Maxim starts toward me on the fourth yank and it springs open on the next try.

I slowly peel them down, not really knowing what he wants. A tease? No. His jaw is clenched, so I yank them down and kick them off my ankles. Once naked, I stand with my arms at my sides.

"Beautiful," he grits out as his gaze settles between my legs. My inner thighs throb; he's staring at the bruises. "Come."

I start forward on cue, and once again, I know instinctively when to stop: just beyond his reach.

"Turn around, *kotyonok*."

I do, feeling warm air fan the back of my neck seconds later.

"Raise your arms."

The moment I comply, something soft and flimsy grazes them. A dress. It's black, lacy, and loose-fitting. The V-shaped neckline plunges between my breasts—one of the few things I didn't inherit from Melanie was her cleavage.

"You are thin," he says near my ear. It doesn't sound like a compliment. "I will have Lucius find you things that are more suitable."

"Thank you," I croak out. I don't know what else to say. It's not a gift. Something tells me that my personal style won't matter a damn bit in what outfits I wear. He has a wardrobe already picked out; I'm no better than Ainsley's Barbie dolls.

"Do not thank me," Maxim says as if to drill that point home. His hand encircles my neck from behind, his thick fingers resting over my windpipe. "Never thank me."

"O-okay—"

"And now," he says over me, his fingers tightening their grip just enough to make it harder to speak. "Are you ready for your punishment?"

My blood runs cold. He's flipped a switch again and another man has taken his place. One who speaks in grunts and grumbles rather than a suave tone. A man who digs his nails into my skin so hard that I flinch before he shoves me toward the bed. I lose my balance halfway and wind up on my knees. The carpet cushions the blow. At the same time, it turns pain into fire as momentum drags me forward.

"What did I do?" I can't help the question. Not even the prissy, bitchy, whiny tone to it.

My guess is wandering his home without permission.

"You disobeyed me, didn't you?"

His footsteps form a foreboding melody: light and soft. Steady. He's taking his time, as if savoring the way I jump with every vibration running through the floor.

"Earlier today, in the café. Do you know how?"

It's the world's most dangerous version of a pop quiz. I always failed those in school, which is one of the many reasons why I dropped out. "I…"

"Think." A tiny bit of skin on my shoulder is pinched. Hard.

"You t-told me to wait?"

"Yes," he says. "And for how long?"

"T-ten minutes—"

"And how long did you wait, *kotyonok*?"

I swallow hard as the answer sticks in my throat. "Fifteen."

"Fifteen," he says. His fingers run through my hair again, smoothing the back of it flat. "Five minutes too late. When I give you a command, I expect you to obey." He rakes his fingers against my scalp and turns them into a fist. "Do you understand?"

My eyes start burning, blinking back moisture. "Yes! I understand."

"Good." His hand withdraws. "Your first punishment will be simple. Get on the bed."

My pussy starts to ache. It's still sore. His voice in my ear reminds me of his cock. Thick. Big. Too damn much.

"Now." He doesn't touch me, even as the slight way he raises his voice hits me like a slap.

I jerk forward on my hands and knees and crawl onto the bed. The comforter is soft beneath me. Softer than anything I've ever felt. In a sick way, it's the polar opposite of the pain I feel on my ass a second later. Sharp. Piercing.

I gasp out, craning my neck back to see the source. Something shiny glints through the air, held in Maxim's fist. It's small. Silver.

The knife.

"On your stomach." His thumb traces the blade, smearing something red all over the surface. "That was number one."

Number two hits my left shoulder above the collar of my dress. It's deep enough to bleed. Deep enough to sting.

I go limp, throwing my arms out beside me, my gaze on the wall.

He takes his time with number three: a long, curved cut along my hip and blood dribbles down after each brutal slice. My heart pounds. Stops. Starts up again. Surges. Stammers. Dies.

"I don't hear you keeping count." His voice is thunder again. I feel it rather than hear it, ripping through my spine.

"F-four," I rasp as the blade bites in again, on my other hip this time. He is more daring than I ever would be, slicing in without a care.

"What's next, *kotyonok?*" His voice sounds deeper. Jagged. "What next?"

I suck in air the moment I feel the start of the next cut. The tip of the knife sinks in.

Oh god.

My bottom lip trembles when he starts to saw. In and out. Over. Over.

"*Kotyonok—*"

"F-five." I can't stop my eyes from welling up as warmth drips down my arm.

"I'm going to fuck you now," Maxim tells me, running his fingers through my hair, tugging them loose whenever they get caught in the tangles. "I will fuck you hard. If you get so much as a drop of blood on the sheets…" His fingers cup my hips, yanking my ass higher until I'm on my knees, face down. "You will be punished. Do you understand?"

I nod into the mattress while his fingers trace a path down the back of my neck, my spine, the curve of my ass. He travels all the way down to my pussy, grazing his nail along my rim. I hear the zipper to his jeans come undone. I feel the bed shift beneath his weight. His hands fan out over my hips, positioning me toward him before I can crawl away.

"You're bleeding," he reminds me. *Don't disobey.*

The cut on my arm is leaking the most. I twist it, feeling the blood run down toward the crook of my elbow instead. The one on my hip is at a tricky angle. I have to tilt my hips slightly to keep the blood from dripping off. I can feel every tiny, warm bead bubbling up, streaking my skin.

And then the bed jerks forward and I only feel Maxim. Inside me. On top of me. I bite down onto the comforter, choking myself with a mouthful of fabric. I won't scream. Won't cry.

But he's so damn big. My body doesn't know what to do with his size. It clamps down tight. Whenever he moves, I feel it in my stomach. My skull. He's pulsing inside me. Pushing through me. Hot. Heavy. Solid.

Fuck.

He pulls out slowly and my body attempts to follow, my ass arching toward his hips to slow the friction and lessen the pain. I have to rise onto my elbows, letting the blanket fall from my mouth in a trail of drool. *The blood.* I twist my arm even more. My heart beats faster. The blood flows harder.

"You are tight, *kotyonok*," he tells me, gritting the words out against my skull. "But not out of fear."

How he knows as much? I can't focus enough to care. Again, he doesn't sound happy about it. Just annoyed. Irritated. I'm too tight. He has to ram his way back in.

Holy fuck. His weight throws me forward. The top of my head smacks off something hard, and I have to choose between being silent or tracking five different streams of blood.

Something gives and I cry out. And then he moves again and I learn an entirely new way to scream: in hoarse whispers and squeaks.

"Not a single drop," Maxim warns somewhere during his fourth thrust.

I squeeze my eyes shut and stop resisting. I let him fuck me and tune into every inch of my skin. I feel it all. The parts where it's gaping and open. Where it's slick with warmth. The pain is a constant buzz running through my veins. Boiling over in places. Ice cool in others.

I have to move: flexing my thigh or clenching my arm to keep the blood from flowing. But sometimes tensing up so that I feel every ridge of the body slamming into mine. It's white-hot agony. One taste of it and my thoughts go crystal fucking clear.

Then numb again.

Clear.

Numb.

Clear, clear, fucking clear. There's one position where I feel him the most. Where he slams into me so hard that I just see white each time. I taste his violence in my throat. In my blood.

And then I don't feel anything…

And I feel everything.

Oh God.

My muscles clench up. Tighten. Clamp down over his cock in ways I don't tell them to. I don't want them to. I gag on my own screams. It's too much. Too raw. Too hard.

The only way to save myself is to throw myself against him until I don't feel anything. No pain. No fear. Just clarity washing over me like a goddamn storm, ripping me open and tearing me apart.

I need it.

I crave it.

I'd sell my fucking soul to make it last.

But it doesn't.

I crash back to Earth and find an animal fucking me mercilessly hard, growling words into my skin with every thrust. They sound angry.

"You bitch." The world shatters into pieces when he pulls out of me and flips me over. I land on my back, blinking up at a devil crouched beneath a canopy of shadow. His eyes flash, his jaw clenched. "Do you think you can get inside my head, huh?" He grabs me by the throat and drags me closer, nudging my thighs apart with his knee. His fingers tighten, lifting my head just far enough so that

I have a view of him entering me. The way he slams in. The mess he makes.

Fuck. My eyes roll back into my head—it hurts that much. It's consuming. Swallowing.

It feels.

It feels…

It *feels.*

I lose my voice. I lose my fucking mind. He fucks my brains out. Fucks me in a way that any other john could ever dream.

I'm cold. I'm numb. And then I'm on fire—like the bastard doused me in gasoline and lit a match. My legs burn up. My hips. My cunt. My soul.

I'm dying. Rigor mortis sets in fast: I stiffen, every muscle clenched so tightly that I can't breathe. Maxim is the only part of me that's still alive. Still moving. Still fucking. Striking the same deep, distant part of me over and over and *over.*

Obliterating it.

I taste blood. I'm drenched in it, rocking back and forth, side to side, until I can't breathe.

And as my vision goes black, a single thought sneaks into my fading mind. For the first time in my fucking life, I feel nothing.

Maybe this is freedom.

CHAPTER SEVEN

He's gone. I know that even before I wake up. Maxim is gone.

And I failed. I got more than just blood on the sheets. Me. Sweat. Drool. I smell it all lingering on the air beneath a masculine musk. While he may not be in the room, he's not far. My body senses it, reacting to the cues my other senses can't pick up.

My heart is already racing even before I hear the footsteps. Heavy. Unsteady. I drag myself upright the moment he appears in the doorway, staring down at me with ice-cold eyes.

"I changed my mind," he tells me, sounding almost human once again. His pants are back up, but blood is splattered on the hem of his shirt. A few lethal drops, still dark. Still wet. "Get out. Now." He jerks his head toward the hall.

I try to move and everything goes *black*. My teeth clamp

over my bottom lip, trapping any noise I want to make. Words break through anyway. "W-what did I do?"

The pain isn't strong enough anymore. I can't think. Fear claws through my brain. Money. Money. MONEY. I bet that bitch came back and Daisy probably handed her the rest of the cash. Mikie was probably letting them all run fucking wild. Ainsley and Eric probably killed each other.

There are so many fucking *probably*s.

I shift my weight toward the end of the bed and the pain comes back. Like a bitch-slap. I can think for a split-second: *Run.* He grabs me before I can even move an inch. His fingers clench my right shoulder, tugging the arm nearly out of the damn socket.

I slide from the bed. Feel air. Hit the floor, all still held by him. Dragged by him.

"Get out."

I'm moving too fast. Burning carpet. Ice-cold marble. It's a shock when I finally land at his feet, the leather of his boots nudging my hip.

"Get out," he repeats, digging the toe of his boot into my thigh.

It hurts too much to stand. But I'm too terrified not to move.

I find a way to my knees as a compromise. My stomach keeps nudging the back of my throat. The room is spinning. My lips part and something warm trickles down my chin. Throw up? *Oh.* I glance down as the liquid in question drips down onto my thigh. Blood.

"What is it?" he demands. It's like I'm hearing him while my head's under water. He sounds loud, but not loud enough. "Money? Is that it? Or were you sent to me? To tempt me, is that it?"

I can barely follow what the fuck he's saying, but for the first damn time in my life, I don't want to lie. "Money," I say, the letters running together into one sloppy sound. "I need the money."

"Hmph." Maxim draws himself up to his full height. Some of the darkness in his eyes clouds over. He's thinking. I try not to look away, but my head's too heavy. He has to tilt my chin with the pad of his thumb. "Do you want to stay?"

My throat ignites as I swallow. *No.* "Y-yes," I tell him. "I need the money."

He frowns, stepping back enough that I can make out the door to the suite behind him. "Give me your hands." His own go to his waist, tugging something free from the belt loops. A strip of leather. Dark. Thick. "Your hands."

They shake as I raise them from the floor as high as I can. They barely go above my chest. Maxim has to bend in order to wrap the end of his belt around them and tug, tying them together.

"Stand up," he tells me next, watching as I crawl to the wall and lean against it to find enough leverage to haul myself upright. Inch by goddamn inch. Sweat breaks out over my forehead, gluing my hair to it and basting my skin. "Look at me." I follow the direction of the cool fingers that nudge my jaw. "Up, up. Good."

Black eyes watch me without a shred of empathy. Mercy.

"Do you want to stay?" he asks me again.

I just nod. I don't know why. It's the pain—it sucks my common sense away. It drowns my fear.

"Then stay here, just like this. All night. Until I come for you." He pets me just once, his fingers lingering in my hair. "You move so much as an inch and when I'm through, you won't be able to walk for days." His thumb caresses my cheek, the nail grazing the skin. "Do you understand?"

It hurts to suck in enough air to reply. "Y-yes."

"Fine." His thumb traces my mouth before he pulls away. With one hand, he yanks the door to the suite open—just enough so that anyone walking by would catch a glimpse of me. Just enough for me to run. "Goodnight."

He returns down the hall, heading deeper into the maze of rooms. Minutes later, I hear a door open and shut.

At least ten minutes of silence pass before I realize he's serious. Stay here, standing, all night. Just because he said so.

I leave, he'll let me go. I think it's what he really wants me to do anyway.

But I stay.

The kids are probably sleeping. Melanie probably crawled her way back into the house. Money. Money. Money. It makes the world go 'round. It makes my world stop spinning.

I stay here, like this, for *money*.

Not because of the pain. Not because of the fact that, even with my knees knocking together and my body weak with abuse and exhaustion, I can think. I can feel. *Everything.*

I submit to him for the money.

Nothing else.

He wakes up at the crack of dawn. I hear him moving; slow and lazy footsteps drifting through a maze of rooms. He's taking his time.

I desperately try to stay conscious even as my eyelids become too heavy to lift. I don't know how the hell I'm still standing, but I cling to whatever senses I have left until he finally approaches.

"You're here." He almost sounds surprised as he rounds the end of the hallway.

Warm fingers brush my chin, lifting it the moment he comes close enough. I can't make out his face clearly—

just those eyes: dark slits where a normal human's would be. He watches me struggle to obey his previous commands. My entire existence is a *struggle*, fighting to stay fucking upright.

I suck in air as he lets me go and my toes start to slide against the marble.

"Go get some rest." He loosens the belt before finally turning away, heading toward the room with the statue.

I hit the floor on my knees, choking on the air that floods in. Was I holding my breath all night? Or only for those tortured few seconds of his touch? I can't tell, and my body is already shutting down. My eyes are closed when his voice reaches me from the sculpture room—a warning.

"In your room. On the bed."

I tense up. He can't really mean to fuck. Not this early. Not again.

"Get some rest," he adds, as if reading my mind. "Though I suggest you move quickly, if you wish to sleep for long."

I don't even try to stand up. I crawl. On my hands and knees at first, and then just with my fingers, dragging myself down the hallway. It feels like I never move. Hours have to pass. I'm dripping with sweat.

I'm still in the fucking entryway.

Move, damn it. I give in to the pain, pushing through it, suffering every fiery jolt of it. I don't stop until my fingers strike wood. I have to rise onto my knees to get the door open, and I use the last bit of strength I have left to close it behind me.

My mind goes blank after that.

I DON'T JUST WAKE up. I'm resurrected—that's what it fucking feels like. Like that scene in Frankenstein: I'm electrocuted into existence by the cold reality that someone is in my room, standing over me, breathing their poison into my skin.

"Wake up," Maxim calls almost gently. "You've slept long enough."

Slept? It feels like I've had my eyes closed for only a few seconds before I'm peeling them open again. I can see him standing in front of me, his polished boots reflecting my appearance. Pale and broken.

He moved me onto the bed, I realize when the mattress shifts underneath me. I'm on top of the comforter, but it no longer feels as soft as it did before. It's crusty now.

"Wash yourself," Maxim tells me, running his fingers through my hair. "Lucius will arrive shortly. I will be gone for most of the day." He withdraws his hand and seems to float over to the door; my eyes blink too fast, turning the motion into a series of broken images, like a beautiful, terrifying slideshow. "When I return, I expect to find you properly dressed for the evening. Do you understand?"

"Yes..." My lungs heave to suck in enough air. "I understand."

In the twisted silence after he leaves, I try to remember how to make my goddamn body move. I flex my toes. My ankles. When I try to roll onto my side, I overshoot, falling off the bed altogether.

A bathroom is attached to my room. I find it by accident when I crawl to the first door I see and pull it open. There's a tub and a separate shower stall. Marble counters line one wall, and the floor is a cool, gray tile like the kind in the entryway.

I leave red over it with every inch I drag myself forward.

Hours. I spend most of them in the shower, trying to wash the blood away without studying the injuries left behind. I can feel them anyway. Every pinch, bruise, cut, and ache.

I find a towel and manage to pull myself upright, using the counter for balance. The bitch I find looking back at me in the mirror isn't worth the effort it would take to examine her. So I just run the faucet and swallow mouthfuls of cold water to wash the taste of blood from it. Afterward, I tear my fingers through my wet hair and dry myself. Once the towel is too red, I drop it.

When I open the door to the bedroom, a stranger is waiting for me, his arms crossed over his chest.

"It's all right, Ms. Marconi," Lucius says, stepping out from the opposite end of my room before I can panic.

"This is Mr. Bartley, the tailor."

As if on cue, the man opens a case at his feet. Rather than clothes, it has a bunch of fabrics inside of it. Silks. Satins. Lace.

Lucius watches while Bartley drags a tape measure around my hips, his eyes narrowed.

"We should start simple for now," Lucius suggests.

"Of course." Mr. Bartley nods and then packs up his case once he's taken my measurements. "I will send up a few items Mr. Koslov should approve of," he says before heading for the doorway.

"Thank you," Lucius calls after him. "Please send the doctor in."

He turns his attention to me and gestures to the bed. The bloody sheets are missing, replaced by a new comforter. White. Pristine. It's like slapping on a Band-Aid: You can't see the mess underneath, but you can still sense it.

"Have a seat, Ms. Marconi," Lucius urges. "It should be a quick examination."

The doctor is an old man with balding, black hair. He pokes and prods at me with a stethoscope and then draws blood—several tubes of it. Lucius steps forward to take them and then leaves the room, while the doctor grabs a sheet of paper from his briefcase and rattles off a million questions.

"How old are you?" he asks.

"Nineteen."

"Have you ever had children?"

"No."

"Any illnesses that you know of?"

"No."

"Use of any illicit drugs?"

"No."

I'm sure he's going to start asking questions about my fucking family history any minute, but he folds up the page after scribbling a final line down and shoves it into his briefcase. Just then, Lucius returns with several garment bags slung over his arm.

"These should last you until the custom work is finished," he says, setting them down beside me. He unzips the top one, revealing a plain, black dress with a lacy neckline. "Wear this tonight," he says, but I almost feel like he's warning me. *Please. Or else.*

"Okay."

"Until then, you may wear the clothing you brought." He gestures to my suitcase, which is still where I left it. He grabs it for me before I can attempt to stand on my own and fishes out a pair of sweatpants and an oversized tee shirt. Smart man.

He turns around while I get dressed and doesn't hesitate to offer his arm for support when I attempt to pull my pants up. I can tell he's not being nice for the hell of it. It almost seems routine to him, and once again, I have to wonder…

Just how many other *women* were there?

"You have a few hours before the evening meal," Lucius says once I sit back down, fully dressed. It's not hard to grasp the implication: *before Maxim comes back*. "I suggest that you get acquainted with the layout of the suite."

He pauses, as if waiting for me to say something. Ask something.

I finally manage to croak out, "Um, didn't you already give me a tour?"

He nods. "Yes. The rooms I showed you are the ones you are permitted in without Maxim's permission, barring the carving room, of course."

I flinch, remembering my punishment for exploring that particular area alone.

"I suggest you learn every inch of them," Lucius adds. "Know your boundaries. I will return sometime tomorrow."

He looks me over once, trailing his gaze along my damp hair and the bruises the sleeves of the shirt don't hide on my arms.

"Good day, Ms. Marconi."

When he leaves, I force myself to stand. Move. Walk. I take Lucius' advice and explore every inch of the suite that isn't behind a closed door. I learn my boundaries. This house must be a temporary one—someplace apart from where he actually lives. It smells different than it should. Too clean. Too *empty,* much like Maxim himself: perfectly fucked-up flawless.

Maybe that's what Lucius wanted me to realize: the level of control it would take for someone to live like this. With rooms organized by color scheme, in a home without an ounce of dust in sight. The devil is in the details, after all, and Maxim Koslov seems to take perfection to the extreme.

Only now am I starting to wonder why he would fish prostitutes from the street for sex.

"I only want to hurt you."

Rather than think on it too much, I keep searching. Keep moving. I wind up traveling the same three rooms over and over, memorizing the placement of every expensive piece of furniture. They all seem unworn and unused. Just decoration. I swear some even have the price tags still on them.

I run my fingers over the leather couch in the living room. It's too firm, having never been broken in. The pillows feel stiff.

The dress, however…

It's not new. Not really. I head back into the room just to be sure, running my fingers over the fabric. Someone wore it before I did. Maybe once. Maybe twice. Not long enough to really make an impression or truly call it hers, but enough times for her scent to sink into every thread.

After my stint at Penney's, I know a damn thing or two about borrowed clothing.

Biting my lip, I head toward the closet and go through the clothes again. I sense the same thing from every single fucking item. They've all been worn before, some more than others. By different women. Different ages. Sizes. I register at least twenty different body types before I force myself to step away and turn my focus to the bed.

It's the only thing in this damn place that doesn't feel used. No matter how many women he's paraded through this house, the bed—go figure—isn't as broken in as the closet. Not as many women have bled on it or slammed their foreheads on the headboard.

I wonder why. Though it's not like it's that big of a mystery. How many ran away after the first night? How many dumbass bitches came back for a second?

I try to wash my thoughts down the sink of the bathroom, scrubbing at my teeth with my toothbrush that tastes more like Ainsley than anything else: days' old sugar and cookie bits. I drag a brush through my hair without looking at myself. I dig my nails into whatever part of me they can reach whenever the panic manages to break through and threatens to ruin everything.

Money.

That's all that matters.

It's what makes the world go 'round.

I *need* this fucking money.

When I finally pull the dress on, it fits me a little better than the last one. It's clean as well, but I can still feel the traces of the woman who wore it last. She was taller than I am by an inch, with bigger boobs and longer hair to frame the scalloped neckline.

I bet she didn't sweat as much as I am now. She didn't bite her lip so hard that she bled and dripped blood into the delicate fabric. I know for a fact that Maxim never tore it off her.

He's home. I sense his arrival, even from this deep inside the suite. I hear the lock of the front door click followed by the thud as it slams shut. In the resounding silence, his voice rings out, cold and demanding.

"Come here."

I take two steps before I realize I'm barefoot.

"Now."

Fuck it. I risk meeting him wearing the dress and nothing else. I can't tell if he's annoyed by the fact when I finally find him pacing the length of the living room.

"Come." He jerks his chin and leads me into the kitchen. There, he directs me to stand in a corner while he drops a paper bag onto the counter and pulls out everything inside it. There's a hunk of fresh meat like the kind bought directly from a butcher, along with onions, celery, greens, and bread.

He seasons the meat and puts it into the oven with potatoes before starting on a fresh salad with the greens. The bread he slices carefully with a blade taken from a butcher's block at one end of the counter.

When he finally strolls out of the kitchen, I don't know whether to stay or follow. So I stay, driving my nails into their respective palms. Over. Over. Over.

"Kotyonok."

I spring away from the wall and find him in the dining room. He opens the drawer of an ebony sideboard, revealing a stack of ivory plates and a box of silverware.

"Set the table," he tells me before leaving the room again, probably to return to the kitchen.

My hands shake as I grab two plates from the cupboard. I set one at the head of the table and the other close by. I find fancy-looking wine goblets and add those as well. A fork. A knife. A spoon.

But I can't tell which size is needed—or what goes where. Shit. I never had to worry about it before. In my real world, setting the table meant throwing a paper plate down and grabbing the least filthy piece of silverware from the pile already in the sink.

I keep fiddling with my placement, moving each different fork and spoon around. I don't stop until I hear him finally come in. He chuckles when he sees my progress and drags his thumb along the edge of one of the goblets. Almost in slow motion, the rest of his fingers fan out, knocking it off the table so hard that it shatters on the floor. He swipes at the place setting just as easily, leaving only one plate behind. *His.*

"Remember, *kotyonok*," he tells me without bothering to explain what he means out loud.

He leaves the room again, and I drop to my knees, picking up the broken glass with my bare fingers. But I'm too clumsy. I grab the pieces too hard and cut myself. On my palm. My wrist.

I bleed.

My blood paints the shards of the broken plate as I pile the rest of the glass onto the biggest piece—but I don't dare leave to find a trash can to throw it away. So I wait, still on my knees.

When he finally returns, he's holding the steaming roaster with the cooked meat and veggies inside. He places it at one end of the table and returns with the bread and the bottle of wine. Without making himself a plate, he sits at the head of the table, reaching for his goblet with one hand. He spies me as I lurch to my feet and nods toward his plate. *Serve me.*

I grab the wine first and circle around to his corner. I tip the bottle and pour until his eyes flash, warning me to stop. Then I lift his plate and take it to the roaster. I don't know how much meat to serve, but I don't dare ask, either. So I cut my losses and slice off two pieces, trying to make them as neat as possible. It's only when I start to transfer them onto the plate that I realize my hands are still bloody. Still bleeding.

"It's all right, *kotyonok*," he calls from his end of the table. It's like he's inside my head, feeding off my fear.

I serve him a single potato and a few slices of onion. I drag the knife through the bread next and lift the cut piece without touching it with my fingers. When I set the plate down in front of him, Maxim eyes it carefully.

Finally, he nods. "Sit."

I start for the chair, but the way he shakes his head stops me dead in my tracks.

His eyes cut down to the floor. "Sit."

I drop to my knees beside his chair, feeling his fingers come to brush the top of my head.

Another chuckle rumbles from his chest, deeper this time. "Not here…" He seizes chunks of my hair, pulling me upright.

Through streaming eyes, I see him nod again. To the table.

I scramble to haul myself onto the edge of it, wincing as my body starts to throb. The pain isn't deep enough to help me think. I'm thoughtless as I watch him sigh and casually reach for his dinner fork.

"You need training," he says while palming a knife with his other hand. He stabs the end of it into his meat and starts to cut. Once he's sliced off a piece, he spears it onto the fork and brings it to his mouth. Those dark eyes cut up to mine, reducing me to slivers in the same damn way. Before I can react, he grabs my hand, smoothing out each finger to expose my ruined palm. His attention is given to every cut, every scar—both old and new. Carefully, his thumb traces a bleeding wound as his eyes drift up to mine again. "Do you know what you did to offend me last night?"

The way he says *offend*. My blood turns to ice. My toes curl. I can't breathe. Can't think. God, I need to think.

"I never want to offend you—"

"Do you know what you did?" His voice dips to that dangerous level. He's barely human now, seconds from becoming a monster again.

"No," I breathe. I breathe and breathe and breathe, but air never seems to fill my lungs.

"Oh?" He raises the meat to his mouth and takes a bite. "You orgasmed," he tells me after swallowing.

Self-preservation kicks in. My answer is automatic. "N-no I didn't."

"You *did*. The only woman ever to in these circumstances." He slices off another piece of meat and wipes the blade along my bare thigh. It's hot. I suck air in through my teeth at the burning sting. "Pleasure is one thing not addressed in the contract. In fact, it takes true depravity or true *skill* to do so while in agony. So can you tell me, *kotyonok*? What got you off?"

I don't know what to say. I don't even know whether or not to lie. Why?

I don't orgasm. Ever. That's what the fuckers who pay me for sex do. That's what Melanie does whenever she screws someone over. It's apparently what Maxim does while fucking me half to death—and it's something he thinks requires *skill* in my case.

The only defense I have is the truth. "I don't do that."

The knife lands against the edge of the plate, spraying steak juice over the table's pristine surface as Maxim laughs so hard that his head falls back. His eyes find me again a second later, but the longer he stares, the angrier he seems.

"Do not play games with me." His hand finds the knife again, allowing the tip to brush my thigh. Once. Twice. "What was it, hmm?" The blade teases the flesh above my knee. Beads of blood bubble up and drip down. Drop by precious drop. "The money? You can admit that. Maybe you think you can swindle more out of me than you've earned? Or something else?" He digs the blade in so hard that I jump and choke on a strangled cry. "Do you have something planned? Some game? Some trick? Some secret to get you off even while being used like a whore?"

"No!" Liquid spills from my eyes, hotter than blood. "I don't know—"

"It seems that you need a demonstration." With a sigh, he tosses the knife aside. His hand lands over my waist before I can react, pinning my back flat against the table. "Lie still," he warns.

His touch is like the IV they stuck in Melanie the last time she OD'd, dripping fear into my veins as he takes my thighs in either hand and drags me toward him. The hem of the dress rides up. My hip knocks his plate to the side, dangerously close to the edge of the table. My right elbow brushes the tip of the knife. His fork is in between my legs.

So is his mouth. Hot breath splashes against the inside of my thighs—the only warning before his tongue flicks out to graze my pussy. I can't even come up with a coherent way to describe it, just broken, random words. Wet. Hot. Strong. God, his tongue is *strong.* He batters me open with it, and I whine at the pain. Too much. Too rough.

I've heard about this. Never experienced it for myself. Never wanted to. Putting my mouth on strangers' cocks was bad enough. I never wanted any of their mouths on me.

Trapped beneath Maxim now, I know that my original fears were fucking legit. The things he does. The way he moves. Nibbling. Sucking. *Biting*—really biting down there. So hard that I see white. I can't feel. Can't think.

I just exist. As gross as it is, the slang for this act seems to fit now more than ever: He's eating me out. Piece by fucking piece. He growls at the taste of me, his nails piercing my skin, his teeth grazing my flesh.

It's awful.

It's incredible.

It's disgusting.

It's fucking insane.

"S-stop," I choke out even though I know that the plea means nothing. I can't refuse him. Can't say no.

Surrender leaves me paralyzed as my brain swirls with every lazy flick of his tongue. There is only one way out. What was it? Three words. *Happy? I'm...*

A wave of pain hits me all at once like a punch to the chest and my thoughts shatter. *Pain,* because it knocks me under. It sets me free. I can think. I can feel. I can scream. Really scream.

I'm flying.

I'm falling.

I'm drowning.

I'm crashing back down to Earth.

He doesn't catch me; he just watches me burn.

"*That* is an orgasm," he says while I blink up at the ceiling and listen to air wheeze in and out of my throat. "Do you remember now?"

I shake my head. That wasn't an orgasm. Not fireworks, or sparks, or the toe-curling, mouthwatering pleasure described in those fucking stupid-ass romance novels Melanie used to read—the ones Daisy does now, hiding them under her bed.

That was pain. That was death.

"Your cum." Maxim drags a thumb between my legs and holds it up for me to see through blurred, unfocused eyes. It's glistening. Wet. With blood. With something else. After a moment, he brings it to his mouth. "Sweet," he declares after his first taste. It's not a compliment.

Several more seconds pass as he stares, waiting for me to confess something. Come clean. Admit it: *I orgasmed.*

But I can't. I need to think. My fingers flex, rubbing against the open wounds on my hands, but my thoughts never clear.

I'm not sure exactly when it happens—but his face changes. Maybe it's after the tears already welling in my eyes fall faster. Or when my entire body tenses up in the face of his slow-building reaction. I've been hit before. Beaten. Slapped. None of those blows packed the punch of his rage.

I jump as he pushes back from the table without warning, rising to his feet. "Go to your room," he tells me, turning to the nearest window displaying a shadowy view of the city. "Lie on the bed. Wait for me."

I haul myself upright and nearly fall off the table in my rush to reach the door. I don't stop running—but I'm going in the wrong direction. My unsteady footsteps don't take me out of the suite like they should.

I'm in my room.

On the bed.

I'm waiting. He told me to lie down, so I do, counting the seconds that pass, trying to breathe. I can think at least. Fear acts like pain, swirling through my veins, making every breath feel white hot. Suffocating.

I can't move an inch. Not even as I hear him pacing in the other room. Fast. Faster. A violent crash echoes off the walls as if something was knocked over. Then another, followed by the chime of breaking glass. Again. More.

It's like a twisted fucking soundtrack is playing as he starts in my direction, bringing a wave of chaos all the way up to my door. A thud ricochets off something close by, resonating through the walls. I feel the vibration race up the bed, joining with the massive slam the door makes as it flies open.

Maxim took the knife from the dinner table.

The edge sparkles as he approaches the bed, step by step. "I know who you are," he says, his voice an unstable rasp. "So I suggest you come clean."

CHAPTER EIGHT

"Francesca Marconi," Maxim bites out as if reading off a piece of paper. "Age nineteen. A poor goddamn whore from Horn Hill. Her price is sixteen thousand." He chuckles to himself, and I have to crane my neck back to see his face: a twisted mask of rage. "Maybe it's the money that gets you off," he tells me, nudging my outstretched leg with his knee. "So cheap. So pathetic that you have to sell yourself to any man willing to pay for it. Or so you want me to believe." He drags his thumb along the knife. "Is that it?"

I nod, more tears spilling down my cheeks. "Yes. I-I need the money—"

"So you keep saying." He frowns, tapping the knife's edge against the mattress, inches away from either thigh. "But I'm not entirely convinced."

The blade drifts higher and my hand flies out to block the tip, but I don't dare sit up. I just breathe. In and out. Out. In. "P-please!"

"You have children. *Siblings.*" His eyes flicker back up to mine and the look twisting his mouth could almost be called a smile. "Did you think I wouldn't look into that? Did you think I would truly believe that this tight fucking cunt"—he gestures with the blade—"produced children?"

I can't breathe. My thoughts get harder and harder to grasp. No. God, no.

"There are six of them," he says, adjusting the blade so that the edge of it ghosts my hip, drifting down. Around. Up again. "Michael—"

"P-please." A retaliatory cut to my thigh can't shut me up. I don't even feel the pain. Just fear, all-consuming. "Please!"

"So then *tell* me."

Tell him what? I don't even know. I'm so fucking stupid. I left them alone. I left a sixteen-year-old in charge.

"Who sent you to me? Maybe I should ask Daisy-Rae?" Maxim wonders. "Or Oliver, Raymond, and Eric."

The knife dips into the flesh of my belly, slicing easily through the fabric of the dress, but the pain doesn't wake me up. It kills me.

"Perhaps, Ainsley?"

He digs the knife in deeper. His eyes never leave mine and I realize it now that this man…

He's a monster.

He could have killed them.

They could already be dead.

I couldn't even protect them.

"S-stop. P-please—"

"You move so much as a goddamn inch." His hands go to his fly, ripping it open, freeing his cock. "And I'll kill them. *All* of them, one by one in front of you. I will make you watch. Do you understand?"

My body shuts down as he takes a condom from his pocket and pulls it on. Fear pins me in place and I let it. He could cut me, burn me, do whatever the fuck he wants to me.

But not to them.

"You have five seconds to tell me the truth. Who do you work for? Who planted you, hmm? They have to be powerful, because you are fucking *convincing.*" He waits, and my eyes go to his knife. One. Two. Three. Four. He sighs, tossing the blade onto the floor. "Fine. Spread your legs."

I have no choice but to obey. My legs drag themselves apart—just enough for him to force his way in between. I cry out when he enters me. It's not like before. My body resists. It hurts, it *hurts*. And, for the first time, the pain doesn't take me away. It doesn't clear my head. It breaks me. Thrust after thrust.

This isn't hooking. No amount of money is worth this. It doesn't sink in until I hear him groan, his hands positioning my hips so that he can pin me flat with his weight, filling me up, ripping me open—getting off on the pain he causes. I can't hold it back. I scream. I cry.

The same way I cried for Melanie. The same fucking way I cried the first time I peeled my pants down for fifty fucking dollars. The tears that only cutting myself can hold back, along with that sickening thought I can never seem to escape: *I failed. I failed. I failed.*

All at once, the world shifts as the unbearable pressure inside me relents.

"Look at me." Warm fingers grip my chin. "Look at me!"

I have no choice. He hovers over me, still wearing his shirt, his eyes piercing through my skull. That anger is gone. All I find is…

I don't fucking know.

"Look at me," he growls before I can even start to turn away. His hand cups my chin so hard that my teeth clip together. The motion tilts my head from the bed, forcing me to meet his gaze. For what feels like hours, his eyes search mine, hunting for something—but finding nothing. Slowly, his mouth falls out of a snarl and back into a cold, emotionless line. "I will never, *never* hurt your family. Do you understand?"

Tears drip down my chin. I'm still crying. All this time. I thought it was background noise—maybe he left on a television somewhere that was playing a horror movie where the dumb bitch being murdered just couldn't fucking stop whimpering.

"Look at me." He tightens his grip and shakes, making my body jolt over the mattress. "Do you understand? You never have to fear that from me. Do you understand?"

He's lying. I can't believe him. I shake my head, stammering, "Don't, don't, don't, don't—"

He stands up. His hand goes for the knife and he throws it onto the bed. When I lunge for it, he watches me, his eyes cold, his arms at his sides. He doesn't move when I curl my fingers around the handle.

I point it at him, and he turns for the door.

"Come."

I don't want to. I *have* to; my body makes me, obeying the warning tone in his voice. I step off the bed and hit the floor, blinded by more goddamn tears. Fear and pain— my brain doesn't know which drug to give in to.

Strong hands curl beneath my shoulders, ignoring the way I'm flailing around with the knife. When he hauls me upright, the blade falls. I'm in his arms a second later, being carried through the rest of the suite and out into the hall.

"Trust me." He brings me down a stairwell and out into a dark, enclosed space. A parking garage?

The sounds I make echo off the walls of it. Choking. Gasping. Gagging. Screaming. Strangled sounds.

The next second, Maxim approaches a black car and shoves me into the back seat. As the car begins to move, I'm thrown forward by the momentum, smacking my head off the front seat so hard that I taste blood. My vision blinks in and out. I see lights. Colors. A million different sounds flood my ears: sirens, shouts, laughter.

"Look at me." Maxim stands over me, his body leaning in through the open door.

The car stopped moving. It's dark wherever we are. After two days in his suite, I almost don't recognize the shitty street corner I find myself on when he hauls me out of the car and makes me stand beside him.

My house gleams in all of its fucked-up glory. The lights are on. Even from here, I can hear Ainsley screaming— but before the fear can bite deep, I make out what she's saying. Curse words. Apparently, Eric got to her stupid-ass dolls again.

"I cannot say the same for you, but I will never hurt *them*," Maxim tells me, his voice trickling into my ear, louder than anything else. "Do you understand? Say it."

I can't trust. However, with this man standing so close to the only shit I've ever worked for, I can't afford not to.

He drags me closer to him as my legs shake and my knees knock together. His arm goes around my shoulders, pinning me to his side—not for support.

"I…" My voice is a rasp. He has to lean closer just to hear me, his lips like ice on the side of my throat.

"Say it."

"I believe you. You won't hurt them."

"And?"

I inhale a ragged breath. "Only me."

Satisfied, he turns back to the car, and I climb woodenly inside, fastening my seat belt this time.

The tears still fall as he pulls away and returns to the high-rise. From fear or pain?

I can't tell.

He doesn't carry me this time. I'm left to limp up the stairs behind him, and he's already in the suite when I finally catch up.

"Get some rest," he tells me, his eyes between my legs, tracking the blood dripping down them. He closes the door behind me, watching as I cling to the wall in order to pass him. "I know now," he says as I start down the hall.

I look back and find him rubbing his jaw with the pad of his thumb. "I know now what gets you off. Masochism." He frowns like it's a dirty word.

One that I don't know the meaning of.

Sighing, he tells me, "It's the pain you enjoy."

He turns away before I can tell if that annoys him or not.

Honestly, I'm not even sure which answer I'd want to find anyway.

A KNOCK on the door wakes me before the sky has turned gray around the edges. I haul myself upright, clinging to the nearest support for balance: the bathroom door. Once I'm on my feet, I blink, slowly bringing the rest of the room into focus. The bed is across from me, the blankets rumpled but still mostly intact.

I didn't sleep on it.

I didn't sleep at all.

In a daze, I head for the closet and find the clothing Lucius gave me hanging inside it. I pull on a dress at random, too exhausted to examine it. Day? Evening? It's white, I think, with a lacy collar. Once I peel the black dress off my body, I fold it and leave it on the floor, unsure of where else to put it.

When I stagger into the bathroom, I look at myself in the mirror this time. Really look.

What a pathetic bitch.

She watches me with bloodshot eyes, her hair a mess, her bottom lip bloody and swollen. She's so damn pale. Her pretty fucking dress can't hide the bruises on her arms. Or the cuts. The blood.

But the injuries aren't the worst part by far. Her greedy fingers seek them out, rubbing the open sores, chasing every bit of clarity like an addict with a high. Pathetic.

I turn away from her and attempt to wipe myself clean. When I drag a washcloth between my legs, I can't silence a gasp. A groan. A scream. *He broke me.* It's not even an understatement: I feel like a goddamn virgin again. A virgin who took a sledgehammer first.

Biting any noise back, I wash myself the best I can, and the rag comes away bloody. I set it down and rinse my hands in the sink. I don't know why, but I sit on the edge of the bed afterward, waiting, rather than leave the room on my own. His footsteps return not long after, stalking a lazy path to my door. He tests the handle first, almost as if he expects to find it locked.

"*Kotyonok?*" The door opens without resistance and Maxim steps in.

My entire body reacts to his presence; I sit straighter, my gaze honed in on every inch of his bulky frame. He's wearing gray today, slacks with a long-sleeved shirt. His eyes drift over in my direction, but rather than command me to change, he jerks his head toward the end of the hall.

"Come."

I trail him into the kitchen, where he makes breakfast, the same way he did dinner, pulling the ingredients from another brown paper bag. Eggs. Bacon. Herbs. He works silently for a few minutes before seeming to remember I'm here. When he looks back at me, he's still holding a frying pan.

"Set the table, *kotyonok*."

He cleaned the dining room, or someone else did for him. It's pristine again, every piece of glass swept from the floor. There's even a new plate to replace the broken one, and I set it in front of Maxim's chair, placing a fork and spoon on either side.

My fingers twitch in and out of fists as I stand in the corner and wait. Almost an hour later, he re-enters the dining room to place a pan of eggs and a tray of bacon onto the far end of the table. The moment he directs his gaze at me, I jump forward, ready to pile the food onto his plate.

When he beckons me to sit, it isn't on the table this time. He nods to the chair beside him and draws it closer once I obey, his hand gripping the sliver of cushion right between my legs.

"Today is your last day with me," he tells me before starting in on his eggs. He stabs a chunk with his fork and raises it toward me. "Open."

I pry my jaw apart to accept the food he shoves onto my tongue. My stomach growls: I'm hungry. I'm starving. The food goes down before I can even taste it. Silently, he offers me more. A piece of bacon. A bite of biscuit. All of it eaten directly from his hand.

"Have you had enough?" he asks when he finally sets his fork down.

When I nod, his eyes flash darker.

"Do not lie." He lifts the plate and holds it out to me. "Get more."

My fingers shake as I add another pile of eggs and a few more strips of bacon to the plate. This time, he feeds me all of it, commanding me to open on cue and demanding with his eyes for me to swallow. Obeying him is like rewiring the nerves in my body so that they no longer take their cues from my brain. Only from him.

He stands when I choke down the last bite and gathers the dishes himself. The next few seconds pass while I watch him wash the plate in the sink and then carefully dry each utensil before putting them away. He wipes his hands after he's done and directs his gaze toward my feet.

"Go put on some shoes."

I scramble toward the bedroom, sensing him on my heels. The moment I open the closet, he's behind me, observing which shoes my hands brush over. He makes a low sound in his throat when I thumb a pair of gray flats, so my fingers jump to a pair of black heels instead. Nothing—a sign I take as silent permission. I rush to pull them on, surprised when he lowers his hand to help me back to my feet.

"I will not fuck you tonight," he announces as the nail of his thumb lightly brushes my palm. "So you can stop clenching your thighs together whenever I look at you."

My cheeks heat up as if the observation were a slap. I look down. He's right: My knees are kissing, my legs shaking. I didn't even realize I was doing it.

"I'm sorry—"

"Sorry?" His mouth takes on a different shape than the stern line I'm used to: a slant. The next second, he drops down on one knee.

Fear rockets through my veins as both of his hands go to the skirt of my dress, winding it up to my waist, revealing the pink cotton underwear I stole from Melanie.

"Hold," he commands, and my fingers race to keep the wad of fabric in place.

I can only stare while he reaches into his pocket and pulls his knife out. The blade hisses as it springs free, stabbing at the air.

"Don't move," Maxim warns as he brings the edge of it against my inner thigh, right below my entrance.

A whine trickles out of me as the blade edge kisses my flesh, slicing a single line no longer than a fingernail. I still feel it bleeding, drop by drop.

"*Now* you have something to apologize for," he tells me as he tucks the blade into his pocket and stands. "Or you will if you get so much as a drop of blood on that dress." He lets the threat hang there while motioning for me to lower the skirt. Then he jerks his chin. "Come."

I follow him back into the hall, squeezing my thighs together with every step. The skirt of the dress swishes out, away from my legs—but he cut me too deep. Blood drips down.

"This way, *kotyonok*." His voice leads me into the sculpture room. The one of the woman is gone, replaced by another block of stone: a darker-colored gray this time. After grabbing a smaller chisel and a hammer from the selection on the wall, Maxim sets to work, hammering the shit out of it while I watch.

Within minutes, I can see why he wanted me to wear shoes. Bits of stone and dust go flying, coating the floor. I back myself into a corner, just watching him. I scan the rest of his body before my brain can register what a bad decision it is to take my attention off the weapons in his hand. His shirt ripples beneath the repetitive motion of chiseling. It starts to bunch up around his waist, revealing a sliver of something that isn't skin: black fabric. An undershirt? Maybe.

But, when he lunges into another blow, the cotton shirt shifts. I can make out the ridge of something along his abdomen, like the top of one of those girdle belts Melanie uses when she likes to pretend she didn't pop out seven children. Going off the muscle shaping the rest of his body, I don't think he's hiding a beer gut.

I drift my gaze back to his hands and let myself become hypnotized by the way he hacks away at the hunk of stone. With anger. With rage. For hours and hours and hours.

In the process, he makes something beautiful: a face, delicately roughed out in the middle of the shapeless chunk. Just like that, he's beaten life out of nothing with only strips of metal and his goddamn fists.

Am I impressed?

Horrified?

I don't know as he finally turns to face me, wiping his hands on a rag snatched from the table along the wall.

"Come here." He reaches out when I'm close enough, kissing my cheek with the pad of each finger. The bite of a probing nail erases any gentleness from the gesture. My heart starts to race, even before he nods toward the wall. "Turn around."

I do, feeling his eyes scan the back of my skirt, hunting for blood. I'm holding my breath.

"Lucius gave me the results of your testing last night," he says. "You are clean."

That should be a good thing. Especially considering what he did with his mouth last night. But, once again, I get the feeling that he isn't happy. Just irritated. Confused. I'm beginning to realize that a puzzled Maxim is a very dangerous thing.

He clenches his jaw and seems to chew over the words he wants to say. "Most women in your position are not."

I flinch at the thought of it: him fucking and sucking a million different women, infected with god knows what.

He laughs as if seeing the thought cross my brain the moment I think it. "I know what precautions to take. A man with my tastes cannot be choosy." The laughter dies off. "But you are young," he adds, frowning. "You are clean. There are other men who could pay regularly for sex should you know where to look. You haven't."

He pauses as if waiting for an answer, but I don't know which one to give.

Maybe that I've been there, done that. No amount of money is worth my pride—or so I used to tell myself.

"I've had women prettier than you come to me before," he says. "With tighter cunts than yours. Women who suck cock better than you could dream." He drags his thumb across my cheek in a gentle caress. "I've fucked them harder than I have you. I enjoyed them more. None of them lasted the week." He takes a step forward, urging my head back so that I meet his gaze directly. "You will not last the week. Get on your knees."

I sink without breaking eye contact, obeying the command he doesn't issue out loud. *Look at me.* One of his hands fists itself in my hair, holding my head in place, while the other tackles the clasp of his pants.

My heart slams against my rib cage as I crouch in a layer of dust while he pulls out his cock, already hardening, and aims it toward my mouth like a bullseye. I open. He rams in, deepthroating me without warning this time.

I choke. I gag. I breathe in through my nose and suffer through it. He groans with every inch he claims—but I'm too sore. Too raw. He can't fit himself in all the way, only getting half of his length in my mouth at one time. He finishes anyway, grunting out.

It's only when I feel the first spurt of cum hit the back of my throat that I realize he didn't bother with the condom this time. My throat clenches up on instinct, trying to spit him—*it*—out.

His hand comes from nowhere, the fingers pinching my nose shut, his voice a husky, hollow rasp. "Swallow it." He thrusts again. Another hot burst floods my mouth, threatening to spill from my lips if I don't take it down. "All of it. You lose a drop and you will be *punished.*"

The tone of his voice chills me to the core. So I gulp, gagging with him still in my mouth, fighting to swallow everything he gives me. All of it. His fingers tighten with every attempt, his breaths fanning my forehead. "That's it. Fuck, take it."

He thrusts so hard that I see black, and my throat woodenly jerks to accept the final load he has to give. He doesn't make me savor the taste at least, but I know better than to let myself throw up when he finally wrenches himself out.

I hit the floor on all fours, breathing in. *In. In. In.* My stomach lurches, pissed off and full. It's something I've never done. Ever. Something dribbles down my chin and I swipe at it in a panic. Drool.

"That was just a taste," Maxim says above me. "The next time I fuck you, you will clean me of every drop."

My body jumps at the mention of fucking. I can't move. I just watch his shadow flicker on the wall as he steps over me and heads for the door.

"I want you gone after midnight, if I don't return before then." He cocks his head for one last glance at me. His eyes settle over my hips and narrow. "In fact, I *will* return," he adds, "to administer your punishment."

I follow his gaze to the front of my dress and feel my heart sink to the pit of my stomach. A tiny pinprick of red has seeped through the fabric, but I don't move, even after he leaves. I just lie here, counting my heartbeat. Too fast. Too slow. Faster.

The room's dark by the time I finally decide to run. Escape. I go back to the bedroom first, even though I don't plan on taking the suitcase. I just stare at it, Melanie's shit in a place she would love. Would it bother her, having her brains fucked out every night?

Probably not. It wasn't like she had much left anyway.

I back myself into the hallway, closing the door behind me, and take a step toward the entryway. My only way out. Freedom.

But something makes me turn, and I follow the hallway deeper into the suite, taking the path Maxim's footsteps do whenever he storms away after leaving me half conscious and bloodied on the bed. They lead me to a closed door at the very end of the hallway. My fingers shake as they grip the knob and twist it open.

I see black. Everything, from the walls to the floors, is the same shade. So is the massive bed placed against one wall. The pillows, the sheets. The lamp shades. The wardrobe in the corner. The doors leading off to either the closet or the bathroom.

All of it is black, with no ounce of color other than the silvery glow of the light bulbs.

I thought my room was creepy with its closet of borrowed clothing. But it, at least, seemed lived in, even if for only days at a time by numerous people.

This room is a crypt. It has that heavy, stale air the show floors in furniture stores do: completely untouched. Unlived in. My house has more signs of Melanie than this room does of Maxim. The man isn't just fucking insane. He's a goddamn ghost.

I can't reach the front door fast enough. My fingers pry at the handle, wrenching it open. Then slamming it shut.

Stay.

Go.

Run.

My head aches as it tries to process several different options at once. He knows where I live. He already threatened my family once. The fear that has grown since the moment he first ordered me down to my knees spills over. It rides a single thought I don't want to face: *He'll kill me.*

And I need the money. Money. Money. Money.

Rent is a black hole I am only now beginning to climb out of. One month here could give me enough money to scrape my way out of debt for good—or long enough to breathe. Think. Do something other than fuck, cheat, and steal to get by. This money could give me *hope.*

Most of his women lasted only a week, but I need a month. One fucking month.

You need to leave, a part of me urges. But it seems to know the same thing I do.

I can't, and he finds me there an hour before his deadline, still standing in front of the door.

"You've made up your mind," he says coldly, his gaze sweeping me over from head to toe. "If you continue to ignore my generosity"—he steps over the threshold, leaving the door open behind him as his hand cups the side of my face—"I will no longer extend it. Leave."

He gestures to the open door with a wave of his hand and even steps aside to let me pass.

I don't move. "I need the money." It hurts to say it, worse than any thrust he could ever inflict on my throat or my pussy. Knowing how pathetic I am hurts. It's the only kind of pain I'd rather suppress than feel.

"Fair enough." He reaches back to close the door behind him and steps in farther, cutting into my personal space. He smells funny: like spice. Like food. He must have eaten somewhere else.

My stomach grumbles.

He laughs. "Hungry, are you?" His hand leaves my chin, goes to my throat. "My seed wasn't enough to satisfy that greedy little mouth?" He cradles my windpipe, still brushing my jaw with the pad of his thumb. "Let me discover for myself just how greedy the rest of your body can be."

He steers me back. Back into the living room, shoving me onto a firm surface. The couch. I tense while he nudges my legs apart with his knee before his hands claw at the front of the dress.

He rips it up. Off. I wait, panting and half-naked, while his eyes trace out a small path up and down the length of me. Down my throat. Between my breasts. Over my stomach.

"Lie back for me," he commands.

His body is stone against mine, crushing me against the leather. His lips trace the line of my throat and then part slowly enough for me to feel his teeth nip at my flesh before they sink in.

"You're fucking sweet," he grits out once he releases his first bite. Again, he doesn't sound happy. Just angry. Just hungry.

He bites me again. Harder, this time. On my shoulder. My collar. Lower…

I breathe out sharply when his breath fans my left breast. His fingers come up, cupping it. Squeezing while his thumb brushes the nipple.

The things I feel…

It's all pain. My throat goes dry. Each touch ripples through me like a pulse, jolting all the way down to my pussy. Stronger. Faster. More.

"You enjoy that?" Maxim wonders as he seizes my nipple between his thumb and his forefinger and pinches again. "My desperate little *kotyonok*?"

He does it again. Harder. Punishingly.

My next inhale turns into a gasp.

"You do." He hovers over me, his tongue swiping. Licking. Another bite.

Oh god.

My fingers grip the couch, fighting for enough leverage.

He licks again before sucking a nipple between his teeth. Then he bites down.

My head flies back, striking the rim of the headrest. My pussy is on fire.

And he does it again. So hard that I can taste the pain. I see it. Feel it: It's like steel, thick, immovable. The surface doesn't have an ounce of give, even as my fingers twitch against it. His chest? If so, the theory of him having a beer gut goes *bye-bye*: He is solid muscle. At least until I feel something softer underneath, stretched too taut to be skin. Elastic?

"Don't."

His tone alone warns me to make my hands fall—but not fast enough. My punishment is a bite so deep that it breaks the flesh. I can't even suck in enough air to scream. I just writhe, choking on agony, trapped at his mercy.

"Your blood is sweet too," he muses, capturing a bead with his tongue. "Sweet and greedy like the rest of you."

He watches it continue to fall, seeping around my nipple. Several tiny, weeping ridges circle it—the imprint of his teeth.

I'm on pins and needles when he starts on the right. He's rougher with his tongue, grinding my nipple into a sensitive, burning point. My body jerks every time he touches it. Looks at it.

I can't even stand to feel him *breathe.*

I nearly thank God out loud when he finally draws back, but his hands go tightly to my hips, sinking beneath the waistband of my panties. I shiver as he tugs them down, eyeing the ravaged flesh of my pussy underneath.

His eyes cut up to mine, narrowed, glowing. "You're fucking *weeping* for me, *kotyonok.*" He raises his hand so that I can see his glistening fingers.

With blood, I tell myself when my eyes don't bother to focus. *Nothing else.*

Nothing else.

A ragged shudder racks my body, ripping the thought away. His fingers are back, running along my inner thigh, grazing my pussy, slipping inside. He groans. I gasp, struggling to *look* as he growls the command. But I can't. My head is too heavy; he's moving too slowly.

"You like this?"

I don't. I can't think. I—

"You *like* this."

A nail grazes the sorest part of me and the reaction resonates like an electric shock. Muscles I didn't even know I have cramp up and tense. My nerve endings explode. And there's clarity. Brief. Harsh. It's like a whisper of calm through the chaos of my mind.

I see him clearly for a split second. I smell him. Taste him, his breaths fanning the skin of my throat. A muscle in his jaw twitches. What feels like a thumb brushes me open, making way for a longer, thinner finger.

I say something. Something broken and forbidden that earns me a sharp pinch on my hip. The pain is almost worth it as the fire building in my blood gets a drip of gasoline to feed it.

"More?" Maxim wonders, his voice harsh, shattering against my skin like broken glass.

I didn't ask for it. I know I didn't. I couldn't have.

He gives it to me anyway. His thumb rams in to join the first finger. Thick. Full. But not full enough.

"I would tear you apart with my cock tonight," Maxim says as a watery, broken sound trickles out of my throat. He growls in response, swirling the pad of one of the searching fingers along my inner walls, making them shake. "So delicate you are."

The pain is still there. Still screaming through my system. He's right. He'd break me. Rip me apart. Tear me open.

"And yet the thought of it"—another searing thrust and brutal caress—"seems to make you even wetter."

He laughs. It's too loud. Insane. Each booming chuckle ricochets off the inside of my skull. I try to shake my head. I don't want it. I'm not...

His fingers spread and I go silent. Limp. My body starts to rock with the force of each rough, bruising thrust. He won't use his cock, but he'll fuck me just as violently with his fingers. And somehow I feel more. Too much. He's pinching, twisting, touching, taking, tasting.

Fuck.

I see lightning as the pain hits me all at once. It's so sharp, it drowns me. Desolates me. This is all I am. All I know. Fucking and being fucked. Right into oblivion.

But it doesn't last. He pulls the fire away just when I'm about to tip over the edge. Lose it all. When I finally blink my vision back, he isn't laughing. A frown shapes his mouth as if it'd been chiseled there, beaten in with every sound I made.

"I've given you enough for tonight," he tells me, sliding his fingers free, ripping away my only lifeline to sanity.

My thoughts cloud over. Can't think. I'm forbidden to move—but my hand jumps anyway, the fingers grasping at the air.

"You want more?" His voice… I've never heard it so thick. It's like he's breaking every word off of stone—hammering humanity out of the monster he really is. "Say it, then. You want more." He snaps his fingers, shining, bloody. "Beg."

I don't want more. I shake my head, biting my lower lip.

He steps back, starts to turn.

I whimper. It's the only sound I can make. Not words. I can't say it.

"Do you want it?" He steps forward, bracing one knee on the cushions of the couch beside me. His fingers come to circle my throat, tilting my head back so that I'm forced to stare into those swirling black holes he has for eyes. "How badly do you want to come?" His fingers sweep down, catching a swollen, bitten nipple between them. "Do you need it?"

Fire licks through my veins, but it's nowhere near strong enough. Harsh enough. I *need* more.

"Y-yes."

When he bears down, I can't hide the scream that rips from my throat. It's too soft. Too damn close to a moan.

"Then fucking ask for it—"

"P-please."

His eyes disappear, narrowed into slits. The next second, he's on his knees, his hands on my hips, dragging me forward. His mouth catches me.

And my body does the screaming for me. It explodes. Ignites. Blows up.

Kaboom! It's a scramble to reassemble myself in the chaos. Nothing in the world compares to his tongue. It's soft. Strong. Licking. Sucking. Breaking. Breaking. Breaking.

This time, I don't get just a taste of clarity. I get a full fucking dose. My thoughts go so clear that, for the first time in my life, I don't feel anything. No fear. No pressure. No stress.

Just *nothing*.

The relief is almost enough to soften the blow when I come crashing back down, face-to-face with Maxim. His lips are wet, his eyes glowing. I can't move, even as his tongue flits out to graze my cheek.

"What I wouldn't give to fuck you right now." His tone is a warning. A threat. "To teach you just what a mistake you've made. To make your body regret every ounce of pleasure you stole from me."

He grinds his hips into me and I feel his erection, straining and heavy. Fear eats away at the pain. At the same time, it fans the flames higher.

"But not tonight." He runs his wet fingers through my hair and then pulls away, rising to his feet. "Tonight, I will have mercy on you."

He sounds too soft—way too gentle. I'm almost fooled until the moment he reaches into his pocket and draws a knife out. I swallow hard at the realization that it's a different shape from the one he normally carries. A leather sheath covers a blade that stretches nearly the entire length of his palm. The handle is thicker, almost as if it'd been carved to fit his grip alone. Casually, he tosses it into the air and catches it by the covered tip. The handle gleams, a dark polished wood. My eyes have trouble focusing on it, even as he crouches on one knee and drags it along my inner thigh.

Mercy? That fucking word taunts me as the cool tip of the handle grazes up and down my flesh, inching closer and closer to my pussy with every stroke. Just like that, my head clears. I'm on the razor-sharp edge of clarity. Literally.

"I would cause damage if I took you with my cock," Maxim says in a husky rasp, almost as if to remind himself of that fact while the front of his pants bulges and strains. "But, if I let you rest completely, *kotyonok*, it would be nearly impossible for you to take all of me again."

I inhale raggedly as the knife handle grazes my outer lips.

"It's happened before. I need to make sure that you remain…stretched."

Tears burn behind my eyes. I blink them back. They sting even worse. I can't help it. My knees twitch, aching to slam together and never let him in. As if he can read my mind, one of his hands palms my right thigh.

"I suggest you don't resist," he warns as the wooden edge bats the rim of me once. Twice.

Air leaves my lungs as it slams in without warning, stretching me apart in ways his fingers could only dream. He doesn't hold back, thrusting so deep my vision fades. The fullness is second only to his cock. I can't do anything other than gasp for air, my fingers flailing for leverage. My nails grip the leather couch, digging in, tearing.

"Let it in," he growls as he thrusts again. Harder. Slower.

I don't have any choice but to relent. Muscle and flesh are battered and stretched into submission. Rather than push the handle out, they tug, pulling it deeper, allowing the invasion.

The gruff sound Maxim makes at the back of his throat betrays his satisfaction with every awful inch. "That's it."

I'm so damn sore. So raw. I barely hear him. It takes all of my energy just to breathe. My chest heaves, almost as if mimicking every inch of me he claims with the knife handle. In and out.

I think the violation is the worst of it. Being fucked with a knife—it can't get any more humiliating than this. But he proves me wrong when the callused, heavy pad of his thumb drifts up to the flesh above the knife. Teasing.

Rubbing. One brush and every fucking muscle in my body tenses. The knife feels bigger, impossibly huge inside me. My skin feels hotter. *Fuck.*

"Look at you. Even this gets you off," Maxim remarks, his voice low and gravelly. Angry.

A part of me tries to react to it and muster up a shred of fear. But my nerves are mush. The motions of the knife churn my insides into a hot, boiling ball of sensation. I can't focus on anything else, just this. His thumb is too fast. Too slow. I'm floating. The angry, gravelly sound that revs up in his chest when I arch my hips sets everything off. Like a match.

But right before it hits the nearby puddle of gasoline, he douses everything in a fire extinguisher.

"No." The handle twists, its curved edge pressing against my inner walls, driving a howl from my lips. "Remember this lesson, *kotyonok.*" He withdraws the handle, leaving me gaping and open. But the hazy warmth in my stomach turns to dread when I hear a dangerously soft hiss. My eyes flutter down and I find him sliding the sheath off, revealing the blade. "You come only when I say you can," he tells me. "Do you understand?"

I nod. I don't think I'll ever fucking stop. Not until he puts that knife away.

"Do not move."

He lowers the blade between my legs. Icy kisses of pain graze the swollen lips of my pussy. Teasing. Prodding. I wish I could say that it feels worse than the handle. I wish. I wish.

"I don't think you are ready for this just yet," Maxim admits before he pulls the knife edge away. His eyes flash a heart-stopping shade of black. "Yet."

I try not to let myself dwell on the promise in his tone as he stands, re-sheathing the blade. Weak with relief, I just collapse into a puddle against the cushions, watching Maxim's features become a blur.

"Our time is up," he tells me before retreating down the hallway. "You can go."

I want nothing more than to do just that. Leave.

But despite how hard I try, I can't summon the strength to even lift my head.

CHAPTER TEN

I'm ripped from oblivion by the howls of someone ranting about their decapitated baby.

"You killed her!" the thin, high-pitched voice accuses. "I'm going to have Frankie beat your ass when she comes back—"

"She probably won't come back," a boy counters. "Maybe she's glad to be away from *your* fucking ugly face—"

"Hey! Knock it off!"

The trickle of authority sounds out of place in a voice not quite deep enough to have come from a grown man. I blink my eyes open as I hear the staircase tremble a second later. A shadow flickers along the wall. Tall. One of the older kids. They reach the bottom step before they find me. Going off the scent of stale corn chips, I think I'm on the couch. Ainsley always left crumbs between the cushions.

"Shit!" I startle at the voice and my vision returns in bits and pieces as Mikie comes closer, a backpack slung over his arm. "Frankie? You scared the shit out of me! Hey, you okay?"

"Fine." I turn my face toward the musty cushions, curling the rest of my body into a ball. I'm not wearing the dress. I know that even before I look down and find that someone dressed me in my sweatpants and one of Melanie's tee shirts. The word *juicy* is written in pink glitter across my chest. Considering how much effort it takes to suck in air, I doubt I was the one who did this. Which brings up another interesting question: I can't remember how I got home. Or how I even left Maxim's suite.

"Where the hell did you even go anyway?" Mikie asks.

I force myself to turn in order to watch him cross over to the front door. My suitcase is beside it. Even from the distance between it and the couch, I can still make out the thick, black envelope sticking out from the front pocket.

"What's this?"

"Don't touch it!" I croak, flinging my hand out as if to physically shove him back.

"Damn, Frankie." Mikie lowers his hand and backs away. "Okay, okay I won't. By the way, I tried calling you when you were gone."

I flinch. The phone. I left it in my bag. By accident. Maybe…

I'm lying. Deep down, a part of me knows the truth I don't want to face: I wasn't given permission to use one. So I didn't.

Guilt hurts worse than whatever my body feels.

"I'm sorry," I force myself to blurt out. "I was…busy."

"You sound like shit." He opens the fridge and grabs a bottle from the very back, holding it up to the light. "I replaced your stash," he says before dropping the bottle onto the sliver of cushion beside me. "Here."

I'm too tired to ask or care how he got the booze or how he knew about my stash—let alone what happened to the bottles already there. I lift the bottle and let him rip the cap off for me, but I'm so fucking tired that he has to lower the rim of the bottle to my mouth before I can even take a sip. I manage to gulp down three times before he pulls it away and sets it on the floor.

In the cool, gray light wafting in from the window, he looks more like Melanie than ever—the only one of us who really does. He has her eyes, which are known to shift from blue to green. Her chin. Her laugh. Her dimpled smile. He doesn't wear it as much as she does though. Not now, at least.

"Frankie…you're bleeding," he whispers as the staircase trembles again beneath several different footsteps.

Shit. I cut my eyes over to the busted armchair in the corner of the room. There's a blanket draped over it, the remains of someone's toy fort. Mikie races over to grab it and barely has me covered by the time the rest of the kids make it downstairs.

"Shut the fuck up," he hisses when Ainsley cries out my name. "She's sleeping. Everyone get your shit and let's go."

He sounds so stern. So damn mature. And no one argues as they march across the living room, fishing backpacks and homework from under chairs and on top of tables. The front door opens, the screen door slamming against the outer siding like usual.

One by one, the kids stream out. The only argument is put up by Ainsley, but Mikie silences her with a hissed, "You can talk to her after school." When the very last kid has jumped off the porch, he says to me through the open doorway, "I'll try to stall them after school. Long enough for you to put makeup on or something. I don't want Ains seeing your face like that…"

I reach up, feeling along my lower lip. It's sore. Pulsating. Swollen. When I peel my eyes open again, Mikie is gone and a Teenage Mutant Ninja Turtle blanket is covering the worst of me. My toes stick out from under it though, crusted in dried blood.

It takes me hours to crawl upstairs and into the bathroom. I shower. I scream. I drag a brush through my hair and even steal Daisy's makeup from under the sink to do what I can to minimize the dark circles under my eyes.

My bitten, cracked lips are a hopeless cause though, so I come up with a lie. I tripped and bit myself there. Once.

Twice. Oh, and I fell onto glass and cut my hands. And my back. I smoked too many cigarettes and burned my throat. I'm limping because…

The lie loses water after that.

It's not like I have the time to put it into practice anyway. Somewhere between searching Daisy and Ainsley's room for spare clothing, I wind up on a bed. So I sleep. For hours. Ages. I'm barely conscious when they come home, screaming and shouting and racing up the stairs. Someone shakes me. Tries to talk.

But I still can't move.

I can't speak.

I just exist, trapped within a cocoon of pain.

I wish I could say that it is an awful way to feel—more than enough of a reason to never go back to Maxim Koslov. But the truth is…I've never felt more at peace.

Never.

FEAR IS A FUNNY FUCKING THING. Three days without him is like someone spending the same amount of time wide awake. It's fine at first—hypothetically speaking. You regain the energy your nightmares sucked out of you. You might even feel hopeful—maybe you won't have them anymore. Maybe this is the start of something different.

A brand-new day.

A brand-new reality.

But as the hours wear on, each second steals a little more of your sanity away. The worries you can't escape gnaw at your psyche like buzzing flies, growing louder and louder. Eating you up.

Money. Money. Money. Moneymoneymoneymoney.

You sing yourself that tired old lullaby, but the sleep doesn't come. Your eyes stay open, seeing every goddamn thing with no shadows to block it out. You can only find snatches of peace again when you doze off, pinching yourself, cutting yourself. Slicing your inner thighs open for one taste of clarity.

But it never lasts no matter how desperately you chase it like an addict begging for a high. You even begin to crave it. The silence. The freedom. The fear. Suffering through a nightmare starts to look better and better in contrast to the thought of having to go another hour painfully aware.

Then finally, you nod off and the nightmare takes over, flickering around the edges of your conscience. It swallows you up before you even realize you've fallen asleep.

And you begin to understand that the only thing more terrifying than the monster you find lurking within it is the fact that…

You've missed it all along.

Because the fear feels more familiar than anything else.

A BLACK CAR comes for me on the third day at the ass crack of dawn, right after the kids have left for school. I have a frying pan in my hand, in the middle of scraping burnt eggs out of it from Daisy's attempt to cook breakfast.

The moment I happen to glance out the window, it falls out of my hand, landing over my left foot, and I can't even cry out. I just move. It's like my body's on autopilot. I grab the suitcase waiting by the front door and snatch up the envelope sticking out of it for the first time. It's heavy. I wind up shoving most of the cash into my stash with a note for Mikie to use it while I'm gone.

Before I head out, I make sure to slip the cell phone into my pocket, and I already have the front door open by the time Lucius mounts the top step leading to the porch.

"Ms. Marconi," he says with a nod. "Mr. Koslov is ready for you, should you choose to return." He pauses as if he's waiting for something, not actually climbing the last step to reach me.

He expects me to say no.

But I say, "Yes." My hands shake as I drag the suitcase behind me, close the door, and lock it.

Lucius only stops to take my suitcase from me and pack it into the trunk before ushering me into the back seat.

The driver takes off. My heart starts to beat again and the sleepy feeling that clouded my thoughts for three damn days eases up.

I *wake* up.

It's a rude, violent return to awareness.

The first coherent thought to cross my brain is, *What am I doing?*

Far too soon, Maxim's high-rise appears on the horizon before I can figure out an answer to that question. I'll go with the safe option: *money.* That's right. I'm here for the money. Nothing else. No one else. The money. Money, money, money, money.

"Ms. Marconi?"

The car's stopped. Lucius is standing out on the curb, holding the door open for me. I swallow hard and follow him out before he can voice the question lingering in his eyes: *Are you sure?*

"You'll meet him alone today," he explains instead after retrieving my suitcase from the trunk and gingerly placing the handle in my grip. "His request."

Something about that wording makes me flinch. It takes me a second to regain control of my body, but I'm still numb when I start forward, toward the main doors of the building. Somehow, I manage to pass through them without turning back. I reach the elevator the same way and ride it up. It comes to a stop way too soon, leaving me no choice but to cautiously approach the lone entrance at the end of the hallway.

My fingers curl into a fist, but I don't even have to knock. I'm just inches away when it flies open to reveal the monster lurking behind it, his hair hanging loose to frame his face, his eyes darker than I remember.

"It's *you*. Lucius didn't say…" His mouth twists into that dangerous frown of confusion as he beckons me closer with a wave of his hand. "Strip."

The fact that there is no one else around somehow makes the command seem more degrading. My heart starts to pound, hammering against my rib cage. To stall, I lean my suitcase against the wall and unbutton my jacket first, which I borrowed from Daisy. Before I have to wonder what to do with it, Maxim holds his hand out.

His fingers clench the fabric, bringing one of the sleeves to his nose. "This doesn't belong to you," he declares after a sharp inhale. Then he tosses it away, somewhere inside the suite. His eyes seize on my shirt next. It's Melanie's, tight and low-cut the way she likes. On me, it's shapeless, and it doesn't take much effort to slip it off, over my head.

Dark eyes track my every movement, and I shiver. Go fucking figure. Almost a year of fucking strangers should have hammered into my own psyche that I'm no delicate, innocent little flower. *He* does this to me, breaking every single wall I've built up simply by impatiently flexing his fingers. My teeth start to skewer my lower lip as I hand the shirt over, and he sniffs that item as well. Frowns. Tosses it.

"The rest," he commands.

I strip down to nothing while he observes every piece of me. My pants next. My bra. My sneakers. Finally panties.

Those he inhales more than once, grinding the fabric between his fingers, growling at whatever he senses. Whatever he tastes. "These belong to you," he tells me before balling them into a fist and shoving them into his pocket. "Come."

He steps aside and I follow him into the suite, shivering as he closes the door behind me.

The layout hasn't changed. It's just as dark. Just as cold. Just as perfectly clean as ever. Though on second thought, the couch is off-center by a hair. There's a dent in the middle, so slight that no one would ever notice it. But I do.

"You're shaking." Warm fingers graze the length of my spine before fanning out along my collarbone. "Having your regrets already?"

I want to say yes. Regret. I *need* to feel that. It would be better than this. This ache. This itch I don't know how to scratch.

One of my thumbs inches toward a cut on my wrist and rubs until the skin burns. The brief sting does nothing to clear my head, and Maxim frowns when I don't answer.

"Are you that desperate to earn more money for yourself, *kotyonok*?" He cups my chin, forcing me to meet his gaze.

I nod. It's the only thing I can do.

In response, he flashes that dangerous half-smile. "How much are you worth?"

We both already know the answer. After all, he said it himself.

"Sixteen thousand." I have to drag the words out. It sounds like such a pathetic number when said out loud. Even Melanie would have a higher price tag. "Sixteen—"

"Enough." His thumb presses down over my mouth, sealing my lips shut. "I will not fuck you tonight," he tells me, easily switching topics as his eyes drift down my naked torso. "Not while you smell like—" He leans in and sniffs—a dangerous omen. I'm left paralyzed as his features quickly twist into that terrifying trifecta: narrowed eyes, crooked frown, and slightly clenched jaw. "*This*."

It's a sin in his world: smelling like burned eggs, and toast, and tears, and crayon wax, along with Ainsley's vomit from two nights ago when she ate too much pizza and threw up. Like life. Like reality. Free from him.

"I need to wash you," he adds. It's a lethal promise. A threat. One that tightens around my throat like a noose as he turns and heads down the hallway, commanding with his posture alone that I follow. He doesn't lead me to the bathroom attached to my room, but into another I know instinctively to be *his*.

It's bigger. The floors are granite, the walls polished wood. A massive bathtub is sunken into the center of the floor— the kind of thing Daisy would kill for, lined in black marble and adorned by silver fixtures that sparkle like knives.

"Get in." He jerks his chin toward a series of steps built into the sides of the tub.

I reach the middle of it by the time he switches the water on and it pours in like a waterfall from a single faucet.

"Sit," he snaps.

I do, tucking my calves beneath me so that I'm on my knees, facing his direction. A heartbeat later, warm water laps at my hips. Too warm. Scalding.

Maxim just watches as steam bubbles up and my skin turns red. It's like I'm boiling alive, and it's not even the temperature of the water that's doing it. It's the look in his eyes. For a rare, brief moment, the man is an open book: He didn't want me to come back. At the same time, he never really thought I would.

I guess he expected to train a new toy tonight, and that forces him to compile a new lesson for me on the fly. His thumb drifts up to stroke his chin as he thinks. After a second, he frowns—a bad fucking sign. Whatever he's come up with could probably be summed up in one word: *punishing*.

Once the water reaches my stomach, he shuts it off and approaches my end of the tub, seemingly satisfied. Relief creeps into my muscles as he removes his boots and tosses them aside. His socks go next. Finally, he rolls each pant leg up to reveal the toned calves underneath and then enters the tub, sloshing water with every step.

"Give me your hands."

My throat contracts with a frantic swallow. His voice… It's too deep. Too soft. My brain has no input as my body reacts solely on instinct. I wrench my hands into the air, extending my arms toward him.

Slowly, his fingers entwine within his belt loops, working the strip of leather loose. I'm unprepared for just how roughly he wraps the length of it around my wrists. It's like he wants me to feel every variation in the leather— every groove in the surface. My sick mind skips ahead, wondering which end would hurt more if he ever decided to use it like a whip.

The sad part? Something tells me he one day will.

"Keep them like that." Grunting, he pulls the ends so tight that I lose sensation in the tips of my fingers as the leather bites in. But the physical pain doesn't even come close to whatever I feel as I watch him cut a lazy path through the water to snatch a rag from a marble countertop.

When he returns, he snaps the length of it into the air to command my attention. Once. Twice. While I watch, he wets the end of it in the water and drags it along the tops of my shoulders, bathing me of everything that isn't him.

"I'm disappointed," he tells me once he sees the scabbed-over marks his teeth left on my breasts. The fingers of his other hand trace one of them, pressing down on the skin hard enough to make it bleed. "You heal too quickly."

If only that were true. My skin feels nothing but raw as the rag travels to the worst of the injuries. Rubbing. Twisting. Ripping them open again until the draining water turns pink. Red. I'm already gagging on smothered cries when he lowers the rag, swiping my hip in scarlet, painting me with my own blood. Marking me as his.

Finally, the cloth slips from his fingers and splashes somewhere beside me. I almost think it's over. That I'm clean enough to satisfy him. But he's still frowning as he scans my torso.

"Open." He curls his thumb against my lower lip, using it to pry both apart when I don't obey fast enough.

One-handed, he undoes the clasp of his pants and slowly peels his boxers down like a magician in one of those TV shows building up to his final and most mind-fucking trick. Watching me like this—bleeding, bound—has made him harder than I've ever seen him. Or maybe it's the fear he's breathing in from my skin. The knowledge that I know, deep down, coming here, back to him, was wrong.

"I'll make this quick," he tells me, cradling my jaw in one of his massive hands.

I'm not sure why he warns me, though I brace myself anyway, and he doesn't hold back, seeking out the tightness of my throat on the first thrust.

Four days of rest and silence weren't enough to prepare me to take him. My throat closes up, my gag reflex going haywire with every forced inch of me he claims. His eyes glow brighter at the resistance, his touch harsher. Brutal fingers rake through my hair and gather chunks of it to control every bit of him I'm allowed to take—and how much I have to swallow.

All of it.

Too much. My nose starts to burn. He's in too far. Too long. I can't breathe, so I choke, feeling warm, salty wetness trickle from my nostrils before he finally tugs himself away, grunting with the effort.

"I told you not to lose a single drop," he warns.

There's no use in trying to explain. My body has become his tool. His *weapon,* betraying me just to get a rise out of him.

A literal rise. I don't know how it's even possible. Maybe he was never really finished after all. He's still hard, straining, erect. He doesn't take his eyes off me, even as both of his hands grip the base of his shaft. He tugs. Strokes. My face heats up as I turn away, staring down at the reddish water instead.

"No," he growls. So I have no choice but to look up. Stare. Watch.

He handles himself roughly—almost as roughly as he handles me. He grinds his fingers along the underside before making long, brutal strokes with his fist. I jump as my pussy clenches in sympathy. Sympathy…

"This excites you. Watching me?" He makes it sound like a question, but there is no right answer.

Once again, I've confused him. I shake my head, and he frowns as his fingers slow their assault.

"Stand up."

It takes me five tries to without slipping on the bottom of the tub. Once I'm on my feet, Maxim approaches slowly, still stroking his cock.

"Is that so?" His free hand reaches between my legs, tracing the outer rim of me along the damp, dripping skin. *That's* the only reason why I'm wet down there—the water.

As if to prove me wrong, he curls a finger, stepping in closer, teasing my entrance with it. He's almost gentle at first, grazing the skin in a featherlight sweep. I don't even expect the moment he rams the entire digit in too deep.

Too easily. God, I can feel his nails contrasting with the thicker shape of his knuckles. The sound he grits out into my ear as he feels me quiver beneath his touch? It's inhuman.

The next second, my trembling knees are forced to support my weight alone as he steps back. I lose my balance and land sideways at the edge of the tub. My nose is in water, sucking in a lungful. I can't even move before my hair is used like a leash: first to push me down, then to yank me upright and shove my body against the steps.

My vision clears and I find him hovering above me. The look in his eye issues the command he doesn't say out loud. My legs spring apart as he palms his cock and grinds the tip through my pussy, rubbing me open.

"Wait." I gasp at the air, struggling to form words. "I thought—"

One brutal thrust sends water sloshing around us. Warmth sears through my pussy, but nowhere near as deep as it should. I glance down and see why: he only managed to fit a fraction of himself inside me.

"You don't think," he tells me, lifting my hips from the water so he can ram in another inch, so hard that I see stars and shadow. White. Black. Yellow fucking fireworks. "You never think. Not while you are with me—"

Another thrust and my eyes roll back. I swear I can see the inside of my skull, my brains being whisked to mush.

"*I* think. You listen. You obey. You feel."

Feel…

I wish he would just fuck me—I could survive that. I could keep my brain intact the way I have with any other man. Any other john. I knew how to save myself, just as long as I *couldn't* feel.

But he's on a mission to destroy me. Sex is a tool to him; he controls every touch, the same way he beats sculptures out of stone. The only difference is how he speaks with every battering thrust, growling the words in a language I don't understand. Sentences. Phrases. God, they sound like promises. Brutal, lethal promises. And then he switches to English.

"…string you up. Make you regret. So tight," he grits out in a throaty rasp. "Fuck, so fucking greedy. *Too* tight." His thumb catches the top of me, rubbing, pinching.

Fuck. Sparks shoot through my body. My knees bend, inching closer to his waist, hugging him, sensing the ripples of every muscle as he drives himself in. In. In. Deep. Deeper. I can't breathe. My body turns into a vise, wrapped around him, tightening.

"You're coming," Maxim hisses before biting my neck in punishment, drawing a noise from me I can't classify. "Without permission."

Thwack! The flat of his hand flies out to strike my hip so hard that sparks dance before my eyes. I'm going to bruise, and the added pain hijacks whatever reaction had started inside me. I grit my teeth against a scream. It's too tense. Too hot.

"You will come when I say you can." He wrenches himself out and flips me over, forcing me up onto my hands and knees.

In this position, he goes even *deeper*. Harder. The friction doesn't just burn—it sets me on fucking fire. I inhale the flames, mindless and numb as my body explodes around me.

But he never lets me fall over the edge. Just when my thoughts start to clear, another slap stings my hip. My ass. A nip on my shoulder. A pinch. A deeper bite. He anticipates every hit of clarity my body seems to be chasing and slaps it away, further out of reach.

I'm on the edge. I can't possibly feel any more swollen and greedy. But he pulls out right when my inner muscles start to spasm and drags me by my hair over to the sink.

"Look at yourself." He's strong enough to cup my hips and lift me right off the floor, spreading my legs so that I can see our reflection in the mirror. His straining cock weeps from the tip, dusky and swollen. The pink flesh it aims for doesn't look anywhere near wide enough to take all of him though. He's too damn big. "Watch." He jerks his hips and sinks inside me anyway. Up this close, I can see his muscles cord as he works his way in, battering through any resistance. "Watch your face change," he growls into my shoulder as I bite a cry back. "Those fucking greedy eyes."

I look away, staring at the floor when I feel another slap on my hip.

"*Look*."

The woman he's fucking is a goddamn whore. Her brown eyes are glazed over. Her mouth is open, releasing tiny gasps as her body jerks back and forth. She's too pale. Too needy. Too desperate. When I look into her eyes, she's not thinking about money.

When he's in to the hilt, my arms go limp, and without the support, my cheek hits the counter. I lie here, letting him ride me. Use me. Fuck the living shit out of me. Too much. Not enough. I'm shaking, my mouth watering, my toes curling.

Maxim is all I know. Inside me. Around me. Huge, relentless, and powerful.

"Beg for it, *kotyonok*," he commands before I even know what it is my body seeks. It craves it. Needs it. If he doesn't—if I don't—I'll go insane.

My inner muscles clench down, gripping him so hard that I feel every pulsing ridge of his length, every strained and throbbing vein. All of it slammed up inside me.

All mine.

"Fuck, not yet." He punishes me with his full weight, bearing down, ramming in before I can savor a full dose of clarity. "Beg."

"Please—"

His hips swivel, and this new pain takes me higher than the fucking ceiling. Higher than any hit of heroin or cocaine. So damn high I won't ever come back down.

Ruthless, Maxim sinks his nails into my hips, extending the pain, making me float. "I need to hear you say it."

Hearing him *need* anything from me—it shatters my mind. My soul. I'm pieces of a person falling at his feet, and he shoves them back together however he sees fit. Any control I had fucking disintegrates. A stranger takes over my throat.

"Please, please, please—"

"Please what?" He pets me, running his hand along my hair. The gentleness contrasts with his next bruising thrust. I'm a rag doll at his mercy, cherished and abused all at once. "Speak to me. Beg. *Umolyat.*"

"Let me come."

He bellows out more words I don't understand while using his thumb to reach between us. Flicking. Rubbing.

Shit.

My back bows, arching my hips into him, riding him, every last thrust. I can't speak. Can't moan. Can't move. I suffer his invasion. I let him break me into pieces. When he comes, the pressure spills over as he yells out, biting into my shoulder. I scream. Sob. Whimper.

And then all sound dies off as he jerks inside me, spilling everything he has left to give. So much. Never enough.

I'm numb when he pulls out, leaving a warm, thick trail down my inner thigh. Only now does it strike me that he didn't wear a condom.

"*This* is how it will be from now on, *kotyonok*," he tells me, his voice gruff as he uses his grip on my hair as leverage to pull himself upright. "I am clean."

I'm not brave enough to even question that.

Other fears cloud my thoughts, washing away the oblivion he fucked me into. Like the fact that I'm not even sure if I'm up to date on birth control—the one selfish thing I always tried to save money for. "I'm not—"

"I had you injected with a serum on your last night here," he says. He looks at me expectantly, and I have to assume he means some kind of contraception. "It is effective in only a few days. You will not get pregnant. That is the one thing you never have to worry about me inflicting upon you."

He steps away from me, his cock somehow still semi-hard, and I don't know what shocks me more. The raw *pain* in his voice? Or the fact that he had me injected with a hormone-altering drug without my permission? *Or* the fact that he came inside me and I'm not disgusted. I don't *feel* disgusting.

Just exhausted. Sore. Empty.

"Don't break on me now."

I feel his breath on my neck, his fingers gliding through my hair. He grabs a lock of it and tugs my head until I face him from over my shoulder.

"You aren't finished yet." He nods to his cock, which is still glistening.

Oh. I suck in air to find the strength to sink to my knees, twisting around.

He palms his cock with one hand, angling the tip of it toward my mouth. "Clean me off. Every last drop."

I part my lips, creeping closer on my hands and knees. Watching me, he narrows his eyes, his breaths coming faster. Harder. I don't swallow him whole this time. I lick. Every drop. Every bitter, strange, musky flavor that coats him.

He lets me work quickly without having to savor—for now. His posture doesn't relax until my tongue captures the very last drop. By then, he's already erect again, dripping precum from the swollen head.

"That's enough." He runs his fingers through my hair, pushing me away from him as his fingers curl around his shaft, stroking it again.

I just stare as a tortured groan builds up in his chest. His knuckles turn white and his cock jerks, spraying cum into the air. On me. I know better than to flinch away. I just sit here on my knees and take every last spurt, letting him paint me with them. Mark me.

He growls when the final drop splatters my chin, satisfied, and adjusts his pants, redoing the clasp. "*Now,* you are clean," he tells me, snapping his fingers for me to stand.

When I do, he removes the belt and leads me to the door of my bedroom. The moment he opens it, I know that something has changed. The bed is still there beneath the black canopy, the white sheets neatly made. But attached to each post of the bed frame itself are four black strips of leather secured by delicate silver strings.

Chains.

CHAPTER ELEVEN

Maxim approaches the bed and gently thumbs one of the straps open. It looks like a bracelet: a bracelet with a metal clasp.

"Come here."

I have no choice but to step toward him, swaying on my feet. I can't tear my eyes away as he lifts the cuff, allowing me to see every inch: the silver buckles to lock it shut, the silken lining, the sturdy, ebony leather around the outside.

"Lie down."

The mattress creaks beneath my weight, definitely softer than before. The slight change proves more than anything that this bed was rarely used for fucking in the past. One night and our bodies have already made an impression in the padding.

"Lie back."

Impatient, Maxim arranges me himself when I don't move quickly enough. He pushes me down and steers my ankles toward the foot of the bed. When he seizes the wrist closer to him, he secures it into a cuff, snapping it tight. He moves toward the ankle next and binds it too, his jaw clenched in concentration while his seed dries over my skin. When the other ankle is secure, he finally turns his attention to my last remaining limb. I sense his hulking shape from the corner of my eye, watching me writhe as much as the bindings will allow.

He curls his fingers around my free wrist and lifts it. "You so much as think about getting free and you will be punished," he tells me as his thumb brushes the back of my hand. "You will wait for me, until I return. You will think of me. Only me. Do you understand, *kotyonok*?"

"Y-yes." I have to force the word out.

Maxim grunts, unconvinced. His fingers lift my chin, tilting my head back against the soft pillow beneath it. "This is not punishment," he says softly, nodding to my outstretched limbs. "This is a gift. I want you to savor how good it feels to be clean."

I hear him drift down the hallway, his footsteps steady and sure. Hours pass, though I sense him wandering the rooms of the suite: eating, sculpting, doing whatever else it is he does as the hours trickle away deep into the night. My muscles are already cramping from misuse when I finally sense him approach my door again—but he continues past it, toward that room at the very end of the hall.

Left without a distraction, my mind plays a dangerous game; it pictures him inside that lifeless, black room. How he might strip down in the silence and climb into the massive bed alone. Oddly enough, I can't imagine him actually sleeping. Just waiting, lurking beneath the covers.

Fear alone doesn't explain why my stomach bunches into knots at the thought of it. His body vulnerable, his eyes shut, that face set like a statue's.

My loose hand twitches, the fingers flinching against my stomach. He told me to think of him—only him. By the time I lose sensation in my toes, I'm in danger of breaking that one rule.

I have to pee. So badly that my stomach hurts, my legs straining against the cuffs, desperate to clamp together. I know better than to wet the bed. The only way to buy more time is to use my fingers, sliding them down between my legs, rubbing the flesh of my pussy.

Only like this can I remember my task: think of Maxim. Just him. Only him. Nearby. Around me. Inside me. Always.

But the wrong reaction takes over; the air I breathe in becomes laced with gasoline. Every touch is a match, fanning the flames higher. I writhe, trapped and helpless, a slave to the motions of my hand. It's like I can hear him inside my head, commanding me, taunting me.

Only me, kotyonok. Only me…

I gasp as the doorknob to my room twitches—then the door flies open. A monster draped in shadow lurks behind it. His eyes hone in on mine, bathed in the glow of the hallway as he inhales sharply, tasting me on the air.

I drop my hand, but it's too fucking late.

Muscles ripple beneath his skin as he steps forward, his fingers flexing. "I said you could think," he tells me softly. "I never said you could touch what is *mine* without permission."

Fear paralyzes me. I just lie here, staring up at the ceiling beyond his head as he approaches. I don't dare look at him directly. I can't.

"Do you need something from me?"

The question makes me flinch as his nails tease my tender flesh. Need… My pussy clenches.

"I—"

"Spit it out," he scolds, but the anger isn't there. He almost sounds amused.

"I have to use the bathroom."

He nods and turns toward the cuffs on my ankles. I hold my breath as he slowly—*slowly*—undoes the clasps on the right one before deliberately moving over to the next.

"Give me your hand."

I raise my free wrist, but my stomach drops when he lifts the empty cuff. I know better than to argue, even as my bladder threatens to rip its way out of my stomach. He snaps the latch closed, but then his fingers grab the chain, following it all the way to the nearest post of the bed frame. I crane my neck to watch him unhook the loop securing it, using the free length like a leash. He lets it fall and dangle beside me over the edge of the bed. Then he casually strolls around to the other end and does the same to the opposite cuff.

"Up, *kotyonok*."

I can't scramble to the edge of the bed fast enough. I stand on throbbing legs, but I hesitate to move without permission. Permission he doesn't give, not even when I sense him beside me, his breath heavy on my neck.

"Put your arms behind your back."

I obey, wincing as they throb at the awkward angle. Cold metal brushes my hip as he gathers up the dangling chains, linking them together before grabbing the loose end. "Come."

He nudges me toward the bathroom and watches me sit on the toilet. Just when I'm about to let my body relax, he shakes his head…and then leaves the room.

I never knew my body could be in this much pain. My eyes sting, filling up with moisture no matter how quickly I blink it back. I curl my toes, kicking them against the floor. My nails claw at my wrists. Control. *Control.* I need to keep it.

But that's impossible. Maxim has all of it.

He doesn't go far, just into the bedroom before the closet. I can see his shadow sway against the wall as he thumbs through clothing and shifts hangers. When he finally returns and nods, I nearly cry with relief.

The desperation to pee is enough to wash away the embarrassment of having him watch. Having him listen. When I'm finally finished, he comes up beside the toilet and gestures for me to stand. I expect him to unhook at least one of my wrists so that I can wipe myself.

Instead, he does it for me, snatching a wad of toilet paper and dragging it between my legs without warning. Once. Twice. There's nothing sexual in his touch, which somehow makes it worse. Once done, he flushes it and washes his hands in the sink.

"Kneel," he tells me, jerking his chin toward the tub.

This one is smaller than the other. There's only enough room for me to sit lengthwise, so I tuck my knees beneath my chin. He runs the water lukewarm this time, letting it get as high as my breasts.

I don't know what to expect when he leaves me here and returns with a rag and a bar of soap. It smells: spicy, flowery. Roses?

I don't ask and he doesn't say a word as he runs the rag over my skin, cleaning every inch of me. My back, my shoulders, my belly, my hands, my face. He even wets my hair, combing it with his fingers before lathering it up with shampoo. As the water drains from the tub, he towels me dry while I sit on the edge of it. Then he dresses me in the clothing I assume he got from the closet.

I can tell, even before he begins to drag a pair of black, lace panties up my legs, that these items aren't like the others. They've never been worn. They don't carry any other smell. Just his. Just mine.

The bra matches the panties—black lace—and I find myself staring down at it as he adjusts the straps. I've never owned a full set of underwear before. Not one cut from the same cloth, tailored to fit only me. It's not really a good feeling to know that I'm the first one to wear these clothes, including the red sleeveless blouse and the black skirt he dresses me in next. It's like being the first convict to sit in a brand-new electric chair.

More people will come after me. Even as the various pieces are tightened to fit my body, it's not out of love or kindness. I won't ever own a single goddamn stitch.

"Stand, *kotyonok*."

When I do, he directs me over to the mirror and somehow finds a brush to tackle my hair with. He's surprisingly gentle—surprisingly good. He tames my damp, wild curls in no time and slicks them back to reveal my bruised, bitten neck. I'm stupid enough to breathe out a sigh of relief when he finally unhooks the cuffs from my wrists and leaves them open on the sink.

It isn't until I follow him out into the living room of the suite and spot the black box resting on the couch that I realize my mistake. It's square, with a red ribbon draped over the top. Maxim opens it for me, displaying a dark leather circle on a scarlet pillow within. A chain of gold dangles from a hook set in the center of what looks like a longer cuff at first.

Make that a collar.

"Raise your chin." He lifts the collar and sets the box aside. He loops the leather around the back of my throat, fastening the clasp without tearing his eyes from mine. "Beautiful." He steps back, fingering the length of golden chain. It nearly reaches my waist, swaying back and forth with every move I make.

"Come." He starts for the entrance of the suite, pulling the door open as I stagger at his heels. When I'm close enough, he snags the length of golden chain to steer me after him. There is no one in the hall beyond his suite to witness or in the private stairwell he takes to the garage.

Once we reach that infamous black car, he ushers me into the passenger's seat this time, fastening the seat belt over my chest. I just stare as he circles around the car and takes the wheel, sitting tall in the driver's seat.

It's overcast and dreary, I see once he pulls out onto the street. Rain falls, splattering the windshield, creating a strange, muted backdrop as the car drifts through the thick of traffic. He never switches the radio on. Never speaks. The silence seems to suit him just fine, so I take his lead and keep quiet.

I try not to wonder where we're going—keyword being *try*. Dread sinks in any way, making my throat contract against the collar as my breathing picks up speed. Wherever he's headed, it's out of the city, over a bridge. I watch the buildings grow progressively smaller and then disappear altogether. In the blink of an eye, we go through a tunnel and enter a world of shadow and trees. Swaths of land pass by, but after maybe twenty minutes, Maxim turns onto a deserted stretch of road, following it deeper into the woods—though, despite all appearances, this place doesn't seem too far off the beaten path. The road is paved, for one, and the farther down it we go, the less untamed the wilderness seems and more beaten into submission.

I don't know what to make of it all until I finally catch sight of a structure at the top of a hill. I must gasp or make some other noise, because I sense Maxim's gaze on the skin of my throat.

"You are impressed, *kotyonok*," he says with the hint of a laugh.

Maybe I am: a building rises from the foliage as if formed from the shadows. Given that, before this, my idea of *classy* consisted of the nicest department store in the mall, I don't have many words to describe it. Just that it's big. Beautiful. Foreboding—the shiver racing through my body insists on that part. Made of black stone, the place resembles a mansion, but I doubt that its true purpose is just as someone's home. Maybe it's the way Maxim is dressed: a sleek black suit and a blood-red tie. I doubt he's on his way to a house call.

So it's not *just* a mansion. With every inch we travel toward it, its silhouette looms bigger, square in appearance when seen from the front. I think it's at least three stories, stretching nearly double that length over the expanse of the hill. If Dracula suddenly developed Maxim's flair for sleek, modern design, he'd probably build this place. Turrets twist at the sky, while huge glass windows reflect the muted backdrop of the forest, adding hints of emerald to the ebony façade.

The entrance, by far, is the most breathtakingly elegant thing I've ever seen. It makes the front of his high-rise look like a shack, no better than mine. Stone columns frame a black door, its edges trimmed in gold. A path made of dark stone leads to it before forking into a massive circular driveway. Maxim stops the car in the center of it, and a man dressed in black comes from nowhere to take his keys and drive it off, presumably to park.

"Come." When Maxim takes the length of my chain, I don't have a choice but to follow him up to the front of the mansion and then inside.

Three adjectives march across my brain to describe what I see: Impressive. Breathtaking. Clean. Make that four, as a shiver dances down my spine and conjures up another term: *Cold.*

The entrance reminds me of him in every way, from the granite floors to the steel-gray walls. The design holds the same layer of icy intimidation. Three silver Xs placed above a curving archway across from the entrance don't provide any clue as to what this place represents. Neither do the two other archways composing the rest of the circular space, each leading off into different directions. Left. Right. Forward. I can't see much of either path: just darkness stretching on.

"This way." Using my chain like a leash, Maxim leads me through the right one and into a room with an open floor plan.

I blink, taking in every inch. A long ebony-topped bar dominates one end, and an L-shaped stage divides the room in half on the other. Crowning the space is a row of floor-to-ceiling windows overlooking what seems to be the valley down below.

The decor reminds me of his suite: black leather with bright drops of blood-red accents. Circular tables cover a corner of the room, though the place seems mostly empty except for a few men milling about, dressed in dark-colored suits meant to blend into the shadows. My mind skips ahead, picturing this place once night falls. It would make for one hell of a club—the kind I certainly wouldn't want to sneak into though.

"Come." With a sigh, Maxim pads over to a table nearest the windows and sits, resting his head back against the top of a leather chair. "Sit, *kotyonok.*" He nods to his knee.

I mount him, facing the rest of the room, feeling unseen eyes on me. On him. Just by being here, this man commands the entire space. At the same time, he demands privacy and not one member of our audience is brave enough to break it. He's almost like the sun: You know he's there, though you know better than to look at him directly.

You'll go fucking blind.

"Relax." His thumb curls around the length of my chain before I even register tensing up, drawing me into him so that I feel the contours of his chest against my back. His breath tickles my shoulder, heavy and spiced. "I will not be long. I just have some business to attend to." His tone doesn't have the hard edge I'm used to.

So fuck it. I take a risk and lick my lips until I'm brave enough to spit out a question. "Is...is this where you work?"

"Work?" Another chuckle rumbles from his chest, jolting my body with the aftermath. "*Kotyonok*, this is where I *play*."

As if on cue, someone new enters the room, briefcase in hand. Lucius. He's wearing gray today, a shade that almost blends in perfectly with the floor. When he spots me on Maxim's lap, he nods in greeting. "Sir. Ms. Marconi."

Maxim waves his hand through the air, dismissing the pleasantries. "Do you have the reports?"

As he approaches the table, Lucius flips the briefcase open, pulling the contents out for Maxim's inspection. Folders—a lot of them. "It's as you suspected…" He trails off, his eyes flickering in my direction.

Maxim nods, though I sense it rather than see it. "Go on."

"Someone's tipping off the Xi syndicate to the distribution channels. They're there at our every turn, destroying what little inventory they don't steal. And that's not all." His breaks off again. "Perhaps it's better if—"

"I said you can speak freely, Lucius." The teasing pull on my collar becomes a violent tug. My head flies back, striking Maxim's shoulder. I don't even think he realizes how tightly he's pulling. I wheeze. My eyes sting, forced to blink up at the ceiling from this angle.

"Levoi Malkov demanded an audience with you," Lucius says flatly. "Tonight."

All of a sudden, the pressure on my throat lets up and I nearly slide off Maxim's lap as my lungs flood with oxygen. My hand flies to my neck, which is throbbing.

"That's quite the word to use," Maxim says, rubbing his chin. "*Demanded.*"

I can't name the emotion lurking inside his tone. My nerves spark, my muscles tensing up in warning.

"I know." Lucius sighs again and runs a hand over his bald head. "I've tried to explain that you are busy, but he *insists*—"

"He knows something," Maxim says, clasping his big hands together, leaving me just a sliver of space to remain on his lap. "Three hits on my distribution in three days. That bastard knows something."

Lucius nods. "And you can be sure that your grandfather is aware of every minor hiccup, as well."

Maxim stands. I fall. My knees strike the floor as I scramble for balance. I know better than to move, even before I feel the solid, unmistakable nudge of his boot against my neck.

"Stay down," he tells me, applying just enough pressure to make my hands shake as they struggle to support my weight.

Just when my wrists feel like they're on the verge of giving out, he withdraws his foot, but doesn't move. I can see the shape of him from the corner of my eye: rigid, hard. It's like watching a tornado swirl to life right in front of my goddamn face.

"Where?"

I hear Lucius ruffle through loose papers. "I'm not sure—"

"Make it be here." Maxim storms across the room like a living, breathing bolt of lightning, sending anyone and anything racing out of his path.

Lucius follows him, and seconds later, shouting echoes off the walls—Maxim—followed by softer, stern murmurs. They talk for what feels like hours while I just sit here, kneeling. My kneecaps throb. My toes feel smashed in their heels. I don't know how much longer I can take this before Maxim finally returns.

"Come," he says to me, reclaiming the seat he left behind. He flicks his fingers when I don't move fast enough, and I scramble onto his lap. Lucius is gone, but Maxim takes his time flipping through the stacks of paperwork he brought. His *sweet* time. Hours. My eyelids are drooping by the time he finally nudges me with his elbow, prompting me to stand. "Come."

I follow him across the room, limping as blood returns to my limbs. More people are here now, rushing about like workers, carrying trays, pouring drinks behind the counter. Around the bar is a hallway stretching back into what seems to be another section of the house. Closed doors line most of it from what I can tell. Maxim stops at one of them, pulling it open to reveal a small room with gray walls. A vanity sits at one end, beside a wooden wardrobe. Some sort of dressing room?

To strengthen that suspicion, Maxim leads me over to the vanity and makes me sit on a tiny black stool before the mirror. Then he heads for the closet, fishing out a length of scarlet material; a dress.

Silently, I pull my current outfit off and let him dress me. I expect the new gown to feel borrowed or loose—but it fits. Too well, and that's not all. Unlike the clothing I found in the closet in my room, this dress has never been worn. As with my current outfit, there is no other scent— just mine.

"Look at me," Maxim commands before I can focus too much on the implications of what that means. He runs his fingers through my hair, frowning. Then he unpins the curls altogether, letting them fall down to my shoulders. "You're from Horn Hill," he says, naming the notorious strip of the city. It's not a question—he knows my address.

For whatever reason, he wants me to acknowledge as much out loud.

"Yes."

"A slum," he says, still adjusting my hair. He teases a single lock, twisting it around his finger. "Maybe that explains it."

Again, his pause feels expectant. He's waiting for me to fill in the blanks.

"Explains what?" I croak.

"Don't pretend you don't know." With a calculated focus, he tucks that stray piece of hair behind my ear. "It explains your familiarity with violence. Such as why I beat a man half to death in front of you and yet—even days later—you haven't asked me about it. Or why you ignore what I *know* you can sense about me."

His suspicions conjure up a million examples. Like the day he attacked someone with a chisel for no apparent reason. Or the mystery around his name—such as why Benny seemed relieved that I'd never heard of it—and Lucius' mention of a strict nondisclosure agreement.

I swallow hard but an icy dread continues to crawl up my throat. "D-Do you want me to?"

His jaw clenches. I've said the wrong thing. "I mean—"

"It is smart that you haven't," he says over me. "Almost *too* smart. Anyone else would have run by now. Look."

He guides my gaze up to my reflection in the mirror and it's easy to allow myself to be distracted. I don't recognize the bitch staring back at me now. She looks like a doll— and not the flawless, porcelain kind. She looks like one of Ainsley's after Eric has gotten his hands on them. Roughed up and glassy-eyed, wearing a pretty dress that doesn't match.

"Beautiful," Maxim says gruffly, one of his rare compliments, but his eyes are on my hands, scabbed-over and bruised.

When we reenter the main room, darkness has already consumed the horizon and blood-colored lights cast a disturbing glow over the black marble.

In less than an hour, it's been transformed; *now,* the open space resembles a club more than anything. An exclusive one, tailored to the kind of people who aren't surprised to find a man leading a woman around by a leash. Though, to be fair, Maxim could make any sin seem acceptable: wrath, lust, gluttony. As he strolls the floor with a predatory grace, it feels like he's already mastered them all.

CHAPTER TWELVE

Here, his cold smile looks different outside the confines of his suite—it doesn't waver as much. He could almost pass for at ease. At least to those who aren't close enough to feel just how much tension his grip contains.

Tension that *cracks* with every step I take in his shadow.

In the dim lighting, the other people in the room look like blurs decked out in fancy suits—the type of men and women who wouldn't ever give me a second look outside of this place. Filthy fucking *rich*. And, I realize as my gaze falls over a few women wearing outfits no better than mine, filthy fucking *filthy*.

Maybe Maxim's allure rubs off on me, because their eyes flicker in my direction more than once, as they toss him murmured greetings. Too much. With every inch they claim, Maxim's grip on my chain tightens, drawing me to his side. Close. Closer. I don't even think he realizes he's doing it. Not until a guy dressed in black eyes me up and down, his gaze settling over my chest. He smiles at me, and out of habit, my lips flinch limply in return.

Shit. I know, even before I feel the telltale pressure on my throat, that I made a dangerous mistake.

"Look at the floor, *kotyonok*," Maxim murmurs into my ear. "Now."

I dart my gaze to my feet, eyeing the heels he picked for me, nothing else. No one else. Fear churns through my veins like poison—and something sharper. Something I can't fucking name. I don't want to.

Either way, my punishment comes swiftly; his free hand cups my breast, clawing at the fabric and opening the barely healed wounds. I shudder, hypnotized by the sight of his tanned flesh on blood-colored fabric. Stroking. Claiming. Even if I wanted to slap him away, I wouldn't fucking dare. One by one, darker splotches seep through the silk around his touch. It's almost like my body itself is desperate to please him. Even if I have to bleed to do it.

"Look. Only I can give you *this*." His fingers clench, grinding tender flesh between them, and my gasp is drowned out by the sound he grunts in response. One almost too terrifying to classify: low, guttural. A growl.

"Only me, *kotyonok*," he warns as his thumb tugs on the strap of the dress, letting it fall to reveal my nipple. Right in the middle of the room. In front of everyone. While I watch, Maxim's hand tugs at the other strap and in a slow dance of scarlet fabric the whole thing falls to pool at my feet, leaving me naked except for my black panties.

Vulnerable.

Utterly his.

To drill that point in, he makes me stand here, feeling several pairs of eyes on my bared skin. The sad part? There could be millions, but none would pack the punch his nearness does. His possession runs deeper than anything he could tether to my collar.

It's the money.

"Come." He yanks on my chain and I nearly stagger into him as he takes a seat at a leather booth near the stage, pulling me down beside him. On *top* of him. Pulsing, his erection stabs at my ass, barely restrained by the fabric of his pants or the flimsy lace of my panties.

It's not my body that gets him off though. He's thinking of his punishment. *My* punishment. I picture the knife and my thighs clamp tighter together.

Gradually, soft music plays and Maxim's lap becomes a sensual, devastating cage. I have no choice but to either go insane from the isolation or stare from the bars of it.

Elegantly dressed women and men flicker past our table, preening for Maxim's attention, though I avoid looking at any one person directly. The rest of the club seems like the safest bet, and it's an odd mixture of vulgar elegance. Girls dressed in strips of black leather and lace carry wine on trays, circling through the crowd as the night wears on. Overall, it's not a rowdy shithole like the kind I'm used to. It's quiet. A low, dangerous hum seems to permeate everything beneath the casual murmurs and sparse bits of laughter.

The atmosphere makes me feel like I'm in a giant fucking jack-in-the-box. Any second, the ominous music will wind down and something will explode. Maybe Maxim's cock? His fingers find my open wounds again. Every time I flinch, he grows thicker, harder, prodding my lower back. It's a struggle to focus on the rest of the room: silvery spotlights over a brilliant black stage dominated by a single stool. When a woman prances toward it wearing nothing but two piercings through each of her nipples, no one bats an eyelash.

Not even when a larger man with a matching set of piercings climbs onto the stage after her and grabs her hips, positioning her over the black stool in the center of the spotlight. He palms his cock, veiny and throbbing. Aims it between her legs. Thrusts in deep while she howls out a breathy moan.

It's nearly a full minute before my mind accepts what I'm seeing: sex. Violent sex.

"You're uncomfortable," Maxim remarks, his voice low beneath the pulse of the music and the moans of the performers. He doesn't sound concerned. If anything, I've learned to fear the raspy edge to his voice. "Out of everything I've put you through, *this* unsettles you?"

Slowly, his fingers slide from my breast and blaze a trail to my hip, dipping beneath my panties. Rough and assured, he finds my entrance and circles it once. I only manage to suck in a single breath before he plunges inside. "Or *curious*," he grates into my ear, thrusting what feels like a thumb in and out. "Are you, *kotyonok?* Though I don't have to fuck you in such a way for the world to know that you are *mine*. Do I?"

His free hand gestures to the crowd around us, all of whom ignore our corner of the room. Even as I gasp. The power he holds over people—over me—is an entirely new kind of pain, more potent than the brief hits I'm used to. He proposes humiliation, and my body begs for clarity.

"Not that I would be opposed to it."

My mouth goes dry at the mental image: Maxim fucking me senseless in front of everyone. No amount of money in the world would be worth that.

It wouldn't.

"Give me a reason to," he commands against my throat. "One reason."

I know better than to say anything. So I just watch through blurred vision, tortured by the man beneath me. The two actors don't slow down as more people approach the stage and sip their wine as they climb into booths. If anything, they amp up their actions, their grunts and groans competing with the music. They don't care that people are watching—in fact, the audience seems to turn them on *more*.

Which is fucking disgusting. *Disgusting.*

And I don't think I take my eyes off them once.

Excitement and fear mingle in my blood as Maxim keeps a mocking pace, matching every thrust. Every brutal fuck. Hard. Fast. Rough. My thoughts swim, impossible to decipher, as fire trickles through my veins. *Shit.* My eyes flutter, my breath catching in my throat, as I find myself writhing against his hand.

It's sick. God, I wish they'd move *faster*.

"You're early tonight." The unfamiliar voice counters the ache building in my body.

Just like that, I'm slammed back to Earth, slumping against the table. I blink and find a man standing at one end of the booth, casting a shadow that obscures most of his face. He's tall, I know that much before I turn away to eye the wall of the booth. Dark-brown hair gleams in the glow of the lights, matching the color of his elegant suit.

I feel Maxim shrug, his fingers withdrawing, and I risk his wrath to peek out of the corner of my eye.

"I'm *angry* tonight," he says, his teeth flashing in a beautiful, heart-stopping smile.

The man matches the expression, and even though I can't see his face clearly, I can tell his grin is just as chilling. "I can see that," he says, the hint of an accent giving his words a musical edge. *British?* "I gather your friend is aware of our policy?" He inclines his head to me.

Maxim twists his wet fingers through my chain again, just enough to make it harder for me to breathe. "Of course. What about yours?"

The man glances over his shoulder, toward a woman standing a few feet away. She looks younger than I am, but not by much. She's slender, with blond, curled hair, pale-blue eyes, and full lips. Her beauty doesn't erase the darkness in her eyes, highlighted by the black dress clinging to her frame. I guess she's seen as much evil as I have.

"Yes, she knows, all right." There's an underlying meaning to the man's words when he faces Maxim again. The fingers of his left hand fiddle with something on the middle finger of the right: a gleaming bit of metal. A ring? He turns away before I can make it out clearly. "I'll leave you to your fun. I would say try not to make too much of a mess, but I beat you to it already." With the eerie grace of a predator, the man drifts off, gliding through the crowd while Maxim turns his attention to the stage.

His jaw is clenched, his eyes narrowed. He wasn't bluffing: He *is* angry.

"You know what I am, don't you?" he asks, catching me off guard by the heat in his tone. Instinct warns me not to speak, only listen.

But on the surface, a part of me has to obey and I try to stammer out a reply as a million potential answers flood my mind. Who is he?

Psychopath.

Criminal.

Murderer.

"Don't speak," he warns. "Just nod. Yes? No?"

My head jerks in some semblance of agreement and he looks away, his brows furrowing. "And yet you continue to play this game," he murmurs, though I think he's talking more to himself than to me—a terrifying fucking monologue. "Let me ask you something: can you handle it? You've lasted this long." He barks out a chilling imitation of a laugh. "But I think that's more due to naivety on your part. If you really saw…if you *really* knew, you'd run—"

"Sir?" Lucius appears before us, leading another man to our booth. He's pudgy and balding, with dark, cold eyes that linger on my collar. A gray suit strains over his beer gut. If I squint a little and ignore the price of his shiny boots, he almost looks like one of my regular clients: the typical arrogant Fuckface.

"Levoi," Maxim says, his tone flat. He lets my chain go and jerks his chin to the bar in a silent command. *Go.*

He doesn't have to tell me twice. I scramble to my feet as the other man sits, and I don't stop until I'm at the counter. The bartender looks at me but never offers up a drink. Maybe he knows my age, or maybe there's some unspoken rule about Maxim's toys. Alcohol makes you bleed more, after all.

But I'm too fucking chicken to test that theory. So I wait until a firm hand grazes my lower back, urging me to follow.

My spine tenses as I turn to face the rest of the room. The person who touched me is only a few feet away, his blond hair gleaming in the scarlet glow. Only now, as I come up behind him, do I understand the purpose of the round tables I noticed earlier. Each one sports colorful roulette boards, tended by a man dressed in black. Maxim heads to the table by the window, the man called Levoi in tow. He doesn't command me to sit on his lap this time. I just stand, my arms crossed over my chest, while the two men take up opposite seats and place their bets.

They begin to speak in Russian: a low, terse conversation that seems oddly polite at the same time. Every now and then, Maxim will nod or flash a dangerous half-smile, but the other man almost seems bored. His eyes keep flickering around to the scantily clad waitresses or the newest sex show on the stage. A busty blond and an energetic redhead are at it now, gyrating their bodies to allow the audience to see every angle of their... performance. I don't even notice the creeping sensation along my hip at first. Then the touch becomes firmer— unfamiliar. Maxim's fingers aren't this stubby. I flinch, caught off guard by the flash of yellow as one of the men suddenly lurches over the table.

"*Nyet*." The tone is a whip, though mostly level. The piercing, dark eyes directed my way don't leave any mistake however. It was a command. "This one is mine," Maxim says, switching to English—a jarring change. "If you want a girl for the night, I am more than willing to supply you with one. *After* we come to an agreement—"

"Agreement." Levoi throws his head back and laughs. The unsteady sound cuts through the music, and suddenly, the current actors on stage fall silent. The whole damn room does. "You think I'm here to compromise, *boy*?" he wonders in an even thicker accent than Maxim's. "You don't understand. Anatoli sent me here himself. Apparently, he thinks that you don't have what it takes to run his operation. He's on his way back to the States. If I were you, I would worry less about your toys." He claws at my side, dragging me closer without warning. I stagger, sprawling onto his lap, my face inches from his crotch. "And more about what will happen to you when your grandfather calls you to heel."

"I will only warn you *one* more time," Maxim says softly. Too softly. Fear coils in my belly, but it has nothing to do with the thick, rough fingers tangling in my hair. "Respect where you are and take your fucking hands off what is *mine*."

"I see you need to learn your place," Levoi says.

The flat of a palm connects with my ass so hard that I jump. *Thwack*!

"Is that so?" Maxim questions.

Then chaos ensues. Nearby, something crashes onto the floor. The next second, the table goes flying. A cold grip snatches my arm, yanking me upright and shoving me aside before I can make sense of any of it.

And then pounding. Over and over—every bit as brutal and calculated as the hammering of the chisel. It's only when I find my balance and glance down that I see just what masterpiece Maxim is working on now.

Levoi's face is a bloody pulp, his body jerking with every blow as Maxim pummels him with both fists. Blood flies. No one moves. The room starts spinning.

"This way." A steady grip on my arm makes me turn. Lucius is standing beside me, his lips set in a stern line. "Trust me," he says when my eyes flicker toward Maxim's back. "You'll want to come with me, Ms. Marconi."

He drapes his own jacket over me and steers me out of the mansion altogether. A different car than the one Maxim drove is waiting, and that familiar driver is already in the front seat. Once we reach the high-rise, Lucius walks me all the way to the door, letting me inside the suite. He doesn't follow me in.

"What was that?" The question spills out of me as my brain reboots, reconciling the horror I've just witnessed.

Rather than answer me right away, Lucius rubs his chin and glances over his shoulder at the gleaming closed doors of the elevator. It's almost like he's waiting, checking that Maxim really isn't there.

"That was *business*," he says finally, turning to face me again. His voice dips, giving the word a chilling double meaning. "I suggest you forget about everything you've seen tonight. Everything you've heard. Though…"

"Yes?" My breath catches in my chest. I can't shake the feeling that whatever he's about to say, it's a warning I need to hear.

"I strongly suggest you avoid mentioning anything of what you heard to Maxim as well. Especially his grandfather. Goodnight, Ms. Marconi. Oh, and your clothing arrived the other day," he adds, before heading to the elevator. It's such a jarring change in subject that I just stare at him, blinking twice. "I had it placed inside the closet of your bedroom."

"Th-thank you." After he leaves, I swallow hard, my mind already hesitant to imagine the type of clothing Maxim prefers his women to wear.

Lace and black seem to be recurrent themes, I find once I reach my bedroom and throw the closet doors open. At a glance, it doesn't look much different than it did the other day. The clothes are still organized into three separate sections, each one with a slightly different color scheme. But, when I look closer, I realize one major difference: Every single item of clothing is new. Tailored for one person. One woman.

Even the shoes are all the same size: mine.

I know better than to read more into it than the obvious; every woman probably got her own wardrobe for however long she lasted. I bet Maxim only kept a mixture of different sizes just in case he had to buy a new toy.

Just in case.

I feed myself that lie as I settle on a black, plain dress for dinner and wait while the hours pass by and the shadows creep over the edges of my room. It's nearly midnight when I pull on a lacy, gray night dress and climb into bed.

Without permission.

But, by two a.m., I'm convinced Maxim won't be returning any time soon. So I risk it, and I've barely drifted off to sleep when the first ear-shattering crash echoes throughout the suite.

It came from his room—I can tell that much. I hear another crash. Another. It sounds like someone is throwing something—a lot of *somethings*. Stomping footsteps mingle with the chaos. And shouting. Yelling.

Brutal, violent noise.

I'm out of bed when glass starts to shatter, and I stagger toward the door, opening it just enough to peek out into the hall. I don't smell smoke. Nothing's on fire. But the shouting grows louder.

The chaos beckons me forward, step by step, while my hand trails along the wall for balance. Another crash resonates through the floor the closer I come, and I find the door to his room already open, swinging as if on broken hinges.

Beyond it, the once completely black room is a collage of broken color. Lighter clothing is strewn over the floor. One of the end tables is in shambles, pale wood spilling out from the flawless façade. The closet is open, the racks within broken and twisted.

In the middle of it all stands Maxim. He's breathing heavily, his head lowered, his body shirtless—and it seems to be the most damaged thing of all. Tattoos and scars riddle the taut flesh stretched tight over coiled muscle. Near the ridge of his abdomen is something that almost looks like a wound at first: a circle of pink flesh. I have to blink before I recognize it, only because of a stint of working at a nursing home a year back. One of my patients had colon cancer and had to get a colostomy. He has the same wound-like area on his stomach: a stoma, I think it was called.

"You should have stayed in bed, *kotyonok*."

I'm already turning to run. My fingers brush the doorknob—too damn slow.

"Stay."

I feel the weight of his command like a slap. My heart starts pounding as I have no choice but to step over the threshold of his room. The carpet feels dangerously soft at my feet, and it's disguising the way they tremble.

He makes me come closer to him than I ever have. Close enough to touch. To breathe him in. Rather than command me to stop, he shoves me down to my knees.

"Do you know the first rule of obedience?" When I don't answer, his eyes darken and he heads for the dresser, wrenching open the only drawer left intact. From it, he withdraws a length of black material and what looks like a plastic pouch. Carefully, he places the pouch around the stoma and then wraps his entire abdomen in the black material: the binder I noticed before. "The first rule," he says after a moment, "is to never question. You submit."

He paces, seeming to grow larger with every step. Angrier. When his hands go to his belt, I assume he'll channel his rage into sex, make me suck him off. My mouth is already open when he yanks his belt free and curls it around one fist.

Then he lashes out with the loose end.

Crack! The flat edge hits my knee in a fiery splash of pain. I can't even attempt to hold back a gasp.

"The second is suppression. You feel nothing. You *are* nothing. Turn." He grits the word out and I have no choice but to obey.

I face the bed on my hands and knees as he comes up behind me. Rough fingers seize the back of my nightgown, yanking it over my hips, and the next blow strikes my ass. I see white—he didn't hold back.

"You fall and I will make this worse for you," he warns as my body sways, sweat beading over my skin. "Do not move."

The whip cracks again. Another burning sting assaults my system. Again. Again. My arms shake, fighting to keep me up. *Keep me up. Please. God.*

Another hit to my lower back draws a cry from my lips, mingling with the drool dripping from my mouth. A lower strike. He lashes away at my calves before finally nudging me with what feels like the toe of his boot.

"Spread your legs."

The carpet bites into the skin of my knees as I wiggle them apart before I sense the next rush of air. I feel nothing at first. Maybe he missed?

Then *stars*. One by one, they float across my vision. My pulse surges through my skin, drowning out whatever Maxim is gritting out above me—it's that damn loud. I can list off every single searing welt on my body: twelve. My thoughts are *that* goddamn clear. It's terrifying to float this high. An overdose of agony.

"Don't move." He hits me again, this time growling out words with every blow. "And finally, the last pillar is honesty. So admit it. You're toying with me. Why? Do you enjoy it?"

Thwack!

"Did you like mocking me?"

Crack! Crack!

"Answer me!" His next blow hits me so hard that I taste blood.

"N-no—"

"*Nyet!*" A string of Russian cuts me off, followed by another hit to my back. "Maybe he planted you, huh?" Maxim growls, switching to English. "Anatoli. Another test. You are just like the rest. Selfish." *Thwack!* "Reckless." *Thwack! Thwack!* "Careless! I've always seen through you. Fuck him. Fuck *you*. Fuck! FUCK!"

He strikes my shoulder and both arms give way, pitching me facedown into the carpet, my ass in the air. I don't know if it's part of my punishment, but he doesn't slow. I hear the whistle of leather. Feel the bite of pain. Over and over and over.

It's all I am. All I fucking know. It will never end. I'll die like this. My eyelids flutter as the blows trail off. He's done. He has to be done.

I've barely taken stock of the damage he's left behind before his fingers dig into my hair, tugging, pulling. He hauls me upright and shoves me forward, onto the bed. I hit the mattress face first, jostled by the shift in weight as

Maxim climbs on behind me. His fingers find the back of my collar, tugging it tight. Too tight. Choking.

Blood rushes to my head. My arms jerk, weak and useless, clawing at whatever they can, trying to reach his hands. It's too much. Too much pain. Too raw.

I'm dying.

And he's inside me, thrusting deep and hard, manipulating my body like a rag doll. I'm only conscious for the first three thrusts. I feel them all the way up to my throat, suffocating me from both ends, but I lose myself after that. Clarity comes only in bits and pieces before I go under again. I hear him grunt. My airway closes. The world goes black. Gray. He groans. Climaxes. I breathe.

The ordeal doesn't end, even when he finally climbs off me. I hear him pace, still throwing off rage like heat from a bonfire. I know the moment he picks the whip up again and the last coherent thought I have is of the safe word. Remembering it.

My lips tremble, fighting to say it. "I'm hap—"

"Shhh." The mattress vibrates as Maxim finally collapses beside me. And the world goes black again before I can say a damn thing.

CHAPTER THIRTEEN

"She's alive."

The voice is familiar. I recognize the accent, but it isn't Maxim's. Shadowy features come to mind instead: dark hair, imposing build.

"She'll heal," the man continues. "There doesn't seem to be any internal bleeding. You must have held back."

"Good."

My body reacts to that gruff, raspy tone. *Maxim.* He sounds close. Maybe his fingers are the ones I feel on my lower back. My mind loses track of the conversation as I register the pain. It hurts—all of it. My skin. My muscles. My arms. My legs.

"You seem concerned about this one. It's not like you to lose control," the other man says, but it comes out more like a question. "Though something tells me that you aren't worried about the money—"

"Thank you," Maxim says, sounding farther away as the touch on my skin disappears. "I'm sorry if I interrupted your fun tonight."

"*Fun*," the other man echoes with a chilling laugh. "You're not the only one who wants to kill, dear friend. I'll be having my fun later. Anyway, while I'm here, how are you on supplies? Has there been any bleeding? I would usually warn most patients in your condition against heavy lifting."

"It's fine," Maxim growls.

"*Right.* Just so you know, I disposed of the body," the other man adds. "And you don't have to worry. Any witnesses were *persuaded* to forget. But your grand— Anatoli will be another matter. You know this."

"You should have strung the bastard up on the wall," Maxim growls. "Use him in any fucking way you wish. As for *him*? I'll handle it."

"Well, just promise me that, next time someone crosses you, you'll leave the poor fool alive. I'd have more use for them then."

They laugh, two dangerously beautiful sounds that chase me as my thoughts scatter once again.

"CAN YOU HEAR ME, *KOTYONOK*?" Maxim's voice trickles around the edge of my consciousness, mingling with the fingers running through my hair. The caress is a mocking omen of the pain seeping through my veins.

Too much. The moment I regain feeling in my limbs, I groan. But that isn't enough. I have to suck in air and cry out. Scream.

My back is on fire. My legs. My pussy.

I've never felt this sore. This swollen. This broken.

I've never felt so painfully clear, either. It's like my thoughts are jagged glass, hurtful and sharp. What do I remember? Maxim pacing. Another voice. Bits and pieces of a hushed conversation: *distribution, Anatoli, the States, Maxim's "condition," pain.*

There's too much in my skull to decipher. Is this better than fog? I don't know. I don't want to know.

"Look at me." Maxim is sitting on the opposite side of the bed when I finally peel my eyes open.

I can't see his face, but I don't have to in order to picture it. Stern, cold expression. Haunting, soulless eyes. He brushes the hair back from my clammy forehead with his thumb, dragging the pad of it along my skin.

"Do you want to say your safe word, *kotyonok*?" He eases his finger beneath my chin, turning my face up toward his.

I flinch at what I see. The rage has drained from his system, leaving his eyes a steely shade of coal. I'm not sure which is worse in him: fire or ice?

My throat jerks to swallow. Spit and blood, according to the taste. Every inch of my body begs me to do it now. Say the damn phrase. As if to make it easier, Maxim's thumb traces my lips, nudging them open.

"I will let you go now," he promises. "If you ask."

Ask. I only have to breathe out enough air to bring life to the words. *I'm....*

The seconds pass. Too long. His hand slips from my mouth, falling somewhere within the twisted sheets that drape my body. *He* must have done it, covered me.

Out of concern? I can't tell as his gaze takes me in. He grabs my hand, unfurling the fingers, and raises a single digit to his mouth, running his tongue along the ruby smear coating the pad of it.

"I misused these tools, *kotyonok*," he tells me, setting my hand aside to lift the leather belt for me to see. His jaw clenches when I flinch and he runs his free hand down my side, bringing bruises to life. "I've used them before you were ready. I've conditioned you to associate them with fear." His searching hand fans out, stroking me from hip to navel. His eyes follow the motions of his fingers, his pupils swollen and hungry. "There is so much more to it than that."

He manipulates me so that I'm on my back. I see white. My lips flutter apart. "I...I'm ha—"

"Relax," he scolds, twisting his body so that he's hovering above me, all I can see, all I can breathe. He drags the sheet away, revealing my bruised, battered skin.

I only catch glimpses of it before I settle my gaze on the ceiling instead. Dark, purple splotches. Angry, red welts. He fingers one and the sharp, burning pinch warns me that part of the mark is gaping. Open. Bleeding. I don't know what I expect him to do…

Pet me isn't it. His heavy palm explores the length of my battered skin. Touching. Claiming. Comforting?

I shiver, too weak to move. I suffer. The softer his touch becomes, the more featherlight brushes of pain I feel. It's like being cut by a million razors all at once in the same damn spot. My thoughts grow fuzzy with every sweep of his fingertips, drugged on the agony he delivers. To my breasts. Between my legs.

I moan when he eases the tip of a finger inside.

"You had your chance to run. You didn't," he says, his voice thick with that lethal emotion I've come to dread: confusion. "So trust me." It's not a command. It's a request: the most dangerous one he's made so far.

My body shivers beneath the weight of it. Trust.

I won't.

I can't.

As if to prove me wrong, his fingers dance over broken skin, capturing my left breast and squeezing until my back bows. It's like pouring sugar over wounds packed with salt. I still feel the pain—all over, everywhere. But he's relentless, stroking and teasing my nipple until it has no choice but to react to him. My hips shift, captured beneath his palms as he moves lower, positioning me so that I'm flat beneath him. One of his big hands cups me beneath my legs, and I gasp, still sore. Still on fire.

"Look at me." His eyes, dark and narrowed, capture mine, pinning me in place as his free hand finds his belt, cinching the leather. He lifts it, letting the very edge drag across the flesh of my stomach.

I go numb with fear. Paralyzed. But then his hand starts to move between my legs. Back and forth. Deeper. Harder.

I don't feel the first pinching slap—not initially. It isn't until I actually *see* him bring the end of the belt down, striking the flesh of my hip, that I connect the two sensations. I don't even have the time to flinch before he slides a finger inside me, slowly, savoring the achingly tight fit.

"Fuck." He breathes out between clenched teeth. "You're hungry for me already."

He flicks the belt again, letting it hit my hip almost gently as that searching finger curls to rub my inner walls.

Shit. My head swims. Thoughts splinter. He hits me again: softer, harder. Harder. Softer. The entire time, his thumb fingers my clit, grinding it into my flesh. It's pain. It's something else. Raw. Hot. Molten.

He strokes the reaction out of me, not even retaliating when my eyes drift shut, disobeying his command to watch. I just feel. He rocks into me with one hand. Teases my flesh with the other. Hard leather. Thick, beautiful callused skin.

More. More. More. I don't even know which one my body craves the most.

"Trust me, *kotyonok*."

I feel his hand pull away. Something needy and broken rips from my throat: a moan.

"Greedy," he scolds, his voice tight.

I feel the mattress shift beneath his weight as he nudges my thighs apart, far enough for his body to fit in between. Something larger than his fingers bats at my entrance as his breath bastes my throat.

"Open your eyes."

My eyelids drift open until I see his face, inches from mine, while his fingers trace a path up my torso, gliding over my neglected breast, reaching for my throat. I'm still wearing the collar, and something about the way my neck must look makes him change tack.

"Hold your breath," he tells me as his hips jerk, his cock sinking in. "Don't let it out until I tell you to."

My cheeks fill with air as my body becomes full of him. I fight to hold it in as he starts to thrust. Slow. Hard. Harder. Harder.

"Not yet," he warns when I gasp, swiveling his hips, making me choke.

My head buzzes. My thoughts blur. My lungs are screaming. My body is on fire. Tightening. Clenching.

When his thumb returns to my clit with devastating strokes, my eyes roll back in my head. I see lightning. I feel it.

"Now."

I gulp at the air while my body comes, riding his length as a million sensations hit me at once. And all the while, he just keeps thrusting.

"Fuck."

My eyes flutter open the moment he throws his head back, blond hair streaming out behind him, his eyes heavy-lidded. His hips roll, grinding his cock into me. I'll feel him for days. For weeks. Forever.

It seems like it will never end, but the next second, he collapses, pinning me flat with his weight. His mouth clamps down over my ear as my body rides the final wave of his release, delivering another dose of agony.

"This is pain, *kotyonok*," he tells me gruffly, releasing the lobe. "This…is all I will ever give you. This?" He grinds his deflating cock into my clit, sparking off another scorching chain-reaction. "This is all you will ever need."

At least the first part is the truth. I know that as my body screams the moment he rolls off me and moves to sit at the edge of the bed. This is pain. This is what I signed up for.

But it shouldn't be what I want.

And it definitely shouldn't be what I *need*.

PAIN IS the only thing I'm sure of when I regain consciousness—that and a featherlight touch against the back of my neck. A finger? No. Goosebumps prickle my skin in recognition of the callused, rough surface. *His* finger. My heart is already pounding against the wall of my rib cage by the time that guttural voice trickles into my ear.

"I know you are awake."

I feel the heat from another body first, before I even sense the hulking shape stirring beside me. *Maxim.* In the dim lighting, he barely even looks human: just a beast glistening beneath blood and sweat.

I'm hypnotized by the predatory way he moves as he stands and approaches a doorway that I assume leads into his bathroom. I hear water running for a few minutes before he reappears with his entire torso bare.

Drool slips between my dry, cracked lips. What was that saying? *Be careful what you wish for.*

If, even for a second, I wanted to sneak a peek at what lies beneath Maxim's shirts, I've learned my lesson. He's grotesquely beautiful, adorned by countless scars that riddle his skin. Some look clean—surgical maybe, like Melanie's C-section scars. The rest are jagged. Broken. Sloppy.

Like mine.

The crowning jewel of his injuries is the circular stoma on his abdomen: a bright, beefy red. Maybe this is why he uses that color as an accent so much? Taken altogether, he *is* one giant contrast of red and silver—with those eyes filling in as the signature black.

Ignoring me, he approaches the ruined dresser and withdraws a clean plastic pouch that he secures around the stoma before wrapping another binder around his waist.

"More than twice," he says, breaking the unnatural silence as he finally turns to face me.

"Y-yes?" The reply instinctively sputters out of me. Though, to be fair, I don't know what he means at first. More than two times that he's rendered me unconscious?

"I've never fucked the same woman more than twice." His shadow flickers over the sheets as he advances on my side of the bed. When his face comes into view, he's frowning.

"Rarely more than once. Most void the contract by then. To them, the money isn't worth the pain or inconvenience of staying with me." He sits, and as the mattress dips beneath his weight, I register for the first time how *heavy* he actually is—like those blocks of stone he likes to beat the hell out of. "You're bleeding." Before I can react, his hand hooks beneath my thigh, flipping me onto my back.

Shit. That simple motion triggers an avalanche of pain. I gasp, but he doesn't hesitate to take an ankle in each hand, baring every inch of me to him. My cheeks heat up at the thought of what I must look like.

As if reading my mind, he jerks his chin toward my splayed legs, his mouth slanted into one of those dangerous frowns. "Look."

I crane my neck on command, gazing down at the dark curls between my legs and the slick wetness along my inner thighs. His seed. My *blood.* A deep, searing burn inside me warns that he was right.

Without taking his eyes off the mess he's made, Maxim lets me go and rises to his full height. "Get up."

I try to move—*try* being the operative word. My body is mush. I barely make it an inch before my brain forgets how to communicate with my muscles and I double over. My eyes stream, my nerves throb, but I'm not stupid enough to admit as much out loud.

"Come," Maxim repeats. The warning in his tone is crystal fucking clear and every nerve in my body registers it: *Get up.*

I swing one of my legs out in a desperate bid for balance —and wind up on the floor. My knees smart, bitten by the carpet, but before I can move, a firm hand grabs my arm and hauls me upright. Off my feet, into his arms. Without a word, he carries me into the larger bathroom himself.

I shudder at the icy contrast as he sets me on the edge of the tub with my feet dangling inside it. Without saying a word, he runs the water, warm this time, and leaves me to grab a rag from the counter. As the water rises, he wets the cloth and swipes it across my shoulders and then down between my breasts. It's such an intimate motion, but he doesn't even ask for permission. Though why should he? I'm the bitch who signed the contract, after all; here, I'm just property, his to bathe as he sees fit.

His hands move slowly, carefully, brushing over every bruise, every single cut—taking stock of how much uninjured skin I have left. While he works, a smell floats up to tickle my nostrils: more of that rose-scented soap. It's strange how much he seems to like that scent on me. Maybe it's the combination: floral and blood.

Anticipation chokes me as he sets the rag aside and his fingers sink into my hair next. I wince, expecting him to grab and pull. Instead, he lathers. More rose scent scatters on the air as he guides my head back into the water in order to rinse, and then he works his fingers through the damp strands again. I don't believe it until I feel the result slap against my shoulders a few minutes later—he braided it. Afterward, he drains the tub and dresses me in gray fabric. It's too soft to be one of the day dresses and too light a shade to be one for evening. Another nightgown.

I'm in a daze as he leads me back into my room, sets me on the bed, and tucks me beneath the covers.

Lying there, I feel like one of Ainsley's dolls again, rescued from my torment for a brief moment. The crayon and dirt have been scrubbed from my hair. My head is screwed on correctly again. But both my owner and I know the truth, even as he carefully puts me away: I'll just get broken all over again tomorrow.

"Sleep, *kotyonok*," Maxim tells me before leaving the room. His parting words drift back to me from the hall, both a promise and a threat. "You will need it."

I WAKE up choking on a scream, but the image in my head isn't one of Maxim, go figure: just an empty room. No razors. No pain.

Just silence.

Always.

"You're in my suite," a cold voice reminds me, jarring me back to reality.

My eyes fly open and I find Maxim in the doorway. Any fear lingering from the dream is instantly demolished by something stronger. Harsher.

Confronting his toys in the throes of a nightmare must be a normal occurrence for him, because he waits until I stop gasping for air before jerking his chin in a silent command. "Get up."

I contort my sore, throbbing limbs so that I'm sitting upright by the time he reaches my side. He pushes the rest of the blankets back from me, hissing at the sight of the welts on my legs. His thumb grazes one, his eyes glowing brighter with every strangled cry I fight to swallow down. I'm starting to recognize his few, if signature, emotions: lust, rage, malice.

"Keep making those noises, *kotyonok*," he says in a warning tone before I can hone in on which one he might be feeling now. "You will not...you will not make this quick."

My pussy twinges as my eyes drift to the front of his pants. He's straining already.

"Come."

I limp after him into the adjacent bathroom and cling to the rim of the tub. This time, I'm allowed to wash myself while he watches, directing with his eyes as to which part of my body I should clean next. My arms. My stomach. Between my legs. There again. I can't shake the feeling that he's not just watching—he's *teaching*. Making sure I'll remember what he likes. How to scrub myself clean so that his scent always remains. For the next day, and the next, and the next.

When he seems satisfied, he takes the washcloth from me and sets it aside. My throat contracts instinctively as he unhooks his belt and lowers his pants. God, he's steel already, jutting into the air. Before I can even mentally prepare myself, his fingers come to pry my jaw apart.

"Open."

I hollow my cheeks around him and fight the urge to gag as he thrusts in. Once again, his sheer size catches me off guard. It doesn't even seem possible that I can take him in all the way. So deep. Over and over.

With a grunt, he pulls out, sending drool down my chin. One of his hands captures mine and guides me to his shaft as I sputter, my eyes streaming. He's rock hard and pulsing at the same damn time. My spit makes him slick and my grip moves easily as his fingers encircle my own, guiding just how hard I squeeze him with every stroke.

Once again, I'm learning more about him without trying. With this method, he likes it hard. He likes it slow. Within minutes, he's pulsing against my closed fist, and only his grip keeps mine intact. Harder. Slower. Fast.

I don't know what does it in the end—maybe the way I swallow hard as his stare reconnects with mine. The next second, his jaw clenches. His eyes flash. My only warning is a low groan before his cum spills onto my lap, dripping down between my spread thighs. One burning spurt. Another. Each lash feels like a blow from his belt. Violent. Painful. Addictive.

"Get dressed," he tells me after he cleans himself off and returns to my bedroom. Once again, he picks every item for me to wear himself, handing me a white, lace pair of panties first. He doesn't offer me the rag, and I'm not stupid enough to reach for it myself. Then again, in his eyes, I guess I'm *clean.*

"Put them on," he prompts as if reading my mind.

I obey and pull the panties up, trapping part of his seed underneath. I don't even question as he hands me a matching bra and then a simple white dress also made of flimsy lace. I just suffer his possession and push every other logical thought out but *this.* My shoes today are cream-colored heels. To complete the look, he unbraids my hair and arranges it into loose waves that drape my shoulders.

Finished, he beckons me down the hall and into the sculpture room, where he snatches a chisel and a hammer from the wall. I stand in the corner while he returns to the half-finished block of stone and channels his rage into something other than me—whatever still lurks within him since the other night. The edge of the blade gleams as he swipes it through the air. The hammer follows. It's not long before he's grunting with the effort, throwing his weight behind every single blow.

Wham!

Wham!

Wham!

The only time he stops is to enter the kitchen and prepare dinner while I watch: chicken, which he seasons before placing into the oven. Then he returns to the sculpture room. An hour later, the baking timer sounds just as the door to the suite opens from the outside.

"Who is it?" Maxim keeps a tight grip on the chisel as he storms to the doorway to meet the intruder. Lucius. The tight expression he wears chills me almost as much as the way Maxim stiffens at the sight of it does.

"It's urgent," he says.

"It can wait until after you explain," Maxim counters.

Lucius squares his shoulders and faces him, sighing. "The east warehouse was torched. Everything lost. It appears that someone else in the syndicate felt the same way that Malkov did. The heads request a meeting with you. *Now.* And that's not all."

Maxim cocks his head, his eyes radiating fire. "Oh?"

"Anatoli is on his way back to the States," Lucius says, frowning. "I tried to request a timeline, but I was blocked from every attempt at communication. However, I assume that he will want to meet with you the moment he arrives."

"Will he now?" Maxim laughs: a broken, harsh sound that trickles out of him, softly at first. Then louder. Eventually, he throws his head back, bellowing out each chuckle. When the sound finally trails off, his teeth flash in a feral smile.

"Eat alone," he tells me, stalking toward the door. "Then get to your room. And I suggest you stay in bed tonight, *kotyonok*."

Without another word, he follows Lucius out into the hallway, slamming the door behind him.

I don't hear Maxim return to the suite this time. When I wake up, he's already standing at the foot of my bed, casting a shadow that swallows up every ounce of nearby light. He's wearing black from head to toe today, his hair hanging loose and unbrushed around his face. For some reason, my first instinct isn't to scream when I see him.

It's to wait, my heart pounding, my breath trapped in my throat. Already my thoughts solidify, chasing away the incoherent nightmares that haunted me all night. Is that a *good* thing or bad?

The question remains unanswered by the time I fully wake up. After a long minute of silence, Maxim commands me to dress and then leads me to the sculpture room, where he spends hours beating the hell out of the block of stone. He's so brutal that he winds up cracking it, ruining the half-finished sculpture, and I spend the entire day waiting for his inevitable cue to open my mouth or strip. Maybe he'll fuck me raw? Beat me with a leather strap again?

Something.

But he storms about the suite instead, shouting orders into a cell phone—mainly in Russian. What little words of English he sprinkles in stick out to me like jagged shards of broken glass: *Find them, any means necessary. Now.*

Afterward, he commands me to bed, and the next two days play out the same way. Apart from washing me in the morning, he never fucks me—and the anticipation is somehow worse than anything he's dished out so far.

Waiting is a brand-new torture he seems determined to inflict.

By the time the final day comes to an end, the only break in the relentless routine is when Lucius comes to take me home. I'm in the corner of the sculpture room, watching Maxim work. When Lucius beckons me toward him, Maxim's only form of acknowledgment is a single command that chases me on my way out. "Have him give you the bonus payment."

It's a second before I realize what he means. A quick glance over my legs alone reveals numerous welts, way beyond the scope outlined in his contract. *Ten inches. Twelve…*

I try to mentally tally up an estimate and choke. Too goddamn much.

"The rate will stay the same if," Maxim adds, turning his back to me, "*when* you come back."

I wait, paralyzed in the doorway, but that's it. He doesn't say anything else, and Lucius has to touch my shoulder to get me to move again. It isn't until after I've stumbled through my own front door sometime after midnight that I realize just what this means.

I survived another week with Maxim—with a few extra thousand padded to my paycheck, too. I only have to last two more in order to make it a month. After that, I would earn my sixteen thousand dollars.

The number is my lullaby as I fall asleep on the couch and wake up to find Ainsley climbing onto my chest, demanding to know why I have so many booboos.

Sixteen thousand dollars: It's a fitting price tag for any whore.

Two days home should have seemed like a godsend. A break from hell.

In reality, they felt more like that sleepy twilight between dreams and waking. When your thoughts are all jumbled and it's nearly impossible to tell up from down.

So you float.

Maybe it's the love that leaves me so disoriented. It tugs at my chest every time Ainsley or Daisy fusses over me.

Every time Mikie slips me a beer once the others have drifted off to bed. When they hug me. Climb onto my lap. Drag kisses over my cheeks.

It's such a contrast to Maxim's cold darkness, and ironically, it's harder to bear than the pain. *Love* just feeds on my fear, dragging up that worn-out mantra.

Money. Money. Money.

I can't escape it, but ignoring the cold reality seems easier now than ever. I'm too tired to ask if Melanie came back or brought along her new husband. I just restock the stash, refill the fridge. Enough to last. Enough to replace me for five more days.

When Lucius comes for me on the morning of what would be the third day, I leave the house without looking back. I don't even bother to pack a bag.

There's no point.

It's not like I have a single thing to my name anyway.

I REACH the penthouse through a haze of rain. Without a word, Lucius drops me off near the front of the building, and I ascend to the suite by myself. I'm only yards away when the door swings open on its own.

Dark eyes rake me over from the shadows of the interior with every step I take, and I instantly know that something is different. A shiver runs down my spine, chased by a single realization that makes me swallow hard. Just by coming here again, I've crossed some sort of invisible line that can't ever be undone.

Not with money.

Not with a signature.

Not even with some stupid safe word.

"Get in," his gruff voice commands when I'm only a few steps away, sealing my fate. Impatience laces the air like the scent of roses, and he doesn't have to say the second part of that statement out loud this time: *Strip.*

Without daring to take my eyes off his shadowed silhouette, I remove my clothing piece by piece: sweatpants of Daisy's and Mikie's old shirt. When I finally reach my panties, sliding my fingers beneath the waistband, he steps forward and a tendril of light from the hallway reveals how he shakes his head.

"Not yet. Come."

He steps aside, and my heart jumps as I follow him deeper into the suite and directly into my room. It looks the same: a haven of white in a world of shadow—but a few key changes stick out, impossible to miss.

The air smells like roses this time. Nothing else. No *one* else. I can tell at a glance that the bed hasn't been touched, either. He hasn't had anyone else in here while I've been gone.

In fact, he's been waiting for me. Two sets of leather cuffs have been neatly laid out over the white duvet.

"Sit," Maxim commands, pointing to the bed.

I obey, folding my hands on my lap to hide how they're trembling. I'm still sore from the last time leather came into play; my legs are purple with bruises. I've felt him every second I've been away: sitting, standing, walking—nothing brings relief.

"Behind your back, *kotyonok*," Maxim instructs without a shred of empathy, reaching for one set of cuffs.

When I contort my arms, he circles my position and fastens the cuffs tightly over each wrist. Once I'm bound, he drags my panties down my legs, allowing his fingers to dip inside me. One, two, three all at once. *Shit.* I'm nowhere wet enough; it burns, and he goes deep as if to make sure of that. Feeling. Searching. Whatever he finds makes him…frown.

"How long were you a prostitute?" he asks, drawing his hand back while I cringe.

I'm no shrinking violet, but call me old-fashioned—I'm not used to being asked something like that at point-blank range. The sad part? I don't even know the right answer. Did he mean in the sense of selling my body or selling my soul? Is one even worse than the other?

"*Kotyonok—*"

"Um, six months," I stammer, rattling off the timespan that I guess is nearest to the truth. Six months ago is when I started working for Benny almost every night. "Just to pay the bills."

I can tell from Maxim's icy, uncaring stare that he's heard it all before. Every fucking excuse under the sun. I could play up the sob story, but something makes me match his honesty with a bit of my own.

"It pays the bills."

"You haven't had many." He swipes his finger along my entrance again to prove it, but I'm too sore, too exhausted, to hold a cry back. If anything, his jaw clenches at the sound. "And still, you're already broken in," he adds softly. "For me."

A single question escapes my doped-up brain. "Huh?"

There must be another term for whatever he means in Russian. Something that doesn't make the person on the receiving end feel like a pair of worn-out jeans. *Broken in.*

"You will never feel tight to a smaller man." He sinks into a crouch beside me. His breath fans my bare thigh as he rams a thumb in beside the first finger, stretching me further. "How many have you been with?" he asks, sounding miles away as his fingers keep tweaking bruised, battered flesh. A pinch here. A swipe there. Then a *brutal* pinch that drives the air out of my lungs.

My blood runs cold at the thought of coming up with a solid number. It's definitely higher than three. "Um, thirty."

Maxim chuckles at the amount as he perches himself between my outstretched legs. He's too big. I have to lie back and fling my thighs apart for him to fit, which stirs an ache that travels through my entire body. Being trapped beneath him like this feels different than anything else. He doesn't even have to touch me; my body stiffens, paralyzed by the sting he dishes out.

"Who was your first?" His palm returns to my hip and I know he feels how I flinch at the question.

My first. That title is supposed to hold some kind of honor, isn't it?

As far as achievements go, *Maxim* takes that crown, in a sense: the first man whose name I actually remember.

"Some guy my mom was dating," I blurt out, not bothering to sugarcoat it. "Climbed into my bed when I was fifteen. They ran off to Vegas the next day. By the time she came back…he was gone."

There's no emotion in my voice. There are no memories in my head. Yet. I dig my nails into my palms, as I much as I can despite the bindings, to make sure. I've only just broken the skin when I sense a deeper, harsher burst of agony along my thigh. It's too sharp to be from one of the previous cuts. Sure enough, I look down and find his thumb nearby. He pinched me.

"Never be ashamed of your past, *kotyonok*," he scolds.

"I'm not." The words are already out of my mouth before I realize what I've done. *Argue.*

His eyes flash and my punishment comes swiftly; he leans forward, hovering above. The soft cotton of his shirt teases my stiffening nipples and chilled skin—but his aim isn't sex in this moment. My only warning is a dangerous, creeping heat as his mouth latches onto my shoulder. I feel teeth next. Teasing. Warning. *Biting.* Deep. Air squeezes from my lungs in a gasp. God, he broke the skin.

"My first woman was a prostitute," Maxim says as he pulls away while wiping at his mouth with the back of his hand. That one word catches me off guard as my brain attempts to reboot in the aftermath of his assault.

His first *woman*—not his first time having sex. Maybe it means nothing. Maybe my head is too fucking clear, jumping to conclusions: anything to humanize him.

"She was older than you are," he adds, fanning his fingers out to stroke the site of his bite, mingling comfort with pain. "I was even younger. My grandfather hired her, you see. To make me a man." He chuckles. It's a chilling sound. *Ha. Ha.* "She reeked of cologne and the several other men she'd been with that night. I was…untried. Untested. The entire duration, my grandfather berated me. He made sure to watch from the end of the bed, you see. To judge."

The darkness in his words shatters even the clarity his touch delivers, making everything too sharp. Raw. Revulsion churns through my stomach. He's lying. He's joking. He has to be.

"When my actions did not satisfy him, he hired more women," Maxim continues without revealing the butt of the joke. "Sometimes he would 'demonstrate' on them. How to make them scream. He only ever completed if they screamed…" He trails off, glaring into his fucked-up past even as his fingers continue stroking me. Soft. Softer. All at once, the nails return, drawing blood when I least expect it.

I jump as pain floods my system, but just as I start to lose my mind, Maxim drags his fingers between my legs again, staving off another trip over the edge.

"I learned then that fucking is just a game, *kotyonok*. But you do not seem to comprehend the rules."

My head continues to spin, even as my heart stops beating at the tone of his voice. Low. Guttural. Confused. It's like he can't grasp the concept of it: that it was possible to get off *not* at the expense of someone else. Suddenly, he reaches down and seizes my chin in his grip, forcing me to face him directly.

"Understand, that even in a game as twisted as Russian Roulette, there can only be one winner."

He doesn't reveal just what he means, but my intuition is more than happy to fill in the blanks as he lets me go: At the end of the game, there is only one survivor. As far as this round is concerned, the odds aren't even slightly stacked in my favor.

Yet Maxim still seems determined to play.

His hand returns between my legs again, and a searching thumb slides along my inner walls as if in punishment for making him feel even a shadow of human emotion—even one as primal as greed. Finally, he pulls away, but I don't even have the chance to feel relief before he flings another command my way.

"Get onto your stomach."

His voice alone affects me like nothing else—not even the pain. I scoot back over the mattress and roll onto my belly, my ass in the air. When I look up, Maxim is holding another strip of leather I instantly recognize: the collar, its chain winking in the daylight streaming in through the windows. All this time, he must have had it in his pocket.

"Lift your chin."

Once I've complied, he fastens the strip around my throat, this time so that the chain dangles against my back rather than my front: an icy reminder of the power he holds over me.

"Lift your legs," he commands next, "so that your heels are near your head."

The moment I do, the tension in the chain becomes unbearable, forcing my head back farther…farther. Going off his calculating expression, I know instantly what he's done.

If I try to lower my legs, my head follows. Just like that, he's turned me into a spit-roasted pig. The only thing missing is the apple shoved into my mouth.

Apparently, he intends to improvise on that detail. "Open," he grits out, coming to stand before me.

My lips spring apart as he finds the clasp to his jeans and rips it open, revealing his cock, pulsing and straining, underneath. Before I can even begin to imagine how this will work, he nudges my lips farther apart. Farther. Only now does the reality sink in.

He planned this, with only one goal in mind.

"Open wide, *kotyonok*."

He doesn't even have to try to deepthroat. He slides right in and there is no way I can move to even try to regain leverage. If I throw up in this position, I'll choke. So I stop breathing. I stop thinking, and the tugging of hungry fingers on my hair is my only tether to reality.

"Fuck," he growls.

His thrusts become faster. Harder. I have to breathe in through my nose in order not to suffocate. Which is fucking impossible. He's reckless. Rough. With every thrust, he tilts his hips to explore another crevice of my mouth or to plunge deeper down my esophagus. There is no mercy. Just pain.

And I can feel every single drop of it.

All at once, he pulls out, leaving a trail of drool over my chin just as my muscles sear, white-hot. I vaguely see him twisting around to mount the other end of the bed. The chain is suddenly loosened and I'm shoved onto my back, both of my hands still tethered behind me. Maxim hovers above, positioned so that he's facing the opposite wall, his cock near my mouth, his head dangerously close to my lower body. In one frantic sweep of my eyes, I take him in: rippling muscle covered in golden skin. I know this position…

"Open," he commands, his breath scorching the inside of my thighs.

Wait…

"Take me in, *kotyonok*," he grates when another second passes and my lips remain shut. I don't think I've heard this edge to his voice before. Broken. *Unsteady.* "Open and I will show you how to use that greedy mouth."

Impatient, his cock nudges my lips, seeking entrance. When I open wide, Maxim rolls his hips, teasing the back of my throat with his length in one stroke. At the same time, his fingers drift between my spread legs, roughly rubbing me open to make way for something wetter. Warmer. Thicker.

Oh! His cock muffles any sound I might make. All I can do is swallow, stroking the underside of his shaft with my tongue. He returns the favor, sinking his own inside me. Hard. Soft.

Shit.

"You like that, *kotyonok*," he mutters into my skin when I stiffen in shock.

I stop sucking, desperate to catch my breath. And my punishment comes swiftly. He seizes a bit of flesh between his teeth and bites down so hard that I see stars.

"Do not stop."

Left with no choice, I hollow my cheeks around him, taking him in as far as I can, while he copies every action with his tongue. Ramming into me. Fucking me.

Driving. Me. Insane.

I've only just gotten the hang of the motion when he comes, spilling himself down the back of my throat. The moment I feel the initial hot spurt, my thoughts drift apart and scatter. I lose my sense of fucking gravity—the climax hits me that hard. I feel it in my chest. My stomach. My fucking soul. Like a freight train.

I expect him to stop, let me come back down gradually, but his tongue only moves faster. Swallowing. Licking. Taking. Swirling, consuming.

All the while, his hips buck, driving every ounce he has left into me. I taste blood when he finally pulls out and slides off me while I blink up at the ceiling and try to remember how to breathe.

My lungs heave for air, but nothing trickles in—just out: gasps riddled with moans.

I vaguely know when Maxim leaves my room without a word and closes the door behind him. But I can't do anything but lie here as the pain in my throat mingles with the icy-hot, ravaged ache of my pussy. I don't know which one is worse to bear. Or which one pushes me closer to the edge of sanity first.

I can taste the first hint of madness when Maxim finally returns. Shadows paint the edges of my room now, making his hair stand out like a halo.

"You may eat, *kotyonok*." Heavy footsteps approach the bed, and when I crane my neck, I find him holding a tray. He lowers it, allowing me to make out the bowl of soup and crackers on it.

It's a trap. I'm sure of it; those haunting eyes are far too soft.

"Sit." Without revealing any sinister motive, Maxim unhooks the cuffs on my wrists and hands me a spoon. I hesitantly feed myself as he watches, but halfway through, he drags my bowl away. "That's enough."

I know better than to ask questions as he fastens my ankles to opposite bedposts before picking up the tray and leaving my room again. When he returns, my heart stops.

He brought me a present: a single flame flickering on the wick of a long, white candle.

As if taunting me, the flame dances on the wick while Maxim approaches the bed and sets the candle on the bedside table. The single bit of light serves as the sole source in the room. Hell, it would almost make for a romantic touch, if it weren't for the tension lacing his body. Stiffly, he steps back, and the orange glow spills over his silhouette, throwing his shadow against the wall.

God, he seems bigger now. Huge. Strands of golden hair fall across the chiseled planes of his face, clashing with the darkness clinging to him as he moves to stand before my spread legs. While I watch, he places something else down between them, but I can only make out the vague shape of it once I crane my neck.

A bowl?

"How do you feel, *kotyonok*?" he asks, drawing my attention.

My heart lurches at his tone—it's too soft. From this

angle, the firelight illuminates the cold gleam in his eyes. I *know* that look, and I can only lie still as ice runs down my spine.

It's the same subtle change in him I saw the other night. Like something broke inside him. Inside his head. His *soul.*

"I…" Any words die in my throat as he runs a hand along my outstretched calf. His fingers feel callused yet insanely soft. Like silk and sandpaper all at once.

"Sore?" he asks.

I force myself to nod. "Y-yes."

His hand slides between my legs again, lifting something that makes a delicate clinking noise… Something shiny. He lowers whatever it is to my skin and the first brush of it hits me like a jolt of electricity. Cold. Frozen. Like ice.

Actual ice.

Shit! I react out of pure instinct, clawing at his fingers.

He only has to say one word. "Stop."

I do, just like that, lying back against the mattress. My hands go limp and he continues his assault. Almost lazily, he slides the ice along the outside of my pussy first, pressing so that I feel every firm, curved edge. My knees buckle, and I can't keep myself from shaking. Both hands clench, my nails digging into the duvet beneath me with every swipe. Just when I think I can't bear it for a second longer, he begins to thrust his fingers, working the ridge of ice inside me.

All. The. Way.

"Trust me, *kotyonok*," he growls as the world falls to fucking pieces around me. The room is a blur, and his face is the only thing I can make out clearly. Pink lips move slowly, stretched tight over ivory teeth. "You will thank me for preparing you."

Prepare... The ice is still inside me when he steps back. I know that much. My muscles tighten, numbed by the frigid chill. My stomach cramps. I have to shove my fingers into my mouth and bite down hard just to keep from reaching down again.

From the corner of my eye, I see shadows dance across the room, flickering. I blink once and realize why: The flame is in his hand now.

"Look at me."

The moment I do, he extends his arm over me. Slowly, he tilts the candle, sending a stream of hot, clear liquid onto my stomach. Fire. Ice. I'm drowning between two consuming sensations.

"I want you to ask me something, *kotyonok*. One of those questions I see burning in your eyes." His fingers return between my thighs, sliding the ice back and forth. Deeper, harder. "But in return, you will relinquish something to *me*. There is no choice," he adds before I can choke out a refusal. "You *must* participate in this."

Why? My heart hammers out a warning. Talking with him is just as dangerous as fucking. But still, self-preservation wins out. I know better than to refuse.

"Ask me something," he commands. The words seem bitten out. Impatient.

Okay.

"Why do you call me *kotyonok*?"

It seems like a harmless question. To me. However, Maxim's eyes narrow.

"It means kitten," he admits. "It is simple."

Simple. I take it that it's not a unique nickname, either. What number "kitten" am I on the spectrum of the countless toys he's played with? My tongue twitches, unwilling to travel down where that question might lead.

"But that is not the question you want to ask," he adds.

Shit. He caught onto my trick. No harmless topics. He wants me to ask him something real. Personal.

This time, I think I know what.

The moment my gaze drifts down to his torso, his posture changes, stiffening. Tensing. *Bingo.*

"Ask," he grates when the seconds pass in twisted silence.

"I…"

His hand returns between my legs. One thick finger rams its way into my pussy and then curls at the last minute, hurting me. *Waking* me. My thoughts spark, way too sharp.

"Y-your stoma," I croak, using the actual term. If he's surprised I know it, his expression doesn't reveal it. "How… Do you have cancer?"

"No. Intestinal. Damage," he says finally, chewing on the words. "I've been this way since I was a child."

Before I can even start to wonder why, he has the candle again. One flick of his wrist and more hot wax drips onto my belly, throwing me off-balance. "Next question."

My brain scrambles to process his words in addition to the searing pain. *Next question.* But what the fuck are words? It's all I can do just to clench fistfuls of the duvet on either side of me, if only to keep from reaching down.

The longer I wait, the more impatient Maxim becomes. He lowers his hand, making the flame dance through the air. I feel that dangerous heat draw close, kissing my hip. Closer.

My only warning is a stinging warmth across my side before skin actually sizzles and burns. It *hurts*.

He's ruthless.

"Ask."

"How did it happen?" I stammer, struggling to phrase something coherent.

"Punishment," Maxim says, withdrawing the candle from my skin. His tone is flat, his eyes distant. In this moment, he's colder than the ice he tormented me with.

And I prefer the first torture.

"To teach me." Suddenly, his hand lashes out, spilling wax onto my inner thigh. Too much. Too close to my entrance.

A scream tears its way out of me, too broken to hold back, even as I slam a hand over my mouth. But it doesn't seem to irritate him. Rather, Maxim's features freeze over at the sound. And just like that, I know why he's doing this.

Something upset him again, and for whatever fucked-up reason, my agony is his drug of choice to numb the pain.

"Another," he grits out, sparring the use of wax this time —but it's not a reprieve. He's saving up for one brutal punishment.

And I have no choice but to dig deep and find something else to ask. Something easy again. Simple. *Why do you live here? Why do you like black so much?*

I try to phrase one of those softball questions, but a different one trickles out over my tongue in the end. "Why me?"

He frowns, still holding the candle at enough of an angle for fresh wax to drip down, splattering the sheets inches away. Searing-hot backsplash speckles my skin, and I can't stop myself from straining my binds, scooting away.

One heavy palm over my stomach pins me in place before I get very far. "Explain."

"You don't like it when I come," I stammer. "So why—"

"I never said I didn't enjoy it," he says over me. "But it is offensive. *Everything* about you is offensive."

As crazy as it seems, that doesn't sound like an insult. Just fact. Fate. He may be the tormentor in this equation, but he makes my sins seem so much worse. Unforgivable.

"There is something broken in you, *kotyonok*. Something damaged. Most men have no trouble leaving out food for a stray kitten every once in a while," he says—a terrifying analogy, given his own nickname for me. "The creature provides him a companion. The beast eats the mice. Both benefit. But when the cat keeps returning…" His hand drifts above me, delivering more droplets of wax. Hotter. Higher.

Shit. I whine when heat sears through my nipple. I can't move. Can't breathe. Everything glows crystal fucking clearly.

"The master forgets his end of the bargain, *kotyonok*," Maxim continues, his gruff tone driving the severity of the warning in—like a hammer. "He forgets that the kitten was always meant to be free, no matter how briefly it might reside in his barn. It isn't long before his new possession receives a collar. A name. It will never leave the prison it's so innocently wandered into." He shakes his head, and I don't even want to fully name the emotion shooting down my spine. It's become a familiar friend lately: *terror.* "But do you want to know the worst part, *kotyonok?*" Maxim wonders as his eyes meet mine again. "The silly little kitten still believes that it is free."

I jump as he reaches for me, but he only grabs one of my ankles and undoes the cuff. After setting the candle on the end table, he lopes around the bed and uncuffs the other. Then he kneels, both of his hands reaching beneath the bed to drag something out from underneath it. A box, I see as he sets it beside me on the mattress.

"And now it is time for *you* to be taught a lesson, *kotyonok.*" With a wave of his hand, he commands me to sit upright, though I'm still spread eagle and bound by both ankles.

My eyes burn. I can't tear them away from his chest—no, his stomach. The twisted hints from his childhood circle my brain on an endless loop. That word he used. *A lesson. A lesson?*

Slowly, he angles the box toward me so that I can observe the tool arranged on a pillow of black silk. Sharp. Glittering.

A knife.

It's beautiful in a way: long, with a slightly curved edge. It's not designed for cutting—it's made to *carve.* When I don't reach for it myself, Maxim picks it up and hands it to me, forcing the hilt into my grip. Nothing has ever felt heavier. Not even him.

"You seem determined to keep coming back," he says, frowning as the words leave his mouth. Like the thought of it is so offensive. So wrong. It requires a punishment. "Perhaps I should make sure that, even when you are gone, you will never forget for a second…"

"Forget what?" I rasp when he trails off. My vision is a blur now, and warmth trickles down my cheeks. How fucking hilarious—I never cry. After everything I've been through, I thought I wouldn't have any tears left.

His hand falls over my shoulder, anchoring me to the bed. To him. That simple, possessive touch echoes the words he growls into my ear. "Who you belong to."

My head jerks in a refusal. I can't control it or the words that slip from my throat. "I…I don't."

I don't want anything from him. I *don't*. Just money. Only money. My fingers shake as if to betray me, threatening to drop the knife altogether.

"My mistake," Maxim corrects. Hot breath trickles across my bare shoulder, closer than before as one of his hands captures mine. As if to prove me wrong, he flips my hand over, revealing the scarred palm. All those cuts. Those "accidental" wounds—some are still open and bleeding. His thumb finds one, stroking the raw flesh. "To you, this wouldn't be a punishment, would it? No." He nods to the weapon in my hand. "*This* is what you want."

Want. Too much power lurks within that single word. My brain short-circuits. Whenever I blink, warmth spills down my cheeks. I try to wipe whatever it is away, only to have my wrist seized in a stronger grip.

"Like this…"

One minute, the knife is clutched in my fist. The next, its sharp edge grazes my skin, creeping across my inner thigh. The slightest bit of pressure sends the tip right through the skin. I jump at the feeling, even as my wrist flexes, extending the damage. Two more sharp lines. More. More. *More.*

His hand guides me, but I'm the one doing it. Me. Bit by bit, he makes me sign an entirely different kind of contract. In blood. In pain.

M

A

X

My fingers tighten over the handle of the blade and it's like I can feel the heat of the flame from across the room, scorching my skin. My hand slips—the edge cuts deeper. Harder. More. The room spins. I have to squeeze my eyes shut to keep from going under and focus on breathing in. In. Out.

Maxim grits out a harsh sound between his teeth before growling something else in Russian. Somehow, I know it's not an admonishment when he sprinkles in two guttural bits of English. "Fuck…fuck."

One more mark. Another. Two more. Only one thought flutters across the murky landscape of my brain: *More.*

"Enough."

The knife is snatched away and my eyes flutter open to reveal the monster staring back. His eyes glow, tinged dark with bloodlust. There isn't a shred of humanity in them.

And a part of me—some sick, twisted part—sighs in relief. *Finally.*

He tosses the bloodied weapon back into the box and then stares down at the mess we've made. My vision is too blurred to focus. I just see red when I crane my neck, tiny strips of it seeping in a perfectly straight line. M A X I M

"On your back."

I let my body go limp, leaving me at his mercy as he brings the candle directly over my fresh wounds. *Drop. Sizzle. Drop. Fuck!*

Each sensation is too violent to comprehend. I have to close my eyes and ride it out: every searing lick of fire and every salty, burning bit of blood cementing his name into my skin.

My teeth chatter. Sweat slicks my inner thighs. Too much. Too much.

The heat from the wax sinks into my veins, creating an entirely different brand of pain: hellish heroin. I'm barely conscious when I feel another sensation against the searing wounds on my thigh: ice. For what feels like hours, he runs it along my skin, numbing me.

Without warning, he blows the flame out, leaving hot wax to dry on my inner thigh. I hear the sound of a zipper being undone. The bed moves. His weight crushes my body into submission as one of his hands circles my throat. Tightens.

In a sinking, icy panic, I realize I can't breathe. Dark eyes stare into mine as the seconds trickle by, daring me to react. One. Two.

Five.

The world blurs; I can't see. I just feel. Him. Heat. Pain. Agony. In one fierce thrust, he's inside me, fucking deep and hard until I forget everything but the sensation of being filled. I forget my name—and just like he promised, he gives me a new one, grunted into my ear.

"*Moya.* Mine."

I forget my fear.

Every goddamn thing.

When he comes, I'm barely conscious. Just a shell, used and filled up.

Only by him and the air he finally allows me to breathe in.

CHAPTER SIXTEEN

The next four days are a whirlwind of fucking and tension. It's like he *knows*. My own, internal deadline is a blown secret, and Maxim Koslov is determined to rub whatever emotions he can into my skin before then. If I leave, he'll make sure there's nothing left of me to walk out the door.

I bathe only with his permission. Eat. Sleep. Breathe. We rarely leave the penthouse—and if we do, he only takes me to the club, making me sit at his feet while he holds court like a self-proclaimed prince in a kingdom of his own making.

In a way, he makes it easy to feel. To exist. He makes it *terrifying*. What used to take multiple slices of a blade to find, he gives me in one brutal dose. An *overdose* I don't even have to ask for.

I beg.

But the most terrifying piece of the puzzle is for how

long? That's the kicker, as they say. Hell, Maxim all but warned me himself, and as the days trickle by, the final clause of the contract is beginning to feel less like a safety net and more like a promise.

In the case of accidental death.

"Did you hear me, *kotyonok*?"

I wince as a chunk of my hair is yanked, my head jerking back so that my gaze connects with the figure looming above me. Reality returns with a whisper of cool jazz that reaches the farthest edges of the room, contrasting with the gruff voice resonating through my skin. I'm crouched on the floor at Maxim's side, but how long have I been here? Two hours? Longer?

"I told you to come." Using my hair like a leash, he hauls me upright, dragging me backward so that the tip of his knee digs into my ass—a violent invitation.

I have no choice but to lower myself onto it, sinking back against his chest. He feels like stone beneath the soft fabric of his gray cotton shirt. He's dressed casually tonight, even though we're at the club and he made me wear a dress. Oddly enough, he doesn't stick out like a slob among all these well-dressed people.

Wearing jeans and a shirt, he's more magnetic than any other man could ever hope to look in a suit.

"Your mind is wandering tonight." Warmth clamps over my right earlobe, setting every nerve in my body on edge: his teeth, nipping just once. "You were thinking about something," he growls, leaving out the obvious crime: *something other than him.*

"I…" Any pathetic attempt to save my ass sticks in my throat. There's no use.

The people watching us from every corner of the room seem to know the inevitable. They glance away. I think some of the bastards even smirk. It's a full house tonight, but the rest of the club seems to hold more interest for the guests; I guess they're all used to Maxim's quirks.

I don't feel so lucky. It's late. Darkness paints the windows black and the only source of light comes from those blood-colored sconces set into the wall. Across the dark marble, shadows and reflections glimmer like flames of hellfire. Once again, the club has come to life around us —and I didn't even notice.

"There you go again."

This time, my hair is pulled hard enough that I see stars. My head falls back, leaving me no choice but to meet his gaze fully. Two empty eyes track my facial expression, glowing brighter every time I wince. Suddenly, I'm shoved off his lap and hit the floor on my hands and knees. The marks on my inner thigh burn, ripped open, but before I can move, my dress is hiked up by a firm hand, leaving my ass bare—he didn't give me any panties today.

"I called your name *three* times," he tells me on the cusp of a sigh. He stands, his boots thudding against the floor, and the hiss of leather edges his words: like that of a belt being ripped from belt loops.

"Do you understand?"

I can't see his face, just the boots of someone walking past, but they're shiny enough to make out my reflection: wide-eyed, dazed, *pathetic.*

"Do you?"

I nod frantically, clenching my teeth even before the first thwack of something hard strikes my ass. It's flat. Unyielding. His palm? Whatever it is strikes me again so hard that my teeth clatter together. Again. Harder.

It's a warmup, I realize the moment the telltale crack of leather hits the air in the wake of the blow. The first sharp hit to my thigh is merely a warning. The next is the real deal. *Shit!* I barely manage to choke a cry down, but the brief sound acts like a lit match struck against a pool of gasoline.

With the next strike, he goes to town.

Two lashes. Three. Each one sets my body on fire, rocking me down to the goddamn core. Mangled cries slip out before I can even think to bite them back, and I'm punished for every last one.

But, even as my eyes water at the sting, I know it's not the brutal, ruthless beating he dished out in his suite. He's careful, almost methodical. None of his blows break the skin. I'm painfully aware of that—*too* aware. It's like being given drips of water from a bottle but never the whole thing.

"I do not hear you counting."

My teeth clatter together as I struggle to catch up. "Ten… f-fifteen—" *Thwack!* I see white and lose track of the count for a few precious seconds. "Eighteen. Nineteen—"

"Twenty," Maxim finishes off for me after the final violent crack.

Panting and breathless, I look up through a messy fringe of my hair. I was wrong—the others *are* watching. The blood-red lighting shields their faces, but the sudden hush beneath the music gives their attention away as I suffer every blow.

My ass is on fire, my knees rubbed raw, my palms so slick that I can barely keep myself upright. In a desperate bid for leverage, my nails scrape against the marble flooring— but nothing can save my soul from a brutal fall. It crashes through the floor. Breathing heavily, Maxim lords over me, still holding the belt. I can see the shadow of it swaying across the marble. Close. Away. Closer.

"Look at me."

I have to twist around in order to be able to. Our gazes reconnect and my heart stops beating. I know that look: *confusion.* It twists his cold features with every second that passes. My chest constricts, clinging to what little air I manage to suck in. Some deep-down instinct warns me to look away. *Now!*

But I can't. And the eye contact only seems to confuse him even more. Frowning, he clenches the belt tightly, the other hand curled into a fist. His eyes are glowing, his breathing heavy and ruffling the strands of hair that fall across his face.

God, he looks insane: an angel in his very own fucked-up corner of hell.

The muscles in the arm holding the whip jump and something inside me flinches in response. But it *feels* all wrong. I don't shy away. My hips arch instead, my sore body preparing itself for another round. The tendrils of pain encase me, flickering white hot. I almost can't stand it; it's *that* fucking intense.

At the same time, though, I've never felt this fucking clear in my life. There's no fog—just *him*: clarity in its rawest, most twisted form.

And I crave it.

"Turn over," he grits out, nudging me with his foot when I don't comply fast enough.

My gaze falls to the floor, my hips rising to meet the next blow he dishes out. And then another.

Tears sting behind my eyes, but for the first time all damn day, my mind is open. I can't think about anything but him. This. Submission. I surrender to my punishment, and he doesn't let up until a brutal lash draws a cry from my lips and my hands buckle beneath my own damn weight.

"Come here."

It takes me too long to contort my throbbing limbs in order to turn around. He already has his belt looped back around his pants when I do. His hands hang at his sides, clenching and unclenching with every second it takes my eyes to drift up to his. They're swollen in blackness, both pupils dilated and endless.

Something wet dribbles down my lip and my tongue attempts to chase it, licking at the edges of my mouth. His gaze tracks every single motion and his eyes narrow before I even manage to snap my jaw shut. Too late.

"Come. Here." I've never heard this tone from him. Guttural. Gritted. Primal. "Now."

He waits until I stagger to my feet and then grabs my arm, dragging me after him down the hall behind the bar that leads to those closed doors. He picks one somewhere in the middle and shoves me inside it. Then he slams the door behind us.

It's too dark to see anything clearly. My hands fly out in front of me, my fingers grasping for something solid. Before I can take note of my surroundings, my back strikes a hard surface. Then I smell him. Feel him. His body forces its way between my legs, grinding his erection into my pelvis. I taste him as something warm nudges my lips, coaxing them apart. Something wet. His tongue? His *teeth*, biting down brutally hard as he shoves me back farther. The cold surface behind me is a shock against my searing skin and my brain doesn't know how to process it.

So it short-circuits, and I can only stare as Maxim wrenches my dress up to my waist and tears the fly of his pants open. I see the head of his cock, rigid and straining. Then I take him: every fucking inch, slammed inside me. No mercy. No restraint.

No *control.*

I can't even think. I just arch my hips to let him in instead, feeling my body struggle to register his length. His first thrust alone triggers a million little explosions: raw, bitter friction. He's never felt like this...

My eyes roll back in my head once I process just how deep he is. *Fathomlessly.* He dominates every fucking inch of me. Everywhere. There is no separating the sensation from reality the way I could with anyone else.

He is *everything*—squeezing out even the air to make room, drowning me in his scent. It's too raw. Animals fuck like this: mindlessly. Hard fingers dig into my ass, holding me in place for every punishing thrust. His teeth rake my neck, sink into it before a guttural growl revs up in his throat and I'm flooded with his release.

He should pull out now—but he doesn't. He lingers inside me, reaching down with his thumb to stroke my clit, setting off sparks. Fireworks. A goddamn explosion. I'm already on another fucking planet when his thumb drags over my open wounds, using fresh blood to add even more wet friction.

Holy shit. My toes curl. My feet lose contact with the floor, which forces him to support my weight as I lose my fucking sense of gravity. It's only when I finally come back to Earth that I register what kind of room we're actually in: not a bedroom, but an office, just a few feet from a polished wood desk that gleams in the light drifting in from the crack beneath the door.

Is this room his? When I finally look at Maxim, I can't tell. His expression is closed, his eyes flashing. All at once, he withdraws from me, wrenching up his pants and turns for the door.

"Come."

My cheeks are red when we finally reach the main room and Maxim returns to his seat at the table. Knowing eyes track our every movement. I can't stop my gaze from straying over to the stage, where a naked couple is currently going at it in plain view. The man fucking the hell out of a busty blond is a pale imitation of what I now understand no-holds-barred sex to be.

"*Kotyonok*," Maxim snaps.

I know without him even having to say another word to kneel beside him, lowering my eyes to the floor.

He doesn't acknowledge me again, not even as my inner thighs ache and something warm trickles down my left leg. It isn't until nearly an hour later that I realize why. It's a dangerous thought, but it trickles into my brain anyway as a new man joins our table.

Every other encounter we had contained some element of control. Every one but what happened in that office.

"It's a rare night when you want to talk business," a man says, his voice thick with amusement.

The back of my neck prickles at the sound of that accent. It's familiar. I lift my head as much as I dare and make out the dark hair of the British man from last time. I don't see the pretty blond around anywhere, not that I'm stupid enough to scan the entire room to be sure.

Beside me, I sense Maxim stiffen. All at once, his hand is in my hair, grasping, feeling. This time feels different than the brutal tugs I'm used to. Like the absentminded way someone might pet a cat that has crawled onto their lap. He *pets* me.

"I need your help," Maxim says, his voice cold. "It will require one of your more specialized talents—"

"Done," the man replies without an ounce of hesitation. "Tell me who, where I can find them, and what you need to know."

Maxim sighs. "Anatoli is returning to the States—"

"Your grandfather," the man cuts in, his tone knowing.

Somehow, I manage to bite my tongue rather than gasp out loud. Anatoli is his grandfather. Going off everything he's already told me about him, I doubt this return has the makings of a happy family reunion. As if to prove it, Maxim's nails graze my scalp. *Hell no.*

"I think you'll understand that it is imperative that I find out who is behind the attacks on my distribution before then," Maxim continues without acknowledging anything else about Anatoli. "Lucius will tell you which man to target. He's a mutual enemy, so you might be able to get something out of this exchange."

The other man laughs. "Always the multitasker."

He leaves, and not long after, Maxim stands as well, beckoning me after him. He doesn't say a single word as I follow him out to the car, and the drive to his suite is just as silent. The moment the car comes to a stop, though, his hand lands on my thigh, every finger clenching tight, his nails piercing my flesh.

"You." He grits the word out on a ragged exhale. It's laced with an emotion that makes my hair stand up: confusion. "You wouldn't be stupid enough to try and deceive me, *kotyonok*? Would you?"

My heart rams itself against my rib cage. This time, I don't even know what I could have done wrong. So I shake my head and say nothing while my racing heartbeat counts the seconds. One. Two. One Hundred.

Finally, Maxim sighs. "Come here." He barely allows me enough time to unbuckle my seat belt before he hooks his hand around my wrist and drags me over the center console and onto his lap. The steering wheel digs into my lower back, and I have to slump against him to keep my head from smacking on the roof of the car. Hot breath trickles between my breasts as his hands grab my waist, anchoring me to him. "Look at me."

When I do, his eyes are cold. Thoughtful. Calculating.

"I never ask where Lucius finds the women," he says softly. One of his hands drifts up my back…higher… Thick fingers settle over my shoulders and inch toward my neck. "I only know what little he tells me about them or whatever I care to find out on my own. But you—" Pain jolts up and down my spine as his hand encircles my throat from behind, tightening. Squeezing. "You will tell me everything."

Somehow, I manage to keep breathing. Air wheezes in and out of my lungs, propelling my heaving chest closer and closer to his chin. He could open his mouth and bite me if he wanted to.

"Like what?" I choke out when the seconds have passed without him saying anything.

His free hand reaches for the lever that operates the height of the chair, letting it fall back a few inches and sending me sprawling against him. "Everything," he tells me. "How did Lucius find you?"

The question is laced with suspicion, and my instincts go haywire. My thighs twitch against his lap, desperate to follow the only command my brain seems capable of issuing: *Run*. "He asked my"—my tongue shoots out to moisten my dry lips—"my pimp B-Benny and he said he had a job."

It feels so fucking strange to refer to Maxim like that now: a job. Was this ever really that simple? Deep down, a part of me knows the answer: not since the first moment he ordered me down to my knees.

"And that is all?" His fingers loosen their grip on my throat and creep up into my hair, seizing chunks, pulling tight.

"Y-yes."

"Why sell your body for sex?"

I flinch. "I need the money."

It sounds so pathetic when said out loud. I've told him this before.

But his mouth twitches into that dangerous frown; *this* time, he doesn't believe it.

"And your clients?" he demands next. "Were any of them recurring?"

In the blur of faces, a few stand out. "Yes," I admit.

The fingers in my hair tighten, causing my eyes to water from the sharp, pinching pain. "How many?"

"I…"

He tugs once and my scalp erupts into flames.

"Three or four."

"And none of them mentioned me? *Koslov?*"

I shake my head as much as I can despite his grip. Every tiny inch earns me a brief bite of pain. "N-no—"

"And you…" He tilts his head to observe me, his eyes glowing in the shadows of the car's interior. "You have been a submissive before."

Alarm prickles through my skin. "N-no." *Bad idea,* a part of me whispers as the words leave my throat. Challenging him feels like straddling a lit stick of dynamite. One wrong move and *kaboom*!

As if to prove it, his free hand moves to my hip, every finger clenching tight, daring me to flinch. "No." He seems to taste the word, digesting whether or not it's a lie. "Never?"

I shake my head a little easier this time. "Never."

He scoffs, shifting beneath me so that our bodies are more in line. He doesn't have to crane his neck back to meet my gaze anymore—I'm swallowed up by the dark, gaping irises. "Are you sure, *kotyonok*?" His tone sinks into my veins like the foundation of a trap; one wrong move will spring it.

Over my body or my soul? Who knows. That's the risk of playing roulette.

"You've never been trained?"

I see his hand move from the corner of my eye, and a sharp tug on my hair draws my head back, baring my throat to him fully.

"You've never been taught how to turn your pain into pleasure?"

My heart sputters as his teeth graze my neck, preceded by a warm burst of air. One lick. Another brief taste. My skin is still damp when he finally draws back.

"You've never had a man whip you senseless, only to turn around and look at him *in a way that begs to be fucked?*" The words end in a growl, bitten off and coarse.

I don't expect the first bite—not even the second. It's a primal assault. He sinks his teeth deep into my collar, biting down hard when I whine. I see stars. A fucking million of them. My only conscious thought is to scream as searing heat floods my veins, spreading.

Suddenly, Maxim draws back with a guttural hiss. "Even this gets you off." His gaze is aimed between my thighs; they're clenched.

Still numb with shock, I can't even defend myself. I can't muster up an excuse. I can't deny it. I just breathe, and he watches me, trailing his gaze over my heaving chest.

After what feels like an eternity, he wrenches the door on his side open and jerks his hips to buck me off. "Get out."

My trembling legs can barely support my weight as I scramble off him—not that he bothers to wait for me to catch up. I'm forced to follow him all the way up to his suite, where he slams the door, making me answer one question without ever having to mention it out loud.

Do you still want to do this?

My fingers shake as they form a fist. I can make out my reflection in the door's polished surface, but I don't recognize the girl gaping back at me. She's a shell of her former self, too desperate to give a damn as to how she might look.

For money. It's only about the money.

In the end, I only have to knock once before the door is opened from within.

Then I step inside.

CHAPTER SEVENTEEN

Muttered voices draw me out of a pathetic excuse for sleep. The moment I peel my eyes open, pain returns with the grace of a one-two punch, flooding my veins like blood.

I'm alone; that's the first thing I'm sure of. I'm also bound —something I notice second. Going off the tension in my arms, they're stretched above my head, my wrists linked together and fastened to the center of the headboard. I flex my hip and remember that my ankles are splayed, tethered to opposite bedposts.

It's a grim bit of *déjà vu*. He left me like this all night, trapped in the perfect position to feel his aftermath. Inside me. *On* me. My inner thighs are sticky with his release. His sweat still bastes my skin, and the right side of the bed—below my calf to be exact—feels warm.

Like he watched me afterward, lingering beside me until dawn.

All things considered, this encounter was tame compared to the rest. He only tied me up.

But I don't have to wait long for him to return for round two. From beyond my room, the hushed voices trail off, closed by a single statement that sounds as if it were growled into a cell phone. "Give me time."

The gruff accent sends panic surging beneath my skin. *Shit.* Just like that, I'm fully alive, electrified into awareness. My muscles tense as I lift my head from the pillow and my heart pounds out a frantic soundtrack against my rib cage. Through the shadows painting the room, I watch the door just in time to see the knob turn. Slowly.

When the door finally opens, a monster is revealed lurking on the other side. His body feeds off the shadows as he stands beyond the doorway, surveying the damage of me he left behind. There's plenty to take in. I'm sore. I'm bleeding.

He smells it; I hear him inhale, and it's a long time before an exhale follows. Without a word, he crosses the threshold and approaches the bed, letting the weak daylight wash over him. I suck in a breath and blame the reaction on lack of sleep. Today, he's dressed in shades of gray. His hair is wild, barely tamed by the brush I assume he ran through it. His eyes are narrowed again, prowling my bare body to seek out the bruises that mark it. On my hips. My ass. My back.

The cuts on my inner thigh sear, on fire. It's been longer than twenty-four hours since he made them, but they still feel open, unwilling to heal—his name branding me for eternity.

While I'm trapped, Maxim takes his time. A part of me expects him to leave again when he's finished. Make me wait. Make me suffer. Instead, he comes closer and unlatches every cuff, watching on in silence as I rub my sore wrists once they've been freed.

His hand lashes out, the rough palm grazing the length of my ass, making me shudder. When I look up, he's staring down, his eyes fathomless shadow. "Can I trust you to bathe yourself today, *kotyonok?*"

It's not a question. I know better than to let him see me flinch. Nothing unnerves me more than when he changes his rigid schedule—and *washing* me seems to be his favorite pastime, right after fucking. He shows my body the same care he does his tools in his studio: wiping them down, rubbing his ownership into every new scratch and scar. He's the hammer. I'm the chisel, at his mercy. Always.

So what changed?

"Go," he tells me without explaining his reasons why. He just nods toward the open bathroom door.

I scramble to my feet and stagger into it, running the bath water first. Moving on autopilot, I grab the rose-scented soap from under the sink, along with a washcloth.

By the time I finally look back, he's gone and my bedroom door is closed again. Another bad sign. My stomach clenches in that familiar, terrified feeling of being caught in an instructor's crosshairs. This is a *test*.

Failing isn't a fucking option, so I do my best to remember the method he likes: washing myself down with the rag in a way to preserve his scent before braiding my wet hair. From the closet, I play it safe and pick a gray dress with white lace trim. My shoes are black flats, and I've only just pulled on the second one when I hear him.

"Come here."

His voice beckons me down the hall—all the way down to that infamous black room. The door is slightly ajar, gray daylight spilling out over the ebony marble. I have to push it open with my palm in order to see him standing before the bed, his hair loose and untamed, his body shirtless.

"Come." He never looks up. Not once as I creep over toward him, wringing my hands together over the front of my dress. He's had the place cleaned since that infamous night. The furniture has been replaced, the carpet cleaned.

God, I hate the way my gaze skips the warning signs— like those flashing, dangerous eyes—and goes right to his body instead. He's showered. The binder is wrapped tight around his abdomen, but lying on the bed are what look like a fresh pouch and a cloth. The moment I reach his side, Maxim just waves toward the assembled objects, no orders given. I have to interpret what he means.

Clean me.

And it's almost terrifying how I know almost instantly just what he wants. I sink to my knees at the foot of the bed, aware of him watching my every movement. The back of my neck prickles the way it does whenever I'm prone before him. Like, at any minute, he'll sink something into it. Mark, beat, claim. My hands flutter when I finally manage to reach for him first, finding the strip of Velcro holding the binder together.

It's delicately soft. There's only the slightest resistance when I start to pull. Tug. Gradually, it comes undone and I unwrap him. Up this close, he's a collection of old scars and wounds. They paint him. Sculpt him. Every little nick in his flesh adds definition to each ounce of muscle. My aim is just to *look*. I don't even realize I'm actually *touching* him until I feel him flinch beneath me. God, he's soft. Warm, rigid.

He stiffens further, and panic locks my body into place, but he never moves. Never retaliates. And, for whatever reason, I can't tear my fucking hands away. They rebelliously trace a path all the way down to the right side of his abdomen, circling the area where the used pouch is still attached to his skin. When my fingers creep too close, he bats them away and peels it off himself before stalking toward the bathroom. I hear the toilet flush, and when he returns, his stoma is bare.

Standing before me again, he waits, and I lunge for the cloth, dragging it carefully along his skin without him having to tell me to. When he's dry, I reach for the pouch, but once again, he takes it from me and secures it himself. His movements are slow though. Deliberate. I recognize the motion; he's teaching, and I do my damned hardest to pay attention. When he's done, he makes me wrap him back up, pulling tight.

And this is when the sheer intimacy of the situation sinks in. Something tells me that this is a ritual most of his toys never see. Never take part in. The look in his eye, once I finally gather up the nerve to peek, cements that suspicion.

He's frowning again, his eyes narrowed into that terrifying expression: *confusion.*

"You're not disgusted," he says softly as he tugs the binder into place. There's no embarrassment in his tone. No shame. Just a question I'm not sure how to answer. Something tells me I just stumbled onto the reason behind this encounter: It *was* a test. To see how I'd react to this. To him.

Would I freak out? Run? I think, deep down, he *wanted* me to run. I've caught him off guard and a part of me instinctively knows that it was the worst possible thing I could have done.

So my first impulse is, like always, to lie. "I've seen worse."

"Have you?" A low sound trickles out of him, bit by bit. A laugh, I realize with a shudder. As the sound finally trails off, his fingers curl into my hair, jerking my face up to meet his gaze once again. "Do you fuck cripples routinely, *kotyonok*?" The way he says that word…

Crippled. It makes something inside my stomach curl up into a tiny ball. I know better than to let him sense the reaction—I try to hide it—but the tight line of his mouth seals my fate.

He picked up on it anyway.

His grip tightens, dragging me closer. "Or is it *pity* that keeps you near?"

"N-no." I shake my head so firmly that the damp braid clinging to my shoulder starts to unravel.

Without warning, he reaches down, curling his thumb around a loose strand. One firm tug and my head is yanked in his direction. The ice in his gaze freezes me solid. "Then what?"

"I've seen worse," I wind up blurting out. Though, this time, maybe it's not a lie. I'm thinking of Melanie and one of the many times I saw her OD. How pale she looked. How dead. The most fucked-up part of all? Each time, I'd wish more than anything else in the fucking world that she really *was* dead.

That, this time, we were finally free.

"Tell me."

My scalp is on fire, manipulated by a heavy hand. When my answer doesn't come quickly enough, he drags me upright, forcing me to sit on the edge of the bed while he stands in front of me. From this angle, he looks more stone-like than ever. Shadows dance over the sculpted planes of his face, illuminating the darkness in his eyes. They glow, daring me to deny him.

My teeth clench together. This is a story I don't want to tell. But, when his hand comes to cup my jaw, I know I don't have a choice. So I spill. Another truth, another twisted piece of my past, drips over his fingertips, more precious than blood.

"My mom was—*is*—a heroin addict," I admit. And that's the most respectable of Melanie's many goddamn flaws. "I can't even tell you how many times I found her passed out. Thought she was dead. And…"

His frown tightens. He adjusts his grip, drawing me closer so that I'm forced to drag his scent into my lungs with every frantic inhale I take. Two quick breaths and I'm the bitch overdosing this time—no amount of Narcan can ever bring me back.

"And when you realized she wasn't?" Maxim asks.

"I…"

Two of his fingers trail the length of my cheek as if he's deciphering my emotions through touch. Only he can make me feel like this: like an open book. His mouth tilts —were he a normal person, he might even yell out *bingo*.

"You were disappointed…weren't you?"

I have no choice but to respond. "Y-yes. I was."

A heavy thumb batters the corner of my lip as if testing the weight of every single word. "And why is that?"

My heart starts pounding, every nerve in my body on red alert. *Mayday, mayday.* This confession bites too deep. My eyes sting. This tiny part of me that still recognizes the creature I call my "mother" doesn't want the truth to come out.

"Tell me," Maxim demands, stroking my jaw.

Just like that, my brain ceases to hold any control. The confession is ripped out of me, dragging up old memories I don't want to face. "Because I hate her."

It's one thing to think it to yourself every minute of every damn day—but it's another entirely to fucking say it. My nails dig into the palm of my right hand, seeking clarity from the racing thoughts. Hard. Harder.

But nothing. My head doesn't clear. My body's grown accustomed to a different brand of pain, and when I look up, it receives another brutal dose. Maxim's fingers leave my face and rake through my hair, wrenching my head back as his body forces its way between my legs.

I fall back. He prowls over me, his mouth catching mine, his teeth nipping the tip of my tongue. Shock renders me paralyzed. Men like him don't kiss; he fucks me with his mouth, crushing my body into submission—tongue-stabbing, drowning, choking, lethal *submission.*

It's hungry.

It's punishing.

I taste copper when he finally pulls away, rolling off me—but his sudden grip on my braid keeps me tethered to his side. Enslaved.

"This pains you to admit," he says, grinding the words out as if through clenched teeth. I can't see his face—just his back. Golden skin is stretched taut over rippling muscle. He radiates tension. Hoards it.

Warning bells go off. I know where this emotion leads when it comes to him. My mouth waters in anticipation, even as my throat goes dry. I'm a wind-up doll, ready to unravel when he finally turns to face me, controlling the direction of my gaze with his grip on my hair.

"You loathe the fact that you hate your own mother," he tells me, his eyes piercing deep into mine, seeing what I can't admit out loud. "You think this makes you…broken. But do you even know the true meaning of hate, *kotyonok*?"

His fist twitches, winding my braid around the scarred knuckles, drawing me closer to him. Inch, by inch. Rising onto my hands and knees I have to crawl toward him as the pressure on my scalp becomes unbearable. My face comes close enough to his that I can feel his breath on my parted lips.

"True hate is being bound only by duty. By blood. It is not even being allowed to feel anything else." His free hand seizes my chin, forcing my mouth open. In a fluid burst of muscle, he raises his head, flicking his tongue along my lower lip. Seconds later, he seizes that same bit of flesh between his teeth and bites down, swallowing my gasp. "I was never allowed to feel," he growls into me: a twisted confession. "I never *wanted* to feel. And you. *You* mock me for it, don't you?"

All at once, I'm pushed back. The force of the blow sends me flying off the mattress and I land on my side. The loss of his heat stings like a slap, even as the taste of my own blood lingers on my tongue.

"In my family, weakness is smothered out," Maxim declares from the other side of the room. The broken, guttural baritone sucks every ounce of oxygen from my lungs. "It is beaten into submission, fucked, cut, killed, betrayed, sold, coveted. It is *ruined.* So comfort yourself." His gaze sweeps over me from across the length of the bed —I sense it. "Had you my father, you would have been forced to kill your mother, rather than merely *hate* her. And if *I* felt anything for you?" He laughs and I've never heard a more twisted fucking sound. "I'd pity you."

Just like that, he leaves the room, slamming the door behind him.

And I don't dare move.

Not one fucking inch.

THE WEIGHT PRESSING on the back of my neck jars me awake. I jolt into awareness, my fingers digging into the carpet beneath me. One inhale warns me to keep still because the scent filling my lungs is the first clue as to the identity of my tormentor. It's followed by the harsh breaths catching on the air.

Maxim. Anger wafts from him like perfume.

I know better than to struggle, so I wait, feeling the warmth imparted by the limb at my throat. His foot? He smells like sweat, and when I open my eyes again, darkness shrouds the already black room.

"Get up, *kotyonok*," Maxim tells me before withdrawing the pressure and walking away.

I hear him cross over to the other side of the room, each step heavy and aimless. Restless. When I finally turn to face him, he's already switched a free-standing lamp in a corner on. The harsh light contrasts with the ebony walls, illuminating the sweat glistening on his skin and seeping through patches of his shirt. He's been sculpting, I assume.

But the physical exertion hasn't helped his mood that much. His eyes fucking glow, stalking my position as I warily climb to my feet. The moment I find my balance, he jerks his chin, sending a fringe of hair across his face, obscuring whatever expression is distorting it.

"Come here."

I swallow hard and force my trembling legs to obey. He lets me come almost a foot away before his hand lashes out, shoving me back onto the bed. I scramble to get my bearings, both hands fisting into the comforter on either side of me.

"If I gave you the full amount specified in your contract tonight, would you return?" he asks.

"I…" That's right. The final day of this week is approaching fast—and the sheer amount of money combined with the insanity of the question overloads my brain. *Shit.* Logic goes to war with what little bit of sanity I have left. Do I lie? Come clean? The answer is obvious though.

Hell no. I wouldn't come back.

"I… Yes," I choke out. But it's *wrong*. I'm lying.

He knows it. With a step closer, he's able to brush my chin with the tip of his thumb, setting every nerve in my body on red alert. "And why would that be, *kotyonok*?" he wonders mockingly, humoring me for once. "The sex?"

Once again, I know the right answer.

And *again*, fear makes a fool of me. "Yes… No." I swallow hard, grappling on the edge of panic and terror. "I don't know—"

"You don't." All at once, his hand falls away, leaving my chin burning in the aftermath of his touch. That unnerving twist to his mouth returns, stopping my heart in its tracks. I've more than just confused him; I've pissed him off. "Fine, then." He backs away, turning to face me fully. His expression alone makes my stomach sink even before he issues his next command. "Touch yourself. With your *fingers*," he adds with harsh emphasis when I just blink up at him. "Get yourself off."

One of my hands dutifully uncurls from the black duvet. Reaches down…hesitates.

"Do not make me tell you again," he warns from the corner, casting a shadow that swallows every ounce of nearby light. He's on edge again, tossing off sparks of anger like electricity. His fingers flex at his sides, curling and uncurling in and out of fists.

He's a live wire.

And I know better than to test him now. My fingers find my pussy and sink into the folds. I feel nothing. Just dry, sore flesh, throbbing and tender. It's like my own body rejects me—and I don't know what the hell he expects me to do.

After a few awkward minutes, he steps forward, his gaze fixated between my legs. "Spread them," he grits out, the muscles in his shoulders flexing as his hands clench again. "Wider. *Wider*."

I fling my thighs apart, forced to prop my upper body back on my elbows while Maxim stalks closer, observing the motions of my fingers.

"Remove the panties," he says. "Give them to me."

When I do, he crushes them in a fist before tossing the wad of lace into a corner of the room.

"Now, get yourself off," he repeats, "but you tell me everything you think. Everything you feel. Don't fucking pretend like you don't know damn well what I mean."

Maybe I do.

Images pop into my head and I instinctively bite my lip to push them back. Away. I don't want to focus. I don't *want* to feel. But fuck, it's like he's in my head. I hear him growl, and the floorboards creak beneath the weight of two dangerous steps.

So I panic. I give in. One of my fingers drifts up to strike my clit. *Shit.* The reaction that swirls in my belly serves as a match—but the image that worms its way into my head is the gasoline. Just like that, the air gets harder to breathe: I pant.

"Tell me," Maxim growls, his tone alone warning me not to lie. "Is it the money? I know that's it, you greedy little cunt. Say it."

It's disgusting how even his hate feeds the flames. My fingers move faster. The fire grows hotter, and the image in my head? It gets sharper. More detailed. *Him. The floor. The bed. His hands. His teeth.*

"Tell me!" Two more ominous thuds snap my thread of concentration.

I blink, my vision unfocused until I find Maxim looming above me.

"What is in your head?" he wonders, his voice a tenuous rasp. Control, his favorite drug, is running out. I sense it, and suddenly, my fingers are so goddamn slippery that I can't get any leverage. His nostrils flare at the increase in arousal, his eyes flashing, demanding an answer. "What the *fuck* is getting you off?"

"You…" I squeeze my eyes shut, hating the sound of my own voice. So fucking pathetic. High-pitched, needy. If he were anyone else, I'd know the right shit to say: *You get me off, baby. You drive me wild.* It would all be fucking lies.

But him?

Maxim.

Koslov.

Drives.

Me.

Wild. Wild like a thunderstorm with deadly lightning. Wild like a fucking tornado. He rips me to shreds. Tears me apart.

And I never stood a chance.

CHAPTER EIGHTEEN

"I see *you*," I croak out again, relieved that I don't hear another cruel advance—just silence and my own frantic breathing. Does he believe me? Does it even matter?

"*Me*," he echoes in a heart-stopping undertone. "Then show me."

Alarm jolts through my skin, clashing with the building orgasm. I'm obeying him down to the fucking T: I'm getting myself off with touch alone. Something I've never, ever done in front of another person. Or *because* of another person. My head swims with the conflicting sensations. I can't think...

"Look at me."

My eyes fly open and, this time, I watch him approach. He comes directly between my spread legs, staring down at my still-moving fingers.

When his eyes meet mine, my hand quakes, presses harder. Faster.

"You're thinking of *me*?" He laughs in that sinister, awful way, slowly shaking his head. "What *about* me?"

He flings the question at me like another test, but this time, I know the answer by heart. My eyes drift shut again and I focus on the image taunting me, feeding the heat building in my blood. God, there are too many fucking answers. My mouth opens, but only a million broken words and fragmented sentences spill out.

"Your face," I hear myself croak. But there's more. "You with the belt—" My entire body jolts as if remembering the biting sting of each lash. The look in his eye. The sounds he made. "Your voice...your—"

"*I* get you off?" He phrases the statement differently this time: colder, harder.

The mattress shifts. Suddenly, my hair is in his grip, and when I open my eyes, his face is inches from mine. Those eyes are midnight, his mouth a snarl of bitter confusion.

"I get you off?" he repeats. "Or is it the *pain*?" His nails dig into my scalp, drawing a gasp and making my eyes well up and sting.

Fuck. The burning pinch alone is too much. I shiver, feeling my own finger slide inside me, desperate for friction—only to be violently ripped away.

"Do I get you off?" Maxim asks, snarling the words into my face one by one as his grip threatens to snap my wrist.

All I can do is nod. "Y-yes."

For the longest time, he stares into my eyes. Stares through me. Beyond me—maybe as far as his fucked-up past. I don't know what finally drags him back. It could be the moan that sticks in my throat when his weight begins to press into my lower half. One of his knees nudges my inner thighs. God, the friction. I can't take it.

"Prove it," he commands, his breath harsh against my earlobe. "Let me see that greedy fucking cunt weep for me."

His voice…the gritted cadence of it sets me off. Like. A. Bomb.

I explode. My head flies back, my teeth seizing my lower lip to trap every strangled cry threatening to break free. I fail. I fall. My spine curls, my back arching, my fingers thrusting in a poor imitation of his cock. Two. Three. Four. It's never enough. Not thick enough. Violent enough.

I need…I need…

Teeth. I feel them first, grazing my outer lips before his tongue plunges inside me. He swirls. Tastes. I glance down and see him on all fours, crouched between my legs, devouring me. Three brutal thrusts and I'm higher than the fucking ceiling, shooting off into orbit. I see stars, galaxies, but when I finally come down, nothing matches the sight of his eyes glaring up at me from over the ridge of my belly: two gaping black holes, swallowing me whole.

He lunges, ripping his jeans down. I go limp and find myself pressed beneath him, his hips between my thighs, pistoning… He doesn't even have to batter his way in—my body *drags* him deeper. Too deep. I have to wrap my legs around him to preserve the fit, riding every hard, sharp thrust. They start off brutal and punishing: a devastatingly timed tempo. Deep. Hard. Deeper. Every bit of raw, sliding friction makes me see stars. My mouth is open, my tongue slithering along my bottom lip in a frantic search for air—but it's a bad move. I wind up tasting sweat, salt, skin. *Him.*

I drown in his scent, and each thrust gets sharper with every taste, slamming back, back, back until my head hits the headboard—his hand flies up and slams down over the ridge of it, clenching the wood.

"Fuck," he growls, his voice gravelly. Then his hips start to roll, forsaking control in exchange for speed. Depth.

Insanity.

Mangled Russian trickles against my throat, giving way to thickened English. "Beautiful," he grits out, pressing his chest against mine with the next shove inside me, feeling my nipples graze his flesh. "So tight. Greedy…bitch. Fuck you. Fuck you. Kill you…"

His hand leaves the headboard and clutches my throat instead. Air becomes a commodity he controls: fucking it out of me, no matter how desperately I suck it in.

Fuck. Fuck. Fuck.

It's not a game this time. It's fucking survival; I cling to him, trying to breathe.

His other hand palms my ass, yanking me from the mattress, slamming me into him. Violently. Again. Faster. Nails break the skin, drawing blood. I feel it fucking up his grip. He has to kneel, propping me up with one knee, the other braced beside me on the bed, my body slammed against the headboard.

Sounds I never knew a human being could fucking make tear from my throat. Moans. Whimpers. I break his unspoken rule: I grab him; I have to. My hands cling to his shoulders while fireworks explode inside me. The orgasm starts up like a controlled demolition, but the moment I clench around him, Maxim slams into me. It's brutal, unsteady. A low growl tears from his throat—one I've never heard from him before.

It's primal. And then he bites me, his teeth sinking into my shoulder as if to prevent himself from making any more of those sounds. He fucks me in a frenzy to finish himself off. When he finally comes, the first few spurts spill inside me. Then he pulls out and flips me over. Two hot lashes strike my lower back, every bit as painful as the whip.

I'm in a daze when I feel him hovering over me, finding my ear, and nipping the lobe.

"You are a good liar, *kotyonok*," he breathes into my flushed skin. "This time…" He licks me, drawing a whine I can't suppress, before rising to his feet and heading for the door. "This time, I almost believed you. But know that, if you lie to me again—" He cocks his head back at me. Then he smiles in a dangerous array of porcelain teeth and dark, confused eyes. "I will kill you."

He leaves me here, breathless and senseless on his bed.

And I don't dare crawl out of his room until the next morning.

WHEN THE FIFTH day comes to an end, it's like being kicked out of a nightmare without being allowed to fully wake up. Maxim barely acknowledges me. The only time he does is when Lucius arrives. He stalks his way across the foyer to shove something into my hands: an envelope.

"Count it," he tells me before turning away. "Every last cent. Think carefully before you come back."

He leaves the room, entering his studio without another word. All I can do is follow Lucius out of the suite, and like always, the real world returns like a bitch-slap hello. The moment the car pulls up to my battered house and I step over the threshold, I know that something is wrong.

First off, Daisy's seated on the couch in the middle of a goddamn school day. There's a man beside her, and not only that, but the fucker has his hand on her thigh. She's too pale, staring down at the floor.

Rage washes through my body. I don't think. I just head for the baseball bat we keep under the sink. No. Fuck that. The knife. My only coherent action is to spit out a question on my way into the kitchen. "Who the fuck are you?"

"I'm your new daddy, girlie," the man says as I wrench the knife drawer open and grab the biggest one. When I turn around, he's smiling, revealing a mouth full of crooked teeth.

"You have five seconds to get the fuck out," I tell him. "Whoever the hell you are."

The bastard laughs. He looks like the same brand of asshole Melanie usually goes for: greasy hair, dirty jeans. She must be with him for his money. He probably got a settlement from some dumbass lawsuit or money from his dead wife—something good enough to make her fuck him. A man after her own heart.

"And what are you going to do if I don't?" He looks me over, licking his lips, and I can't help the way I cringe.

I'm wearing one of Maxim's dresses. I still smell like roses. Today, he even braided my hair, leaving my neck exposed —the perfect doll.

"You want to find out?" When I lift the knife, only Daisy is smart enough to jump up and back away. "Four seconds," I tell him. "Three."

Laughing, he stands and swaggers toward me, raising his hands and flexing the fingers. *Come at me.*

Any other day, I might have called the police instead. Thought about the consequences. Today, I go at the motherfucker with the blade, swiping it through the air.

Laughing, he dodges, quicker on his feet than I was expecting. "Your mommy was right, little girl," he tells me. "You kids need a *daddy's* touch."

I see black. This time when I swing my hand out, the knife catches him deep, tearing through the flesh of his arm.

"Bitch!"

I see his fist come for me from the corner of my eye. The next second, I'm on my knees. Wham! My vision blinks on and off, but I don't let the blade go. I keep it raised, my teeth gritted, my eyes narrowed.

"You want to go for round two?" I croak, spitting out a mouthful of something that tastes like blood. "Get the fuck out!"

Clutching at his arm, the bastard finally heads for the door. "You better watch yourself, bitch."

I lift the knife even higher so that his blood gleams on the edge. "Likewise, buddy."

The moment he leaves, I toss the knife aside, hearing it scatter across the tile. Then the world starts spinning. I can't get my bearings and wind up on my hands and knees. *Shit.* Pain throbs through my skull. I reach up and run my trembling fingers over my right eye. *Double shit.* It's tender; the sucker's going to bruise.

"Are…are you okay?" Daisy's standing by the couch, wringing her fingers together. I don't see a mark on her, but she's wearing a sweater, so I can't tell much.

Still, I've never felt this kind of fear before.

"Did he touch you?" I jerk my chin to the door.

When she shakes her head, the breath I didn't even realize I was holding escapes in a rush.

"Good." It's the only thing that fucking matters. I can't waste energy on anger. I can't…

The money. That's all I focus on as I stand and stagger over to the fridge. I yank open the door and reach for my stash —but it's gone. All of it. I feel around the back of the fridge. I look under a carton of milk but don't turn up even a fucking penny.

"You gave it to her." The words stick in my throat. I have to spit them out, but hearing them out loud stings worse than the itching suspicion I've had all month. "You gave that bitch more of my money."

"I'm *sorry.*"

Sorry. It seems to be the only fucking thing Daisy can say. There are tears in her eyes when I turn around to face her. Her bottom lip trembles. She looks like Melanie now more than ever. Guilty as shit.

"You're sorry?" I can't stop myself. Can't contain the anger. I'm in front of her in an instant, my hand flying out, striking her cheek. "You're fucking sorry! Do you know what I had to do for that money?"

What I sold.

Who I became.

"Frankie—"

"Shut up!"

Think. Think. Think. I can't. Not when I dig my nails into my arm. Not when I bite my lip. I have to snatch another knife from the drawer, swiping at my wrist. Deeper.

Fuck.

"Frankie! What the hell are you doing—"

"Go pack your stuff," I snap when a hint of clarity peeks through the chaos in my mind. It's enough to help me refocus. Bright-red drops drip down to splatter the floor, but I squeeze my eyes shut rather than notice them. Breathe. Just breathe. "Now!" I add when I don't hear her moving. "Ainsley's and the boys' too. Go!"

Knowing Melanie, the bastard she was shacking up with now probably had plenty of "friends" who wouldn't hesitate to help him beat his new "wife's" family into submission. They'd come back. Take the house. Take the rest of the money.

Everything.

And.

I.

Don't.

Fucking.

Care.

When Daisy finally staggers down the stairs, carrying a pile of bags slung over her arms, I don't go through it all. I just lead the way out and hail a cab once we've reached a main road. Then I head in any random direction until I find a hotel. I go pick the other kids up from school myself, and that night, the seven of us wind up sharing one room. Ironically, it doesn't seem to faze them too much that we don't head home.

But, when the others have fallen asleep, Mikie creeps over to me and presses something into my hand: a wad of cash.

"I kept most of it on me," he whispers. "Daisy only gave Mom a couple hundred."

I swallow hard, clinging to the bills like they're the only fucking thing I have left to hold on to. Maybe they are. "Thanks…"

In the end, a part of me knows I shouldn't even care about the money. My latest envelope from Maxim is in my pocket. By the end of next week, I'll have even more.

But it's funny how money never seems to fix things—whether you have enough or too little.

It just makes them fucking worse.

ON THE DAY when I'm supposed to return to Maxim...I don't. I stay in bed. My right eye is swollen, my head throbbing, and somehow, this injury aches worse than any Maxim delivered.

I don't want to move. Don't want to feel. Don't want to have to think. I just lie here in a pile of twisted sheets while the kids watch cartoons and fight over the free shit they want to stuff into their bags before we leave.

Maybe I *forget* my deadline.

Maybe I think that, away from home, he won't be able to find me.

Hell, perhaps he wouldn't even care? I'm sure I wouldn't be the first girl who disappeared on him, given his tastes. And he all but told me to take his money. Take a hike. Leave. So I don't think much of it when one of the kids races to answer a knock on the door. I assume they ordered room service—until I hear the voice of the visitor.

"Hello," the man says in a soft, warm tone. Only the unmistakable accent gives his identity away—and my entire body goes cold. "Is Francesca here?"

"Frankie!" Ainsley calls.

My heart sinks. My right eye is too sore to even open properly…

Shit.

I crawl out of bed. My eyes cut over to the bathroom adjacent to the room. Daisy's makeup bag is on the counter, but there isn't enough time.

I feel his gaze on me before I even look over my shoulder and see him lurking in the doorway. Dressed to kill in an ebony suit, Maxim is wearing a smile for Ainsley's benefit, though his fingers clench into fists the moment he sees my face. Two words are ripped from his throat, chilling me to the fucking core.

"Hello, Francesca."

CHAPTER NINETEEN

Francesca. Nothing in the world has terrified me more than hearing my name come out of his mouth. Nothing. I rock back on my heels as every cell in my body urges me to slam the door. Grab the kids. *Run.*

But I'm drawn forward purely by the look in his eye— that dangerous gleam I've come to know so well: confusion. It's like he doesn't know exactly why he's here.

"Can we talk in private?" He's still smiling, his voice deceptively casual. For Ainsley's benefit, not mine. And a part of me feels *grateful* for that.

He can do whatever the hell he wants to me. Just not in front of her.

"Y-yes." In the end, I hesitate only a second before stepping out into the hall and wrenching the door shut.

The moment we're alone, he lunges. One of his hands circles my throat, pressing me back against the wall. I already have an excuse on the tip of my tongue when his fingers drift up, the knuckles grazing my swollen eye. One brush of his thumb and I lose my train of thought.

He doesn't prod the way he examines the injuries he inflicts himself. He just feels. Acknowledges. When he draws back, there's blood on his fingertips and his eyes reflect murder.

"Explain."

That raspy baritone… It sinks into me. Corrupts me.

It wakes me up.

But maybe it's better to remain in the nightmare.

"I don't want to go back to you," I insist, shaking my head. His jaw clenches, but he doesn't move, watching me. "I don't. I don't! I can do this on my own. I always do everything on my own!"

My voice echoes back to me like a stranger's and I deflate against the wall. I was screaming. My throat aches and I can't bite back the sob that rips from it. "Just leave me alone. Leave me alone! I don't need you." I meet his gaze, willing him to listen to every word despite the hitch in my voice. It's the truth. It *has* to be. "I don't want you—"

"Tell me what happened." His voice resonates like thunder, easily overpowering mine but it's the look in his eye that leaves me stunned. There's no anger. No hate. Just a primal, raw understanding that cuts me right to the fucking core. "Tell me."

Like a switch being flipped, my lips part. Words spill out —I tell him everything. Melanie. The money. Her stupid new husband. Everything. He drinks in every rambled truth with no reaction. No frown. No narrowing of his eyes.

Nothing at all.

When I finally trail off, panting, he uses his grip on my throat to angle my chin back, forcing me to meet his gaze fully. "Get…home—to my suite."

I suck in air. It's the first time I've ever heard him speak in anything but polished, completed sentences. His eyes widen once he realizes, and his fingers shake—and even clench—closing off my windpipe.

"Now," he commands as I wheeze. "The car is waiting out front."

I cling to the wall when he lets me go, my legs already twitching to obey. But something holds me back, strong enough to outlast even my fear of him. I can hear Ainsley laughing at the television from here, completely oblivious to the danger lurking at her doorstep.

"My family…"

His eyes darken, swallowing up the shadows in the hall. "Go. Leave it to me."

"But—"

"That wasn't a request, *kotyonok*." His posture alone promises one hell of a punishment should I dare disobey. "Unless you want to use your safe word."

He waits, but I don't say a damn thing.

"Then go." He jerks his chin toward the end of the hall. "Now!"

I shouldn't. I should stay, fight on my own, handle shit alone, the way I have for so long.

But go fucking figure, Melanie's genes kick in this time: I leave. I put my trust in a man who likes to keep me on a leash. I put my family's *lives* in his hands.

I'm a terrible sister. A terrible person. The worse offense of all?

Even as I escape the hotel and slip into the back seat of the car waiting out front, I don't feel a single ounce of regret.

I don't feel anything.

He does the thinking for me.

I just obey.

I WAIT IN MY ROOM, but he doesn't return to the suite until after midnight, storming into the foyer like a creature ascending from hell. I hear his loud unsteady footsteps over the marble flooring. Wait, make that *two* sets of footsteps.

Is Lucius with him?

"Come here."

The command draws me out of my bedroom and into the hall. I'm still wearing the pair of crumbled sweats from this morning and an oversized tee. There's no time to even consider whether I should change. Maxim is waiting for me at the mouth of the hallway, but behind him…

Rather than his trusted butler, a trail of red paints a path toward the sculpture room. My nostrils flare, recognizing the telltale hint of salt on the air.

Oh shit.

"Come," Maxim growls when I stop moving.

Dread floods my stomach. I can hear my pulse in my ears —it's *that* damn loud. The steady thump plays like a backdrop to every slow, deliberate step I take. The only other thing I seem capable of doing is watching him. He's wet, dripping moisture onto the floor. It must be raining outside. The dampness slicks his hair back away from his face, leaving every feature in stark detail. Like always, his eyes are the most beautiful, terrifying part of all: they're narrowed, his mouth tight. When I'm close enough, he grabs me by the throat, dragging my body against his chest, lowering his mouth near my ear.

"You know what I am. *Who* I am." Without waiting for me to respond, he growls, "So do you want to see what happens to someone who dares to touch what is *mine*?"

My heart shrivels up at the grated quality to his voice. He sounds barely fucking human. Before I can answer, he steers me around, forcing me to face the mess streaking the marble. Together, we follow the ruby smears all the way to the mouth of the studio.

A pool of orange light cast by a chandelier illuminates the scene before us. There's a man crouched in the center of the floor, bloodied and bound, both hands tied behind his back. His forehead is bleeding, marred by a single gash that looks fresh. Other than that, he doesn't seem too worse for wear, though a bit of red has seeped through the sleeve of his raggedy tee shirt. I guess I cut him deeper than I'd thought.

"You bitch," Melanie's Fuckface snarls at me the moment he sees my face. He spits at the floor, aiming for my bare feet, and misses. The act is all for show though; he's scared. He keeps cutting his gaze over to Maxim, watching him warily.

I take it that their introduction wasn't a pleasant affair.

"What the fuck is this?" Fuckface demands. "Do you know who the fuck I am?"

"Your mother has chosen a Skinhead as her lover this time," Maxim says behind me. His voice is a cruel imitation of its usual polished cadence. He's a wolf, barely fitting within the sheep's clothing he's trying to wear—but it's all part of the game. There is no honesty in Russian Roulette.

Like an expert player, he steps around me, cutting a breathtaking silhouette. Black and gold gleam against red: his trademark colors. I expect him to glower, as in control as always, but when he finally turns to face me, I don't know how to process the look on his face.

So I dissect it in tiny, bite-sized pieces. Haunted, empty eyes. Hollowed-out expression. He's a ghost. A monster. A demon.

I take an instinctive step back, but deep down, I know there's no use in running. I've already sold my soul to him, after all. Still… A question wheezes out of my dry, sore throat. "What is this?"

"It was easy to find him," Maxim says without elaborating. "I tracked him down but I had Lucius arrange to bring him here, just so that I didn't kill him too soon."

My heart stops beating when he laughs, each bellowed sound trickling to the farthest edges of the room.

"He belongs to an upstart MC," he adds. "The Saints. They typically run in street drugs, but lately, they've taken to rounding up young women and selling them off for sex. Pretty girls."

I think of Daisy and flinch. My mind skips ahead: her face. This motherfucker. Her eyes without their typical innocent gleam. He had his hand on her leg. If I hadn't come home then, only god knows what would have happened. But that's a lie; I know.

She'd have wound up just like me, and it fucking *hurts* like nothing I've ever felt to picture it. I can't.

"So tell me, *kotyonok*," Maxim says over Fuckface's shouted curses. Those black eyes find mine, hollow and endless. "How should he suffer? The choice is yours."

I can taste the dare lurking behind his expression. The taunt he doesn't voice out loud: *You think you can crave me? Fuck me? Accept me? Think again. This is what I am. A monster.*

I know the reaction he expects from me. Maybe at any other moment, I'd give it to him: shiver in the corner, shake my head, cower, scream. I'd beg him not to do the big, bad things I know he's capable of. I'd make a game of it.

But tonight, my mind is too damn fuzzy. I attempt to rake the hair away from my face and realize I'm shaking. From head to toe. I can't stop.

"Tell me," Maxim warns, sounding miles away. "Tell me what is in your head."

What a fucking question. My lips part on command, but a torrent of nonsense spills out.

"Melanie's done this before," I croak, hugging myself tight. "That stupid bitch. She did it before—"

"Did what?" he presses, suddenly patient. That uncharacteristic note in his voice sets my nerves on edge like nothing else. It's…*comforting*.

"She has messed with a drug dealer before," I say in a rush. "Or fucking gang member. When she cuts them loose, they never stop. For months after, they'd come by the house, looking for her, looking for payback. Once…"

I swallow hard and stagger aimlessly as the room starts to spin around me. *Shit.* My hand flies out, my palm flattening against the wall for enough leverage to stay upright. Only now does the memory descend with full force.

"Tell me," I'm commanded.

Voice shaking, I obey. "Once, three of them came looking for her and found me instead, sleeping on the couch while the others were passed out upstairs."

The words die as I re-live that moment in chilling fucking detail.

They wanted fun and there were too many of them to fight off alone. Mikie was only a kid back then, Daisy even more naïve than she is now. I had no choice but to let them in. No choice but to do whatever they wanted just to make them leave. No choice… So I shoved a sock inside my mouth to muffle my own screams. I survived. I always fucking survive.

But once again—like always—there is another threat. And I know that, no matter what Maxim does, it won't be enough. This new Fuckface will always come back. His friends will return. And considering how long it's been since I've done laundry, I don't have any clean socks left.

And Daisy…

She will never be put in that position. Ever. Not if I can fucking help it.

"*Kotyonok*." Maxim's tone sounds different now. Less mocking, more curious. Even more unnervingly gentle.

I look up and find him watching me, his eyes narrowed, his mouth twisted up in confusion. I haven't run. He isn't sure why, and this time, his question isn't a taunt.

"Tell me what to do."

After everything he's dragged out of me these past few days, there are some secrets even he can't command me to tell. I have to show him.

My hand slides up along the wall until my fingertips brush something sharp hanging from a hook. I grab it, pulling it lose, and when my eyes drift up, they meet midnight. Once again, he does that thing: seep into my brain without permission, picking apart my thoughts and my fears before I've even admitted them to myself.

He stiffens when I take a step toward him, his nostrils flaring, his fingers flexing. The moment I come close enough, he reaches out, ready to take the offering in my hand.

But somewhere along the way, I mess up. I keep going, turning my attention to the man on the floor. Obeying Maxim would be the easy way out; I'd keep my conscience intact. But then I see that motherfucker's face and he's grinning. Laughing at me.

So I think of my sister.

And then I stop thinking altogether. I do what I always do: I *survive*.

My arm flies out and the blunt end of the chisel hits bone. Skull. The sound it makes: sharp, cracking. God. Someone cries out.

Him or me? I can't fucking tell. The next blow smashes one of his eyes in its socket though. I know that much. The third hits his mouth. The next… I lose count. I lose my fucking mind. My arm throbs as I strike over and over and over. The air is thick with salt and copper. My face is wet.

But I can't stop—not until someone grabs me around my waist, dragging me back and lifting me off the floor. The chisel falls from my grip, scattering into a distant corner. And Maxim…

His mouth is on my neck, his fingers running through my hair—not tugging this time. Petting. Through blurred vision, I see our shadows flung over the wall, like one distorted monster.

"*Moya*," he rasps into my skin when I try to pull away. "*Moya angel.* You were made for me. Mine."

I don't know what he's saying, but I recognize how he says it. His voice is thick. Gritted. Strained. It's the rare bit of emotion I've seen from him other than anger, and I don't know what name to put to it.

"Shhh," he murmurs, turning me around to face him before I can try. His eyes scan my face, his fingers stroking away the fresh drops of blood and tears. Is he angry?

I wait, shivering, but he caresses me, dragging his palm over my tangled curls.

"Mine. You were made for me." He's rambling, speaking to himself more than anyone else. "I knew it. I didn't want..." He shakes his head, cutting the thought off. Both of his hands come to land on my shoulders, dragging me closer so that his mouth can hover over my parted lips. Close enough to touch. Inhale. "You are mine," he tells me, sealing the confession with a harsh, bruising kiss that leaves me gasping for air. "Mine."

When he draws back, I look over my shoulder, too numb to process any of this. I see the man lying there. What's left of his fucking head. *Oh god. Oh god.*

"What did I do?" The question spills out of me, a broken howl. I'm on my knees, rocking back and forth. "What did I do? What did I do? Oh my god, what did I do?"

I look down at my hands. They're red. No matter how hard I rub them into the cotton of my shirt, I can't clean them off. *I can't get it off!*

"Look at me."

I blink and he's there, sinking to one knee while his hand cups my chin. His grip is strong; I can't turn away. I just stare up into his gaze and drown.

Golden hair frames his features like a halo, while his shadow stretches over the floor in a way that resembles broken wings.

My devil.

My deliverer.

My doom.

"You killed him," he tells me, shaking his head when I moan in disbelief.

No no no no no.

"Yes." His grip tightens over my chin before I can turn away, forcing me to face him. "There is no denying that—you would only hurt yourself. You *killed* him. In your mind, I suppose you had to. But do you know the secret behind committing sin?" This time, he doesn't wait for an answer. "It is absolution. Punishment in exchange for release. So let me deliver it to you." He tilts my head back, exposing my wet face to his gaze. "Tell me how."

The gist of his words resonates with what little sanity I have left: *Pick your punishment.*

My eyes go to his belt, and he stands and nearly rips the damn thing in half, wrenching it from the belt loops. I'm already on my hands and knees when he gets it free. I drop to my elbow, my free hand reaching back to wrench up my shirt.

He doesn't bother with tearing my pants off. The first blow hits me through them, biting deep down into the skin. I cry out, wailing into the flesh of my wrist. The slapping pinch isn't enough, and my teeth clamp down, causing enough pain to help me ride it out.

He doesn't hold back. I'm punished, blow for blow. Sin for sin. Each lash rips flesh open, making me bleed before I'm stitched back together. With pain. With agony.

That word he chose makes crystal-clear fucking sense now —he *absolves* me. And I can think again, feeding on the burning ache, blocking out the mental image of everything else. Nothing in the world exists but *this*. But him.

I'm lying flat on the floor when he finally ceases his assault. My eyes overflow with tears, my sobs catching on the air. I've never cried like this. Never felt like this. Broken. Damaged. *Free.*

"Come here." Rough fingers fist in my hair, dragging me upright and into the living room. When he lets me go, I hit the leather couch facedown, too weak to hold myself upright.

"You have a lot to be punished for tonight," Maxim tells me, breathless and ragged. The gruff tone doesn't match the reverent way his fingertips rake my flesh though, aggravating old bruises. "Do you know for what?"

I can't help the laugh that trickles out of me and ends up smothered into the leather. I know. My heart lurches, but I don't say anything until he flattens his palm against my throbbing ass. "I didn't come—"

"You came back to me the first time," he tells me, his big body resonating with the words, driving the vibration of each one into me. Through me. "Then the second. I could have thrown you away, even after the second." He flips me over so that I'm facing him fully. "Even the third time," he says as he scans my body. "I believed the lie that I could let you leave whenever I fucking wanted."

I'm prepared when he reaches for the hem of my pants and yanks them mercilessly down my legs.

He sniffs the fabric. Growls. Tosses it aside.

"But the fourth?" His fingers dip into the waistband of my panties, dragging. Tearing. "No. The fifth? *Never.* It's too late now."

His fingers bat my thighs apart and plunge inside me. He's ruthless. My thoughts splinter, my hips jerk, and my spine curls. Even as my head detaches from my body, I hear every word he says.

"I will never let you go now. Do you hear me, Francesca? You belong to me."

There's no chance to resist. His body moves over mine, his hands stripping me down to nothing but bare skin. One thrust takes him deep. My body surrenders, letting him in, clinging to every inch of his cock. With each brutal shove, he takes me higher.

Fucking me. Biting me. Swallowing me.

Even after he finally comes, filling me up, he doesn't stop. He flips me over. Rams in with his fingers. Makes me cry out. Makes me scream.

It isn't until I'm shaking, brainless, and half-numb with pain and lust that I realize just what he wants from me. Something he can't even ask for.

It has to be given.

"Maxim." His name tears from my throat as he enters me again, sinking in to the hilt. Deeper than I ever thought he could reach. He's beyond my body. He's in my soul. "Max…Maxim."

After one last bone-shattering thrust, he collapses on top of me, pressing me into the couch with his weight, breaking in the leather surface once and for all. "You are mine, *kotyonok*," he swears into my ear. "I will never let you go. Even if… Even if they rip you from my goddamn hands. *Never*."

They? My splintering thoughts can only come up with a faceless army of enemies. Melanie and her future fuck-ups? His mysterious Anatoli?

"Mine," he says, smothering every other concern but him.

Deep down, I know this is not a heartwarming confession.

It's a promise.

A threat.

This man will never let me go.

And maybe…I don't want him to.

OBEY

Obey

Obey By Lana Sky

Copyright © 2019 by Lana Sky
All rights reserved.

No part of this publication may be reproduced, distributed, or transmitted in any form or by any means, including photocopying, recording, or other electronic or mechanical methods, without the prior written permission of the author.

This is a work of fiction. Names, characters, businesses, places, events and incidents are either the products of the author's imagination or used in a fictitious manner. Any resemblance to actual persons, living or dead, or actual events is purely coincidental.

Cover Design and Interior Formatting by Charity Chimni
Editing by Mickey Reed Editing
Proofreading by Charity Chimni

CHAPTER ONE

I used to think I'd die before reaching twenty. Maybe I'd overdose on something? More realistically, I'd wind up stabbed to death by some shady-ass john.

Fairytales with shitty endings appeal more to me, anyway. The real Little Mermaid turned to dust in the end, and Snow White got buried in a glass box, all without getting the prince. I'm definitely not some fairytale princess—far from it, in fact. But maybe, just once, I want to know what it feels like. To dare to dream for something more than the inevitable unhappy ending. To want something so badly that you'd die for it.

After all, I've already killed for less.

"What are you thinking?"

The question rumbles against my eardrum. When I don't answer fast enough, warm lips part against the nape of my neck, releasing nipping teeth that demand obedience.

Answer me.

"S-something stupid," I croak, remembering where I am. Not a storybook setting, but a devil's lair. Black sheets conform to my exhausted form, soaking up sweat.

I risk looking over my shoulder from behind a fringe of my matted hair. A predator lies beside me, his skin glistening with sweat. Pale moonlight streams in through the window, casting him in a silver glow. If I squint and ignore the stench of salt in the air...

This moment could be normal pillow talk. How people in those shitty rom-com movies act after sex. Panting and still with limbs that almost touch.

One of those people wouldn't be bleeding though. They'd probably be closer in age, too. Not to mention, there wouldn't be a body in the foyer of their fancy high-rise— no, that would be a whole different genre. The kind in which the lead actor utilized a whip, left discarded somewhere on the floor.

"*Kotyonok.*" Maxim's tone snaps me back to the present. I've kept him waiting for a response for too long.

"Nothing," I say finally, licking my bitten, sore lips. "I'm thinking of a stupid game I used to play."

Or one my siblings and I used to, anyway. Proposing hypothetical wishing scenarios only poor brats could envision. Like: *Would you ever kill a man?* Or: *What would you do with a million dollars, Frankie?* For shits and giggles, we'd add a downside, just to make it harder to answer. *Hey, Frankie, what would you do if you committed murder with a man who had a million dollars?*

Well…

I'd probably be in bed with said chiseled Adonis who seemed to own the whole fucking world. He'd have blond hair. Wild strands of it might fall across his forehead, casting a shadow over his piercing gaze. One look and my heart would clench as if jolted by a defibrillator. *Zap!* It's pathetic to admit, but only he would have that kind of power over me.

I'd let him have it.

Being so close to him would sting—worse than any bruise or cut I could ever inflict on myself. At least a knife would have a human impulse controlling it. Logic. Mercy.

But he wouldn't.

He'd be different. A beautiful, soulless contrast of ivory and shadow. All mine and yet so far out of reach. But, like the idiot I am, I'd forget that. Just for a second. I'd stare, eyeing the contours of his jaw in search of a hint of softness.

Maybe I'd find some, right *there* lurking within dark irises. I'd reach for it, my fingertips grazing flesh and muscle. Then he'd open his mouth and say…

"You slept." His voice resonates through my skin, his breath hot on my shoulder. "The first night I killed, I didn't."

I stiffen at the reminder, and then my hand falls to the sheets beneath us. Blood, violence, death. The memories circle my brain, forming a tornado of panic that almost drags me under—almost.

Like a good dealer, he already has another dose of my chosen poison on hand to keep me afloat. Rather than a bite or pinch, my antidote lurks in more violence, uttered like a bedtime story.

"I was a child then, the first time. My father would beat my mother, you see." His tone is so casual that he could be talking about the weather. Not death. "It was common among them," he adds. "His brothers. His father. It was even expected that I should hit her, should the feeling strike me to." He blows out a sigh that ruffles my hair. "But she was kind. Gentle. She barely raised her voice to him, and yet he would attack her just because the wind was blowing. There was no reason. No purpose. He just could."

His confession puts everything he's done to me in a newer context. The contracts. The safe words. Each layer is constructed to differentiate his preferences from those of an abusive prick. To prove to himself: *I'm not like him.*

Maybe it's enough of a difference. Or a lie. The same one I tell myself every damn day: I'm not like Melanie. I whore because I have to. I steal, cheat, lie, and fuck—all because I need to.

Like that makes it any better.

Like that makes it any easier to look at myself in a mirror.

"One night," Maxim continues, "he stormed into the house in a rage and struck her once. Just once, but she died instantly. Brain hemorrhage. Even as a child, I knew what he'd done. How little he cared in the aftermath—he kicked her when she didn't get up. Then he poured himself a scotch and headed up to bed, muttering how he'd make her pay in the morning. So I followed him." He remains silent for so long that I start to think he won't finish. Finally... "I don't even remember what I called him. He turned around and struck me across the face. In retaliation, I pushed him. He didn't die instantly, not like her. He was still alive, howling at the bottom of the stairs. He'd struck his head, but not hard enough to kill him. So I took a poker from the fireplace..."

Oh god. I squeeze my eyes shut as if the pathetic act can stop my brain from conjuring an image to match his tale. "Why are you telling me this?"

He sighs, breathing out harshly against my spine as I open my eyes again. "So that you will understand. Contracts aside, I am who I am. *This.*" He raises his hand, extending each finger as though his true nature is tattooed on each knuckle. "I will never hide this part of myself from you."

From someone else, I think the confession would sound romantic. Out of his mouth, it's a terrifying promise.

And he makes me chase it, staying silent until I ask, "What happened next?"

"I spent days in that house alone with their bodies. My grandfather was the one who found me. Found his son. I was afraid." No one would ever guess as much now. His voice lacks any true definition—just hoarse, emotionless words. "In my family, you can kill and abuse anyone *but* blood. The penalty is worse than death. But rather than punishment, he gave me my absolution: I was to head the division of the syndicate my father had. My family had a long heritage in running guns in and out of Russia, along with gambling. Overnight, I was given control of it all, with the same punishment my father faced should I fail: death. I was ten years old."

Heat prickles behind my eyes. Blinking doesn't push the tears back, and for the millionth time this week alone, I'm fucking crying. I can't stop it. In a way, I don't *want* to stop it. The moisture spilling down my cheeks tethers me to reality, far away from the twisted past he's reliving.

But not for long.

"I was weak," he says, continuing the thread of this fucked-up fairytale. "I still mourned my mother. Wept for her. And my grandfather was not pleased. To him, my actions were pathetic. He feared that I would never grow into a man. That I was too soft. Nothing should matter more to a man than his name. No *one* else. In his mind, he only saw one way to 'cure' me of those instincts."

His hand drifts down his torso to the edge of the binder shielding his stoma.

No. I'm holding my breath. My lungs are screaming for air, unable to take any in until he finally delivers the final piece of his story.

"He hired men," he says into my shoulder.

A sharp pain makes me jump: He bit me, giving us both a dose of the drug we've come to crave—but this time, it's not enough. I'm in the void with him, sucked into the past, forced to relive his horror to the very end.

"A group of them. To teach me why it would not be in my best interest to continue acting 'like a faggot,' as he put it."

Oh god.

I can't. I shake my head and then push him off. Away. In a rush of unfurling limbs, I try to crawl to the end of the bed, but he catches me, fisting his hand in my hair.

"I learned the truth about pleasure and pain that night, *kotyonok,*" he says in a chilling monotone. It's like once he's started talking, he can't stop. "You can never have one without the other, and I ensured that I would *never* be on the losing end again. I came to America. I built my own corner of our empire with my own fucking hands. I found people I could share it with."

He doesn't mean a family. Something more. I think of the British man, and Lucius, and the aura he's cultivated in his club. He built a new life.

"But *you.* I never planned for you."

Hot, searing pain splashes across my scalp as he yanks on my hair, drawing me into him.

"You are disgusted," he says, but he doesn't sound angry. Just resigned.

I crane my neck and find his mouth twisted into that terrifying emotion: confusion. His fingers trace my jaw as he studies my expression: my gaping mouth, my weeping eyes and what I know he finds in them.

Pity would be one thing, but this is different, unlike any agony he could ever dish out with a belt or his teeth. Something deeper than physical pain—it's understanding.

And it's fucking horrifying to feel it for someone like him. To feel it at all.

"I'm so sorry," I blurt as his frown deepens. "I'm so sorry—"

"Sorry?" Darkness clouds his gaze, and my heart sputters to a stop in my chest. When he reaches out, I'm frozen solid, but his fingers merely graze the length of my chin, tilting my face toward his. "One would think that, by now, you would stop surprising me, *kotyonok*," he says. Then he rolls toward his edge of the bed and stands. "I want you to answer this question honestly: Do you trust me?"

"W-what?"

"Trust," he snarls. "Do you know what it means?"

"I…"

I don't. Trust—that's a make-believe concept. I grew up being taught over and over that you only had one bitch on your side: the same one you saw in the mirror.

No one else was needed.

But him…

I know the word I want to say. I try to spit it out, but my brain scrambles it, turning the answer into something else. "I don't know."

Maxim nods. He's already dressed, and one of his hands dips into his pocket and withdraws a familiar object tucked into his palm: a knife. He flexes his wrist, springing the blade to its full length.

"My family thrives on 'trust,'" he says, mutilating the word like it's some sick inside joke. "On honor. Obedience. I am expected to follow any command given to me. No questions asked. No hesitation. Could I expect the same from you?" He takes a step in my direction, sending every muscle in my body into a frenzy. "The will to let me approach you with this blade and not so much as flinch because you trust whatever I will do with it. To you. Could you give me that?"

He smiles when I don't answer: a dangerous flash of teeth. "Stay here," he says, changing the subject. "I need to clean."

I swallow hard. Clean. In other words, remove the body. I can smell it from here, lingering beneath the musk of sex. Blood. Death…

"Get some rest, *kotyonok*."

When he leaves this time, there's no uncertain anticipation of what he might do next. I know: He'll come back.

And for whatever insane reason…I'll be here.

CHAPTER TWO

"Trusting" begins with a simple lesson, more basic than any so far. Wake up in his arms, breathing in his scent: a giant who holds me like a doll he doesn't want to break. Yet. The moment he senses I'm awake, his grip tightens, trapping me here. Beneath him. Beside him. Possession laces his touch, but it feels different from before.

My old collar was leather and gold, but this time…

Secrets bind me to him, forming a noose around my throat—one I'll never be able to remove. I can only endure it. Feel his skin molded against mine, sinew and muscle coiled with enough strength to kill. Take in everything Maxim Koslov has to offer…

And not flinch.

I last two seconds—the longest stretch I've ever gone with him. When I finally react, he pulls away and stands.

"Get up." After crossing over to a dresser, he removes a crisp white shirt and a pair of black slacks from it. "Up, *kotyonok*," he warns, frowning. I haven't moved. "As much as I'd love to punish your insolence—" His eyes rake over me and his tongue traces his bottom lip. Meeting my gaze, he sighs. "I'm taking you home."

Home. A part of me recoils even as I scramble upright. I can't imagine stepping foot back in the fucking shack again. The one place where I'm easy bait for Melanie the next time she comes knocking.

"Not there," he says as if reading my mind. "I'm taking you *home.*"

The subtle inflection in his tone adds a terrifying new connotation to that word.

"What about my siblings?" It hits me that I don't have any idea where they are now. At the hotel? Somewhere else? My throat constricts. How could I have been so fucking selfish? "Where are they?"

"Safe," Maxim says. His tone paired with the knowing gleam in his gaze gives me an idea that he's handled it, taking all decisions right out of my hands.

Should I feel insulted? Petrified?

Still numb from last night, I can't decide. Absolution is a funny fucking thing in practice. It takes something more than the submission he craves—it takes desperation. I could fight back against his smooth insertion into my life or demand to know more.

Or I could say that fucking safe word and end it all now.

And he wants me to. That is why he's taking his time unfurling his shirt and pulling his pants on, waiting for the exact second I'll challenge him. When that moment never comes, he stands, fully dressed, his head cocked slightly to the side.

"Get dressed," he says and I lurch from the sheets and stagger to my feet.

He follows when I head toward my room, lurking in my wake. A glance down the hallway reveals that the center of the foyer is pristine, free of blood. Terror seeps in for a brief second, rooting me in place. My hand trembles, and for a moment, I let myself relive it.

The lack of resistance after the bone was crushed. The rusty smell of his blood painting my skin. The life draining from his eyes…what was left of them.

"*Kotyonok.*" Maxim's hand lands on my shoulder, nudging me into the room down the hall from his. "Come."

With him in tow, I approach the closet and observe the clothing within. I don't even put up the pretense of choosing an item on my own. Sure enough, he reaches around me and flips through an array of hangers before settling on a black dress with a lacy collar. I start to pull it on, but he stops me, running his hand across my cheek.

"I need to wash you."

My stomach churns as I follow his gaze downward. My rust-colored hands reinforce a grim reality: I'm still covered in blood. So is he, though he doesn't seem bothered by the faint red streaks along his jaw.

In my bathroom, he guides me into the tub and washes me with his usual hyper-focused attention. My legs garner most of his care. He wrings the cloth directly over the worst of the cuts marring the pale skin—a savage array of lacerations on my inner thigh.

Reading the name they form over and over to myself doesn't make the ownership sink in.

Only when he roughly drags his thumb over an open wound do I feel the tug of that invisible chain.

You were made for me.

Once I'm finally dressed, he leads me to the front of the suite.

"I've had your belongings moved to a new location," he admits, confirming my suspicion: the home he referred to isn't the shitty two-story dwelling in Horn Hill that I've busted my ass all these years to protect.

Wherever he's taking me is a new realm. His.

My lips part, though I'm not sure why. Maybe I'll gather up the nerve to ask him more? Any words die in my throat as a buzzing tone draws his attention, and he withdraws a cell phone from his pocket.

"What?" he snarls, pressing the receiver near his ear. Whatever he hears from the other end makes his eyes dart in my direction, his jaw clenching. "No. I didn't know *he* was in town. Fuck—I'll be there." He shoves the phone into his pocket and heads for the sculpting room. "Go. Lucius will meet you out front. I'll join you later tonight."

It's funny. His tone is as cold and measured as always, but he's switched again, shedding any resemblance to the man who held me throughout the night. My brain processes his transformation in mockingly slow motion. How his eyes lose what little light they had. His mouth twists into that stern, haunting frown next. He's Mr. Hyde in the blink of an eye.

When I don't move, he jerks his chin toward the door. "I said go."

As expected, Lucius meets me in front of the building. Rather than head for Horn Hill or the hotel, his driver takes us to a townhouse in an upscale section of town, not too far from the high-rise. A block away, to be exact. It's a gated community right in the heart of Vermillion Heights —one of the most expensive sectors in the city. At first, I assume that Maxim wanted some other errand run first, but no. This is "home"—and it is way too much: an extravagant dollhouse fit for a toy.

"Here it is," Lucius announces as the car pulls into the driveway.

All I can do is stare. Overall, the house is made of stone, three stories tall, with old-fashioned fixtures. It's slightly beyond Maxim's sleek, modern style—more classic. It's beautiful. It's impossible. It's *borrowed.*

I tell myself that as I unbuckle my seat belt and step out of the car. When I see the house up close, my internal musing slips out. "He can't be serious."

"This way, miss," Lucius prods, as unshakably calm as always.

Shaking my head, I follow him up a path leading to the front door. Before Lucius can even knock, a beaming blond opens it and introduces herself as "Nancy," the new au pair. At my confused glance, Lucius shrugs—the most casual act I've seen from him yet.

"Mr. Koslov spared no expense in assuring that your family would be well taken care of," he explains.

What exactly that means remains to be seen.

The moment we step over the threshold, I hear screaming.

"Ainsley?" I rush toward the sound, but before panic can even set in, I register the scene unfolding in front of me: Ainsley and Eric are wrestling in the middle of a breathtakingly huge living room with a real fucking fireplace. The older kids are lounging on leather couches. When they see me, it's a stampede, and I'm suffocated beneath hugs and a million fucking questions.

"Frankie, what's going on?"

"What is this place?"

"Is this all ours?"

Rather than answer them, I shrug and force my lips into the shadow of a smile. "Can I have a tour?"

Ainsley takes charge to lead me through the house. It's huge. They each have their own bedroom, and I can't ignore the knowing shiver that runs down my spine once I see the décor of each one.

He knew—Maxim. He knew that Ainsley likes pink and Daisy prefers purple. He knew which room to supply with Teenage Mutant Ninja Turtles sheets and who to equip with an enormous dollhouse.

All of it feels too carefully catered to detail to seem accidental. No, he researched me. My life. My family.

And he chose a place Melanie will never be able to sneak her way into.

"Are you all right, miss?" Lucius asks once we return to the foyer.

"Yeah," I lie. My heart is racing, my palms slick. I'm not okay. Fear is a new kind of poison dripping through my veins. It doesn't make my thoughts feel any clearer. I'm just on edge.

As Maxim warned me himself, there was only ever one winner of the game.

So when is he going to finally pull the trigger?

All I can do is hope that the bullet comes before I get used to this. Before I get even more stupid—let my guard down any further.

I rarely pray, but here goes it: *Please, God, let him end this before this goes too far.*

Before I forget that this was only ever a game.

CHAPTER THREE

Maxim doesn't arrive until after sunset, but the sound of him prowling across the foyer contrasts sharply with childish shrieks and bits of laughter drifting from the living room behind me.

I race to meet him, and my heart goes haywire as I watch him dominate the doorway. His shoulders are back, his posture neutral. If I didn't know any better, he could be a kind neighbor welcoming a new family into town.

Not the devil who owns me, body and soul.

"Stay," he says when I start for the door. "We're having dinner here tonight."

"W-what?" By the time I finally remember how to move, he's already halfway across the room. "Wait—"

"Who's at the door?" Ainsley demands, her cherub face peeking from around the doorway to the living room.

Oh god.

A suffocating pins-and-needles feeling comes over me as I observe Maxim towering over her tiny frame. When she spots him, she creeps to my side, her arms like iron bars around my waist.

"I'm a friend of your sister's," Maxim says, but there is a noticeable difference in how he responds to her versus me. For one, a warm smile unfolds over his mouth and his eyes lose a bit of their natural ice. When he sinks to one knee, I nearly jump out of my skin—but he only extends his hand, his expression one of pure charm. "I am very pleased to meet you."

Ainsley, who's painfully shy around strangers on a good day, manages to smile back. She even shakes his massive hand with one of her own.

Score one Maxim Koslov.

I watch awkwardly, unsure of what to do. "Should… should I give you a tour?" I ask as Maxim rises to his full height.

"No." Shaking his head, Maxim advances down the hall with an unnerving familiarity. "I'm sure dinner is ready."

"Dinner?" I ask, creeping in his wake, Ainsley in tow.

He must have called ahead. Planned this. The table in the dining room is already set for eight—by Nancy, I suspect. I hadn't even noticed.

After a whirlwind moment of introductions, I find myself shoved into a chair while all six kids take turns shouting over each other in a battle to narrate their week. What a difference a few fucking days of security can make. It's almost like we're a normal family for once.

There are no requests for new shoes or field trip dues. Just "I made a friend at the new school. Her name is Suzie."

"I actually passed a damn test."

"You look tired, Frankie. You look so tired…"

Alone, I'd have to fend the questions off by myself. Laugh on cue, smile, pretend. That was the price of security in the old days. I smothered my yawns of exhaustion and took one for the team. I sacrificed, even if it meant lying.

I'm not tired. The words are on my tongue, but for the first time ever, someone beats me to the punch.

"I am terribly sorry to have kept your sister away," Maxim says, his voice smooth and self-assured. "I've been keeping her busy these past few weeks."

Considering his sleek, black business shirt, red tie, and slacks, he resembles the type of man who might mean those words in the platonic sense only.

God, how appearances can be deceiving.

"She works for you?" The question comes from Mikie. His eyes are sharp, resembling how I guess I did whenever Melanie brought a new patsy around.

I don't know whether to panic or be proud. My heart is a swollen ball of nerves exploding in my chest.

"Yes," Maxim replies without missing a beat. Seated beside me, he dominates this section of the table, dwarfing me and Daisy, who is sitting on the other side of him. Though his blond hair may be neatly slicked back and his hands free of blood, he's imposing.

I can't ignore the way the kids are mysteriously quieter around him, either. It's like they can sense what I would have in their place.

Nothing about this man broadcasts normal.

But, as if to prove me wrong, he shifts in his seat and his bulk suddenly seems less intimidating and more ungainly. The smile he's wearing helps. A little. To someone on the outside looking in, the expression might seem friendly. To me, it's a warning.

The scary part? I'm not sure of what. His glance in my direction conveys a silent message: *Relax.*

"Is it illegal?" Mikie demands, placing both hands flat against the table. Good boy. Stupid boy.

I try to meet his gaze. Shake my head. I'd be giving myself away, but what the fuck does stealth matter now? I know what happens when Maxim is pushed too far. The thought of him going at my brother with one of the polished steak knives from the table steals my breath away and my eyes dart to the door.

"Would your sister participate in anything illegal?" Maxim wonders.

His voice is neutral enough to draw a nervous laugh from the others, and the sound simultaneously drowns out my gasp as his hand settles over the small of my back. Thick fingers caress my spine, imparting a simple message: *I told you to relax.*

The room spins as a new voice joins the fray, announcing dinner. A maid? Whoever she is, she's smiling, but her pretty face drifts in and out of focus as she places a platter of food at the center of the table.

The kids attack in a blur of flying plates and silverware, and the chaos provides enough cover to disguise the warm lips that graze the side of my neck.

"Breathe. As I told you once before, I will not hurt them."

I didn't realize just how much I needed that reassurance. Some of the tension leaves my body in a sigh—some. Despite everything, one bastion of Maxim Koslov's character seems to hold true: He isn't a liar. At least, not intentionally—but any second the game could change.

Then again, believing him is the only shred of comfort I have to hold on to.

Dinner passes in a blur. Afterward, I juggle Ainsley on my lap, but I'm barely tethered to the warm, casual atmosphere everyone else seems to be feeling. My eyes don't leave Maxim once.

I'm hunting for the usual hallmarks of his anger: flashing eyes, clenched jaw. Instead, I find a new discovery that blows my mind. He keeps smiling, but it doesn't seem forced. He speaks when someone initiates a conversation with him—which, of course, is everyone, all at once. They flock to the relative newcomer, feeding off the novelty of a strange man who doesn't seem to be a criminal. Not outright, anyway.

They aren't up in arms like the way I've taught them to be around Melanie's conquests. I could write it off as just another part of Maxim's strange charm, but I know the truth. And it hurts.

They trust *me*.

And, what's even stranger, Maxim doesn't seem to forsake that. I can sense it in the way he keeps his posture open and relaxed even though such a stance doesn't come naturally to him. Neither does the small talk he endures.

"...and then I punched him," Ainsley says proudly, concluding her narration of one of her escapades on a playground. She eyes Maxim, her mouth wrinkled thoughtfully. "Have *you* ever punched someone?"

Maxim furrows his eyebrows as if seriously considering the question. Then he shrugs. "I prefer other methods," he says.

It's like being in the fucking Twilight Zone. I don't know how to react. So I just watch. I suffocate.

And, as if it's easier than breathing, Maxim Koslov effortlessly manipulates my family the same way he does me.

There's something seductive in the way he speaks when he's not growling out a command or a warning. His rich baritone caresses every word, making them ring out like musical notes.

I've never seen Daisy so relaxed around a stranger. He flatters Daisy with gentlemanly compliments, and he even gives Ainsley a "pony ride" around the living room when she demands it. He jokes with Mikie and the boys too.

I've never seen a man go out of his way to encourage this reaction in them and the shock of it all chokes me.

Torturing me aside, this is the most terrifying weapon that he's ever used. Pain is fleeting, but this? Normalcy is addictive—a drug I've never had. One that's too dangerous to ever indulge in.

"That's it. It's getting late," I blurt as the time creeps toward midnight.

When I finally usher the kids off to bed, it's like I can breathe again—and the instinct that took root the moment he arrived flares at full force. "You didn't have to do this."

"Do what?" Maxim doesn't miss a beat as he takes me by the arm and steers me toward the entryway, far from any listening ears—some of the kids must be watching from the stairs.

"This," I croak as the door closes behind us. I don't think air trickles into my lungs again until we've gone halfway down the front path. "I didn't… It's not good for them—"

"I didn't come here for *them*." He's dropped the charming act. All that's left behind is tension, which gnaws at the air between us. "This is what I can give *you*. More than pleasure. More than pain. More than sin."

I lick my lips, priming them to ask a dangerous question. "Like what?"

"More," he snaps. "Safety. Financial security. Support."

My brain instinctively shies away from those three words. I've never had them. Never needed them. Do I want them? I shake my head, my hair flying. Hell, I don't know if I'm trying to convince him or myself.

"Why?" I ask.

The contract, he should say—trading brutal sex for his money. Instead, he raises an eyebrow. "You can always tell me to leave."

It's a warning. I see his posture from the corner of my eye: broad, stiff, unmovable. His scent floods the air, filling my lungs. There is no escape.

Just surrender.

"Thank you," I croak. "But it's not good for them. Getting attached to someone. When this is over…"

"Ah." Maxim releases a low, rumbling chuckle that chills me to my very core. "You are still under the impression that this will be a temporary arrangement?"

"Isn't it?"

At least until the moment he gets bored, anyway. When he finds another woman to play with. Still, his words keep echoing in my head. *I will never let you go.* A part of me expects him to say them again. Reinforce it.

Never.

"Temporary," he says. A shadow flickers across his gaze as his fingers spread, gripping me tighter before releasing me. "If you say so."

He turns away, leaving me to follow him to the car. But while I walk, I can't shake the feeling that he laid down a trap.

And I stepped right into it.

CHAPTER FOUR

He makes me sleep in my room alone, but in the morning, his voice draws me awake.

"I need to wash you."

Later, when I'm dried and dressed, he enters the sculpting room and a terrifying thought sinks in. Despite everything, it is possible to forget what Maxim is. For five minutes maybe, when his shoulders aren't tense and his face is relaxed as he performs a hobby he obviously enjoys.

Something other than fucking.

But then, as if the universe has a vendetta against letting him appear human, something or someone quickly makes him raise his guard again.

This time, it's the door to the suite flying open and two men barging inside the studio. Make that *one* man, and he's dragging the other. I recognize the first's features before his voice rings out, tinged with a familiar accent. The British man from the club.

"I have a gift for you." He inclines his head at the man he's holding by the collar of a tattered sweatshirt. "My biker friend here may have some information that can help you with your…problem."

A scruffy beard obscures most of the blood streaming from what I think is the man's badly broken nose. One shove from the British man and he falls forward on his hands and knees. His dark, beady eyes flicker anxiously to Maxim. I wonder if he's from the same "biker" club as Melanie's last bastard.

"I know who you are," he says, spitting out blood. "You think you can kill me? The whole crew knows what you did to—"

"Good," Maxim says over him. "I didn't hide it. And unfortunately for you, I won't kill you. Yet." He sinks down low, still dangling a chisel from one hand. "First, I have a few questions I need to ask."

The biker goes three shades paler, but he bares his teeth, keeping up the tough act. "Like what, you motherfucker? We didn't fuck up your shit if that's what you're asking."

Maxim's eyes narrow and his hand flexes, tapping the edge of the chisel against the floor in a slow, lazy rhythm. "Oh? And you wouldn't happen to know who did, would you?"

The man chokes out a laugh and then grunts, clutching his nose. "And you don't?" he mumbles around his fingers. "Funny, because the fucker is one of yours—"

"Go on," Maxim goads, his jaw clenching.

"Yeah. Blond guy. Same fucking accent as you. He your boy or something? From what I hear, he's been going around to everyone, ratting out your positions on everything."

Maxim goes rigid. He and the British man lock gazes and I get the sense that they're having a full-blown conversation without a word spoken between them.

"Him?" the British man asks, his tone hard.

Maxim says nothing. Before him, the thug grins, too smug to notice the alarming shift in his captor's posture. "Your warehouses," he sneers. "Where you do your runs. All that shit. I even heard that he's been asking about some bitch you fuck with by name." He nods in my direction. "This her? Francesca—"

"Go." Chisel in hand, Maxim is instantly transformed. His eyes darken, icy and flat. I can see my soul reflected in them as they gloss over my position in the corner. "Now, *kotyonok*," he tells me. The muscles in his forearms flex, a dangerous omen.

I start to move, but I only take a step before something in me falters. I stop. Maxim shoots me a glance, his eyes like midnight. There's a warning in them. A dare. *This is who I am.*

A monster.

Can you really accept me?

Seconds pass before my body makes the decision for me. I stay.

Turning from me, Maxim extends his arm, clenching his hands into fists. *Wham!* The violent thud of flesh striking flesh echoes like a gunshot, churning my stomach. In a sick arch, blood flies, painting a trail over the marble.

"Tell me more," Maxim demands as the man before him cowers, coughing up scarlet liquid. "Does he have a name, this 'fucker' of mine?"

The biker shakes his head. "I dunno," he croaks.

"Shame. Then I suppose our conversation has concluded."

Silver streaks the air and my mind takes a belated second to identify what it is: the chisel. *Thwack!*

It strikes skull. Bone. Flesh.

Again.

Again.

Again.

Maxim and his victim congeal into a shapeless blur of black and red as my eyes lose track of the violence. I can hear the noise. Taste blood.

Then it's over, and a harsh touch on my shoulder snaps me back to reality.

"When I tell you to leave, you leave."

I blink to find Maxim in front of me. His thumb shoots out, stroking my cheek. It's red, smelling of salt.

"Or do you think now that you've had a taste, you can handle this, *kotyonok*?" His eyes hone in on my quivering throat as I swallow to fight back bile. "You can't," he decides tonelessly. The chisel flies from his grasp as he turns away. "Go. And this time, do not make me tell you twice."

When he returns his focus to the helpless man on the floor, I dart into the hallway before the next blow lands with a sickening thud.

Then I run.

"You know it's him." The British man's voice chases me, a low, contemplating murmur. "Must our past keep haunting us because of your family?"

HOURS PASS before the whimpering finally dies off. From my position on my bed, I hear the front door open and then slam shut, which creates a chilling prelude to the slow, steady steps advancing on my room a second later.

He takes his time, turning my heartbeat into a rapid melody of surging blood and a hammering pulse. Just as it reaches a crescendo, my door opens.

These four white walls can't contain his bulk. They strain at the seams like an overstuffed birdcage and I'm the fucking canary. The half of my prison he dominates becomes a shadow, swallowed in darkness. My little corner contains the only hint of light seeping in through a nearby window, while my racing heartbeat floods the air. Only one of us can survive the impending collision.

Him?

Me?

What a stupid fucking question.

My knees knock together, but I can't move. I just wait. In a vain attempt to ground myself, my fingers flutter over my white duvet, cinching chunks of it.

"Look at me." One step brings him closer.

I smell him, choking on the scent of sweat and lust as my eyes adjust, seeking his shape out. His eyes glow, adding a chilling contrast to the bulge straining against the front of his pants. Instinct warns me that he's erect. Violence gets him off. So does fear.

So does *this*.

"You didn't run," he tells me, anger deepening the words into a guttural hum. "Not even when you saw the worst. You stayed. Do you think that makes you brave?"

I blink. The worst? He must mean torturing people in front of me, apparently—more than once.

But he's wrong.

The worst horrors he inflicts on me are what he's doing now: switching personas like hats. One man claims I was made for him. And the other? Made to spite him.

The only weapon I have in my arsenal is deflection. "Why did he say my name?"

He frowns, his head cocked. Just as quickly, he recovers, crossing over to the bed. With a well-placed swipe of his thumb against my lip, my body shivers, resonating with his possession. It's the strangest feeling imaginable—terror and need. It's like being on the edge of a high. Like bleeding out. Hemorrhaging.

"He was mistaken." His accent chops each word into several harsh syllables. "Forget him."

"What about that guy?" I croak. "The one I..." God, I can't even say the rest.

"Are you worried?" he counters. "Do you think I won't protect you?" He makes it sound so dangerous, doubting him.

A reply I can't swallow down springs to my lips. "What happens now?"

"Now..." He rolls his head along his shoulders, the closest I figure he can get to a casual shrug. "Have you consider what I asked you before?"

"What?"

"You can watch me beat a man to death…but can you give me your trust?" The way he speaks—strained and guttural—makes a part of me tremble. "Could you trust your life to me? No, I don't think you could." He shakes his head. "But the day you give me your trust—your full trust. There is nothing that I would deny you."

A dare? It's easier to focus on the mocking dip in his tone than the rest. His honesty is like a shotgun blast—lethal at point-blank range. I could test him like he said. Ask for something insane. Outrageous. Make him give me a response.

"So…" I swallow to clear my throat. "So, if I asked you for a million dollars—"

"You ask me for what you need. I will give it to you," he warns.

So, in other words, *yes*. If I needed a million dollars, he'd give it to me, in theory. The thought of that blows my mind.

He can't possibly mean it.

But the funny part is that, the longer I stare into his gaze, the more it seems like he does.

"So…how do I?" I croak. *Trust you.*

He comes to stand before me, his head cocked slightly to the side, those eyes fathomless. "Come here."

Holding my breath, I stand and approach him.

"Trust means nothing more than surrender," he explains. "I'm not asking for anything more than that. You. So get on your knees. Prove it to me."

On my knees. Prove it. He doesn't have to spell it out. My tongue slides along my lower lip, even as my instinct goes to war with logic.

Instinct wins: obey. I sink to my knees and shift toward him. He stays standing, though he spreads his legs wider when I reach for the fly of his slacks. With one tug on the zipper, his cock springs free. He's hard already. I can barely fit my lips around the swelling crown.

The moment my tongue cradles his shaft, I realize that this isn't like all the other times I've sucked him off. I hesitate for the space of a second, but he never grunts out any harsh commands. No orders to deepthroat. His hand grips my scalp instead, more for reinforcement than anything, driving the truth into my skull.

He's here. My goal is to pleasure him. Nothing else…

There are no dollar bills to mask my shame with. No salary to make it worth it. Just the slim knowledge that as long as I give him what he wants, he'll do the same.

Trust, I guess.

Slowly, I let my tongue drift up and down his length before spreading my lips around him again.

"Fuck," he grunts, the vibration rumbling through him.

With each suck, his grip tightens, pulling loose strands of hair. Ripping them *out*. It isn't long before he's pulsing at the entrance of my throat, demanding I take him in. All of him. Deep. Deeper…

For the second time, I have the same suspicion: Violence *must* turn him on. He's even thicker now. Straining. Some rabid impulse spurs me on, making me hollow my cheeks around him. I know he's at the edge when a burst of precum floods my tongue, ripe with his taste. Just when he starts to tense beneath me, his grip on my hair becomes a vise.

"Enough."

Before I can let him go, he drags me upright. My eyes flutter, taking in bits and pieces of the room—but he's already shoving me face down onto the mattress.

"Stay like this," he growls into my ear.

Drugged on anticipation, my brain struggles to interpret what he means. *Oh.* Like this: prone, at his mercy. *His.*

"Just like this…"

A sharp nip on my earlobe sends a jolt through me as his erection throbs against my inner thigh. Grasping, his hand travels down my hip to nudge my legs apart before guiding his length inside me.

One hard thrust and he's as deep as this position will allow. Fathomless. I can't even begin to silence my cry. So I don't, letting the sound ring out.

I squeeze my eyes shut, surrendering my body to the pace he sets. Fast. Slow. Slower. I come even before he spills himself inside me, and then I float back down to Earth just in time to feel the bed shift with his weight.

With his fingers in my hair, he tugs me toward him. Gnashing teeth meet my lips in a flurry, prying them apart, tearing me open. Kissing him always feels more penetrating than the sex. More intimate.

I'm breathing his air, inhaling his scent, and there is no boundary to negate the intensity.

He crushes me down, claiming my mouth with more ruthless need than he ever has my body. Harder. Deeper. I'm a writhing mass of sensation as muscle and bone react to his touch like a magnet. We're intertwined, skin on skin. Eager for more, I shift against him, sinking my fingers into his hair.

His words echo in my skull, a mocking taunt. *I can give you what you need.*

And maybe I want it: all of him.

Every inch.

Everything.

Something broken and unwarranted slips from my lips, mingling with his satisfied growl as his teeth nip at my jaw. "Maxim…"

Panting, he draws back, his gaze meeting mine, and my heart stops. He's beautiful like this. He's terrifying like this

—because he's too close. My thoughts scatter and I almost forget the truth of why I'm here. Why he's kept me with him.

Necessity.

This is just a game, but I can't stop myself from dragging my fingers along the planes of his face anyway, adding more bullets to the barrel of this dangerous round of roulette. There's no pain in this moment to get me high. No thoughts of money in my head. Just him. And he's enough. I'm not just a desperate hooker anymore.

"Maxim—"

"No!" Suddenly, he wrenches back as if electrocuted. Within seconds, he's at the other end of the room. His chest heaves, muscle rippling with every breath he takes.

Our gazes reconnect and my blood runs cold at what I find in his: nothing. Not lust. Not hate.

Just shadow, dark enough to paralyze me despite the haze of sex weighing me down like a cloud.

His lips twitch, preparing to say something.

But, without a word, he turns and leaves, slamming the door in his wake.

My heart won't stop pounding and sweat pours off my skin, dampening the sheets beneath me. The man is bipolar—I know that.

Even so…I did this.

Someway, somehow, I crossed a line.

And I know he'll punish me for it.

CHAPTER FIVE

I wake up alone. Without Maxim.

Without anyone.

When the sunlight starts to stream in through the windows, I get dressed, picking out a simple gray dress that seems like the safest choice. For what feels like hours, I sit on my bed, waiting. The second I hear the door to the suite finally open, I'm on my feet, creeping into the foyer—but rather than Maxim, I find Lucius waiting for me.

"Mr. Koslov thought you'd enjoy spending time with your family today," he says, smiling.

It's funny. I've almost forgotten what it feels like: spending time with them.

When I finally reach the house, they're sprawled over the living room, spilling snacks all over the floor—crumbs that Ainsley promptly grinds into the floor as she rushes to greet me.

"You're back!"

Back. Like I was away long enough for my absence to be noticed. But maybe I was…

Ollie and Ray clear a space for me on the couch while Daisy and Mikie launch into descriptions of their new school, and the reminder cuts into my psyche like a lance. Maxim.

All of this is possible only because of him.

They're safe, only because of him…

Hours later, Ainsley's in the middle of reading me a story when Lucius receives a phone call. One look at the screen and he chooses to answer it in the hallway—but even from the living room, I catch snippets of his conversation.

"What? So soon?" He sounds startled, and he lowers his tone. "No. You shouldn't go alone, but I will go with you. Sir, I—you know that these matters are private. Delicate. No, I'm not questioning you, sir. I… Are you sure?"

He repeats that last phrase at least three times. *Are you sure?*

To Lucius' credit, he's smiling when he appears in the doorway and motions for me—but it's one of those strained smiles typically worn by a used-car salesman who knows that the old Buick he's trying to sell you might blow up if you take it for a test drive.

"Mr. Koslov requests your presence," he says, leading the way to the door.

During the ride over to the suite, he says nothing. Though, when I finally climb out of the car, I find him watching me through the windshield. He's frowning, his mouth taut, and recognition runs down my spine as I trip onto the curb. It's an expression I've seen only once before: after Maxim beat a man to death in front of an entire roomful of people.

That helpless, resigned sort of look. "Goodbye, Ms. Marconi."

My stomach is in knots when I stagger into the building, but I try to shake the feeling off as I head up to the suite. A minute later, the elevator doors part to reveal a figure pacing in the hallway.

Maxim snarls, each syllable reverberating like thunder. "Do you think *you* can dictate to *me*?"

Instinct overrides everything else. I stagger back, but before I can choke out a pathetic defense, I notice the cell phone pressed against his ear. He's dressed casually— another warning sign. On second thought, maybe the look is more ironic than anything. The black shirt and slacks help him cut an imposing silhouette against the wall and accentuate his blank, hard expression: a fallen angel in limbo.

"I'm not a dog," he growls into the speaker of the phone, directing the venom at whoever is on the other end. "*No one* calls me to heel. Tell him that I will come in my own time." In a violent motion, he winds his arm up like a baseball pitcher and hurls the phone. A second later, it shatters against the wall. "*You.*" His gaze hones in on me, trapping me against wood and metal.

I swallow hard, rocking onto my heels. There are so many things about this man that I'm beginning to understand. Like when he's furious. Or when he's uneasy. Surprise, surprise, *both* emotions waft from him now. Which one is more dangerous?

Who the fuck knows.

"Come." Without another word, he heads for the private stairwell rather than the elevator. One of his hands wrenches the door open so hard that it slams against the wall, which startles out the breath I didn't even realize I was holding. "I said come."

My fingers rush to smooth the skirt of my dress as I follow him down to the bottom level: the garage. Rather than approach his own car, Maxim leads me out to the front of the building, where Lucius' driver has pulled another vehicle around. Without hesitation, Maxim claims the back seat, motioning for me to as well.

"Sir?" the driver asks once the door closes behind us.

Minutes tick by before Maxim answers. He sprawls out over his end of the seat, glaring at the nearby buildings and streets the same way he eyes his battered blocks of stone, chisel in hand. That cold frown tugs on his lower lip; it's the one he typically displays when he's looking for a weak spot to pummel into submission.

"The house in Black Briar," he says before the suspicion can finish unfurling in my mind. His eyes flashing, he rests his head back against the seat, radiating exhaustion and annoyance in one swift motion. "You know the one."

"Yes, sir." The driver nods, and not even ten minutes later, we arrive before an imposing brownstone—this one in an even more exclusive part of the city, secluded behind an iron gate.

From the front of it alone, I can't tell what sort of person might live here. Just that they value their privacy. *A lot*, judging by the men lurking around the edges of the estate. They eye the car warily, their hands on their pockets.

If I thought Maxim might explain why we're here, I was wrong. He simply observes the property before finally climbing out of the car. One of his hands snatches my wrist, pulling me after him.

"Come."

It's a short trip up a narrow stone walkway to reach the front door. Maxim knocks once. Not even a second later, a woman wearing a black uniform opens the door. Her graying hair neatly tied back into a bun.

"Mr. Koslov." She bows her head in respect and then scurries deeper into the house. A whispered statement floats back to us, uttered cautiously. "He's expecting you."

Maxim's shoulders stiffen as he pulls me along, rippling with tension not even his cold, expressionless mask can hide.

I can barely see my hand in front of my face—it's *that* dark in here. It's as if the person who designed this place wanted to make sure that, even on a sunny day, very little light would reach the interior. Dark walls and polished wood create a harsh contrast between light and shadow. Very few items of furniture or decoration add any definition to the rooms we pass, either. Just winding hallways that make each footstep echo for what seems like miles.

Finally, the woman, who I assume is a maid, stops near a doorway and then darts away. I catch only a glimpse of the room from over Maxim's shoulder before he drags me inside.

It looks like a study. Shelves of leather-bound books frame an open space where a man is sitting behind a mahogany desk. He's handsome in a harsh way, with stark features framed by blond hair, streaked with gray. Like Maxim, he's wearing black: a tailored suit with flashing silver cufflinks.

He spares one look in our direction and it suddenly feels colder here than it did outside.

"Maximov…" His voice is raspy, distorted by a heavy accent. "I was wondering when you would finally scurry before me." He extends his right hand, displaying a silver ring on his thumb.

Maxim says nothing. Does nothing. Frozen in place, he stands at the mouth of the room, still holding me by my wrist. There's no life in his touch. I might as well be held by a goddamn statue. Looking at his face, I can't discern anything from his gaze. Not anger. Not even fear.

He's soulless.

An icy dread washes over me. It is the same feeling I got when he nearly beat me to death with a belt. And when he spilled the dark secrets of his childhood. Like he's not really here but far away, reliving a horror no one else can see.

"Did you hear me?" The man raises his hand again, reaching out over the surface of the desk this time. Two of his fingers flicker in a silent command. "Show some respect, *mal'chik.*"

That name cuts through Maxim like a knife. One ragged inhale and he's alive again. In one smooth motion, he crosses over to the desk, but his grip on me doesn't let up and he hauls me forward as well. Once he's close enough, he lowers his head in order to brush the surface of the ring with his lips.

"Grandfather," he grates out before returning to his full height.

Terror smothers my shock. His grandfather. The one responsible for his stoma.

Anatoli.

Does he hate this man? When the two finally lock gazes, I can't tell. Maxim seems farther away than ever.

Chilled and distant, his voice rings out. "You called for me?"

Anatoli scoffs. "Men are *called*. But boys?" He rises to his feet and has to stoop to keep his head from brushing the edge of a hanging chandelier—he's *that* tall. "Boys are whipped into submission." There's an unexpected grace in the way he moves from behind the desk and advances on our position.

With every step he takes, the tension coiled in Maxim's grip gets tighter...tighter... Like a fucking powder keg ready to blow. When the man places a hand on his shoulder, the pressure on my wrist intensifies. Fuck, I swear for a second that he might break it.

"It's been a long time," the man says softly. "But your current results have disappointed me. Perhaps you need another lesson on how to be a man, *mal'chik*?"

Maxim's entire body vibrates. His grip becomes iron, his nails piercing my skin. I can't swallow my gasp—and then Anatoli finally seems to notice me here.

"You brought a toy." The disapproving tone cuts through me, but just as quickly, he returns his attention to his grandson. "After all this time, one might think you'd learned your lesson. Are you aiming to insult me?"

The question strikes like a knife. To bear the impact, Maxim grits his teeth, his expression blank.

"Or maybe she's a toy for Sevastyn?" Anatoli wonders. "A thank-you for cleaning up your mess."

For a brief second, shock disrupts Maxim's hardened mask. "Sevastyn?" he says, grating the name between his teeth. "You requested an audience with *me*—"

"Don't play the fool, Maxi." The voice comes from a man who appears in the doorway, and I have to blink just to dispel a sense of déjà vu. With long, wild, blond hair and dark eyes, he is Maxim's twin—just as massive and just as intimidating. His face is thinner though, bonier, and where Maxim scowls, he smiles. "Don't pretend that you don't know what this is about." He runs a hand along his black suit, flicking away invisible dust. "Or perhaps the rumors are true? All these years have made you soft."

"Grandfather," Maxim says, focusing solely on the man near the desk. "If you want to discuss business, you speak to me. In private—"

"Oh?" Sevastyn chuckles. "And what *should* be private, Maximov? The mess you've made within the past month? Or the punishment that awaits should you fail? Again?" His lips pull back from yellowed teeth as he flicks his thumb along the stubble on his chin. "Perhaps my father is right and a lesson may be in order? I still remember a trick or two to bring you to heel—and you certainly need reminding of your place. Rumors have spread. That you've made an enemy you shouldn't have."

"I have the right to defend my interests," Maxim says coldly.

"Do you?" Anatoli waves his hand dismissively. "Or are you too busy settling personal scores? Send your toy away. Now."

Maxim steps forward, nudging me behind him. "Go."

I don't think twice before escaping into the hall. The door closes behind me, but my ears pick up noise they shouldn't: low murmurs dominated by a raspy growl I know to be Maxim's. Most of the conversation is too distorted to make out—Russian, I think—but I can tell from the insistent tone that it's an argument. A heated one.

When the door finally opens again, Maxim looms behind it, leaning against the doorway as if for support. His lack of stability isn't what sends my pulse racing, however. It's his eyes; they're fixed ahead of him, hollow and black. Dead.

Behind him strolls Sevastyn, his teeth bared. "I hope you understand, dear nephew," he says, placing his hand on Maxim's shoulder. "Blood may be blood, but business is business. Though I'm not averse to mixing it with pleasure." His gaze cuts to me. "Is this one of the morsels from your club? A bit scrawny—"

"She's no one," Maxim replies in haltingly clear English. "And I do *understand.* But"—a shadow flickers over his face and he stares down at his shoulder and violently shrugs off the hand on it—"Anatoli or not, you touch me again and *I will kill you.*"

"Is that so?" A mocking laugh chases him over the threshold. "Next time, leave your toys at home, *mal'chik*. Perhaps then you can face me like a man."

When Maxim's gaze finally focuses on me, I tremble. From head to fucking toe. The instinct to run is almost too strong to swallow down, rising up the back of my throat. My legs twitch, my knees knocking together. His expression…

I only saw him like this one other time.

That very first day when, to him, I was nothing more than a nameless whore.

Replaceable.

But I'm not. The pathetic assurance comes from some distant, naive part of my brain as he steps past me and advances down the hallway. His hand shoots out, snatching me forward. Like iron, his grip dominates my wrist, radiating possession and I can breathe again. I'm the only one he's kept.

The only one to stay.

Despite the contract.

Despite everything.

CHAPTER SIX

He takes me back to his suite. Without a word spoken, he storms into his sculpting room and I linger in the foyer for hours, listening to him work. Hammer. Pound.

Destroy.

Only God knows what set him off this time. Eventually, he calls to me, his voice a rasp. "Come here."

I step toward him, fighting to keep my fear from showing on my face. Then I fail. My bottom lip trembles, and the corner of his mouth flicks down in response: a dangerous frown.

"Do you know what you saw today?"

It takes me three tries to suck in enough air to reply. "No."

"Of course not." His eyes lose their hungry gleam as that beautiful mouth straightens into a cold, lethal line. It's only now that I realize he's covered in dust. The grayish sheen makes him look frozen in the cold air around us. "My organization was nearly ripped from my fucking hands. *My* business." He stares down at his fingers, flexing them in and out of fists. "Everything I've worked for. Why?"

He lets the question hang in the air, but in the end, he comes up with his own answer.

"Maybe I've been distracted…"

It's dark in this room, but the glow from the sculpture area gives definition to his body, highlighting the sweat and signs of exertion I didn't notice before. His hair is damp, his body rippling with tension.

"Look at me."

I don't even notice him move until it's too late. Upon grabbing my chin, he wrenches it back so that I have no choice but to meet his gaze again. His fingers creep down to my throat, tightening. Squeezing.

Choking.

This isn't a sexual game. His eyes don't hold a shred of warmth or lust. Just ice.

Alarmed, I use my hands to claw at his grip. "M-Max—"

"I could kill you," he says, dangerously soft. "I could. Maybe I should?" His grip tightens to cut off my windpipe entirely. "Before they do it for me."

I wheeze as my pulse surges in a futile rhythm. He's holding too tight. Too long. Just as spots speckle my vision…

He shoves me back.

Weightless, I crash into the leather chaise on the other side of the room. Air wheezes in and out of my chest as my eyes burn and overflow. My throat is on fire. For what feels like an eternity, I can't stop gagging until I bring up bile that coats the floor. When I finally get my bearings, he's gone, slamming the door behind him.

And I'm left alone in hell.

Around me is a mess of disheveled pillows. A lamp was knocked over and is in pieces on the floor. The chaise is askew.

Unease twists my stomach into knots and I have to curl up on my side as I process what happened. Something tells me, even before I reach up to feel the tender skin along my throat, that his grip will leave a mark.

"I could kill you," he said.

How close did he come to doing just that?

You don't want to know, a part of me warns as more burning tears spill down my cheeks. *You don't fucking want to know.*

WE HAD a cat a few years ago. Some stray Daisy had let in and Ainsley had enough heart to name. Whiskers, or something like that, I think. Something stupid. Forgettable. I only let her stay around for as long as she did because she'd go after the mice or roaches every now and again.

I saw her trap one once. For the longest time, she watched it scuttle around, just out of her reach, before swiping at it with her paw—but she didn't kill it. Not right then. For what seemed like hours, she wounded it bit by bit, letting the poor thing get just far enough away to tease escape before capturing it again.

It was only when it gave up the fight that she put the poor bastard out of its misery. Sometimes she didn't even eat it. The game was enough to fulfill her—until it wasn't. Boredom was her prey's final sin, and only then would it face the ultimate punishment.

It's funny how those warning signs witnessed in a wild alley cat can translate over to a much larger beast. A monster with black eyes, golden hair, and maybe half the patience of old Whiskers. A part of me knows the awful truth, even before his fingers roughly graze my inner thigh, jolting me awake.

"Look at me."

He's empty when I do, but it's not like any other time before. Except maybe that first day I met him in his suite… Once again, I'm just a hole, used up without an acknowledgment or foreplay. He sinks into me roughly, grinding my body into the mattress.

His hand grips the back of my throat throughout, like a noose capable of cinching off my windpipe at any moment.

He's testing me. No, it's worse than that. He's testing himself. I can almost trace the twisted trail his mind wanders in the resounding quiet. Fear rides my spine, paralyzing me on sweat-soaked sheets.

But I'm too fucking chicken to run.

How dangerous this man is when he *thinks*. When he broods. He mulls over his thoughts the way an assassin polishes his weapons. Slowly. Carefully. He can't let so much as a sliver of metal lose its lethal edge.

So he becomes obsessive in his meticulous routine, wielding sanity like a switchblade.

Flicking it on.

Off.

On.

Night brings out the worst in him, but I'm realizing I fear the day more. It's the quiet after the storm with no shadows to disguise the damage left behind.

I'm dreading the moment I have to peel my eyes open again, despite the fact that I never slept. Not really. My stomach aches with the threat consciousness brings: clarity. I bury my face into the pillow beneath me, hoping to linger in oblivion for a few seconds longer.

Too late.

His heavy sigh shreds the oppressive silence. Then he stands, still gloriously naked. Uneasy, I watch him, slack-jawed from over the crook of my elbow. The moment his feet hit the floor, he's untouchable, miles away from me in a world where I don't exist.

He takes his time reassembling the cold exterior I've come to associate him with. His shirt goes on first, and he buttons it the whole way up. The pants are next. Dark eyes gazing at me from behind a fridge of wild hair are the last detail he arranges. They narrow, hardening like winter ice. He heads for the door—but the final look he casts my way might as well be directed at the wall.

And then I know.

Maxim.

Is.

Bored.

He's a lot less subtle than my cat. He never pretends that escape is an option. If anything, his suite becomes my prison even as he spends most of the time somewhere else. His brief absences become hours. Then days at a time.

By the end of the week, I'm not his *kotyonok*. I'm not even Francesca. I'm just a slave, beckoned by snapping fingers and the unzipping of his fly. Those brutal, violent fucks become snatches of oral sex.

Until one night…

He doesn't return to the suite alone.

I smell her first: cheap perfume like the kind Melanie wears. Just enough to hide the scent of sex from other men, but not enough to cloak her desperation. Stumbling in Maxim's shadow, she's skinny, wearing cheap high heels and a low-cut dress in a tacky zebra print. A long, tangled wig obscures most of her naturally brown hair, framing a face that's almost pretty. Her eyes widen when she sees me standing at the mouth of the foyer.

"Double-team is gonna be extra," she slurs, her voice high-pitched and breathy.

I'd peg her age at a year older than I am. Maybe even two. She's been around the block more than once. Still, there is something unnerving in her smeared lipstick and unfocused, brown eyes. The desperation reeking from her in waves feels familiar. She even *looks* familiar. Like me with a bad dye job, viewed through a blurred mirror. A more broken, more fucked-up Francesca.

Without a word, Maxim steers her to the leather chaise in the center of the main room. He sits, and she stands, trying to look sexy while he palms her tiny waist in his hands and hikes her dress up to her hips. Her bare ass is sporting a handprint—some john wasn't very nice. I wonder if that's why she's consented to let someone like Maxim take her back to his private suite. How desperate is she? How much money does she need?

What has he promised her?

Or maybe she's not doing it for the money at all. Her moan is real as Maxim drags her closer, his head lowering toward her waist. Whatever he does makes her sway on her feet, her back bow…

"What are you doing?" I don't even sound like myself. That soft, weak whisper could never come out of the Francesca Marconi I knew.

"Get out." Maxim doesn't even look at me. "I said get out!" There's no mercy contained within the syllables. No lust. Just a command: *Go.*

I try. I *do*, taking a step toward the hall. My vision blurs. The hooker becomes a multicolored smear as her moan deepens, and the room starts spinning.

As if from far away, a woman gasps while a man growls, his anger rippling to the farthest corners of the room like thunder. I'm transfixed by my shadow, how it sways back and forth. Back and forth.

"Did you hear me?" He's practically snarling.

Maybe it's pathetic, but my mind searches desperately for an explanation. Shaking, I blurt out the first one I can come up with. "Is this because of what that man said?" His creepy, blond doppelganger Sevastyn. His attention still burns, making my skin crawl. "That I'm—"

"Stop." He shoves the girl aside so hard that she trips into the wall, not that he spares her a passing glance. Like honed missiles, his gaze seeks out mine, ripping through me. "You think you can even question me?"

"I thought you wanted…" I can't even say it out loud. *Trust.*

"What I want?" He stands and advances on my position while fastening his slacks. "I *want* you to learn your place." He lunges, grabbing my arm.

Before I can react, he turns and marches to the door, dragging me from the suite and into the stairwell. My heart hammers as I stagger down the steps after him, forced into the garage. When we reach the car, he heads straight for the passenger's side and shoves me in before claiming the driver's seat for himself.

The moment he closes the door behind him, Maxim takes off, plunging headlong into the thick of traffic. He's reckless, as if the speed limit is nothing more than a design tacked onto the signs we pass.

He heads deeper into the heart of the city. Far beyond the bars and strip clubs and into the land of icy business and jaw-dropping wealth—all unfamiliar territory to someone like me. This paranoid part of me can't help thinking the destination is on purpose: *Even if you manage to run, you won't get very far…*

I swallow the fear back and put all of my effort into trying to decipher our surroundings. Gray skyscrapers tower above, blocking out what little remains of the overcast sky. Suddenly, the car turns and the interior plunges into darkness before I can make out what exactly he entered. A parking garage? The place appears to be a single level, devoid of any other cars.

"Come." He parks and climbs out, leaving me to follow him through the metal fire exit that opens onto a narrow hallway.

The air tastes like rust here, and I find myself shivering as he leads me through a maze of corridors and finally into a large, open room I don't recognize.

The walls are black. The floor is bare cement, and in the center of it, someone spread out a large square of plastic tarp. Not just any quality, either—it's the kind butchers use when they cut up an animal. I know only because Melanie dated one once upon a time. The back of his shop resembled this room in a way: cold and semi-dark. The only difference is that, instead of carcasses of cows, hunks of stone in various stages of sculpting linger around the corners.

"Strip," Maxim tells me as my eyes blink rapidly to adjust.

Confusion weighs my veins down like lead; I'm too slow. It feels like an eternity before I finally manage to bend and remove my shoes first. Then my dress. Panties. Bra. When I'm naked, Maxim leaves my clothes untouched and jerks his chin toward the tarp.

"Lie on it."

I'm allowed only two seconds to comply on my own before he grabs me by the shoulder and drags me closer to the edge of the tarp himself. One shove and I go down hard, landing on my side, tasting blood. I must have bitten my cheek.

True terror creeps beneath my skin as I watch him through a jagged fringe of my hair. With an almost beautiful elegance, he heads for a corner of the room, where tools hang from the wall. They're sharp, glinting in the dim lighting. After a moment's observation, he grabs one seemingly at random—but it just so happens to be the sharpest: a knife. When he turns to face me again, my entire body tenses up in recognition.

I *know* that look.

"Face the wall," he commands, his voice strained and gritted. His boots thud against the floor as he advances step by goddamn step. His shadow dances over the floor behind him, beautiful broken wings. "Now."

Choking a question down, I obey, facing the darkness. The only light comes from a naked bulb dangling from a chain in the ceiling. Even so, I can still make out his silhouette—every thick, brutal limb. Every ounce of lean muscle. Looming over me. Swallowing me.

"On your knees." His footsteps trail off a few feet away.

My ears pick up a noise my brain races to identify: something moving through the air. Cutting through it. I flinch before I feel the burning sting between my shoulder blades.

"Ah!" My gasp slips out despite how I bite my lip to seal it back. Already, something warm drips down my lower back, pooling at my waist. God, I can feel it.

Drip.

Drop.

"I said *on your knees.*"

Another rush of air ruffles my hair, but I still don't expect the second blow. It catches me across my hip, biting deeper than the first. Another cry escapes my throat, and a second later, I hear a metallic cling as if something struck the floor. From the corner of my eye, I catch the knife rolling into a corner. The brief moment of distraction costs me: Maxim lunges. One firm nudge against my ass—his foot—and I lurch onto my hands and knees, slamming my forehead on the floor.

"Now..." He breathes heavily as pain shoots through my skull. "Open your mouth."

He circles around me, wrenching at the fastenings of his pants. His jaw is clenched, his eyes shielded by his wild hair. He pulls twice on his fly, and I brace myself when he finally frees his cock. Like always, he's breathtaking—but this time for an entirely different reason.

Nestled in that thatch of golden hair, he's not hard. I blink to make sure. Again. Nothing changes before the pressure on my hair tightens. He yanks my head back, forcing me to meet his gaze. The crazed expression I find is nothing like the cold Maxim I know. I don't think he even fucking sees me.

"I told you to open your goddamn mouth." He drags me forward, forcing his limp cock against my parting lips.

I try to obey, take him in, but…it doesn't feel right. He cringes from the contact, even as he pulls me against him, shoving his length deeper into my mouth. My tongue reacts instinctively to cradle him, and vibrations run through my teeth—he's shaking.

When I try to suck, he shoves me away.

"Fuck!"

The shout rings out as I fall back, hitting my head on the floor. Stars dance before my eyes, obscuring the figure hovering above me. Or maybe it's the tears? I still see the shape of his arm move though. It whistles through the air like a missile a heartbeat before the bitter sting sears through my cheek. *Wham!*

Shock renders me paralyzed. Pause. Rewind. Play.

He hit me.

My brain barely registers the blow before his fingers are in my hair again, tugging, pulling. He grabs my hand in one of his, forcing me to grip his cock. A growl rips from him at the contact, but it's not out of pleasure. His hips buck away from me. His fingers tremble, struggling to maintain their grip. When he attempts to make me stroke him, he lurches back on the balls of his feet, knocking me away again.

"Stop! *Do not touch me.*"

I blink, staring up at him as every ounce of air in my lungs shrivels into nothing. His eyes are wild. Haunted. Insane. They drift over my body and find the knife again. He steps toward it and I know that this time…

This time, just drawing blood won't be enough. My screams won't be enough.

God, I know that look. It's hatred, violent and unrestrained. It's the way I look whenever I think about Melanie. It's loathing. It's pain.

My lips flutter apart. I mean to say the safe word. I try to choke it out—but different words spill from my tongue instead.

"You hit me." I sound so goddamn pathetic. So fucking surprised. A man who pays me for violent sex hit me when he felt like it. So hard that I bit my tongue. So hard that I saw black. So damn hard. "You hit me."

He blinks, caught off guard, and staggers back a step, staring around the room as if seeing it for the first time. Then his eyes return to me, resigned. "So what if I did? You are a whore. *Suka.* I give you money, you do anything. Do you really think you mean more than that?"

Do I? Did I?

My head is an endless rush of a million different thoughts. It hurts. The world isn't spinning anymore—the merry-go-round is in fucking flames.

He's not the first man who's hit me. He won't be the last.

But he's the only one—*no.* I dig my nails into my palms to cut the thought off, but it's too late. Too painful. Too pathetic.

He's the only one I didn't expect it from. Not like this.

"I'm…" I suck in air, struggling to choke the words out. Just two. "I'm—"

"Happy?" he finishes for me. "You think that will be enough? That it will be *that* easy?" He laughs, throwing his head back with every broken chuckle. "You think I really give that much of a damn about some stupid little bitch? I will kill you, and do you want to know what I will do after that? I pay off the police. I dump your body. At most, it will cost me a day. Nothing less. Nothing more."

He's still laughing as he says it. It's the truth. Knowing that churns my stomach. It cuts me into pieces. And I wish it were because of fear. I'd give anything to scream. To run. To say that fucking safe word.

I'm in his head again—and I know why he brought me here: the sick, violent reasons. I know what he wants to prove to himself. Like the night when Melanie left again,

Daisy was sick, and Ainsley was a baby. When *I* was a fucking baby. I didn't know what to do. How to cope.

So I turned my pain on the only fucking person who deserved it. I took a knife from the kitchen sink. I cut myself deeper than I ever have. More than I ever have. I lost so much blood. I even lost consciousness.

The only thing that saved my life was that I didn't nick an artery.

And even after all that, the next morning, all I could do was wrap an old pair of stockings around my wounds and get the kids ready for school. I kept going. Kept living.

Maxim Koslov isn't living. He's playing with the edge of the knife, toying with how deeply to cut himself this time. How much of a mess can he make before it all becomes too much? Game over.

Whatever happened within the past few days snapped something inside him. He'll kill me now. I know it.

But I can't run. So I wait, letting those black eyes stare dead into my own. With every second that passes, they grow brighter. Crazed. Maddening.

It's like looking into a goddamn mirror.

"Do not..." His voice shakes as if he's struggling to maintain control. "Do not think that I will not hurt you, *kotyonok*." He lashes out, grabbing my throat before I can react. Gradually, his grip begins to tighten, cutting off my windpipe. "Because I will. Make no mistake about that."

More pressure is added to prove his point. "Weakness is always exploited. Never forget that. Before you could ever be used against me, I would eliminate you myself."

As soon as I begin to sputter under the pressure, his hand jerks free and I'm left panting, trying to grasp what the hell just happened.

Weakness. The word reverberates through my mind. *Weakness.* His own words break loose from the tangled mess of my thoughts. *To teach me. I was too soft. He hired men…*

"Your family…" I choke out on another gasp of air as more twisted puzzle pieces fall into place. That distant look in his eye. The way he reacted when I mentioned his uncle. The violence now. "You think they will hurt me."

Maxim goes rigid. His arms fall flat at his sides, his eyes wide like I slapped him this time. Two steps backward carry his body into the wall and the blow resonates throughout the entire damn room. Slowly, he sinks into a crouch, his back braced against the wall. His voice cracking, he commands, "Get out."

But I can't fucking stop.

"They hurt you before—" Horror robs me of my voice. I just whisper, dragging my gaze down to his hip. *Oh god.* His pain seeps into me and everything feels too clear. I picture the way he reacted when that man—his uncle—touched him, and my stomach starts to crawl up the back of my throat. "Did he do that to you? Your uncle—"

"*Leave!*"

I should. My limbs unfurl as blood sticks the tarp to me. When I finally gather up the strength to rise on my hands and knees. I'm shaking too badly to even attempt to walk, so I crawl.

In the wrong goddamn direction.

He watches me with every inch I gain, like a volcano ready to erupt. My cheek still stings with the memory of his slap, but I can't stop. The moment I'm close enough, his hand flies out, clenching my throat instead. Tight. He chokes me so hard that I see black. I'll bruise. Seconds pass. I'll die…

"Am I supposed to cry now, *kotyonok*?" he asks me mockingly, sounding miles away. "Tell you my sins? Beg for your forgiveness?"

Air floods my lungs as he shoves me aside like trash. I go limp, my cheek pressed against the ice-cold floor, his hate basting my skin. It feels different this time—everything. It's too real. Too sharp.

His voice inflicts more pain than any knife. Go figure.

"Please…" My throat aches in the wake of that word. What it means: pleading. I've begged before. I've begged Melanie not to go. I've begged men not to hurt me. I've begged landlords not to kick us out.

No one ever listens.

Maybe I never really meant it before now.

"What?" Maxim demands. "Please don't hurt you? Please don't kill you?" He laughs again and the vibration runs through the floor as he stands. Two steps bring him close enough for his foot to nudge my side. Hard. "Pleading didn't save my mother from her fate—"

"I'm not her—"

His foot rams into my side, knocking me onto my back.

Gasping, I can only stare up at him as he glares down. "You're not him."

"I'm not?" Slowly, his eyes track over the length of my body, narrowing as they reach the space between my legs. One of his hands reaches down to palm his cock, while the other…

From one of his pockets, he pulls out a knife and flicks his wrist, springing the blade free. Then he sinks to one knee, capturing my thigh in his other hand before I can attempt to scuttle away. In retaliation, his nails dig in, his breath searing my flesh, and he drags the blade between my legs.

There's no teasing this time. No taunts. He slides the blade along the outside of my pussy, nudging me open. A strangled gasp trickles between my lips as my hand flies out to bat his away.

"P-please."

He jerks his grip on the knife and the blade bites into my inner thigh, drawing a stream of blood that dribbles down, slicking his way.

"Spread your legs," he grates, his voice ragged. A hiss of anger leaves his mouth when I don't move quickly enough, and the blade cuts me again, another fiery line. "Do it."

The tarp clings to my skin as my legs drift apart to let his bulk fit in between them. He risks letting me go to grab his cock again, but even from this angle, I know he's still not hard. Not even when I flinch. Not even as tears sting behind my eyes and slide down my cheeks.

There's no way around it: Since meeting him, my pain alone isn't getting him off. His eyes are too haunted. I don't even think he's really here, but in the past. Trapped. Furious...

Terrified.

And I should say the goddamn safe word. My lips move, but nothing comes out, just whimpers. He lifts the knife and I raise my hand, pressing my palm against his cheek in one last bid for mercy. It takes everything I have to meet his gaze—to stare into his eyes and not cringe away at what I see.

"I don't want you to hurt me like this. I don't...I don't want to be afraid of you."

Confusion shatters the bitter expression, matching the emotion surging through me. It makes him look even more lost. Even more terrifying. More dangerous. He drags me beneath him, his weight crushing me against the hard floor.

"Do you think I won't?" he growls into my ear.

"*Don't.*" My knees rise up on either side of him while my other hand grabs his hip, breaking that unspoken rule. Bit by bit, some life returns to his eyes, but he doesn't pull away.

"Then do not let me go back there. To that place," he grits out. His eyes flutter, unseeing one second and alive the next. "Keep me here. I don't… I'm not him."

I don't know what he means until he lunges. His lips latch onto mine, kissing me. Biting me. He's ruthless, shoving his tongue into my mouth without giving me a chance to come up for air.

Benny only ever gave me one piece of advice when I started working for him: "*You want to get it over with? Let those fuckers think you want it. That you need it. It'll finish them off and you'll probably get a tip while you're at it.*"

I could never really pretend.

I've never been that desperate.

But this time…I don't have to think. Maybe I'm just too fucking chicken to die. I let myself cling to him, dragging my fingers through his hair, kissing him back—knowing that, at any second, he'll push me off. Kill me.

But all he does is come back to life. Restless and ragged, the fallen angel returns from hell with a vengeance. My body is his tool. His anchor. His altar.

Maybe it's way too easy to arch into him. Either way, I don't give myself the chance to think about it.

When he flips me onto my stomach, his kiss becomes something else. The lips pressed against the back of my shoulder don't reveal nipping teeth. They just graze my skin. They feel. They taste.

I don't know how much time passes before something else stabs between my legs, guided by his hand. I barely register the familiar shape before he's sliding inside me, fucking me deep with a groan: one part pleasure, one part relief.

Sweat and skin wrap me inside my own corner of the universe: a tiny sliver of hell. Warmth spills down my cheeks like fire as he finally thrusts in earnest.

Each slow buck of his hips desolates me. I was wrong. This isn't fucking—it's something else. Something more twisted than any torture he's inflicted upon me so far: *desperation*.

"You keep falling deeper," he murmurs into my throbbing skin, so softly that I probably imagined it. "Every fucking time I try to give you a way out. You refuse to take it."

Any reply escapes me as my stomach bunches into knots, my insides swirling into jelly.

"And I've tried to show you mercy." A hard, deep thrust sends my eyes rolling into the back of my head, making me cry. Making me scream around mouthfuls of plastic and blood. "I've tried… But if I can't eliminate you myself, I'll have no choice…"

With one last thrust, rivulets of heat spill into me.

All of him.

I'm swirling in a daze as his lips find my ear again, his voice rough. "I'll have no choice."

CHAPTER SEVEN

I wake up in my bed. No…*his* bed. When I finally peel my eyes open, there is no mistaking his domain. Ebony walls encase me, blending in with the black sheets and duvet that shield my body from the still air. One sharp inhale and I'm drowning beneath his scent.

Literally. Musk and sweat are a noose that asphyxiates me against layers of silk and satin. And blood.

I'm still bleeding from the cut on my back. Every part of me feels tender and sore. As cliché as the boast sounds, I won't be able to walk right for a few days.

Because he cut me.

My fingers slide beneath the blankets to feel the wounds for myself. The marks still smart, weeping and fresh. Only a few hours must have passed…

Which gives me plenty of time to come up with a new plan of action. When all else fails, there's always good old reliable plan B.

Run.

I roll onto my side first, biting a groan back as sores and wounds rip open. It's dark in the room. Maybe just after dawn, before the sun has fully risen. I know at a glance that Maxim isn't here, lurking within the corners. To be sure though, I crane my neck, straining my ears against the silence, and don't hear the sound of anyone in the rest of the suite, either.

Logic warns me to crawl into my bedroom and wait. Ride the contract out for as long as I can.

But, at the moment, my brain feels too fucking wrecked for logic.

Bit by goddamn bit, I wrestle my limbs into submission and crawl to the edge of the bed. When I finally manage to peel the covers back, I find that he left me naked. A quick scan of the room doesn't reveal my clothes anywhere. I have no choice but to limp over to his closet and wrench the sliding door to it open.

Any bravery I managed to muster up drains from me in one go. Even his clothing intimidates. Crisp dress shirts hang neatly in shades spanning black, navy, gray, and the purest white. My fingers shake as I grab one at random along with a pair of boxers. I pull both on while simultaneously staggering for the door.

He isn't in the foyer when I tiptoe across it. Neither do I hear him working in the sculpture room. His absence leaves an almost eerie, unnatural silence, broken only by my ragged breaths and the slight click of the front door when I finally pull it open.

I take the stairs down to the first floor and slip through a fire exit. Barefoot, I flag a cab down before realizing I don't have any money to pay the fare.

Go fucking figure.

Maybe the driver takes pity on me, because he sighs when I paw through the pockets of Maxim's shirt in a half-assed search for cash. "It's all right, miss." His eyes skim over my bruised, battered face and he quickly looks away before letting me off near a random street at the edge of Horn Hill. "Consider it on the house. Just take care of yourself out here."

This area is close to my old house. I should go back and regroup—think of a way to get the kids back home, if Maxim doesn't kick them out first. Or worse…

I start heading in that direction. But, somewhere along the way, I take a wrong turn and wind up in a back booth of some rundown diner. It's a slow time of day, right before the midmorning rush. A waitress patrols the aisles, brandishing a fresh pot of coffee. She offers to pour me a cup, but I shake my head and pray she'll walk away without looking at me twice.

Unlucky for me, I can't ignore my own fucking reflection. It's splashed over the metallic border of the window beside me. Splotches of blue and purple. Bits of garish red. I'm a fucking smorgasbord of color and wounds. I try smiling and look even worse.

It's only once I finally start to warm up beneath the building's artificial heat that I realize exactly what I'm doing: hiding out in the shitty part of town, wearing a madman's stolen dress shirt, and why? Because he hurt me. He scared me.

He's *scaring* me.

He's haunting me…

I look up when the bell above the door chimes and it's like his entrance is perfectly timed to create the most impact. At a glance, it's easy to tell that the figure entering the diner isn't the typical patron. His head is bowed, his face partially obscured by the hood of a gray sweatshirt, but his clothing is of the highest caliber, and his black boots are polished to a shine, clean enough to eat off of.

I'm already scrambling to the edge of my seat when his voice reaches me, a low but irresistible rasp.

"Don't run."

I've never heard him this coarse, absent of his usual poise. When I freeze, he jerks his head toward the table.

"Sit. We will talk. Can you give me that much, *kotyonok?*"

Can I?

My arms shake as I wrestle them around me, struggling to hide the shape of my body beneath his shirt. I picked white, of all fucking colors. Despite its quality, it's thin enough to see my nipples through. I've already stained it, too; streaks of red are blooming along my hip. Though maybe he won't miss it, considering how he switched up his style today.

I track every motion of his body as he claims the bench across from me and adjusts his bulk to fit within such a small space. His legs reach my side of the table, and he hunches over the width of the booth, his face so close that his breath scalds my cheek. That sweatshirt isn't the only change in his typical attire. Underneath it, he has on a gray tee-shirt that's soaked through with sweat. Drops of it glisten over his forehead as well and slick his hair back. Wherever he's been, he's been sweating. Sculpting? Working out?

His raw, bloodied knuckles give the answer away.

When he notices the line of my gaze, he casually tucks his hands into fists and moves them beneath the table. "So this is how you run, *kotyonok*?" He tilts his head just enough for me to see his face clearly through the shadow cast by the hood. "Frankly, I'm surprised. You seemed more like the type to press me for money before voiding your contract."

He's devastatingly polite, even in his harshest insults. *Press.* I know what he really means: *blackmail.*

But is he that far off base? Maybe not.

Any other time, I'd try to deny it. I'd pull out the main tricks Melanie always used in her arsenal. Bat my eyes. Feign ignorance. I'd promise, never intending to keep a single goddamn word.

"You are afraid." The statement comes as the seconds tick by and I don't answer.

He's right. Fear is wired through my every nerve, and I nearly jump out of my skin when he reaches across the table. The pad of his thumb hesitates near the side of my face.

"I hit you," he says, eyeing the swollen welt beneath the black eye already there. "I apologize for that."

Shock could be blamed for the way I shudder, which makes him pull away in response. It's not every day that men—*anyone*—apologize to me.

The most terrifying part though? I think he means it.

Or maybe I'm just dumb enough—*desperate* enough—to believe him despite everything my life has taught me about the pervasive nature of violence. Apologies don't mop up blood. If my throbbing eye accounts for anything, they don't make your boo-boos magically feel better, either.

Though who the fuck knows? Again, I've never been presented with one before.

"I was rough," he adds, drawing my attention back to him. "But I don't think it will scar—"

"That's not the point." Of all the things clawing up my throat, desperate to be said, I don't expect what winds up spilling out. "I...I didn't sign up for this."

He sits up straighter as my voice breaks.

"And not the violence," I add as warmth spills down my face, impossible to stop. "You're a man. I've learned my whole life that men are violent pieces of shit—"

"We all ready to go?" Oblivious, the smiling waitress appears beside our table. She makes a show of convincing Maxim to order a cup of coffee, and—whether because he needs the caffeine or rather to just make her go away—he accepts two mugs, which the woman places between us.

As I watch the steam waft from the drink on my end of the table, I consider throwing it on him. Taking my chances. Running. But my own imagination isn't even on my side: I wouldn't make it very far.

His eyes narrow, honing in on the way I'm huddled against the back of my bench, as far from him as the space will allow. "Something tells me that this is about more than my..." He seems to mull over the nicest words to describe it: *more than my fucking loss of sanity.* "My brief lapse in composure."

Despite everything, I nearly choke out a scoff. *Composure* —that's what he calls it.

So what do you call it, Frankie? a part of me wonders. *What has you so fucking spooked? All you have to do is say the magic words...*

"I've shown you worse."

I stiffen at the accusation lurking within his tone. Almost a challenge: *I nearly beat you to death before and you stayed. Now, you run.*

"You threatened to kill me. You tried fucking someone else in front of me." My throat threatens to close up against those words. Gritting my teeth, I force more out. "I may like pain, but not like that."

"So," he says, his tone low and careful. "Are you saying you want to end this?"

He doesn't sound angry—that's the observation that worries me most of all.

"You don't throw away the people you say you want to keep." More tears. They come down like a fucking waterfall, blurring my vision. Within seconds, Maxim Koslov is a massive, indistinguishable shadow over red vinyl. "You told me... You said you'd never let me go." His words rasp over my tongue, nearly drowned out by the sudden laughter from a group of truckers seated two tables over. I let them linger in the air regardless, tasting their impact. Hearing them said out loud should mean something. It should resonate with some stubborn part of me that wants to bide my time.

He's a monster.

"I did," Maxim admits. Seconds pass without him saying anything else and I shift, attempting to stand.

"I-I don't know what you want."

"Wait—" His hand slams onto the table before I make it to the end of the booth. Gone is his blank mask of politeness. A feral fire flickers underneath, growing brighter with every word he grates to me next. "Let me explain. That night… You never looked like her," he rasps almost as if to himself. "Not until then. Like how she did. Her eyes…"

What are you talking about? That's what I try to say. A gasp crawls out of me instead. His face is in shadow, his body heaving, his breaths mingling with mine. My heart slows to a crawl; I've never been more terrified of him than I am right now.

He's never looked more human.

"I spent years telling myself that I wasn't like him," he says haltingly, as if picking the words one by one from some place deep inside himself. "It's the lie we feed ourselves as children, you see. The one we tell ourselves every fucking night. The same damn lie: *It could have been different. If they* were different. The world. You. Fuck, who knows? But you say it anyway, like a prayer: They could have changed. It could have been different…"

That dangerous, unstable edge creeps into his voice, triggering every flight response my body possesses. *Run, Frankie!* He's not talking about us in this moment. He's far away, beyond this room. Just when the panic becomes unbearable, he blinks and reality reels him back.

"Only now do I realize that it was just a fucking lie—" He forms a fist and smashes it against the table. His heavy sigh negates the violence of the act though. It's like he's too tired to feel a damn thing. So he just bleeds, spilling more of himself in words than he ever could of my blood. "She would never leave him, even at his worst. She was broken. So was he. So am I. And so are you. You still hear that little voice yourself, don't you, *kotyonok?*" he wonders, flicking his gaze to my face. "'*Maybe I can change,*' it tells you. '*Maybe I won't be like her.*'"

I know just who he's referring to. *Melanie. Maybe I won't be like her...*

No. I want to shut him out. But he's speaking to a part of me too primal to control. The one place inside my soul that still thrives?

Unsatisfied with throwing me away, he has to kill the one thing of value I have left.

Hope.

"It's a lie, *kotyonok,*" he says as if reading my mind. "You know it. So do I. It's inevitable. This is who we are. We're fucked, just like them. We will end, just like them. And do you know what else?" He laughs. "We will never change. Why? We do not want to. Hell, even now, you've yet to say your safe word."

"I want to say it now." The confession feels like the equivalent of striking a match over a pool of gasoline.

One wrong move and the world will erupt in flames. Not for the first time, I have Maxim Koslov's full, rapt attention.

But, as the seconds race by, I'm starting to realize that the infantile plea wasn't directed at him. *Say it,* a part of me begs. Pleads. Desperation sets my throat on fire, burning no matter how much I swallow.

"I…I'm—"

"No, I owe you an explanation," Maxim says over me.

My eardrums pick up the subtle distinction, and curiosity steals my voice. *I owe you.* Not: *I want to give.*

"I forget that you are not used to this arrangement. You don't understand how it works." He makes it sound so complicated. So clinical. I'm a faulty piece in his cold, brutal machine of a life. "Your body is all I ever required from you," he clarifies. For a second, he gets that lost look again. Then he blinks, his gaze settling over my chest as if he can see my rapid heartbeat through paper-thin skin. "Nothing else."

His meaning takes an eternity to register. My body. *Sex.* Just sex. No moaning his name during said fucking, unbidden. No understanding his fucked-up childhood. No pitying him. Crying for him.

I wasn't supposed to glimpse the human beneath the monster's mask.

A funny sensation leaves me feeling dizzy—like he flipped the world upside down when I wasn't looking. Only he can do this to me: make me risk breaking my own damn rules. His past shouldn't matter. His fucked-up reasoning shouldn't matter. The pain that crosses his gaze for a brief moment *shouldn't* catch my attention.

Too late. My mouth opens. "So why keep me?"

He frowns, flexing his fingers as if flicking the question away. "I will make you an offer." In the blink of an eye, he's composed again. He scans the brightly colored upholstery behind my head as if the conversation is starting to lose his interest—but I'm not fucking fooled. One of his hands clenches the edge of the table, and the knuckles are stark white.

He waits, letting the gravity of the temptation sink in. Like the greedy bitch I am, I wait too, taking the bait. The devil is about to offer me another deal—and God, I should run.

"I'll let you go," he tells me, his eyes cutting into my own. "You can take the full amount in your contract, along with any extra owed to you. You will keep the house, and our arrangement will be null and void."

"Why?" I nearly choke on my confusion.

"I'm through with you," he says. "Don't think too much of it. It eventually happens with every woman I am involved with. Again, I will fulfill the payment promised in the contract."

It's a better offer than I could have ever asked for—in theory. But it doesn't feel that way. My chest aches like something tore through each rib, muscle, and bone. Maybe logic. Nothing in life comes without a pesky caveat: There's always a catch. I lick my lips, feeling them scrape against my tongue like broken glass. "If?"

He sits back against the booth, folding his hands before him. "Your pimp's name. What was it?"

Of all the people to be mentioned now. "Benny," I say.

"I remember now. Benjamin Ireland." He nods and steeples his fingers. "You will tell him that you will never work for him again. In exchange, you may stay in the home I've bought for you. However, I expect you to maintain our confidentiality."

I know what he really means: I stay away from any other man and keep his dirty, bloody secrets.

"And if I don't?" My breath catches, and my imagination takes off again. I picture him taking a new toy, fucking her on my bed—no. *His* bed.

Would he call her *kotyonok*?

"Tell me something." He leans forward, his accent thick, his breaths drifting across the table, heavy and hot. "And you do not want to lie to me now." He reaches out, cupping my chin, holding me captive, and I can sense the danger coiled in his touch, barely restrained. "What you said. That I'm not like… You were pretending, hmmm?"

I flinch as his thumb grazes a path over my throbbing cheek, deceptively soft, as if to coax the truth out.

"To save your life. I can forgive you that much," he says, "*if* you admit it."

My heart lurches in my chest. Of course I was lying. I *was...*

"I see." His hand withdraws, curling into a fist that he quickly shoves into his pocket. "I will give you a week to make your decision." He stands, leaving his untouched cup of coffee there on the table. "You can have the money in the meantime. My protection. The house. All of it. Return to your normal life if you want. Live as you would away from me."

I'm holding my breath—even before he tacks on the dreaded *but*.

"*But* I ask that you obey my request." His eyes find mine, drilling in the unspoken threat.

This isn't a negotiation. I know there's no point in arguing. Still, I lick my lips and choke out, "Can I ask why?"

"You are naïve," he says as though it's the most obvious explanation. "My enemies wouldn't be above fucking you for leverage."

In other words: *You're a liability.*

"And what about you?" My teeth chatter as if they're fighting to keep this line of questioning locked away. It's a dangerous, stupid game to play. But fuck it, he's the one who called me a masochist. "Will you get someone else?"

To fuck.

To toy with.

To beat?

He looks away while rummaging through the pockets of his sweatshirt. After a few seconds, he tosses a bill onto the table. "Stay. I'll arrange to have you taken home. Consider the house yours to do with as you wish. Lucius will settle your finances." He lingers near the booth, casting a silence that seems to ensnare the entire fucking café in a net of tension. There is more he wants to say. Confirmation of my suspicion?

No matter what he wants me to do, he *will* get a new woman.

He *will* fuck someone else.

And there isn't a damn thing I can do about it.

Why?

He is the dominant master, drawing eyes from every single patron as he heads for the door.

I'm the invisible, worthless submissive: a cheap whore, easily thrown away. He may have let me keep my dollhouse, but that's all I'm worth to him.

A bribe.

Hours must pass after he leaves, but I just sit here, staring at the empty seat across from me. When I finally slink out of the diner, it's dark out.

But there, idling just alongside the curb, is a familiar black car. The driver meets my gaze through the windshield and nods just once in a silent gesture. *At your service.*

I've been thrown away so many times.

This latest trip to the figurative dumpster should be nothing new. My own mother didn't want me. What difference should the whims of a psycho billionaire make?

Not a one.

Despite knowing that, I can't escape the pins-and-needles sensation stabbing at my spine, warning me that something isn't right. This time *is* different. Psycho billionaires just don't throw away their wayward pets who scratch too deep and leave a mark—no, they put them to sleep.

And every passing second feels like the tightening coil of a trap. I know it will spring without warning. Maxim will step out from the shadows and demand some cruel punishment for ever leaving him.

I'll lose this twisted game.

In the meantime, I spend each night sleeping in an unfamiliar bed before wandering around an unfamiliar house to get the kids ready for school. A new *private* school they were mysteriously enrolled into, despite it being the middle of the fucking school year. I expect them to resent me for the change. To hate me for ripping them from the house—*our* house—without any real explanation.

Ainsley should be pouting.

Mikie and Daisy should be bitching about missing their old friends or their old neighborhood.

Ollie, Ray, and Eric should be pining for their old beds, their old rooms.

Instead, it's like we've lived here all along. Like we weren't fighting over scraps of pizza just a few weeks ago. Like they *always* could relax on their front lawn without worrying about some gangbanger cutting loose.

Survival is a funny thing.

"Frankie?"

I jump as a hand lands over my shoulder and the plate I'm holding falls back into the water-filled sink. It smacks the edge wrong and promptly breaks into a million expensive chunks of porcelain.

"Shit!" I shut the water off and try to fish the broken pieces from the sink, being careful to avoid cutting myself. The jagged edges are sharp. The slightest nudge with my fingertip causes a faint echo of pain. A hint of it —but a firmer nudge sends a tendril of agony shooting down my spine.

"Are you okay?" Daisy presses when I don't acknowledge her right away. Little does she know, she just asked the question of the fucking day. "Frankie?"

"Yeah…sure," I hear myself croak as my fingers plunge into the soapy water and clumsily grab at another chunk. It cuts me deeper this time and a brief flash of red fades through the water. "Why?"

"You've been washing the same three knives and plates for the past hour. And," she adds, her voice quivering as she watches me wrench my bleeding hand from the water and shove it into the nearest dish towel, "That's the fifth plate you've broken since you got here."

"Oh." I let the word hang there, a perfect summary of the past few days.

Oh, my fingers slipped.

Oh, I'm bleeding.

Oh, it doesn't hurt.

"I'm okay," I force myself to choke out when Daisy doesn't move, her unsaid questions itching my skin. "It… it doesn't even hurt."

"Okay." In her small voice, a heavy sigh somehow sounds louder than even the few times she manages to shout.

"Well… I have to finish my homework…" Her eyes drift hopefully in my direction. "Are you busy?"

Busy. My brain toys with that word. Busy? For once, I'm not. I'm not scraping by at some shitty job for low wages. Or on my knees pleasing a horny stranger for cash. It's been so long since I've been able to stay in the same house with the kids and not race to get ready for the next dead-end job.

"No." I step away from the sink and wipe my hands on my shirt. "Sure… I can help."

"Cool!" Daisy beams and I catch myself staring. It's the first time I've really seen her smile in so damn long. "It's just math," she says, leading me to a section of the dining room, cordoned off by a pink backpack and a mound of books. "Algebra." She rolls her eyes and gestures to an open workbook. "Think you can help? I hate equations."

I scan the scrambled mixture of numbers and letters printed on the sheet and squint. Algebra? It's like another fucking language.

"What about this one?" Daisy points to a cluster of symbols. "I need to solve for X but I have no idea where to start."

"X?" I raise an eyebrow. "Isn't math supposed to be about numbers?"

"Never mind." Daisy closes her workbook and starts to shove it into her backpack. "I'll ask Mikie—"

"No! I can help." I practically snatch the notebook from her hands and flip to a random page. None of it makes sense. "I… Do you have a calculator—"

"I said it's fine." Daisy grabs her book but rather than put it away, she clutches it to her chest, eyeing me warily. "Can I ask you something?"

"Sure," I croak. But I look away and eye the table rather than her. "You can ask me anything."

"Okay… Well, you've been acting really weird lately, you know?"

"Weird?" I choke back a laugh. *Weird,* or just too fucking stupid to solve a math problem. "How?"

"Weird like bringing a scary guy home," Daisy says. "Weird like moving us into a mansion overnight. Weird like—"

"Hey!"

I look over my shoulder and see Mikie there, a game controller in hand.

"You coming back?" he asks Daisy. "I'm about to crush this level."

"Not yet." She sighs again. "We were trying to do homework." She's still smiling, but it's lopsided. Strained.

"I can help," Mikie says, strolling over. "Let's see it. Oh yeah, this shit is easy. X is twelve." He pumps his fist in triumph. "Need help with more? Come on. I'll help ya. I bet Frankie's too tired for algebra anyway."

"Thanks for trying," Daisy says, following in Mikie's wake. "Night, Frankie."

"Night," I echo, but when I finally turn around, I realize I'm alone. Which is a funny emotion to feel in a house with six other people.

Our new house isn't the only change the kids have seemed to easily overlook.

Apart from Daisy, it's like they don't even see the battered, bruised excuse they have for a sister, either. I'm dripping blood, spouting off excuses like Band-Aids. The lies I tell to explain the injuries away are easily accepted, too—but with a catch. They avert their eyes and nod a little more than necessary, which is the same way I used to accept Melanie's lies. The ones I was too damn tired to challenge. Even Mikie doesn't question me. As far as they're concerned, I'm still the same old Frankie. The same old nagging, sole-providing, fight-breaking, rule-setting fucking Frankie.

Barely five minutes go by without me having to separate Ainsley and Eric, clean something, fix something, or wipe something from the floor. I bust my ass to erase every speck of dust and dirt they leave behind.

Because we don't really belong here.

I don't belong here.

But at least money is the furthest thing from my mind now, right?

I try to tell myself that over and over, hoping that it might stick this time. Maxim may be a lot of things, but I don't think a *liar* is one of them, at least where finances are concerned. And if I am anything like my mother, I'll milk him for all he's worth for as long as I fucking can.

In the end, I last three days. Three damn days before the walls of the house start closing in. Three days before my own skin starts to shrivel around me. Three days that I can't even fucking look at myself in the mirror.

I'm a sleepwalker in a dream, observing myself in the bathroom for cracks in my porcelain skin.

Then I hear it—a sound that shatters my daze: crying. Screaming.

"Frankie!"

Horror sends my stomach plummeting as I race downstairs into the entryway. "What's wrong?"

I find Daisy huddled on the bottom step. Spotting me, she lurches to her feet, tears streaming down her pale cheeks.

"What's wrong?" I demand, grabbing her by the shoulders.

Her eyes dart to the front entrance and reality returns like a bitch-slap. We're not alone.

Two men dressed in blue police uniforms guard the open door while another man in an impeccable suit stands in the middle of the room, radiating authority. Lucius.

My heart stops. *Me.* They're here for me. Maxim may be a self-professed crime lord, but I'm not.

And I committed murder.

"Ms. Marconi." Lucius steps forward, his dark eyes laced with concern. "I apologize for this sudden—"

"She's dead," Daisy blubbers over him. "Mama... She's dead."

I blink. My first thought is who? It's almost like one of those game show songs is playing as my brain slowly connects the dots. *Mama. Mom. Mother.*

Oh. Finally, my tongue wrings out a name. "Melanie?"

"Yes. They found her this morning!" Daisy wails against my shoulder. I have enough sense to throw my arms around her neck, holding her close. She's still wearing her pajamas, her hair in two braids. "I-I don't know how—"

"It's best if we discuss this in private," Lucius interjects. "In fact, I would have preferred to deliver this news myself." He cuts his gaze to the officers.

"It's an open investigation," one of them curtly replies.

Like it's that hard to guess the cause of death. I've had at least ten previous overdose scares to serve as a dress rehearsal for this moment. Some concerned passerby found her dead on a bench or in an alley, I bet. She slipped away high off her ass, without a concern to bother her pretty little head. My only consolation is that the kids didn't find her.

"Go to your room." I slide my arms from around Daisy and nudge her toward the stairs. "Go. I'll be up in a bit. Everything's fine."

Even I can hear the lie in my voice. Still, she heads for the stairs, and Lucius moves to stand beside me, taking her place.

"I suggest you say nothing, Ms. Marconi," he says.

"Is that really necessary?" One of the officers sighs. "We would just like to ask a few questions—"

"I suggest you direct all inquiries to Ms. Marconi's legal counsel," Lucius interjects. "I can facilitate a meeting, but as for now, gentlemen, I'm sure this family would like privacy."

"I don't think we can leave just yet." The other officer steps forward, twisting a pen between his fingers, a notepad in hand. He's young, with dark hair and piercing eyes. "Can you tell us the last time you saw Melanie Ryder alive, Francesca?" he asks. "We have a witness that claims the two of you had an argument recently. Can you elaborate?"

My mind goes blank, and I don't know how to describe the emotion that washes over me. It starts in my stomach, pinching like hell as I try to identify it. "I—"

"I suggest you save the questions for another day," a newer voice cuts over mine.

Both officers share wary glances before eyeing the newest figure to enter through the doorway. Dressed in black and shrouded in an ebony coat, Maxim Koslov exudes an aura of intimidation not even they can ignore.

"Sorry to interrupt." His gaze passes over me, finding Lucius. They share a silent nod, and Maxim crosses his arms. "But if you wouldn't mind, gentlemen, I believe Ms. Marconi should process this devastating news alone."

"This is an open investigation," the man with the notepad counters. "I can't just ignore protocol…"

Maxim doesn't say a single word, but the officer grits his teeth and then shoves his pen into his pocket. "Fine."

The other officer concedes with a curt nod. "Goodnight."

As they leave, Lucius follows. "I'll handle this," he says to Maxim.

The door closes behind them and I'm trapped. Within seconds, his scent easily overpowers that of six kids and a nanny. Three days without him have strengthened it. My pathetic brain hones in on the chilling familiarity of it over all else. Primal, raw musk. As long as I breathe it in, there isn't room for anything more.

"For now, I think you should avoid the police," he says, his voice low—out of respect for the kids, I realize. "I wanted Lucius to tell you before they could."

Belatedly, his words register—and what they reveal.

He wanted Lucius to tell me. Not *him.*

I cross to the other end of the foyer and eye the view beyond the window. It's late, way past sunset. Storm clouds darken the ebony sky, and lightning flashes between them. Of all the days to die, Melanie sure picked a winner. Though, there goes my park bench theory; Melanie hated the rain.

A motel then, I surmise. They found her sprawled out in one with a needle in her vein. I've entertained that scenario as well, though not as often as the others— because a motel overdose means publicity. Her name might show up in the paper. Publicity means investigations, long and drawn out.

Investigations during which a dumb, worthless whore might say the wrong thing, casting suspicion on her billionaire client who relishes his privacy.

That's why he's here.

"I'm not going to say anything about that guy I…"

Killed. The word sticks in my throat. I still can't say it out loud.

"I won't go to the police," I confess to the window. "That would bring my sister into it. I'd never do that to her."

Even if I were spiteful enough to mention his name.

There. He should be satisfied…

But his footsteps don't echo to signal a retreat.

"Do you need me to sign something?" I ask, wringing my fingers together. They're shaking, and each nail nips at any bit of skin it can reach. A pinch here. A scratch there. I watch the blood bubble up from miniscule scrapes, but it's strange. I feel nothing.

"No," he says finally. "Lucius will handle your legal counsel."

"Okay." I sound like the perfect obedient hostage, meekly abiding by his rules. "Thank you."

I turn to face him, ready to keep up my act. Go upstairs. Lock myself in my cage. Let him see how well I can play the role of damaged, unwanted toy.

But his face is all wrong. His gaze is solely focused on me, his posture rigid, his eyes unnervingly sharp. A million secrets lurk in them, daring me to question.

"How…how did she die?" I croak before I can bite the words back.

"She was stabbed. They found her in a home in Horn Hill. The coroner will rule it a homicide. There are no leads…" He trails off, a blond eyebrow raised. "Hearing this upsets you."

No. I shake my head, unable to push a denial past my thickening throat. Upset? I'm not. Those aren't tears searing my eyes. Just dust. He must have been sculpting before he came here. The air is fucking thick with heavy, cloying residue.

"What else?" I ask.

"They will not release her body for a few days, at least until the investigation is concluded. However...I believe it would be best to schedule a memorial service anyway. Closure for your siblings. If you'd like, I can make the arrangements."

Closure. Siblings. My siblings.

The strangest thought makes me laugh brokenly. "You knew. Of course you knew!" Exhaustion robs my voice of its dramatic flair. I just sound fucking tired. "For how long?"

"Since yesterday morning." He doesn't even deny it. "She was initially a Jane Doe, but I had my suspicions. They identified her officially late last night."

"But you didn't tell me then. You were going to have Lucius tell me instead." And not out of oversight. I've become well-versed in the nuances of Maxim Koslov lately. He does nothing without calculated interest. "Like I said, I won't go running to the police. So you can stop pretending like you even give a shit—"

"You're upset." A warning laces his tone, soft like a trip wire waiting to be sprung.

"No." I exhale, running my fingers through my hair. "I'm… *You* ended our contract. That means you don't get to control—"

"I wanted to give you more time." He grabs my wrist and I flinch as every nerve goes haywire beneath my skin. *Zap!*

It's funny. Melanie always went back to heroin no matter how many fucking times she overdosed, and I hated her for it. But now, with his touch on my skin, I think I know why. Oblivion is so much better than cold, cruel reality—and it takes everything I have in me to pull away.

Even more shocking? He lets me.

"Time to what?"

The answer lurks in the tentative way he held me. Not hard and punishingly like I'm used to. Softer. Gentler. Comforting?

"Time to think."

I shake my head. "I don't want to think!"

I need to act. Do something. Hug the kids, maybe? Call around for funeral homes. Normal people send out announcements when a family member dies, I think. Go figure, I can't think of a single person to announce Melanie's demise to. Maybe the deadbeat boyfriends eager to pay their last respects? Or all the bill collectors that will undoubtedly come calling? Or I bet she has a mound of debt waiting to be shackled to her next living descendant.

"Breathe—"

"I'm not upset." My voice falls flat, echoing in the cavernous room around us.

Shadows stretch across the floor, swallowing us in their path. Thunder echoes beyond the walls, faint but distant. Like memories, in a way. Those old, blurry ones from my childhood, back when I might have felt something other than hate for Melanie. Something instinctual and pathetic that I assume every child has either nurtured or squashed by those around them. Love?

My love for her, if it ever existed, is now long gone. Dust.

Like the particles swirling in the air, making my eyes water and my throat constrict. This fucking dust.

"I'm fine—"

"Fine," he says without argument.

My heart pounds harder. Thoughts race. Too many things battle for attention. Melanie. Death. Melanie. Funerals. Arrangements. The kids. Maxim. Maxim. Maxim…

"I'll handle the arrangements," he says, flicking the collar of his coat. "Goodnight."

He heads for the door before I can say anything else.

When he leaves, he doesn't look back.

Not once.

DING, dong, the witch is dead. I should designate the date a personal holiday. But Mommy dearest always had to have the last laugh: I'm the one still paying for her mistakes.

Lately, it feels like there are two Francescas, both superficial copies. One is a lapdog who used to pine at her master's feet. The other is a pseudo *mother-chef-referee-office worker-consultant-grief counselor-banker-always-has-everything-together, no-shit-taker.*

I'm not sure which woman is easier to be. I'm not even sure which one I like being more. Maybe it's the mask that requires no real effort on my part to wear?

The pet who just lies there as she's walked over, used, and screwed.

Or maybe it's the performance that makes me feel—even for a little while—like someone worth being.

As long as I continue to *do*, and *be*, and *have* everything.

At least in one of those roles, I don't have to smile as much. Here, trapped inside the house Maxim bought for my family, my lips are always contorted on cue. Voila. I'm caring, loving sister Frankie, ready to comfort, and hug, and offer reassurance that everything will be okay, as long as I'm here.

We don't need *her* and never have.

I approach the living room, determined to put on a convincing act. I can hear faint sobbing even from here—

Daisy probably. Sure enough, I round the corner and find her slumped on a leather couch, with Mikie by her side. At her feet, Ainsley is body-slamming Eric to the floor, while the twins, Ollie and Ray, trade insults over a video game playing on the television.

"Bet you can't beat my score—"

"Bet your ass I can!"

"Fuck off!"

As the bickering continues, I sense my nails dig into the inside of my wrist, pinching. Gouging. I look down, recognizing the bright-red substance seeping from the tiny scratches, but the burning sting I should feel is nothing more than a dull ache.

Am I dreaming? Inside a parallel universe? One where up is down and down is up and dead mothers still exist?

"Hey, Frankie," Mikie calls, drawing my attention. A frown tugs at his mouth, but otherwise, he looks fine.

In fact…everything feels so fucking normal.

Except Daisy. Her sniffling could signal yet another of her daily dramas—if it weren't for what she has clutched to her chest.

My eyes hone in on it, narrowing. It's a photograph, framed in one of those popsicle-stick frames you make in kindergarten. A photo only she would keep, long after I'd tossed out every other picture of this person in particular. The strange woman smiles up at me from between Daisy's splayed fingers. With dark, curling hair and brown eyes, she looks like me—long before she took to dying her hair and caking makeup over her face. She looks so damn young. I can't stop staring.

I can't stop seeing that handmade frame as a goddamn mirror, reflecting everything I am now back at me.

Tired. Desperate. Pathetic.

"Oh, look!" Eric exclaims, ramming his elbow into Ainsley's stomach. "Suck it—"

"Mikie!" Ainsley whines while the twins burst into a shouting match over their game.

All I can think to say is, "I… Can everyone shut up?"

Silence descends as suddenly as if I flipped a switch. I can think, finally. I can hear. Daisy's sniffling. Ainsley muttering. Mikie standing.

"Frankie?"

"You...you do know that she's dead?"

They all stare up at me, six blank faces, only one streaked with tears.

"*Melanie*," I correct harshly. "You know Melanie is dead, don't you?"

"Yeah." Mikie nods and glances at the younger kids. "It's sad, but I don't want us to focus on it—"

"She was stabbed to death," I spit out. Oops. It's the wrong thing to say.

"Frankie!" Mikie slaps his hands over Ainsley's ears.

She immediately attempts to shrug him off. "Let go!" she shrieks, only to have Mikie slap his hand over her mouth, too.

"Are you really doing this right now?" he asks.

"Why would you say that, Frankie?" Daisy lurches from the couch, still clutching that damn picture to her chest. "Why the hell would you say that?"

"It's the truth." God, I don't even recognize the sound of my voice. I'm not used to sounding this cold. This callous. Like…

Like Maxim.

"She's dead—"

"Shut up!" Daisy's voice rises to a whistle-like pitch, her cheeks splotched and red. "Why are you here? Why is she even here?" she demands, turning to Mikie. "It's not like you really give a shit anyway, right, Frankie? You're never fucking here!"

"What are you talking about?" Genuine confusion has me frowning. "I'm always here."

Always. Even when most people my age would have bailed on the responsibility. Long after Melanie *did* bail. I've always been here.

"Are you?" Daisy steps in closer, her arms wrapped tightly around the picture frame.

Up this close, I'm struck by just how different we look—not like siblings at all. She's blond-haired. There are no cuts on her wrists or scratches on her fingers. She doesn't share the empty, dull expression of the woman in the photograph.

I can't stop myself from reaching for it. My fingers only manage to snag the end of a popsicle stick before the whole damn thing snaps.

"Stop it!" Daisy rears back. "What did you do?"

"Everyone calm the hell down!" Mikie positions himself between me and Daisy, his palms outstretched to opposite ends. "Everyone just relax—"

"No!" Daisy pushes past him, her arms wrapped around that goddamn picture. "I don't want her here. It's not like she really cares anyway," she blubbers. "Do you? Or maybe you're glad, huh? Maybe now you can stop trying to be her—"

I don't register the slap until the moment my palm connects with the smooth skin of Daisy's cheek. The resounding thwack echoes like a gunshot. Suddenly, it's too damn quiet.

"Frankie, what the hell?" Mikie rushes toward Daisy, dragging her back.

She stares at me, her mouth open in shock. Even now, she's still holding that goddamn picture.

You don't care, do you?

But does anyone, really? I glance around the room and surmise the answer on my own. No. No one really gives a shit. Our mother is dead, but it might as well be another day. Another fucking Sunday. Another goddamn, grueling, unbearable day.

Do I care?

I should. The shackles that have weighed me down for so damn long should have fallen off the moment she drew her last breath. Daisy's right: I don't have to be her anymore. I don't have to fill her shoes. I don't have to wear her mask and be all those things she never was.

The bitch is dead; I *should* be free.

"Frankie?"

The soothing color scheme of the living room blurs into gray as I whirl on my heel and ignore the hand that paws at my shoulder.

"Where the hell are you going?"

I open my mouth to answer, but nothing comes out. Somewhere.

Anywhere.

I just need air. Ironically, I don't find any when I finally wrench the front door open. My lungs expand on nothing. I can't catch my breath, no matter how quickly I race down the walkway. Up ahead, a car waits and the driver stands at the back seat door, ready to usher me inside.

"Ms. Marconi?" He clears his throat pointedly when I start past him, reminding me of my unspoken boundary. Even thrown away and exiled, I'm still on a leash. "Ms. Marconi?"

I walk faster, inching toward the gate that bars this wealthy community from the outside world. Then I keep going, following a path that cuts through a scenic park, toward god knows where.

I'm not running.

Maybe I'm still looking for that elusive fresh air? Everything I breathe in feels tainted. Dirty. Dusty.

A bit like my soul.

Melanie was always a stain inside me, seeping through flesh and bone. Like a fool, I always believed that her inevitable death might act like soap and scrub it clean. Everything I've done—the worst, most disgusting acts— has been because of her.

Or has it?

Desperate to regain my bearings, I collapse on a random bench, cradling my aching head in my hands.

She's gone.

I have to say it out loud, just to hear the way it sounds. Hollow—that's how. Melanie is dead, but I...

I'm not.

"Here."

I flinch as a white strip of fabric appears in front of my face, offered from above by someone behind me. A shadow fans out before I can react, painting the pavement black as I sense a presence settle onto the narrow bench. I look over and find Maxim seated there, staring resolutely ahead. It stopped raining hours ago, but the stench of it still taints the air. Odd. I can finally inhale it now, tasting the nuances of the past storm and the evening chill.

"I just needed some air—"

"You do not have to lie to me."

My lips seal together, a slave to his command. Don't lie. I might as well say nothing ever again. It's all I fucking seem capable of lately.

I'm fine.

I'm fine.

I'm fine.

"Are you going to be watching me forever?" I wonder. "Waiting to jump the second you think I won't play by your rules?"

I don't receive an answer. Just as well, I'm used to responding to myself these days.

"I'm so tired of everyone treating me like a punching bag, or a piggy bank, or a toy." Oops. The confession spills out of me, hot and raw. I grit my teeth, biting back more—but it's like a dam breaking. Boom. Everything spills loose. I'm on my feet before I realize, pacing on the path of grass beside the pavement. "How could she do this to me? How could she be so fucking selfish?" A strangled sound cuts off the tirade. God no. My eyes are on fire. I reach up to rub them, but shit, the motion just triggers an avalanche. I'm sobbing in no time, gasping. "I hate… I hate her!"

Someone grabs me harshly, spinning me into a wall of muscle. Maxim. His smell trickles down my nostrils, tripping every nerve on the way down. The nearness stings, like touching a hot stove, and I instinctively jerk out of his reach.

"Get off of me!"

He doesn't move, but a slight tensing of his jaw conveys a silent warning. I'm making a scene. Even now, there are people out strolling the paths, enjoying this quiet hour just before dusk. They giggle and gossip, oblivious to the crime lord casting a shadow over this secluded corner.

He's a demon painted red in the glow of the blood-red sky. The sinking sun ignites the horizon, adding a chilling backdrop to his gaze. It's beautiful. And terrifying. Taken altogether, he's a striking contrast: smooth ebony silk and impenetrable flesh.

"You're in shock," he murmurs in a tone that makes my blood run cold. Maybe he's talking that way because he's never seen me like this: crying, sobbing. He's never seen the disgusting shell of Francesca Marconi his pretty dresses and bruises used to disguise.

"I'm fine."

"Look at me." His nails capture the underside of my jaw as his body moves in, nearly knocking me over to keep me close this time. Trapped.

My lips part, ready to deliver my customary response. *I'm fine.* It's right there on the tip of my tongue.

"I-I'm so tired." *Fuck.* My cheeks burn, but nothing can snatch the answer back. It's there, lingering on the air. "I'm so fucking tired. I'm so tired."

Of what?

He doesn't need to ask the question out loud—his grip tightens, wringing the confession from me.

"I'm so tired of pretending and being everything for everyone. I'm so..." Another sob triggers a burning rush of tears. They sink into the front of his shirt, alerting me to just how close he is—no longer entirely of his doing, either. My hands snuck against his abdomen without my realizing, seizing handfuls of his coat. I flinch, forcing my fingers to open, letting him go.

"I just… I don't want to be like her!" I'm channeling Daisy in her most dramatic of fits now, choking back sobs and sniffling snot. "I don't want to be like her anymore."

Lost.

Useless.

Worthless.

"I'm so tired of taking care of everyone all the time. I just want—"

"What?" He grabs my chin again, forcing it back so that I have no choice but to face him.

"I want…to be free," I hear myself croak. Though what the fuck does that mean? "I want…" My brain overloads and stalls like a crashing computer. Rebooting takes a few breathless seconds as I watch him watch me. "I just want something that's mine. Something that I can have for myself. I don't have to pretend. I'm not her. She never did anything useful. All she did was screw people over and…"

Survive. Just like me.

There are so many things she wasn't. Successful. A good mother. Happy. "She never went to school. I couldn't, either. She never made something of herself without fucking someone else over. But what have I done? Bedtime stories, money for field trips, the rent! She never took care of any of these things and still Daisy thinks she walks on water. I sacrificed everything! And for what? To be someone's whore? A pet? It's not like I'm made for anything better. God! I couldn't even help Daisy with Algebra—"

"Education," Maxim says over me. "Is that what you want?"

I blink. Like any delinquent, I have my GED, but beyond that?

Before I can answer, he sighs. "Consider it done. As payment for your continued silence. Stay here." He steps away, adjusting his coat. "I will have Lucius come for you."

He turns and advances down the path without an invitation for me to follow.

And I've never felt more alone.

CHAPTER NINE

Melanie never spoke about what she wanted when she died, at least not around me. Funny, because we damned each other to hell on a daily basis, but I don't even know if her body belonged in a church.

We could be Jewish for fuck's sake.

Regardless, Maxim takes over the "arrangements," leaving me blissfully in the dark. Good. Would knowing she's in the ground, tainting the earth, be any better than having her ashes on the mantel while the kids played on the floor beneath?

It's one of the myriad of things I don't want to think about—but Maxim's taken careful steps to reinforce his previous promise: he handles it all.

I can hear the kids being marshaled, presumably by Lucius, and ushered out the front door of the house. So I stay, trapped within a room like one from a fairytale. A deranged, twisted story in which the innocent victim isn't really all that innocent. Her monster prepared a special place for her in his substitute lair: one with white walls and carpeting and a bed with a gossamer canopy. But in the end, it's nothing more than a cage. A way to keep her separated from his real dwelling.

She's expendable.

"Ms. Marconi?"

"Coming." My heart pounds furiously as I follow the direction of the voice and find Lucius in the living room.

"The au pair took the children out for dinner," he explains. "I hope you don't mind. Also, Mr. Koslov asked me to bring you this."

He extends an object in my direction, and I warily accept it. It's flat, like a book. A brochure? On the front is an ivy-covered building underneath text proclaiming a name I vaguely recognize. One of the city colleges?

I look up, eyeing him warily. "He's serious?"

He can't be.

Lucius nods. "Should you accept, he will handle the tuition. Pick your courses. Tomorrow, you go for the preliminary tests."

"He can't be serious." I sound like a broken record—emphasis on the broken. Something seeped into my voice without permission. Terror?

Men like Maxim do nothing without expecting more in return.

Looking at Lucius' stoic expression, I can't tell what the price is this time.

"He doesn't have to bribe me to stay silent," I say in a rush.

Lucius raises an eyebrow. "I'm not sure what you mean, miss."

"I...I don't even know what to study." I never had the time to wonder before. In fact, the only "educational pursuit" I'd probably be good at is business management, all things considered.

"Have you changed your mind?"

I stiffen, shaking my head. "N-no. I just—"

"Then I will come for you tomorrow." He nods curtly and heads for the door. "Oh, and my condolences for your loss. Your mother's memorial service is tonight." An uncharacteristic emotion colors his voice. Hesitation? "All you have to do is arrive."

Arrive, most likely, to a funeral home, where some priest will give her the pomp and circumstance she never gave me, let alone any of the kids.

"Don't you think this is moving too fast?" I hate how fucking breathless I sound. Weak. "I mean, d-do the police even know who killed her—"

"Mr. Koslov thought it would be best to move quickly to give your siblings closure," he explains. "Her body hasn't been released, but a drawn-out investigation can be... taxing on some. He thought this way would be easier. Unless..." He furrows his eyebrows. "Do you not want to go?"

My teeth descend into my lower lip as I rebel against the obvious answer. Good daughters would attend their mothers' funerals, even if they hated them. Even if they wished them dead on a daily basis. Even if...

That "good" daughter sees her mother's smug fucking face wherever she looks, haunting her. Taunting her. *Don't you see, baby?* she croons from the grave. *We're the same...*

"I can convey your wishes to Mr. Koslov if that is so."

"No." My cheeks burn in the aftermath of the confession. It's like I've said a dirty word. "I don't think I need to. I mean..."

"All right." Lucius nods. "That just gives you more time to study." The reminder is paired with a deliberate nod toward the brochure still clutched in my fist. "Have a good evening, Miss Marconi."

After he leaves, I curl up on a leather chaise, tucking my legs beneath me. At first glance, the brochure looks like a typical overview of the average college campus. Numb, I flip through the first few pages, only to realize that the latter half is a summary of information for an entrance exam. English. Math. Spelling. All those subjects that feel like distant relics from high school.

Because I did so fucking good back then. My eyes squint as I run over the various subjects. Some jackass had the nerve to insert "general knowledge" in there somewhere, as if geography and the shape of fucking clouds are something everyone knows. The only thing that makes somewhat sense is math. Maybe because it's all I ever excelled at—a bitch who couldn't count her money right had no business hooking, after all.

I try my hand at the practice questions at the very back of the booklet. Wrong. Wrong. Wrong. It's like playing a game of how badly I can fuck up, proving something I've always known. Hell, even Melanie told me once that I'd only ever excel at one thing: lying on my back.

And plain fucking lying.

CHAPTER TEN

I would sell my soul in a heartbeat to keep my family safe. I used to tell myself that. I used to say it out loud. Once, I even shouted it at Melanie when she'd had the nerve to bitch about the sacrifices she made, having her children so young. "High school," she'd scoffed. "You had it easy. I didn't get to do any of that shit."

Fuck her. That bitch never knew the meaning of sacrifice. But do I? It's turning out to require more than I ever thought it would. Surrender is beyond enduring someone else's abuse, apparently.

It's having them ask you to *like* it.

It's believing that you might even *need* it…

It's letting yourself fall without even trying to safely land.

Only now am I starting to understand that I never really had to sacrifice anything, either. Nothing that really matters, anyway. Despite all the hell I've been through,

I've always still been Frankie. Jaded, bitter, desperate, defiant, fucked-up, fucking Francesca Marconi.

No one had ever asked me to stop *being* her before. They never had anything to offer in exchange: namely all the shit I always told myself I never needed. Security. Safety...

I've given up so fucking much for my family over the years, but I'm not sure if I can leave that girl behind. Go figure. She's been the only bitch I could rely on.

Hell, Maxim easily found another toy.

And yet I remain in his dollhouse.

The obvious expense of the place seems eerie now. Alone in the living room, my breaths echo: shallow rasps echoing off the walls. I see myself. No matter where I look, my reflection gazes up at me from the polished floors. Only it's not *mine* entirely, but a woman who looks like me. Her eyes are wide and mocking, her hair a tangled mess.

Don't worry, baby, she tells me, snickering. It doesn't seem to faze her that her throat is slashed open and bleeding. *At least now you know what to look forward to.*

Fuck her. I turn so that I'm lying flat on my side, but my hair drips over the edge of the chaise, spilling onto the floor like blood. If I squint, that's what it looks like. Carnage. Death.

Murder...

He said she was stabbed. Did she even see it coming? Did she suffer?

I doubt it. Melanie *never* suffered the consequences of her actions. She wouldn't hesitate to put me or the others in her place, either.

So. She. Shouldn't. Matter.

God, I wish she was here. I'd punch her. Hit her. Say all those things I had enough tact not to while she was alive. I'd give her a real fucking sendoff.

She'd never have the last word...

And she still won't.

I shake my head as if the act alone can drive her out and rise from the chaise. Enough. She's dead.

She's *dead.*

Gritting my teeth, I escape into the bathroom and run the bath water as hot as I can stand it. The noise helps somewhat in drowning her out—but not completely.

I see her on the water's surface. She's smiling. Smirking, taunting me from the grave: *You call this struggling, sweetie? You've had it easy.*

Fuck her. Closing my eyes, I submerge myself beneath the water, counting the seconds.

One.

Two.

Ten.

Gasping, I resurface, only to find a stranger watching me from the mirror's surface. Her eyes are bloodshot. Straggly brown hair clings to her shoulders, a far cry from Melanie's multicolored wigs. But the haunted quality of their expression is the same.

Like mother like daughter…

I STARTLE to awareness in my room, blinking back the remnants of a nightmare. One of the shapeless phantoms chases me into the real world. When I leave my room, intending to make breakfast, he's standing at the base of the stairs.

Dressed in a gray suit, he takes one look at me and inclines his head. "Get dressed. I'll be waiting out front."

My fingers sneak to the inside of my wrist, pinching hard —but I don't wake up. "You're taking me?"

It's obvious. I think I just need to hear him say it.

His eyes sweep over me, revealing nothing. Turning on his heel, he approaches the door. "I'll be in the car."

Unease has me swallowing hard. Aware of him waiting, I wash up in record time and wrestle my hair into a ponytail. Minutes later, it is a surprisingly normal trip down to his car.

No dead mothers make an unwelcome appearance. No unspoken tension ruins the odd familiarity between us. Hell, it could be just a normal day in Maxim Koslov's world—until I spot the uncharacteristic clutter lying across the car's front seat.

I'm stopped in my tracks, vaguely aware of the frown tugging on my mouth.

"One of the children must have left them behind last night," Maxim says, sounding miles away.

Them. Soft, red petals spill from a dying set of roses, tied together with white ribbon. They're cut short, the perfect length for placing on an altar.

Or a coffin.

I shake my head and wrench on the handle, opening the passenger's side door. "How... How was it?" The memorial service. God, just pairing that word in the same context with Melanie makes me snicker.

"It went well." He sounds so cold. I can't parse anything unspoken he might be hiding.

"G-good." With one hand, I grab the roses. Freeze. Their delicate scent taints the air and I can't help but picture Melanie. The artificial version was her signature stench— one so ingrained that it's like she's here, reeking of cheap, flowery cologne.

"I'll take those." Maxim snatches the roses from my grasp and tosses them onto the back seat. "Get in."

His voice sinks into my bones, jolting them into submission. I slump onto the passenger's seat, inhaling the air as shallowly as possible. I imagine my pores closing up in protest, refusing to absorb so much as a fucking ounce of him or the roses.

Breathe it in, baby, a woman's voice taunts, sounding so close that I swear I can smell cigarettes. *We might as well smell the same...*

"We're here."

I flinch, noticing our surroundings. Minutes must have passed without me realizing. *Here* is a parking lot surrounded by a lush, green lawn and towering stone buildings. I only have movies to compare this scenery to —one of those shitty thrillers taking place on a college campus. The lead female would be a beautiful, normal blond who grew up in a beautiful, normal family. Her tuition was paid for by a scholarship or some shit. Not by a man with seemingly more money than God.

She might be one of those bookish types too, who outsmarted the killer in the end and lived happily ever after. Such a good girl would never sell her soul to him in exchange for the kiss of his blade.

Sucks for her. To each his own.

"Your preliminary session is in that building over there," Maxim explains, nodding to a castle-like structure directly ahead. Without warning, he reaches across me and flicks the glove compartment open. "Here—" A new, glossy brochure lands on my lap, along with a slip of paper. "The room number is on it. I'll arrange for your transportation afterward."

"I can get home on my own—"

"I'm not going to hurt you." His stern glance makes me bite a retort back. He doesn't sound like the ruthless dominant demanding a concession. He won't hurt me.

Not intentionally, with whips or knives.

Supposedly not unintentionally, either.

"Fine." I swallow hard and wrestle for the handle. As I scramble for the curb, I find myself croaking, "B-bye."

His watchful gaze seers a hole through the back of my neck, tracking my every move across the deserted campus. At a second glance, this place holds little resemblance to the bustling college set from that movie. There are no students racing to their next class. No professors juggling books and supplies.

There is no one else *at all.*

Even inside the building, it's too quiet. The only other inhabitant I find lurks on the third floor, in a room marked 301—the same printed on the slip I'm holding.

The room itself is a narrow classroom with a view of a small, picturesque grove. Unlike in my movie—only one desk dominates a space obviously meant for many more. Across from it is a larger desk that I assume belongs to the professor. A woman is sitting behind it now, her blond hair neatly swept back into a bun. Spotting me, she stands up, tucking a piece of hair behind her ear. It's her most striking feature, considering that a beige dress and loafers barely distinguish her from the plain walls around us.

"You must be Francesca. I'm Gemma." She smiles, extending her hand. "It's nice to meet you."

"Likewise," I croak.

Her nails are manicured and pink, her skin flawless. No marks. No cuts. If anything, *she* resembles the bright-eyed protagonist from that fucking movie. Cast alongside her, I'd be the brunette slut who dies running from the killer in high heels.

"Shall we begin?" She nods to the empty desk, her hands folded primly over her lap. "This is more of a counseling session than anything. We'll go over a basic review first, and then you'll take the entrance exam. It's mainly to see where you place—"

"You're the professor?" The fact that she's a woman doesn't shock me. Knowing Maxim, I'm not surprised. But she's young. I'd peg her as only a few years older than I am, if that.

She's pretty too.

Not to mention that she doesn't exude the same twisted, business-like aura of Lucius or anyone else in Maxim's orbit.

As weird a term as it feels to use in this context, she's...*normal.*

"Think of me more as a private tutor," Gemma explains, her lips quirked in an amused grin. "Let's get started."

I perch myself on the smaller desk, placing the brochure in front of me. With all the gusto of some of my most eager high school teachers, Gemma directs me toward a set of review questions on the back page.

Ugh. Dread forms a knot in the pit of my stomach, tightening the longer I scan the assorted topics. Math. Science. Grammar. Each one triggers an unwelcome flashback to high school—the worst being the many fucking times a teacher would demand an answer to a question, but I'd be too damn tired to respond. Working the night shift wasn't conducive to learning, go figure.

"Let's start with some simple equations," Gemma suggests. "Think you can try this one?" She scribbles a series of numbers on the blackboard.

"I..." My brain stalls. In the end, I spout off a random number.

"Not quite," she says, tilting her head thoughtfully. "Let's look at it from another angle." She turns to the blackboard at the front of the room. Picking up a piece of chalk, she maps the problem out. "We can tackle it in pieces," she offers. Strange. I don't sense any mocking in her tone. Patiently, she guides me to the right answer and claps once I reach it. "Awesome! Now, let's try another."

A RED FUCKING pen can seem more menacing than a bullwhip or a leather belt in the right circumstances. With my final score in question, Gemma wields her tool as expertly as Maxim does his, manipulating it across my scrawled answers.

The final tally could lead to praise or potential punishment. Which one do I crave more?

My nails bite at my wrist in anxious nibbles. I can't decide on an answer.

"Relax," Gemma says, glancing up. Her eyes widen, honing in on my mouth. "Are you all right?"

I'm biting my lip. I don't realize that until warmth drips from my chin and seeps through the delicate collar of my dress. Absently, I swipe the substance from my neck. It's red.

"I-I'm fine," I say, rubbing my fingers along the side of my dress.

"Good, because I'm all done." Gemma presents my marked-up booklet to me and beams. "You passed. Good work."

"What?" My eyebrow shoots up into my hairline. "How?"

She laughs. "Don't sell yourself short. I'm going to recommend maybe some remedial English, but mainly for grammar."

"Maybe I should learn Russian while I'm at it," I blurt out. "I already know the word for kitten, anyway."

"Oh?" She inclines her head thoughtfully. "What is it? Though I'm afraid all I know is English."

A sharp, pinching sensation stabs through my stomach. "*Kotyonok.* That's the Russian term."

She shrugs. "I've never heard it before—" Then she breaks off suddenly, rising to her feet. Ivory displaces the pink in her cheeks, making her resemble that horror movie heroine even more.

The "murderer," I suspect, is standing in the doorway, casting a shadow that dampens the daylight streaming through the windows.

"I don't mean to interrupt," he says.

"I… We were just finishing up."

My stomach tenses, but I don't know why. She's startled— Maxim is certainly the type of man to inspire that reaction. I'm reminded of the first time I met him, how intimidating he seemed.

How intimidating he still is.

It's the odd hint of recognition that I find in Gemma's expression which confuses me. Obviously, they met before —he hired her. But there's more to it…

She stiffens, unconsciously brushing a hand along her throat, as if remembering a particular touch. The suffocating clench of someone's fingers.

His fingers.

Blinking, she shakes her head and forces a smile. "We're all done here. I'll do some research and then we'll discuss potential majors, Francesca." She's still smiling, but her cheery tone falls flat. Forced. Glancing beyond me, she nods. "It was good to see you, Mr. Koslov."

Maxim says nothing. Turning to face him, I'm not sure what I'll find. He's still wearing his suit from earlier, his hair slicked back instead of wild. Cold, his gaze is unreadable as ever. But…

I sense something lurking just beyond that stoic expression. Another revelation, maybe. Or another bombshell. About Melanie?

Or maybe *this*.

The curious reason why he brought me to be "tutored" by a woman he used to fuck.

CHAPTER ELEVEN

I've been in confined spaces with dangerous men before. Hell, thanks to Melanie, I've lived with them. Hid from them. Suffered at their hands.

Men who violated my life and my body in unforgivable ways—and I survived every last one. No matter what, I was always unbreakable, unshakable Frankie.

But this new monster...

He changed my name and invaded my soul. He turned me into a pet—a replacement. Simply one of a hundred.

"I could have enrolled on my own," I say, breaking the silence for the first time since we left the campus. "Found my own teacher. My own school—"

"Was Gemma not satisfactory?" The hard note in his voice makes me grit my teeth. It's defensive.

Around us, traffic flows smoothly, unaffected by the suffocating tension robbing the air from my lungs. For whatever reason, he's decided to drive himself again.

"She's nice," I admit, but that word has a hollow ring to it.

One he doesn't miss.

"You're wondering about my relationship with her." His eyes are on the road as he masters the steering wheel, his jaw clenched.

"I think I know." God, I sound so calm. Strange, when I feel anything but. My heart is trying to beat its way out of my chest, hammering against my throat in the process. "One of the women you referred to before?"

How did he put it? Women more beautiful than me.

Better than me.

"I was her client once, yes," he admits.

I wince, startled by the pain ripping through my wrist. I'm doing it to myself: scratching so hard that I break the skin.

"She came to me four years ago," he adds as if in afterthought. "But the position didn't suit her. I saw her potential in other avenues."

My brain takes that statement and runs with it, inferring what he doesn't say. The beautiful, scholarly Gemma came to him as a hooker, but he—good old Maxim—saw her *potential.*

"She couldn't do it?" I ask, staring at the streets racing past.

"No. She didn't belong. She voided the contract."

"Did…did you ask her why?" We're nearing the house. I sense the car pick up speed as it lunges through stoplights as if he can't wait to dump me there.

Still, he plays along.

"She needed money for her education. Her parents had declared bankruptcy, leaving her with a debt to pay." He almost sounds genuine. Like someone with an ounce of pity to spare. "Now, she has tenure at the university and knows a variety of subjects."

"You didn't call her *kotyonok,* did you?" I didn't mean to ask him that, but it's too late. Deep down, I already know the answer anyway. "She didn't know what it meant." Maybe all this time, I thought that name was a universal term he applied to all of his pets. But not her, Gemma. He calls her by name.

She was more than his wayward kitten—maybe they *all* were. The other women smart enough to leave him before he threw them aside like trash.

And that's all you are to him, baby. Melanie's voice slithers through my thoughts, tainting them. *Trash. Just like me. You think any man might feel differently? Think again.*

"You're upset, aren't you?" He phrases the statement as if doubting it the moment the words leave his mouth. "Look at me—"

"Goodbye, Mr. Koslov."

We're in front of the house now, parked in the driveway. A yellowish glow illuminates the windows; the kids are home. My lips twitch, fighting to remember how to smile as I reach for the door handle.

"No—" The car lurches backward and then veers onto the road so fast that I have to brace myself against the window.

Heart pounding, I look at him from the corner of my eye. He's rigid, hunched over the dashboard, his eyes on the blurring streets.

"What are you doing?" I ask.

"We're not done."

I can taste his anger, more potent than the perfume of those fucking roses.

"I asked you a question."

"Let me out," I rasp. But if he replies, I hear nothing. Just my pounding pulse and ragged breaths. One. Two. Ten. Fifty. The faster I inhale, the more lightheaded I feel.

He's zooming through traffic, running red lights…

With no fucks given, he veers across oncoming traffic and a barrage of honking horns deafen me as my stomach lurches to the back of my throat.

"Stop!" I tug at the handle, only to realize he's engaged the locks. "What are you doing?"

Seconds later, his high-rise seems to come from nowhere, looming above for a heartbeat before he turns into the garage. After he parks and switches the car off, I can breathe again.

"What are you doing?" I repeat, my voice shaking.

"Get out." He doesn't even face me before exiting the car. The door slams shut behind him, echoing like a gunshot. "We need to talk."

"I'm done talking."

So why aren't I running?

I'm copying him instead, approaching the elevator. Maybe I really am in that damn thriller. There's a monster on my trail, though he keeps his distance, calling out in a dangerously soft cadence.

"Did you hear me?" he wonders, his voice chasing me as I pull ahead of him.

Yes. I hear him. Just like I've heard a million others throughout my life. Teachers. Boys. Men. My mother. My sisters. My brothers.

You're too stupid to do anything but scrape, Frankie.

You have to take care of us, Frankie.

You're worthless, Frankie.

All you're good for is lying on your back…

"Look at me."

My spine curls at the lethality contained in just a few terse notes. Shit. There's no ignoring him. The entire elevator car crackles with tension, feeling impossibly small. Crushing myself in the corner can only buy me a second's reprieve. What the hell am I doing here?

I start for the closing doors and try to wedge my hand between them. "Take me back—"

"Look at me."

A violent crack rips through the silence. The door slamming shut? No. His fist meeting the control panel so hard that a chunk of metal flies off and ricochets across the floor.

It misses me by mere inches, and I cringe, pressing myself against the wall out of instinct. But when I finally process my emotions, I only feel…pain.

Sharp and searing agony claws through my stomach, but my nails aren't the cause this time.

Poor baby, Melanie taunts. *You thought you were the special one? Ha!*

The room blurs, reducing Maxim to a golden blur on black canvas. No matter how hard or fast I blink, nothing holds the tears back.

"Are you bored?" I ask him. In the narrow space, I sound dangerously loud. "Is that why you brought me here? To fuck? To terrorize? Whatever it is, let's just get it over with." I claw at the front of my dress, undoing the buttons beneath the collar. *Ping!* They fly off one by one, dancing across the floor. "Should I bend over? S-stand? Just tell me where you want me—"

"Stop." He watches my pathetic performance without a shred of emotion.

"Here, then?" I'm already trying to shove my arms from the sleeves. "Just tell me—"

"Stop it." He's closer in an instant, grabbing me by my throat, clenching hard enough to cut off any sound I make.

I'm forced to stare up, but from this angle, his eyes burn. Like glimpses of hell smuggled in the gaze of an angel.

"Tell me what this is about," he demands.

"About?" I croak—the loudest reply I can force through his grip. None of this should be surprising. His real feelings shouldn't hurt. I should take his money like a good girl and perform whatever song he wants in return. "Just tell me how you want to use me. That's all I'm good for. Isn't it?"

He laughs, and never in my life has a sound ripped down my spine with such intensity, resonating in my bones. Like thunder, that first warning herald before one hell of a storm.

"I see it now. You're jealous." He lets me go and steps from the elevator, leading the way down the hall. "Of her," he calls back.

I should deny it. Shake my head.

Lie.

"Tell me," I choke out instead. "I just... I just need to hear you say it."

God, why do I sound so weak? Breathy. Desperate.

"Oh?" His tone rings with warning, begging me to heed it. *Stop this.*

Hell, every nerve in my body screams at me to do the same. *Get a hold of yourself, Frankie!* I bite my lip. Gouge at my wrist. Nothing clears my head. Instead, the same damn thought keeps echoing over and over. *Her potential. Her potential...*

"Was I that much of a whore?" I ask in a rush. I can't stop spitting each word out despite how his shoulders stiffen, his posture tenses. "Is that why you made your offer?"

Why you threw me away.

"Enough of this." He whirls on his heel without warning. His hand latches onto my skull, dragging me deeper inside.

I try to back away, but he's relentless, grasping me even tighter.

"Whore? Yes," he snarls. "Just like the rest. And to you, I was just a job. Look at me—" He tugs even harder when I try to turn away. Goosebumps swell over my skin, feeding off the tension radiating through him. It's like he's a fucking inferno—even though his voice chills me right to the fucking bone. "You want to know about *her*?"

He shoves me onto a leather chaise face down before I can reply. I twist my hips, fighting his grip—but his knee lands on my lower back, easily pinning me beneath him.

"The trembling little girl who came to me in a goddamn prom dress?" he hisses. "Who vomited on my cock before she could even take the damn thing in her mouth? A girl who wouldn't have lasted a day, let alone a night with me? And what about *you*?" He yanks my head upright, ripping tiny hairs from their follicle beds. My scream can't drown him out; he's that loud. "You came to me no better than she did. I showed you mercy. I told you to leave. You *disobeyed*—"

His voice rasps as if the concept confounds him, even now: I came back to him.

Again.

And again.

And again.

Suddenly, the pressure on my scalp loosens. Through streaming eyes, I watch him back toward the center of the room.

"I gave you what you wanted—more than all those fucking women combined." He's still shouting, straining the cords in his neck. I *feel* each bellowed word like he's hammering them into my skull. "Gemma has a husband. A child. The first time I spoke to her in four years was to request her services. For *you*. Fuck, the things I've done for you." He sounds awed. Disgusted. "The things I'm still doing. For *you*. Even when it costs me more than you can imagine. And you want to play this childish game? Like a mouse chasing the cat's tail. You enjoy this, don't you?" Amusement flickers across his expression, but it's mixed with something else, visible only in his stern frown. Something too heart-stopping to name. "Don't you?"

"Enjoy it?" I choke out. His madness is contagious. *I'm* going mad. I tear at my hair, rocking back and forth as the pain barely registers. "I hate it! Stop toying with my head. *You* threw me away—"

"Did I?" He glances around the massive room as if taking stock of each possession. The luxurious leather chaise. The polished, pristine floors.

And finally me, trembling at his mercy.

"Bored. You used that word. And I *should* be bored of you." He takes a step closer.

I jump back, but he advances again, another step. Another. His movements are jerky, devoid of the grace I'm used to. Almost as if he doesn't even realize he's doing it. Prowling. Hunting. Closing me in near the wall, eliminating my only escape route with a mere shift of his weight.

The second I flinch to the balls of my feet, it's already too late.

"You want to know about *kotyonok*—" His hand sweeps out, capturing a fistful of my hair again.

One ruthless yank makes me stagger into him, my hands grasping for leverage. I can feel his heart beating like this. It's fast. Unsteady. Manic. He doesn't care when I stiffen. His fingers just readjust their hold, crushing me against him.

"You were the only one whose name I didn't bother to learn at first. Just you," he admits, murmuring the confession into my hair. In a sick way, he sounds softer than before. Gentle. "You were right to be jealous. If you and Gemma both came to me that first day, I would have picked her."

Fire shoots through my chest. Is that pain? No, it's too sharp. Too raw. It doesn't numb me—it makes me reckless. "Get off of me!" I try to turn away, but his grip tightens.

"Don't." His teeth nip my earlobe as he snarls the warning. "I would have picked her," he echoes, an octave softer. "I could smell the desperation on you then. To you, I was a wallet. A job. A necessary evil. But I didn't judge you for that."

He doesn't sound angry. Merely crisp. Clinical. Like a scientist mulling his most puzzling experiment out loud, inviting anyone to offer insight.

"I knew you only wanted money. It's why I let you stay. It's why I didn't take the same pity on you that I did on the others. You were too young. And when you came back the first time…I knew exactly why. For money. And the second. And the third. All you wanted was fucking money."

He chuckles in that cold, chilling way, making goosebumps rise over my skin. We're too close. There's no escape from everything that makes him Maxim Koslov: the smell. The bulk. Those eyes glaring into my soul as if he knows everything I've ever tried to hide.

For what feels like an eternity, he stares into me. Through me. Whatever he finds just hardens his features further. He's stone within an instant, impossible to decipher.

"Believe it or not, I could stomach your greed. I have more than you've seen in your fucking lifetime. Enough to make you choke on it—" His free hand flinches for my throat as if he's intending to do just that. Choke me.

This time, for good.

Instead, he twists me around, shoving me face-first against the ice-cold wall. He's brutal. Unbearable pressure pins me in place: a prison made of flesh, and bone, and skin.

"It's not the money, is it?"

Warmth tickles the back of my neck: his mouth, nuzzling me. Biting me. Another gasp claws up my windpipe, but he's already licking the pain away before I can voice it.

"No… Something else keeps you coming back now."

There's no answer. None that I can give, and none that he'd believe. There's just silence, and a heartbeat—his and mine, hammering out a violent, unsteady rhythm in sync.

"I don't even think you know," he declares, sounding thoughtful again. "But it's wearing thin, Francesca… Though damn, maybe *this* is what you want?"

His fingers creep up my hips, groping through my thin clothing. Up my rib cage. To my breasts. The tighter he grips me, the more disjointed this moment feels. I'm in a parallel universe, where oxygen is an afterthought.

My body subsists only on *this*. His touch. His hate. Without warning, his nails sink into my skin. Lightly at first. Then firmer. Viciously. The tighter he holds, the harder I squeeze my eyes shut.

Harder. Harder. Light flashes before my eyes by the time he finally relents. Judging from the fiery welts stinging on my chest, he drew blood.

"I'm losing my patience," he admits, exhaling against my shoulder. "I'm losing my goddamn mind. Gemma, I could let her fuck someone else. She doesn't matter. I don't fucking care—but you?"

A shadow along the wall is my only warning before he wrenches my head to the side, baring my throat. A part of me lurches, anticipating teeth. Instead...I just feel the unstable gusts of his breath.

"I should bite you," he says against my skin. "Taste you. Make you bleed. More. Take all of you until there's nothing left."

He turns me around, capturing my throat in both hands, and yanking me onto the tips of my toes. Though my fingers fly out for stability, my nails catch the material of his jacket, accidentally seeking the flesh underneath. Bone.

He doesn't even flinch.

His hand cups my scalp, pulling me toward him, and I'm frozen. Blood. That's what we taste like as he forces his mouth to mine. Blood mingled together over bitten lips. Salt from my tears. Heat from his rage. Lust. Our tongues clash, his clambering to steal it all without sharing an ounce. And a terrifying thought starts to take hold: Maybe this is the only way I'll ever know how to let him in.

Through violence.

Because deep down, we're the same.

Selfish, twisted creatures.

CHAPTER TWELVE

Just as quickly as the kiss began, he ends it, shoving me back. "Get on your knees." Each word crackles with barely concealed tension as he looms above, his hair obscuring part of his face.

I know the look in his eye, however, and I'm already staggering backward, rushing to obey the command. My knees strike the floor, bare beneath the hem of my dress.

I stare down at the bruised flesh, not looking up even as I hear him circle my position. My brain scrambles to take note of every nuanced emotion from him. He reeks of sweat and something else. Something sweet that drips from his fingers and taints the air like perfume.

"Your dress. Panties too," he grates out amid the telltale crunch of leather over fabric. His belt.

I picture it being wrenched from belt loop after belt loop. Impatiently. A shiver runs down my spine as I contort my arms behind my head and struggle to lift the fabric. The cool air kisses the bruises already there, but I barely feel the ache. By the time I rise onto my hands, the first crack of leather hits the air.

And the only thing I can do is *feel.*

He's reckless. A grunt rips from him with every brutal lash, mingling with the groans I barely manage to smother. In a twisted semblance of harmony, we create a symphony of muted agony and sadistic satisfaction. What feels like seconds later, it's over. His belt hits the floor with a thud, his breaths unsteady over the air.

"Get…up." His hand sinks into my hair, guiding my head back just enough so I can find him staring down on me, his eyes feral and unfocused. One hard yank and he has me on my feet, staggering down the hall, into his room, toward the bed.

I land on my back, my legs spread apart just enough for him to fit in between. He palms my waist, wrenching the hem of my dress up farther while pinning me flat against the mattress. With one hand, he reaches between my legs, cupping me in his palm.

I can't stifle a gasp. He feels hot. On fire. His fingers are slick as well, and I cringe as I wonder why—or maybe the moisture is from me? He hasn't touched me in days. I shouldn't crave that rough, bitter sting only he can deliver, but my hips are already arching into it, extending the torturous seconds.

"Still greedy," he bites out, stroking me with a callused finger. The anger is gone, and the teasing pinch on my clit is my reward. I think. He curls a thumb inside me before I can be sure, purposefully stroking my inner walls. "Roll over."

When I do, he smooths my hair along my back, guiding me upright. The other hand is still inside me, slowly churning my insides to mush.

"Your knees."

My thighs jerk apart, anticipating the moment he mounts the mattress behind me, his breath on my throat. Wet heat precedes the warning nip of his teeth. A tease. The next bite goes deeper, easily breaking the skin.

My lips fly apart, a moan caught between them. As if in punishment or encouragement, he bites down harder, tearing…grinding. My fingers sink into the sheets, straining the cotton. It isn't enough to anchor me though. My head floats, my thoughts drifting.

Clear. Crisp. Real.

"You're hungry for me. Aren't you?" Maxim growls into my ear, banishing the dark suspicions.

My body agrees with that assessment. Both nipples feel like razors teasing the inside of my dress. Each brush heightens the heat building in my blood. I'm starving, but he just might be poison and my body is torn between the risk of dying and the promise of instant gratification.

"Aren't you?" He nips me again, soothing the wound with a lick from his tongue.

The mattress sinks as he settles in behind me, throwing me off-balance. The hiss of a zipper being undone pierces the air, and then his fingers are between my legs again, nudging them further apart.

He breathes out after the first experimental thrust of his thumb. With the slightest bit of pressure on my clit, he has me lunging toward the headboard, bucking into his hand. He wields me like a tool this way, stroking and pinching to make me squirm. Make me scream.

Make me submit.

His broadness teases my entrance. Stretches me open. Wakes me up. My inner muscles clench, hungry for his length, but he doesn't thrust. He lingers, giving me the briefest taste of the fullness I crave.

It's maddening.

My legs shake, my fingers grasping for leverage. Just when I start to sway, he thrusts another half of an inch. Another. A burst of wetness coats him, easing his way— not that he takes advantage of it. It's like he's getting off from the anticipation of fucking me alone, thickening against my entrance. Driving me fucking insane.

Maybe this is his way of apologizing.

When he finally does thrust, it's a slow-burning chain reaction of friction and force. I'm on fire with every inch of me he claims, and I can't even tell how deep he really is when he slows and groans against my ear.

"You're shaking, *kotyonok*." Suspicion thickens his already guttural tone and snippets of fear mingle with pleasure.

He finds enough leverage to fist a chunk of my hair again, trapping me right where he wants me: back bowed, ass presented to him. When he pulls out, it's a sharp jerk of his hips that leaves me empty without warning. Not for long. I don't even have the chance to blink before the bed lurches and I'm full to bursting. I see white—he forces himself *that* deep. The feral grunt rumbling from his throat betrays his satisfaction. Control may get him off, but so does this: raw, primal fucking with a hint of restraint.

"Tell me why."

An answer I can't bite back springs to my lips. Lying is impossible when he's this close—dominating me. "A… Afraid."

"Why?" Confusion makes his voice shake. Makes *me* shake.

Another thrust, painfully slow. His free hand claws at my hip as if that much control is a struggle for him to achieve in this moment. He's straining at the seams again.

I wail as he lunges, sinking in so deep that I can't breathe. Pain. It paints the world black. It makes me desperate; I'm an addict itching for the only drug that gets her high. When he wrenches his grip, raising fire over my scalp, I'm thrown onto the dangerous precipice between sanity and clarity.

Can't think.

"Why?" he demands again.

The answer leaves me in a rush. "Because I shouldn't want you."

And I *do*. My body is a glove, gripping him so tight that I can feel every pulse of his cock. His chest heaves against my back as his mouth nudges my jaw. Within seconds, ravenous lips find mine. Crush them, battering me into submission. His tongue swipes. Invades. Subdues. It's not a kiss. It's a sampling. He'll devour me later, but like any predator, he toys with me first.

"Say it," he growls before nipping my bottom lip, eliciting a moan I can't smother. "What is it you want?"

Drugged on him, I can't lie.

"...to keep me," I gasp as my cheeks heat with shame. But there's more. *I want you to smother me. Capture me. Collar me. Break, break, breakbreakbreakbreakme.*

"Why?" he wonders, biting me harder when I don't answer.

Copper trickles between us and his tongue hungrily chases every last drop. I can't even feel disgusted. My body is on fire, aching on the devious edge of pain and fear. Horror and need. I feel like that fucking French queen, about to be beheaded, only I'm eager for the blade to come down. I *need* to feel it slicing me to pieces.

"Why?" Maxim questions for a second time, his voice colder. He's stopped moving, leaving me unbearably full, right on the edge of *real* insanity.

My brain stalls. "I…"

He shoves me down when I can't choke an answer out, flipping me onto my back. Cold silk rasps over my skin, alerting me to the fact that my dress is bunched around my waist. Only vaguely do I remember where we are. His bed.

And he doesn't seem to give a damn.

He takes my wrists in his hands, forming painful manacles out of his fists. Using his weight as a prison, he pins me down, grinding his pelvis just where I need him the most.

"I'm done toying with you, *kotyonok*," he hisses. At the same time, he thrusts, ramming his erection between my legs, aided by the teasing friction of cotton and silk.

It's torturous.

Desire curves my spine as my thoughts meld into one overriding sentiment: *Holy fuck*. My limbs liquefy. My breath catches. Just as the pleasure scrapes me raw, his nails gouge my inner wrists and the pain bites deeper, keeping me tethered to my body. To him.

"You want to be kept," he reiterates, still crouched above me. "Why?"

"I…" Another brutal assault centered near my clit stimulates my nerves into painful awareness. My lips part, spitting out words at his command before I can properly compose them. "Because…feel…with you."

"Again," Maxim snarls against my throat. Shock doesn't color his tone. Just impatience. God, it's like he's in my head, seeing what I can't, ripping me apart to seek out the secrets I thought I was so good at keeping. "Say it." Pinching teeth startle me into obedience.

"Feel," I breathe. "You make me feel."

The Frankie Marconi I know and hate would never utter those words. She'd never whimper them while twisting her hips for another hint of agonizing ecstasy. She'd never fucking mean them.

And Maxim would never push her like this. Punish like this.

"How?" He thrusts his hips again, taking another moan from me.

He's different with this woman who's so eager to be his doll. He's reckless with her.

Bruised and battered, she'll never fucking forget who she belongs to. He'll handle her roughly and glue her broken parts together.

The worst part? She'll be grateful for every new crack.

My thoughts form the words more quickly than my tongue can push them out. "Something. Anything…"

Maxim laughs, swallowing my words with a bruising pass of his lips, and I have no doubt that he will make me regret every word.

He'll make me regret every twisted minute I continue to play his game.

And I'll never feel more fucking alive.

Bound to him, I won't have a damn choice…

And maybe the promise of that oblivion is what I really wanted all along.

I let myself sink into the brutality of his kiss and the violence promised within every harsh brush of his lips. His fingers bite into my ass, yanking me closer with our mouths still fused.

Rather than slow, he rocks his hips, slamming into me. Again. And again. And again… Heat builds, even though I don't want to acknowledge it. Sore flesh melts beneath his assault. Nerves spark. Catch fire. The air in my chest becomes liquid. My thoughts are smoke.

He's an inferno.

Gritting his teeth, he holds nothing back. Two thick fingers sink between my legs and find my clit, grinding the bundle of nerves into fucking oblivion. Stars. Tension. *Fuck!*

It isn't an orgasm that rips through my body—it's an entirely new reality. Sweat and skin become my universe. Everything else ceases to matter.

Breathless and spent, I watch him finish seconds after I do. His hands grip the headboard on either side of me, his head rearing back. Guttural, broken noise rips from his chest: a demon's growl. It reverberates through marble and chilled air. Seconds later, his release floods me, dripping down my thigh as he abruptly pulls out.

He's still hard somehow. Like a battering ram, he nudges my inner thigh, painting me in streaks of cum and sweat.

I WAKE up with three fingers inside me. Twisting, curling, maddening fingers. They swirl along my inner walls, drawing a cry from my throat. It's promptly swallowed by the warm surface that nudges my mouth open. *Lips?* I don't have any time to be sure before I'm consumed. Deep, hungry pulses of a tongue push me further to the edge. *Off* of it.

I'm clenching, swipe by swipe like a windup toy. Before my thoughts can reassemble, they're scattering apart toward different sides of the room.

"Look at me."

My eyes fly open on command and I find the devil hovering above. His black eyes trace my own, which watch on in satisfaction as they glaze over and then roll into the back of my head. *Shit.* My back bows, and my lips stretch around a moan.

The physical pleasure is maddening. But when his free hand latches onto my hip, his nails sinking deep…

Explosions. He rips me to pieces, melds them all back together, and calls it a "climax."

My body protests as he eases his fingers from me. Already, he's reaching for his cock, stroking his hand along the rigid shaft. He runs the crown along the length of me. The first thrust stretches me wide. The next, he's in to the hilt.

His name rips from my throat, hoarse and broken. It's the only coherent word I can manage, and for the moment at least, it seems to be enough. He growls in satisfaction at the sound, rolling his hips as he fucks into me. Thrust after thrust after thrust…

I'm mindless. My thoughts consist of an endless loop of only one word: *Shit…shitshitshit!*

It feels like an eternity before he finally comes, lunging against me—*into* me. Seconds later, he's rolling away, leaving my body naked on his bed.

His bed. It feels important to drill that point home. These sheets reek of him; the mattress has conformed to his body's imprint. But I'm the only woman to ever lie on it —I know that terrible truth without even having to ask. The walls inhale our combined scent, tossing it back at me like a flashing neon sign.

You're the only bitch who's been fucked here.

I'm the only bitch dumb enough to stay. I have to dwell on that fact as my blurred vision focuses on the ceiling. I blink twice to clear it, enough to make out his shadow pacing in the center of the room.

He frowns, looking me over. His jaw is clenched, those eyes like midnight. Anger is a familiar expression on him, but even that doesn't come close to describing this one. It's an unknown characteristic to his features, more terrifying than rage.

"I called you *kotyonok* because from the second you came to me you were on your guard, ready to pounce. Ready to bite." Still pacing, he frowns, raking his hand through his hair as if rearranging his thoughts. He's been thinking about this, I realize. "The other women were hardened. Most of them. Even Gemma knew what to expect. But you? So eager for your reward, you didn't even read the rules." He chuckles at that, grating the sound off his teeth. "Few lasted a night. Fewer an entire day. As I have told you before, you are the only one to stay. Contract or otherwise…you are the only one to stay."

He lets it sink in. Before, he was vaguer in his generalizations. He never came right out and told me that I was the only one. Or maybe he did. Maybe it was easier to ignore him then, in the cold, lifeless cage of the suite— before he showed me parts of himself that had been previously off-limits. Before he waltzed right into my home and made a mark on my family.

Maybe, in his own way, Maxim even tried to warn me.

"I told you," he says as if reading my mind again, consuming my thoughts the same way he has everything else. "Coming back to me was your first mistake."

"And the s-second?" My heart plays a pathetic pitter-patter pattern against the inside of my chest. I don't want to hear the answer, but my ears won't shut. My hands don't move to cover them, either. I'm at his mercy.

Where you belong, a part of me taunts. *Where you want to be...*

Maxim sighs as his footsteps slow. "You came," he admits. "Around me. For me." The raspy note in his voice makes the tiny hairs along my arms stand on end. "I told you that no one ever has. I *told* you." I know what he really means: *I warned you.* "But even that was a forgivable offense. Do you want to know what the final nail in your coffin was, *kotyonok?*"

"What?" I whisper, fighting for air as my heart swells, squeezing the breath from my lungs.

He sighs. "I don't think you'd understand, even if I told you."

He advances on the bed, climbing onto the mattress before I can blink. His hand cinches my waist, dragging me toward him.

"Sleep," he commands near my ear. "Tomorrow... Tomorrow we will talk."

CHAPTER THIRTEEN

"He's baiting me. No. I'll let him play his game." Nearby whispers meld into a deafening hum as snatches of reality gnaw away at my psyche.

And then it hits me. I'm in *his* suite. In his bed. His bite marks are on my neck.

And his words are in my head: *I don't think you'd understand, even if I told you.*

No. I shake my head to banish the thought, but the motion only betrays me.

"I'll handle it later." The murmured voices trail off and footsteps advance in my direction. Finally, a man commands, "Get up."

I peel my eyes open and witness his face in the dim glow of a nearby lamp. God, he truly resembles the devil. His eyes gleam red, his expression fierce, his lips glistening. There is something clenched in his fist.

Without warning, he throws it at me: soft, silky fabric that rasps over my naked skin. "Put it on. Then meet me out front." Then he's gone before my eyes even fully adjust and dread sets in.

Talk, he said—but my brain comes up with another word for it: regress. We'll meet in another secluded diner. He'll take back all the things he said.

And I'll be tossed in the trash again.

For a second—just one—I toy with the idea of running. Leaving him there and letting the master with all the cards know what it's like to be left holding a shitty hand.

Then logic takes over. Groaning, I pull myself upright and creep down the deserted hallway, entering "my" room for the first time in what feels like an eternity. I wash up quickly and stagger to the closet before I remember that I've already been given my costume.

The dress is black, I realize once I return to his room and fish it from the twisted sheets on the bed. It's low cut but relatively modest. After grabbing a pair of heels from my closet, I leave the suite and take the stairs down to the first floor. His car is idling out front, but this time, the driver is occupying the front seat and Maxim is dominating the back.

Upon spotting me, he wrenches the door open from the inside and beckons me with a wave of his hand. It's earlier than I thought. The sky is a coal-colored shade of gray and darkness floods the car's interior as I climb inside and close the door behind me.

My eyes dart toward him, but his face reveals nothing. He stares forward as the driver navigates toward a destination he and the driver must have already discussed between them.

Minutes later, we arrive before the elegant mansion I recognize as his club.

"Come."

Darkness still spreads across the sky as he unfurls himself from the car, rising like a goddamn giant. He's wearing a suit, black and crisp. It accentuates his muscles as he starts past me, advancing toward the entrance to the club.

I follow, partly unnerved, partly enthralled.

It's unfair how beautiful he can seem like this. With his hair wild and slicked back, his posture blazing confidence.

I'm not the only one entranced by him, either. A hush falls over the club as we enter. It's packed to the brim with its usual blend of scantily clad women, powerful-looking men, and pulsing music. Maybe he'll do it here?

Cut me loose and then choose another woman from this harem.

I tense as he slows his pace. Just when I start to suspect the worst, he turns in a different direction, ignoring the main club entirely. I'm not sure where he's heading, just that we pass through swatches of people before all other sounds finally die down.

We're in a hallway. He travels down to the very end and disappears through a doorway. When I finally gather up the strength to follow him, the air leaves my lungs.

It's a bedroom, I think. At the same time, it's so much more. His room back at the suite, if it could even be called that, is a crypt—detached of all semblance that it could have ever been inhabited by a human being. This room though…

It's bigger, for one, but it seems more cramped somehow. Lived in. The walls are that iconic shade of black, the floors marble. A minibar dominates one end of the room, and stone dust streaks the floor, leading to a section of the wall where a row of finished statues gleam in the glow of a silver light fixture. Most of them are abstract figures, with a few recognizable shapes sprinkled throughout: a wolf's head, a doe's, a woman's. *One* woman. Her face appears a few times, her features similar: a plain face with a simple nose and empty eyes without pupils. She's always naked. Always contorted into some unnatural position: her arms reaching toward something that isn't there.

If I squint, she almost looks familiar…

Turning away, I focus my attention on anything else.

At the center of the room is the strangest sight of all: a massive bed, the blankets rumpled, the pillows disorderly. My nostrils instinctively flare, but I only sense one scent.

Musk and sweat. Maxim. No one else comes into this room, I suspect.

Not even to clean. Never to fuck.

It's *his.*

My heart pounds as he crosses the threshold and nudges the door closed. That quiet thud shoots through me like a gunshot. I feel like I'm breaching the sanctity of this place. An intruder.

Apparently, the suite is just a temporary rest stop. *This* is where he lives.

It's like he realizes it too, once he sees me here, occupying a space I don't think he's let anyone else invade. Which is funny, given that more people probably run in and out of this club than I care to imagine. The fact that he can commandeer something so private speaks to the power he carries over this place. Over people.

A hint of it lurks in his muscles as he draws back and observes me. "We are going to play a game."

He gestures to a small table I didn't notice before, tucked into a corner of the room. It's black, and on it is a pack of cards with glossy, ebony backings.

"A game," I echo, creeping as close as I dare. The more I twist the prospect around in my brain, the more horrifying it seems. I don't think he plans on playing Go Fish. "A card game?"

A rare smile quirks his lower lip, gone in a second. "It's something one of my associates dreamt up. A bit childish, but for now, it will serve my purpose."

What purpose, exactly? I wait, my heart in my throat, but he doesn't say. Instead, his eyes flick over me, narrowing as they take me in.

"Sit."

I obey in a mass of trembling limbs. My muscles throb. Everything aches. My thoughts are way too clear. I'm aware of *everything.*

His nearness. My thudding pulse. More than that, even. Like the subtle way his breathing changes once I look up and meet his gaze. He's panting, inhaling my unease. Getting high off every drop, I suspect.

"Look." He takes the seat across from me and lifts the deck. One by one, he lays an array of cards face up. For some reason, I expect the typical arrangement: kings, queens, hearts, clubs, etc.

I shouldn't be so damn surprised by the designs I find printed on each card instead. One sports a bloodied heart in vivid detail. Another displays what I think is a flogger, with tiny metal beads dangling from the ends of it. There's also a pair of handcuffs, and a whip, and—of course—a knife.

"The game is simple," Maxim says while cutting the deck in half. He places one stack before me and keeps the other for himself. "You draw a card and I will guess which one it is. You do the same to me."

I lick my lips. It sounds so fucking simple, but nothing ever is where he's concerned. "And if I lose?"

His eyes flash, displaying a fleeting emotion that disappears before I can name it. "If you fail, I decide your punishment."

He waits, almost daring me to ask, *And if I win?*

He shrugs. "You do the same."

Again, it sounds too easy. "How am I supposed to—"

"Draw," he commands, nodding to the cards on my end. "I will guess first."

My fingers shake as I brush them over the topmost card. Slowly, I flip it over, concealing my selection from him: a whip.

He eyes me for so long that I start to wonder what the real purpose of this "game" is. To unnerve me, obviously. To make me sweat and squirm. To keep me guessing, even if he's supposedly the one in the hot seat, trying to decipher me.

"You drew a whip," he says finally. When I gasp, he clarifies, "You look too eager."

Eager. I marvel at that even as my stomach twists into uneasy knots.

"For your punishment, you give me an answer." He shifts slightly in his seat, leaning forward, his hands braced over the polished wood of the table. "How long do you see yourself staying with me, should I rescind my other offer?"

In other words: *If I dust you off and pluck you from the trash, how long before I toss you aside again?*

An answer springs to my lips almost too quickly. "A month, maybe."

He frowns. I answered wrong.

"Guess," he snaps while fishing a card from his own deck. Coldly, his eyes scan the surface, impossible to read and unbearable to decipher.

Seconds tick past before I give up with a halfhearted guess. "A knife?"

"No." He flips his card over: another whip. "I win again." Lifting the card, he observes it in the dim lighting. Then he places it apart from the rest. "Your punishment."

A shiver runs down my spine. I can't breathe. Only sheer force of habit makes me obey when he commands me, "Draw."

I do, but my eyes barely register the object on the other side of the card before he says, "A knife."

"How?"

"You are easy to read when it comes to the things that excite you."

My heart skips a beat. Excite?

He doesn't elaborate. Instead, he reaches out and snatches the card from my grip. Laying it beside the whip, he sighs. "I win again."

And I've supposedly earned my next punishment. I eye the knife warily as he draws another card. When I scan his face, however, something itches across my skull. Recognition? I know this expression.

I blurt out a guess without even thinking it through. "A heart."

He stiffens. Then, very carefully, he flips the card over, revealing the image printed on it.

"I win," I rasp in shock.

But beating him was the easy part.

His eyes meet mine again, more piercing than before. "And my punishment?"

Only he can make something so harmless—a childish game—seem so damn serious.

"The truth," I demand. "Why did you throw me away?"

He sits back, running his fingers along his chin. I'm caught off guard by how casual he makes the act appear. Almost like he planned for things to end like this all along. When his eyes flicker knowingly, I'm sure of it.

This whole game was an elaborate ploy for this: He needed a reason to talk. And a way to ensure I was ready to listen.

"You see yourself staying with me for a month," he says, twisting my words against me. "But maybe that would be for the best. Because being with me. *Truly* being with me… You would be risking way more than an occasional injury. In my world, you do not *keep* anything you're not willing to kill for. Money. Power. Prestige. You must be willing to lay your life down for it all. But a woman?"

He looks down, eyeing the table as if it offends him. Clenching a fist, he sets it down over the image of the heart, blocking it from sight. "My own father couldn't provide that protection to my mother. She was cattle. Do you understand what I mean?"

No. My brain isn't deranged enough to imagine exactly what he's implying—but it comes close.

"His own brothers could touch her," he says, confirming the worst. "Hit her. Abuse her. And he would let them. Why?" He lifts his shoulder in a heartless shrug. "Because to defend her with his life would mean defending her from *them* and he was too selfish, even though he plied her with lies of love and affection. My methods may seem harsh, but when a contract is terminated, there are no loose ends. No possession to protect."

"So…if they thought you cared for me—" My voice breaks. Even suggesting it seems unnatural. "You think they might hurt me."

"I *know* they would."

My stomach churns. I feel sick. "And you'd let them? You'd let them do those things to me?"

He doesn't say anything.

Sweat creeps across my palms as I reach for my deck and peel another card from the top. Without fanfare, I flip it over and slam it onto the table. How fitting. Another knife, just like the figurative one I feel twisting in my chest.

"So why even bring me here?" I demand, blinking rapidly. I won't… I am. Tears spill down like acid, eating through my skin. "You want to keep the stupid contract? Fine. But why do you keep toying with my head—"

"Because I can't let you go." He raises his fist and slams it over the heart. Once. Twice. With each blow, the entire table shakes. "I won't. And I should. That motherfucker is already asking about you."

My brain stalls. Sevastyn?

"I don't…I don't understand—"

"If he touches you, I'll kill him," he growls. "But I *can't*." He unfurls his fists and upends the entire table. *Bam!* It slams to the floor halfway across the room and every card goes flying. A flicker of shadow from the corner of my eye is my only warning before his hand captures my chin. "If I kill him. I'm done. Everything I've worked for. Everything I've slaved for. Gone. Are you really worth so much? Though, fuck, maybe it's not even *you* I want, either?" Laughing, he shakes his head, sending golden hair falling across his shoulders.

The locks obscure his face. Good. I can't even imagine an expression to match the grit in his voice. He's thinking out loud—and that's the terrifying part. Nothing unnerves me more than the brief glimpses I've had inside his mind.

"Maybe it's the idea of it," he says through gritted teeth. "The idea of having someone to fuck when I want. Hurt however I can. Someone foolish enough to stay so that I don't have to constantly look for someone new. That could be it…"

Frozen solid, I'm a slave to his touch, interpreting every fucking detail that I can from his coarse fingertips. They graze my skin, a heart-stopping caress. Eventually, he cuts my reprieve short, tilting my head back, forcing me to meet his gaze directly.

Dark, swollen irises convey so much in one glance. I can't interpret it all. Just that I'm in danger. Horrible, lethal danger.

And not because he might choke me.

Because he's confused. He's thinking. Without ever giving me the fucking chance to have any input, he comes to a decision within seconds. Like a door slamming shut, his expression shifts into a hardened mask.

"Could you stay, then?" he wonders. "With no contract? No promise of protection?"

And, if he were the kind of man to even offer such a thing, no love.

I know what he wants me to say—what I should say.

Of course not.

"My own mother didn't want me," I hear myself argue instead. God, I sound so old, aged a million years in just a few goddamn seconds. "I'm used to rejection. Hell, maybe I don't want you, either—"

"Don't lie to me."

I flinch as he shifts his stance and drops to his knees. With his height, it's easy for him to block me in. I brace for an assault, but his forehead meets mine without malice, his breaths scalding my cheek.

And this is worse than violence.

"Not now. Don't fucking lie to me. I wish it were just the sex." He laughs. Growls. "Any other man could fuck you. Keep you. But you haven't seen a client a fraction as often as you've been with me—this unnerves you. Any other woman could give me her body for a price. But no…" His fingers sink into my hair, gathering strands of it in a brutal fist. "It's *your* skin. My marks on it," he hisses near my ear. "Your scent. The way you move. Your fucking voice—" He tugs and stands, hauling me to my feet as well. Trapped by his bulk, I'm crushed against the wall, forced to endure every word of his confession. "It's you. And *you* threaten everything I've built. Everything I've worked for... But I can't let you go."

"Then don't." My face is buried against his chest and I pray that the cotton of his suit muffles every fucking word. Because once I've started, I can't seem to stop. "I just want..."

"What?" he demands.

"To submit," I say in a rush. "*One* aspect of my life when someone else takes complete control of everything for once. Someone who won't throw me out or push me away. I don't care about the rest. I just want to *stay*."

My nails dig into the fabric, biting into the tender flesh beneath to convey what I can't put into words.

"It's out in the open now," he says, his voice rough. Strong hands grip my waist, bunching up the skirt of my dress. "You know my limits. I've hidden nothing."

His limits: I'll never be worth fighting for. His club. This room. His world. All of it takes precedence over me.

Can I live, knowing that?

His lips brush my jaw before I can decide and every thought vanishes. "Everything else I can give you," he swears. "Money? Fine. However fucking much you want. An education? A home for your family? I'll give you that."

And all of it tethered to a contract, nothing more.

Which is fine. I don't need anything else. I tell myself that over and over as his teeth nip at my lower lip, pry my mouth open, and claim every inch for himself.

I tell myself that as he backs me to his bed and crushes me to the broken-in mattress.

I chant those fucking words: *Material things are all I need.*

Maybe if I repeat it enough times…

I'll finally believe it.

"GET UP."

The husky voice, paired with a fiery splash of pain on my hip, draws me from a dreamless, heavy sleep. Peeling my eyes open, I find Maxim sitting beside me, his palm hovering over my smarting skin, ready to strike again.

"Come."

I crawl after him to the end of the mattress, groaning in a mixture of pain and exhaustion. It has to be some time in the afternoon, judging from the sliver of sunlight seeping beneath the black curtains that shield the windows. He's kept me here for hours.

Was this part of my punishment? Getting fucked into oblivion?

I bite my lip as a pang shoots through my belly. It wasn't hope. It *wasn't*.

"Come here."

He leads me into a nearby bathroom. Gold fixtures and white marble are a chilling contrast to the darkness of his room. After steering me into a sunken tub, he runs the water hot and watches as the liquid rises, lapping at my skin.

Looking down, I don't even recognize myself. A patchwork of cuts and bruises stand out in brutal contrast to pale skin. Only now can I feel the sting and ache from each little injury. My left eye throbs the most.

"Don't—" He stops me from reaching up to touch it, capturing my wrist.

I can't breathe as he lowers my hand to the water and then flicks his thumb along my cheek instead.

"When I sculpt, every strike must be precise. Controlled," he says gruffly, observing my wound like he would a cracked bit of marble. "The slightest chip can often be smoothed or polished—but a crack is irreparable. I can only start over, move onto something else. But *this*…" He lightly teases his nail against my skin, just enough to bite. "I can't start over new."

His jaw clenches in the dangerous way it does when he's thinking. Contemplating. Plotting.

"I suggest another game," he says, lowering his hand. When I stiffen, he shakes his head. "Not like that. This one… If I ever hurt you again, you have my permission."

I'm cold despite the steam wafting from the water around me. It's up to my chest now, and the gentle flow from the faucet adds a haunting backdrop to his low, careful tone.

Hurt. He doesn't mean via the lash of the whip or the sting of his blade during foreplay.

"Permission to what?" I croak when seconds pass without an explanation.

His fingers leave my hair and move to my hip, this time with a washrag caught between them. "Permission to render your own punishment," he says. "I will give you that."

Shock lances through me. Punish him how? I'm not brave enough to ask. His promise lingers, tainting the air as he washes me up in earnest.

There is no rose-scented soap here. Instead, he lathers me with a scent that smells like him. Musky, spicy, and masculine. I don't know how long he bathes me in total— just that he takes his time, extending every touch and caress.

I wouldn't call it gentle. More resigned. The same way the drug dealers in my old neighborhood used to wash their expensive cars out in the open, daring anyone to touch their property. As the water drains from the tub, he disappears, slipping into the hallway, and I finally let myself process the snippets of what happened last night.

So much about his bipolar mood makes sense now—and that's the fucking terrifying part. He makes perfect sense. I can easily guess what will happen next. For now, he'll keep me around, but the moment I get too close. Push him too far. Draw too much attention from his fucked-up family.

He'll cut me loose again.

"Lift your arms," Maxim commands, snapping me back to the present.

He got a dress for me while I was lost in thought. With little fanfare, he redresses me in the black shift I wore here. Together, we return to the now deserted main hall of the club and then out front, where his driver awaits.

It's only when we're halfway across the city that I stop to consider how dangerous this game of roulette has become. It's one thing when the bullet is an unknown number of pulls on the trigger away. It's another entirely when the bullet is in your goddamn hand.

Safety. Security. Sex. I've bled for those things before. But maybe that's the point. Who am I *without* the constant, soul-numbing struggle I've known my entire life?

That's the real question.

HE TAKES me home and I find the kids in the living room. Dread weighs me down as I linger in the foyer, listening to their laughter drift through the doorway. This time of day, I can't scurry past them or hide from sight.

Inhaling, I start forward, taking stock of the battlefield before me. Ainsley and Eric are trying to stab each other with the ends of expensive-looking fake flowers while Mikie and the boys shout at the television, game controllers in hand. I spot Daisy lurking into the shadows. The moment I enter the room, she's already sneaking out before I can say a word.

Sighing, I start after her. "Daisy, wait—"

"She's okay," Mikie says without looking away from his game. "Give her some time to cool off... You look like shit." His eyes sweep over my damp hair and my wrinkled dress. "Sorry," he says a second later. "I just meant—I mean. Hey."

"Hey," I choke out.

Ainsley and Eric are watching me, frozen mid-fight. Ollie and Ray stare too, while Mikie turns back to their game, his shoulders hunched.

I don't know what else to say other than, "How…how are you guys holding up?" The neckline of this dress is too damn low. Awkwardly, I cross my arms over my chest in a pathetic attempt to disguise the bared flesh. "Everything okay?"

"Fine," the twins say in unison.

"Fine," chirp Eric and Ainsley.

Mikie sets his controller down. "We're all good," he says, flashing a crooked grin. His eyes meet mine, unusually sharp. He's trying to tell me something, but he doesn't say what out loud—for their benefit, I realize.

Then it hits me, a figurative punch to the chest: He's playing the role I used to, keeping the kids calm while the deadbeat mother makes her occasional appearance.

"Get back to the game, you dummies," he barks to Ollie and Ray. "Let's see how many times I can kick your asses!"

I back out of the room, heading for the stairs. My eyes sting. My throat is on fire, but this time, I'm not sure why.

Relief? They're doing fine without Melanie.

Or me—which is a good thing...

"The police were here again, you know."

I look up and find Daisy standing at the top of the steps, her arms crossed, her pink lips in a flat line. I don't even recognize her voice, so dull that she might as well be whispering.

"That bald guy scared them off. But they said some stuff."

"What?" My heart races, my palms slick. "What did they say?"

"That guy Mama married is dead too. Did you know that?"

My eyes widen before I can school my expression. "No," I rasp. "I didn't."

"He is." She squares her jaw, something she does only when she's upset but trying to save face. A trait she picked up from me. "The police said he was in a gang. They said more stuff, too."

"Like what?" I reach out, grasping the banister for support. The walls are spinning. The spacious house feels too damn small, like the foundation might crack beneath the pressure.

"They asked if you and Mama had a fight."

"Oh." I struggle to keep my voice even. "And what did you say?"

"The truth." Her eyes gleam, harder than I've ever seen them. Then, without a word, she turns and disappears down the opposite end of the hall.

"Daisy, wait!"

I mount the rest of the stairs, but I don't follow her. It's only when I'm in the room designated as my own that I finally notice something tucked into the folds of my dress like an afterthought. It's stuck to the fabric—a black card sporting the image of a bloody, beating heart.

I stare at it as my eyes water and burn. Gasping, I bring my opposite hand to my mouth and bite down so hard that I taste salt.

Of all the things a billionaire psychopath can promise to give me, he keeps the most dangerous item of all for himself.

But at least he has control of his—my heart is in six pieces with nothing left to share for anyone else.

No matter what price he'd be willing to pay.

CHAPTER FOURTEEN

He gives me one night with my family. One miserable night spent hiding in my room while the sounds of their laughter drift up through the floor.

The next morning, Lucius is waiting for me before the kids even leave for school. Rather than to the suite, he brings me to the college and another lesson with Gemma passes in relative normalcy.

Whatever that means.

"You did good," she says when our time is up. I don't miss how her eyes cut up to my bruised, ravaged neck. "Take care, Francesca."

A black car is waiting for me out front of the building, driven by a man whose gaze meets mine through the windshield. *Zap!* It's like I spent the entire day sleepwalking—now, I'm awake, electrified into awareness.

Clarity paints Maxim Koslov in terrifying detail as he exits the car and circles around to my end while I approach. He opens the door to the passenger's seat, but the look in his eye raises the hairs on the back of my neck.

It's determined.

"Get in," he tells me.

I swallow hard as I perch myself on the leather seat and he closes the door behind me. Five seconds are my only reprieve before he re-enters the car on the driver's side. Palming the steering wheel, he sighs.

"You are going to stay with me tonight." Gritting his teeth, he shakes his head and tries again. "I…I want you to stay with me tonight."

My breath catches inside my lungs. I'm suffocating even as my brain desperately tries to process his question. Our new understanding demands new rules, apparently.

It's not enough for him to command, or for me to obey.

I have a choice this time.

Choose to play the game despite knowing how it'll inevitably end.

"*Kotyonok*," he prods when my silence stretches too long. Tension coils his posture, and his knuckles are white.

"Okay," I rasp in response. "Okay."

When the car comes to a stop, we aren't in front of the house. Or his suite. A tall brick building looms above. A window framed in dark-colored drapes displays an empty dining room, the sight of which raises goosebumps over my arms.

Once we pass through the main doors and a smiling hostess rushes to meet us, I remember. *This* is the place where we first went over the terms of his contract. In bloody thorough detail.

I can't suppress a shiver as we're led toward that exact same table. It's set for two, the silverware flickering a dangerous, burnished gleam.

"Have a seat, *kotyonok*," Maxim commands.

He's already seated, his eyes tracing my body. He's wearing gray today, matching my outfit either by accident or intention. The color brings out the harshness to his features in a way black or white never could. He's beautiful, polished stone, set with eyes of obsidian that warn anyone caught in their glare not to disobey.

I stagger toward the empty chair and collapse onto it, scooting in as close to the table as I dare. The moment our gazes reconnect, Maxim reaches under the table and withdraws an item that must have been in his pocket: a folded slip of paper. Without explanation, he rips the document in half and then slides both torn ends toward me.

"Our previous agreement," he tells me, his eyes fixated on mine as if hunting my reaction down. At the same time, he grabs a bottle from the table and pours a layer of scarlet liquid into a glass on his end. Without a word, he does the same to a glass near me.

My fingers jerk against the white tablecloth. I almost can't control the need to reach for the torn contract and press those broken pieces back together. Memorize that monetary amount and cling to it like a fucking prayer.

"So, now?" I force myself to ask, my voice faint. "What happens next?"

A lethal smile quirks his lower lip. Or maybe it's a frown, exasperated and terse. "When I do business, I never renege on my terms." He's not referring to the shadowy dealings of his empire. Oh no, his tone is too guttural. "I know what I want from the outset. Always. I never want more. Now?" He nods to the glass beside my trembling hand, a silent command to drink.

I do, choking down a single sip. If his aim was to help relax me, it backfires. My throat is a fucking desert. Swallowing doesn't ease the dryness at all. "I don't know what you mean."

"This is an unusual situation," he admits, sounding partly amused and partly…not. "I don't make a habit of discussing my intentions with someone like you."

"Well, I don't make a habit out of sleeping with criminal billionaires." My cheeks flame when I realize how fucking bold that sounds out loud.

Even more insane? He doesn't look insulted.

"Criminal?" His eyes flash, his tongue tracing his lower lip. It's like he tastes the word, melding it with his next sip of wine. "And what might give you that impression?"

I can't tell if he's joking or not, but his stern expression demands a response. "You kill people."

He laughs. "Am I so obvious?"

He *is* joking. My heart lurches as my thoughts stall. Reacting to him should be harder than this. "No," I finally say. "I'm just not as naïve as I pretend to be."

"Like your sister? *Don't*," he warns as my heart sinks through the goddamn floor.

My fingers grip the table, and it takes everything I have to stay seated. So this is what he meant by "discussing my intentions."

"I won't hurt her. But I must say, she is very perceptive."

"What did she say?" God, I can't breathe.

"She told the police you had an argument with your mother and that you intervened when her husband cornered her," he explains. "I paid off the officer in question so the news never made his report. You can relax."

"Can I?" My shoulders slump despite me, my body deflated. "My sister thinks I had something to do with the death of our shitty, deadbeat mother—who, for some reason, Daisy thinks still walks on water."

He tilts his head, unnervingly thoughtful. "I've handled it."

"I don't think you can control the entire world. You *can't*. And you can't control my family. Just like you can't control yours."

"Ah." His gaze sweeps over me. "So now *you* are the criminal mastermind?"

I flinch at the insult. "Maybe I'm just being honest."

"Honest?" he echoes. Only now do I remember that he doesn't like being challenged. He relishes in it. "Your siblings. Do you feel loyalty to them?" Before I can nod in agreement, he adds, "Even if they make your life harder? They weigh you down with their squabbles and indecision. They drain you. Now, say one of them tried to undermine you, ripping away piece by piece everything you sold your soul to gain. What might you do?"

"Slap her," I blurt out. "D-Daisy, I mean. She's… It doesn't matter."

"I see." He nods thoughtfully. "And let's say that *Daisy* owned half of your family's assets, and that by slapping her, you'd be declaring war."

He's talking about more than just my sister. Sevastyn is on his mind again.

Could I declare war on my family?

In a way, I have done just that. Who did Mikie stand by when Daisy and I fought? It wasn't me.

"How would you handle that?" Maxim demands.

I think it over, gazing into my wine. My imagination takes the shade and deepens it into a bloody scarlet. Blood is thicker than water—isn't that how the saying goes?

Or is it *poison* in his case, weighing down your veins and tethering you to a world you might have never chosen for yourself. That's the dangerous part, honestly asking yourself: *if I had to do it all over, would I?*

"I'd try to remember who I am," I say, returning to his dare. "What I've done. Why I've done it. I know that I'm not perfect, but I've never been selfish. I've always been willing to give up everything…"

"And that sacrifice gives you the right to risk upsetting them?" he wonders.

My mouth opens, but I close it and mull the question over. "I deserve to have *something* for me," I finally say. "Even if it won't last. Even if it hurts."

And even if it costs me more than I was ever willing to lose.

"I see." He sits back and drains his own glass. Just as quickly, he pours himself more wine from the bottle. "And if what you want doesn't matter in the grand scheme?"

I think about everything I've done in the name of replacing Melanie. "Does anything really?"

He's quiet for way too long. Nearly a minute. When I finally look up, his expression is unreadable.

"I should start keeping a tally of the times you surprise me."

It's not a compliment, and my heart seizes up in anticipation. Mr. Koslov, terror of the criminal world, doesn't like to be surprised. Least of all by me.

"Tell me something. If you could have one thing in the world, what would it be? Something material," he adds.

"I…" My brain goes blank. "I don't know."

"Don't lie." He palms his wine glass, making the liquid within swish, matching motions of the unreadable emotion flickering in his eyes. "Name it."

"Someplace that's mine, I guess," I stammer. "Where no one could kick me out, or overrun, or rip away."

He processes that in silence, his jaw clenched. Finally, he sits back, placing his hands on the table. "You—" His gaze cuts to something beyond my head and anger distorts his blank expression. "What is it?"

I look back, surprised to find Lucius crossing the deserted dining room. "I tried to stop him, sir," he says, his tone uncharacteristically strained. His eyes cut to a figure entering behind him. "He was persistent."

The entire table jolts as Maxim rises to his feet. "To seek me out…you must have a good reason, Uncle," he says coldly.

The intruder laughs, clapping his hands as he approaches. Sevastyn. His hair is slicked back into a low ponytail, adding a casual contrast to the elegant black suit he wears. Once again, he and Maxim look eerily similar: two halves of the same twisted coin.

"That I do," Sevastyn replies. "But I must say that I didn't expect to find you *here*. And with a toy…" His eyes drift in my direction, inching up my body. Recognition paints them a dangerous shade of black. "So *this* must be the mysterious Francesca." He looks at Maxim, an eyebrow raised. "I didn't realize she was the same—"

"Get out," Maxim growls.

"What, no introductions? I thought you were taught better manners than this, Maxi. Maybe you need another lesson?"

"Do you really believe that you are in the position to order me?"

I jump at the subtle change in Maxim's voice. Gone is the hint of restraint he displayed with me.

He's icier than ever in the blink of a fucking eye. "Now, get out—"

"Be a good boy and send your toy away." Sevastyn dismissively flicks his fingers. "Now."

"No." Maxim slams his hand on the table, knocking his wine glass to the floor. It shatters into a million pieces, and I swear I can see myself reflected in each one, broken just as easily with much less force. "Do not test me."

"I think it's you who forgets your position," Sevastyn replies, dangerously soft. "To refresh your memory, it is a precarious one."

"I will ask you one more time to leave—"

"Oh?" his uncle counters. "So the *boy* thinks he can give ultimatums now? I thought you were too busy fucking your pet while our enemies nip away at your pathetic little enterprise. What? Don't look so surprised, Maxi. I've heard the rumors."

"Rumors?" Maxim echoes. "Or maybe *you've* gotten too bold, Uncle? Sloppy. You're not as careful as you think you've been."

"So challenge me, then," Sevastyn counters, his head cocked. "Or not. Continue to be the little boy who cowers in the corner as he is forced to learn what it really means to be a man—"

"Enough!" Maxim snatches something from the table.

Bam! Air whizzes past my head. In the distance, glass shatters as red liquid explodes against a wall on the other side of the room. Belatedly, my brain makes out the pieces of the wine bottle, raining down like jagged snowflakes.

"I'm not the one who is getting sloppy, Maximov." Sevastyn steps forward, flicking the collar of his jacket, unconcerned by the red liquid staining his white shirt.

"The next time you lose your childish little temper, I would encourage you not to miss. Oh, and by the way, consider yourself relieved of the western sector of the city. Anatoli has decided to bestow it upon me instead. Goodnight."

He leaves, chuckling the entire way to the door.

"Get out," Maxim snarls.

I stiffen, still frozen on my chair. That time, the vitriol could have only been directed at me.

I instantly rise to my feet and stagger toward the doorway. Halfway there, my steps change direction. I'm on my knees by the table instead, picking up the shards of his wine glass. I'm not even sure why I'm doing it. Just that I have to. One by one by…

"Enough!" Maxim grabs my wrist, yanking me upright. Fury deepens the black of his irises as he reaches out.

I cringe, covering my face with both hands. I'm braced for a blow, but a heartbeat later, warmth grazes my cheek instead of pain. His finger, I realize as I cautiously let my hands fall.

Meeting his gaze directly is like throwing myself into an inferno, knowing it will burn. Destroy. He peers into my battered shell, staking claim over what shriveled parts of me he hasn't bothered to mark yet—but there's a restraint lurking there. Desperation? Like a diver, clawing his way to the surface, fighting for air. The deep won't drag him down just yet.

It *can't.*

Eventually, his eyelids flutter and the tension drains from him as he yanks me close, grasping my hips. Our foreheads meet and my nostrils flare to breathe him in. Every goddamn inch of rage and muscle and terror. Then, slowly, he pulls away and heads for the door.

With his back to me, his voice lashes out, as sharp as the sting from a whip. "Come."

When we make it back to the suite, he reaches into his pocket and withdraws a cell phone. I suck in a breath as his eyes cut in my direction. For once, he's open.

I can read him like a book, able to decipher every single page. They're all blank, but in a way, it's more telling than paragraphs of text.

In his gaze, I see a warning.

And a plea.

Know your worth, Francesca, he tells me without having to say a fucking word. *Because I've already calculated it.*

"I've made up my mind," he says into the mouthpiece of the phone, turning his attention to the figure on the other end of the call. "We will meet in person to discuss this in full, but…" He looks back at me, his gaze searching mine. "I know where I stand now."

And in a way so do I.

CHAPTER FIFTEEN

It's funny how being a prisoner warps your entire perception of reality—especially when the bars are in your soul. The first time you wake up, you still feel free. Alive, even. Your sanity may be gone, but you're the one who locked it up and threw away the key.

There's power in that, I guess. Surrender. For the first time in for-fucking-ever, when I peel my eyes open to a darkened room, money isn't the driving force on my brain.

It's panic. It's an instinctive awareness of the man who corrupted me. It's calm. It's fear.

It's *Maxim.*

He's not here. For what feels like hours, I lie still, breathing in his scent, drowning. Eventually I hear the door open but I don't know whether to move or wait. Too many questions linger, demanding to be asked.

Either way, I won't have a real choice in the end.

Huddled beneath the sheets, I listen to his footsteps. Slow. Unsteady.

Unsure?

He circles the foyer like a shark and starts down the hall before changing direction.

An icy dread congeals in my throat. The way he moves is different than the confident prowl I'm used to. Not Maxim.

Lucius, then?

No. My heart pounds as I jump to the next conclusion: an intruder. I dart my gaze to the dresser, but I don't find Maxim's knife. Or even his belt. Desperate for a weapon, I lunge from the bed and grab one of my heels instead.

"I know you're in here," a man calls from down the hall. Something in the raspy, thick accent conjures a terrifying image: Maxim with an older, thinner face and longer hair. "Where is he hiding you, little mouse?" One by one, the foreign footsteps advance in my direction.

Run. The instinct is almost too strong to choke down. Before I can even contemplate hiding, a shadow falls over the doorway and a single thought chases all logic from my brain. *Caught.*

He's tall, the intruder, his face achingly familiar. Sevastyn. "Here you are," he murmurs, leaning against the doorway, his arms crossed. "Maxi's little toy. I have to say…you are beautiful." His eyes flit over what little of my body isn't covered by the sheet. "I'm sure he's told you the opposite. Diminished his attraction to you, even. Maxi always was protective of his trinkets." Standing to his full height, he takes a step closer and I instinctively inch back. "Don't be shy," he scolds, but his smile betrays his enjoyment. "He's kept you busy, I see. I'm surprised he brought you *here*." He glances around the room, his upper lip curled in disgust.

My pulse surges with every second I watch him. "What do you want?"

"Ah… So you are feisty." He chuckles, roving his gaze up to my face. "I knew you were different the moment I saw you, you know. I've only seen him so open with his weakness once before. He's always been a sentimental boy. With toys. With pets."

His tone scratches over my skin, and I draw the sheet tighter around myself. Maxim isn't here. I know that without even looking. Hoping.

"I said, what do you want?"

"Patience." Sevastyn licks his lips and advances a step. He laughs when I flinch and advances another. "You should know exactly why I'm here. My dear nephew deserves nothing less. It's business, my dear. Little Maximov must learn his place." He bares his teeth in a chilling smirk. "I thought making problems for his little enterprise would be enough to get my message across. But it seems he's more…distracted than I thought." He shrugs. "To be honest, I always thought Maxi was much too repressed for a mouthy whore—"

"Get out!"

"Oh, I wish I had time to play with you." He hones his gaze over my throat and I see a hint of the malice he and his nephew share—but it's different in him. Sevastyn lets his darkness consume him, whereas Maxim fights it. "Alas, Maxi must be taught his lesson quickly. I won't violate you," he adds as my nails dig into the fabric of my sheets. "I prefer, let us say, a select breed."

Bile claws up my throat as an image pops into my head, though I'm not sure why. It's how he said that phrase. *Select breed.* Like a little boy with white-blond hair, aching for his mother. Until one horrible day when a monster made him fear showing any ounce of emotion at all.

"I must make my point, however." His hand lashes out so fast that I only catch a flash of shadow before *pain!*

My vision goes black, and when it clears, I only know that I'm on the floor, tasting blood.

"So I apologize if things get…messy. It can't be helped." A heavy hand slams against my lower back, pinning me flat, while another hooks around to capture my throat. Grasping. Squeezing. As if from underwater, I hear Sevastyn murmur, "If you beg, I'll make it quick—"

"No!" Kicking out with my feet is purely instinctual—but my heel connects with bone.

And the man just laughs.

"Oh, you would be so much fun," he murmurs, loosening his grip enough for me to gulp in air. "I can see it now. Why he's kept you like a dog with a bone. Look at me. *Look at me.*" He yanks my face in his direction.

I blink rapidly to clear my vision. Gradually, his face comes into focus.

"Oh yes. There it is." He drags his thumb across my cheek. "That weak hint of desperation. Little Maxim couldn't resist, could he? No." He laughs, shaking his head. "No, I suppose he couldn't. Why? He probably sees himself in you. A desperate, pathetic mutt accustomed to being used by others. Did he ever tell you?" he wonders, lowering his mouth near my ear. "How he became a cripple? I know you've seen them, his injuries… Yes," he decides from my expression alone. "He did. But not all, I suspect. Just the little pieces he can live with. Maximov always was like that. Prone to biding his time like a scheming little mouse. He probably used vague, broad terms to describe it, but shall I tell you the whole truth?"

He shoves me aside and I barely manage to brace my hand against the wall to keep myself from crashing into it.

"His mother was an *artist*." His nostrils flare as if the word is something filthy found stuck to the bottom of his shoe. "She taught him to paint and sculpt. I think he still does.

She used to make him little trinkets. Toys." He chuckles, reliving the memories of Maxim, young and innocent. "When she died, he kept one—carried it everywhere, despite how it annoyed Anatoli. A little stone cat, I think it was. He called it his '*kotyonok.*' Until one day my father made him smash it using his bare hands. And then…" He looks at me, chuckling, and my stomach churns in grim anticipation. "He had him beaten, but it wasn't enough. Not far enough. Not memorable enough. A boy like that, he needed a different kind of…" A twisted smile shapes his mouth as his tongue traces his bottom lip. "Touch."

No. My mind shies away from what I think a part of me already suspected. I picture the day Maxim brought me to that empty room with the tarp. The pain in his eyes. How lost he looked. Afraid—I can apply that term to him only now.

Not for himself.

But for me.

I will kill you before they do it for me.

"Don't be so surprised," Sevastyn says, still standing above me. "I don't think he even told Anatoli what—"

"You're sick," I croak. "You're a monster."

"I am," he says.

My eyes catch the motion of his shoulder tensing—but it's too late. I can't even brace for the blow. *Wham!* Agony rips through my chest, knocking the air from my lungs. I cough, thrown to my knees, knowing he's behind me.

"What a shame." He crouches and grabs my wrist, rubbing his thumb along my palm. I wrench my arm back and his grip tightens as his gaze latches onto mine. "I'd hate to ruin you too much. You really are a prize. But every good lesson has some cost."

He stands, dragging me with him to the bed. I claw at his grip with my free hand, but he lifts me like I weigh nothing and slams me onto the mattress. Like stone, his weight lands on my chest, pinning me down. Crushing me.

He hits me again, drawing a gasp from my throat.

Nails drawn, I swipe out. Flesh catches beneath my fingertips and I dig as deep as I can, breaking flesh.

Roaring, Sevastyn hits me again—hard. My head lolls as the nerves in my body lose contact with my brain. As my senses return, I find him swiping at his shoulder. His fingers come away red and he frowns, gritting his teeth.

"Feisty little bitch," he snarls, gripping my throat. "He'll throw you away after this, so you know," he gloats as dark spots speckle my vision. Just a few at first. Then an inky coating obscures my sight. "So secretive our Maxi is. In fact, I suspect he'll kill you before you can spill his little secret. But if he doesn't…you can always come to me. I may make an exception…"

He releases my throat, but as I gulp for air, an unfamiliar touch traces my inner thigh. *No!* I buck, clawing at anything I can reach, but he's too heavy. Immovable. *Nononononono!*

A sharp crack cuts the air before I feel the fire painting my cheek, the result of a slap. Another. My thoughts flood, impossible to decipher.

And all I feel is pain.

CHAPTER SIXTEEN

Hushed voices battle the darkness weighing me down. I'm somewhere enclosed, where everything echoes, way too loud. A room? My eyes won't open. Trying to form a coherent thought is like trying to catch smoke.

I'm floating, but eventually, I can make sense of the words being spoken around me.

"She hemorrhaged," a man says, his voice clinical and unfamiliar. "I doubt there's organ damage, but—"

"When will she wake up?" another man interjects, his tone more strained than I've ever heard it sound. Maxim?

My heart pangs. Something is wrong. Really, really wrong —he's never sounded so cold.

So empty.

"I'm not sure," the first man replies. "All we can do is wait."

"Can you hear me, *KOTYONOK*?" Sensation bleeds through my consciousness for the first time in what feels like an eternity: warm fingers gently parting my hair. "Open your eyes. Look at me."

It's not a request.

I try to obey. But each eyelid weighs a million pounds, impossible to move.

"Francesca." Those creeping fingertips smooth over my forehead and travel down my cheeks. Pain flares in their wake, disrupting my thoughts like a flickering flame. "Look at me."

It's no use. There's no connection between my brain and my mouth. I'm just a conscience tethered to an immovable body. Am I dead?

No. My heart wouldn't be aching if I were.

"Look at me," Maxim commands, but his touch fades away, leaving nothing behind but an empty chill. "Please…"

"She's waking up!"

The high-pitched voice sounds out of place here, insanely loud. Peeling my eyes open takes too much energy. I have to do it in stages, taking in my surroundings via snippets at a time.

"Frankie?"

Something warm lands on my arm. A hand? I blink as a face comes into focus. Small. Round with bright, wide eyes.

"Can you hear me?" Ainsley asks. "Are you okay?"

"Get off of her, Ains!" someone scolds. Mikie. He comes from nowhere and picks up Ainsley by her waist. Then he sets her down in the corner of a spacious room. A hospital room, I think, going off the crisp, clinical smell.

"Where…" My voice is a stranger's rasp. I lick my lips and swallow to strengthen it. "Where am I?"

Mikie glances at someone beyond my line of sight. "The hospital."

"You had an accident," Ainsley says and my stomach sinks. How much do they know?

My memories are a blur, but a few details stick out. *Sevastyn. Pain.*

"That old guy, Lucius, said they were going to sue the other driver," Ray pipes in, coming into view, Ollie in tow. "What a dick—"

"Watch your mouth," Mikie scolds.

"A car accident." I taste the term on my tongue and cringe. So that's the lie he came up with.

"We should let you get some sleep," Mikie says. Like a general, he marshals the others to attention and they stream out one by one. "We'll be back, Frankie. Just get some rest."

My "ACCIDENT" caused contusions over my entire body and left me unconscious for two days. Realizing that puts a million hazy memories into perspective.

The first being Sevastyn. Bits and pieces of that day flicker in and out of my thoughts like a horrifying slideshow. He hit me. Forced me onto the bed…

My brain refuses to show me anything after that.

Deep down, I don't think he raped me. In some ways, his violation was far worse—he marked me. Brutalized me. Toyed with me.

All just to make a point.

And Maxim…

Was he really here or did I just imagine him?

Every minute he stays away, I start to settle on imagined. My only visitors in the next three days are the kids and the odd doctor or nurse. They discuss my care in vague, simplistic tones that give the rouse away. *It's out of my hands. Someone else is pulling the strings and paying the bill.*

Yet he never comes by once. Instead, Lucius appears near the end of the third day, his briefcase in tow.

"Miss Marconi," he says, inclining his head respectively. "Mr. Koslov wanted me to inform you that he is currently out of the country." He pauses as if to let the words sink in one by one. "Any attempts to contact him may go unanswered for a period of time. Meanwhile, if you need anything, I will be able to assist."

He waits as if expecting me to say something. Do something.

When I don't, he inclines his head and leaves. His voice reaches back to me as I finally remember how to move. "Goodnight, Miss Marconi."

A DAY LATER, I'm brought "home" with fanfare. The kids make a show of bringing me lunch in bed and fluffing my pillows.

But the first night passes in dreamlike slow motion.

And the next.

The next.

It's as if the world continues: a boring-ass play, minus one key actor. He disguises his role in my new life, but his interference is painfully clear. Gemma comes to the house to continue my lessons and the bills are magically paid. A mysterious driver appears to chauffer the kids wherever they need to go.

And I'm still a prisoner.

But, as the hours pass, my captor can't even visit my cell once. Days turn into weeks.

My body is a bruised, scabbing mess of flesh, yet...I don't feel a damn thing. I can't feel anything.

"Frankie?"

I look over my shoulder and find Daisy creeping through the doorway.

"You've been in here for hours," she says, glancing around the wide, empty room. "You didn't even eat lunch or dinner—"

"Oh, you're talking to me again?" I snap, only to sigh when she flinches. "I'm sorry. I didn't mean it like that—"

"You've been different," Daisy says. Her eyes well up and she sniffs, swiping at her cheeks with the sleeve of her pink sweatshirt. "It's like you're another person. A zombie. I miss Mama—and I know you hate that," she adds. "But I miss *you* more."

"I'm still me," I rasp, even as I scan my battered limbs without a hint of recognition. "I'm still the same Frankie."

"You're not." Daisy shakes her head, crossing her arms over her chest. She's shaking, sniffling harder as more tears paint her cheeks. "You barely leave the house. You stare into space all the time. Ainsley's afraid of you. She thinks you're dying—"

"I'm still here," I insist. But my voice sounds so fucking weak. I don't know if I'm trying to convince her or myself.

"I miss you," Daisy says. "More than Mama. I miss you—so much. You were always strong, even though you cursed too much and worked too hard. I miss *you*." She lunges, wrapping her arms around my neck, squeezing tight.

She's a little kid again. The one I always had to spend extra time comforting after one of Melanie's fuck-ups. The one so naïve that she never saw the trouble coming.

Or maybe she just pretended not to all this time.

"I'm sorry," I croak into her hair as my stiff limbs cradle her awkwardly. "I'm sorry."

"Just come back," Daisy blubbers. "Come back. Be the old Frankie again. I can't take this anymore."

The old Frankie.

What was her motto? Anything to survive. Even if it meant scraping, and fighting, and stealing.

She would never let herself be thrown away.

She'd fight back.

How?

By beating the master at this own goddamn game.

CHAPTER SEVENTEEN

"You're on fire today!" Gemma exclaims as I hand over a sheet of test questions. She heads to her desk at the front of the classroom and fishes a red pen from a drawer. A few minutes later, she returns the test to me with a score scribbled in the corner: 80%. "You keep this up and you'll have no trouble acing your preliminary finals. Then we can discuss options for majors. Have you thought of any?"

I shake my head. Resurrecting yourself requires baby steps. Waking up. Forcing yourself to breathe. Making yourself focus.

Relying on the relenting passing of time to tide you over, other than a steady pulse of pain. If I focus on that—just moving, and breathing, and living—there isn't room for anything else.

"Well, I think you'll have a great base to build on." She crosses over to her desk. A pinging noise cuts the air, and it must come from her cell phone, because she fishes it from a drawer and eyes the screen. "Oh, my husband is such a nerd," she says, smiling. "It's our anniversary."

Something in her tone cuts through that insistent chorus circling my brain—don't think about him. Anything. *Everything* but him.

"Francesca? Are you all right?"

Crack.

I look up, meeting Gemma's startled gaze, and I can't stop myself from asking, "What was he like with you? Maxim."

Even the sound of his name makes her jump. Her fingers flutter to her throat and she reflexively clutches her cell phone like a child with a teddy bear. Her eyes dart in my direction before lowering to her phone. With a trembling finger, she traces the screen. "Terrifying." She inhales raggedly and looks at me again. "He was terrifying."

She's not lying. Her face is ten shades paler than before and she wobbles to her chair, collapsing onto it. "I was a stupid, desperate kid. I didn't know what to expect. He took one look at me and just...I felt cold." She stares through me, years into the past. "I couldn't go through with it, and he told me to leave. To be honest, I thought he might...I don't know, hurt me or my family. When I received a letter in the mail, I nearly had a heart attack. But it was a check, no strings attached."

For her education—I remember. Maxim Koslov may have trouble keeping the women he claims to crave, but he has no problem being strictly transactional.

"Are you okay?" Gemma stands and approaches me, placing her hand on my shoulder. "Is he...Is he hurting you?" She glances around the room, still clutching her neck. "Maybe we can—"

"I'm fine," I say, rising to my feet. Her concern feels far too real. Earnest. Her wide eyes hone in on my bruises and I know the conclusions she jumps to. Abuse. Violence. From him.

Any sane person would think the same damn thing.

Maybe they'd have a point—though the only true damage Maxim Koslov has inflicted on me is on my psyche. My fucking soul.

"Frankie?" Gemma brushes her hand along my shoulder. "Are you sure you're okay?"

"Y-yes." Swallowing hard, I force myself to smile. "I really am fine. Thanks for everything."

I leave her staring after me in a daze, but I don't have any room left in my head to care. He warned me: I'm not worth fighting for. Dying for.

But fuck it.

He can tell me as much to my face.

CHAPTER EIGHTEEN

The first place I go to turns me away. I look too young, they say.

Too young. I almost laugh until I catch sight of myself in a reflection on a glass window on my way out. A wide-eyed stranger stares back. Shit. It's like my time with Maxim has aged me backward, stripping away the battle scars I've built up over the years. I've lost that spark in my eye. That gleam that made any man I walked past do a double take and clutch his wallet. That hard-as-fuck, tough-as-nails glimmer that warned bitches like Melanie to back the fuck off.

I've lost myself.

Now, I just look pathetic. A little girl lost, caught in the wake of a monster who dishes out the only candy worth having. *Pain.* She's grown addicted to his bitter sugar and can't stop licking her lips for more.

But, already, I'm remembering what it feels like to go without it.

It feels like desperation.

The second place I go to doesn't turn me away.

"You start tonight," the owner tells me as he leans against a barstool and flicks a disapproving glance at my plain, white dress. "Make sure you fucking change first. We don't do the kiddie shit here. Thongs and lace."

He slaps my ass on my way out, and it's only now that it sinks in. This is *real*. I'm in the real world again, and the pain here doesn't feel so good. My ass smarts. My throat tightens.

But no one steps from the shadows to avenge the assault and I just keep walking.

I waste the day lurking in another bar until the hour of my first shift. When I return to the club, I'm directed to an older blond woman who glances me over and sighs.

"This way."

She turns on her heel and cuts a path through a barroom packed with sweaty motherfuckers clutching loose dollar bills and jostling for better seats around the stage. They whoop and holler while a woman wearing a bad wig strips her skimpy lingerie and shakes her ass to the tune of a rap song blaring through unseen speakers.

It's nothing like the dangerous displays of flesh Maxim puts on in his club.

Not that it fucking matters.

I cut my teeth on places like this. You've been to one strip club, you've been to them all. Unless it happens to be owned by a psychopathic Russian…

Snap out of it. I shake my head to clear it as I follow the woman into a narrow room lined with mirrors and clothing racks.

"Pick something," she tells me, nodding her chin toward a rather paltry selection of silk and lace.

None of it is hand-tailored or of the finest quality. It's cheap, bargain bin stuff, probably from JC Penney. When I finger a black bralette, it chafes.

"You sure you're up to this, sweetheart?" the woman asks, frowning as she looks me over for the second time.

The mirror in front of me reveals just what she sees: a skinny bitch with wild hair and haunted eyes. Her face is bruised, and cuts litter her body like the glitter my tour guide has sparkling on her skin.

She's pathetic.

She's not *me*.

But when I speak, her lips move. "I'm fine."

"Whatever you say," the woman says warily.

To prove her wrong, I strip my dress and start to pull on a set of black lingerie.

Rather than look impressed, she winces. "Oh, honey!"

Her gaze is on my upper thigh. Mainly the name carved into my skin.

"Your man doesn't play around, does he?"

He doesn't.

But he isn't mine, either.

I know without having to search the corners of the barroom that he's not here lurking when I take my place on stage. As the lights dim, I'm left alone in a puddle of dingy, artificial glow, unguarded by my master, who doesn't seem interested in claiming me anymore.

Instinct guides my movements as I gyrate in a circle to some sleazy pop song. They claim they don't want "kiddie shit" here, but that's what I feel like: a kid sticking her fingers into electrical sockets, waiting for the moment I'll be scolded…

Only that moment doesn't come as jeers and taunts rise from the crowd, demanding I strip. "Take it off!"

My fingers shake as they creep up my rib cage. I finger the edge of my lacy bra once. Twice. The tease earns a round of groans, but I'm not playing the same game they seem to be.

I'm more attuned to my body than I've ever been. I wait for the telltale hitch in my throat. That uncanny ice-running-down-my-spine sensation that warns me I'm being watched. The cold, chilling realization that a predator is nearby with me in his sights.

I'm breaking his fucking rules for everyone to see.

But I'm never punished for the transgression.

I strip the bra to applause and cheers. The money flying in my direction is only a fraction of what Maxim could offer.

Maybe I'm stupid for spitting on that.

Or maybe…

I'm just fucking insane.

I DON'T GO HOME. I don't even call the kids to let them know where I am. Instead, I use what little money I earned my first night to rent a motel room, the cheapest I can. The walls are as thin as tissue paper, the door even thinner. But they hold the entire time I toss and turn on the crappy bed.

Alone, I return to the club and dance the next night, scraping my meager wages together.

I do the same the next night.

And the next.

Four nights in and only now does it sink in. Reality. This new, cold world I've found myself in, where I'm numb to the drooling looks of horny men. Only on this night does someone touch me, hooking their fingers into my thong when I stray too close to the edge of the stage.

Asshole. My thoughts short-circuit as I wait for the disgust I should feel. The instinctive need to scurry away or fight.

Instead, I feel…

Fire? It sears through my veins as a warning. The first real fucking thing I've felt in so long. Greedily, my fingers fly out, desperate to chase it. Extend it. I find a meaty, groping hand that clenches mine in shock and nearly drags me off the stage and onto some asshole's lap.

He chuckles, clenching my ass so tightly that I gasp. He smells like beer and sweat, and my heart races, pounding out a frantic melody.

Air sticks to the inside of my lungs. God, it's like I'm waking up. I feel everything. Sharp, ragged fingernails scraping my flesh. Harsh, unsteady breathing on my neck. The sweet, terrible clench of foreboding in my belly that warns me of danger like nothing else.

Alarm bells go off in my mind. *Mayday! Mayday!*

I'm shaking before I spot him in the corner of the room. He's dressed casually tonight, a realization that makes my throat tighten. A black shirt is lazily buttoned to reveal a sliver of the muscled chest underneath. Flashing eyes meet mine and the full breadth of my fear slams into me like a freight train. Have I gone insane?

Maybe.

He leans against the wall, his head tilted appraisingly. The pad of his thumb strokes his chin in a spine-curling rhythm. Slow. Steady. He watches me the same way he observes those beaten, broken chunks of marble left over from his sculpting sessions. Which is the fastest way to sweep the mess up and toss it aside?

Most nights, he just leaves it there for a maid to clean, I assume.

But now?

His jaw isn't clenched in the way I've come to expect. His shoulders are relaxed, free of tension. The only ominous clue I have to latch onto are his eyes. They smolder in the glow of the stage lights, fixated on my position without revealing a shred of what he's thinking.

But I just *know*.

My eyelids flutter at the feeling. It's raw, like I sliced myself open on a jagged piece of glass. A million things rush to pour from the wound all at once. Vital things. Pain. Fear. *Sanity*.

But at least I'm fucking feeling something. Tears prickle behind my eyes as my head swims beneath the aching burn of emotion.

"You gonna move or what, baby?" the asshole whose lap I'm on asks.

I move, all right. Arching my hips back and forth doesn't earn a single reaction from the only client who matters. He could be watching paint dry as far as anyone else is concerned.

But with every slow, deliberate motion, my heart threatens to beat its way from my chest. Save itself. Flee. An overwhelming sense of danger descends like a cloud, looming above me. *Doom. Doom.* It's like someone is here, whispering the word into my ear the longer I grind on the sleazy stranger.

The longer I extend my disobedience.

The perv hisses in anger when I finally climb off him and blindly stagger to the stage.

But it's too little too late. The music trails off, followed by one terrifying sound that cuts through the murmurs of the crowd and the hammering thud of my pulse.

Thwack.

Thwack.

Clapping? The racket is made by just one man, who's leaning against his chosen corner. The slow, deliberate crack of his palms meeting matches the way my heart thunders and slows. His eyes hone in on my own, *seeing* me.

Punishing me.

Stripping me bare with a soul-crushing promise.

I've broken our "arrangement."

And the feral gleam in his eyes reveals that he's more than willing to devise a fitting punishment.

CHAPTER NINETEEN

He pulls away from the wall with the agility of a wolf. Heedless of anyone watching, he mounts the stage, swallowing the distance between us with slow, deliberate strides. He comes close. So fucking close… My nostrils flare to capture his scent. *Ice, winter, danger.* Cotton grazes my bare skin, sparking the urge to fight or flee. Before either instinct can win, time runs out.

He leans in for the kill and I'm paralyzed as warm lips brush my cheek and raise goosebumps in their quest for my ear. He inhales, tasting my sweat mingled with the stench of a stranger.

And I tense as I wait for retribution.

"That…that was a beautiful show," he murmurs instead, his tone level with each word. Flat.

There's something I didn't notice before in his hand. As he draws back, he lets it fall to the floor at my feet without explanation.

My gaze lowers, seeking it out as my fingers quiver. He brought me a rose. Its petals dot the floor as he leaves, taking the fire with him.

The damn thing consumes my attention, even as someone tries to motion me off the stage. Material is wrapped around it, mangling the lower petals. It's a tiny strip of paper, tied with a scarlet ribbon. An address is printed on it, along with a simple message.

Wear the dress.

I stagger backstage and find a strip of silk waiting for me, draped over one of the vanities. Another folded note rests beside it, graced with crisp handwriting. *Refuse me now and I'll end this.* My heart skips as I read those words a second time. Again.

End this. I should crave that outcome. An end to this pain. This tumultuous hell. No more feeling him in every pore.

The promise haunts me as I scan the page and notice all the little details I didn't before. His hand shook as he wrote this. He pressed down hard too. Hard enough to slice the paper beneath the strokes of my name. *Francesca.* It's scribbled there at the bottom, and each inked letter glows, a searing reminder of the brand on my thigh.

The dress itself is beautiful. Too beautiful. A plunging neckline shows off what the dominant male I know wouldn't, giving a greedy glimpse of my cleavage. Too much. However, apart from the daring cut, it's shapeless. Just thin silk rasping over battered flesh. A sudden realization makes my chest tighten.

It's made for ripping. For tearing.

I might as well be wearing nothing at all.

I'm tempted to take it off. Walk away. He's given me so many chances before. Maybe this is the one out I'm finally willing to take? Or not… I swallow hard as my fingers graze the material gathered at my hip. I flick it once. Twice. With each touch, I wrestle with the obvious question.

To stay or go?

Unsure, I turn and observe myself in the mirror. My mouth curls into a snarl of disgust. Fuck. Maxim's pet is a creature I hate. She looks nothing like me. The girl staring back is too thin. Too fragile. Too broken. Her brown eyes are dilated and desperate. *Hungry.*

And not for food.

Not for money.

I turn my back on her and leave the club, pushing through anyone who stands in my way. It's only when I'm outside that I start to wonder just what I'll do. Run? The thought doesn't even finish forming before a black car pulls up alongside the curb, cutting my escape off.

Maxim isn't the one driving, and the stranger says nothing as I hesitate. Slowly, I reach for the handle. Pull back.

Eventually, I climb in, and he takes off the moment I'm seated, pitching me headlong into another dizzying nightmare.

This one begins the same way our first official meeting did. I'm brought to a restaurant in the richer part of town, where the price for valet is more than a month's rent.

Goosebumps prickle my skin as I eye the grand exterior. Sleek glass gives a breathtaking glimpse within. Dark walls. Dim lighting. The perfect lair for a beast who craves discretion.

I know how this part of the story will unfold. I'll wander down this new rabbit hole and find my monster waiting for me within. He'll give me a new ultimatum. Only this time…

This time, I'll refuse. Walk away.

I won't crawl into Wonderland again.

Where did this newfound resolve come from? I don't know. It races through my veins like smoke, nearly impossible to catch and identify. God, I try. I want to cling to it. But the moment my eyes focus on the figure approaching my side of the car, that frail emotion dies.

Someone scribbled into the margins of this chapter, adding in things that shouldn't exist. Like Maxim, opening my door and offering a hand to help me out. He shouldn't be here. Not like this. Waiting for me. Claiming me with no time for me to compose my thoughts.

"Francesca."

I shudder at the grated cadence to my name. He grinds it between his teeth, the only clue as to the emotions smoldering beneath the icy exterior. His face reveals nothing. Dressed to kill in black, he could almost pass for a normal man.

Almost.

But those eyes belong solely to a predator fixated on my bared skin and fluttering pulse. I stare at his palm without reaching for it. The smooth skin disguises so much potential for violence. The fingers quiver ever so slightly, echoing the unsteady energy running through my entire body. I'm a live wire. He's a fucking lightning storm, threatening to overload my fragile senses.

Obliterate me.

A breath I didn't even realize I was holding escapes in a rush as he stands back, returning his hand to his side. A quick jerk of his chin, however, conveys the command he doesn't issue out loud. One I don't dare disobey. *Come.*

I scramble out onto the curb. After two frantic steps on my own, I think he'll let me walk unaccosted. Yeah, right. The heavy hand settling against my lower back shatters that delusion. His heat radiates into my skin. Figuratively. Literally. I'm breathing in flames, exhaling smoke, smoldering from the inside out like the electrical fire that destroyed our house a few years back. None of us smelled the stench of burning until it was too late.

"You're back." I don't know how I manage to question him considering that my lungs are devoid of air.

His palm flexes, guiding me toward the restaurant's entrance. From the corner of my eye, I see his jaw clench for a second and then loosen, which betrays effort on his part to stay in control.

"For how long?" I ask, goading him.

He doesn't give me an answer as he leads me inside what appears to be a private dining room, away from the front-facing windows. Burgundy wallpaper decorated in golden designs forms a beautiful prison. There's only one table here. Two chairs. *One* dinner guest, who's standing beside me. His hand presses impatiently against my flesh, withdrawing only when I'm close enough to a chair to sit.

But I don't. Not even when he takes the seat opposite me and rests his hands over a pristine, white tablecloth. At a glance, a naïve woman might mistake his expression for one of calm.

But those hands betray him. They flex against the table's surface, the knuckles whitening with every second I stay standing.

"Sit, Francesca." He nods to the chair before me.

I don't move. "I'm…" I trail off, unable to put into words just what I mean to say. In the end, I blurt out the argument circling my brain in a morbid loop. "You left. I thought you were done with me—"

"You are making this…difficult."

My throat hitches at the unmistakable strain in his voice —the first slip in his façade. "Good," I say hoarsely. "Because it's been *hell* for me." I flinch at the vitriol tainting my own voice. Fuck it. "Tell me why I shouldn't leave—"

"I know you're upset." His eyes only reflect more tightly controlled restraint. "Sit."

I bite my lower lip. It's not quite the dangerous octave I've come to fear, but it's close to it. In the end, I perch myself at the end of the chair and brace my hands on my thighs.

"We will talk, and this time, no one will interrupt us," Maxim says, speaking each word deliberately. Almost as if he's hammering them out between his teeth, sculpting the illusion of calm the way he does marble. "How do you feel?"

I blink. On cue, I should spit out my tired line. *Fine.* "Someone hurt me," I croak instead. "And you weren't there."

He flinches, punched. Just as quickly, he cocks his head and his eyes flash. "No. I wasn't."

"And now? What?" My eyes water, overflowing within seconds. "I'm supposed to just…sit in a cage like a good little pet, while you—"

"I needed time to think," he says over me. "Time to reassess my priorities."

"Priorities," I parrot. "Maybe I've reassessed my priorities, too? I think I need a new client—"

"I made a mistake in thinking you'd be patient," he says before I can finish. "I should have known better than to underestimate you. Again." As he speaks, his hand drifts toward a polished set of silverware spread out in front of him. His thumb dances a slow path from the tines of a fork to the edge of a silver butter knife as if deciding between the two. A tool or a weapon? "But you're not angry that I caught you." He nods, seemingly to himself. "No… You enjoy this. You enjoy pushing me to the fucking brink."

"Stop!" I cringe and push back from the table, ignoring the telltale clenching of his jaw. "You're insane."

"And *you* live for it," he counters, still seated, still eerily calm. His thumb continues to stroke the edge of the knife. Faster. Harder, leaving streaks of sweat along the metal. "I saw the truth tonight. That look in your eye. You're wet already, thinking of the things I will do to you."

He's lying. My body feels heavy because I'm afraid. So afraid that I'm aching. Burning. Dying from anticipation.

"And the things I *will* do to you," he muses, his voice thickening. "Whatever punishment you think you've earned, I can assure you that you won't come close."

My mind skips ahead, conjuring a million horrific tortures. Whips. Chains. Pain.

"Then," he says as if factoring in every single fantasy, "we will be, as they say, *even.*"

Even? Something he said weeks ago sticks in my brain. *If I hurt you again, you have my permission…*

"Like you have the right—" My breathing hitches and a guttural sound cuts into my thoughts, setting every nerve in my body on edge. It came from him, ripped right from his chest. A growl.

"I can smell you from here," he warns, his throat jerking around a harsh swallow. His eyes flash and train on my throat, tracing every nervous swallow I take. "You deserve to be ripped raw for what you've done. Bitten until you know you're mine. Fucked senseless for every man who's seen you. One hundred and fifty-seven. I've been keeping count."

He says it all without a damn given for any waiter or waitress who might overhear. But we're alone by design, I realize after a quick glance around.

This display of domination is solely for me.

"You *want* me to," he declares coarsely. His knuckles whiten further as his fingers flex, bunching the tablecloth with every tense motion. "So ask for it."

"Why? So you can leave the country the second you feel like it?" My knees are shaking, knocking against one another. My thighs are clenched together so tightly that sweat drips between them. God, I hope it's sweat. "I thought you were done—"

He laughs and the rich sound startles me into silence. "You know, any other pet would take that as a mercy," he says. "A sane woman. They'd be relieved."

His tone is too hard. It's not a joke.

"But not *you*," he continues, his lips parting into a dangerous shadow of a smile. He's never looked more terrifying than he does now: painfully, insanely honest. "You don't want to share your pain. So fucking greedy, you are. You want my sole attention, *kotyonok*. You want to be the only little doll I get to fuck."

My cheeks flame. "But you don't want to keep me."

"*Oh?*"

I've barely processed the motion of standing when his hand strikes the table so hard that his knife goes flying and slides across the wooden floor. His sharp intake of breath is my only warning before I feel him. His hand cinches around my wrist, imparting a strength that makes me gasp. Groan.

A monstrous crash shakes the room to its core. The table being shoved aside? No, a giant, barreling toward me.

Pain. Nails sink into my flesh as he grabs me by the shoulder and yanks me back, lifting my feet from the floor. I kick out, but it's no use. He spins me around and crushes me to the wall. His chest feels hard against my back, his teeth catching my earlobe and biting down. It's merely a taste of his anger, and the brief, sharp pain has me writhing against burgundy wallpaper.

But it's not enough. Never enough.

"I will give you what you want," he swears. "But first, you admit it. Tell me, little *kotyonok*. Tell me what you need."

My brain shies away from the question, chanting an answer that's become a mantra. *Nothing. Nothing. Just money. Nothing else.* But the lie doesn't leave my throat, and I go limp, sandwiched between him and the wall. What do I need?

I scrape my nails against the harsh surface beneath me, seeking the delicious burn. Any pain I can find on my own. Clarity. I crave it. Whatever I feel is only a faint echo of what the creature behind me promises. His breath alone is a tempting burn against my flesh.

Too. Fucking. Real.

"Say it," he coaxes, destruction promised in every grated syllable. Thick fingers fist through my hair and tighten, making tears burn behind my eyes. He tugs his fist. "Tell me—"

I groan, smearing drool along the design of a gilded fern. "You tell me," I choke out.

He pulls on my hair so hard that I'm forced to arch my back and focus my blurred vision on the ceiling. A scream escapes my throat, but it's in vain. No one's coming. Not a waitress or another diner.

I'm alone in hell with him.

And this time, he won't let me escape.

My heart hammers at the chilling realization. My lips moisten. Throat swallows. Legs tighten…

"Fuck, even the thought of it arouses you," Maxim accuses. He barely sounds human anymore. Just a pained creature who communicates in growls and grunts. Primal. Ruthless. Animal.

He's unashamedly harsh, grinding his erection against my ass, teasing me with the brutal fullness. Moist heat floods my inner thighs, readying for the violence promised. If I let him, he'll break me. Ruin me.

A thought races across my mind before I can smother it: *I want him to.*

"I'll tell you what I want. I promise I'll…" His teeth seize the skin along my collar and bite down to the point where it stings. But not enough to bleed. Not enough to really hurt. Not enough to make me feel how only he can.

Sharp.

Clear.

Alive…

"I'll say it first. Is that what you fucking want? I want *you*," he admits, his voice a nearly unintelligible octave. "You…begging me to stop. Knowing I won't. I want you raw. Wet. Fucking. Screaming. Fuck, I crave *you*—"

He stops making sense and just mutters nonsense. Violent things. Brutal things. Tempting, fucking, twisted, insane goddamn things.

"But you…" Ragged breaths slice my words into gnarled bits. "Let me go. Again. You're always letting me go! Do you want to know what he said? Sevastyn?" I twist, spitting the words in his face. "He said you wouldn't want me after. And he was fucking right!"

"No." Without warning, he wrenches the sleeve of my dress down one arm, baring my breast to the mercy of his fingers. Heat. Tearing. Ice. He cups me in his palm, capturing my heart through layers of flesh and bone.

Groaning, he squeezes.

"Never. You are mine." He finds my nipple between the pads of two fingers and crushes it.

My moan drips from me in heaving, disjointed cries. They nearly drown out what he says next. What he breathes into me. What madness he confesses.

"I will *always* crave this tight fucking cunt. This greedy little whore who screams my name when she comes for me. On me. I want to own her. One day…I will destroy her. I'll rip her into fucking pieces—"

"Stop lying."

"Enough!" he roars deafeningly. It's a sound I've never heard him make. His hands grip me tighter than ever. Bruising. Breaking. "Do you know where I went? I needed to think. Are you worth it? My money, my world, all of it—"

"Stop!" I go limp, choking on tears. "I get it. I'm fucking not. I get it! I'm fucking worthless."

He draws back too suddenly. I have to cling to the wall for balance and wind up sinking to my knees. My throat aches, but that voice didn't come from me. No. Not that pathetic fucking plea. I haven't heard that girl in so damn long. Not since she uttered the same words to a shitty-ass mother who never cared.

No one ever cared.

But he listens, feasting on every whispered word and sob.

I'm cutting myself open on the remnants of his soul.

And. It. Hurts.

Like nothing else.

"But I don't care if you think that. I...I'm tired. I'm done." I try smothering the words into my hands, but he's there, crouching behind me to tear them away. "I'd rather walk away for good than constantly have you rip me *open*."

"When I learned what he did, I realized something." His palm captures my throat, tightening. "Nothing is more important than family."

"Stop." I pant. My cheeks are wet, my chest aching. But there's no use fighting him now. Squeezing my eyes shut, I surrender. "I...I can't—"

"But *they* are not my family." His voice resonates in my bones, unbearably deep.

The only way to block him out is to cover my ears like a fucking child. "Please stop."

"I don't have the right to, but I'm asking. Give me one more night. One more day. If you can do that, you know where to find me."

He steps back and I watch him through blurred vision.

"Wait—"

"I need you to come to me one last time," he says. "One last chance for you to decide…"

Decide what exactly?

He leaves without saying.

And I'm too fucking tired to guess.

CHAPTER TWENTY

As the hours pass, I can't ignore this little voice in my head telling me that I am losing the bet already. He said that, when I'm ready, I would know where to find him, but with a man like him, there is only one domain where he would cement a deal like this: the closest equivalent he has to hell.

I'm shaking as I finally drag myself from my motel room, dressed in a shirt and a pair of jeans, and find a car waiting for me out front. One word and the driver knows the way. Twenty minutes later, he brings me right up to the mouth of the club and that shimmering entrance.

There's no one waiting for me out front. I have to enter alone, pushing the main door open before wandering through that cold, foreboding archway. The intensity of the club hits me all at once: murmured voices, low music, sex crackling in the air.

My eyes are automatically drawn to the stage, just in time to witness the climax of the current show. A buxom redhead is lying across a dais while a man wielding a whip flogs the hell out of her ass from behind. She's pretty, making enough noise to sell the performance.

But it's her costar who commands the stage and steals the limelight.

He's bathed in the scarlet glow of the club, and I've never seen anyone look so menacing. So fucking powerful: a creature of sin and perfection with a devilish temper to show for it. His hair streams back from his face like a mane, his expression feral as he gives the redhead another brutal taste of the whip.

She throws her head back sensually, howling in pain.

The crowd fucking drools.

But then the show abruptly comes to a halt. Every bit as revealing as a spotlight, two black eyes hunt me down where I'm standing. His hand falls, the whip striking nothing but air as a frown twists his mouth. There is no ounce of shame in his expression: just a dare I'm not brave enough to answer.

Why are you here, kotyonok?

I don't know what draws me forward, forcing me to sidestep a well-dressed couple intent on creating their own show. The closer I come to the stage, the more impressed I am by the setup, despite myself. Three black steps built into the side of the structure allow someone to mount it seamlessly from the audience.

The moment the sole of my sneaker strikes the first step, a shadow falls over me and I find a monster impatient to dish out my punishment. He doesn't say a fucking word. His eyes merely track my ascent as I mount the second step and cling to the wall for balance. Somewhere within the past few minutes, the redhead disappeared. The dais is empty: a slab of black marble beckoning me closer.

Beyond the stage, the entirety of the club stretches out, and every patron watches with avid interest as a heavy hand cups the back of my throat and herds me forward. I'm blinded by the blood-red glow of the lights as Maxim trails a thumb over the corner of my mouth.

When he nudges me forward, I comply, resting my upper body over the cold slab of marble, both hands braced on either side of me. The moment I'm prone before him, hungry fingers wrench up the back of my shirt and tug on my jeans, baring my ass. A weighted second passes, as if he's giving me the chance to resist. Run. I don't, and not even a second later, something whistles through the air— it's like he can't control the whip fast enough.

The first blow isn't a love tap. The leather bites deep, leaving a stinging pinch I feel all the way in my goddamn core. The answering cry rips out of me, too raw to be held back.

Not that I even try to.

The next blow jolts me forward onto the tips of my toes, forcing my fingers to scramble for purchase over the marble. I'm bleeding: a searing welt too shallow to drip. The blood ekes out slowly instead, smearing my skin, tainting the air like perfume. Another hit draws a real cry out of me, one that echoes above every other sound.

And for the first time in so long, I can think. I can feel.

Everything.

Pain returns like an old friend, assaulting me at the urging of a sadistic master—and he makes damn sure I suffer for every second he had to wait for me.

It feels like an eternity—and every stinging blow only feeds the fire surging through my skin. Consuming me. My cheek is pressed flat against the marble when I finally sense him staggering closer, his hips brushing the back of my ass. Unrelentingly hard, his erection pulses against the fabric of his pants, hungry for my skin. For me.

Another sound tears out of me before I can choke it down. Wet heat clamps over my earlobe as I writhe against his hardness.

"Did you think it would be this easy?" a demon growls into my ear, yanking on my hair when I don't answer. He maintains his hold, even as I stagger to regain my balance —but it's a damn good thing he does.

I've never felt this unsteady before; it's like I'm drunk, intoxicated by his scent. The rest of the club is a smear of blurred features and meaningless faces. My sole focus is on the creature behind me.

With little care for my modesty, he wrenches my jeans down my legs. Panties next. My shirt, he rips from my collar down, baring my breasts and leaving me naked. In front of everyone. One firm yank on my shoulder twists me around to face him. His eyes probe my own as he steers me back, forcing me to climb back onto the stone slab, his body between my legs.

I get the briefest taste of his erection brushing my inner thigh before he kneels. *Oh god.*

His palm flattens against my stomach, pinning me down and throwing my upper body across the marble altar. My head dangles off the edge and all I see are scarlet and shadow before I feel the splash of his breath on me— followed by his tongue. His *teeth.*

My eyes roll to the back of my goddamn head as the noise from the crowd swells with murmurs of interest. This isn't the typical act they're used to. With ruthless, brutal determination, Maxim Koslov shreds the script.

Right here, on his knees, in front of what feels like the whole damn world, he fucks me with his tongue. Eats me out. Devours me.

There's no preamble like last time. No point to prove.

Two of his fingers spread me open while his tongue strikes deep, and my entire body jerks as it registers the invasion: thick, hot, burning…too much…*god.*

I buck my hips, chasing the sensation, and the nails of his right hand dig into my ass in retaliation. The burning sting has barely coursed through me before he changes his tactic and aims higher, going for the jugular. Pain and pleasure are my only clues to illustrate what he's doing to cause that harsh, aching sensation in my core: grinding my clit between his teeth.

And then my brain ceases any coherent thought altogether. I stop tracking his movements and I just fucking feel…

Everything.

In the end, he doesn't let me come; he drags me to the edge. Right when my toes curl. When my chest heaves, my nipples stabbing at nothing. Right when I can't think or *do* anything else but explode…

That's when he pulls back, his lips glistening, his eyes on fire. One of his hands shoots into the air as if beckoning someone closer.

Or something from the ceiling…

I catch the glint of silver from the corner of my eye before I witness the object being lowered on a rope as if on cue. It's a hook, the end pointed toward me. With one hand, Maxim grabs it while the other manipulates the whip. He turns his wrist clockwise, winding the leather strap around his knuckles.

Somehow, I know to lift my arms, raising them high above my head. A shiver runs through me at the harsh contrast of his heat and the cold leather as he wraps the loose end of the whip around my wrists, binding them tightly. I have no choice but to scoot forward to the edge of the slab as he lifts my bound wrists so that the hook catches the center bit of leather between them. Then he steps back and the pressure in my arms grows taut. I have to strain on the tips of my toes—until even that isn't enough. Within a matter of seconds, I'm suspended by my hands, dangling completely at his mercy.

Higher and higher, my body is hiked by the hook, until I have to stare down to meet Maxim's gaze. His narrowed eyes trace my captive form, honing in on my heaving chest, my breasts swaying for his attention.

I try to close my eyes. Block out the tension swirling through my veins, growing hotter with every step I hear him take—but he is a ruthless master. Callused fingers grab my hip, holding me steady as his body edges in closer. Too close. The ragged vibration of every inhale he takes electrocutes me. My skin is paper, his touch a ravenous fire threatening to burn me alive.

And the worst part?

My inner thighs are already slick, craving the destruction.

"Look," Maxim commands into my ear. With one hand, he manipulates my body just enough for me to see the shape of the crowd lurking behind us. "They're watching you. They smell you." He inhales too, the sound reverberating down my spine. "How you weep for me. *Fuck,* I can taste you."

The raw lust in his voice steals my breath away. I've never been this terrified. This damn *alive*, on the edge of pain and insanity. Too many men have had my body to even count, but none have made me crave them back. Like heroin. Like air. Deep inside, muscles I didn't even know I had clench and unclench, desperate for something to cling to.

"Look at me."

His gaze is feral when I do: all teeth and those eyes crazed with hunger. I nearly choke on the cry that threatens to break free as he muscles his way between my legs, jarring my precarious balance. The rasp of his pants against my inner thighs clashes with the throbbing pain building in my shoulders. It's too fucking much.

"I will not play with you tonight," Maxim tells me, his voice gritted. "There is a reason why you came back to me. Can you tell me?" A cruel thumb nudges my chin, forcing me to meet his gaze again, our frantic breaths mingling. "Hmmm?"

My body jolts. I *know*. Every cut in my flesh stings in a mocking symphony. Away from him, none of it feels strong enough. *I'm* not strong enough…

And, damn it, I don't want to be anymore.

"Say it," he goads, nipping my throat, a taste of what I crave. "Your safe word," he adds when my brain stalls, unsure of what he means. "Say it now."

If it was hard to say it before, it should feel impossible to now. My leverage. My sanity… All of it is tied to two little words that spill from my tongue on command. "I'm…happy."

His unstable chuckle swallows up the words and it's like I never said them at all. "Now, beg me to fuck you. And know that, the moment I enter your cunt this time, there will be no more lies. No more games."

No more safety net, a part of me cries, filling in the blanks of what he doesn't say.

"You can still run." Another dizzying kiss lands on my shoulder, giving way to raking, biting teeth. "Maybe I'll even let you go. But we both know…" His hand slips between my legs, batting the dangling limbs apart and gliding along the outside of my pussy. One thrust of his thumb and I'm jerking on the hook, swaying back and forth, a scream trapped in my throat. "We both know the truth, don't we, *Francesca*?"

Hearing my name come out of his mouth, thick with need? It shatters me. Suddenly, even the brush of his fingertips stings like the touch of a live wire. I can't breathe. Can't think. I'm so damn close…

"I will only tell you this once." His tongue blazes a trail along my jaw, inching toward my mouth. Once he reaches his destination, his lips settle over mine, allowing me to feel every uttered word. "Tell me why you're here."

"Because… Because I'm yours."

One minute, he's holding me steady in the air. The next, he's ramming into me, with one brutal hand on my ass while the other sinks into my hair, forcing my mouth against his.

We don't fuck.

We come un-fucking-done.

I scream.

He growls, pistoning his hips until the friction sets me on fire. I'm eaten alive by the flames, watched by countless people, consumed by the only man who matters.

"This"—he thrusts, stretching me wide while his free hand assaults my throbbing clit—"is"—another thrust—"pain. I feel it…" Awe chokes his voice as he thrusts again and the motion triggers his release, which draws out a roar he bellows into my skin. "*What have you done to me?*"

I'm on cloud fucking ten, but I still know I'll always remember those words. How he said them: raw, without a damn for who could hear.

"What will I do to you?" he rasps next, sounding crazed. Mindless. One last pump of his hips grinds the rest of his release into my ravaged pussy and I go under. Maybe I only imagine the words I hear next. "You are mine."

He lets his ownership hang in the air, which is every bit as powerful as the orgasm ripping me to pieces.

CHAPTER TWENTY-ONE

Survival is something you can't ever regret—I know that better than anyone.

Whatever it takes. No matter the cost. You lie, cheat, and steal if you have to. Your actual feelings never matter.

Until they *do* and it's all you can do to just lie there in a daze, hemorrhaging something more vital than blood.

I've never felt this kind of pain before. It's consuming, biting deeper than anything physical. It's in my soul: a wound left gaping open and I don't know how to staunch the flow. Something tells me that Band-Aids won't work in this scenario.

Maybe it's pride I'm losing—the one thing I always told myself I still had. Not even hooking deprived me of it. Neither did Melanie or any of the shit she put me through. I was still Francesca Marconi through it all, one tough-ass bitch.

But without even trying, Maxim Koslov made me surrender the only thing of value I had left. The worst part?

I gave it to him willingly.

Ain't that one for irony.

My exhausted psyche can't admit defeat just yet and clings to any other alternative. *This is just a nightmare… It isn't real.* As if to prove me wrong, reality returns in full force. It's cold here. I'm numb. It's loud, a million sounds battling for supremacy. Murmurs. Music. My head spins, struggling to piece it all together from the chaos of my memory. *The club. The stage. Maxim.*

Too late.

Ruthless fingers rake through my hair, electrocuting the nerves along my scalp. My shoulders are on fucking fire—I feel that first and nearly choke on a gasp as my eyes fly open to a hazy blur of red and black. I have to blink a few times before I can make out anything of substance, but in the end, only one sight registers: two dark eyes.

"Look at me." He must come closer, because the shadows recede, allowing me to make his face out clearly.

Just like that, I stop inhaling what little air my lungs managed to suck in.

It will never cease to amaze me how this man can turn something like confusion into the most devastatingly violent thing to witness. His jaw is a chiseled line, his mouth stretched tautly. Sweat glues his shirt to his body, his muscles rippling as his hands wrestle his cock beneath the zipper.

I know, even before he says the words, that this isn't over.

"Tell me to release you."

Shivers run down my spine at the strained tone. I'm still on the hook: still naked, my arms stretched above my head. I can feel his seed drying on my inner thigh and our sweat slicking my skin.

Without the high from the sex, the position is agony. Unbearable. Dried, my lips spring apart. "P-please."

Satisfied, he muscles in, cupping one massive hand against my ass. "Hold on to me."

A whine rips from my throat as the tension in my body suddenly snaps. He's already there to catch me when I fall, holding me close. I do my best to dig my nails into the fabric of his shirt, but even that seems damn near impossible. My muscles are jelly. Breathing is a struggle.

I should be terrified, I think. It can't be good to be this disjointed. So dizzy. So tired. So fucking *real*.

For the first time in my life, there is no fog threatening to descend. Just cold, harsh reality.

And he gave it to me—this man who lifts me like I weigh nothing, cradling my body in his arms.

Seconds later, he lays me onto something soft. Through heavy-lidded eyes, I recognize his second room.

"Are you in pain?"

The knowing tone in his voice quickens my already racing heartbeat.

"Yes," I admit into the silken sheets.

His next words come thickly. "Tell me where."

I flinch at the question, unsure of how to respond. Would *my fucking self-worth* be an adequate answer? I doubt it. So I improvise and blurt out an area on my actual body.

"My back…"

I hear him grunt in acknowledgment. Footsteps follow, but I'm too damn exhausted to turn my head and see their destination. I just have to wait and listen. Something that sounds like a drawer opens and closes. More footsteps.

When he's close again, my nostrils flare, catching the familiar aroma of his musk mingled with something sharper. Spice. It's like my body knows when he's near before I even do. It tenses up, every nerve on high alert, before the mattress dips beneath his weight, and his breath fans the back of my neck.

"Spread out your arms," he tells me.

When I obey, a warm substance falls onto the middle of my back and I have to smother the urge to shudder. Whatever it is feels like liquid. Hot. Oil? Something heavier descends before I can be sure, rubbing the substance into my skin. His hand? His *palm*, each finger fanning out along my spine, nudging tense muscle underneath.

I suck in a breath as he presses hard, setting off a chain reaction of sore muscles and aching nerves. He performs the same manipulative stroke three more times before I actually realize what he's doing. Massaging. Tugging. Pulling. I'm at his mercy, and my brain anxiously tracks each touch, anticipating the moment a fingernail might stab through my skin. Would that ruin this? Make it better?

"You will have some muscle tenderness for the next few days," he warns me without an ounce of guilt lurking in his voice. "Next time, I will better prepare you before using the hook."

I stop breathing, hung up on so many implications of that statement.

"I *will* do this to you again," he promises, reading my mind. There's a slight tremor in his voice: impatience. Like he can't wait to string me up a second time.

Tonight? I press my cheek against the sheet beneath it and tell myself that I wouldn't want him to. *Because…*

"Do you know why you came back to me?" he asks, interrupting my quest for an answer. His free hand sinks into my hair, wrenching my head back so that I can face him directly. "Do you? You said it once. Say it again."

I swallow hard and resist the urge to shake my head. Lying—that's Melanie's trick. The one thing I've always been able to fall back on. You lie to the patsy you're planning to screw over. You lie to yourself. To do otherwise is fucking suicide.

It should be easy to lie now, but looking at him…I just nod once.

"Say it," he prompts, tugging on my scalp when I don't comply quickly enough.

Freedom should be a good thing, but my body doesn't think so. Both lungs seize. "Because…"

I trail off.

He waits.

In the end, I guess there's only one real answer. "Because you make me feel wanted."

A low sound rumbles from his chest. It's only when he throws his head back that I can put a name to what it was: a laugh, unlike any I've ever heard. Beautiful, fucked-up noise.

Rather than say anything else, he releases his grip on my hair and continues his massage, moving along my lower back before digging into my arms.

I can't escape the mental comparison to how he handles his tools: wiping them down after a brutal sculpting session, rubbing oil into each scratch and imperfection.

"Wanted," he finally echoes after one last manipulation of my wrist. His tone is less gruff. I guess he's agreeing with me. "That is one way to put it."

The mattress shifts as he stands and circles the bed toward the direction I'm facing. Step, by step, by step…

"But I will tell you the real reason why." He stops just beyond my line of sight. While I stiffen in anticipation, his shadow falls over me, painting the edges of my vision black. "The real world doesn't keep you here. Not always. It can be too…harsh. Too cold." He's speaking from experience, his words losing their polish again for a brief second. "You go numb."

My hands twitch weakly at my sides, desperate to clamp over my ears. He shouldn't be making sense. Not now, when I'm too tired to counter him. Those weeks alone flicker across the inside of my skull like a slideshow of emotion. How it felt—or more like how cutting myself *didn't* make me feel.

"Look at me."

I must have closed my eyes, because they flutter open as something brushes my chin. His finger. With surprising gentleness, he uses it to steer my face up in his direction. Darkness has swallowed his pupils again, but this time, he doesn't seem inhuman. Just fucking insane.

"I can make it better…can't I?" His voice is rough, like he's unsure of the words even as they leave his mouth.

Like…he wants them to be true. "In a way that even you cannot."

He nods toward my wrist and I instinctively draw the hand closer to my side, bunching my fingers up to hide the cuts slashed across my palm. I can't disguise the other marks though. Ironically, they look even worse than the mess he's made of my skin. His marks are precise blows from a chisel. Mine are just sloppy. Not artful.

And that's just it: He turns agony into *art*.

"Coming back to me… You know what this means, don't you, *kotyonok*?" His head is cocked to the side, those eyes unreadable for once.

I have to take a risk and guess what emotion might be filling them now. I know anger on him. Confusion. Hate.

Maybe this is something different: pity.

"No," I croak, the truth.

Rather than punish me, he strokes his hand along my cheek. "I will release you, and you will stay because you want to."

My eyes start to burn. Blinking just makes it worse and hot liquid spills onto my cheeks. *Damn it.*

Slowly, I nod. Swallow. "Y-yes…"

Watching him this way, I finally see a shadow of the creature he must have been on stage. Tall. Imposing. Blond hair wild, eyes blazing, body radiating tension.

No wonder that little redhead looked so eager to be near him, even if it only meant being flogged. No wonder the entire fucking room of people stopped to watch him at work. If I wanted to take pity on myself in this moment, I'd go a step further: *No wonder you've gone fucking insane.*

It's impossible to judge your own mental psyche when looking at him. He's fucking psychotic, but he doesn't even begin to hide it.

He paints the world with it, not giving a damn for the lives he might stain with his twisted brand of madness.

"Sleep," he tells me once he finally reaches the door, feeling along the wall to shut the light off. He doesn't have to say the rest.

You'll need it.

CHAPTER TWENTY-TWO

He doesn't take me back to the suite.

I'm eerily familiar with our destination anyway: a desolate, dank parking garage. Dread congeals in my throat, making it harder to breathe as he exits the car. The door slams after him—and it all clicks.

He made up his mind, all right: If he can't fight for me, he'll destroy me.

"No." The refusal slips out of me unbidden, impossible to bite back. My fingers grip the handle tight while I try to find the lock. "N-No—"

"Come." His voice reaches me through metal and glass, faint but still laced with authority. There is nothing in his tone to give me a hint of what he's feeling or why he's brought me here.

But it's obvious: to kill me for good this time.

"Just let me go," I croak. "Please let me go—"

"*Kotyonok*…" He advances toward the door and wrenches it open from the outside as I cling to the handle. "Come with me."

He pries my hand loose, yanking me to my feet, and my brain goes blank.

"No!" I lash out, nails drawn, desperate for any part of him I can reach. Skin. Cotton. Anything. I kick and I hit with everything I fucking have.

But he's stone, impossible to outmaneuver.

"Enough!" He grabs my wrists, pinning them both to the hood of the car. The harder I try to escape, the tighter his grip becomes. "You have nothing to fear." He frowns, as if the thought only just occurred to him.

I can barely contain my scoff even as he releases me and holds his hand out for me to take.

"Do I really need to say it after everything else that's happened tonight?" Irritation makes his tone even harsher than anger—but his expression softens in the same instant. "Fine. I will not hurt you here. I need you to trust me."

Panting, I eye his fingers and consider running. Trust? Why, when all he's done is prove why I shouldn't? My blood pistons through me, making my entire body jolt with each frantic beat of my heart. If I listen hard enough, the thrum sounds like a warning. *Run. Run. Run.*

"Can you give me that?" he wonders, consuming my focus. I look up, unnerved by the uncertainty I see in his gaze. As if, for the first time, he can't predict what I'll do. He's just as unsure of me as I am of him.

"Come," he prompts, flexing his fingers. "I'm asking for your trust."

This time, I reach out and let him grasp my hand. He tugs, guiding me step by step down that dank, dark hallway. My nostrils flare. It still smells like rust, but now an even worse stench lurks underneath. Something rotten? Decaying.

The closer we come to the back room the more sweat slicks my fingers and it's easier than ever to slip from his grip if I have to.

Even his reassurance can push me only so far.

I stop dead in my tracks just beyond the doorway as my eyes warily trace the interior. The tarp is gone, at least. But in the center of the space lies a reddish stain someone tried very, very hard to get up with bleach, if the acrid stench left behind is any indicator.

They failed.

"Come here." From the doorway, Maxim watches me, his face partially hidden by shadow. "I will not hurt you here," he stresses. "So trust me. Come."

His eyes track my approach. When I'm close enough, he captures my entire hand in one of his own, his eyes honing in on my heaving chest.

Only now do I realize we're not alone.

A man lies in a far corner of the room, beyond the view from the doorway. Someone stripped him naked, and my stomach threatens to crawl up my throat as a sliver of light gives his flesh definition. A rainbow of violent, grim color. Purplish bruises and red, gaping wounds form a collage that covers him from head to toe. Some of the cuts bleed and ooze, still fresh.

The stench assaulting my nostrils warns that whoever he is, he's been here for days. Beaten for days…

My gaze fixates on a particularly nasty row of scratches along his shoulder and both eyes widen. It looks as if someone dug their nails in with all their might without giving a fuck as to the damage they'd cause.

"Back so soon…Maxi?" A hoarse, ragged sound fills the room. A laugh. *His.* He's alive. *Sevastyn?*

I flinch back, wrenching out of Maxim's reach. "What did you—"

"Look at me," Maxim commands. His hand latches onto my chin, giving me no choice but to obey. "You wanted to know why I left…" He waits until I nod.

"I went to Russia and met with some of my uncle's old acquaintances. Some of them were hostile to me. But others had axes to grind." His eyes flash, displaying every ounce of ruthlessness I know he possesses. "In the end, most gave me their loyalty. So if Anatoli wants retribution…he can have his war."

My head spins. "But—"

"As for *you*." He returns his attention to Sevastyn. "I thought even a dog like you should be shown mercy before you die. I'll let you plead for your life, even." He cuts his gaze back to me. "So beg her for it."

I sway. Maxim's lips continue to move but all I can hear is the whoosh of air leaving my chest and the thrum of my pulse hammering through my eardrums. I try to speak. Refuse. Scream—anything.

The moment my lips part, more maniacal laughter drowns out whatever I intend to say.

"Mercy?" Sevastyn wonders, his voice wracked with pain. "For me, Maxim? Or her?" His eyes seek mine out, red and swollen but gleaming. Burning. "You think I'm the monster? He'll destroy you worse than I ever could. You never could protect your toys, could you, Maxi?" He spits out each word, spraying blood. "You are pathetic. Still just a soft, pansy little fa—"

"Enough!" Maxim lunges, a blur of shadow, and something silver arches through the air. Sevastyn grunts and I turn away—but not fast enough to avoid seeing the blood splattering the gray floor.

And then silence descends like a noose.

I can't move. My eyes sear with the horror of what I've witnessed, but in a sick way I can still pretend that it was just a trick of the light. Or a nightmare.

That this isn't real.

But the man crouched before me *is*, and for some twisted reason my brain doesn't shy from his violence. Not the blood streaking his pale hands, or the harshness in the grunt he releases, throaty and raw as the metal object in his grip falls to the floor.

"He's wrong," he murmurs, rising to his feet. "Protect you? I'll do so much fucking more than that." The air hitches in my throat as he faces me, sweeping his gaze along my body. "I've thought of so many ways. So many ways to mark you. I've considered them all. Branding," he says musingly as he wipes his scarlet fingers onto the front of his expensive slacks, "with ink or with fire. A collar. A leash. Something so that the world knows you are *mine*."

That dark gleam in his eye greedily strips me down to the bone. Like he could devour me, body and soul.

"But none of those methods were enough," he continues while advancing on me another step.

I stagger in the opposite direction out of pure instinct, but my back strikes the wall and there is no escape.

"It isn't enough that the world knows you are mine, if you still have doubts."

Shaking his head, he approaches a table overrun with stone dust and worn tools in the corner and lifts something from the piled-up chaos.

"Here." He extends his hand. Warily, I wrestle my limbs into submission and cross over to him.

My fingers shake, grasping at the air as he drops a single object onto my palm. It's small, whatever it is. And yet oddly heavy. I almost can't bear to unfurl my fingers. So I don't. I tremble, observed by the man before me, and for some reason he allows me just a few moments of disobedience.

"Look at it, *kotyonok*," he commands finally.

The tone of his voice snaps me into action and I crane my neck down while peeling my fingers apart.

A small circlet of black marble rests on my palm. Streaks of silver embedded into the stone catch the light like stars in the night sky. It's beautiful. I can admit that—despite the way my stomach sinks to my toes as a gasp escapes my lips.

There in the center of it, etched in gold, is a single name, shining with ownership. MAXIM.

"You wear it when you are ready," he tells me. "When you can give me your trust... Can you give me that? Can you prove him wrong?"

"H-How?" I rasp.

"It is simple." He almost seems to shrug despite the tension radiating off him conveying anything but nonchalance. "Francesca Marconi must die—"

"What?" I rock back on my heels but he grabs my arm before I can attempt to run.

"You give me everything," he says, tightening his grip as he braces against me from behind. "Your body. Your life. Your name..." His fingers grasp mine, curling them around the ring I'm still holding.

"And you take mine." He breathes heavily against my throat, painting me with fire in every exhale. "As a Koslov, I can protect you. Forever."

And *now* I know exactly why he's brought me here. In shock, I eye our entwined fingers, his rough and tanned, mine trembling and pale.

Ink.

Blood.

Marble.

They are all just symbols—but a man like Maxim doesn't mark his ownership with something so simple. A man like him won't just claim any soul he craves. It must be offered.

With complete surrender.

SURRENDER

Surrender

Surrender By Lana Sky

Copyright © 2020 by Lana Sky
All rights reserved.

No part of this publication may be reproduced, distributed, or transmitted in any form or by any means, including photocopying, recording, or other electronic or mechanical methods, without the prior written permission of the author.

This is a work of fiction. Names, characters, businesses, places, events and incidents are either the products of the author's imagination or used in a fictitious manner. Any resemblance to actual persons, living or dead, or actual events is purely coincidental.

Cover Design and Interior Formatting by Charity Chimni
Proofreading by Charity Chimni

CHAPTER ONE

God has a twisted sense of humor—and for some reason, he seems to enjoy testing my sanity, especially for his amusement. With chaos. With violence. And with scenarios that force me to ask myself questions like—*what do you do after a man proposes marriage while towering over a dead, mutilated body, Francesca?*

The answer turns out to be relatively simple. You stand rigid in a corner while said murderer makes a single phone call, and then you watch him pace circles around his handiwork.

He can't seem to *stop* moving. Raging. Thriving on the stench of blood and the taint of death. He's like an inferno of brutality, burning so bright it hurts to stare at him for too long.

Ironically, I'm frozen in place, incapable of looking away.

The only part of me seemingly alive is my heart, beating in tune to his every footstep. *Thump. Thud. Thump.* Amid the ominous soundtrack, I'm riveted. I'm numb.

Though I should be terrified.

Of him.

Of myself.

In this moment, Maxim Koslov lives up to the worst aspects of his identity I could minimize until now. The criminal who deals in violence and death. The mob boss, dripping blood in his polished suit. The murderer.

As if reading my mind, he inclines his head in my direction, his gaze unreadable. "Leave, if you want. Go."

But he utters no further instructions. Deep in my soul, I know that his driver isn't lurking out front either, and he never offers the keys to his car to drive myself.

The command was a test. Namely, of the fragile promise linking us together amid this chaos. One forged in blood and a vow. My finger aches beneath the figurative weight of it—a marble ring with a single name etched into its surface.

It's so simple in its beauty and so damning in its symbolism.

Marriage.

Corruption.

Surrender.

"I told you to go." Maxim stands by the wall now with his hands braced before him, his back muscles taut. I could trace the line of his spine even through his clothing; he's so rigid. Stone. "You won't want to see what happens next…"

Next. Implying the ultimate fate of the body lying on the floor a few paces away.

I can't look at it. Or give it its proper name in my head. Nope. It's just a thing.

"I won't shield you if you stay, *kotyonok*. I won't. If you run now, I will not judge you, either."

Real urgency laces his words this time. He truly doesn't want me to see this—the twisted aftermath of his violence. The real Maxim Koslov.

But I can't run.

Move.

Breathe.

And with a sigh, he finally acknowledges that fact, though his muscles bulge against his skin as if threatening to explode from it. He's angry. And in some ways, I think he's resigned, too. If I can stomach him at his worst then…

We're *both* fucking insane. It's why I hear footsteps that shouldn't exist, advancing with confidence in our direction.

Then a voice rings out, far too stern to be a figment of my imagination.

"I'm here." We both turn to face the figure who appears at the mouth of the hall. I flinch against the nearest wall, but Maxim looks unsurprised.

"Finally." He nods in welcome. "You came. I was afraid you were away on one of your little trips."

"You were lucky. I just got back." Dressed in a black suit, the tall man cuts a startling figure against the bare walls. Dark hair frames a strikingly familiar face as his eyes latch onto mine before settling over the body on the floor.

"Shit," he says simply. Two bold strides bring him closer, and he nudges Sevastyn with the tip of his boot. I cringe from the sight, slapping my hand over my mouth in grim anticipation. A wave of gagging contorts my throat, but nothing comes up. Yet.

"You could have waited," the man adds. "I would've come sooner if I'd known you were planning this." Disapproval colors his British accent, and I finally recognize him—the figure I saw in Maxim's club during one of our first trips there. The same man who also examined me the last time Maxim lost control. "You know *this* is something I would've enjoyed watching…" His eyes narrow, disrupting his composure. Then he shakes his head, and all traces of emotion vanish. "We have to move quickly."

"How should we dispose of him?" Maxim asks while turning from the wall. His eyes find me again, even as he continues to speak to the man. "It needs to be clean. I suspect we have less than a few hours before his spies come looking for him."

"*You* shouldn't be anywhere near this to be completely honest." The other man reaches into his pocket and withdraws a cell phone. "Leave. I'll call one of my men—"

"No." Maxim steps forward and grabs his wrist before he can raise the phone to his ear. "No one else. Anatoli has spies watching his own fucking spies. *We* handle this. Alone."

"Fair enough." The other man's eyes narrow, but he slowly returns the device to his pocket. "What do you suggest?"

"I don't fucking know." Maxim turns to the table strewn with tools and grabs one item at random, testing its weight over his palm. As the light glints off a sharpened edge, I realize what it is—a knife. "Whatever we do, it needs to be done quickly."

"And this is a brand-new suit." The other man must know what he intends without him having to say it out loud. Sighing, he snatches his own makeshift weapon from the table and then crosses over to Sevastyn's body. "You can replace it." With clinical detachment, he examines the contorted, battered limbs. Then he looks up. "What about her?"

"Her?" Maxim echoes. He eyes me as well, but his gaze is so distant…

I suck in a breath and press myself against the wall. In the space of a heartbeat, this man becomes as much of a stranger to me as I seem to be to him. His icy glare alone warns me Maxim is gone, replaced by a creature tormented by his past, consumed by the violence of it— all those horrible things his uncle's return dredged up. My lips part, a plea building between them. *Don't.*

But right before I voice it, he blinks…and Maxim reappears, his knuckles stark white over the handle of his blade. Eyes narrowed in concentration, he rips his gaze to the weapon in his hand. "She… She stays."

Without another word, he crouches beside the battered, bloodied mass that used to be his uncle's head. Metal flashes as he lowers his hand…

Desperate to escape the image, I squeeze my eyes shut. I can't watch. *I can't.*

"No," comes a grunted demand, too stern to ignore. "Look. Look at me."

It's not an order—his tone wasn't that whip-like growl. Even more unsettling, I think he meant it as a request, one so dangerous my heart flutters in the face of it.

No, a tiny voice inside me pleads. *Don't.* But as if against my will, my eyelids lift anyway. I fixate on the floor first before inching closer toward that gruesome corner…

Until splatters of glistening red are all I see.

Fucking red everywhere.

"*Kotyonok.*" Blinking, I snap back to awareness as the rest of the room comes into focus. Maxim is still crouched before me. Watching me. Our eyes meet, but something deep inside won't let me flinch away. Perhaps I'm in shock?

The intensity of his gaze is, in some ways, more alarming than the pool of scarlet congealing at his feet or the mass of flesh just a few feet away. One look conveys more than he could ever say. A promise. A threat. *This is what I'd do for you,* that expression declares.

Kill. Maim. Cut. For you. Can you handle that, Francesca?

"Maxim?" As if from miles away, a deeper voice intrudes. "Have you thought this through? You know he won't be missed for very long. I'm sure Anatoli is already calling for his favorite pet," the British man says. "You do realize what this means?"

"It means war," Maxim replies to him. "It means I make my claim now or let that motherfucker win. It means I end this *now.*"

Eyeing his blade, he positions the tip against Sevastyn's neck, right below his skull. Nausea makes the room spin around me, but I can't help but register how surely he moves. No hesitation. No queasy unease. Only one explanation makes sense as to why—he's done this before.

"Though how long was it before Anatoli made the first strike anyway?" he muses. "Sevastyn wouldn't dare attack me without his master's permission. He came after me first. He drew first blood. No one can blame me for this."

"Sevastyn…" The other man frowns. "You think he was behind the attacks on the network?"

"He all but admitted it," Maxim hisses, his teeth bared. "As for Anatoli, I'm sure the bastard already knows what I've done. If I know him—and I do—he has half of the family assembling on the next fucking plane. He'll see this as an insult."

"An interesting theory." The other man raises an eyebrow while adjusting his grip over his blade as he scans Sevastyn's pale limbs. "But the man isn't omniscient—"

"He knows." Maxim shifts to nudge the body with his foot, rolling the corpse onto its back. "He knows the same fucking way that piece of shit knew where to strike to provoke me. The way they *all* know."

"Right." The other man's eyes cut in my direction. "I can admit that it is…*unlike* you to keep a companion for so long. But are you sure that they will—"

"Sure?" Maxim laughs, still eyeing the weapon in his fist. "Go on, ask me why Milton. I know you've wondered.

Why I would risk everything. My business. My standing—"

"Don't assume. You don't know what I've thought, my friend," the other man says swiftly. "But I'll tell you what's on my mind. We need to get rid of him. Now."

Maxim grunts in agreement. With surgical precision, he lowers the tip of his blade to Sevastyn's throat.

And utilizing the palm of his other hand like a hammer, he rams it straight through the flesh and bone.

CHAPTER TWO

I n reference to the dismemberment of a human body, I discover that "now" isn't as speedy as it sounds.

It takes *hours* to render the body to nothing more than bloody chunks haphazardly shoved onto a sheet of plastic for easy disposal. Maxim and Milton work ruthlessly in sync to sever muscle and tendon and bone.

At the very back of my skull, I know the gruesome nature of what I'm watching. I know that the lifeless pieces collecting onto the floor once belonged to a living, breathing human.

I just *pretend* they're nothing more than inanimate chunks of meaningless matter.

Time and space blur into one dizzying realm as I watch the grim display. I'm only aware of the passing hours at all because Milton takes meticulous note of them. "It's been two hours," he says at one point. "Another hour, you think?"

Maxim merely grunted in acknowledgment—though by then, the sound of my pulse surging through my eardrums drowned out any other noise.

I should have vomited at some point. A normal, sane human would. Maybe I did.

By the time the final, grisly piece is shoved out of sight, my knees are buckling. My stomach is a fucking mass of Jell-O balanced between my ribcage. I can't speak. Move. Even scream.

I merely stare as, together, Maxim and Milton bundle the mess between them and haul it to the door.

The sound it makes…

I'll hear it forever. A dragging hiss, followed by a wet, heavy thud.

"Fuck." Maxim hisses, eyeing a trail of ruby speckling the concrete in their wake. He starts to lower the morbid parcel, but I'm already at his side. The world jolts as I sway, off-balance, and clumsy.

I don't know what possesses me. Shock? I'm a mass of trembling, quaking limbs as I wrench my dress over my head and sink to my knees. Wadding the fabric between my fingers, I start scrubbing and scrubbing.

But the stains never disappear. Instead, the red drops multiply into an endless stream.

They're suddenly everywhere, coating everything within sight—blood-red blood.

"Enough!" Maxim rips the fabric from me, and in one quick motion, the red streaks vanish, easily swept away. "Where the fuck do we dump him?" he wonders, directing the question beyond me. "The river? The landfill?"

"We destroy it," Milton calls from the doorway. "I know a guy who runs a furnace. He's good. We won't be traced. I'll make the arrangements while you work on crafting an alibi. Anatoli won't take long to suspect the truth, but you don't have to make it easy for the old cunt."

Coldly and calmly, he wipes most of the blood from his hands with a handkerchief and casually drops the soiled cloth onto the plastic mound at his feet. "And to stop your paranoia from going bat-shit, I'll make some calls to my people. Plant rumors to stall the inevitable. Anatoli isn't a fool. Sevastyn was a loyal bitch, and his master will notice when he no longer comes to heel with his fucking tail wagging. With a little more planning, we could have crafted a more believable disappearance..."

"Go on and say it," Maxim scoffs. "I shouldn't have killed him. Not like this. It's fucking sloppy."

"You shouldn't have killed him," Milton agrees. "But that isn't why I'm concerned."

"Oh?"

A frown distorts Milton's otherwise emotionless visage. "You claimed *Sevastyn* was the one disrupting your supply lines. You sure of that?"

"It makes sense." Maxim returns to his full height and tosses my bloodied dress aside. Concentration consumes him, tightening the line of his jaw. He doesn't even seem to notice or care that I'm entirely naked, without even a pair of underwear. "Why? Have you learned new information?"

"Maybe." Milton looks down at his hands, flexing them one by one. "I didn't want to bring this to you until I was absolutely certain, but my men may have made headway in discovering the true culprit..." He looks up to meet Maxim's gaze directly. "I don't think it was Sevastyn."

"Fuck. Then who?" Maxim's upper lip pulls back from his teeth as he strokes a bloodied finger along his chin. "A rival? No. If it were someone well known, I would have narrowed it down by now."

"Someone we both always seem to underestimate." Milton's gaze drifts toward me and then back to Maxim. "Someone who might enjoy disrupting your supply lines if only to prove that he could."

"No..." Maxim shakes his head. "No. Even he wouldn't dare."

"Wouldn't he?" Amusement tilts the corner of Milton's mouth. "You never could predict Vadim. Though, maybe it's about time you finally set aside your—"

"I said no." The crunch of clenching teeth cuts the silence like a gunshot. "Don't even say his name—"

"Which is why I wanted to be sure," Milton says smoothly. "But even if it is him, he won't take it further."

"Or he could be working for Sevastyn?" Maxim interjects, his voice rasping. "Don't pretend like you haven't kept tabs on them both this entire fucking time."

"No." Milton inclines his head, his lips pulled tight. "He's a clever son of a bitch, I'll give him that, but if anyone wanted to drive a knife into Sevastyn more than you, or myself, it's Dima—*Vadim*."

"I told you not to say his fucking name."

"*Fine*." Milton extends his arms in a gesture of surrender. His bloodied hands are a chilling reminder of the current situation, almost appearing like a ghoulish pair of gloves to compliment his ebony suit. "Consider the discussion over. For now. We have more important things to do, like focus on getting rid of this wanker. The sooner we finish, the sooner I can call in a team to erase any physical traces."

Wordlessly, he and Maxim refocus their attention on the grisly mass nearby. They both take a corner of the plastic tarp and drag the body into the hall inch by inch, grunting with the effort.

I'm left behind, trembling in the frigid air, naked without my dress. Before I can attempt to move, Maxim's voice reaches back to me. "Stay."

I do, my vision blurring. The only sounds are my ragged breaths scratching at the air as I inhale. Exhale. Faster. God, salt is all I can smell. All I taste.

Maybe I'm overreacting?

Because despite Maxim's comfort with death, this isn't my first time facing it either—a terrifying concept I can't dissect just yet. *No.* So I wait, listening to the scraping of plastic over concrete, desperate for relief.

I find my escape in snippets of murmured conversation.

"You're sure about this?" Milton says, his accent distinct. "We could always attempt to stall. Forge rumors about his whereabouts."

"Like you said, Anatoli is no fool," Maxim replies. "After tonight, it's not like I have a choice regardless."

"So, what now?"

"Now..." Maxim sounds fainter, his words interspersed with muffled grunts and more hissing plastic. "Now, we beat the motherfucker at his own game..."

When approaching footsteps return moments later, I recognize their heavy, ominous cadence before their owner appears alone in the doorway. Bathed in shadow, Maxim inclines his head for me to follow. "Come."

I lurch after him on unsteady, jellied legs. My thoughts are too scattered to make out our surroundings—only he has any definition against a formless, colorless landscape of shadow. Hunched over with my arms around myself, I'm freezing until a layer of warm fabric falls over my shoulders —his jacket, reeking of salt and damp in places…

I gag—but his scent dominates the luxurious fabric despite the wetness. Somehow breathing it in keeps my roiling stomach at bay.

I can resist the terror. He alone is my anchor to sanity, guiding me in deliberate commands and stern touches.

"*Kotyonok*," he prompts as we reach a familiar destination, his car. "Get in."

He opens the door on my end, and I climb woodenly into the passenger's seat. Once we're secured within the confines of black leather and metal, I can finally breathe normally again.

But I'm not brave enough to ask more questions. Like where the body is. Or Milton. Or what happens next.

I close my eyes to shut out the world entirely as Maxim starts to drive. Only now do I realize that I have no fucking clue where he's headed. Despite everything—even the ring on my finger—paranoia sets in, gnawing at my fragile composure. There is one fear I can't ignore when it comes to him…

The unsettling knowledge that he's always on a hair-trigger. Is this the moment when I meet my own end on a wad of sheet plastic? The fear of that fate should bite deeper into my psyche than it does, though. This stupid, internal voice resists it, too naïve to believe but persistent, nonetheless. *He won't hurt me…*

"We're almost there," Maxim declares, breaking the string of morbid thoughts. Like a puppet master adept at his craft, he knows just when to reassert his presence. "Look at me."

When I reopen my eyes, I don't recognize the cluster of buildings around us. They're too tall. Too bright. So we aren't heading toward his usual suite, then. But this isn't the neighborhood where my family is either.

Though, I'm not left to wonder for very long.

As if on cue, he turns a corner, and the car comes to a stop amid unfamiliar scenery. Gripping my seatbelt, I race to piece together our surroundings. Somewhere dark. Enclosed. A garage? Fresh panic sets in, scattering imaginary butterflies in my stomach. Dark spaces have terrible connotations where he's concerned. Especially when he looks like this…

Smoldering in silence. Tense, harboring fire within his gaze as white-knuckled fingers clench in and out of fists.

"Come." He's already exiting the car, oblivious to my reaction. Either that or he's deliberately ignoring the terror I know is etched on my face.

"Come," he commands again, but his back is to me, and he starts across the garage without waiting for me to move.

Before he can leave my line of sight, I stagger after him, a slave to his whims even as my brain stalls.

The garage exits into a darkened hallway closed off by a single elevator. When the doors part several floors later, they reveal another door at the end of a carpeted corridor. Here an eerie sense of déjà vu washes over me. I recall that very first day weeks ago when I arrived as a prostitute before a mysterious, wealthy client who lived in a building much like this one.

Beyond this black door lies a fittingly similar suite—but it's larger than the last. Or so I assume from the echoing, cavernous interior that multiplies our footsteps into a deafening clamor. This layout differs from his old residence in more than just size. The furniture scattered across a spacious entryway is simpler when glimpsed in the dark. Practical.

"We will stay here for now," he explains as he crosses the drawing room. A series of closed doors line a short hallway leading deeper into the interior. His confident steps betray a knowledge of the layout that makes me suspect he didn't just buy it on a whim. "I've already had your things from the old suite brought here."

As he speaks, he opens the door to a room that I assume at first is a copy of my old one. But it's larger. And instead of white or his preferred black, these walls are painted a simple shade of gray. An odd feeling of relief eases some of the stiffness in my limbs.

At least it's not red.

When I breathe in deep, I smell still, scentless air—no salt.

It's a welcome change from that cold, concrete room dominated by a table stocked with weapons. Here, the main piece of furniture is a massive bed positioned near a breathtaking view of the city. It's nearly twice the size of my old one—but it's the open closet that draws my interest.

Of all things to pop into my head, the first thought is fittingly childish after a night filled with death. Daisy would *die* to own a closet like this—one large enough to fit our entire old house in with room to spare. I can't take my eyes off of the clothing displayed in meticulous order for some reason, though. Most of the options on metal hangers consist of his customary dark shirts and slacks.

But they only take up one half. The other side of the space contains an array of delicate, lacy gowns and dresses recognizable at a glance. *Mine.*

And a dangerous thought threatens to disrupt our previous boundaries—this room is *ours.*

Maxim barges into the closet without explanation—as if that little detail means nothing. Sighing, he strips his shirt, and the cadence of his voice snaps me out of my shock. "Take off your clothes. Put them with mine. I'll dispose of them later."

He does the same, but tension contorts his body into a series of rippling muscles. And I'm hypnotized. His scars gleam in the glow of moonlight, betraying a mere hint of the horror he's lived through.

I still haven't moved by the time he throws his wadded shirt to the floor, and wrenches open his slacks. "Did you hear me, *kotyonok*?" He cocks his head in my direction, his gaze indiscernible. "Move."

I jump, too enthralled by his appearance to turn away. Blood speckles his chin. Even more paints his fingers in violent streaks. When he notices me staring, he turns and reenters the bedroom. There must be a bathroom nearby because I hear water running. A few seconds later, he returns, and the blood is gone.

"Look at me," he demands. But I already am.

He hasn't bothered to turn a light on, and only the glow from the floor-to-ceiling windows bathes him in bluish definition. The contours of his body create organized chaos from the hulking mass of bulk and muscle that shape him. He's beautiful, as if hand-carved by an artist intent on crafting a creature somewhere in between a devil and an angel. The only detail out of place is the black binder cinching his waist, obscuring yet another traumatic souvenir from his past.

"*Kotyonok...*" His eyes meet mine, and my heart seizes up at what I find in them. More rage? No. Something far more unsettling. In fact, when his nostrils flare with my scent, it's the most alarming sight I've been faced with all night, and I stagger back a step in the opposite direction.

Lust.

In him, it's an emotion comparable to a match striking a pool of gasoline. Volatile. Like a predator, he advances, herding me into a corner. Within seconds, my back is against the wall, and he's towering above me, rage smoldering off his skin.

But I'm not terrified of what the anger itself does to him. In a way, it's beautiful to witness its impact up close.

His features shift and meld, seamlessly transforming him from man to beast. Gone is the cold, dispassionate mask. Teeth bared, he eyes me with a ruthless flick of his gaze, and I know he's here with me fully—not trapped in the past. But then he laughs, and the sound resonates all the way down to my fucking core.

Sevastyn wasn't the only one to stoke his temper, it seems.

"It's always as though it's the first time. How you look at me," he murmurs, reaching for my chin. His thumb brushes my jawline reverently, even as his eyes glow with that unsteady gleam that heralds disaster. My heart lurches with every careful stroke, and I know better than to say a damn thing. "Whenever you see me at my worst," he explains, lowering his gaze to my throat. "You stare at me, with your eyes so fucking wide. Always as though it's the first time. The first day..."

He laughs again, but it's a bitter sound.

"Those fucking eyes haunt me. I shouldn't even give a damn if you're afraid." He bares his teeth in torment as his finger presses harder, seeking out the bone beneath my flesh. The second I wince, he withdraws. "But I still see what he did to you. What I *let* him do."

My barely healed injuries throb at the reminder, but I don't welcome this biting sort of pain. It burns, summoning tears I have to fight to keep at bay.

"I close my eyes and see it," he adds thickly. "I can't sleep without fucking seeing it. Even now, I can still hear that motherfucker, taunting me with the threat of you."

In a sick way, he resembles someone fighting to stay awake. Like Ainsley when she's resisting a nightmare—but the phantoms in his head consist of horrors no child should ever face. In frustration, his hands unfurl, the nails drawn like claws, and he resorts to the one tool he's relied on until now.

Anger.

"Did you take my ring out of fear?" he wonders, his accent thickening, his baritone deepening. He's hunting for a line of attack, I think—desperate for anything to feed his rage. To distract from the truth—he's losing control. "Is that it?"

"No." He flinches at the sound of my voice, but I finally regain control of my limbs before he can reply. There is only one way to reach him when he's like this—the only language we both understand.

A startled grunt escapes him as I brush my hands over the front of the jacket draped over me. A tailored silk, the fabric easily slides from my shoulders to the floor.

His eyes narrow, tracking the flesh bared with ravenous interest and that wavering darkness slowly fades in favor of a new emotion. He's here again, alone with me in this room—not the past.

I swallow back my relieved sigh and brace. Maybe he's right. In some ways, it really does feel like that very first day all over again. My first exposure to the taste of his brutality. I'm unsure of what to expect from this massive creature who radiates power and control.

And yet for whatever reason, I'm drawn to the flame, even if it burns.

This pain doesn't hurt the way it should.

"Say it," he demands, recapturing my chin in his grasp. With gentle pressure, he pries my jaws apart. "You are mine. Say it."

I rush to obey. "I'm yours—"

"Body and soul," he prompts, each word grated through clenched teeth. His tone alone betrays that they mean more to him than a selfish boast of possession. So much fucking more. They're the reason why I can watch him at his worst, on the brink of madness, and keep what little shreds of sanity I still have left. Why his hands shake as they grasp handfuls of me—whatever he can reach. Nails drawn, he claims every inch of flesh, his eyes fluttering as I flinch.

"Body and soul," I tell him, fighting to form a coherent response.

"And you won't run from this? From me?" He grinds his hips into mine, igniting a tendril of fire in my core. Clamping my thighs together is the only way to stave off the inevitable inferno.

"I won't."

In a blur of motion, he moves in, claiming my mouth as his hands grip my waist. His tongue barely slips between my lips before he draws back and wrenches me around to face the wall. I suck in a breath, the sound nearly drowning out his appreciative groan. His palm smooths over the flat of my belly, aiming between my legs. In an expert motion, he spreads me open, teasing me with the broadness of his thumb.

I barely adjust to the substitute before the real thing batters against my throbbing skin.

One thrust, and he's so deep I can't even cry out in response. I gasp instead, my lips parted, air trapped in my lungs. Overwhelmed with the feel of him, my brain conjures a million words to describe the sensation—*full, so full. Thick. Heavy. Everywhere.*

Then he moves, bucking into me, forcing my cheek against the ice-cold wall as his body pins me in from behind. He's slow at first, ensuring every thrust stings. Burns, so deep I'll feel him for days. Just as the pain fades into a delicious ache, he moves faster. Harder.

The rhythm lacks the brutal tempo I'm used to. My world narrows to sin and skin, and the wet heat of his mouth latched onto my shoulder, muffling the animalistic grunts he makes with every single thrust.

My nails uselessly scramble over the surface before me, seeking out stability. Security. Anything.

I find neither.

Nothing in the world is stable enough to anchor me against him. I have to endure—every ounce of frustration and fury, slammed into me, straining the confines of my body. The emotions roused by the night's events seep from him, betraying more than words ever could.

Sevastyn rattled him.

Infuriated him.

But what happened after confused him.

And the sight of that marble ring on my finger...it scares him?

There's almost too much to make sense of—too much for him to process alone.

So he spills them all into me one by one, until his release drags both of us under. His grip on my hair tightens painfully as he rams into me one final time, so hard my knees buckle.

He's left holding me, sweeping his hand beneath my knees as he pulls out and lifts me into his arms. Boneless, my head lolls against his shoulder as I find myself focusing on his face first, marveling at what I see. Gone is that twisted, pained expression. I can't resist stroking my fingers along the corner of his mouth, tracing its shape when devoid of a scowl or frown.

For once, he moves free of tension, crossing the room to another door that I hadn't noticed. The bathroom? He shoulders the door open, and I realize that my suspicion was horribly off base.

"I will admit that I prefer to use the club whenever I can," he admits as he steps over the threshold. "But in the interim, *this* will make do for when I need you."

This. A space enclosed by ebony walls and gray marble floors, containing more careful details than the rest of the suite. There are no windows to the outside world. Just closeness and shadow and him. The only real item of furniture is a table in the center made of solid black marble, polished enough for me to make out my reflection as he sets me onto it.

It's cold. A hiss escapes my mouth, and he tugs me closer in response, dominating the space between my legs. Leeching off his heat, I watch him silently explore the surface beneath me. For my benefit, I realize—it's a silent tour of sorts.

Beneath my position, a small ledge extends from the side of the table. I follow the line of his gaze as he runs his hands over the objects strategically placed there, all within reach. One article is a pool of thin, black fabric.

A blindfold? Alarming enough—but the other items are seared onto my psyche even if I don't dwell on their purpose for now.

An unlit candle.

A pair of metal handcuffs, lined with black leather.

And lastly, a knife, sharpened and ready. Maxim grasps the weapon first, testing the weight against his palm.

"Do you know when I first knew it?" he wonders against my scalp. "That you were mine? Do you?" His finger returns to my jaw, urging me closer with a beckoning caress. "It was that first night you climaxed. Do you remember?"

I do, and my throat goes dry at the memory.

"It's not the fact that you got off that made me consider snapping your fucking neck right then and there." His thumb teases the throat in question, tracing the hollow of it as I suck in air, too enthralled by his words to release it. "I could feel it…your greedy cunt gripping me tight. For the first time, fucking wasn't satisfying an urge, no more intimate than pissing or breathing. Your body wanted more than a fuck, wringing every ounce it could from me."

The awe in his tone resonates down to my core. Deep inside, muscles clench in response, my brain buzzing.

"You don't understand it." He looks down at his hands and curls them into fists. "What it feels like to go your entire life satisfying those primal fucking urges out of necessity and nothing more. Before you, I rated the quality of sex based on how efficiently I could get it over with. How much blood I could draw and gasps I could wring from the whore beneath me just to know…I was still there. Still alive. Still connected to my body. Pleasure didn't matter. Lust was a mere byproduct of biology. I was always in control. But that night with you…" His lips purse as he lowers his hand to his glistening cock. "You forced me to feel it, didn't you?"

His eyes cut up to mine accusingly.

"You made me see you. Even now, at the edge, when I can feel myself so fucking close to slipping. When all I should crave is to go numb. To rage, and maim, and kill. *You…*" He laughs in disbelief, shaking his head. The manic gleam in his eye reassures me despite how my heart seizes up. The terror is still there, building in my blood, but that one, searing expression keeps me from succumbing to it.

Because it means he's still here in this moment. Still Maxim.

And he reaches for me like a lifeline, his nails biting into my skin, sealing in his possession.

"I still feel you," he admits. "Like no one else. So hear me now—"A searing pain in my ear is my only warning as he bites down over the sensitive lobe. "Mine," he rasps. "You were made for me. And I will ensure the world knows it. No matter the fucking cost."

CHAPTER THREE

My memory goes hazy after that, devolving into snippets. More sex. Restless sleeping. Waking. More sleeping. When I fully regain my senses, I'm lying on a substance so soft that I swear I'm floating. Falling. My fingers fan out, scrambling for purchase against something solid. And I find it.

Warm, flexing, heavy…

Confused, I open my eyes, enthralled by the vision before me. Maxim Koslov, in stark naked glory, save the black binder around his waist. Golden hair fans over his forehead, obscuring his eyes. But they're closed and his chest rises and falls in a steady rhythm. He's asleep. And that fact alone transforms him into another fucking person.

My breath catches as I find myself inching closer, riveted by his face when devoid of a glare or scowl. Someone like him can never be at peace—not fully. But this may be the closest I've seen him come to it.

And the sight leaves me stunned. My fingers fan out without my brain telling them to, smoothing over his cheek. I barely touch him before the moment shatters. He springs into awareness, grabbing my wrist, but when his eyes finally open, his fingers relax, releasing me.

We're on the bed, I realize.

Our bed. Sweat and musk flood the air—me and him combined into one indiscernible aroma. Gone is the distinct, invisible barrier that always divided his old suite, separating him from me.

This place is different.

And he's still here, lingering beside me in a way he rarely has. Nostrils flared, he inhales my scent as his other hand grazes my waist, dragging me closer to him. Like a dog on a leash. I arch into the touch, savoring the satisfied grunt resonating in his chest.

"So much like a kitten," he murmurs thickly. "My *kotyonok*. Snuggling close to me when she should turn tail and run. Now more than ever."

For once, he doesn't sound angry, and he doesn't roll me beneath him in a sexual frenzy either. *This* is somehow more unsettling. Him lying here with me. Breathing me in. Feeling me. Torturing me.

"I scared you tonight," he says, his cold eyes blinking once. "I saw how you looked at me. Like I lost my goddamn mind. But, you were not the catalyst for this… I used to dream of killing him." I marvel at the raspy cadence of his voice, devoid of hostility. I think he's half-asleep still, but for whatever reason, he feels compelled to share. Something. Anything.

So I hoard every scrap he's willing to give.

"I planned it down to the last fucking detail," he continues, absently stroking the side of my hip. "How I would make him suffer. Make him scream. For over twenty years, I've dreamt about it. But there are rules when it comes to revenge. I alone was never worth the risk…"

He settles the palm of his free hand against my cheek. Though he may have cleaned them of blood, violence resonates in his fingertips, impossible to erase. I can feel the power weighing down every inch of flesh and nail and bone. It's intoxicating in its potency.

But intimacy shouldn't feel like this—like a drug—I know that. Going off depictions in movies, I should crave heartfelt embraces and passionate cuddling.

I should crave normal, wholesome affection.

Not the caress a murderer can impart just as easily as ruthless brutality. He frowns, seemingly just as confused as I am by my reaction. My chin tilts, seeking out the contact, extending it.

"So greedy," he admonishes. "You take only what you can in the moment. Maybe it's for the best," he adds. "Dwelling on the past is for the weak. Don't make the mistake of assuming that's why I did it. I didn't kill him because of what he's done—but because of what he was. A wolf too much of a fucking coward to hunt in the light, so he thrived in the shadow, picking off weak prey. *You* appealed to him. He hurt you, and yet you look at *me* with pity."

His voice catches on a dangerous, unstable note I know too well.

"I don't crave your pity." I flinch as his fingers brush over my cheekbones, but I don't pull away. Nails drawn, he probes me mercilessly. Whatever he seeks must lurk in the corner of my mouth. He slides his thumb along the seam, blinks…and he's back again.

"And yet you offer it, anyway." His nostrils flare, his voice hollow. "It's the one thing you give me freely, other than submission. Your pity." I can't tell if that angers him or not.

In the end, he merely sighs and eases the hair from my face with the tip of his finger.

"That motherfucker didn't make me. I made *him*. I ended him. He didn't fucking win. They won't win. And whether I seek out Dima or not, nothing changes."

"Dima?" I risk asking. He's mentioned that name before to Milton. "Who is—"

"No one," he snaps, but the viciousness in his voice warns of the opposite. "The past cannot be undone. So there is no point in regret. I never owed him a damn thing. I still don't."

My lips twitch. I need to say something else. Comfort him, I think.

Before I can get a word out, he rolls onto his side with his back to me. I barely mourn the loss of his touch when he hooks his arm around my waist, dragging me to him.

Tethering me to him.

"I chose you over him. Over them." I can feel the vibrations rumbling through his back with every grated word. It's more than a boast. More than a promise. It's a warning. "Don't forget that. Don't ever forget that. I chose *you*. I will fight for you."

Saying it out loud must comfort him in ways that even bashing Sevastyn's skull in didn't—because within minutes…I know he's asleep.

I wake up again to golden daylight flooding in through the window, but I don't have the strength to even move, let alone get up. I'm so fucking tired. My muscles ache, my mind exhausted. For a second, I think I'm still dreaming, imagining the snippets of conversation drifting on the edges of my consciousness.

"…A message came this morning," a man confesses, his tone cordial. *Lucius?* "You won't like it. Should I convey it regardless?"

Someone grunts in response. That guttural baritone needs no introduction.

"Anatoli has demanded your presence," Lucius continues. "Far be it for me to make a suggestion, sir. But if you were planning to declare your independence from him, now might be your chance. My contacts have already picked up on chatter within the network, speculating on Sevastyn's sudden absence over the past twenty-four hours…"

If Maxim replies at all, I don't hear him, imagined or otherwise. It could be because my brain shuts down, cringing from any mention of that name. *Anatoli.* If I'm still dreaming, the image creeping into my mind would surely reinforce this moment being a nightmare—a man with cold, lifeless eyes so similar to Maxim's it's chilling. Like he's doomed to one day reach the same level of callous, inhumanity.

I squeeze my eyes shut, blocking out the memories. Rolling over, I press my face against a mound of silken sheets. Just as I start to drift off again, a familiar command cuts through the exhaustion like a knife. "Come."

Still half-asleep, I scramble from the sheets and find a black robe draped over the end of the bed. It's silk, tailored to my size. Made for me.

Cautiously, I enter the hall wearing it and find Maxim in an enormous dining room adjacent to an open floor plan kitchen. A row of windows displays the city of Fair Haven from its very heart. From the bay to the glittering center, all the way to a glimpse of the slums on the very outskirts.

Attacking his uncle may have been the opening salvo of a so-called war, but Maxim certainly isn't in hiding. This bold, new residence makes one fact painfully clear—he's ready for a fight.

And this view serves as the perfect backdrop for the breakfast of a man hell-bent on domination. What might fuel such an enigmatic figure? Two plates before him contain the answer—poached eggs over a rare steak sliced to perfection.

"Sit." He nods to the chair beside him. When I comply, he picks up a fork from the table, twisting it between his fingers. He's been up for a while, already fully dressed in a black suit, his hair damp and freshly washed. The sight of him makes me keenly aware of the grime still clinging to me. Namely, the rust-colored gunk caked beneath my fingernails.

I try scratching it away, but the stain remains no matter how fiercely I dig. It hurts, but I can't stop scraping. Probing. Bleeding.

"I have business to attend to," Maxim informs me, and I look up, forcing my hands flat against the table. "Meetings. I'll be gone until tonight."

I nod absently, still processing the past twenty-four hours. My brain struggles to digest the tonal whiplash. Murder one moment. Breakfast the next.

And brutal sex replaced by casual conversation.

"Lucius will accompany you today," he continues. "But you will be on your own for most of it."

That sounds like more than an afternoon spent here waiting for him. I brush my tongue along my lower lip before replying. "For what?"

Rather than answer me immediately, he drags my plate toward him and cuts the meat into even smaller pieces. Then he nudges it in my direction with a grunted command, "Eat."

As I shovel a piece of steak into my mouth, I catch him watching every fucking move I make, missing nothing.

"Swallow," he prompts, once I've taken a few mechanical chews. Satisfied, he adds while my mouth is full, "I'm sending you for a dress."

A dress. Maybe his penthouse and our relationship isn't the only thing that has changed after last night? He thinks I need a new wardrobe as well. I'm partially through chewing another slice of meat when I finally process the deliberate way he pronounced that word, however. Dress.

A dress.

The dress.

I swallow too quickly and wind up choking. Eyes streaming, I gulp at a glass of water shoved in my direction. Once I stop sputtering, the only thing I can think to say is, "But I haven't even told my family."

About the true nature of my relationship with him.

About why our lives have changed so drastically.

About…

"Did you change your mind?" he wonders, his tone eerily level. "About marrying me."

I flinch and set my fork aside. Even thinking in those foreign terms heats my skin. It sounds unnatural. Me *married* to Maxim. Him, waiting for me at the end of an aisle. Signing up for forever at his whim.

It sounds fucking insane.

"If your siblings are your main concern, we can arrange for you to tell them before then," he suggests while stabbing at his own piece of meat.

I feel my brows furrow. "Before what?"

"The ceremony." He pauses to chew a bite of steak. As he swallows, he dabs at the corner of his mouth with a white cloth. Then he continues, "I've arranged for it to take place by the end of the month."

"So soon?" I sound more panicked than surprised. So soon. A wedding.

"The sooner, the better," he insists while slicing off another piece of his steak. He makes it sound so simple. Like a walk in the park. A necessary chore. Business—but the more he broaches the topic, the harder it is for my brain to comprehend. "It is not enough for me to merely claim that you are mine," he says. "I must prove it. Publicly, in terms that men like my grandfather will understand. In my family, your worth only extends to the power of the name attached to it. If you are to be protected from now on, you must take mine. Eat."

I force down another bite while observing him. It's going to storm today—literally and figuratively. Already, dark clouds shroud the sun, choking out the daylight. A cold, overcast gray replaces it, reflecting off the angular features that make his face so expressive and so beautiful.

Even while he's brooding.

Aware of me watching, he shifts, angling himself toward me. "A month might seem 'soon' from your position, but trust me, it's a gift. Even a week's delay is wasted time." He takes a sip from his own glass of water as his eyes flicker over mine suddenly guarded. "The sooner you become a Koslov in name, the better."

Though, in a sense, I already have his name. Absently, I trail my fingers along my bare inner thigh, tracing a series of healing welts. Lines. When viewed at once, they proclaim ownership. His. "Why so fast?"

I'm not brave enough to mention the conversation I may or may not have imagined. Could his accelerated timeline have something to do with his grandfather's demand?

"Why?" He cocks his head and observes me from the newer angle. "Consider it like another transaction. I give you security. In return, I know you are protected."

"But why rush?" I say, probing him as much as I dare. "We barely even know each other."

Which is a goddamn lie. In some ways, he knows me better than I know myself. And as for him…

I know that he's someone who would never offer a "transaction" like this to any other woman.

"Your feelings or mine have nothing to do with it," he says, scoffing at the prospect. "This would be a transaction. Nothing less, nothing more."

"Okay, but…" I shake my head. "What about my family?"

"It's simple. They become *my* family."

"And the house? Will we stay there—"

"Nothing else will change," he snaps, shoving his plate aside. "Think of it as merely an extension of our previous arrangement."

"Through marriage…" My head is spinning. I lean over the table and cradle my temple against my palm. "A wedding," I repeat, tasting how the word sounds out loud.

Terrifying, that's how. "Are you just going to take me to the courthouse or something?"

"I don't think you understand the situation." His tone softens a fraction, sounding damn near gentle. "Killing Sevastyn didn't end this. It started it. If I don't make my intentions known now, they won't just kill you. They'll take pleasure in using you against me any way they can. They'll sell you. Beat you. Destroy you." He glowers into the distance, seeing his hypothetical threats unfold. "So, trust me when I say that a month isn't soon enough. Regardless, you still have time to tell your family."

"And then what?" There are ways to sugarcoat it—but I doubt Daisy and Mikie will buy that I would meet a man and marry him in less than a year. They *shouldn't*—even if said fiancé purchased a new house and enrolled them in schools, we could have only dreamed of them attending a few months ago.

Melanie did shit like that. Not me.

"Then…" Pulling his plate back, he glowers at the meat before slicing through it. "Then you'll be protected. Nothing else will change. And Sevastyn can rot in the ground like the rat he is while Anatoli twiddles his thumbs in the front fucking row before the altar."

I flinch at the imagery. I don't think he even realizes the irony of it—in one breath, he makes being a Koslov sound synonymous with envious security. But in the next, he refers to his own family members in terms most people would reserve for mortal enemies. Melanie had a habit of hitching up with men she barely knew—but here's the funny part. I know even less about Maxim or his past.

But some topics are better left broached when he doesn't have a knife within reach.

"I'm guessing I can't just wear a dress from Kmart?" I say, clumsily changing tact.

He raises an eyebrow. I caught him off guard. No, it's stranger than that—I've amused him. "Not exactly." His hand shoots out, and he snags one of my curls. As I watch, holding my breath, he tucks the strand behind my ear. "My wife deserves something a bit grander than that."

Goosebumps rise over my skin at how dangerous that word sounds coming from him. *Wife.* His tone caresses it like a noose, strangling any warmth from every single syllable. It's not a title. It's a life sentence.

"You're serious about this," I rasp.

"More than serious." He grasps my hand, extending the fingers for his inspection. The one wearing his ring trembles beneath his scrutiny. "I told you once, in so many words—I do not offer what I am not willing to give." He strokes his thumb along the gleaming marble for emphasis. "I am offering you this."

This. Him. Our lives. The possibility of those two things no longer being mutually exclusive.

The possibility of tethering myself to him in ways more binding than a stupid piece of paper.

The possibility of complete and total surrender beyond the boundaries of sex.

"It's a lot to consider overnight," I croak—but it's another lie. I've had days to reconcile my relationship with him well before now. Hours of dwelling on him. Endless minutes of contemplation of what my connection to him means.

And I've avoided thinking of anything beyond the here and now.

"Did you think I was lying?" he wonders as if reading my mind. "Or making a boast in the heat of the moment?"

"No," I say quickly. "But…"

"Or perhaps you don't understand just what it is I'm offering. Do you think I was my father's only child?" He stands and storms over to the windows. With every step he takes, tension ripples down his spine, enhancing his bulk until he appears ten times larger. Massive. "Of course, I wasn't. He had more bastards than a stray mutt drawn to any bitch in heat. But *I* am the one with his name. I was the one legitimate enough to supplant him. I am a *Koslov*." He makes it sound so much more than a title. It's his identity. In a way, I think he's proud of it as much as he hates what that very name makes him.

He is Maxim Koslov. In his world, that gives him meaning. Purpose. Enough for him to adhere to its archaic rules.

And prize its twisted perks.

"Even Anatoli cannot deny that fucking birthright. Once you are my wife, no one will be able to touch you outright. No matter who I kill or what I do. You won't have to fear a fucker like Sevastyn ever again…" He frowns as if unconvinced of his own words, but the subtle tensing of his jaw reveals that he's already made up his mind. "I would like your permission," he adds, clenching his hands so tightly the knuckles crack in unison. "But don't presume I need it. If need be, I can drag you to the altar."

"Really?" I feel hot. My body reacts to the warning, tensing up. Unease thickens my throat. All I can choke out is a stupid, pathetic question. "Is that what you really want?"

"No," he confesses—and for what it's worth, I believe that he means it.

Regardless, I can't take my eyes off his ring. Like magic, it morphs, becoming a ball and chain, making my hand impossible to lift.

"Don't forget that you've already accepted this," he points out. "You've accepted me. And yet there it is. Those eyes —" He glowers at me from over his shoulder. "Always so fucking surprised. I kill a man, and you strip yourself naked to assist me with the mess. Only to pretend that you have no idea what staying by my side at all *means.* Have we really come back to this?" He sounds so empty. Maybe because those are the exact words I asked myself last night.

Which brings this whole conversation to a morbid full circle.

Unsure of the answer, I meet his gaze and shiver at the secrets I find lurking inside it. Going off of my experience when he's angry, he should frown, or flash that disapproving glare I've grown accustomed to. Anything but tilt his head away from me, disguising any potential reaction I could decipher.

"Tonight." Turning on his heel, he starts for the foyer, flexing his arms to adjust his suit jacket. One of his hands brushes his collar, smoothing the lapel flat while he shoots me one last searching glance. "We will discuss this tonight. Everything. *After* you return from the fitting."

Even if I felt brave enough to, he doesn't give me the chance to argue. With his back stick-straight, he marches to the front of the suite. A second later, I hear the door slam.

And I'm alone.

Our impending discussion doesn't include the potential of whether or not I'll need a dress—the matter has already been decided. Like always, some aspects of Maxim Koslov are nonnegotiable—what he wants, he gets. Within seconds of him leaving, his trusted henchman is already knocking on the door.

"Ms. Marconi," Lucius greets me with a small smile. "I will allow you to get dressed, and then we can be on our way."

After a quick shower in a luxurious bathroom off the master suite, I change into a simple black dress and join Lucius in the car.

Minutes later, we reach our destination.

"I'll be waiting whenever you're ready, Ms. Marconi," Lucius announces from the driver's seat. He eyes the building straight across from where we're parked. It's simple, made of brick, positioned between some of the more upscale buildings in the affluent part of the city. Places I used to only glimpse in magazines.

My heart pounds as I exit the car and cross the busy street, bustling with the height of afternoon traffic. Trust Maxim to pick such a place—exclusive and excluded, yet unabashedly public.

Through a pair of gleaming black doors, I find an interior of dark walls and plush carpet. A woman comes to greet me from around a wooden podium, her outfit a crisply tailored black. "You must be Francesca," she says, clasping one of my hands. "This way."

She leads me into a wide, open area displaying a rack of fabric along one wall and a row of mirrors along the other. My reflection taunts me from them—an army of pale, wide-eyed figures gaping as the world shifts around them.

"Mr. Koslov had a list of requirements sent over," she explains while fishing a slim black notebook from an apron slung around her waist.

"Requirements?" I sound surprised, but deep down, I'm not. Maxim leave something as personal as a wedding dress up to me? Never. Like everything else in his life, he seems to have it planned to the last meticulous detail.

"Oh yes," the woman gushes, oblivious to my confusion. "The designer can't wait to get started. We drooled over the sketches last night. Not many people opt for traditional gowns nowadays. And attempting a Russian style gown will be a unique challenge, especially."

She pauses expectantly, but all I can do is blink and force a smile.

"Yes…well…" Clearing her throat, the girl steers me before the wall of mirrors and withdraws a tape measure from another apron pocket. "Today, I will just get your preliminary measurements. You don't have to lift a single finger. Shall we begin?"

Eyeing my reflection, I nod. The girl in the glass glares at me, her gaze revealing everything I'm too chicken to say out loud. *Don't be stupid. You're not really surprised, are you? Emotion has nothing to do with it.*

In Maxim Koslov's world, relationships are tethered to contracts. Sex is a primal release, no more intimate than breathing.

And marriage is a business transaction.

Nothing more.

HOURS LATER, and I'm still staring at my reflection—a stranger draped in yards of ivory lace. If I ever were to imagine myself wearing a wedding dress, I wouldn't pick white as the color.

It makes my skin look sallow, and my hair duller than usual. My curls are a frizzy cloud barely able to support the thin, sheer fabric thrown over them as a makeshift veil. Not to mention the dress itself.

Grander, Maxim claimed. Maybe his real meaning got lost in translation—extravagant. Swaths of silk and taffeta extend from my waist. It's the skeleton of a ballgown ripped from one of those princess movies Ainsley loves to watch.

The designer is crouched beside me, sticking pins into a massive skirt. She works efficiently, but one thing is clear—my input isn't needed. While I may be the one meant to wear it, this dress is a token in the same vein as my ring. Maxim has his own plan set into motion. I'm just a pawn being moved across the board.

"We're all done for today," the woman announces, rising to her feet. She swipes imaginary dust from her knees and then helps me remove the pieces of the dress. "Your next appointment is in a week. Mr. Koslov has already made the arrangements."

A week. The timeframe feels like an ominous deadline. One I'm keenly aware of as I exit the boutique and find a black car waiting for me. Before I can take a step toward the curb, a voice calls out.

"Mrs. Koslov? Mrs. Koslov!"

I turn to find the seamstress racing from the boutique, a white piece of paper clenched in her fist, and a shopping bag dangling from her opposite hand. Even as she rushes toward me, I can't bite back the instinctive need to correct her. "I'm not—"

"Here," she insists, shoving the items into my hands. "Mr. Koslov wanted me to pass this message along, along with this dress. Have a nice day."

I stare after her, my heart racing, my throat dry. Inside the shopping bag is a white box tied with a black ribbon. A building sense of dread churns in my stomach as I shove my hand between the edges of the box, just enough to catch a swath of dark fabric inside, nestled within tissue paper. Whatever it's meant for, I doubt it's intended for the wedding. Something less formal, then? Like another meeting with Anatoli…

My grip tightens, and it takes everything I have not to drop the bag onto the sidewalk. The note, however, turns out to be relatively simple once I unfurl it with trembling fingers. *You're shaking now,* he wrote, and the back of my neck prickles with awareness. A glance over my shoulder reveals that no one is there—but I sense the extent of his control, nonetheless. Especially as I read the next written line. *But get accustomed to how it sounds, Mrs. Koslov.*

"Ms. Marconi?" I look up to find Lucius watching me from beside the car. "Are you alright?"

"Y-Yes." I stagger the rest of the way toward him. "I'm fine."

"Good. We have a few moments to spare before Mr. Koslov suggested you return. In the meantime, I can take you by your family's home," he suggests while ushering me into the backseat. "I know that Ainsley, for one, can't wait to see you." A rare grin tugs at his mouth, and I force a smile in response.

"It feels like ages since I've been home," I admit.

Ages since I've had to clean up decapitated Barbie dolls or break up fistfights. Since I've had to confront my family and lie to their faces.

And it feels like it's been even longer since I've had a say in my own wardrobe. The item within the box turns out to be a dress after all—black velvet with a high, modest collar. The kind of outfit someone might dress his supposed fiancée in while parading her before a man who raised a family of monsters and murderers.

"Ms. Marconi?" Lucius asks. "Was that a yes?"

"Y-Yes! Thank you. That would be great." I look down, and my gaze drifts from the black dress to my ring. My ears are still ringing with two ominous words. *Mrs. Koslov.* "I need to talk to them."

"That you do. But if I may make a suggestion…" Lucius eyes me in the rearview mirror, and a frown strains his normally professional expression. "Mr. Koslov can be insistent when it comes to his point of view, but if you are uneasy with the pace of current events, you must tell him."

"Uneasy?" I echo. Though it's no use feigning innocence when I can barely look at the item of clothing on my lap.

Lucius nods while effortlessly melding into the thick of traffic. "I saw your face just now, if I may be blunt. After the fitting. You seemed uncomfortable."

Shock paints my cheeks scarlet. "I... I..." I don't know what to say. "You aren't just talking about the dress," I finally croak. "Are you?"

"I'm afraid not." He clears his throat, and I sit forward in anticipation. Rarely does he reveal snippets of his secretive employer. I think the only other time was during one of our first meetings when he issued a warning—*my client has unusual tastes, Francesca.*

"I've been working for Mr. Koslov for over ten years," he continues. "I would like to think I know him better than most—so when I say that the effect you have on him has been...dramatic, to say the least, I hope you take my words at face value. And I hope I may take this time to impart a bit of advice."

I swallow hard, wringing my fingers together. The note caught between them is crumpled in the aftermath, made smaller and smaller the more I twist and pinch. "What do you mean?"

"While I may have known him for more than half of your life, I suspect that you know more of his past than I will ever learn. More than I care to know, if I'm being frank. He's not an easy man to work for, but he is a loyal and just employer. If he happens to have a few...quirks that may make him seem unapproachable to most, well, that is beyond my place to say. But everyone, no matter who they are, needs an outlet. A release. Someone." His tone deepens with unsaid meaning, and seconds pass without him saying another word. Then he sighs, and that single sound betrays just how old he really is. How exhausted he is. "A life devoid of that simple luxury, can make a man act out in ways he might regret. I am well aware of what happened last night," he adds, shocking me with how unperturbed he sounds at the prospect of murder. "It wasn't the first time he has called me to clean up such... lapses in judgment. Those calls have not stopped since you've been with him, either. But the nature of them has changed. He has changed. You may not notice it. And with everything you've been through, maybe you don't care to. That is your prerogative, to be fair. But..." He sighs again before confessing, "I feel like I sound a bit like a gossiping old woman, but I think you need to hear this. Heed this one piece of advice—be honest with yourself. Be honest with him. It may seem impossible now, but a man like him has built his entire life around rejection. You can trust he knows how to survive it. But deception?" He tilts his head, his brows furrowing. "*That* would inflict a wound I doubt even Mr. Koslov could come back from. And deception can be an innocent thing at first. One might not even realize that their intent is insidious at all. Lying to someone," he adds with a shrug. "Pretending to feel things that you do not—or even worse. Lying to yourself. Misrepresenting your emotions because you cannot face them. Take charge of them. You are too wracked by fear to take ownership of what you desire while understanding what it *truly* is at its core. Do you understand what I mean?"

Our gazes meet in the rearview mirror, and I nod once. A creeping, aching sensation spreads throughout my stomach. *Deception.* Is that what I've been doing?

"I don't want to hurt him," I admit, my voice hoarse.

"Of course, you don't." He sounds like he truly believes that. "But tell me something. A hunter comes across a wolf and learns to care for it. He feeds it. Nourishes it. And then he locks it in a small cage because it is a difficult thing to care for a wild creature. To understand the freedom it needs. To trust that it will always return to you. That hunter may admire its beauty, and its power, and its brutal strength. But how can he trust that such a creature won't turn on him? And the wolf, it cares for the hunter as well, you see. But even such a creature can sense the fear in the other. So it tries to deny its nature and pretend it enjoys its life within captivity. But instinct can only be ignored for so long… Until one day, the wolf lashes out from behind its bars, mortally wounding the hunter. And they both die, each never truly knowing the other."

"What are you saying?" The picture he painted is in my head, replaying in a morbid loop. *Death. Death. Death.*

"I'm saying that love is in trust," he warns. "*Not* fear. Though that was merely a silly story, of course. And you must recall that you're relationship with Mr. Koslov was built on a contract first and foremost. An understanding. From the outside, it might have appeared odd. Imbalanced, even. But was it?"

He waits long enough that the resulting silence demands an answer.

"No," I admit. "I could always walk away."

"And you still can," he warns. "I apologize for the aimless chatter. Nonetheless, I appreciate your time. We should be arriving shortly."

He refocuses his attention on the road, and his professional demeanor returns. In some ways, it feels like he's drawn an invisible curtain between us, cutting off my chance to reply.

Beg for more.

More snippets of a man who hoards his past so fucking jealously.

But I'm desperate enough to risk it, testing the bars of my own invisible cage. "What if, in your story…" I lick my lips, they're so fucking dry. My hands shake, and the crumpled note falls to the floor, bouncing beneath the driver's seat. "What makes you think the hunter loved the wolf?"

Seconds tick by, but he doesn't answer. Only the hum of the engine fills the silence between us—and my heartbeat. It beats faster. Harder. It's all I can hear. *Thump. Thump. Thump!*

Reaching out, I place my hand on the back of Lucius' seat. "Please—"

"A hunter's nature is to kill," he says softly. "*Something* in the wolf made him forsake that purpose, even for a second. Even if his following actions were misguided. Something in the wolf made him, for a moment, question his sole intent. It might not fit the average definition, but why, in his viewpoint, would the mere desire to spare that one wolf, not be worthy of being called love?"

I inhale raggedly, my mind buzzing. "Do you know what—"

A classical ringtone cuts me off, and Lucius fishes a cell phone from his pocket, answering it one-handed. "Sir? You mean... Understood." His jaw clenches, concern clouding his weathered features. "We're already on the way. Yes, sir."

He hangs up, and the car lurches forward as his speed noticeably increases.

"Is something wrong?" I ask, scrambling for my seatbelt.

He doesn't respond.

Within minutes, we reach the building housing the new suite. Lucius takes the dress and ushers me from the car, up to the penthouse. I follow him inside, but my footsteps falter before I truly process the scene before me.

Maxim's thunderous bellow reaches me first. "Find him *now*, Milton," he growls. "I want his fucking head on a platter... No! Don't lie to me. You've always pitied him, coming to his rescue. Little Dima. I *know* you're aware of where he is. Do you think Anatoli is cunning enough to plan this on his own? No. Someone is pulling his strings —don't talk to me about strategy!"

He stands in the large sitting room off the foyer hunched over a black end table, a cell phone held to his ear. His posture alone sets every nerve in my body on high alert. He's trembling, his fingers grasping the edge of the table so tightly it rocks on its axis.

"Find him! I want a location by tonight—you owe me this. But it might be too late, even then. They all know it by now. They'll be coming for her. *Fuck!*" Hissing in rage, he rips the cell phone from his ear and throws it across the room.

I take an instinctive step behind Lucius before I even think to focus on what might be the source of his rage. On the table before him lies a square-shaped object I can't make out at first. It's gray, made of metal. A briefcase?

As Lucius continues to advance, Maxim looks up and his eyes... I don't even think he sees us at first. Just phantoms from a nightmare he can't seem to wake up from.

"Sir," Lucius calls to him, his tone level. I can tell from his careful stance that the words he spoke in the car weren't bravado. He's used to dealing with Maxim in this state—a caged, feral wolf. For one, he wisely keeps his distance. "Can I be of any assistance?"

"Lucius." Maxim blinks and refocuses his attention on the older man. "*This* was delivered to one of my offices," he hisses, gesturing to the case. "It came from Anatoli himself. It seems the bastard couldn't wait for me to come to him. I'm sure you know what it means."

"I believe so, sir." Lucius' jaw clenches in recognition. "I'll review any breach in security immediately. As for this. I can remove it—"

"Like it would do any fucking good. Leave," Maxim demands. "But you—" He turns to me. "You stay."

"As you wish, Sir. I'll make adjustments to your security immediately."

"The house first," Maxim snarls. "They may start there."

"Of course. I'll double the detail." With a wary glance in my direction, Lucius retreats from the suite. In his absence descends a silence so heavy it's suffocating.

"What's going on?" I manage to rasp. *House.* That word won't leave my fucking brain. The only one I know of him owning just so happens to house my entire family.

As I watch, Maxim braces his hands on the table, his expression like thunder. Slowly, he nudges the case, tracing the corner of the lid with his thumb. Then he lifts it, revealing a sliver of plain, gray material and a flash of red. That's all I see before he slams the lid shut. His eyes cut to mine, and I swear my heart stops beating.

It's like my entire body can't function again until he turns away, his shoulders hunched, hands curling into fists. "I changed my mind," he snaps. "Go! I need to be alone."

I flinch toward the door without actually taking a step. The tormented figure who devised the phrase "hot and cold" had to have Maxim Koslov in mind. In some moments, his apparent need for me burns so fucking hot, I can pretend it means more than lust. More than a sadistic whim. But then his gaze can go so cold. Like now.

And it's like I don't even exist.

Lucius referred to a wolf and a cage—but the analogy he should have used was that of a doll and a child who can't decide if he wants to play with it or smash it to pieces.

"Is something wrong?" I ask, taking a cautious step toward him. "What happened—"

"You got your wish," he says, his mouth twisted in a cruel sneer. "There won't be a fucking wedding. So smile. You can remain as nothing more than my whore. What?" He cocks his head as I stiffen. "That's what you wanted, isn't it? Well, now you have an excuse to turn tail and run. Though, I suggest you don't go too fucking far."

He's right. Hurt pride could drive me away from him now. Make me run. It's what he expects.

And it dawns on me that it's exactly what he *wants*.

"What's wrong?" I ask instead. The strength in my voice surprises me almost as much as it seems to surprise him. "You let me go to the fitting," I point out. "So whatever changed, it had to happen—"

"I said leave." He shifts onto the balls of his feet, ready to storm away himself.

"Talk to me," I beg, switching tact. "If something is wrong… If my family is in danger, I need to know. Just talk to me."

"*Now*, you want to talk." He strokes his chin with one hand while the other tears through his hair. "Are you sure you don't want to tremble and stare and cower? Like you don't know *who* I am…"

This is about more than a mysterious case or a phone call.

Images from last night flood my brain in ominous snippets. How easy it is to lose him to anger, contrasted with the only method capable of bringing him back. In some ways, Lucius' words feel more like a warning now than a comfort—*you've changed him.*

But not for the better.

"Tell me what's wrong." Before he can reply, I approach the table containing the case. My rebellious fingers brush the metal surface, and his reaction makes me suspect that I'm not the source of his unease after all. "What does it mean?"

"You want to know?" Finally, he faces me, devoid of any expression whatsoever. No hate. No anger. No mercy either. "Open it."

An ominous thrill shoots down the fingers I use to pry the ends of the case apart. As the lid rises, I hold my breath…

Only to release it in a puzzled exhale. The inside of the box is lined with gray velvet, betraying a formal purpose, but all it contains is a single strip of blood-red fabric. Confusion displaces some of my fear. Enough that I can eye the item objectively. It's silk, cool to the touch, and deceptively luxurious.

I flip it over and notice a design embroidered on the other side in a slightly darker shade of scarlet—an intricate series of conjoined circles resembling a cross.

"What is it?" I ask. A scrap slightly too small to be a handkerchief or anything useful from what I can tell. Almost like a sample swatch, one might use to order a couch or carpet. Or a dress. I look up at Maxim only to find him watching me. But the look on his face now…

His eyes are black holes constricting even darker pupils.

"*That* is a death sentence," he says. "*Krasnyy konets*, the 'red ending.' An old archaic tradition, but one still alive and well in certain circles. Within families. My family." He extends his palm—a silent command for me to relinquish the cloth. When I do, he eyes it with an expression that makes every hair on the back of my neck stand up. I've only witnessed him deploy that glare at his uncle.

Or his grandfather.

"This is a mere symbolic token. At its core, the purpose is to signify a bounty. An insurmountable one, no amount of money, can outweigh." He forms a fist, crushing the fabric within it. "And it should have come for *me*. I was expecting it. He should have… No one would confront *me* out in the open, blood price or not."

I swallow hard, eyeing the case again. From what little I know of his family, I sense grand displays of murderous threats are nothing new. But this… This is different. It's evident in Maxim's hostile posture. The rage spilling from his eyes, barely contained by his obsessive restraint.

He's more than angry. I think…

I think he's terrified.

"What does that mean?"

"It came for *you*. And the bastard doesn't truly want you dead. Oh no…" He exhales a growled chuckle and turns, lumbering toward the far corner of the room. A virgin section of the white wall draws his notice, and he braces his hand against it. Then he forms a fist and strikes the surface, so hard cracks appear in a spidery web. Lashing out a second time, he shouts in a way I've never heard. A howl. A hiss. A broken, maniacal laugh all in one.

His following sigh resonates like the first raindrops falling in a breaking storm. One I'm naked in the face of. My only course of action is to brace at the mercy of the tempest.

And pray, I survive it.

"If it came for me, I could resist him. Fight him," he explains. "He would be declaring war, and no one would get in my fucking way if I went for his throat. I could rip him apart at my own fucking discretion, and not even God could say a damn thing." He laughs again, his body locked in the violent pose, his knuckles trembling against the wall's surface. "But now? He doesn't have to kill you. He doesn't even have to lift a finger. You're already as good as dead. So much for my protection. I couldn't even fucking outsmart him."

He turns, crossing the room in an instant. I don't even have the sense of mind to run.

"No one will acknowledge you," he snarls, snatching my wrist, his focus honing on my ring. "No one will accept you. With this, you will never be a Koslov, and I couldn't even avenge you."

He rips the ring from my finger and throws it so hard it ricochets across the room, its progress tracked by faint musical pings.

"So much for a fucking wedding," he growls amid another unstable bit of laughter. "In my world, you no longer exist."

Fear weighs me down, almost too powerful to overcome. Inhaling shallowly is the only way to combat it. One deep, slow breath right after the other.

Until eventually, words form, escaping my throat before I even register them. "What are you saying?"

"I'm saying that there is no point in a wedding," he hisses. "No point in a ring. No point in a fucking engagement.

Everything my name could give you means nothing now. Anatoli has won. The only thing I can do now is keep you from being killed."

He stalks toward the door, creating a noise comparable to thunder. The force of his rage strains the entire room at its seams, too wild to be contained. A part of me fears the windows might explode beneath the pressure.

Or I might.

"Is that the only reason why?" My voice echoes back to me before I realize I've spoken at all. My words play amid an eerie backdrop of silence as Maxim freezes.

"What did you say?" he demands.

"I…" Instinct warns me to run. Back down. I lick my lips tentatively, but something won't keep me silent. I break. "Is that why you wanted to marry me? Power?"

"No. For *security*. Why else?" he counters, driving that point home. "With my name, no one could touch you. Is there any value in a ring more than that certainty? Tell me you're not so sentimental."

His steps reverberate through the floor, advancing toward me. I couldn't escape him, even if I tried. My body jolts as he touches me. One brush of his finger feels comparable to a hot poker jabbing against the chilled flesh of my throat.

But it's not the sort of pain I've come to associate him with. Whippings, biting, and beatings feel nothing like this—emotions utilized more ruthlessly than any knife. *Is there any value in a ring?*

"You would always be protected as my wife," he says, tightening his grip so that I'm forced to face him. "But now, a few vows will change nothing. As much as I loathe the motherfucker, I can't go against Anatoli on my own—and married to me or not, nothing would change as far as my family is concerned. If anything, they will make a game out of trying to use you against me. And Sevastyn... He was the tamest among them."

I cringe at what that implies. A family of people more evil than a child abuser. People so ruthless even Maxim seems shaken at the prospect of them coming for me. And yet a family he seems desperate to make me a part of. A name he cherishes above all else.

"So, the ring means nothing?" I reiterate.

He inhales as his fingers twitch against my throat. "You're upset." He sounds more confused than alarmed by that realization. "I don't understand why..."

"I'm not upset," I clarify. I've been touching my ring finger as I spoke, something I only realize as I look down and observe the pale naked flesh. "It's just a lot to take in." My ragged laugh proves that I'm not lying. I sound fucking insane. Manic. "First, you want to marry me. Then you don't—"

"And you ask why?" He starts for the door again. "What use is a fucking worthless token without the power it conveys?"

I don't know why I follow him, no match for his ruthless pace.

"So, what happens now?" I ask, watching the muscles in his body coil as his hands curl in and out of fists.

"Now? I need to get you somewhere safe." The callous phrasing conveys a million different meanings. Somewhere safe. Away. Out of his hair. Like a nuisance fly, he has to trap in a jar just to keep it from getting smashed.

"Where?" My brain spins with the possibilities. Somewhere out of the city? The country? "What about my family—"

"They'll be fine. I'm already moving them to a new location. But I… I need to think this through. Alone."

I flinch at the barely concealed warning. Everything about him broadcasts a blazing, ominous warning. *Run. Retreat. Let him brood and rage in peace.*

"I want you to tell me something," I croak instead, still frozen in place. "If this never happened. If what you think your ring means was still the same, what would change?"

"What?" He scoffs. "You would be protected."

"But nothing else?" I don't know why I'm probing him at all. Where I'm going with this line of questioning. What drives me to ask next, "So you would continue to make decisions for me without including me?"

Despite all the appearance of power and security, as his wife, I would be powerless. An animal in a cage like the one depicted in Lucius' story.

"I don't know what you expected from me." He sounds so damn tired. If the threads of his control were visible chains, I can imagine them straining. Cracking. Breaking.

"Our first contract was always prefaced on the understanding that I could always walk away," I say. It sounds so strange to recall that fact after weeks of being at his virtual beck and call, under his mercy always. But Lucius was right. "You laid out the risks and the benefits. You gave me a choice. I could leave if I wanted to—"

"Is that what you want now?" The hollowness of his tone sucks any warmth from the room. I'm shivering. "To leave me?"

"No." I start toward him only to falter paces away. He's still within my reach though, a raging shadow in the waning daylight, but my fingers twitch uselessly at my sides. His anger radiates, forming an invisible barrier too dangerous to breach.

"Then what are you saying?" he demands.

"I'm saying that what we had before is the kind of security I need now." Even if I don't know why. "I want to know the risks if my life is in danger. I want you to explain. I want a…choice."

"Choice?" He whirls on me. "Your only choice is to stay with me or die. The bounty is on your head regardless. I cannot fix this."

And that lack of control is consuming him like nothing else. I've never seen him so resigned. Except maybe once before in the face of his uncle.

Before he beat him to death with his bare hands.

"I want to stay with you," I admit, marveling at the contrast between my voice and his. I should be the one straining, my words faltering. I should be the one trembling beneath the sheer insanity of my fate.

Slowly, I reach out and settle my hand against his forearm. He stiffens as if his first instinct is to shrug me off. I can physically feel the jolt of muscle tensing and then relaxing.

"Talk to me," I beg. "Tell me the risks. I want that choice."

A sound resonates low in his chest. Another laugh? I can't tell as he inclines his head without looking in my direction. "You want that choice? Well, here it is. Anatoli ensured that I can never give you the safety I want for you. Even if I kill him, the fucking mark stands. You will never be seen as a Koslov by the people who matter. To them? You will always be a fucking whore."

And that bothers him. More than he will admit out loud. So much is simmering beneath his surface fury, boiling over in ways he can no longer control. I suck in a breath as he faces me directly and brings his hand to my cheek, tilting my face for his inspection.

"I want more for you than that," he swears, brushing his thumb against the corner of my mouth. "But first, I will get you and your family somewhere safe. Then I will reach out to some contacts in my network. If Anatoli wants to play this game, then we will play. Though nothing I do will really matter in the end. The family won't move against him. Fuck!" The tension drains from him as I watch, and his lips part into a terrifying grin. "He's won this round, I will give him that. To challenge him, I would need another Koslov. I would need…"

His fingers snatch at his chin, stroking the stubble there as he thinks. "I would need an ally who is blood. But would he… No—" He shakes his head, breaking off whatever thought he may have had. "I will make the arrangements for you to leave within the week. It's safer, the less you know."

"Safe?" Again, I barely recognize the woman speaking. Her voice doesn't tremble or falter. Each clear tone resonates as strongly as his does. "I trust you," I race to clarify before he can reply. "I do. I don't even know why I do. But I can't live my life being treated like… Even when I first came to you, you forced me to become a player in your game. You didn't leave me in the dark like this."

"Didn't I?" A wicked, soulless smile shapes his mouth as he balances my chin on the palm of his hand. "Don't fool yourself, little kitten. You were always a pawn."

"Or a bullet," I croak, shocked that I'm challenging him at all. "We were always playing Russian Roulette."

He frowns at the comparison. Against me, his fingers twitch, part caress. Part lashing, his nails nipping deep. "And yet you still want to play?" he wonders.

"I could… If you tell me what you want from me." I try my best to meet his stormy gaze without flinching. Maybe I succeed because he doesn't hiss in disgust. For a second, I can glimpse a hint of the turmoil lurking beneath those dark irises. The pain. The frustration.

"What I want?" He shakes his head as a growl rips from his throat. Within a heartbeat, his entire posture changes. It's like watching a chain on a raging, barking dog snap. He's loose, barreling off in a random direction.

A thunderous sound echoes as he strikes the wall again. Again. Red streaks paint the surface when he withdraws, and the same liquid coats his knuckles, dripping onto the floor. Blood.

"I want to rip that bastard limb from limb. Can you give me that?" he demands. "Can you? I want to set his entire fucking empire on fire and force him to watch it burn. I want the power to destroy him! Can you give me that?"

"No," I admit hoarsely. I sound like myself again, but when I approach him, I don't hesitate to reach out, brushing his forearm. "I can't. But I can give you something else."

"Like what?" he snaps.

Lucius, in his own quiet way, gave me the answer.

"Control," I say softly. "A release. You don't have to keep this in—"

"Release." His gaze cuts to me as calculating as a predator observing fresh, bleeding prey. "You want me to hurt you, little *kotyonok?*" His bloodied knuckles boldly brush my cheek, daring me to flinch. "I'm more than capable of doing so. You want to get off on my anger and then run like you didn't enjoy every fucking second of it? Maybe that is why you stay—"

"No." I reach up and settle my fingers over his scarred, bloodied ones. They twitch at the indignation of being trapped against my skin—but he doesn't pull away. "I want to give you what you need."

"Sex?" His accent thickens over that single word, stressing its pronunciation. Like that, he gives it another connotation that triggers an answering shiver through my entire body. *Pain.* "You think that's what I need? That I won't hurt you? Do you think that in this moment, if you beg me to stop that I will?"

I take in his unfocused, wild stare and manic grin. A part of me whispers in horror, *No. He won't stop. He'll go too far again. He's insane. He'll more than hurt me. He'll kill me.*

For an instant, I'm in that cold, terrifying room with the plastic tarp all over again, watching him brandish a knife, knowing that he's too far gone to reach. He's nearly as unhinged now as he was then.

Do I trust him anyway?

"Yes." I swallow hard and meet his gaze unflinchingly. "I know you will."

His eyes narrow, displacing some of the anger with... shock? I can't be certain because he snatches my jaw the next second, dragging me to him. He slams his mouth to mine, claiming my lips with devastating blows from his tongue. Sharp, his teeth sink into my bottom lip, making me jump. In retaliation, I grip his forearms, sensing the power coiled in every single muscle.

But the balance of power is his to claim this time. To do so, he shoves me back, tearing at my dress in the same ruthless movement.

"There have been things I've wanted to do to you," he chokes out, grasping at any part of me he can reach. My breasts. Hips. Hair. His fingers claw at each additional piece of me, using them as a leash to yank me toward him. Harshly. Harder. Viciously.

"I've thought about it," he adds, finding my ear. His teeth skewer the lobe, sowing another sharp burst of pain, scattering my senses further. "I'll do it now."

He backs away and grips my shoulders. A taste of his strength forces me down to my knees before him. I'm stunned by the shift in position, still struggling to keep up.

But knocking me off balance is his favorite part of the game.

"Stay," he growls, turning on his heel. My heart stutters as I watch him follow the hall to the master suite. I ignore the devious suspicions running across my brain, taunting me with what he could be getting. Seconds later, he returns with something dangling from his right hand. Not a whip or a knife. This is something different. Long and heavy, it drags along the marble floor in his wake.

A rope? No. Craning my neck, I can make out gleaming links of metal forming a slender, but still substantial chain. Alarm prickles through my belly. Only God knows where he had it hidden up until now.

"Up," he commands, bending his fingers in a curt motion. "Look at me."

I look up, desperately hunting his expression for any sign of…something. Malice? Rage? His mouth flattens into a firm, cold line, withholding any hint of his intentions from me.

Slowly, I shift on my knees, wincing as my weight bears down against the hard, unyielding marble. The icy cool contrasts with the heat sweltering beneath my skin, growing hotter, the more my brain scrambles to reconcile his aim with the length of chain.

With one hand, he sweeps the hair from my face and cradles my throat. His thumb caresses my quivering windpipe. It would be so easy for him to crush it. Break me. He strokes me instead, tracing a path from my collar down to my left breast.

A gasp escapes me as he teases the aching peak with the tip of his nail, coaxing the flesh to stiffen. He's gentler than he's ever been—even as his eyes bore into me ruthlessly. My back arches, my body heating to his touch. I can't deny the reaction he inspires within me—burning, vicious need. Aware of his effect on me, he nods, a satisfied hum reverberating through his chest.

Without warning, he crouches and grips one end of the chain. I only make out something small and silver attached to the end of it before he brings it to my breast. To tease me, like he did once with ice?

No. Fire sears through my nipple so intense I cry out, jerking back. I don't even go an inch before his opposite hand snatches a fistful of my hair, locking me in place.

"Don't." The low, dangerous rasp in his voice, spurs my heartbeat into a frantic rhythm. "Don't move. Don't look down—" He captures my chin, smoothing his fingers against the flesh. "You look at me."

Him. A man so alarmingly on-edge that his body sways with every breath. Alight, his eyes lazily dip lower, relishing in the freedom he's denied me. Whatever he sees makes him groan, biting his lip between clenched teeth.

"You are so beautiful," he praises thickly. "Like this. Red. Swollen. Bitten…" He drags his thumb over the stinging wound in my lip, left by his teeth. "Mine."

My body radiates with tension as he reaches down, lifting the chain in his fist. *Fuck.* My eyelids flutter. I feel every twitch in every goddamn link. Through my nipple, down my spine, into my core. Slick with moisture, my inner thighs rub together as my cheeks catch fire. I've never felt… *Ever.* My thoughts dissipate as my breaths feather. Already I'm drugged on this pain.

"You enjoy even this," he remarks, sounding smug. "Fuck, I knew you would. But stay with me, *kotyonok*—" He tugs again…harder. "We aren't done yet."

A whine tears from my throat, high-pitched, and broken. I can't think. His face is my only anchor to sanity. In a beautiful display of flesh and bone, he eyes me reverently, his lips parted, eyes wide and unfocused.

"You can take this for me," he suspects. "You will. So good…"

He doesn't sound angry anymore, but a part of me clenches in anticipation of the emotion that replaces it. Hunger. Excitement. Lust.

His nostrils flare as he fingers the chain again, keeping it raised within my line of sight. Each deliberate caress roils through me, raising goosebumps over my sweat-misted skin. The reaction must cement some dark suspicion of his because he nods. "You can handle more."

Handle… Can I? He doesn't give me a chance to decide. The chain rustles, tugging…pulling. I grit my teeth, hissing out a breath. I don't register what he's done until it's too late.

He lifts the chain higher, displaying it curved around his finger, held taut at *both* ends. And an inferno rips through my body. My head swims, my heart pounding madly. I can taste my pulse in my fucking throat, hammering through each nipple. He did something to them. *Clamped them,* I realize as my eyes rebel against his command, glancing down. Metal beads surround both peaks, crushing them into tiny points.

And the resulting sensation intoxicates me.

"I warned you." Maxim tugs a fraction harder. I whimper, digging my nails into my hips—it's the only way to stop myself from reaching for the chain. Tugging it back. Tugging it more. God, I can't think.

"Do you want me to stop?" he wonders. How his voice cuts through my broken, splintered brain? I'll never know.

"Yes…" I croak, but just as quickly, I stammer, "N-No…"

He winds the chain between two fingers, and I go rigid, shaking my head frantically.

"No! No!"

"You want it." He tugs so hard my body lurches across the marble. As if from far away, I hear a scream echo off the walls, nearly drowned out by my own hammering heartbeat. The next thing I know, I'm quivering in a ball, my head resting against a thick, hard thigh propped beneath it. Soothing and tender, warm fingers run through my hair as a deep voice offers endless praise.

"So good for me. Always so good… More than I wanted —always more I want to do to you. But fuck you make me…"

Crazy. In the same way, he makes me mindless. His words dissolve into meaningless grunts as he slides his hand between my legs, hissing at what he finds.

Soaking, aching flesh—his to claim. His to take.

He has me in his arms within seconds, moving too quickly for me to process his next actions in order. We're racing down the hall. Then crashing inside the bedroom. I've barely regained my senses when I land on the bed face down as his weight slams against my back.

Panic sets in before I can smother it. He's crushing me. But then his fingers sink into my hair, grasping a fistful that he uses to wrench my head back, allowing me to suck in air as he nudges my legs apart. I quake from head to fucking toe, assaulted by too many sensations at once to pinpoint them individually. His weight. His skin rasping over mine. The pull of the chain swaying against my chest, enhancing every single fucking movement to an agonizing degree.

And finally, his cock rips into me, demolishing every other feeling like a wrecking ball.

My eyelids flutter as I focus solely on breathing, allowing my body to adjust to his size. *Massive.* He thrusts in hard without restraint, hissing out his pleasure. Jolted by every bucking motion of his hips, I wind up lying on parts of the chain, straining others, and I lose track of the sounds I make. My throat aches, throbbing and raw as he grips my hips, fucking me in earnest.

If I were a normal lover, he would hurt me, there is no question. But his voice drips into my ear, an awed growl, revealing the difference that makes me just as deranged as he is. "So wet for me." He inhales sharply and then groans with another brutal thrust. "Always so wet for me."

His mouth finds my ear, nipping at the lobe as his mangled, grunted words punctuate the movement of our bodies. "You know what I need, don't you? You give it to me. You take me… Fuck! You aim to tame me…"

I close my eyes, savoring the violent contrast of gnashing teeth, and broken groans, and sweat as his body ruthlessly claims mine. The sex isn't about pleasure—I know that. I'm climaxing anyway, biting a mouthful of sheets to silence my cries as every muscle goes taut. I see stars, speckling my vision as he grunts, slamming inside me one final time.

His release is that in every sense of the word. The tension leaves him as he collapses beside me. His fingers remain in my hair, preventing me from facing him. The heat and sweat of his body assault me in an overwhelming barrage as his mouth finds my shoulder, his teeth teasing the flesh.

"You can fuck me like this," he says, almost amused despite the growl reverberating in my skin. "Let me use you any way I fucking want—" His finger slips beneath me, teasing a length of the chain just enough to make me shudder. "But if I offer you more, you hesitate. And yet when I refuse to give you an empty fucking vow…you challenge me."

I'm too exhausted to move, awed by his tone—part sated lust, part smoldering fury.

"Do you want me to marry you?" he wonders musingly. "Or collar you? State your preference now, so I know whether to offer you a ring or a leash. Say it. No?" He chuckles while I pant, too breathless to reply. "I'll tell you what it is you crave. Ignorance. For years you wore yourself down caring for your siblings. They've drained you—so you chase any vice you can find to take the pain of it all away. To let the world crush you rather than spend your energy carrying the weight of it on your shoulders. I make it easy for you." His lips brush my shoulder, a mocking kiss. "Don't I? You question my intentions for marrying you, but I have no doubts as to what I want. But what is it *you* want from me? Tell me what happened at the club was a lie."

Was it? The other day feels like another lifetime now—coming to him of my own volition. Promising complete and total surrender. Have I been lying all along like Lucius insinuated?

"No," I admit, uttering the truth as much to myself as to him. "I meant it."

"So perhaps it isn't fear then," he suspects with a puzzled grunt. "Tell me what you want from this, if protection isn't good enough to tempt you."

"I want..." Not for the first time, I don't even recognize the sound of my own voice. This new, braver stranger must have been born in the aftermath of Sevastyn's death —like watching the whole gory affair killed something inside of me as well. Or awoke something. Something so deviant it thrills at the agony only he can arouse within my body. "I want clarity," I tell him. "About everything."

Everything I can discover about Maxim Koslov and what makes him tick—and not out of mere curiosity either. Maybe because his anger matches mine—the horrific magnification of the twisted shit I never faced within myself before him. The flaws only he has ever called me out on.

The selfishness.

The self-hatred.

The blind, consuming rage.

I could be the world's most pathetic masochist, thriving off the manifestations of my own internal bullshit. But I'd be lying to myself if I accept that explanation—the easy solution to what exactly draws me to him.

Because even now, I'm not really afraid. My heart may be racing, palms sweating, and my entire body tense on red alert. But deep down, the real name to call this emotion by could be...excitement. Guilt. Jealousy.

As long as he feels the twisted, dark shit festering beneath the surface of his soul...

I don't have to face my own.

"Clarity, how? Answer me." He grips my chin, forcing me to meet his gaze, but there's no real strength in the contact. He merely eyes me as if I'm a mirror, utilized the same way I might be using him.

Is there any true connection mingled within it all?

I want to say no. But my heart pounds against my ribs, hammering out a silent answer—*liar, liar, liar.*

"Marriage is status to you. But…" I lick my lower lip, tasting my answer before I have the strength to utter it out loud. "I don't even know what it is to me. My mother didn't exactly model healthy relationships."

Though what does that say about not only me? Daisy, Mikie, and the others have never known stability either. A loving mother is a foreign concept in our world, let alone a father.

"You value your name, but I value my family. I don't want to make the same mistakes Melanie did."

And what little I know of marriage comes right from her playbook. Melanie had been married at least four or five times. Hell, to be honest, I've lost count. In her view, being a wife was nothing more than a fashionable accessory. A game. A way to chase off boredom.

But I've never even had a serious boyfriend. I've had partners. Clients. Johns.

I've had Maxim.

Only one of those options has lasted longer than a handful of hours at a time.

"Deep, down, I always told myself that I never wanted more," I confess. "That life was enough. Scraping by and depending only on myself was enough. I don't know anything else."

"But I can teach you, little *kotyonok*," he finally says, satisfied by my answer. "There is so much I have yet to teach you."

He nudges me onto my side, tracing my sore nipple with the tip of his thumb. In one swift motion, he releases the clamp, and my head swims.

"Holy shit!" I nearly crawl off the fucking bed to escape the unbearable sting—he has to press on my hip just to keep me in place.

"It will hurt," he warns, soothing the abused flesh as blood rushes back to the area. "I think you might enjoy this more than a whipping." He spares a glance at my trembling knees, fighting to stay together. "Next time, I will..."

He trails off, letting my twisted imagination fill in the gap.

A whine breaks from me as he releases the second clamp, but then his hands settle over my hips, drawing me into him.

"I can show you the lengths a man will go to in order to prove his claim to the entire fucking world," he swears. "But I won't call you my wife without the power that title deserves. I won't." He drags his fingers along the side of my face, down to my throat. "So if you want it…then fight *with* me for it."

"How?"

"There is someone I could use as an ally," he admits, and I marvel at the change in his tone. Gone is the bitter anger. He's the composed, calculating game master again. One with a new strategy in mind. "Finding him will be difficult," he adds. "But if you want a partnership? Then come with me when I eventually do track him down."

"Really?"

"Yes." I shiver as his fingers soothe my burning scalp, replacing the violent tugging with a rare, addicting softness. "He would never agree to meet me alone. And you… You will fascinate him." A growl mangles the words, making them anything but a compliment.

His touch turns possessive as his nails nip at my flesh in a silent warning. *You're mine.*

"Who is he?"

All at once, he withdraws from me and leaves the bed altogether. His footsteps retreat toward the doorway, but I know better than to chase him this time. I merely roll over and watch him go, his body dominating the door as growing darkness shrouds the room in shadow. Near the threshold of the hallway, he hesitates.

"He… He is someone I mistrust even more than Anatoli. And he is the only other bastard crazy enough to stand against him."

He enters the hall, and his echoing steps track his progress throughout the suite—but he never leaves.

And I don't sleep. I just coexist in a silent dwelling that I know he still occupies, fuming in some distant corner. I can smell him. Sense him. It's like my body stays attuned to his presence even if he isn't in the same fucking room.

I'm draped in invisible chains this time, tugged and twisted at his discretion.

And right now, he is twisting hard.

CHAPTER FIVE

For what feels like hours, all I can do is lie still, listening to the cadence of his footsteps echo. He's pacing. It isn't long before his voice reaches back to me, though directed at someone else.

"You found him?" he demands. "I knew it! Where? Don't bullshit me, Milton, your men are more accurate than that. No, I won't kill him. Yet. And why even ask? Don't tell me that after all this time you still harbor some ounce of pity for the son of a bitch? I didn't think you were so sentimental. You were children then, after all…"

He must hang up. After a few minutes of silence, heavy footsteps fill the absence in the wake of his baritone, advancing slowly in my direction. He takes his time, lingering in the hallway, just beyond the door. He's testing me, I think. Knowing I'm awake but wanting to draw out the tension and extend every last second of brutal anticipation.

Unchecked, my pulse flutters beneath my skin, each frantic beat counting the seconds down. *Thump. Thump. Thump…*

"Your family is safe," he finally says. "They're in a property outside of the city. I'll take you to them in the morning. Together, you will be moved to a more secure location."

I sit upright, still draped beneath the bedsheets. The darkness shrouds him well. I have to strain my eyes before I spot him leaning against the wall, his arms crossed. "Thank you."

"But tonight…" He shifts, and I sense him mulling over his next words, debating uttering them at all. "I have a lead," is all he says. "Come with me if you want—"

"Where?" I'm already scrambling to my feet.

"Get dressed. Meet me downstairs within ten minutes. Or not. You have a *choice*."

I flinch, recognizing my own plea being thrown back in my face. Still, I can overlook the jab in favor of the larger prize.

Answers.

For once, tangible, real answers.

What kind of man might someone like Maxim Koslov seek out for help against his grandfather? How does this figure tie into his past? My brain spins with a million potential possibilities as I race into the closet and tug on a dress at random. It's too tight. My nipples throb, forcing me to switch to one with a looser neckline. When I finally join Maxim in the garage, I'm panting.

He, however, sits calmly in the back seat of his car while a dutiful driver claims the wheel. The door on my end is already open, and I climb in without a word, settling beside him.

"If there is one thing you are, it's eager," he murmurs. He reaches for my left hand, and his thumb strokes my bare ring finger. "Perhaps, I may have broached the subject from the wrong angle?"

My heart clenches. Is this an apology?

"I forget… In some ways, you are so young—ignorant," he continues as the driver guides the car into the street. "More often than not, it seems I misjudge you."

He's thoughtful tonight, his expression pensive as passing streetlights illuminate his face in various shades of neon red and green. A lack of tension makes him seem more open than usual as well. I can't stop staring. It's such a contrast to even a few hours ago.

"There are some things I don't have to explain to you. But others…" He runs his fingers along my shoulder and parts my tangled hair. "You have no idea as to the lengths I would go to keep my word. Do you? Just know that when all is said and done, God himself won't be able to dispute my claim over you. Do you understand? I need you to say it out loud—" His hand cups my chin, gently lifting it higher. "Can you give me this? Time?"

I have to inhale deeply and form each word in the base of my throat. "Y-Yes. But—" His hand stills against me. "I need to know everything. I don't want to be *ignorant* anymore."

"Fine." He turns away, letting me go, and my entire body slumps in the wake of his touch. "But first, you promise me one last thing."

"What?"

He leans forward and grunts something to the driver. Simultaneously, the car lurches forward with a sudden burst of speed, and I scramble for my seat belt.

"I'll let you ask what you want. I'll answer your questions. But you keep those wide eyes in check," Maxim warns. "If you think you can stomach my world, then you accept it. All of it. No more flinching. No more running."

"Okay."

"So now, ask your questions."

"Where are we going?" I ask—a neutral enough starting point.

"Outside of the city. I have a general area of where to look," he admits, eyeing the world racing past beyond the window. "But no key destination. Admittedly, one could say that I'm shooting in the dark."

"Who are you looking for? One of your uncle's men?"

"Not quite." He leans back against the seat, tilting his head away from me. "Sevastyn was never interested in surrounding himself with *men*."

Mayday. Unease floods my belly, and I flick my tongue along my lip to delay posing another question. Dealing with him sometimes is like pulling the lever on a slot machine—I never know what prize I'll get.

Such is the risk when it comes to roulette.

There is no time to think.

Or regret.

"Tell me about him," I ask, pulling the trigger.

"Sevastyn?" He makes a sound in his throat somewhere in between a grunt and a scoff. "He served as a liaison between my grandfather and the more senior members of the family. That position made it ideal for him to use blackmail as his weapon of choice. So like any snake, he traded in sin, tempting powerful men and women with the kind of debauchery most only acknowledge on their deathbed to a priest…"

He told me more than he meant to. Confusion disrupts his icy gaze before he refocuses it on the road. Around us, the buildings gradually decrease in height. We're nearing the city limits.

"How do you know Milton?" I ask, aiming my focus at a less volatile target. Or so I think.

"Milton?" He grits his teeth—a habit I'm starting to connect to when he's suppressing an instinctive need to lash out. Evade. "You could say our upbringings were similar," he admits to my shock. "I've known him since I was a child. As it turns out, our goals in life converged as well. I trust him."

It's a surprisingly chilling concept—a child Maxim forging a friendship that would include future bonding experiences such as the dismemberment and disposal of a body. I try to picture him as an angry boy with flashing dark eyes and white-blond hair.

But I can't.

I recall how he interacted with Milton instead. In some ways, he seemed more at ease than he is even around Lucius.

"He's your friend?" I ask.

"He is my partner." His tone gives that word far more reverence than the one I used. "Apart from my family's holdings, everything in my business was built between the two of us. Everything."

"Like the club?"

He nods. "It's as much his as it is mine."

Given how comfortable he feels there—especially in his private room—that simple acknowledgment conveys so much more. The place has more value to him than some piece of random property.

"What does the name stand for? XX—"

"An X for every partner with skin in the game." He flexes his fingers, observing them one by one. "We combine our resources. Think of it as an alliance."

"Three men for three Xs," I deduce. "You, Milton, and…"

"Another investor." He shrugs, crossing his arms. "I don't know his identity. Everything goes through Milton. As long as the money flows and our business interests remain unchallenged, I don't need to know the details. The third member has remained anonymous since the start."

"Milton knew Sevastyn." Or so I'm assuming from his apparent disgust when he saw the body.

"He did," Maxim says. A dare lurks in the ensuing silence. *Do you really want to know how?*

Given what little I know of Sevastyn already, I don't. Two men with similar upbringings—one of whom I know was caught up in the web of a child molester.

Ignorance may be preferable in this instance.

"I believe it's my turn to ask some questions of my own," Maxim says, reclaiming the reins of the conversation. His inflection doesn't change, but I recognize the shift in subject as a warning. A plea. "I never asked you about the dress. What did you think of it?"

"It's…white." I gauge his reaction in glimpses snuck from the corner of my eye. "I don't know much about religion, but I don't think someone like me is allowed to wear that color in a church."

"Allowed?" He raises an eyebrow. Have I surprised him? Or annoyed him? A searching look later and I'm still not sure. "I don't think you understand the irony. As my wife, no one will dictate what you are *allowed* to do. Not a priest. No one."

"No one but you?"

"You think I tell you what to do?" He laughs, but there's no warmth in the sound. "You… Who stayed when I first told her to run? Who questions my intentions to give her the highest thing of value I possess in my name?" I jump as he grabs my hand, dragging it onto his lap. His heat floods my blood like poison, enhancing my awareness of him. He sits rigidly, but not out of annoyance. His thigh muscles tense in a way that makes me suck in a breath. "The woman who, with one look, can make me fuck her like an animal when I desire control," he adds softly. "But yes, I control *you*. Starting with keeping you alive. You will leave the city tomorrow night. I've already contacted Gemma so that you may resume your lessons while away."

I grit my teeth, unsure of how to respond. "I—"

"Stop here," Maxim snaps, directing the order to the driver. Just like that, the brief display of intimacy is over. As if a switch is flipped, his jaw tightens, eyes narrowing. He's in business mode, fixated solely on whatever motive drew him here in the first place.

Here, being a seedy-looking bar on the edge of the highway. We're just beyond the city limits. In the distance, skyscrapers pierce the horizon, pointed like daggers. The imagery makes me shiver. A poetic observation, or an omen?

"Come." Maxim exits the car and extends his hand for me to follow. I step out onto a narrow curb in his wake, taking in whatever I can.

At a glance, this place is no match for his elegant club XXX, that's for damn sure. Made of brick, the building itself is square-shaped with a broken neon sign reading *Money's*, instead of the intended *Montey's*.

Inside, plumes of cigarette smoke choke the narrow barroom, so thick I can barely see the figure beside me. Dressed in a crisp, black suit, Maxim stands out among the shadows—an angel in hell. Coifed blond hair and a blood-red tie give him a harsh definition against the monochromatic backdrop.

Which only confuses me more when my own appearance is factored in. Given his usual obsessive attention to my clothing, he must want it this way. My dress is a plain, shapeless gray. Still mussed from our stint in bed, my hair is a mess. If I wanted to be self-deprecating about it, I look like I belong slobbering over one of the truckers camped out near a pool table at the back of the room— not on his arm.

His palm cups my waist possessively regardless, forcing me to match his pace as he draws up to a chipped, wooden counter. A man stands behind it, rubbing a filthy glass with a filthier dishrag.

"Can I help you?" he wonders without looking up. It's funny how, after all this time in Maxim's world, seeing someone dressed casually in a pair of jeans and a T-shirt stands out as odd. At least in comparison to the polished suits everyone down to his drivers seems to prefer.

"I believe you can." Maxim reaches into his pocket and tosses something onto the bar. My eyes widen as I identify it—a wad of cash, neatly constrained by a silver rubber band.

"I'm looking for someone," he continues. "Calls himself Vadim. *Dima.*"

The bartender's movements slow as he assaults the same crusty stain over and over. Finally, he looks up and shrugs. "Don't know anyone by that name. Sorry."

"Is that so?" Maxim laughs and returns his hand to his breast pocket. This time, he withdraws a second wad of cash, noticeably larger than the first. "Does this refresh your memory?"

The bartender glances over his shoulder. Then he swipes his hand across the bar, dragging the money toward him. "Heard of a Dima," he admits while stuffing the cash into his pocket. "Showed up a few weeks ago, I think. Didn't cause a lot of trouble. He owe you money or something?"

"How do I know your memory isn't faulty?" Maxim wonders. His upper lip curls back from his teeth, and the other man flinches, nearly dropping a wad of bills before he can fit it all into his pants. I don't blame him. Maybe I flinch too. It's chilling how easily the figure beside me can switch from suave to menacing. "Describe him to me."

"Tall, um… Lanky. A bit of an oddball—" The bartender twirls his finger beside his head and raises an eyebrow. "Kept to himself, like I said—"

"How do you know it was him?"

"His name," the bartender says, shrugging. "He didn't exactly make a secret of it. And he was damn good. That's why I asked about the money. He would come in some nights and fleece the shit out of my regulars playing pool." He nods to the table in the corner. "Damn smart, that guy… He might have looked scrawny and all, but I ain't never seen anybody play like that. It was like he was reading fucking minds and shit. And tough, too. One of the guys tried to have a go at him after he won. But that Dima guy, he just gave him a look, ya know? Billy went to prison for attempted murder, so he ain't no chicken shit. I never seen him back down from a fight like that." He shakes his head and snatches up his rag. "But he hasn't been here in a few days."

Scowling in concentration, Maxim braces his hand against the bar. "And you're sure of that?"

The man nods. "Positive. But ah, if you want, I can keep an eye out." He eyes Maxim's bruised, bloodied knuckles and swallows. "Let you know if I see him."

"Good." Maxim fingers his lapel and turns his attention to a nearby booth. He moves boldly, drawing attention from every patron in the entire damn room. "I'll have a drink."

He sits, pulling me down beside him and withdraws a cell phone from his pocket—a different model than the one from the other day.

"Lucius," he snaps, bringing the receiver to his ear. "Switch out with Victor. We need to talk."

He hangs up and eyes the silver watch on his wrist and then refocuses his gaze over the center of the room in a way that makes my stomach twist into knots.

One by one, he eyes the few other patrons huddled in the bar, scanning their faces with ruthless focus. The longer he stares, the harder his expression becomes. After about an hour, he stands, tugging me after him.

"Come."

Once we return to the car, the other driver is gone. Instead, Lucius patiently inclines his head for instruction. "Where to, sir?"

"I don't fucking know." Maxim swipes his hand through the air as he reclaims the back seat. He looks ready to pounce through the windshield, hungry for a fight. "Drive around. And as you do, you can explain why Dima has been here for weeks, and I haven't heard a fucking word."

"That is news to me as well, sir." Lucius calmly pulls into traffic, heading toward the main road. "I know for a fact he hasn't been spotted in the city." A rare note of sternness colors his tone. He's confident of that. "But if he has been on the outskirts, I will have my men extend more resources immediately. Any lapse in vigilance is unacceptable."

"I should have known it seemed too damn easy," Maxim hisses. "The bastard knew I was coming. He's probably in fucking Moscow by now. I should have known Milton would protect that piece of shit... But you are no lazy hack, either," he adds, speaking to Lucius. "The only way for this to go under your radar was if someone *helped* sweep it under. I paid one of the men off, but I could tell the fucker's been bought before. Only one man I know is cunning enough." He strokes his chin, his eyes gleaming murderously.

"Sir?" Lucius inclines his head. "You don't mean—"

"Milton has always had a soft spot for Vadim. They were in the same batch, you remember? In Europe. Kept like prized rats in a cage to be bought and sold amongst the same fucking 'clientele'..."

He glowers, staring beyond me, and this car and anyone else. The past surrounds him, and he bares his teeth against it.

"I thought time may have broken that pathetic sense of pity in him. But I was wrong." A single twitch of his frown betrays just how deeply that fact unnerves him. "When it comes to Vadim, I can no longer trust him."

"Sir?" Lucius inclines his head. "What would you like for me to do?"

"You have full reign," Maxim replies. "Do what you must to hunt him down—but don't kill him. I want you to give him a message." He laughs in a way that will haunt my fucking nightmares. "Tell him to stop hiding like a boy and face me like a man."

His voice resonates with more vitriol than usual—even for him.

"Let's see how the rat reacts when presented with a pile of cheese."

"As you wish, sir. But Ms. Marconi?" Lucius clears his throat, and Maxim flinches at the subtle reminder.

"Bring her to her family," he commands, returning his attention to me. "Then take me back to the city."

"Yes, sir." Lucius nods. "Right away."

Dawn paints the horizon as the city skyline looms in the distance. Fair Haven, as a whole, looks surprisingly cold when viewed from here. A lifeless jungle of concrete I've been stuck in for my entire life. Before Maxim, I think I would have sold my soul to escape from it.

Maybe I did, shedding my old life and neighborhood for something new.

Glimpsed from the perspective of a brutal billionaire, Fair Haven contains a darkness far more terrifying than the prospect of wasting my life as my mother did. It reminds me of Maxim in a way. Beautiful from afar. Terrifying and cold while up close. Impossible to leave for reasons I can't really explain.

The fact that our destination is beyond the city limits unsettles me in more ways than one. It's symbolic, in a sense. I've craved my freedom from the place for so damn long…

But as it turns out, the world beyond my home is flat, boring, and devoid of the chaos I've grown accustomed to. When we arrive at the property, I assume my family is sequestered in, I'm even more unsettled. No one would ever guess the true owner of the quaint dwelling enclosed by a wrought-iron gate. Hell, add in a white picket fence, and the place would look tailor-made for some rich soccer mom and her brood to inhabit.

Not a crime lord with a preference for penthouses.

The only glitch in the façade is a security booth guarding the entrance, staffed by two men dressed in black. They nod solemnly as the car advances past them, down a paved driveway and up to the front of the house.

"The extra security measures are temporary. As for the house, I admit it's not my usual taste, but it's secure," Maxim explains as I take in the white mansion with black trimming. He must sense the skepticism my expression can't disguise. "Get some rest. Your family is already settled in. I've asked the guards to remain out of sight. Lucius will come by later."

He doesn't bother to explain what will happen after that. He doesn't have to, considering that my experience with his controlling nature is enough for me to fill in the blanks—tonight, we'll be on a plane to only God knows where. Though, to be fair, in Maxim's world, God himself sits beside me, so convinced of his own power. Any slight violation of his wishes equates to a mortal sin.

Like daring to question him. "What about their school?"

"The arrangements have been made," he says, prepared for me. My punishment is his thumb tracing my lower lip as if savoring my rebellion. "As for your siblings, they've been told you're going on a surprise family vacation."

Surprise. Our first trip from the city ever is anything but a "vacation."

It's petty to focus on that point. To be irritated by it. After all, what is a trip somewhere new in relation to a pre-designed wedding dress, or a disposable ring? Petty, fucking concerns. It's even pettier to needle him for no damn good reason. "What if I don't want to leave?"

A low sound resonates in his throat. "Don't." He meets my gaze directly, his stare fathomless. "You feel comfortable enough to question me. I can respect that.

But don't ever doubt me or my intentions toward you. When you are safe, I can turn my attention to Anatoli without any distractions."

"So, you're staying in the city?"

"Keep the car running," he tells Lucius before exiting the car. To me, his tone is far more curt. Another warning. "Come."

I trail him up the walkway, allowing him to take the lead. Beyond the front door is a layout similar to that of his previous house. Faint noises from various directions betray the presence of other occupants, awake despite the early hour. Running water. A muffled television. High-pitched bickering over toothpaste.

A sense of relief nearly barrels me over, and I forget my annoyance. I've spent these past few days so wrapped up in myself. I didn't have the time to truly fear for my kids —or feel the gratitude for the man who has kept them safe all this time.

I glance at him only to catch him observing me in return. Dark, his eyes brim with an unknown emotion. One too dangerous to decipher on a whim. Rather than try, I reach out, brushing my fingers along his forearm. "Thank you—"

"Frankie!" I turn to spot a tiny blur of pink and blond racing down the stairs in my direction. "I missed you!" Ainsley declares while throwing her arms around my waist. "Where are we going? I've never been on vacation before!"

"Um, it's as much as a surprise to you as it is to me," I confess. But I force a smile and try to bite back any doubts. "Are you excited?"

"Why do you look so funny?" She wrinkles her nose and tugs me along. "Never mind. Hurry up. I want to show you my new doll. Are you going to stay over?"

"I think so…" I look back for confirmation, but Maxim is already gone, vanished without a goodbye.

And I barely catch the door closing behind him.

CHAPTER SIX

It's scary how easy it is to fall into an old routine. To take on another persona as though it's a well-worn role in a tired play. I've been away from the kids for days, but in little over an hour, I've broken up two fights and played referee during three shouting matches.

Some things never change. And in Maxim's world, maybe that's a *good* thing.

"Damn, Frankie," Mikie grumbles from across the living room. He lies across a couch so expensive it probably belongs in a fancy boutique rather than here. His bare feet are propped on one of the armrests, and I nearly rip his legs from their sockets as I knock them off.

"Have some fucking manners," I snap at him. "We don't live here." And I can't shake that fact no matter how comfortable they seem. The beautiful, priceless furniture serves as a mocking reminder that it's not truly ours. It's borrowed.

"Chill," he says, laughing. "I almost forgot what it sounds like to hear the master utilize ten different curse words in one sentence. Bravo."

"Fuck off, smartass." My jaw aches, but when I rub the sore muscle, I realize why. I'm smiling.

Maybe because this feels good in a way I don't expect. No talk of weddings or gowns. Normalcy.

But there is always an undercurrent that reinforces one thing—this newfound security is possible at the behest of one person. The man who pays the bills. The puppet master who ensures that I don't have to craft a lunch of burned macaroni and Pop-Tarts like I used to.

In my new reality, a chef appears from nowhere to announce that brunch has been served in a dining room set exactly for seven. In lieu of paper plates, fine cutlery and expensive china adorn each place setting. No roaches are scurrying in the corners to set the mood. Instead, a bay window overlooks a meticulously crafted garden of fancy, colorful flowers.

Trust fund babies, eat your heart out.

"Hey!" Mikie snaps, slapping at one of the twins' hands as they reach across the table. "Use your goddamn manners and say please. Right, Frankie?"

Something inside me aches as he eyes me as if for permission. While I've been gone, I have no doubt as to who had to step up to fill my shoes.

"Right," I croak.

"Taste this," Ainsley squeals, shoving a forkful of her food in my face. The menu ironically consists of a fancier version of macaroni and cheese with vegetables on the side instead of sugar.

I choke down a bite. "It's good."

"Yeah! I didn't know anything, but pizza could taste so good," Ainsley chirps in agreement.

"Pass me the bread, *please*," Mikie says while reaching for a porcelain saucer. "So where are we going, Frankie? I never thought we'd be the kind of people who 'go away' for summer break."

I can't tell if he's horrified or excited by the prospect.

"It's a surprise, right, Frankie?" Ainsley pitches in.

"Do I have to eat this? I read in a magazine that dairy isn't good for your skin," Daisy muses, eyeing her plate. "Though the sun isn't either, so if we're going to a beach—"

"What's a little more acne, pizza face?" One of the twins snipes.

I sigh and reach for a fork. "Cut it out. Let's just have a nice, normal fucking…"

Something in the window catches my eye. A shadow, displacing the pretty flowers and manicured lawn. No. A person…running?

"Frankie?" Someone taps my shoulder. "You okay?"

"I…"

Suddenly, two men race into the dining room and lunge toward the window. One of them bites out a shouted command, "Get down!"

And everything goes to shit.

Glass shatters. Screams echo. Something slams into me from the side, knocking me to the floor. I scramble for balance, dazed as a million different things happen at once.

Racing footsteps. Another monstrous, echoing sound. Noise. More screams, high-pitched and deafening. I can't see. Think.

Then a hand comes from nowhere, yanking me to my feet. "This way," someone commands into my ear, their tone familiar. Lucius. He throws his arm around my shoulder, pinning me to his side. "Keep your head down. I've got you."

He nudges me toward the exit, but I turn back, barely recognizing the room behind me at all. Glass decorates the table like confetti. One of the chairs is broken, and flailing bodies clamor for the doorway. It looks like a fucking bomb went off.

"Ainsley?" Panic breaks my voice into a hollow rasp. "Daisy?"

"Come!" Lucius grabs my arm. "Everyone is safe, but we need to move. Now!"

I follow him blindly. Wherever we go, we move too quickly for me to track our progress. All I know is that when Lucius finally stops, we're in an enclosed space illuminated only with fluorescent lighting. A basement?

One by one, the kids stream inside, flanked by several men I don't recognize. They're dressed in black, each openly sporting a weapon. Guards.

"What's happening?" Ainsley demands. I look down to find her clinging to my waist. Her eyes are wide, staring blankly. "Frankie, what's happening?"

"A minor gas leak," Lucius explains calmly. "It most likely caused a small pipe explosion. Nothing to worry about. Ms. Marconi, if you don't mind, may I have a word?"

He heads into the hallway, past the guards. The second we're out of earshot, I reach for his hand, forcing him to face me. "What's really going on?"

"Someone just tried to kill you," he explains, his tone eerily blunt. "It was a lazy attempt to be sure. A warning more than anything, but Mr. Koslov will want you brought to him immediately."

"No." The world spins. I have to hunch over and cradle my head in my hands just to keep standing. The floor sways beneath me as a tattered giggle escapes my throat. Maybe I'm in shock. From here, I can hear Mikie demanding answers amid a thin, terrified cry. *Ainsley.*

God, she's never sounded so frantic before. Standing upright, I start in their direction. "I'm not leaving them—"

"Trust me, it will be for the best," Lucius insists, grabbing my hand before I even make it a step. Frowning, he withdraws a handkerchief from his suit pocket. "You're bleeding. If I may—" He dabs at a patch of flesh above my left eye, but I don't feel anything. The cloth, however, comes away red. "Don't be alarmed," Lucius says, stowing the stained fabric within his jacket. "It's merely a superficial laceration. Nothing too serious. Still, I'll have a physician meet you at the club."

"The club?" My thoughts congeal within my skull like jelly. He's speaking too quickly. I can't keep up.

"Yes." Lucius nods. "I need to get you to Mr. Koslov immediately. And I know you're concerned for your siblings. I will stay with them. And, if I may be blunt, they'll be safer apart from you for now. Tomas?" He directs his attention to one of the men dressed in black who steps forward. "This is the head of security," Lucius explains to me. "He will bring you to Mr. Koslov. Now go."

But I never have a choice. Tomas takes my arm and steers me into another room before I even realize what's happening. I start to protest, but one last look from Lucius makes me go limp, resigned.

It's the same way he looked at me in the car after dispensing his "advice."

Without judgment or irritation. No anger, either…

Just pity.

TOMAS DRIVES me to the club in a vehicle I don't recognize. Rather than a sleek sports car, I find myself in the back seat of a bulky van with tinted windows that paint the world beyond in dark obscurity. Rather than to portray luxury, its purpose is far more utilitarian—safety.

And urgency.

Forgoing about a million traffic laws, Tomas whips the van over the courtyard of the club and parks mere feet from the entrance. A heartbeat later, he's already at my door, moving to shield my body with his. "This way, Ms. Marconi."

We barely enter the building before Maxim appears as if conjured from thin air. Wild with rage, his eyes trace my face, narrowing over the blood drying on my forehead.

The next second, I'm in his arms, my head on his shoulder. His pulse hammers madly beneath his skin as he carries me down a darkened hallway and into the secluded bedroom, I know to be his.

"You're bleeding… Damnit." He makes me sit on the edge of the mattress, his focus on my forehead. "Are you alright?"

"No," I croak, but the blood dripping down my chin barely fazes me. In fact, the only thing I can seem to care about is a simple statement Mikie said. "It's almost summer break."

Maxim frowns, scanning my face. "How do you feel? Is your head—"

"I mean, my kids should be in a fucking amusement park or something." My hands are shaking. Balling them into fists isn't enough to stop the tremors wracking me from head to toe. My teeth chatter, breaking my words into a series of jagged syllables. "They deserve a normal vacation. School. A *real* home. Not getting s-shot at—"

"Breathe," Maxim warns, stroking the uninjured side of my face. "You're in shock—"

"You think I want protection?" I'm babbling. I can barely make sense of my own damn words—but I can't shut up, either. "I want normalcy! I want my sisters to grow up in a normal fucking environment, and my brothers shouldn't see me covered in bruises... I want them to have bedtimes, and allowances, and take walks in the park. Shit normal people do. I want them to have what I didn't. Not this." My eyes burn, and moisture spills from them the second I blink. "Not borrowed mansions, and fucking fear."

Maxim watches me cry, his expression unreadable. Then he crouches before me, and his heavy sigh ruffles my wayward curls. "You were right to question me," he admits, bringing his mouth against my ear. "Separating you from me was foolish. It won't happen again."

"Who was it?" I ask as the chaos replays in my mind over and over. "Was it your grandfather?"

His upper lip pulls back from his teeth. "I don't know," he snarls. "But I will find them. They will pay—"

"Sir?" The door opens, and Tomas enters.

"What the hell is it?" Maxim whirls around, but before he can utter another word, Tomas approaches him and whispers something into his ear. Whatever he says makes Maxim's entire body stiffen. The next second he's barreling into the hallway, and I have to run to keep up.

At first, I don't know what makes him stop at the edge of the club floor. His erect posture is alarming, but nothing compared to how I'd assume he'd act in the face of an armed intruder. For one, he doesn't draw a weapon. Instead, his body ripples with barely concealed tension— but that's the odd part. He's trying to *hide* it.

I discover the answer to the mystery once I spot the lanky figure leaning against the bar, admiring a bottle of liquor. He's tall and alarmingly thin. His body barely shapes the gray sweatshirt he wears paired with light wash jeans. Wild dark hair obscures his face from this angle, but his pale fingers betray an unusual grace as he twirls the bottle between them.

"I hear you've been looking for me," he says without turning around. "Well, you've found me, little Maxi. What do you want?"

Maxim observes the other figure in a way that can only be described as hostile. His fingers flex at his sides as if he has to consciously keep them from forming fists. "It's about damn time you've crawled out of hiding, Vadim."

"Oh?" Vadim cocks his head, still facing away from us. "Unlike you, I don't dwell in the lap of luxury. I am, in the open, as they say. Easy to find." He has an accent as well, though it's less pronounced than Maxim's and harder to place. British? Russian? French? He speaks with a blend of several different inflections. "And it's funny that you sought me out. Considering you threatened to kill me if I ever set foot in your precious city again. I took your sudden change of heart as an invitation to visit. Nice place—"

"You know what the fuck I want." Maxim advances a dangerous step, but Vadim doesn't seem to notice. Or care. He lazily tosses his bottle into the air, catching it one-handed.

"Enough games," Maxim warns. "Let's cut to the heart of it. Stand with me against Anatoli. You know I will make it worth your while."

"Is that so?" I jump as Vadim barks out an unexpectedly harsh note of laughter. Compared to the musical quality of his voice, the sound rings like an off note in an otherwise pretty piece of piano music. "You think I give a damn about your money?"

"No." Maxim flexes his arms, adjusting the fit of his suit. "But did I say anything about money?"

"What else could you be willing to offer? Hmm?" Vadim finally inclines his head to observe us with the same scrutiny Maxim inspects him with. I feel my mouth fall open as I take him in. He's beautiful—but in a different way than Maxim could ever be.

Instead of harsh, violent appeal, this man could only be described as *delicate*. His swanlike throat and graceful jaw are comparable to meticulously crafted glass in contrast to Maxim's powerful bulk. But his eyes…

They're a shade so dark they seem to glow, even from this distance.

"Do tell," he prompts, waving his hand expectantly through the air. "You have my full attention."

"I'll give you a piece of my so-called empire," Maxim replies, crossing his arms. "That's what you crave, isn't it? That which was always *mine*."

"Oh no…" Vadim leans back against the counter, still fiddling with the bottle. The motion displays him from a different angle, making it apparent how young he is. Maybe in his early thirties, like Maxim. Or even younger —but whatever his age, he's nowhere near naïve. A guarded calculation shapes everything from his perusing gaze down to the quirk of his chin. He's ready for an attack at any moment. "Crave? I think the correct phrasing is 'what I'm owed.'"

"Discuss my terms, and you can have it," Maxim suggests. "What little scraps I'm willing to give."

"Scraps…" Vadim runs a hand through his hair, parting the thick black strands. He observes a particularly long section, his nose wrinkling in disapproval. "You must think I'm stupid, Maxi," he says, returning his attention to the other man. "A stupid fucking prick, huh? Even from my little hidey-hole, I've heard the rumors. That lately you've started collecting your dolls, rather than just fucking them." He eyes me pointedly and sighs. "An amusing little anecdote. Following in the footsteps of our dear old man, I see? What is she? Some obscure countess you aim to impregnate before chopping her to pieces—"

"Is that what the rumors say?" Maxim interjects—but my brain remains stuck on three words. *Our old man…* I barely comprehend what he says next, "I knew you were wallowing in your shame, Vadim. But obsession? It's beneath you."

"So is lying, Maxi," the other man scolds, wagging his finger. Was his insinuation a joke or something more? I can't tell. The only similarity I can find between the two is icy, ruthless confidence. "But you've always been good at that," Vadim adds. "Lying. Scheming. Backstabbing. How does the saying go? You can take the boy out of the whore, but not the whore out of the boy—"

"Enough." Teeth bared, Maxim advances another impulsive step. "Watch yourself."

"I've *also* heard that someone's pissed off the old man," Vadim says, seemingly unconcerned. "He doesn't seem to care who you fuck, but the day little Maxi decides to take a wife? The old man issues a bounty. Have you stopped to wonder why? It isn't like him to panic so easily. Not to mention, his favorite doggie's gone missing. Though you wouldn't happen to know anything about that, would you? While he may let you run your little empire on the side—" He gestures around us with a wave of his hand, indicating the club itself. "Anatoli wouldn't react kindly to a direct challenge. And you've been such a dutiful servant all this time. Why risk it now?"

Maxim says nothing, but Vadim nods as if he has.

"Ah... I see. You were *sloppy*." He grins, displaying perfectly white teeth. "Sloppy and reckless. If I can suspect as much, you can believe the old man has. It's why he's gone out of his way to bring you to heel. Oh yes, you've been a bad boy, little Maxi—"

"And you need to decide what role you want to play, *Dima*," Maxim snarls in a tone so harsh I suck in a breath. "As a player? Or as the stray mutt, you've always been? Milton can't protect you forever."

"Maybe." Vadim flicks his tongue over his lips. "Milton wants me to play nice and assist in your little war. What he really wants is for you to break from your chains and claim the city for yourself so he can stop worrying where your loyalties lie. But me? Maybe I should watch Anatoli rip you apart and find another whipping boy to serve as his figurehead? One could say I've dreamt about it..."

"Funny. I would dream about amassing my own power. But some things never fucking change, do they?" Maxim reaches into his pocket and withdraws a small, rectangular item that I recognize as a business card. From this angle, I can only make out a silver letter X gleaming on the front of it. "When you get tired of hiding behind another man's pant leg, you know where to find me—" He tosses the card onto the floor. "Come when you've made your choice as to what role you'll play."

"What about as a spectator?" Vadim laughs again, but there's no mistaking the sound for what it truly is. A growl. "The decision as to 'where I stand' was made for me a long time ago—I am no Koslov. And you've always made sure to remind me of that. Haven't you?" He extends his throat, drawing my attention to a reddish scar stretching from his jawline down beneath the neckline of his shirt. It's nasty, betraying the severity of the wound that made it.

I swallow hard and run my fingers along my own neck. Images sneak into my skull before I can fight them back —the feel of a knife, biting into my flesh.

"Pretty, isn't it?" Vadim's eyes flicker toward me, meeting my gaze directly. Maxim snatches my arm, pulling me to his side, but something won't let me turn away. It's his expression. He doesn't blink, his stare open and raw. With one look, I get the sense he understands all too well. "And I can tell your little friend has already gotten a taste of your...let's call it, *affection*—"

"You speak to me," Maxim demands in a hiss. "No one else."

"If only you listened. But you are right. Let's cut to the heart of it…" Vadim turns his attention to one of the intricate silver chandeliers hanging overhead, his frown wistful. "As much as I'd like to see the old man burn in hell, I don't have a problem with Anatoli. In fact, you could say I've made peace with the idea of letting his time run its course—" His lips twitch in a fleeting smirk. "As for my help, tell me how someone as lowly and worthless as I can be of service to someone so great?"

"Cut the bullshit." Maxim releases me and takes another step in Vadim's direction. Mere feet separate them now, and for the first time, the other man displays a hint of wariness. He sets his bottle on the counter, freeing his hands. "I know Milton has been protecting you—"

"Milton is Milton." Vadim lifts his arms in a casual shrug. "And as far as I know, he's made his choice of alliance *very* clear."

"Then you know as well as I do whose side that is. You've been attacking my network. Don't insult my intelligence by insisting that he just found out recently. He knows your handiwork better than anyone. I'm sure he's been aware of your scheming since day one," Maxim continues. "You must have some resources to hide your tracks so well. Though scheming from the shadows isn't too much of a stretch for a rat."

"What can I say?" Vadim smiles, and the slight tilt to his mouth transforms his face. He's a different man in a heartbeat, charming and bright. "I was taught by the best. You should know—he trained you too. Good old Anatoli.

Tell me something." He strokes his chin, suddenly thoughtful. "When you brought your new 'friend' to him —and I use that term loosely, all things considered—did he fuck her first? Or did you toss her to Sevastyn to have her broken in?"

A roar of anger reverberates like thunder. Maxim. In a blur of motion, he lunges at Vadim, his arm raised, fist poised for a blow.

But Vadim stands calmly in the line of fire. Right before Maxim can touch him, he says, "You *did*, didn't you?" A shadow falls over his face, enhancing the nuances of his expression concealed until now. He's not afraid. He's angry—but in a different way from the furious figure standing between us.

Where Maxim radiates fire, this man is cool, controlled ice.

"You threw her to Sevastyn." Awe paints his tone, mingled with horror. "Either that or you failed to protect her from him. For some reason, Maxim, I never pegged you as a womanizer to quite *that* extent. Even with your quirks…"

Maxim says nothing, his fist still raised, body trembling with tension.

"I thought it was a lie, the last, juiciest bit of gossip fluttering around about you," Vadim adds. "I guess not. Anatoli *has* put out a bounty, after all, merely to spite his golden boy. A hefty one."

"Oh?" Maxim lowers his fist but doesn't back away. If anything, he towers over the slender figure, but the pairing doesn't seem quite as unbalanced as it should.

Maybe because his opponent meets his glare unflinchingly.

"A blood price to be exact. *Krasnyy konets*," Vadim says. "So archaic and dramatic of him, but somewhat fitting in this sense. How else can he better define the rules of that precious family? *Koslov*. Otherwise, it's figurehead may get the urge to induct some unworthy whore into such a stoic bloodline, and the world will fucking end."

"Watch your mouth," Maxim snarls.

"You know it's true," Vadim taunts. "Even in his old age, the man can still read you like a book, Maxi. You *finally* move to declare your independence from him, and he issues you a spanking you can't ignore. A blood price is no small offer considering the old man—bless his soul—could keel over at any moment. I could claim the bounty now, for instance, and earn my place in the family, right over your head. In the event of Anatoli's unfortunate demise, I might even be able to take the reins of the entire precious Koslov empire. Such a prize."

"Am I supposed to feel threatened every time the old man decides to test me?"

"Oh, but I didn't say the bounty was on *your* head." Vadim's gaze finds me again, glinting with renewed curiosity. "Did I? I see now, why you picked this one. A wide-eyed innocent little girl who won't ever question her master. Who stays by your side, even when you toss her to the wolves. How much was she worth? A few grand? You wouldn't pay any more than that—"

"Enough."

"Yes. I've had enough." Sighing, Vadim easily slips beyond Maxim's reach and starts for the exit. "Goodbye for now," he calls with an enthusiastic wave. "But we really should do this again. It's been far too long...*brother*."

Shock nearly robs me of the balance I have left. I almost miss Maxim's reply. "You are nothing to me," he hisses. "You want to play games? Get the fuck out."

"Ah, yes, well, we can't choose family, can we?" Vadim confidently strolls for the archway connecting this part of the club to the rest. "Oh, and I won't be needing the calling card. I'll just name my price outright. Since you like to whore out your woman, then that's what I'll take. An hour with her, alone—"

An object hurls through the air and smashes to pieces above Vadim's head. A torrent of clear liquid and broken glass miss him by mere inches, but his steps don't even falter.

"That's the price," he says, oblivious to the murderous glare Maxim directs his way. "And don't think about having me followed. Your men are good, but they aren't the sharpest tools in the shed, so to speak. Invest in more skilled minions if you hope to find me. I'll await your real answer once you've thought on it. *Dasvidaniya.*"

"Follow him," Maxim growls the second he's beyond view.

"Yes, sir." Tomas leaves, followed by two men.

"Fuck!" Maxim rakes a hand through his hair, his shoulders hunched away from me. When he finally looks back, I can't read his expression. I don't want to.

It's funny in a sick way. These past forty-eight hours have desolated my sanity. My security. My sense of self. But out of all of the twisted revelations I've been forced to reconcile, only one lands the heaviest blow.

"He is your brother." Like a broken record stuck on repeat, I can't stop blurting it out loud. "You have a *brother—*"

"No," Maxim growls with barely concealed restraint. We're alone now, and his voice echoes to the furthest reaches of the club floor, easily dominating my hollow whisper. "My father had a *bastard*. Vadim is nothing more than a mutt. Look at me. Fuck, you're still bleeding—"

"You never mentioned him," I point out. God, I sound so dazed. Like I'm sleepwalking in a nightmare, half convinced that none of this is real. "I've told you everything about me. Everything about my family, but I didn't even know you had a brother—"

"Vadim is not a factor in my life." He snatches a handkerchief from the breast pocket of his suit and grabs my chin, keeping me still. "*Your* family is my only concern. Stay." He dabs at the wound above my eye, his eyes narrowed. "Your pupils are dilated. You could have a concussion."

"I'm fine." I try to turn away, but his fingers skim my hair regardless.

"The doctor will examine you—"

"Just stop!" I cringe from him this time. Alarm renders him frozen, and he doesn't reach for me again. "Please…"

"Alright." He tosses the bloodied cloth aside. The fact that he backed down at all shocks me. Almost as much as how he stands there awkwardly, his fingers clenched into fists. "Lucius sent for a doctor," he says after a second of silence. "When he gets here, let him examine you—"

"I need to go home. I need to… Ainsley was crying. She needs me." More tears spill down my cheeks, startlingly hot. All this time, they've never stopped falling. "I need to make sure my family is okay. I need to comfort my baby sister, who had a bullet whiz past her head. I need to…" A sudden urgency spurs me to stumble for the doorway. "Take me back."

Maxim doesn't move. "I can't."

"Why not?"

"Because…" I look back, and his gaze reluctantly meets mine. "They're already on a plane."

A tattered laugh escapes my throat as I stagger, my knees trembling. Before they give out, my back strikes the nearest wall, and I cling to the cool surface.

"So, you've just kidnapped them." At the back of my mind, I know I'm overexaggerating. Logic can't pierce this fog of sheer, fucking panic. I can't stop shaking. My chest feels like a brick is balanced on my ribcage, crushing it. No matter how quickly I breathe, I can't find enough air.

"You're hyperventilating." Maxim places his hand on my shoulder, but I wrench away from him, and I have to brace myself against the wall again just to keep from falling.

"Don't touch me! You've kidnapped them because that's what it's called when a stranger takes your family members away, isn't it?"

"*Kotyonok*—"

"I don't know you!" I bury my face in my hands, blocking out the sight of him. Something Vadim said serves as a morbid fucking key, unlocking the twisted, horrible memories I've done my best to lock away. "Is that why you wanted me to go with you?" I have to grit my teeth to keep from gagging. Vomiting. "You knew what he'd ask for. You said it—I would fascinate him. Was that it? You wanted… You wanted to w-whore me out—"

"Look at me."

"Don't!" I throw my hand out, keeping him at bay. "I don't know you. I don't know your past. I don't know who your friends are. I didn't even know until five seconds ago that you had a brother. Maybe it's best if you don't marry me." I stare at my bare finger. This pinching, aching sensation in my chest, could be relief—not agony. "I think I'd rather be your whore than your property—"

"Enough!" Eyes flashing, he moves in on my position. Despite how I cringe from his touch, his hand sinks into my hair, forcing me to face him. "Vadim is no one. You care for your siblings, and I respect that. But him? *He* was a tool. One of my father's many bastards. If anything, he was a whip that Anatoli used to punish me, serving as a reminder that I could always be replaced. Our relationship extends to nothing more than the shared blood of the monster who sired us. Do you understand?"

His nostrils flare when I don't respond. Readjusting his grip, he wrenches my head to the side, and his opposite thumb traces the space above my left eye.

"You want to know why I brought you? Because if I didn't, I would have lost my fucking mind, and I would have killed him. I would have lost control..." His voice breaks, followed by a laugh and then a sigh. "You say you don't know me—but you do. You know when to ask me fucking questions I wouldn't tolerate from anyone else. You know how to use those fucking eyes so that I can see myself reflected in them. You keep me here." His tone deepens with unsaid meaning. *Here.* In the present, away from the horror of his past.

"And I know that *you* don't panic easily. I know when I've pushed you too far... And I know that I won't lose you like this. Not because of him." He releases me, only to grab my chin and coax me into meeting his gaze. "I want more than protection for you," he admits, lowering his lips to the uninjured side of my forehead. "I want…"

His nostrils flare, inhaling me, and he says nothing else as if the act speaks for him. He wants my scent—skin and sweat and a hint of blood.

"You want your normalcy?" He finds my earlobe with his mouth, nipping it with gentle pressure. "Then you will have it. No matter what it takes."

But, as if to counter that promise, slow, heavy footsteps advance on our position from the direction of the entrance hall. Maxim tenses just as the newcomer appears in the doorway. Dressed in an ebony suit crowned by a blood-red tie, the man cuts a striking figure against the gray backdrop.

"Milton…" Maxim withdraws from me, lowering his hands to his sides. The posture is a stark contrast from his hostility toward Dima—but not completely relaxed either.

"I came as quickly as I could," Milton explains, fingering his collar. His eyes dart cautiously around the room before settling over the broken glass on the floor. "Vadim was here?"

"Don't pretend like you don't fucking know," Maxim says with a scoff. "I'm sure he didn't learn this location through luck."

"It's your right to mistrust him," Milton says with a nod. "But can I make a suggestion?"

"Like what?" Maxim cocks his head. "Say it."

"Give him what he wants. End this feud."

He makes it sound so simple. So easy. Maxim doesn't seem to know whether he's joking or not. A rugged sound escapes his mouth in response—part laugh, part growl.

"I'll assume that you don't know what he requested," he concedes in a lethal tone. "So, I will let that insult pass."

"And you can't give up anything, not one fucking thing, in exchange for a truce?" Milton's eyes narrow, revealing the briefest hint of anger. A heartbeat later, it's gone. "Dima has vital insight on how to defeat Anatoli—"

"Dima," Maxim echoes, an eyebrow raised. "You still call him that."

Sighing, he crosses to the bar. Putting his palms flat on the surface, he observes the liquor selection with his back to us. "I don't ignore my past. Not that it lets me. Some days it bothers me, I won't lie, but I've made peace with it. I don't let it define me now, and I don't dwell on it. If I choose to refer to Dima as *Dima,* so be it."

"And I do? Dwell?" Maxim strolls toward the pile of glass on the floor and nudges a chunk with the toe of his boot. "Tell that to the mess he's always left in his wake. The past does not define me, either. I have just never made the mistake of forgetting it."

"Anatoli threatens my livelihood as well, or did you forget that?" When he turns from the bar and meets Maxim's gaze head-on, Milton's noticeably colder. "Despite his faults, Dima knows better than anyone how to… let's call it, circumvent overwhelming odds. With his help, you can make Anatoli bow with little bloodshed."

"So, you want to play peacemaker?" Maxim laughs, shaking his head. "Don't talk like a pacifist, Milton. It's beneath you."

Milton flashes a disarming smile. "Alright, then, let's cut the bullshit. You don't have what it takes to defeat Anatoli on your own—" his voice deepens, losing any ounce of congeniality. "You and I both know it. Running from him will only delay the unavoidable. In his arrogance, Anatoli will see it as an opportunity to force you to surrender. The old bastard will get spiteful, placing us *all* at risk. You do realize that?"

"Go." Maxim turns away from him and observes my forehead, frowning in concentration. "Get out. We will discuss this later."

"Will we?" Milton starts toward the entrance, his steps deliberately slow, skepticism darkening the shadows on his face. "I'll leave out of respect for the circumstances—" he points his head in my direction. "But I won't let you ignore me this time. I mean it. You have my loyalty, but I'm not above making my wishes known in ways you can't ignore. Understood?"

He passes through the archway, and the second he is out of view, I remember how to move.

"Are you alright?" Maxim reaches for my forehead, but I recoil, nearly tripping in my rush to back away.

He follows, his eyes narrowed, jaw clenched. "Don't move—"

"I'm tired." My fingers tremble as I brace them against his chest. I'm too weak to push him off, but he withdraws regardless. "I… I just want to see my family."

He eyes me for so long. I'm numb when he finally nods and turns away, his expression blank. "Clean up—" He gestures to the rag on the floor. "I'll bring the car around. We'll leave soon. Together."

I watch him go, storming off to take charge once again.

But I have no desire to follow him this time.

CHAPTER SEVEN

I could never hold onto anger the way Maxim does. At least, in the sense that I don't acknowledge it at all. Feel it. Let it consume me. If anything, I've always been a doormat, swallowing down my emotions. Choking on them. My pain. My hate. If I didn't, I doubt I would have survived up until this point.

Melanie may have been a cunt, but she wasn't stupid—and she wasn't inclined to get arrested for child neglect either. She knew which kid to shoulder her responsibility on. She knew whose personality she could meld and shape and beat into submission.

She knew that as much as I hated her, I loved the kids more. Enough to willingly suffer anything for them. Anything…and devotion was one surefire thing she could always bank on—even when the shitty marriages and stolen money ran out.

And now, she's laughing at me from her spot in hell. *I never got them shot at, Francesca,* I imagine her taunting in that smug fucking way only she could. *I never put their lives in danger. I was a selfish bitch, but I never entangled them in a mafia war. What does that make you?*

It makes me crazy.

It makes me guilty. So fucking guilty…

And it makes me more selfish than she ever was.

I'm blind to everything but the gut-wrenching panic building within me, as Maxim's doctor finally arrives and examines my injury. His determination is a mild concussion, nothing serious. Once I'm deemed able to fly, Maxim ushers me into the car, and we leave for the airport.

The following hours pass by in a blur too dizzying to interpret. I'm left with just snippets of memory. Entering a private jet. Staring blankly from a window, aware of Maxim watching me. I don't even have the sense of mind to acknowledge another of the many firsts I've experienced with him—my virgin plane trip.

I'm numb when we land, and I nearly lunge out of my seat the second Maxim stands. Exiting the climate-controlled cabin for a sweltering, oppressive heat feels like entering a parallel universe. The sun is so bright I have to shield my eyes with my hand and take in our surroundings in bits and pieces.

No city, for one. No skyscrapers and lifeless concrete. Instead, I see endless blue—sky, water—everywhere, reflecting sunlight like glitter. The taste of salt teases my tongue and triggers my curiosity. We're somewhere tropical. Near the ocean?

Maxim pushes ahead without revealing the answer, and I don't ask. As we descend the steps to the tarmac, I spot a black car waiting nearby, along with a familiar face.

"Sir. Ms. Marconi." Lucius nods to us in greeting, but even his warm smile can't disguise the exhaustion hammered beneath his eyes in purplish bruises. I doubt he's slept at all since I saw him last. As dutiful as ever, he opens the door to the back seat. "Once you're settled, we can go."

Maxim extends his hand for me, but I stare ahead and enter the car on my own. He follows me in without a word, and Lucius commands the steering wheel.

"Your siblings are safe and sound," Lucius declares before I can get a single word out. "Everyone is settled in. They know to expect you shortly."

"Thank you." God, I sound worse than he does. My eyes burn as I rest my head against the window on my end. I can't even tell how long I've been awake. An eternity, it feels like.

"Sir," Lucius begins, shifting the conversation. "Mr. Hood has been persistent in his attempts to reach you."

"Milton?" Maxim's voice is a passionless hiss. "Tell him I'm otherwise engaged."

"I have," Lucius admits. "But I will say that he seems… unwilling to be pacified in this instance. I know for a fact he's tracked the jet out of the country, an action he doesn't normally take—"

"Did you make the arrangements I requested?" Maxim interjects, forcibly changing the subject. *Arrangements.* I make a half-hearted attempt at guessing what he means. More security? More shuffling my family around like pieces on a gameboard? More lies?

Wary, I eye him through a crack in my eyelids. Though he sits beside me, we could be an entire fucking world apart. We don't touch, our bodies poised on opposite ends.

"Yes, sir," Lucius replies. "I will admit it was a challenge, but everything is in place."

"Good."

They continue speaking, presumably about business, but I stop listening. I must drift off because when I snap to awareness, Maxim's hand is on my shoulder, and the door on his end is open, letting in a wave of stifling heat.

"We're home." Something in his tone catches me off guard. The softness, maybe?

I inhale in the wake of it, my fingers fluttering toward him. But then I remember Vadim's "price," and I shrug him off and exit the car on my own, clinging to the side of it for balance. His eyes track my every movement, dark and unreadable.

In a bid to ignore him, I focus on our surroundings.

It looks to be late in the evening now. Despite its intensity, the sun has gone down compared to when we first landed. A brilliant, reddish-orange paints the horizon, threatening to swallow it for good. I can't tell how long we were in the car.

Or where we are now, exactly.

Somewhere luxurious, seemingly private, and far from civilization. Around us lies a courtyard enclosed by palm trees and white stone architecture. A path leads off into what seems to be a garden, bathed in shadow. I can just make out a gurgling marble fountain and countless, sprawling plants in the fading daylight.

Behind me looms the real attraction, however. Towering at least three stories, the structure is composed of the same white stone as the courtyard—a mansion expensive enough to star on the cover of some fancy billionaire magazine—the exotic beach home edition. Massive windows promise a view of the ocean I can see looming beyond the trees.

It's breathtaking.

"You and your family have the run of the place," Lucius announces, drawing up beside me. He eyes the house objectively, stroking his chin. "There is a pool. A courtyard. Plenty of rooms. Several acres of property for recreation—"

"I just want to see them," I blurt out, starting forward. "I need to see them."

A passing figure manages to beat me to the front door. Maxim. He opens it without a word to me, revealing a wide entryway.

I barely register the layout at all. I can't fucking *breathe* until several figures rush toward me all at once, shouting my name. Before I know it, I'm assaulted by all six kids, and I gladly allow myself to be crushed within the rush of hugs and the barrage of questioning.

I can't stop touching them. Feeling them—and they hold me even tighter in return. A part of me shatters at that fact. I did this to them. I put them in the middle of this mess.

And I refuse to fail them ever again.

Fresh tears slide down my cheeks, obscuring my vision as I bury my face in Ainsley's hair, inhaling her scent. Even so, I'm painfully aware of a certain figure who keeps his distance from the fray, eventually leaving the vicinity altogether. His absence reinforces the truth I think we both know at heart, and the ache in my chest could be resignation more than anything else.

This is where I belong.

With my family—not him, a man who sees those around him as tools...

And nothing more.

Children are so easy to fuck up. Traumatize. Hell, I should know that better than anyone. Melanie left scars on my psyche that probably deserve intense therapy or some shit.

But history has a way of repeating itself. Of rubbing your nose in your own mistakes and taunting you with the aftermath.

Right before she started talking, Ainsley went through a clingy phase—but without her real mother around, she attached herself to me. *Separation anxiety*, I think one of her social workers called it. Whatever the fancy term was, she'd panic if I wasn't within reach.

At the height of it all, I had to carry her into the bathroom with me. Eat with her in my lap. Bathe with her. Hell, it got to the point where she would only sleep in my bed.

It went on for four months, being her entire world. At

least until I stole a night light from the drugstore, and she stopped having nightmares.

Until now. Roughly a day after being shot at, we're back at square one.

She's the first kid to swarm me when I arrive. With hugs at first—then death grips on my arms and eventually my waist until I can't pull away. It's nearly an hour before she lets me go just long enough for me to escape into the bathroom.

Finally alone, I splash water on my face and inspect the wound above my eye in its full glory. It's a thin scratch, superficial like Lucius said, but I can't stop touching it out of morbid curiosity. It's going to scar, joining the many already scattered on my skin. I've grown accustomed to ignoring my old cuts. The ones made "accidentally" intentionally with a knife or my nails—anything sharp I could get my hands on. They're mostly silver now, faded with time.

My newer wounds are more severe in both number and brutality. Injuries left by Maxim. Bruises inflicted by Sevastyn. And now this…

"Frankie!" The door shudders, assaulted by someone's pounding fist, and I nearly jump out of my skin. "Frankie!"

"Coming!" I leave the counter, passing a sunken tub and polished white marble tile to reach the door. My hand shakes as I wrench it open, dreading what I might find on the other end. Broken glass? Another shooter? Maxim?

My knees knock together as I face the inevitable. "W-What's happening?"

Ainsley is the only one standing on the other end. I barely take a step before she throws her arms around my waist so tightly it hurts to walk, but I don't go far. The bathroom is just off the open living room on the first floor. Whether intentional or deliberate, the color scheme is night and day to Maxim's grim monochrome.

If an insanely rich mafia boss were to read a manual on what décor might less alarm six children, this room would be on page one. Beige walls blend in seamlessly with pale hardwood floors, creating a brighter, cozier interior than that of his penthouse. Instead of a king's perspective from the heart of the city, the view from here is of the night sky, glimpsed from beyond a landscape of palm trees. It dawns on me as I settle Ainsley onto a white leather chaise near the windows, that I haven't even explored the rest of the property yet.

Even if I wanted to, Ainsley claws at my wrist until I finally relent and sit beside her.

"Don't go." Wider than ever, her eyes fixate on the window. "What if bad people come back?"

"No one's going to hurt you." I pull her into my arms and run my fingers down her back. She's shaking. "Ever."

"Is the man going to protect us?" she asks. "Is that why he's here now? He can fight away the bad people?"

"The man?"

She buries her face against my chest rather than answer. I have an idea of who she's referring to, however. Should I be relieved that she associates Maxim with protection? Maybe. Maybe I'm more alarmed that she noticed him at all despite his intermittent presence these past few weeks. I'd been an idiot to hope that they all wouldn't. Not yet.

Not when I have no fucking clue where he even fits into our lives. Or where I fit into his…

"Close your eyes, baby," I murmur, running my fingers through her hair. "I'm not going anywhere. I promise—"

"You should get some rest," a deeper voice suggests. I stiffen, though the speaker's identity is no mystery—his shadow looms over the polished floor beneath my feet, inescapable. "You need sleep. Both of you. Lucius has coverage on the house from every possible angle. A fly won't get inside unnoticed."

"We're fine." I tighten my grip on Ainsley and close my eyes, nestling my nose against her scalp. If I inhale her deeply enough, I can ignore everything else—including the masculine musk threatening to invade my nostrils by the second.

My sister smells sweeter. Like sugar and toothpaste. And…

I recoil, my nostrils flaring. *Shit.* She smells like pee. Like she wet the bed overnight, but no one else had noticed or forced her to wash up well enough. Guilt hits me like a punch to the stomach. I can't even be angry. It was a habit she had grown out of after a year of constant vigilance and enough pull-ups to last a lifetime. We worked damn hard —the two of us—until she stopped.

My eyes burn, but I blink any new tears back without saying anything. I don't have the heart to. Not even to drag her into the bathtub. Not yet.

I owe her one fucking night of peace, at least. For now, she's breathing normally, her hands in my hair, already asleep.

"There is a room for her upstairs," Maxim continues. "She has a bed. Her clothing has been brought from the—"

"She needs *me*." I pull her closer, cradling her in my arms. "I'm not leaving her."

"There is a room for you as well." His tone falls flat, far more level than I'm used to. "You can share it with her."

"Right now, all I need to do is keep her safe. Make her *feel* safe. No one else can do that. A fancy bed or a fancy fucking house, doesn't change anything." My voice rings out, harsher than I've ever heard it.

In the end, I don't know how long it is before Maxim finally retreats. Minutes? Hours?

I force myself not to care, pouring my sole focus into my sister.

What I said to him was the truth. She needs me more than anyone else. *They* do.

And I've already failed them more than once.

I STARTLE AWAKE to the sensation of my skull on fire. More specifically, like someone is trying to rip a chunk of my hair out. Panicked, my eyes fly open, my body hunched defensively—but my only assailant turns out to be the tiny blond curled on my lap. Still asleep, she moans, grasping for any part of me she can reach.

"You're having a nightmare," I murmur, shaking her awake. "Open your eyes, baby. It's morning."

Soft yellow light seeps in through the windows. As Ainsley rubs her eyes, I stand up.

"Don't go!" She all but climbs onto me before I can go a single step.

"You're okay. Hold on—" I bite back a sigh and lift her into my arms. Her smell hits me like a punch. The house is air-conditioned, but a ruthless humidity magnifies every ounce of sweat and grime.

"Where are your clothes?" I ask.

She shrugs, but I carry her up a modern-style staircase to the upper level of the house, recalling Maxim's mention of a room. It doesn't take me long to find the one meant for her and Daisy to share. Daisy's still asleep in one of the beds, huddled beneath yellow sheets.

The whole room is decorated in shades of pink and yellow, somehow suiting them both. A large window overlooks a clearer view of turquoise water and a distant, white beach. Wherever we are, it's breathtakingly gorgeous—like a goddamn living postcard.

Once I shake off my shock, I find Ainsley a fresh pair of clothes from a jumble of suitcases stacked in the corner of the room. Then I take her into an attached bathroom every bit as luxurious as the one downstairs. Oddly, this feels like falling back into yet another routine from our old life. Cleaning her up. Scolding her for not attending to her hygiene properly while gingerly showing her the correct way to.

"No one shows me like you," she says as I drag a washcloth over her back. "Daisy's always too tired. I was *trying*. Honest."

"I know." I brush my fingers along her delicate cheek. "But you should have told me. I would have helped you. You know that."

She shrugs, sending water sloshing over the rim of the tub. "You weren't there."

I freeze, still holding the cloth against her back. "I'm sorry."

Maybe I'd assumed that Daisy would have been watching her more closely all this time. Or that one of the maids Maxim supplied would know how to coax a six-year-old who didn't understand the concept of soap and body odor fully.

Assuming as much might have eased some of the guilt for staying away.

But not anymore.

"I'm not going anywhere," I whisper near her ear. "I'm not going anywhere ever again."

"Really?" A small smile shapes her lips. "Promise?"

"Yes, baby…" I run my fingers through her damp, tangled hair and sigh. "I promise."

After I dry her off, I help her dress in clean clothes and carry her downstairs. Someone else is already in the living room, peering from a section of windows that overlooks a different view of the outside.

"Hey, Frankie," Mikie calls to me despite his face being practically pressed against the glass. "Have you fucking seen this? Holy shit! I know that guy is loaded as fuck, but damn!"

"What?" Alarm spurs me over to him, only for my mouth to drop open once I reach the window.

I don't even have the sense of mind to scold him for cursing. "Holy shit."

The house has a massive pool that pales in comparison to the view of a sandy beach and the ocean beyond it—but I barely notice those features. Because on the lush green lawn below the terrace, someone dropped a random carnival.

I rub my eyes. I'm delirious, that explains it. But when I look again, nothing's changed.

"This is insane," Mikie exclaims. "The twins are gonna lose their shit. They've been begging to go to shitty Fun Mountain for weeks—" He eyes me from over his shoulder, suddenly serious. "If this is your rich boyfriend's attempt at buying our affection, then consider me fucking bought. This is *insane*!"

Insane is one way to put it. Colorful tents stand erect in the morning light, bathed in the shade of massive palm trees. An actual fucking carousel and some kind of spinning ride add to the impossible illusion. Staff in fitting costumes mill about, setting up machinery and equipment.

And standing stoically amongst it all, I spot a lone figure directing the chaos.

"He gets mad points for this," Mikie adds, his voice dripping awe. "Even if he is in the fucking mafia—"

"Watch your mouth!" I flinch, pressing Ainsley to my chest, though she's seemingly too busy eyeing the scene beyond the glass to listen. "What are you even saying?"

"Frankie. I'm not fucking stupid." He shoots me another brutally honest glance, and my cheeks catch fire. "Normal people don't dress like him. He has a private jet. Armed security. And…" His eyes skim the length of me, surprisingly sharp, missing nothing. "You're always on edge around him—"

"Here." I do my best to hand Ainsley to him. "I'll be right back."

"No! Don't go!" She squirms, but Mikie's strong enough to hold her. Regardless, I have to rip myself away, and her nails sink into me one final time, drawing blood.

"Go ahead. I've got her," Mikie insists, wincing as she claws at his arm next. "It's okay. Right? *All of this* is okay?"

I turn away, unable to answer him. My heart pounds as I race deeper into the house and eventually find a set of French doors that exit onto the terrace. A wall of heat hits me like a slap, and sweat instantly slicks my skin. My brain buzzes with the scent of sea salt, and I sway, blinking to adjust. It's like I'm in a different world entirely from the cold, gray realm of Fair Haven.

One presence serves as my anchor to this reality, however. He stands near the edge of the pool, his back to me. Presumably, due to the heat, he wears a crisp white linen button-down and slacks instead of a suit.

"You're awake." I stiffen at the formality of his tone. He barely inclines his head in acknowledgment as I approach. "How did you sleep?"

"Fine." I cross my arms over my chest, self-conscious of my rumpled clothing and messy hair. At his subtle reminder, my back throbs in full force, sore after sleeping upright. "But what is this?" I gesture to the scene unfolding before us. "Where did you even—"

"This?" He sounds as though waking up to find a popcorn machine in your backyard is a totally normal occurrence. A boring one, even. "This is…*amusement*," he says. "Though I hope you realize why a visit to a real park is out of the question."

"What?" I stare, stunned. Then it dawns on me, what I said to him in the club. *My kids should be in a fucking amusement park or something…*

"No." I shake my head, tearing at my hair. "You didn't…" The insanity of it all is harder to process when viewed up close. The scent of cotton candy and popcorn taint the ocean air. It's as if he really has transported an amusement park here, to only God knows where. Just for the kids?

No. A telltale pinch in my chest warns me that isn't the only reason.

"I was just… I was being hysterical," I croak. "You didn't have to—"

"Get dressed. I need to ensure everything is in order." He turns his attention to one of the passing workers, leaving me behind.

I watch him go, my throat tight. A man of his resources is capable of making the unbelievable possible daily. Like committing murder undetected. Or making problems disappear. Moving families across the world on a whim seems to be his favorite pastime lately. But of all of those actions…

I can't fathom this one.

Confused, I return to the house and enter one of the bathrooms. I wash up at the sink, but without any fresh clothes, I keep on the same dress and comb my hair with my fingers. By the time I return outside, all of the kids are already fully dressed, descending on the lawn. Racing past me, they fan out, rushing from attraction to attraction, all while laughing. Fucking around. Taunting each other in a way they did back in our shitty living room while fighting over video games.

I didn't realize until now how long it's been since I've heard them like this…

They actually sound happy.

And the lone figure responsible stands apart from them, silently watchful. The heat is affecting him as well, gluing the hair to his shoulders and making him glisten beneath a sheen of sweat. He doesn't look anywhere near as rough as I do, though. It's like he thrives within the change of environment, dominating the world even beyond the city. Untouchable. Unfazed.

Unreadable.

Lucius stands beside him, speaking intently. From this distance, I catch snippets of what he's saying. "…Mr. Hood called again this morning, sir."

Maxim grunts in acknowledgment, but he doesn't turn his attention from two workers currently setting up some kind of machinery.

"He was insistent, sir," Lucius adds. "He said if you didn't return his call by this evening—and he specifically accounted for the time difference—then he would, and I quote, 'take matters into my own hands.'"

"I'll handle him," Maxim says, still surveying the surrounding activity. When his eyes find me, he stiffens. "That will be all, Lucius."

"Yes, sir." Lucius nods and crosses the terrace, entering the house.

Alone, Maxim says nothing, but he doesn't turn away. An odd feeling thickens my throat as I take a tentative step in his direction. Gratitude? Guilt? I only make it halfway to him when another voice rings out.

"Frankie?" I bite back a groan as Ainsley spots me from near the carousel and races over. The closer she comes, however, the more relieved I feel. Her eyes are bright, a crooked smile shaping her mouth. "Do you see? There's ice cream!" She excitedly points to a booth across the lawn, staffed by a smiling server. "Can I have some now, even if it's breakfast?"

"Yeah… Just this once." I let her take my hand and follow her over. Not only is the ice cream booth fully stocked, but with an impressively vast selection. So much money must have gone into this. And effort.

I remember something Lucius said in the car after collecting us from the airport. *Everything is in place.*

Were they in on this together?

"I don't know which one," Ainsley whines, drawing my attention back to her. "There's so many. I can't pick!"

I crouch beside her, reading the advertised flavors. "Just pick whichever one you like the best, baby."

"Or…" It's only when a deeper voice replies that I realize she wasn't talking to me. "You can try more than one." Maxim stands nearby, just beyond physical reach—and I can finally put a name to his tone. *Cautious.* "As many as you like."

"Really? Okay!" Beaming, Ainsley turns to the server and proceeds to order a cone topped with five different flavors. The resulting creation is a massive stack she struggles to hold upright. After a few careful licks, she turns to Maxim and flashes a crooked grin. "Yummy! Which one is your favorite?"

"I don't know." His dark eyes scan the ice cream menu, devoting far more attention to the deliberation of dessert flavors than I suspect he usually would. "I admit that I've never tried it."

"What? No ice cream? Never?" Ainsley's eyes go bug-wide as melted chocolate dribbles down her chin. "You should try vanilla, right, Frankie? It's my favorite, and it's the safest bet—"

"Ainsley!" Mikie shouts from across the yard. He, Daisy, Eric, and the twins stand before a toy shooting range, complete with a selection of stuffed animal prizes. "Come see this! I'll win ya whatever you want."

"I want that bear!" All thoughts of ice cream forgotten, she races off, a different girl from this morning.

Four months of progress in four minutes. I know this won't last, but still… A wave of gratitude nearly knocks me over. I have to grip the edge of the ice cream counter for balance. In an instant, I sense a presence nearby, and someone's hand brushes my shoulder.

"Are you alright?"

"I'm fine." *Damn.* My voice echoes back to me, so fucking bitchy. "I'm sorry." But should I be? In frustration, I rip my hands through my hair. "I mean, I'm sorry for what I said last night. But I have to think about what's best for—"

"I could leave now," Maxim suggests. There's no anger in his voice. It's not a threat, but an offer. "Say it, and I will be on the next plane within the hour. You can stay here."

Here in paradise, freed from his presence. But would the distance prevent another attack in the name of his grandfather?

"I…" My mouth is suddenly too dry to speak. I have to moisten my lips with the tip of my tongue, weighing my potential answer. And as I do, Lucius' words come back to haunt me once again. *He can handle rejection…*

"Ainsley thinks you can protect her," I rasp, jerking my head in her direction. I could blame her newfound attitude on the random carnival—but that's not it. My sister isn't that fucking fickle. In the presence of Maxim, she feels safe for whatever reason. Safe enough to let her guard down. "Can you?" I demand. "Can you let her get attached to you without revealing what you do in your spare time? Can you give her stability—and you know I'm not talking about an army of strangers with guns camped outside our house, or a million fancy mansions. I come with *them*. All of them. Do you really understand what that means? You won't open up to me—" Gritting my teeth, I choke down my own hurt in favor of what really matters. "But can you include them into your world? If you can't, then maybe it's best if…"

"If?" His eyes narrow a fraction, fathomless in the sunlight. The more seconds of silence that tick by, the dizzier I become. My chest feels tight, like my heart might explode after the events of the past forty-eight hours.

Should he leave? Stay? I'm on the verge of deciding either way when a guttural voice cuts the tension.

"I will try vanilla," Maxim declares. He's speaking to the server, apparently to order a single scoop of ice cream on a cone.

My breath sticks in my throat at the sight. For a man who can wield a chisel as a weapon, it's nearly impossible to fathom how awkward he looks now. He eyes the cone warily as if skeptical of the purpose of dessert as a whole. Regardless, he brings it to his mouth anyway.

"I confess that I never found the appeal of the concept," he says, this time to me. "*Vanilla.*" His tone betrays a different context for that word, far beyond ice cream.

Without elaborating, he extends his tongue. At the same time, his eyes flick up to mine, and something inside me tightens. I choke down a lump in my throat, incapable of reading his expression. Not even as he tilts his hand, silently offering the cone to me.

"I… I'm good," I stammer, shaking my head.

"You don't appreciate the taste of *vanilla*, after all?" He definitely isn't talking about a shitty frozen treat anymore.

"I-I do." My fingers shake as I curl them over the base of the cone, overlapping his. If I aimed to prove him wrong, I fucking regret it instantly. The heat of his hand is a furnace, melding with the scorching sun.

"Then taste," he commands.

Sweat beads over my forehead as I copy him with my own brief lick. *Vanilla?* This is a version of it I've never experienced, that's for damn sure. The taste flooding my mouth feels anything but *safe*.

"It's good," I agree, drawing back.

He samples another taste for himself. "It's sweet," he declares after swallowing. "I could see how some men prefer this overall."

"For some people, that's all they need," I point out. My gaze drifts beyond him to where Mikie and Ray swing Ainsley between them, while Daisy carries Eric on her back. "Boring. Easy. Safe."

"Safe? Appealing to some, yes. Though I think I will always prefer another taste..." A low sound resonates in his throat as he laps up an entire section of ice cream in one ravenous swipe. Another. His gaze doesn't leave mine once, feeding a dangerous curiosity.

What taste could appeal to him more?

The dessert is already starting to melt, dripping in rivulets down his knuckles, conjuring sinful imagery. *Glistening fingers, assaulted by his tongue, coated in a liquid far different from this...*

I exhale sharply as he takes a step back. I can breathe again. But the reprieve comes at a cost. His entire posture shifts. In an instant, he towers above me, no longer the aloof carnival director. In his gaze lurks a dare he doesn't pose out loud.

Come. His chin tilts, beckoning me closer. Closer. Closer.

I comply before I truly register advancing toward him. Eventually, we wind up yards away from the commotion centered around the kids, and I'm faced with the sheer size of the property. A row of swaying palm trees and a wooden shed obscure us from view now. Happy squeals and joyous shouts make me suspect we won't be missed for a while.

"Maybe your sister had the right idea?" Maxim proposes. His voice sounds closer to its usual baritone, though still cautious. "More than one flavor. A mix. A harmony—" He offers the melting cone to me again. "*Taste.*"

I lick.

He inhales, his eyes gleaming in the sun.

"Would you really be okay with that?" I swipe my hand over my mouth. "Adding *vanilla* into your life?"

"I am not unwilling…" He steals another bite of ice cream, his expression contemplative. "But there will always be parts of me that I cannot change. Certain tastes I cannot compromise for anyone. Can you understand that?"

The cone returns to my mouth. I barely feel the chill wafting off it amid this heat. The suffering mass of ivory symbolizes so much more—no match for satisfying Maxim's true appetite. A wolf can't subsist on vanilla ice cream forever.

But the fact of him even trying it at all might be enough…

"Yes," I whisper. "I understand."

He nods to his hand. "So taste."

I lean in, but at the last second, he moves the cone out of reach, and our lips meet instead. I stiffen at first, only to relax into him. Groaning, he shoves his tongue inside me, snatching me against his chest. The cone falls, but he turns his attention to savoring a different taste. Sugar and sin.

Me. He licks at the sweat dripping down my throat. Down my chest. Between my breasts. My dress is a cumbersome obstacle, no match for him. Fabric rips, and his hands eagerly replace the material, groping. Grasping. Taking.

But even from here, Ainsley's laughter tickles the air. Too close.

"Wait—" I barely voice the plea as he tugs me into an enclosed space. Somewhere hot. Stuffy. The shed?

I only make out a row of hooks on the wall, sporting an array of clothing before his fingers are inside me, his mouth near my ear. "Relax," he growls. "We're alone. Fuck... Always so wet for me."

He's right—and the intensity of his touch takes my breath away. There is no restraint to each violent, brutal thrust of his thumb. No care to disguise the lust edging every hoarse sound to leave his throat.

He devours me.

And some sick part of me is desperate to be consumed. My inner muscles clench around him. I'm wetter by the second, melting in his fucking hands.

"My little kitten," he grates as if in agony. "Always so fucking greedy."

Our eyes meet. Lips again. Panting, I tug at his shirt. His pants. The second his cock is free, I rock my hips, and he enters me. It's fire. Gasoline meeting a lit stick of dynamite.

He feels so good. Too good—despite there being no pain to feed off of. No nipping nails. No bitten flesh. Just him, slamming inside me in a ruthless rhythm. Like he's too drunk off the feeling to crave the violence.

His fingers, slick with ice cream, paint a trail up and down my hips, grazing my nipples, heightening every sensation. Marking me.

Maybe it's the heat or the sweat, but I've never been so wet. He's never felt harder. Deeper. We move in sync, my body gripping him in desperate, grasping convulsions. And yet at the same time, there's a rightness to it. A knowledge deep within that every quivering, yearning inch of flesh belongs to him.

I'm offering it to him.

And his answer lurks within the way his release floods me in waves of scorching fire.

He'll take it all.

CHAPTER NINE

"I may become a fan of vanilla yet," Maxim murmurs against my throat, his fingers entangled in my hair. "Admittedly plain, but…" His lips ignite a fiery path up to my ear, down my jaw, and finally, claim my mouth. "Satisfying," he says, pulling back as my lips burn in the aftermath of his kiss.

"Where are we?" I eye a mass of pink sequins dangling from a hook above my head. An unusual design choice in his world.

"On a private island in the Caribbean."

"Oh." I ferret away that bit of information for later. "But, I mean, now?" I gesture to the view before us—a deconstructed clown costume piled against the opposite wall.

"A staff lounge," Maxim explains absently. "Something about occupational code. Lucius insisted I needed one for the workers, even for a day."

Which reminds me of the insanity that is this morning. "I can't believe you did this—"

"Can't believe?" He lifts me and spins me around, placing me on a flat surface that creaks against our combined weight. A table? I'm too distracted to be sure. His eyes track a white bead of liquid dripping down my chest, and he lunges for it, laving a path with his tongue.

"Still so doubtful of my limits. Though, I do *believe* I am a new fan of ice cream. A rare admission," he confesses against my navel. Before I can recover, he crouches down between my legs, wrenching them apart. My cheeks catch fire at the way he eyes me. Like someone starving. Depraved.

I arch my back, craving the act he promises with a pointed flick of his tongue against his lower lip.

But then I hear it. Voices, calling out desperately. For me.

"Frankie? Where did you go?"

"Shit." I lurch upright, and Maxim returns to his full height, blocking me in.

"Relax." He grabs my arm before I can race for the door. "Listen. They aren't in danger."

He's right. The kids call playfully, but they seem close. Too close. Right when I'm sure they'll barge into the shed, their voices fade, sounding further away.

"An hour's absence," Maxim says. It's only when I notice the thoughtful tilt to his head that I recognize the statement as a proposal. "They will not miss you for that long. They have diversions…"

And even Ainsley can survive for an hour without me in a private, personal carnival.

Could the possessive master be asking for permission?

My heart skips at the possibility. Finally, I trace my lower lip with the tip of my tongue as my gaze meets his. "An hour," I concede.

His eyes flash as he stoops and fishes something from the floor. His shirt. Unfurling it, he coaxes my trembling, languid limbs into the sleeves. Then he redons his pants, and we creep to the door of the shed.

Maxim peeks out first. After a few seconds, he inclines his head for me to follow, and we cut across the terrace for the house at breakneck speed. I don't think it dawns on me until we finally pry open the French doors and slip into the air-conditioned sanctuary what we're doing—sneaking around like horny teenagers desperate for a minute alone. That is, if I had ever been a normal horny teenager who did normal teenage shit.

I doubt he was either.

Still, I can see the appeal of it as Maxim takes my hand and pulls me across the living room and up the stairs. In the absence of his shirt, his muscles ripple with his every movement, devoid of tension for once as he heads in a direction different from that of Ainsley's room—and the other kids' for that matter.

Conveniently out of earshot of the rest of the house, this hallway leads into a semi-private wing. A single door opens onto a space that I presume, given its size, to be the master suite.

It's large enough to fit at least ten more beds, apart from the massive one dominating the center of it. Floor-to-ceiling windows display an intimate view of the surrounding landscape, and a clean, simplistic color scheme fits in perfectly with Maxim's taste.

Black, black, and more black.

Sliding glass doors open onto a secluded balcony containing only a lounge area shaped like a bed, covered in a delicate canopy.

That refuge isn't his intended hiding place, however. On the edge of the suite—coincidentally facing a view of the beach the other rooms only hint at—is a bathroom fit for a mafia prince. Ebony marble reinforces his unique tastes, combined with golden fixtures and a huge sunken bath designed to have an uninterrupted view of the ocean.

I'm so entranced by the sight, I barely notice as thick fingers gently remove his shirt from me, tossing it aside. Naked, I'm at the mercy of his scrutiny. Maxim's breath scorches my overheated flesh, growing harsher the more of me he inhales. Starting at my neck, he skims the width of my shoulders and then back again. Despite our self-imposed deadline, he takes his time, and my thoughts dissipate with every passing second.

Eventually, he manages to get the water running and eases me into the basin of the tub. He sits at the edge, and I settle between his legs, aware of the parts of his body he doesn't bother to disguise for once. His binder which chafes against my back. His bare legs positioned on either side of me, riddled with scars. His cock, hardening already, straining against my hip. I'm a glutton for this moment, hoarding as much of him as I can steal beneath the tips of my fingers. They skim him greedily, unrestrained for once.

God, he's a creature formed of beauty…

And brutality.

My heart lurches the more of him I explore—awed and terrified at the same time. I tentatively trace a stretch of his inner thigh, emboldened when he growls in appreciation. But then my fingers catch a gnarled, near-invisible scar, and I recoil. It's so jagged, betraying a long, agonizing healing. God, I can't even begin to guess what could have made it. Something *painful*. So painful…

"A whip," he explains as if reading my mind. His fingers find mine and force me to touch the scar again. It's as if my curiosity enthralls him almost as much as it consumes me. "Anatoli," he adds. "He liked to embed metal in the tip. That time, I served him a meal without showing the proper respect—I didn't kneel deeply enough."

He sounds so cold. Like someone telling a normal, boring anecdote from his childhood. Not a snippet of horrific, traumatic abuse.

"This upsets you," he deduces, fingering my fluttering pulse. "I will spare you any further—"

"No!" I grasp him in return and tilt his hand, revealing the calloused palm. It's as brutalized as the rest of him—a map of a million unknown injuries. "I want to know."

A deep sound rumbles from his throat as if questioning. *Oh?* I sneak a glance at his face, surprised to find him watching me, an eyebrow raised in confusion. Could that be why he's so fucking secretive? Not because he's trying to hide his past, but because he can't fathom the idea of someone wanting to know about it. About him.

"I want to know everything about you." I hate how it sounds when uttered out loud. So desperate and pathetic. But he doesn't scoff or hiss in annoyance. Taking a risk, I finger a scar slicing across his palm and propose my first request, "Tell me what caused this one."

"A blade, I think." The rising water around us sloshes as he shrugs. He's skeptical of this game of show and tell, but still willing to play along. For now. "He made me train with them. It is easy to cut yourself if you aren't careful."

"What about this one?" I finger a crescent-shaped mark across his knuckles.

"Glass," he says without elaborating.

"And this one?" I turn to face him and place my hand over the center of his chest.

He sighs. "That one… Some of them I don't remember the cause of." His eyes darken, revealing his surprise at that fact. I wonder if he's ever stopped to tally up his marks before.

Or those inflicted *by* him.

Another question worms into my mind, and I don't bother swallowing it down. "How did Vadim get his scar?" I'm not brave enough to meet his gaze, but his fingers find my jaw and lift it anyway.

Anger isn't what colors his expression for once as far as that name is concerned. Just exhaustion. "Vadim?" The lines around his mouth strain, more pronounced than ever. He looks so worn. So tired. So alien from everything I know about the depth of human emotions and how normal people express them. He's more wolf than ever.

"Forget it," I croak. "You don't have to—"

"I tried to cut his throat." He lets me go and hones his gaze on the window.

"Why?" I whisper.

"We were children. I had a knife. I won't lie to you—" He snatches my hand, pressing it to the side of his face as if forcing me to feel the truth in every uttered word. "I wanted to kill him. It was only due to my inexperience that I didn't. Why? Because he stood in my way." His tone chills me to the core, despite the steam wafting from the water. "He was an obstacle since birth. A potential replacement always compared to me. Always. By our father. By Anatoli. If I slacked for even a second, Vadim's name was on their lips. In some ways, they preferred him. He was smarter. More cunning. Charming in his own way. But when it came to a direct challenge, he always lacked the strength." He bares his teeth in a feral snarl, still trapped in that competitive cycle—even if it leaves him fighting against a memory. "Only one of us would be deemed worthy of carrying the Koslov name. I couldn't fail, not even for him. I refused to…"

He blinks as if forgetting where he is. Then his eyes fixate on me, and some of the tension constricting them eases.

"My entire life, I have fought for *this*." He nods as if to indicate his entire being. His identity. "I've won—" He grips my chin in return, inspecting my expression. Whatever he finds, makes him recoil in disgust. "And yet, you are the only person in the world to ever look at me as you do. With *pity*."

"It's not pity." I lunge for him before he can push me away. Trembling, my lips brush his chest, sensing the heart racing within. His taste is a world apart from melting ice cream. Dangerous. Enticing. Addicting. Alarming. And I lick my lips to savor every drop. "I do not pity you—"

"So what is it then?" he gruffly demands. "Disgust?"

"I… I feel for you," I find the space above his heart with my fingers—coincidentally where one of his worst scars is. He goes rigid every time I graze the ropey, uneven flesh. Regardless, I can't stop touching him. "I know what it feels like…"

To fight.

To sacrifice.

To suppress.

"Oh?" He laughs. "You know what it's like to stab your own fucking 'sibling'? I respect your intent, Francesca—" His use of my name stings, anything but an endearment. "But, I strongly suggest you avoid comparing yourself to me in this instance."

"I know what it's like to lie to yourself," I insist, ignoring the warning in his tone. "To crave an escape. You wanted to destroy your brother. I… I wanted to destroy myself."

Suddenly, he captures my wrist and extends it for his inspection. Something, in particular, draws his interest, making him stiffen, a curse on his lips. It's a nasty scratch, stretching the width of my forearm, still weeping fresh beads of blood. "Do not tell me that what happened with Vadim caused this…"

I frown at the sudden seriousness of his tone. "No." But it's not like a fresh wound is an unusual occurrence between us. Then it hits me—he thinks I did it to myself.

"These have lessened," he points out as if reading my mind again. His thumb travels down my arm, grazing over countless healed scars and weeks-old scabs. "Since you've been with me. Did you think I didn't notice them?"

I wrack my brain, surprised that he might be right. Apart from a few nicks from my nails, I haven't hurt myself the way I used to. Not with a knife or razor. Not with my teeth.

"You enjoy pain," he says carefully. "But it wasn't until I noticed these—" he fingers another old injury of mine. "That I understood why. You crave the release of it."

"And what do you get out of it?" I counter, though I think I've finally deciphered the real answer on my own.

His mouth twitches, part grimace, part frown. "Pleasure."

A lie.

I can put the pieces together, even if the picture they make terrifies the shit out of me. One example comes to mind.

"You made me kneel for you." I brush my free hand along his forearm, sensing the power lurking beneath the healed, scarred flesh. "When you whipped me. You made me kneel. Like your grandfather made you—"

"Don't. *Please.*" He shakes his head, his teeth gritted. He's quiet for a moment. "I do not take for granted what you give to me. What no one else could, you do—" he returns his attention to the scratch. "But I don't want you seeking control out of fear."

"I didn't hurt myself," I admit. "Ainsley scratched me by accident. She's afraid."

"I know." He shifts, stiffening against me. "I will do everything in my power to prevent what happened from happening again."

"But you can't, can you?"

He doesn't respond.

"She's a little girl." My voice breaks. "She doesn't deserve to grow up afraid."

"I can make her happy," he counters. "Happier than today —all of them. I can keep you content. You can keep me sane."

"Is that what you really want?" It sounds like yet another way of phrasing the give and take of our entire relationship.

"I want understanding with you," he corrects. "No more mincing words. I want you on my side."

"As a partner?"

"Or a lover."

My cheeks burn at the raw heat in his tone. "You don't normally talk like this."

He returns his gaze to the view, eyeing it blankly, unimpressed. "You weren't listening before. Maybe this language will convince you?"

"So what are you suggesting?"

"At night, you give me what I need. And by day…" His eyes rove slowly to my face. "I give you what you want."

And what is that?

He doesn't say, but a few options come to mind. A Maxim who talks. An open Maxim. And unfiltered Maxim.

An unrestrained Maxim.

"What are you thinking?" His thumb slips beneath my chin, lifting it. So rich and deep, his eyes seem to stare right through me, impossible to escape.

"I'm wondering…how you'll indulge without traumatizing my family if we're all staying in the same house." Mikie's right. He's no idiot.

"Is that all?" Maxim's mouth quirks, and it's like the world fucking falters. "I have two methods in mind that should work in tandem."

Something warns me not to ask what they are. Not yet.

"But as for today?" He reaches out, grasping my hand. Raising it to his mouth, he brushes his lips along my knuckles, inhaling deeply all the while. "I will do nothing to alarm your family. You can trust me on that."

And I think I can.

At least for now.

CHAPTER TEN

The house itself turns out to be far more incredible than I initially realized. The open floor plan is centered around a breathtaking view of the square-shaped pool and the ocean beyond it. Wide, open windows allow in a sea-salt tinged breeze that displaces some of the heat, making the air feel more comfortable than the most intense air-conditioning.

There aren't many rooms in total either. The girls share a spacious suite in one wing while the boys share another. I'm struck by the careful planning of the layout as Maxim leads me on this impromptu tour, his hair still dripping wet. Our only detour is a trip to the closet of the master bedroom, where he changes into another linen shirt and plain slacks. There I discover an array of women's clothing hanging alongside his, conveniently coordinated to match. I slip into a loose-fitting white sundress and make a mental note to explore the rest of my wardrobe later.

"It's a fairly new acquisition," Maxim explains as we follow a wide hallway next, accented by windows that look out onto the terrace. From here, I can see the kids, clamoring to ride the carousel. "Even I have yet to explore it fully. Though there are a few…necessities that I insisted upon before closing."

Necessities? I decide to overlook voicing such a loaded question in favor of something far more harmless. "Where is my room?"

"Where? You've seen it." He gestures in the direction of his master suite. *Our* master suite, apparently.

"Oh. But when I was with Ainsley, you said…" A sudden realization chokes me off. He suggested I sleep with her in "my room"—which really meant he would forfeit his own bed entirely.

"Come." I look over to find him inclining his head. "There is one final feature I want to show you."

I follow him warily into the suite. This time, he approaches a door opposite the bathroom, near the bed. Another closet?

"Open it," Maxim says without explanation. "My one request before I would commit to buying the property…"

The grim commentary comes as I reach for the curved, metal handle. I tug, but rather than open automatically, I sense a slight give, and my ears pick up a mechanical sound before the door finally comes loose.

"It is now bio-metrically activated." I look over my shoulder to find Maxim advancing, his expression unreadable. "Only you or I can unlock it."

"Really?" I observe my fingers, too terrified to face what might be waiting beyond the door just yet.

"Come." As if aware of my hesitation, he takes my hand and steps around me, leading the way into the mysterious space. His bulk blocks my view initially. I can only make out a short hallway though the echoing sound of our footsteps alludes to a much larger area beyond it.

"It's still…rough," Maxim says as he maneuvers me to stand beside him. "I had the construction rushed to ensure it would be usable, but it will suffice. For now."

It being a near-identical replica of the "toy" room from his penthouse in the city—only white marble flooring makes the space seem even more isolated than the black. It's a stark canvas in a sense, incapable of hiding any stains; something I suspect he's planned on. A marble altar-shaped platform sports a thin, white pad for comfort, and a row of metal cabinets must contain whatever a man like him might need to indulge his inclinations toward sadism.

"Do you still agree to this?" His fingers slip beneath my chin, guiding me to face him directly.

Do I? Deep down, I sense that the answer is more important to him than the fact that we're standing in a sex room designed for pain and pleasure. He still wants my consent.

"The rules won't change," he adds. "If you want me to stop, you—"

"I know," I say.

"And?" His thumb traces the ball of my chin, making my breathing hitch with every traversed inch. "You aren't one for nuance, but I sense there is more you want to say."

And he's right. I suck in a breath and release it on a single question. "When we return to the city, will things go back to how they were before?"

Him dwelling primarily alone in his secluded penthouses while I live apart from my family.

He strokes my cheek. "Only if you want them to..."

WE RETURN DOWNSTAIRS, and Maxim leads me through an impressive kitchen with a view of the terrace. Without a word of explanation, he proceeds to stockpile several items from the fridge and a walk-in pantry into his arms. Meat. Veggies. Bread. I watch him in silence, intrigued by the potential uses for the ingredients. Fodder for the kids to throw at the shooting game, maybe?

Once on the terrace, he approaches a metal grill and confidently rolls up his sleeves. As he fires up the range, his true intent becomes crystal clear, and I suck in a startled breath.

He plans to cook dinner. For *us.*

As impossible as it seems in theory, the scent of grilled meat wafts across the lawn within minutes—a far cry from the polished, cold dinners I've come to associate him with.

The backdrop of the ocean breeze and the distant murmur of crashing waves create a cozy, casual aura. Even the kids are enticed enough to trudge in from the dispersing carnival, exhausted and dripping with sweat.

"I thought we might try something different tonight," Maxim says while dropping cooked hot dogs onto a plate. "Something…informal." His gaze cuts in my direction, and I squirm. Again, it's as though he's reading my mind.

Or even more unsettling—he's starting to know me too damn well.

"I want that big one!" Ainsley demands, appearing beside him, her eyes fixated on the food. "Or maybe that one. Or that one…"

The rest of us scatter onto nearby lounge chairs. Ironically, it's no different from how we used to eat, but with actual silverware and a mansion backdrop rather than a filthy living room.

And a newcomer whose presence is impossible to ignore.

As if sensing all eyes on him, Maxim tosses a fresh wave of food onto the grill. "Did you enjoy the attractions?" he wonders as the meat sizzles—his attempt at small talk, I realize. It doesn't come naturally to him, at least not in this context. But as stiff as his voice sounds forming the words, they land innocently enough.

"Yes!" Ainsley beams, practically bouncing on her toes. "I had so much fun, though I rode the spinny ride too many times and threw up on Mikie's—"

"No reminders, please," Mikie pipes up from his position near the pool. He cradles his head in his hands, and I notice a damp splotch on his shirt. "It took two bottles of water to get it out."

"Don't be such a baby," Ainsley snipes. Then she turns to Maxim and points to the spatula. "Can I help? Please?"

"Well…" His movements slow as he processes the request. "If your sister doesn't mind, then I suppose so—"

"Ainsley," Daisy says from a nearby chaise, "leave him alone. You're bothering him."

"No, I'm not!" Jutting her chin into the air, Ainsley tugs on Maxim's pant leg. "Right?"

"Right." No match for her, he surrenders the spatula and stoops to help her tend to the sizzling food. Under his guidance, she flips a hot dog by herself and howls in triumph.

"See?" Her impish grin could easily be classified as smug. "He *wants* me to help."

"You don't have to be a little brat about it," Daisy bites back. "But all you're doing is getting in the way."

"Hey!" I stick out my hand, inserting myself as the referee. "I think it's okay as long as she is careful—"

"You would say that, wouldn't you?" Scoffing, Daisy crosses her arms. "Like you give a damn about her safety."

"Daisy…" I resist the urge to groan out loud. "Do we have to do this now?"

"Do what? Lie? Eat dinner like a good little family?" She rolls her eyes at the plate of food balanced on the end of the grill. "Are we really pretending like everything's okay? Like we weren't shot at the other day? Like we aren't missing school? Like this is *normal*? Oh, I'm sorry. I guess we're just going to keep acting like what happened at the other house really was a gas leak—"

"Daisy." I stand and start toward her, fighting to keep my voice level. "We can talk about this in private—"

"Private? Like you give a damn about *privacy*! We don't even know who he is!" She points at Maxim and jabs the same finger at me. "Or who you are to him. Are you dating him? Screwing him? Are you some kind of high-class hooker? His mistress? What the hell is it? Or—" She hisses, her eyes narrowing. "Are you going to act like Mama and want us to call him 'Daddy?'"

"Knock it off!" Mikie snaps, appearing at my side. "Stop being a bitch."

"Don't be so stupid!" Daisy laughs at him, her voice high-pitched.

Whatever triggered this, it isn't about fucking hot dogs.

"She hasn't denied it," she points out, propping her hands on her hips. "And don't pretend like you don't know how she got her money before, Mikie. The slutty dresses? The late nights? Do I have to spell it out? She was a fucking prostitute. And this? It's just a fucking buy-off—"

"I care about your sister," Maxim interjects from his position near the grill. Silence falls instantly. It's as if the entire world stops, heeding the authority he exudes in every word.

Daisy grits her teeth, ruthlessly defiant. "I'm sorry, but what is that supposed to mean to me? Because all it's meant so far is bouncing around from place to place with no fucking clue as to what's going on." Her voice breaks. Tears spill down her cheeks, and it's painfully clear what today, despite all of Maxim's effort, truly was at the end of it all. A Band-Aid. "I'm not the only one who thinks it's fucking weird," she adds. "I'm just the only one brave enough to say it. I've already been through four stepdads, and I'm sorry, but I don't want another one. And it's not good for Ainsley, or Eric, or any of us to have strange men bounce in and out of our lives because they pay the bills for a few months."

"True," Maxim concedes, still tending the grill. "Stability is important, and words are meaningless. Which is why… I've asked your sister to marry me."

His statement is met with more silence. Unbearable, overwhelming fucking silence. I can't even look at Daisy, or the others for that matter. I stare at the sky instead. A swath of orange paints the horizon like fire, burning up the peace of the day, and leaving darkness behind.

"Um…okay." Mikie clears his throat, ever the peacemaker. "Is that true, Frankie?" I force myself to face him, prepared for the worst. But his expression doesn't convey anger or shock. Just confusion.

"Of course not," Daisy snarls, her cheeks red, eyes blazing. "Because you wouldn't do that, would you, Frankie? You wouldn't be dating someone without telling us. Your *family*—"

"Of course, she wouldn't. Which is why she rightly refused my offer," Maxim explains while flipping over a cooked burger. His shoulders are hunched, his posture rigid, and yet his voice doesn't hold a trace of annoyance. The relentless calm neutralizes even Daisy's hostility. Slowly, she sits back down.

"You mean more to her than anything I could offer," he continues. "More to her than any promise of money, or luxury. In fact, she threatened to leave me if I ever questioned that devotion again, and as you can see, there is no ring on her finger. Consider this vacation as my way of apologizing for insulting her. Nothing more. I can only hope that she will reconsider."

He finally looks in my direction, but I turn away and hunt for the first distraction I can find. "I...I'm going to take care of these dirty dishes."

I snatch up the nearest empty plates and cut across the terrace before anyone can recover enough to stop me. My hands shake so badly it takes me three tries before I can pry open the door to the kitchen. *Fuck!* I trip over the threshold in my rush, and the plates fall from my hands, smashing apart at my feet.

I can't even muster the sense of mind to clean the mess. Instead, I approach the sink, panting to control my breathing. Running the water as hot as it can go and shoving my hand beneath it is the only way to regain some semblance of clarity.

So much for our day of normalcy.

I close my eyes, mulling over the potential ways I can fix this mess. Apologize? Slap Daisy a second time? Run?

It's too late. My neck prickles with the awareness of someone behind me, betrayed by heavy footsteps.

"I know that is not how you wanted to tell them," Maxim admits. Before he can come closer, I turn off the water and tuck my stinging hand to my chest. "I apologize—"

"For what?" I force out a broken laugh. I don't know what's more disorienting, this entire conversation? Or the rare hint of regret from him? "You covered for my ass when you didn't have to. Thank you. But…"

"But?" he prompts.

"You wanted me to take your name, but what about them? Daisy's right, we've had our fair share of winners come through. And…have you thought about what kind of relationship you're comfortable with allowing?"

Melanie had her suckers throw around the word "Daddy" like it meant something. I could never do the same to the kids. Even with a description as harmless as *"Maxim, the brother-in-law for protection only."*

He doesn't say anything—but again, it's as though he's reading my mind, waiting for the real concerns to come spilling out.

"And what if…I don't want it? Your name. Even if your grandfather removes the bounty. And not because of you," I add in a rush. "But…he *abused* you—"

"Don't." He grits his teeth and glances at the doorway. Thankfully none of the kids have followed us inside. Yet. Returning his attention to me, Maxim's tone deepens in warning, "He has nothing to do with it."

"Doesn't he?" I rake my gaze over him, sensing the scars lurking beneath the polished exterior. "Your uncle was a pedophile," I add softly. "Only God knows about the rest of your family. You care about the Koslov name, but do you really want Ainsley to share the name of people like that? As you can tell, we aren't exactly the most perfect family to start with."

"You're upset," Maxim concedes. He crouches and grabs the broken plates with his bare hands. After tossing them into a garbage can, he heads for the door. "Come and eat." For whatever reason, his voice still holds that persistent calm. His posture, however, stiffens, his jaw tightening. "Give me this night to prove that I meant what I promised you, and the rest..." He blinks, suppressing whatever emotion might threaten his composure. "We can discuss later."

"That's it?" I wave halfheartedly in the kid's direction. "We just spring a bomb like that on them and then pretend it never happened?"

"You wanted normalcy," he says. "I may not be an expert, but I believe this might be part of it. Honesty. Or have you changed your mind?"

He waits near the doorway of the terrace until I finally leave the sink and follow. Outside, all six kids remain seated, but none of them seem willing to make eye contact. We merely coexist in awkward silence until Maxim reclaims his spot before the grill.

"Who wants another hot dog?" he asks, breaking the quiet.

Easily distracted, Ainsley perks up and raises her hand. "Me!"

"Me too," pitches in Mikie.

Then Ray, Ollie, and Eric all voice their assent.

Finally, Daisy sighs, lifting her hand. "I'll take one, too."

"Alright, then." Maxim continues to cook, and I force myself to reclaim a lounger, watching him. Them. It's a slow, clumsy return to our previous rhythm, and it doesn't come easily by any stretch of the imagination.

But it happens.

Eventually, it happens.

CHAPTER ELEVEN

As night falls, the kids stagger off to bed, exhausted. I tuck in Ainsley and press a kiss to her cheek while Daisy ignores me from the other end of the room. I let her sulk, preferring a tense truce over starting another war.

After checking on the boys, I finally steel myself to approach the master suite.

The sheer distance between it and the other rooms becomes apparent as it takes me a full minute to traverse it. The spaces are close enough that I would hear any bloodcurdling screams emanating from the kid's rooms—but little else. And they, theoretically, wouldn't hear anything in return. Like a cracking whip or a hiss of pain.

Or, more reassuringly, any brutal sex.

Inside the master bedroom, Maxim stands with his back to me and sheds his shirt, tossing it aside. "If you've changed your mind," he begins in a hollow tone, "if you want to stay with your sister—"

"I'm okay," I whisper.

Who cares if it's a lie? We had a deal. But the weight of our trade-off truly sinks in the longer I watch him. He's lost within his head again. Radiating tension, his muscles ripple and coil beneath his skin, threatening to rip from it.

Lucius' wolf analogy returns to mind. A beast can only remain caged for so long—and that's the word to describe how he looks now. Caged.

And I'm the bitch who twisted the key.

"I'm sorry," I croak, advancing a cautious step. "I had no right to mention your past like that—"

"You are ready?" With those three words, he cuts me off, and his façade of control splinters. He gave me what I wanted—peace. And now I have to return the favor.

"I'm ready…"

"Come." He crosses the room and opens the door. My breaths quicken as I approach him, my palms slick with sweat.

He looks so on edge. So fucking haunted.

As I near the threshold, I can't resist touching his forearm. "What's wrong—"

"No!" He wrenches beyond my reach and storms into the room. Deep down, I know the answer anyway. I brought up his past, ripping open old wounds he'll never acknowledge out loud. "No talking. Not now. I just… I need—" He moves to one of the cabinets on the other end of the room and tugs open a drawer. From it, he withdraws a single, coiled strip of leather. My heart lurches as he unfurls it with a graceful flick of his wrist and then turns to face me. "Kneel." When I don't move, he exhales, practically swaying on his feet. Corded muscle flexes in his throat as he rasps a second time, *"Kneel."*

It's not fear that has me frozen. It's shock. This is the closest I've ever seen him come to…begging. And I never want to see it again.

Relief escapes him in a harsh sigh as I sink to the floor, my head lowered in obedience.

His steps resonate like thunder as he approaches me, and here, in this new arena, the rules of the game change once again…

Entirely at his discretion.

A GROAN RIPS from my lips as my eyelids part to a stream of blinding sunlight. It's morning, but I doubt I've slept a full hour. Minutes, maybe?

Or seconds.

Revenge might be too petty a concept to apply to someone like Maxim. Perhaps retribution instead? Whether to exact payment for yesterday's events, or out of anger for what I said, he kept me in the room until every inch of me throbbed in punishment…

I only remember snippets. *The whip. His commands—kneel, kneel, kneel.* I huddle beneath the sheets as one image remains in my skull no matter how hard I try to block it out—his face the few times he allowed me to glimpse it. I'll never forget that expression. Cold. Icy. Detached. The only comparison that might come close to it is the day he took me into that dank room already lined with a tarp.

And yet…

I can't escape the feeling that, this time, he held back. That's the most alarming part of it all. Neither assault broke the skin. He didn't fuck me either. Locked within himself, he merely raged, fighting against phantoms I couldn't see.

And by the end, I realized…he was never angry with me.

Afterward, I vaguely remember him carrying me to the bed. However, his steps then retreated, alluding to a night spent wandering throughout the house. Even now, he's not in the room.

And I don't know whether to sigh in relief or despair. The true cost of our bargain hadn't been put into explicit terms until now. His silence, for my comfort.

Closing my eyes, I contemplate sleeping again, but a scent tickles my nose, and confusion draws me upright. Food? Either Maxim hired another private chef, or Daisy—the only kid brave enough to tackle the stove—is trying to cook again. Though fuck, burning this fancy house down could be her latest act of rebellion.

Morbid curiosity outweighs my exhaustion, and I take a quick shower before throwing on a light linen dress. Then I head downstairs only to find everyone in the kitchen, camped out around a center island.

Everyone.

Maxim stands at the heart of the commotion, as stern as a drill sergeant—though one wearing gray slacks in lieu of a uniform. Armed with a pair of tongs, he dishes out various portions of pancakes and scrambled eggs to the eager troops jockeying for position around him. When his eyes find mine, there is no hint of the coldness from last night. He merely nods in acknowledgment while balancing a platter of food on his opposite hand. "You're awake."

"Frankie!" Ainsley rushes to me and throws her arms around my waist. "He made pancakes! And they were good and not burned like Daisy's—"

"Shut up," Daisy snaps, but she eyes me sheepishly. "Morning, Frankie."

I blink. The lack of a scoff directed my way might even be her attempt at an apology. Is this a hallucination? I resist the urge to pinch myself.

"Have a seat." Maxim pulls out the stool beside him and ladles food onto a plate for me. If I were sleeping, I figure the shock of this moment might snap me awake. He actually made pancakes, not steak, or some variation of bleeding meat. "Eat."

My gaze darts around the room as I chew mechanically, uneasy for reasons I can't name. Maybe the feeling has something to do with the mischievous way Ainsley keeps eyeing Maxim from over my shoulder?

It's fucking weird. Normal even?

Once I've cleared my plate, Ainsley nearly bounces off her seat, and the jig is apparently up.

"So can we ask her now?" she pleads, batting her eyelashes. "Please?"

Maxim eyes her and sighs. "Your siblings were wondering if you would consent to a day at the beach," he says.

And that simple phrase triggers all six kids to start speaking at once.

"Please?" Ainsley whines.

"He said he has a boat," Mikie pitches in. "And a jet ski—"

"And there's a cabana," Daisy adds hesitantly. "I could tan, and—"

"Okay." I hold up my hands in surrender. "Okay."

"Yes!" They race off, clamoring for the stairs while I try to process the concept with more scrutiny. A day at the beach, like a real fucking family. Have we ever had one of those?

It doesn't take long to settle on an answer. *No.*

"Lucius is a trained swimmer, as is Tomas," Maxim explains while piling dishes into the sink. "Both will accompany them for now."

I frown at the phrasing. "We won't?"

"No." It takes me a second to classify his expression. *Wary?* After rinsing the last of the dirty plates, he dries his hands and then heads for the stairs. My only clue as to his intent comes in the form of a single phrase uttered from over his shoulder. "We need to talk."

Left with no choice, I mount the stairs in his wake and trail him down the hall. As we enter the bedroom, I can't suppress a shudder. My eyes find the door to the "other" room. Will he insist on a round two, even in broad daylight?

Rather than head for that door in the corner, however, he steps onto the balcony. It's hot as hell out, and the sun beats down ruthlessly, illuminating everything in view for miles—from the terrace, to the beach, to a good portion of the open ocean.

"We will be able to see them from here," Maxim explains. As if on cue, a stream of tiny figures darts from the house to the beach, led by a taller person with a body shape suspiciously like Lucius'. "We can hear them as well..." His breath scorches the nape of my neck as he leans in closer to add, "But they cannot see us."

I've barely processed what that fact could implicate when his fingers find my shoulders and dig into the sore, tense muscle. Groaning, I relent to the pressure. He's damn good with his hands, kneading stiff flesh the same way he works his stone carvings. Before I know it, we're seated on the wide lounger, and he's massaging me in full.

Despite slipping his hands beneath the neckline of my dress, he keeps the contact purely clinical, focusing his attention where I ache the most.

"You're tight here." A rare hint of emotion colors his tone, leaving me reeling. Sympathy? Or maybe resignation at his handiwork.

This definitely isn't the worst state I've been in after a night with him. As the seconds tick by, I'm faced with the possibility that his hesitation has nothing to do with my soreness at all. Finally, his fingers still.

"Last night may not have been ideal," he starts, "but if you are satisfied with this arrangement, we can continue in this way from now on."

Normalcy for the kids by day, kink for him at night.

I lift my head and scan the stretch of beach until I spot where the kids have made camp. They fan out, darting from the waves to the shore.

"It could work," I say cautiously. "As long as Ainsley doesn't wake up from a nightmare and barge into the bedroom."

What I intend as a joke seems to have the opposite effect.

"Good." He stands, his hands held awkwardly at his sides. "We should go join the others—"

"But can we discuss the rules at least? Boundaries?" I can't forget how he looked last night. Closed-off. Isolated. "If we are to do this. *Really* do this, then I need to know what we keep in the room and what stays out."

He tilts his head thoughtfully and sits back down. "Some things… My past—" His gaze clouds over, distant. "That stays in the room."

The things he can't talk about. Such as Anatoli's abuse or his way of coping with it.

For a second, I wonder if it's worth arguing over—demanding to know more. But then I look at him. He's stiff, glowering at the ocean as if seeing hell where most people would only see paradise. There's so much about him I don't know, but maybe it's not my place to force him to reveal what he's not ready to.

"What about sex?"

He frowns, and I have his attention again. His fingers cross the distance between us, stopping short of my hip. The simple act conveys the power harnessed by him always. "In the room, I will have control."

"And outside of it?"

"Outside…" As he mulls over the question, he sweeps his hand along my thigh. There's no possession in this action. Just touching. Feeling. "Does my kitten crave another taste of vanilla?"

I look away, my cheeks on fire. Do I? Sex with him is one thing when pain is involved—mind-blowing. But without, like what happened in the shed?

It's a different taste entirely. One I'm not sure I want to write off exploring.

"Hmph." Maxim hooks his finger beneath my chin, coaxing me to face him. "I will admit that I am not familiar with this. Being…*domestic*." His accent thickens as though it's a dirty word.

The sinful, unknown kind of dirty—the way someone might sound describing his peculiar tastes. Taboo.

"I suppose that outside of the room, you may decide…" He trails off, seemingly unable to finish the thought. Outside of the room, I could potentially have control.

Over him.

It sounds too fucking good to be true.

"Really?"

"If it is necessary to your normalcy," he counters.

"So, during the day, I can touch you when I want to?" I rise up onto my knees, shifting to face him.

Dare I say he looks…curious. My heart jumps, rebounding off my ribcage.

"Touch?" he questions softly.

"Like this…" My fingers shake as I unfurl them one by one. When I brace my hand over his chest, he doesn't flinch. Emboldened, I undo the buttons of his shirt, and he shrugs his shoulders to help me remove it. Observing him this way is an experience unlike any other. I take my time, determined to savor every second.

His scars look ten times more grotesque in broad daylight. Beautiful too. I finger one, aware of his gaze tracking my every movement. Leaning forward, I press my lips against the most abused piece of flesh.

A low rasp catches in his throat. "You want to touch me in this way?" He sounds so amused by the prospect. As though any warm-blooded woman wouldn't crave a chance to appreciate his body.

I murmur in agreement, too intent on my task to form a coherent reply. But the more of him I inspect, the more doubt starts to sneak in. Could someone like him enjoy sex without control?

Once my hand travels downward, I discover my answer— oh *yes*. Hard, straining muscle pulses beneath the fabric of his slacks, conveying anything but discomfort. My breaths quicken as I press another kiss to an old wound on his chest. Another. I feel as though I'm marking them mentally for more detailed exploration in the future.

I can learn their secrets later.

Learn more of him later.

Right now, he's presenting me with a rare gift I know better than to waste. Patience. Time. Control.

True to our agreement, he doesn't command where I can touch him or how. He merely leans back against the cushions, at my mercy for once.

And I never knew what it could fucking feel like. Having *this* kind of power over someone. Studying them like an open book—far different from being a receptacle for their cock. I can't stop touching him. Kissing various parts of him. Learning his taste. The touch he likes—not what he demands, but truly *likes*. He jumps when I feather kisses over his pecs. Growls when I slide my fingers over his nipples. Inhales, the lower I go.

Lower.

Lower…

A guttural hum revs in his throat when I open the fly of his slacks, finally freeing his cock. This close, I can sense the sheer force of will it takes for him to keep from grabbing me. Forcing me. Controlling the act.

Were this to go his way, I'd never be able to caress him with soft, featherlight strokes. I'd never test the limits of his body, bringing him to the edge. Heavy-lidded, his eyes find mine, conveying the words he isn't capable of uttering out loud. *Witch,* I imagine him hissing. *What are you doing to me?*

I'm savoring him in every conceivable way. Like his taste when mingled with the hint of sea salt and the unbearable heat. His size. How thick he can be when barely aroused —and how intimidating he can become once engorged, his body throbbing for release.

A gasp rips from his throat when I finally part my lips and take him in. It's fucking music, so beautiful. Noise I never knew him capable of making. This new, restrained Maxim comes complete with his own soundtrack—fabric hisses as he fists his hands in the material beneath us, nearly ripping it.

My brain buzzes, drugged on the atmosphere of lust, and the heady flavor of him. What would seem debasing in any other context is indescribable now. I take him deep, moaning at his taste. His feel. Everything. I don't care if I'm forced onto my knees, my ass in the air, my hair fanning out around me like some whore. He doesn't demand a single fucking thing from me.

Not even when he's pulsing against my tongue, practically writhing beneath his skin. I look up, meeting his gaze. Sweat slicks his forehead, his eyes unfocused, his lips parted. God, he's unrivaled like this.

But even now, doubt still sneaks in.

"Is this okay?" I blurt in a clumsy rush.

"I…" His throat cords around a thickened swallow. "I need to be inside of you."

That's all it takes to melt my brain entirely. A simple plea.

And I nearly come before I can even lurch against his chest and part my legs. He groans once he's seated to the hilt, his eyes closing in relief, teeth clenched. His hands find my waist, but he doesn't set the pace. I'm left to ride him of my own volition with no outside influence.

Slowly.

Harder.

Distant laugher and the roar of the ocean create an odd, unsettling backdrop that feeds the pleasure thrumming beneath my skin. This is insane. Fucking him beneath the sun in broad daylight is insane. Kissing him in between every thrust is maddeningly *insane.*

My orgasm hits me before I even register the depth of pleasure. He follows me, hissing partly in satisfaction, partly in agony.

"Fuck!" His hair frames him like a halo as he falls back against the headboard of the lounger. Utterly spent, I land against him, and his hand finds my hip, delivering a reverent stroke. "I *definitely* think I may come to enjoy vanilla…"

We wash up, change, and join the kids on the beach before noon. The youngest four are making a sandcastle at the water's edge, while Daisy and Mikie share a jet ski under the watchful gaze of Lucius, who wears his customary suit despite the heat.

A row of cabanas is positioned with a view of the water, creating a cozy, homey space. Maxim leads me to one, and we share yet another bed-sized lounger—though this time with a safe distance between us.

It should be so boring in theory. Lazing in the shade, watching the kids frolic in the ocean without a care in the world. To some people, maybe it would be. To me, this strain of peace is a new drug.

And I'm hopelessly addicted already.

Just when I think our "normalcy'" has reached its peak, we're accosted by a whining Ainsley who begs Maxim to take her into the water. Which he does, utilizing a gentleness I would have never suspected him capable of expressing. I think he's surprised by it as well. The tenderness in his voice as he shows her and a bashful Eric how to plant their feet to withstand the waves. The playfulness he exudes while chasing them in and out of the water to help ease their fear of it.

A part of me keeps whispering that it's all an act—the real man comes out at night in that dark room. But witnessing him like this easily overpowers the doubt.

And I realize in the pit of my stomach that nothing else could come close to *this*. Not the supposed benefits he promised being with him would bring. Not the money. Not the ring.

I'd trade everything for this.

This moment.

This contentment.

Him, seemingly at peace, even for a second.

THE SUN IS in the process of setting by the time we return to the house. Dinner consists of leftover hamburgers eaten on the terrace while dipping our toes into the pool—another variation of our previous family meals.

I sit on a lounger across from Maxim while the kids chatter about random topics.

"Mermaids don't exist, stupid," Eric snipes in response to Ainsley. "But sharks?" He holds his hands up to his mouth, baring the nails like makeshift jaws. "They do, and they love eating little dummies like you!"

"Knock it off," I scold, but my voice lacks the old authority it used to. It's as though the warmth, and the breeze, and the hum of the ocean rob the atmosphere of everything but peace. Lifting my head to shoot them both a stern, warning glance, is about all I can muster in terms of refereeing.

Luckily, they both retreat.

"Mr. Sir?" Ainsley climbs from her lounger and crosses to Maxim's. Before I can stop her, she's already managed to crawl onto his lap, heedless of the discomfort turning him to stone.

I scramble to my feet, reaching for her. "Ainsley—"

"It's okay." Maxim raises a hand to halt my approach. One of his arms moves to cradle Ainsley's waist, keeping her from falling. The stiffness doesn't leave him, but the way he tilts his head receptively conveys that he's tolerating the contact regardless.

Oblivious to us both, she keeps chattering. "If you did marry Frankie, and you have kids. Would they be our brothers and sisters, or—"

"Ainsley!" Daisy rolls her eyes, shaking her head. "God, you can be such a moron sometimes."

"Not uh!" Pouting, Ainsley tugs on Maxim's sleeve until she has his full attention. "It's a good question, right? Are you going to have kids?"

Mikie groans, burying his face in his hands while the twins suddenly seem very interested in their food. The only person seemingly unbothered by the question is Maxim.

"I… I don't know." His voice sounds neutral enough. None of the kids seem to sense the hesitation in it that I do. From this angle, I can't see his face, just the hard, pulsating line of his jaw. "I'm afraid I can't answer that question."

But I can. That answer is one of the few things he's provided willingly without needing to be prodded—*no*. During my first few days with him, he ensured as much by injecting me with birth control without even asking for my consent. *You will not get pregnant,* he said by way of explanation. *That is the one thing you never have to worry about me inflicting upon you.*

Back then, I'd been more than relieved by that reassurance. But now, with the prospect of marriage looming overhead?

I'm not even sure what I want. But with his past…who knows how much of that affects his viewpoint on the concept of children? Which brings up the very good question as to where my kids fall into the grand scheme that is Maxim Koslov's fucked-up world.

"Oh, well." Sighing, Ainsley scampers off of him and returns to her seat. "I always wanted a baby sister. I hate being the baby—"

"Shut up, *baby*!" Eric balls up his napkin and throws it at her. Squealing, she throws it back, and they dissolve into a silent war while Mikie takes the reins of the conversation, steering it back to less volatile topics.

"How much does a yacht cost?" he demands of Maxim, raising an eyebrow. "Hypothetically speaking, if your only income came from cutting grass in the summer, how many summers might it take to buy one?"

Once again, we somehow manage to pass the awkward huddle and return to a smooth, easy rhythm of conversation and silence.

But as the darkness gradually claims the landscape, I sense a palpable shift in the man beside me. His responses slow to silence. His gaze grows more distant, fixated beyond this moment. Eventually, he stands and enters the house with a polite, "Goodnight."

At the same time, Ainsley starts rubbing her eyes, and I take the sign as a cue. "Bedtime."

The others groan in unison, but I follow them upstairs, surprised by the feeling building in my stomach. It isn't until I tuck Ainsley in bed and plant a kiss on her cheek that I can name the sensation for what it is.

Dread.

That cold, dark room awaits. But it isn't fear that sends my heartbeat surging as I finally approach the master suite. Maybe it's a little grief? The open, relaxed Maxim from earlier is dead and gone.

The figure standing hunched over the foot of the bed is a different creature—the other half of the twisted coin that is this beautiful, broken man.

"It's dusk," he says in a rasping tone. His hand gestures curtly toward the window. Sure enough, the horizon is a bloody, brilliant scarlet mingled with shades of orange. The sun is making its last stand. Technically, it isn't nightfall just yet. "If before… You can ask me one thing. The question I know is burning on the tip of your tongue."

My heart skips. His offer isn't a thoughtful request or a meaningless gesture. It's an olive branch. Reassurance—this is a true give and take. No matter how much effort it requires on both our parts.

"Do you want children?" I blurt out. He's right. That one question has been hovering in my throat, and I didn't even fucking realize it until now.

He sighs, lowering his head. "Would you trust me as a father?"

I'm unprepared for the question—one so different from his usual defensive responses. I think of how he can be with Ainsley, Eric, and the others—so gentle. On the other hand, it seems to take effort on his part. So much damn effort that at night, he needs to lock himself in a room just to express the pent-up violence. And with me…

He's slipped before, going too far, almost beyond reach. Could someone as small as Ainsley or even smaller be able to stop him?

No, a part of me whispers in horror. *But you know that. You've known it all along…*

I shake my head, banishing the doubts. "I don't know."

"Oh?" He laughs in a way that raises goosebumps, cold and distant. "You *do* know."

"Should I?" I swallow hard, watching him. He must have opened a window. A breeze drifts in, disrupting the golden halo of hair brushing his shoulders. For the first time, I toy with dissecting the real reason he's kept me with him, apart from the kids, except during our strained hiatus. I'd always assumed he preferred to live alone, but what if there is more to it than that? "Are you okay with my kids being here now?"

He doesn't answer.

I blink more rapidly, my eyes burning, my throat tight. "If this is all too much…"

"It's not," he says, and it isn't until now that I realize just how much I needed to hear that. My knees buckle at the genuine honesty in his voice. "I don't mind them. I will never lose control around them, I promise you that."

But something is on his mind, gnawing away at his previous composure. Something he can't—or won't—explain, no matter how many seconds tick by.

"Does this help you?" I finally ask, avoiding the real secrets looming between us. "The room. Even if you don't talk about it? Does it help?"

He nods, and it's like I can track the instability building within him. His spine goes rigid, his hands clenching into fists, his body hunched and angular. "Yes," he confesses hoarsely. "I need this… I need this from *you*."

"Okay." I turn to that infamous door, this time freed from hesitation. When I grip the handle, a mechanical noise sounds before it opens. I've barely stepped over the threshold when I sense him on my heels, herding me inside.

"Kneel."

Choking down a hiss, I sink to the hard floor. Every ache from last night throbs, renewed beneath his gaze. With him, pain takes on a sick connotation, enhanced by his reaction to it.

He inhales as if feeding off every flinch and twitch of sore muscle. I track his steps to the opposite end of the room. That one drawer, I suspect.

Sure enough, as he returns to me, the telltale snap of leather cuts the silence. Instantly, a stinging pain bites at my hip—a warning.

"Get on your hands and knees."

I do, bracing my palms over the frigid floor. He must control the air-conditioning in this room apart from the rest of the house. It's colder in here. My teeth are chattering, and yet sweat drips down my spine at the same time, a twisted dichotomy.

In this realm, even logic ceases to matter.

Another blow lands across my lower back. Another strikes my hip. My thigh.

"Strip," he commands.

I do so without bothering to stand up, shimmying from my dress. His footsteps echo, resonating in my bones as he circles my position, eyeing his handiwork. None of the lashings broke the skin, but they came damn close. The one on my hip smarts like hell, and I grit my teeth against making a sound. Attuned to my body like any true predator, he nudges that wound with the whip as if aware of the amount of pain inflicted in each particular spot.

Without warning, the whip hisses through the air and lands in between my shoulder blades. It hurts. I can't smother a groan, even as my thoughts start to dissipate, drunk on the burning sting.

Merciless, he hits me again.

Again.

Eventually, he forsakes the whip entirely and captures a fistful of my hair, wrenching me to my feet. Without explanation, he guides me to the marble slab and shoves me across it. Shivers ripple down my spine as he slides his hand between my legs, hissing at what he finds.

"There are things I want to do to you that would terrify you," he admits, stroking his damp fingers up the curve of my back, leaving a trail of moisture in his wake. "Things you aren't ready for. I've been patient, but fuck… Can you trust your body to me, even now?"

A part of me realizes in horror just what he's doing —begging.

Do I trust him? With his voice thick with lust, his fingers trembling with malice, my body on fire from his lashing…

Slumped against the marble slab, all I can do is nod. The intensity with which I do so makes my mind reel and has him grunting in relief. What dark, twisted fantasies has he held back from enacting?

For whatever reason, I'll take them without asking. Without hesitating.

His fingers dance over the throbbing skin of my ass, lingering there on purpose to heighten my anticipation. I writhe, too on edge to remain submissive. The disobedience makes him hum, and I know he's savoring the thought of whatever punishment lies in store.

"No one's ever fucked you in this way," he suspects, inching lower down the curve of my hip, to the center of my back. Then lower…

Oh. I have a grim suspicion as to what he wants.

"I can tell," he adds accusingly. "You stiffen whenever I touch you here. Why?"

My cheeks catch fire at the intimacy of the question. Because no matter how broke or how desperate I've been, no one could ever make me relinquish that one, small bit of myself. No one. Anal sex was never on the menu to any John, no matter the price.

"Do you trust this to me?" Maxim wonders, invading my thoughts so easily that it's pointless to speak them out loud. He *knows*. More than I should be comfortable with allowing. More than any other man ever will. "I won't take it from you—" He slides his fingers dangerously close to the entrance no one has ever touched. Not even him.

I tremble, my chest heaving. I'd be lying if I claimed I wasn't afraid. What little I know of anal is that it hurts. Like hell. If done too violently, it can cause lasting damage. Unimaginable pain…

And yet, my hips buck—*toward* him, not away.

"You're so perfect for me," he grates against the groove of my neck. It's both a praise and a curse. Perfect for him. Squirming and willing, thwarting the perfectionist in him that craves control. I'm ruining his careful, precise vision of taking my last shred of virginity. I'm far too fucking eager. Voice breaking, he commands, "Tell me I can have you—"

"Yes." The words escape me before he's even finished speaking. "You...you can have me."

He whispers something too softly to make out. An apology? His thumb grazes my lips before I can question. He parts them with persistent pressure, finding my tongue. Slowly, he wets his fingers—but I don't understand why until he moves behind me, urging me to lie higher across the altar.

I nearly jump out of my skin as he guides his thumb between the crack of my ass, finding that elusive opening. One of his hands captures mine, gripping tight as his other pins my hip to the marble.

I only have enough sense to suck in a breath of air before he slips his thumb inside...

Out.

In.

This taking is brutal. No planning. No preparation. Only after a few tests of his thumb does he rub the head of his cock against that untouched opening, hissing when I flinch.

"Say that you trust me," he demands, nipping my earlobe. "Say it."

My lips part, devoid of hesitation. "I trust you—"

"Then take me." He bucks his hips, and the sharp pinch of his invasion takes my breath away. *Fuck fuck fuck fuck!*

I choke on a cry as his length slams into me, crushing me between his bulk and the unyielding marble. My fingers claw uselessly at the surface, scrambling for purchase.

He goes deep. Too deep. So deep.

It should be impossible to find pleasure in this—suffocating, crushing, writhing agony. In some ways, maybe it is. The heat of his breath on my neck burns like fire. He grips my hips without care, driving his nails in, forcing me to take every thrust with no mercy.

I'm convulsing around him anyway.

It's a feeling I could never find in his arms, lounging beneath the sunlight. Something violent and raw and selfish that lingers in the knowledge that only I can give him this.

True submission.

Even if it hurts. Even if the aftermath leaves me trembling on my knees, too exhausted to stand on my own. Murmuring against my skin, he lifts me into his arms, carrying me from the room. Still on edge, I gasp as the atmosphere changes. Warmth displaces cold. The air thins. Moonlight replaces the harsh, fluorescent lighting.

We re-enter the real world like creatures from hell, and it's a slow, cruel readjustment to reality.

He drapes me over the edge of the bed and disappears for a moment only to return with a cloth clutched in his fist. He bathes me carefully, but his touch lingers afterward.

It's like I can read his mind as he weighs the prospect of taking me back into that space. Feeding this addiction with another round.

I've already resigned myself to exactly that when a frantic knock on the door shatters everything.

"Frankie? Frankie?"

"Shit!" I only have enough energy to roll onto my side, facing the door, and pray that it doesn't open. "W-What is it?"

"Can I sleep with you?" Ainsley asks in between sniffling cries. "P-Please?"

Double shit.

"Uh…" I can't even look at Maxim. "Not tonight, baby. G-Give me a minute, and I'll come to tuck you in—"

"It's okay." Maxim enters the closet and tosses me a robe. "Let her in."

He's already pulling on a pair of gray sweats and a shirt. Before I can call Ainsley myself, he crosses over to the door and opens it.

Rubbing her eyes, Ainsley barges in, trailing a pink blanket behind her that I assume came from her bed. She climbs in beside me and burrows beneath the sheets. From the corner of my eye, I notice Maxim already entering the hall.

"I'll be on the couch," he says.

"No!" Ainsley sits up, her eyes wide. "You have to stay in case the bad man comes back. You have to!"

"Ainsley…" I run my fingers through her hair and try to coax her into lying down. "Baby, try to get some sleep—"

"It's alright." Maxim lingers near the threshold before he returns to the bed. I can't read his expression. He circles around to the opposite end from Ainsley and me and then sits on the floor with his back braced against the mattress. "Get some sleep," he grunts. "No one will hurt you."

A faint reply comes muffled from beneath the blankets. "Promise?"

He sighs again. "I… I promise."

Satisfied, Ainsley snuggles against me, and within minutes she's sleeping deeply.

But her protector doesn't budge from his post. Even though he has no real obligation to, he keeps his promise.

He stays.

CHAPTER THIRTEEN

I wake up content—a fact that makes my heart beat faster before my senses fully return. There's no foot in my side, no tiny fingers tangled in my hair. Confused, I feel out with my hand, alarmed to find empty space beside me. "Ainsley?"

"She's eating breakfast," someone calls before panic can set in, their voice raspy with sleep. I look over to find Maxim unmoved from his previous position on the floor, his back to me. A familiar heat stirs as my eyes skim over his muscle, defined in the daylight.

But once I reach his face, the fire dies down, replaced by cold, hard fear. From this angle, I can only make out the stern set to his jaw—he's still in that room, brooding internally. Over regrets? Normalcy by day and BDSM by night could be a game that even he isn't up to playing for very long.

"Maxim?" I tentatively call out, rolling toward him.

He doesn't answer. Then he groans, stretching his arms above his head, and the tension leaves his muscles. "I believe they're having omelets," he says from over his shoulder, his voice neutral. "Courtesy of Lucius."

Slowly, I relax back into the mattress. "Is there anything he can't do?" I wonder tiredly.

"If there is, he'll rectify it somehow," Maxim replies with audible respect. "The man is the best money can buy."

That and loyalty. There's no denying that, their professional relationship aside, Lucius cares for him.

"You should go eat," Maxim suggests, rising to his feet while I shift to keep him in view. "I will shower and…"

He meets my gaze, and whatever he finds makes him trail off. The distraction is mutual. One look from him sets me alight despite the exhaustion weighing me down. I flick my tongue along my lower lip as I follow the line of his gaze downward. *Oh.* My robe fell open when I moved, revealing my breasts. Absently, I start to adjust it, but he lunges, grabbing my wrist.

I'm in his arms before I know it. He takes me into the shower, and we bathe together, saying nothing—verbally anyway. The way he touches me conveys a million different things, soothing over every sting inflicted last night.

A tendril of lingering doubt creeps in, feeding off the memories of him in that room. The anger. The repressed emotions. Again I have to wonder if this little game of give and take is more than he can handle. Is normalcy beyond his limits?

His fingers sink into my hair, grazing my scalp as if to banish all other thoughts but this. His nearness. Our nakedness. Heat. Cautiously, our lips meet. Once. Twice.

"I am curious about something," Maxim confesses, drawing back. My lips burn, mourning the loss of his as he turns his attention to my throat. His teeth knead the flesh along my collar, sending heat churning through my belly with every nip.

Distracted by how his mouth increasingly travels south, I can barely form a coherent reply. "Oh?"

"You didn't argue," he points out before cupping my breast in his palm. With a sinful caress, he squeezes, making me lurch against him. "When I told your family you refused my proposal."

"What?" I stiffen, but his tongue laves over my nipple, and any logic dissipates. "I-I…"

"You didn't deny it either. That I had pursued you—or 'dating' as your sister put it." Rather than annoyed, he sounds oddly…smug at that fact. As though in not refusing him outright, I hadn't closed the door on an engagement entirely.

"I…"

He returns his mouth to mine, robbing me of the chance to argue. Within seconds, he's buried within me to the hilt, and I lose track of everything but the sensation building between us.

Slow, lazy, unhurried sex is another first.

Experienced with him, it feels like some novel, newly discovered concept that I pity every other woman for never getting to enjoy firsthand.

Afterward, we dress, and by the time we make it downstairs, breakfast is long gone, and Ainsley is musing about lunch.

That meal is eventually supplied by Maxim as well—more grilled meat and fresh fruit from the well-stocked fridge. This time, we pack up the food and eat on the beach, wiggling our toes in the sand. That hazy, dreamlike feeling returns and I'm stupid enough to wish this could last forever.

But when Lucius approaches, a cell phone glued to his ear, I know reality is about to descend. Rudely.

Apparently, Maxim assumes the same. He lunges to his feet and races to meet Lucius first. Whatever words they exchange leaves the younger man scowling, and when he returns, he shoves his hand into his pocket and withdraws a wallet. From it, he takes several crisp hundred-dollar bills.

"Who wants it?" he demands, brandishing the bills in his fist.

Predictably, all six kids shout in a deafening clamor.

His voice booming, Maxim easily overpowers them, "Alright. If all of you can make it to that end of the beach —" he points to a spot in the distance "—and back, you can divide it amongst each other. Go now."

Oblivious to anything but their challenge, they take off, jockeying for the lead.

The second they're out of earshot, Maxim grabs my wrist and pulls me to my feet.

"What's wrong?"

He doesn't answer in favor of leading me back to the house. As we enter the living room, I see the cause of the disturbance for myself.

Dressed in a tan suit with a crisp white shirt, a few buttons open at the neck, a tall man commands the massive space. He stands rigidly, casting a cynical glance at the bright, neutral décor. Once he spots Maxim, he inhales as if steeling himself for a battle. "I will explain—"

"Explain, Milton?" Maxim echoes in a dangerously soft tone. "You don't *ever* come to me unannounced. Which means, you've suddenly picked now, the first time in twenty years, to drop by for a surprise visit. Or…" His eyes narrow. "You've decided to spring something far more unforgivable on me. Which one is it?"

The other man inclines his head toward the foyer. "You can come in."

"Many apologies," a new figure simpers with mock contrition. Dima. But in comparison to Milton's polished appearance, I don't know whether to laugh or stare as he strolls into the room. In lieu of a suit or linen ensemble, he wears an array of mismatched clothing as if he picked them out last minute from the bargain bin at Goodwill. A large, oversized pink sweatshirt shrouds his lanky frame, sporting a yellow heart in the center. A gray knitted cap obscures most of his dark hair, and a ratty pair of jeans completes the overall look.

He could easily fit in with the entertainers Maxim hired for his makeshift carnival—except for his expression. It's calculating, matching his easy, cautious posture. He keeps his hands in his pockets and scans the interior of the house in a way that makes me suspect he's memorizing every single detail.

But overall, he looks more cold than comical. *Physically* cold, hunched beneath the sweatshirt as if freezing despite the heat.

"I apologize for my ensemble," he says with a contrite nod. "Oh, how I wish I had the foresight to pack my own priceless suit before dear Milton forced me onto his private plane. Luckily, his sweet flight attendant gave me the use of *her* clothing—"

"Get the fuck out! And you—" Eyes flashing, Maxim whirls on Milton, poised on the balls of his feet. "What the hell were you thinking, bringing him here? Have you lost your fucking mind—"

"My mind? No." Milton smooths his hands along the sleeves of his suit, inspecting the ebony cufflinks, securing each one. When he finally meets Maxim's gaze, there's no hint of fear in the dark irises of either man. They stare each other down coldly, two opponents equally matched. "My *patience*, on the other hand? I'm running out of it. You could have avoided this if you picked up my calls. I made myself fucking clear to Lucius."

"Clear?" Maxim exhales sharply, his body practically humming with anger. "Don't speak in fucking riddles," he commands. "You want to say something, then fucking say it. Start with why you would dare to bring him here. Around my—" He grits his teeth, his eyes narrowing to slits. "You bring him here, knowing the risk you just put me in. Why?"

"Dima won't hurt you," Milton says tiredly, as if bored by the mere thought of it. "No one else will learn of this location. Proven wrong—which I won't be—I will personally fix it." He turns his head in Dima's direction, the politest version of a lethal threat I've ever witnessed burning in his eyes. "You have my word. But you know who *does* intend to harm? Danil. The motherfucker landed in Fair Haven not too long ago. Rumor has it, he's planning an assault, with or without Anatoli's backing."

"All of this over fucking Danil?" Maxim turns on his heel, leaving me at the doorway, his hands in fists. Several thunderous steps carry him across the room, parallel to Milton's position—but no further. It's as if the man serves as an invisible wall, preventing him from reaching his actual target. So he paces. "That bastard can't button his own fucking fly without Anatoli's blessing. You think he threatens me?"

"Your cousin may be a fool," Milton concedes, "but others will follow. Dima is the least of your concerns."

"If you believe that, then you really have lost your fucking mind—"

"I lost my *fucking* mind a long time ago. As *you* did. As Dima did." Milton says through clenched teeth, the unspoken history between them rotting the air. "Do you honestly doubt me?" There's a few seconds' silence. "I thought not. Now, let's get this over with. Give Dima the girl. End this childish idiocy between the two of you. Accept his assistance, and *together*, we can take Anatoli down."

Maxim stops short. "Were you anyone else, Milton, I would kill you for what you've just said."

"But I'm not anyone else, am I?" A hint of irritation disrupts Milton's polished façade. He's just as angry as Maxim, but in a very different way. "These are the facts you need to face. Anatoli has gotten bold in your absence. He's planning to attack your suppliers directly—a full-on assault. And, I apologize, but I don't want an open war. Not now. Not while..." He cuts off, shaking his head. "He and those loyal to him need to be dealt with. I suggest you return to the city as soon as possible."

Maxim laughs. "Give him *your* woman then. What? You thought I didn't notice her? The blond you've kept so close to you? Give her to Vadim, if you are so eager for peace."

A shadow falls over Milton's face, and this room becomes the world's smallest cage despite its size. They're both wolves, snarling for dominance in the center of it, leaving little room for anyone else.

All I can do is pray that none of the kids wander into the house—but I seem to be the only spectator concerned. Meeting my gaze from across the room, Vadim playfully waggles his eyebrows. *"Brothers,"* he mouths with a smile.

I cringe away from him, returning my attention to Maxim. If I thought the hidden room upstairs brought out the worst in him, I was wrong.

"What is it, then?" he demands, cocking his head. "Your little whore is too good for precious Dima, but my woman isn't? In fact, shall we ask her?" He extends his hand toward me. "Francesca, are you my whore to be utilized as I see fit?"

All three men turn to me. Stunned, I clear my throat. "N-No."

"Good," Maxim hisses. "Then it's settled. Unless you want to force her, Milton? Perhaps you and Dima prefer to reenact the very bonds of slavery you escaped from?"

"I suggest you watch your words as well," Milton warns, advancing a single, dangerous step in Maxim's direction.

"As for Dima, you know he won't hurt her—" He nods toward me. "You know he won't hurt *you* either. All he wants is to toy with you. Entertainment. And you're all but providing him the shit show he wants by resisting. I could easily convince him to relent, but I won't. Do you know why?" His eyes cloud over with an unreadable emotion. "You *owe* him. You owe him this one fucking request, no matter how childish and spiteful it might be. We both know why. What was it you called it? The bonds we all escaped from?"

"Is that so?" Maxim clenches his hands into fists, cracking the knuckles in the process.

"*Yes.*" Milton merely observes him, seemingly lacking the energy to match his vitriol. All he does is sigh. "I've humored this grudge of yours for over a decade, but I'm telling you now, I'm *tired.*" Another layer of his persona falls away, betraying his words to be the truth. Worn lines strain the flesh around his eyes, enhancing an expertly disguised exhaustion. Even Maxim's can't compare. "My little blond whore, as you call her? Is under *my* protection. And I won't stand aside and watch Anatoli turn his attention to *her* to get to you. I fucking won't, Maxim. End this fight with Dima—"

"Get out." Maxim storms past Milton, but rather than head for Dima, he comes for me. His hand cinches my wrist, yanking me to his side. "Both of you. *Now.* As for Anatoli, I will return to the city in the morning and handle this myself."

Milton sighs again, more heavily. "You and I both know that you can't."

"So, you've come to insult me as well as threaten me?" I've never heard Maxim's voice so guttural. "I suggest you leave. You want to turn on me? Fine. I don't need you, or your pet—"

"You do," Milton insists. "You need me just like when we were kids, and we had *no one* but each other. Or have you forgotten that, too? I do not doubt your strength or ability to defeat him on your own. You just never had the *will* to. Dima isn't the pet here. *You* are. You've always been that little boy pining under Anatoli's shoe, desperate for his attention. His acceptance. Even if it bloody kills you."

"Don't use your fucking degree on me," Maxim snarls, his lips curling from his teeth. "Go!"

"My degree?" Milton laughs, a disarmingly beautiful sound. With his head held high, he faces Maxim directly and moves to stand within his path. "One of many I got from an education that wasn't free. That I paid in blood for. You want me to use it? Fine. You never hated Dima, not truly. You just can't stand what he signifies. Freedom. Independence. Someone who can live outside the shadow of your grandfather unscathed by his poison. You've let jealousy consume you for over twenty years. Dima never wanted his name—and *that's* what bothers you. Anatoli bred you like an animal, and you don't know a life outside of that brutal, violent existence. Do you deny it?"

He waits, but Maxim says nothing.

"I thought so." Flicking his collar, he strolls for the front door, deliberately unhurried. "When you change your mind, contact me, and I'll make the arrangements." He stops and cocks his head before adding. "What happened today doesn't change anything between us. Not to me, anyway. You know I'll always stand by you—but I won't enable you. I *can't*."

"Well, this was lovely," a cheerier voice cuts in, a surreal contrast to the anger crackling in the air. "A wonderful reunion, much better than I could have ever hoped for—"

"Race ya!" The high pitched, childish shriek cuts through the tension like a knife. It takes my brain a second to identify it as not belonging to any one of the three men before me. Which can only mean…

"Fuck!" I race to the glass door leading to the terrace to find Ainsley skipping toward me, her hair streaming behind her. She waves, giggling even as I shake my head and fumble for the door.

"No! No, no, no…"

Suddenly, a deeper voice calls out, and Lucius appears in her wake, running to catch up.

Whatever he says makes Ainsley turn to him, and he manages to take her hand and lead her away. Relief rips through me, and I brace my palms against the glass just to stay standing.

"Thank God."

"A child? Hers?" The question comes from Dima, or so I assume, given the lightness of the baritone. But his voice sounds different, suddenly devoid of amusement. Surprise colors it instead. Alarm. "You brought a child here. With him?"

He isn't speaking to Maxim.

"No. No one could be that reckless…"

"Come, Dima," Milton snaps, sounding farther away. When I finally have the strength to look back, he's halfway across the entryway. "Now!"

But Vadim doesn't move. His dark eyes remain fixated on me, narrowed with disdain. "You trust him with your child? I'd assumed you were his victim, but perhaps I was wrong. No *real* mother would ever put her children in danger—"

"Maxim!" In a blur of motion, Milton reappears as if from thin air to physically shove the other man back.

"Get out!" Eyes like coal, Maxim pivots, nearly barreling past Milton, who has to grasp his shoulders just to keep him back.

"Go, Dima!" Milton snarls.

Vadim doesn't seem to even notice the commotion. Or care. An expression crosses his face almost too quickly to process. Only my time with Maxim gives me a faint hope at interpreting it—an icy veil of memory, trapping him in the past.

"Your little daughter? He'll carve her to pieces," he tells me softly, while brushing his hand along the scar on his throat. "But you know that, don't you? You *know* he'll see her beaten. Raped. He'll sell her to the highest bidder himself, if his true master tells him to. You know this to be true." He nods as if my expression alone gives him all of the confirmation he needs. "And yet you stay. How dare you put an innocent in harm's way?"

Pain lances through my chest. It feels as if he punched me though he never moves a single inch. My lungs throb regardless, and it's harder to breathe. Think.

Is that what I'm doing? *Selling...*

Maxim bellows something, followed by another frantic warning from Milton.

But all I hear is Dima's calm, relentless murmur, sneaking past the clamor to easily reach me. "If you keep your child around him, you're no better than he is. You condemn her, and any other children you may have. The Koslovs. That name is more than *just* a name," he insists. "It is a creed. A brutality. And you've already sold your daughter to them just by taking his ring—"

"Get... Out!" My chest heaves as I spit out the words one by one, surprised by their ferocity.

From the corner of my eye, I see Milton and Maxim pause, panting in their struggle.

"As you wish," Dima says with another gallant nod. He turns on his heel, strolling for the door. Once he's out of view, Milton follows, adjusting his mussed suit. Near the threshold, he pauses.

"I'm sorry. You may not think Danil as a threat, but you didn't ask why he—of all Anatoli's pawns—would be so desperate to attack you directly. But he wants the bounty, Maxim." He sets his gaze on me and then back to Maxim. "And if you want to protect yours, as I am mine, reconsider this place. If I found you, he will, fool or not."

Finally, he exits the house, and both men leave, taking all hope of normalcy with them.

CHAPTER FOURTEEN

Milton's visit shatters what little semblance of peace we'd managed to cobble together—but the most alarming part in the aftermath is how everyone, from Maxim to Lucius, still manages to pretend like nothing is wrong. At least around the kids. It is "normalcy" pushed to its very fucking limits.

I should be grateful for that.

Maxim doesn't brood around them, becoming a vicious stranger in a heartbeat. He disappears instead, leaving me alone to keep up the façade.

But I'm a sleepwalker, trapped in the nightmare of Dima's insinuation. *How dare you put an innocent in harm's way?*

When the kids return from the beach, we eat pasta around the center island in the kitchen, courtesy of Lucius, who serves as head chef in Maxim's absence. They chatter on about jet skis and swimming, innocently oblivious to the looming danger. Danger, I put them in.

That guilt robs me of my appetite. All I can do is pick at my plate while my mind spins in turmoil. When the kids finally trickle off to bed, I'm on edge, and Maxim is nowhere to be found.

Unease creeps in as I start to search for him.

He isn't in the bedroom or the bathroom, or even the infamous "other room" when I gather the nerve to check. For all I know, he could be gone already, heading back to the city without so much as a goodbye.

Would that bother me? I'm surprised by the ache knotting in my chest at the possibility. *Yes.* It would.

It fucking would.

Even as the fear sets in, I can't ignore the intuitive sense that he's still here—as if there's a taste lingering in the air, unique only to his brand of rage. My nostrils flare as I try to pinpoint his exact location. In a way, doing so feels a bit like some creepy, childhood game. *Find the mafia boss in the haystack.* And yet...

There's a skill to it. Knowing where he'd go to rage in peace. Somewhere where he can presumably do the least amount of damage to avoid alarming the kids—if he truly does care about their comfort. Somewhere open and unconfined, too, like the wild expanse of lawn beyond the terrace...

I slip out through the kitchen doors and cut past the pool, guided by the last shreds of daylight. A blood-red sunset bathes everything in a fiery glow, enhancing every nuance of the landscape.

Namely the lone figure pacing on the very outskirts of the property, far beyond the view from the house.

The dusky glow ignites his golden hair, illuminating the panes of his face and enhancing the rage shaping them. When he spots me, his entire body goes rigid, a creature apart from the man I spent the last few days in paradise with.

Fear nearly paralyzes me. Only God knows what keeps me moving, tiptoeing through the grass on bare feet.

"I'm leaving in the morning," he declares when I approach him. I jump at his tone. His voice resonates as deeply as a roar of thunder, and I half expect lightning to strike. "You and your siblings will be moved to another location. I'll send for you when I'm ready."

My heart lurches. Another move. Another gameboard. Another stint as a pawn. "Please, just slow down," I say. "We should talk about this—"

"Talk?" He whips around so swiftly I stagger an instinctive step back. Alarm stimulates every nerve in my body, urging escape. *Run!* "Do you really think you can dictate to me?" he wonders, his teeth bared.

No, a part of me whimpers in defeat. I'm no match for him when he's like this. Some things can't change. You can't cage a wolf—eventually, it will go for your throat.

The only option is to give in. Surrender to the inevitable fact that we'll always be back at square one. He'll always be a stranger, lost to rage. To him, peace was never worth chasing.

And a future with him will never be normal.

"Go into the house," he growls, resigned to the same outcome. "Now—"

"Please…" I take a step toward him. Then another as he falls silent. Cracks disrupt my brave façade however—my fingers shake when I reach out, finding his chest…

And all of my fear vanishes, replaced by a throbbing, inescapable concern. His heart is hammering, his chest heaving with shallow breaths. Up this close, I can sense everything he uses the rage to mask. He's panicked. He's breaking. He's losing control.

"You believe him, don't you?" he surmises, his eyes narrowed. "That I will hurt you. Hurt your children. I saw your face. You believe *him*—"

"I don't know what to believe," I say, taking another step. "But I want to trust you."

"Go." He turns away, glaring into the distance. "I need to be alone."

"You need *me*," I whisper, surprised by how true that statement seems the more I touch him. I slide my hand up to his shoulder, tracking how he flinches in response. "Talk to me—"

"Go!" He shrugs me off so violently that throwing my arms out is the only way I can keep my balance. "Don't be a fucking fool, Francesca." He toys with the syllables in my name to inflict the harshest sting. "I need you in the sense that I require the use of your cunt at my discretion. Now go into the fucking house—"

"You need me now." This time I step into him, lacing my arms around his neck. Before he can react, I feel along his jaw. It's a reckless move—he could bite me; he looks so fucking unstable. Lost. But he doesn't, and the slightest contact is enough to keep me talking. "You need to talk to me. Tell me what's wrong."

His hands fall to his sides, but he's still staring into the distance, far beyond here.

So I stand on tiptoe, bringing my lips near his ear, so it's harder for him to ignore me. "If you need to leave, fine, but you owe me—us—the chance to hear why. Do I worry about the kids? Maybe. But they trust you. *Ainsley* trusts you…" Emotion thickens my throat. I swallow hard and choke out each confession one by one. "Don't you dare forsake that. *Ever.* We don't deserve to be tossed around like objects. I won't let you throw them away, either. I can't. So talk to me, if you want us to work. This is what real families do. Talk—"

"Family?" he echoes gruffly.

"Yes… That is what I need from you if you want me to stay. More than protection. I need stability. I need my *family.*"

One word, and it's like a candle being blown out. The stiffness leaves him all at once, and he sways, nearly bringing me down with him. At the last second, his hands cinch my waist to the point of pain, but we remain standing. I endure the discomfort, smoothing my fingers over any part of him I can reach. He holds me so tightly I know I'll bruise in the aftermath. At the same time, I savor this pain more than any other agony he could ever inflict.

It's *him* inflicting it, not the monster living in his head.

Cautiously, his fingers creep into my hair, parting the strands as if memorizing every one, using me as an anchor to ground himself. His breathing eases first, and then his stability returns, and I can let myself relax into him fully without fear of falling.

"A family with you…" Soft, his lips nudge my throat, coaxing me to meet his gaze. He's here again, his expression hollowed, but here. His lips brush mine almost in apology before he devours them, demolishing my defenses with his tongue.

We kiss hungrily, heedless of the heat and the chirping insects around us. I don't resist as he shoves me down, pressing my body to the ground.

He slams into me from behind, his mouth at my throat, his thrusts frenzied. Desperate. I don't move when he finally collapses against me, breathless and dripping sweat.

His hands smooth the hair from my face, his lips feathering over my shoulder. "You will marry me," he murmurs, but he sounds crazed. Russian words mingle with more broken bits of English. I doubt he even knows what he's saying. "Marry me. You will. I need you to marry me..."

His hand captures mine, forcing our fingers together.

"I won't lose you," he grates in between pants. "I can't."

It's minutes before he's coherent again, nudging me to face him as darkness fully descends, drenching us in shadow. "We will leave tomorrow," he says. "Your siblings can stay here for a week, long enough to make arrangements for them. But then..." He fingers my chin, ensuring I can't turn away. Visible even in the faint moonlight, his eyes glow. "We stay together. You have your normalcy, but we stay. Like this..."

I nod, unsure if he can even see me or not. "We'll stay together."

CHAPTER FIFTEEN

Maxim leads me to the terrace but doesn't follow me inside. "Sleep," he says. "We'll leave first thing in the morning. I'll make the arrangements."

I don't bother to ask him what "arrangements" could be made alone, outside in the middle of the night. Despite our breakthrough, I know better than to push for more.

So I enter the master suite alone, though I don't sleep. Eventually, I wind up in the shower and linger there for hours until dawn finally paints the horizon.

When I creep downstairs to find two suitcases near the door, I *finally* risk hoping that last night wasn't a fluke. For once, we might have communicated beyond sex.

Unscathed by the recent chaos, the kids are already awake and out on the terrace, still wearing pajamas.

"Are we leaving already?" Ainsley whines the second I join them, fully dressed. "But we're having so much fun!"

"Your sister and I are leaving," Maxim says. I jump and turn to find him exiting the house behind me. His outfit alone signifies the end of his vacation. The customary suit has made a reappearance, a striking shade of ebony. "We all would be returning to the city today, but the gas leak damaged the other house. Do you trust your sister to find a better one?"

Mikie mockingly rolls his eyes. "I guess."

"You have one more week of paradise," Maxim adds. "Then I'm afraid it's back to reality."

He steps back a respectful distance so I can say goodbye to the kids one by one. When I reach Daisy, I wrap my arms around her, but say near her ear, "Whatever you might think of me. It doesn't matter. I still love you. But that also means I expect more from you. Watch out for Ainsley and make sure she cleans up properly. Got it?"

She nods.

"Sir," Lucius calls from the doorway. "The pilot is ready."

Maxim nods and places his hand on my lower back. "We're on our way."

Together we travel through the house and exit from the front door to find a black car already waiting out front. Maxim leads the way and ushers me inside before settling beside me. His hand finds mine, interlacing our fingers.

And with that, we return to the real world.

My second plane ride unfolds a bit more memorably than the first. Like everything in Maxim's world, his private jet is nothing short of impressive. Custom leather recliners are comfortably spaced around the climate-controlled cabin, conveying an aura primarily for business over pleasure. The overall color scheme isn't surprising given Maxim's tastes—black and gray with modern accents.

"We will need to move," he says. His voice conveys a sense of calm that contrasts sharply with his tense, stiff posture. Poised on the very edge of his seat, he keeps eyeing the silver watch on his wrist, his gaze turned inward. But for whatever reason, I recognize his attempts at conversation for what they are—a stab at maintaining our fragile sense of normalcy. "And quickly," he adds. "I'll leave the house hunting up to you, this time. You'll start tomorrow. I have a real estate agent I can connect you with. He works fast, and the cost is no option."

I raise an eyebrow. Compared to the danger looming overhead, house hunting sounds like a rather unusual priority. Not to mention the time frame. "Can you really buy a new house in a week?" I ask, the most innocent of questions to probe him with.

Something that could be a laugh trickles out of him, and he sits back. "*I* can buy a house in a week. But you will need to arrange the furniture as well. For everyone—" Sitting back, his hand falls over the end of my armrest, but he doesn't reach for one of mine. "I don't think I'll have the time to assist you…" He spares another glance at his watch. When he faces me again, his expression is strained, though he flashes a lethal grin as if to disguise the unease. "I have a list of non-negotiable items I require, however. I'll leave it up to you as to how to disguise them."

My head swims at the thought of it—for the first time, I'm the one responsible for the manic move and décor. As well as stocking our sex room, apparently.

The term *domestic* is turning out to have a surprising amount of new meanings when it comes to him.

"The kids will stay with us?" I ask next.

His slow nod is all the confirmation required.

Relieved, I sink back into the leather cushions of my recliner. His responses so far make me bold enough to risk letting a more direct question slip out. "What about your grandfather?"

He stiffens, and I nearly kick myself for bringing up that dilemma too soon.

"I will handle him," he snaps. "Parading you beneath his nose so soon would not be my preferred course of action… But he will not be so bold as to attack me out in the open. As for the others? I can handle them as well."

Such as the mysterious Danil, whom Milton mentioned.

"Why did you bring me, really?" I can't resist leaning toward him to brush my fingers along his forearm. He lets me trace a path from his shoulder all the way down to his wrist before he grabs my hand in return.

"Because of business," he says, his gaze thoughtful. "Apart from me, you are in no less danger. Perhaps more. Some would be emboldened to harm you in my absence."

"Oh." I lick my lips. Does the answer sting? Maybe, but I swallow hard to disguise it.

"And…" He tilts my fingers for his inspection and settles on the one coincidentally meant to bear a specific type of ring. "I could enjoy your presence," he adds tonelessly, as if remarking on the weather. "Your scent. Logistics aside, I could enjoy knowing that no other man could even look at you without my consent. Or that with one glance, one word, one touch, I could have you wet and ready for me."

He withdraws slowly, dragging his fingers along my flesh in retreat. Then he turns his attention to the window on his end and strokes the collar of his suit. "I will let you decide which answer to accept."

Minutes later, the plane descends, and Maxim recaptures my hand, smoothing his thumb along the back of it. "We're landing," he explains as the cabin shudders around us.

It's nightfall when we finally touch down outside of Fair Haven, and it's like waking up from a dream for a grim, colorless reality. The chill hits like a slap as we exit the plane for the night air. A black car waits nearby, helmed by an unfamiliar driver. Unsurprising, since Lucius stayed behind with the kids, ensuring their protection.

"Come." Maxim draws me to his side, and we begin our descent toward the tarmac.

"Good evening, sir," the driver greets as we approach. "The arrangements have been made for—"

"Fuck!" Maxim reacts first before I even process the events unfurling in front of me. The driver stopped talking, cut off mid-sentence. Why? I look at him, trying to discern a reason but nothing makes sense.

He's falling. Red liquid goes flying as his body slumps against the side of the car, but something is wrong with him. His head? It doesn't look right…

Because it's missing.

"Get down!" Maxim shoves me to the ground at the base of the stairs. His weight crushes me down, shielding me entirely.

But I can still hear. Footsteps. They approach in a barrage, betraying more than one person. Judging from the tension radiating through Maxim's body, they aren't friends of his.

"Not so fast, little Maxi," someone calls amid the echoing sounds. "I wouldn't be so hasty. Don't even think about reaching for your gun or calling for backup. Now stand, the both of you."

Maxim stiffens. Then all at once, the pressure pinning me down recedes, and he grabs my shoulder, urging me to my feet. I blink to adjust to the darkness. Only a few spotlights illuminate this section of the tarmac.

But we aren't alone.

At least ten men advance from the shadows to converge on our position. They're bulky, but even as panic sends my thoughts scattering, my time with Maxim made an impact. Several details stick out. For one, they don't move in crisp unison like Maxim's trained men do. They're disjointed. Sloppy. Some wear polished suits, but others—like the man who seems to be leading them all—wear a T-shirt, jeans, and a leather jacket. But all are armed, with weapons trained on us.

"Danil," Maxim says. "What a pity. I always thought you were the smartest of your inbred branch of the family tree, but I was wrong. Obviously, you have a death wish to approach me like this."

"A death wish?" A balding man, presumably Danil, wearing the leather jacket, chuckles, waving his gun casually through the air. His accent reminds me of Sevastyn's, cold and crisp like the hiss of a snake. "Maybe I am just not as mischievous as Anatoli? I don't like to make my prey sweat before I make my move. I prefer to simply—" He aims his weapon at the sky and fires. "Move."

Maxim's grip on me tightens, and he all but shoves me behind him. "What do you want?"

"Don't play dumb, boy," Danil warns with another hearty chuckle. "Anatoli requests your presence, but as for me… I'll take the girl."

"Take?" Maxim cocks his head as a low laugh resonates in his chest. "Is that so?"

"Usually, I wouldn't go after such petty bait," Danil adds with an apologetic sigh. "But, you see, Bruno here?" He reaches behind him and grabs the ear of a thinner, younger-looking man with long blond hair, dragging him to the front. "The fucker screwed up and got himself disowned. Botched robbery." He tugs on the man's ear, forcing him to kneel. "He has prostrated himself before Anatoli to no avail. Perhaps this little bounty will get him back into the fold? As a bonus, I'll let him play with the girl beforehand, so he can finally learn what it's like to fuck a woman outside of his little video games. Yes? *Wait* —" Suddenly, he aims his weapon over Maxim, his eyes narrowed. "Not so fast, Maxi. I've heard of your temper, but even you know when a man is outnumbered, yes?"

The men around him adjust their weapons as well, and Maxim's grip on my arm turns bruising.

"Now," Danil says, shrugging. "I suggest we do this the easy way. You will come with us for your spanking, Maxi." He nods toward an approaching black van. "And the girl will go with Bruno."

"Touch her, and you'll be dead before your withered cock can even enjoy the thrill," Maxim says.

Danil smiles. "If you wanted me dead, I would be dead, boy. But no hard feelings, eh? This is nothing more than the love of a father, helping to right his son's pathetic mistake. Though you wouldn't know anything about that, would you?" The corner of his mouth curls in disgust as his gaze rakes over Maxim, settling over his waist. "I've heard the old man likes to castrate little whelps like you. Render you sterile so that you can't spread your seed without his say-so—"

"I suggest you watch yourself, Danil." Maxim stands rigid, his fingers flexing at his side. "Between the two of us, only one may experience a castration firsthand."

"Hmph. I think you and I will catch up first before I tend to your little friend. *Then* I'll give you to the old man," Danil taunts, his eyes gleaming. He gestures to the men behind him with a wave. "Come on, boys! Let's go—"

"I'm afraid *not*." The door to the back seat of Maxim's car opens, and a lanky figure gracefully climbs out. Like a dancer, he unfurls his limbs, stretching them one by one as if oblivious to the violence surrounding him. An oversized black sweater adds artificial bulk to his slender frame, and his dark curls spill from a knitted hat lazily perched on his head.

Dima.

"What the hell?" Maxim's grip loosens over me for a second, revealing his shock. Dima looks back at him with a wink before he whirls on his heel to address the hoard of men behind him.

"So predictable, Danil," he says mournfully, eyeing the body of the driver nearby. "I mean, I told myself that even you wouldn't be so dreadfully sloppy. So unimaginative. Alas, I was wrong."

"Vadim?" Danil's mouth contorts into a scowl, but he lowers his gun a fraction of an inch. "Have the two mutts reunited? How sweet. The last I heard, you were still selling your ass for treats, *dog*."

"That is the nicest rumor I've heard floating around about me," Dima says, slapping a hand over his chest in gratitude. "Now, your plan sounds marvelous and all, but I'm afraid Maxim and I have a previous arrangement regarding the girl. *I've* claimed a moment with her first, you see. Your wayward son will have to find another way to crawl back into Anatoli's good graces. *Adieu—*"

"Oh?" Danil laughs. "And you'll just wave your pretty little hands and make us leave?" He glances at the men around him. "I've heard you were a crazy son of a bitch, but you can at least count?" He aims his weapon at Dima's head. "You were always a sniveling rat, but Maxi here? I've heard the stories. Any other day I wouldn't dare come to you without an army at my back. But the rumors were right. A woman has made you soft, and I can assure you that Bruno—as well as the rest of us—will surely enjoy fucking her. And then there's Anatoli… I'm sure he'll take what's left, eh boys?"

The men around him laugh, voicing suggestions that churn my stomach.

But the loudest laughter of them all spills out like music and comes from none other than Dima. "Come now, Danil," he says. "You may be the most useless of Anatoli's pawns, but even you must see it?" He gestures around us. "The girl is the only reason you are still standing where you are. Were Maxim any other man, I'd assume he wanted to spare her the trauma. As it stands, I think he's merely biding his time to inflict the most…impact." He brushes his fingers over his heart a second time, his head bowed. Then he raises his hand and cuts the air in a sharp motion. "I, however, have no such qualms."

Maxim grabs my chin, forcing my face against his chest. "Close your eyes," he growls.

It's too late.

Blood goes flying, and Danil falls over, his limbs splayed in unnatural directions. A heartbeat later, his son slumps over as well.

I breathe in, resisting the instinct flooding my veins. I don't scream. I don't go numb. I inhale the salt-tinged air, and when I pull away from Maxim, I don't cringe from the violence at my feet.

I take it all in. Every grisly, horrible fucking bit.

"You can go now," Dima says, dismissing the remaining men with a wave. They continue to raise their weapons, eyeing each other warily. "Quickly, before I change my mind and have my snipers take out the rest of you. And don't even consider firing a single bullet."

The men exchange another round of wary glances. Then, all at once, they turn and pile into the black van. Seconds later, it takes off, its wheels skidding in their haste.

As the vehicle lumbers out of view, Maxim advances a step toward Dima. "Give me one reason why I shouldn't kill you."

"This was fun," Dima exclaims, utterly unconcerned by the other man's nearness. "We should do this again. I mean, who knew sibling bonding could be such a rush—"

"How did you know?" Maxim demands, his throat cording. "I had ten fucking men on the perimeter. Danil and his shitheads had no hope of getting through."

"Yes," Dima concedes with a thoughtful nod. "That is, if Danil didn't happen to bribe the airport manager into calling in the Feds on suspicion that your plane might be smuggling drugs from a foreign country. A smart move. Too smart. I believe his son came up with it, given the plot of one of his rather amusing video games. Have no fear, I was able to defuse that nasty situation, though it allowed Danil enough time to sneak past your defenses—"

"So, you come to the rescue?" Maxim spits at his feet. "Bullshit. Why? And why not warn Jacob if you were so fucking smart?" He nods to the slain driver.

"Hmm…" Dima slips his hands into the pockets of his jeans and shrugs. The simple gesture makes him look even younger than he already appears. A boy in grown-up clothing—but his eyes portray anything but innocence. "I'm afraid that poor Jacob had to be sacrificed for the sake of research. Call it a hunch."

Maxim snatches my wrist and nearly drags me to the car he moves so quickly. "Talk in riddles if you fucking want to. You have five seconds to get out of my sight before I have you killed. Thank Milton for that shred of mercy—"

"You've killed in front of her before, haven't you?" Dima wonders as Maxim wrenches open the door to the back seat of the car. It's covered in blood, and he hisses, wiping his hand on his jacket. Then he slams the door shut and fumbles for the front passenger-side door.

"You were afraid to kill in front of her again. You hesitated, I saw it," Dima insists. "You had every chance to call your snipers to take out Danil, but you *hesitated.*" Awe colors his voice as if that simple fact is the most fascinating discovery. "Were you going to wait until the bastard was right on you before you reacted? By then, she certainly would be scarred for life, considering his brains would be in her lap. And you trust him around your child?" His attention turns to me, his lips quirked in an amused grin. "There is so much we must discuss when we finally have our talk—"

"You will never even touch her," Maxim swears. "Now get the fuck out of my sight."

"Why do you even want to talk to me?" I'm surprised that the steady, level voice is mine.

"Why?" Dima raises an eyebrow as if perplexed by the question. "To learn you, of course. The woman who fucks a beast apparently in the hopes that he may one day become a house pet. You fascinate me more than the concept of Maxim seeing a woman outside of the role of a warm, wet hole. Yes, we must discuss!"

He laughs as I turn away from him, my face on fire.

"Oh, yes. Though I have been waiting patiently, haven't I, little Maxi?"

Maxim says nothing. Finally, he gets the door to the car open and shoves me inside it. Then he storms to the other end and claims the driver's seat while I fumble for my seatbelt.

"Goodbye for now," Dima calls as Maxim slams the car door. Muffled, his voice still manages to seep inside. "I'll be waiting for your call. I am anticipating our meeting more than ever, Francesca—"

Maxim slams on the gas, sending the car lurching forward and leaving Dima behind. At the same time, he snatches a cell phone from his pocket. He must speak to more than one person, switching from English to bellowed words of Russian before he finally tosses the phone aside.

"Are you alright?" he asks me.

No. I think I'm dazed. In shock, maybe. My brain seems delayed, processing everything in comically innocent terms. Like how, as we approach the city limits, Maxim completes his transition from budding "domestic" into a calculating mafia boss. I observe him, noting the shift in his posture and the subtle tensing of his jaw. But before any real doubt can set in, he grabs my hand and places it on his lap.

"Talk to me."

I flinch, recognizing my own words mirrored back to me.

"I..." Tears spill from my eyes before I can hold them back—but I'm not afraid. I'm too tired for that. Too exhausted. All I can do is squeeze his fingers, conveying a million things I can't say out loud.

When the car finally skids to a stop, I'm surprised that we're at, of all places, the penthouse he'd brought me to before we left Fair Haven. In silence, he escorts me from the car and up to the suite. It looks exactly how we left it, but it's a stark contrast to the warm, open beach house and its brighter décor.

I miss it—more than I thought I would. More than the other houses and mansions we've left behind. I miss the man I discovered there, sampling ice cream beneath the hot sun.

I miss the begrudging smile of content he'd tried to suppress after relinquishing control on the balcony. And how he had comforted Daisy and went out of his way to provide the others with what they wanted. What they needed.

A part of me despairs at the memories—we might never get those moments back. That peace. That...normalcy.

A different man entirely, Maxim drags me into the bathroom of the master suite and strips me naked before shoving a washcloth into my hands. He leaves, and when minutes creep by without him returning, I manage to wash mechanically and dress in a thin nightgown and a robe.

The murmur of distant voices creeps into the silence, coming from the front of the suite. Still oddly numb, I wander into the main hall and follow it out to the foyer.

There, my dreamlike haze shatters. I'm in a nightmare now.

Two demons star in it, dominating opposite ends of the foyer like the living incarnations of light and shadow. A violent, gleaming gold, Maxim takes up one corner, while a glowering Milton claims another, clothed in black from head to toe.

"How many more times do I need to tell you to end this? Letting Danil off his leash was a direct message to you. You *know* that," he warns. "For fuck sake, end this. Before even Dima gets bored of this game and decides he'll have more fun watching your livelihood destroyed by Anatoli than trying to make amends with you—"

"Stop pretending like you give a damn about me, or my fucking 'livelihood,'" Maxim bellows, his chest heaving, his hands balled into fists. "Otherwise, you would be the one to grow bored with this game. Bored of humoring Dima. For years, I've let you play the role of the so-called peacemaker. But what fucking use are you now?" He looks around mockingly and scoffs. "You manage our investments, only to withhold them when it suits you just to placate your childhood pet. You put your women and your interests above mine. And now you pretend as though I'm the one abandoning you? Why don't we call in the other investor, then? If I need so many allies? The truth is, you were never *my* ally, were you?"

"You fucking *idiot*," Milton hisses, his upper lip curling in disgust. "Don't talk shit. You're so blinded by fear and hate that you can't hear how bloody ridiculous you sound. You know what…" Tearing his fingers through his dark hair, he lets out a deep breath. "Fine. I'm done. You want to pretend as if it's you against the world? Even after everything we've been through? After everything I've done for you. Be my fucking guest. You accuse me of putting my life above yours, even though I'm the one risking my life every day for *you*. Well, maybe it's about time I did, for once. Go for it, *Max*. Knock yourself out."

He turns and storms from the front door of the suite. He's still visible within the hall when Maxim calls after him. "Don't tell me you're leaving little Dima to my mercy, Milton?"

"Dima?" Milton cocks his head and laughs coldly, the sound more unsettling than any I've ever heard. "Dima can handle himself. It was never *him* I was protecting when it came to the two of you. You're just too damn stubborn to see that."

He presses forward, vanishing into the shadows.

Roaring, Maxim pivots and slams his fists into a nearby end table. It shatters in a violent display of glittering glass. He stands alone in the aftermath, surrounded by countless jagged shards. Blood drips down his left forearm, originating from a gash sliced into the flesh, but he doesn't even seem to notice.

"I'm sending you back," he declares, spotting me standing at the mouth of the hall. "I need to handle this without any fucking distractions. Fuck Milton. Dima can play his little games. I won't let him win. I won't let him get inside your fucking head—"

"Maxim, s-stop." I exhale the plea, but he breaks off, his throat cording. Swallowing hard, I weigh my next words. This is a true Russian Roulette. To pull the trigger, or run away? "I don't think you spook easily," I add, my voice rasping. "So, something had to happen to make you change your mind…"

He cocks his head, his eyes flashing. "I don't want to hurt you," he rasps, as if the words are being ripped from his throat. "I *don't*."

But he has. He's left marks on me that will never truly heal, and I don't think I'll ever fully be able to suppress the lingering fear from that. At the same time, he's done so much for me…

So much it's pushed him to the fucking breaking point.

"You won't hurt me." This time I think I actually believe it. Reaching for him, I take a hesitant step, and he nearly jumps out of his skin in his rush to maintain the distance between us. His blood paints the floor with every step, coloring the monochromatic world of his own making.

"Go," he snarls, and my body shivers in recognition of that deep, resonating tone. He's beyond even the past now. He's trapped within his fucking head, and only God knows what he's seeing.

"Talk to me," I plead, inching another step forward.

"Talk?" He scoffs. "I'll talk. I'll talk about the fact that Anatoli is toying with me. Attacking my business like one would spank a naughty child. The bastard thinks he can *summon* me—" He breaks off, and the tension coiled within his body reveals just how much that simple command is affecting him. "Like I'm still a boy beneath his boot. Should I talk about that? Or I can talk about the fact that Milton has turned his back on me. And I can talk about Vadim, always having the last fucking laugh—"

"Tell me about him." I take another step, narrowly avoiding a streak of blood. God, the wound looks even worse the closer I come. Carefully, I strip my robe and wad the fabric in my fist.

"Vadim?" He laughs again more darkly, his eyes still fixated on a world I can't see. "I was four, I believe, when we first met. My mother must have upset my father more than usual. That day he left and reappeared with another child. *His* child, nearly my age. 'You think that since you have my heir, you are untouchable?' he asked her. 'Well, I have plenty of spare bastards to take my pick from.' He kept Vadim around after that, parading him before us periodically just to prove his point."

"That's awful…" Horror constricts my throat as I finally come close enough to him to risk brushing my fingers along his injured arm. He stiffens, unmoving. Cautiously, I peel back the sleeve of his shirt and wrap my robe around the worst of the wound.

"He should have looked smug then, Dima," Maxim continues, oblivious to the pain. "He wore rags, dragged into a home worth more than his whore of a mother could ever make on her back. In that moment, he had a taste of the mantle of being the heir and what it meant. He should have fucking smirked…" He sways, and I brace my hand over his chest, but my strength is no match for his bulk.

"Come with me." I glance over my shoulder and spot a nearby chaise. Gingerly I lead him toward it, still coaxing him, "What happened next?"

"I killed our father," he croaks, but rather than sit, he goes rigid, scowling beyond this room. Beyond me. "His mother died of some disease. Together, we were sent to Anatoli."

Uttering that one name drains the humanity from him. A darkness falls over his expression, and a stranger appears in his place—someone so cold and emotionless he could be formed from stone.

"I knew what awaited us the second we entered those fucking walls. *Hell*—" He balls his hands into fists, and my heart skips. An instinctive need to back away takes hold, but the second I withdraw, he staggers away from me, still speaking. "I knew. Dima... He didn't. That first night, Anatoli broke my ribs in retaliation for what I did to his son—" He flattens his palm against his chest in remembrance of that pain. "I didn't cry. But Dima? The old man didn't lay a fucking finger on him, and he wailed anyway. He never had what it took—and I couldn't forgive him for that. For weakness..."

He takes another step, teetering dangerously to one side. It's as if he's drunk off the rage, blinded to his own senses.

Renewed concern for him outweighs any fear for myself. I approach him again, keeping my voice as soft as I can. "Maxim..."

He recoils, as if his first instinct is to resist my touch. A heartbeat later, his hand captures mine, pinning it to his chest. When I lead him toward the leather chaise, he collapses onto the edge of it. His arm is still bleeding, and I race to apply more pressure, all while still stroking him. Speaking to him.

Keeping him here.

"*He* was weak," he tells me. "I had Anatoli's favor. I was his preferred heir. Everyone knew it. But Dima... He called the old bastard evil to his face once, can you fucking believe it?"

He laughs, partly amused, partly incredulous.

"I don't know why they didn't kill him then and there. Perhaps it was more fun to toy with him. He sniveled when they beat him. Cried when they whipped him. Cut him. Starved him. Did worse. But he never fought for his place. Not really. And when he looked at me, it wasn't in fear. He knew what failure meant. And yet, Vadim? He always looked at me with...fucking *pity*." His body vibrates with disgust at that word, mirroring his anger whenever he seems to sense it in me. "Can you believe that? As though I was the weak one. When I survived. I won. I took what I was owed and never looked back. I need no one's pity."

"Tell me what happened after."

"Anatoli grew bored," he adds, deflating. "He declared that only one of us would become the true heir, if we were willing to fight for it. The loser would go to Sevastyn..." He inhales sharply, and I press my hand to his cheek before that unsettling shadow can consume him again. With gentle pressure, I make him look at me.

"I'm here," I whisper. "You're with me. You're not there." He blinks, his expression blank, but I maintain the contact anyway. "Talk to me."

"He should have won." His gaze refocuses, fixating on mine. Hints of him return, peeking from behind the dark irises. The more I stroke him, the more of him I see. A man so confused the frustration haunts him. Poisons him.

It's tormenting him.

"He should have." Voice rasping, he insists, "The bastard should have fucking won. He wasn't stronger, but he was faster. Smarter. He could handle a blade better than anyone. He should have won."

I don't say anything. I can't. All I can do is stroke his jaw and staunch the bleeding from his arm, utilizing patience I never knew I had.

Gradually, his nostrils flare, and his expression regains some semblance of definition.

"There it is," he accuses in a surprisingly hollow tone. "*Your* pity. Worse than his in so many ways…"

"No." I shake my head and lean forward, resting my forehead against his chest. "It's not pity. It's never pity. Never…"

He doesn't argue. He's not here fully yet, but his breathing eases, and when I attempt to stand, he tightens his grip as if to pull me back.

"You're covered in blood." I take his hand and tug him to his feet. "Come with me."

Despite everything, I'm shocked when he lets me take him into the bathroom. He sits in the tub, watching skeptically as I gather supplies. I strip him slowly and then wash him inch by inch. When I finally reach his head, he pulls me in, kissing me deeply. The rest of my clothing comes off easily beneath his touch, but he doesn't settle me over his cock.

His hands find my waist instead, his chest meeting mine. He sinks his fingers reverently into my hair while pressing his lips to my collar, right above my breast. "You… Life was never a mystery to me. I knew what I wanted. Money. Power. Control. I took all of it. But never could I imagine you… I won't lose you. But…"

A raw, pained expression contorts his features, triggering an instinctive alarm in the pit of my soul. I've never seen him like this. In agony, but the physical wound isn't the cause—and I don't think he'll ever truly heal from it.

"Dima was right," he croaks. "Can I give you what you need? I don't know. You are young. You will want children —do not deny it. You *will*. And… In my world, children are met with strictness. Violence. What happened to Vadim and me is typical—they are beaten into submission and traded like chattel. And you will not understand, but this did not bother me. It is all I know, and therefore I made a choice. No children of my own."

His voice is a monotone hum devoid of emotion. I don't even think he's talking to me anymore—not really. This is for him—a confession of the things he can't express, even in the dark room.

But he's not alone, forced to use whips and knives to express the pain he won't ever admit to out loud. Silently, I brace my hands over his chest, reinforcing my presence.

I'm here.

"I expected no different," he adds. "Even with your siblings. I knew I would have to restrain myself from beating them if I was to keep you near. I was prepared to. But…" He frowns, and the expression breaks my heart into a million fucking pieces. He looks more confused than ever. So lost—a boy trapped in his memories with no way out. "I didn't. I didn't want to harm them. Not once. I didn't want to beat them down for insolence. I felt no urge to hurt your sister when she defied you. Your brother does not deserve to be whipped for daring to question me. And the youngest…" His voice breaks, hollow and hoarse. "I couldn't imagine hurting her. Selling her. If Dima threatened her that day, I would have killed him."

I believe it. He practically levitates with repressed emotion. Brushing my lips along his shoulder is the only way to ease the tension from him again.

"I've never considered being a father," he tells me. It is honesty delivered as efficiently as one of the blows from his whip. Devastating in its aim. "But now? You think I struggle with this life. I *let* you believe that—" He tiredly meets my gaze, and all I see reflected in his dark eyes is a man pushed to his breaking point, exhausted beyond belief. "The truth is that…I feel clearer, the more I'm with you. With them. At the same fucking time, I feel like I'm losing myself. The man I've been for so damn long." He eyes his hands warily and then lets them fall into the water. "If you leave…who will I be in the aftermath?"

"You," I whisper against his skin, curling myself against

him. I take one of his hands and thread our fingers together. "This is *you*. You don't have to suppress your past with me."

"I don't?" He laughs, but the sound trickles from him as a sigh more than anything. I look up to find him observing our clasped hands. "Dima is a different breed of monster from me, but he is right. You will never be safe in my world. Trying to convince you otherwise was a lie—"

"I like your world," I interject, my voice small. "Not your grandfather's fucked-up empire, or the twisted games, or the lies. *Your* world. A beach house with rules we decided on. Lazy days and vanilla sex, with kink at night. That world."

His expression shifts, and I choke out a startled laugh. He looks comically skeptical, an eyebrow raised. "I will have to fight to give you that world."

"I know. Which is why you need to let me help you." I weigh the danger of pushing him too far. But hell, that's the only game to play with him. Reckless, Russian Roulette. "If it will make a difference like Milton said, then let me talk to Dima—"

He makes a low sound in his throat. "I will grant you anything… But I will pretend you didn't request *that*."

"You need his help," I say, parroting Milton's insistence. "I don't want to come between you and your friend. And…" A part of me shies from voicing more, but I don't have a choice. It's the truth. "If he hurts me, I know you'll kill him."

"And if he toys with your head?" he counters, tightening his grip on my hand. "Plants devious, vicious lies? He is a snake."

"That's why you need to trust me. Like I trust you."

Trust. The line of his mouth softens at the sound of that word, but in the same damn breath, his nostrils flare. "No—"

"Maybe I can help you find the truth?" I suggest, trying a different line of attack. "Learn what he really wants? It's been bothering you, don't tell me it hasn't."

"The *truth* is, he wants to destroy what I have. He couldn't take the Koslov name, so he'll take you from me."

"And I won't let him."

His brows furrow as if the idea of my free will never factored into his thinking.

"You gave me a choice before," I add, recalling how he questioned me in front of Milton and Dima. "Or was that for show?"

Sighing, he repositions me so that I straddle him. It's a devious ploy only a true game master would enact to regain control. His hands feel huge against my hips, cradling me with a gentleness he rarely utilizes. Our foreheads meet, and his teeth tease my lower lip, dissolving my will to argue with every sensual nip.

"I trust you," he confesses as my thoughts start to scatter. "My kitten who can be so affectionate when she chooses, sucking me off for all of the world to see. And ice cold the next, lashing out with her claws. But I will never trust Dima."

Thinking fast, I slip my tongue between his lips, stealing his taste. He groans in shock, his nails grazing my flesh. As the upper hand shifts in my favor, I'm bold enough to propose, "What if we trade?"

A frown tugs on his mouth—he's suspicious. "I am curious as to why you are so determined in this instance. Vadim seems to catch your interest more than marrying me."

"I want to help you," I confess, brushing off the uncharacteristic note in his voice. Jealousy? In silent reassurance, I press my lips against his skin over and over. With each affectionate kiss, his breathing quickens, and the balance of power teeters again in my direction. "I only want to help you."

Can he really not see the toll this is taking on him? Though hell, he doesn't even seem to feel the wound on his arm. I swipe my thumb near it in sympathy. A normal man would be rushing to the emergency room, demanding stitches.

"You think I need helping?" he wonders.

"Maybe we both do? I want a future with you." I sound so damn tired, and I am. This is my last-ditch ploy to win this round—and not for Dima's sake or anyone else's but my own. And his. For him, I have no shame in resorting to selfish begging. Maybe later, I'll let myself examine what that might mean.

"I do," I repeat against his collar bone, cutting my brain off to any thoughts but this. "I'm willing to fight you for it, and if I'm wrong. I'm wrong. We've been through worse. So what do you say? At least consider a trade?"

"I will think about this." His lips find mine before I can argue, silencing me with a kiss so deep my head reels when he pulls away. Robbing me of any chance to recover, he rocks beneath me, settling between my legs. Before I can even steel myself, he's thrusting in deep, groaning at the feel.

"In the meantime, we will trade in this way," he grates through gritted teeth.

A thrust for a thrust. Pleasure for pleasure. A kiss for a kiss. All of it is currency we're both squirreling away for leverage later.

So is the way of the game.

CHAPTER SIXTEEN

Hell doesn't contain an ounce of fire. It's just so fucking cold. Wet. There's red everywhere. Painting the walls, sloshing over the floor, flooding the air with the scent of salt.

It's blood.

Screaming, I try to swim as the level rises higher by the second—an ocean of violence, washing me away.

And I'm drowning in it...

"It's alright," a heavy voice drips into my ear, persistent over my cries. Patiently, the owner coaxes me back to a reality of silken sheets and a darkened room. "You're safe. Wake up. Look at me, Francesca."

For a twisted, painful few seconds, all I can do is struggle to breathe as I take stock of my limbs. I'm drenched—but the liquid isn't blood, just sweat. I'm not in hell either. A nearby window displays a view of Fair Haven bathed in darkness, illuminated with accents of neon.

"You were dreaming," Maxim murmurs, brushing his lips over my forehead with a rare gentleness. He's beside me, his heat like an anchor, giving me strength against the tidal wave of fear threatening to swamp my thoughts. All those memories…

It's getting harder to ignore them. Harder to keep them at bay.

I saw yet another man die in front of me. More than one.

Sooner or later, I'll have to face that fully. I can't hide from the horror forever.

"Sleep," Maxim insists as if reading my mind. He eases his fingers into my hair, parting the sweat-soaked strands. "What happened changes nothing. You'll meet with the realtor in the morning—"

"What if your family tries to attack you again?" I'm shaking at the thought of it, and more terrifying worries sneak into my brain. The constant danger. The crippling paranoia. It will always be like this with him. Always. "What if—"

"I will ensure you have a team of security on you at all times," he says, raising his voice to gently overpower mine. He sounds different, though I can't name how. *Exhausted?* As if what happened in the tub drained parts of him away. His cold baritone resonates warmer than usual as a result, and it sinks into my bones, easing my fear. "As you said, I do not spook easily," he adds. "So sleep. If you trust me as you claimed to, then trust me now. No one will ever harm you again." His eyes scan my face intently, hunting for any sign of doubt. When I finally start to drift off, he sighs, relieved. "I'm here…"

HE'S GONE before I wake up. The mass of sheets twisted around my body reveals that he didn't lay beside me for very long. Just enough to soothe me back to sleep before rising again. Then I suspect he paced until dawn before the windows, mulling over the prospect of his kingdom in peril.

A gray dawn bathes said kingdom, and the room itself, in a soft, neutral glow now. It's such a jarring contrast to the chaos of last night, but I know better than to enjoy it for very long. Instead, I rise from the bed and stretch to wake up my sore limbs. After grabbing a clean dress from the closet, I shower alone and leave the bedroom to find a plate of lukewarm food waiting for me on the dining room table, along with a note.

I will be gone until tonight. The realtor has a list of my preferences. I insist upon them all. — Maxim.

My lips twitch as I fold the note and set it aside. I don't know whether to laugh at the rare attempt at a joke on his part, or…

Shiver. I suspect his "preferences" go far beyond a request for a particular architecture style or double sinks. The more I stress over what he could want, the more I start to second guess going out alone at all.

But intuition warns against the panic. Trust goes both ways. If I want him to include me in his life, I can't attach myself to him forever. I can't always kneel in his shadow.

I need to make a place for myself and determine my own rules as to what I'll allow within it.

So I eat, and when the realtor comes, I'm ready. Hours later, we've explored every fucking mansion within a twenty-mile radius, and some of my previous confidence starts to wane.

Who knew that a "family home" was a foreign concept in this city? Sure, there are plenty of spacious mansions like the few Maxim's shoved my family into before. They look beautiful, with plenty of space and "curb appeal," according to the realtor.

But none of them seem…real. Stable. Like a *home*, not that I'm a fucking expert on those. Even with money being no obstacle, I can't bring myself to sign off on any of the sprawling, lifeless structures I tour with Jonathan, an Italian man who peppers nearly every sentence with architectural terms.

"As you can see, this atrium will provide your family maximum privacy while allowing in some sunlight and the allusion of the outdoors." He beams at the plastic-looking trees and flowers cramped within the narrow space in the center of the last home on the list.

Suffice to say, it's a no.

I'm exhausted when I finally return to the suite. I've spent my entire life in the slums, and yet a day touring fancy homes worth millions has somehow left me feeling filthier than I ever did in Horn Hill. Disgusted, I strip my clothing right at the door and head straight for the bathroom. When I finally emerge from the shower wearing a robe, I discover that someone is already in the bedroom, ripping a suit from his muscular limbs.

"You found nothing," he says without looking in my direction. Am I surprised that he's kept tabs on my progress?

Maybe not.

"No." I awkwardly fiddle with the strings of my robe as he continues to strip, tugging at his shirt next. "Nothing really stood out to me…"

"It's a house," he points out gruffly. "What needs to stand out?"

I bite my lower lip. He has a point. What does a house need?

"Safety?" I ask, thinking out loud. "Someplace that Ainsley can play in, and Daisy can sulk, and Mikie can have his own room for once. A home."

"Hmph." He pauses, his shirt still clenched in his fist as if the concept is as foreign to him as it is to me. Then he snatches a clean one from a hanger and wrenches it on over his head. "I've added more men to the team on you. Lucius is still with your siblings, but I will need time to ensure the security of the new home before they can return. As long as it's secure, I'm sure any place will suffice rather than have their return delayed."

Which makes his week deadline more pressing than ever.

"Are you leaving?" I wonder as he swiftly buttons his shirt and straightens the collar.

"Yes. I've been busy strengthening my security overall," he adds while stripping his pants in exchange for a fresh pair. "Restructuring my assets. Letting Danil confront me at all was a mistake on Anatoli's part." His grim expression reinforces the guttural edge to his voice. "A mistake he will not make again."

Once fully dressed, he marches to the doorway. Only then does he seem to remember my presence enough to add, "I won't be back tonight. Tomas can bring you dinner—"

"Wait." I reach out, brushing my hand over his shoulder. He falters, but doesn't fully stop, rocking back and forth on his heels with barely suppressed impatience. "Is something wrong?"

"No." Without warning, he captures my chin, kissing me hard with an intensity that leaves me clinging to him. Up this close, I can sense the unease bubbling beneath the surface of the stern façade he's crafted beneath the fresh suit and aloof gaze. His lips linger over mine until he finally pulls back.

"I've made up my mind," he says, his voice cold. Final. "I won't let you near Dima. There is nothing worth trading for that risk. Nothing."

I watch him go in a daze, too stunned to argue.

At least he was honest. The man can offer me the world, but there is nothing I possess he deems worth having. Nothing apart from complete possession.

Even the prospect of us living together doesn't seem to appeal to him beyond the surface practicality of it. What he said won't stop taunting me, echoing in my brain on repeat. *"What needs to stand out? It's a house."*

Maybe he's right.

Or maybe...he is capable of viewing it from just one angle. It's not the house itself that matters but what it symbolizes. This cold, isolated penthouse reflects the many aspects of him he's clung to. What's helped him survive in his world for so long. Few personal belongings. A bed he rarely sleeps in. Furniture picked solely for its functionality.

Lucius had a point, but I think I misinterpreted his original warning. You can free the wolf from its captivity, but if all it knows are iron bars, the forest doesn't seem like home anymore.

But no real family can survive within the confines of a cage.

The only way to bridge the gap is to find a compromise. Learn what bait might tempt a wolf…

Enough for him to forget he was ever a prisoner at all.

CHAPTER SEVENTEEN

The next morning, I wake up to the realtor, Jonathan, knocking on the door of the suite. When I open the door, hastily dressed, I find him flanked by two armed members of my expanded security detail. One is Tomas, who nods stiffly in greeting.

"Mr. Koslov strongly suggested we close on a property soon," Jonathan says while tugging nervously at his purple tie with one hand and juggling a briefcase in the other. Crossing to a—newly replaced—end table, he fishes a stack of documents from his bag and shuffles through them. "I believe you'll love a series of homes in the exclusive Knight Heights district—"

"I think I want to look at some places near the water," I suggest, cutting him off.

It's the one feature that separates Fair Haven from most other shitholes in the country—a bay on the outskirts, which serves as both a focal point for what little tourism there is, as well as the main reason why it's such a hotbed for crime in the first place.

We're open to the world in a way that leaves it ripe for the taking by men like Maxim.

Jonathan's brows furrow. "The bay? An interesting choice." His skeptical tone betrays his true thoughts on that front. "I will admit that location holds a more *rustic* charm. You won't come anywhere near to the elegance of say, this property here—" He gestures around us, referring to the penthouse. "Though, I suppose you could always renovate…"

On that optimistic note, we take a car staffed by one of Maxim's drivers. Within an hour, we're pulling up to the first property to fit my preferences. My initial impression is that Jonathan was right. These homes are nothing like the highly modern mansions we toured in and around the city. They look older, like something you'd see in one of those small-town dramas. Still huge and impressive, but in a less obvious way.

The place a mob boss might live, only when retired or under witness protection.

The one we approach now is sprawling, made of sturdy brown wood, and supported by stone accents. Positioned on a hill, it overlooks a quiet, semi-private section of the bay, complete with a rocky beach and a wooden dock.

Inside, the mixture of stone and wooden architecture continue, creating an open, simple layout centered around three large windows overlooking the water.

"There are ten bedrooms in total," Jonathan remarks. "Plenty of acreage if you're into outdoor activities, and there is a pool in addition to a private section of the waterfront. Basic amenities, but they possess a certain charm, I suppose."

I crane my neck back to take in the high, vaulted ceilings above a living room dominated by a stone fireplace. The beautiful, "rustic" design will amplify every single sound the kids make. When Ainsley and Eric fight, it will resonate with the intensity of an army skirmish. Daisy's whining will echo times a million during one of her rants.

And Maxim's voice alone will have no trouble filling the space, reaching every inch of it.

"Ms. Marconi?" Jonathan wonders, an eyebrow raised. "Are you ready to move on?"

"No." I sigh, turning my attention to the view of the water beyond the windows. It's no tropical paradise, that's for damn sure. Shitty Fair Haven can't compare to endless blue waters. But in some ways…

This is so much better.

Turning to Jonathan, I square my chin. "I'll take it."

MAXIM WASN'T LYING about his ability to purchase a home within days. All Jonathan seems to require from me is simple confirmation. Afterward, he devolves into a flurry of phone calls and shuffling paperwork. Before seeing me off, he presses a folder into my hands. "Oh, Mr. Koslov requested I give you this once you'd settled on a property. Tomorrow, I'll connect you with an interior designer to get the furnishing process underway."

My heart pounds ominously as I tuck the folder beneath my arm and enter a car driven by Tomas. It isn't until we're nearly in the city that I finally gather the nerve to open the folder and observe the documents within.

I scan the first line, expecting an explicit, detailed list of sex toys. Instead, I find a series of names with a sentence or two scribbled beside them, denoting that particular person's requests. All of it is written in Maxim's handwriting, with curt phrases implying that he personally interviewed every member listed.

Ainsley – Pink walls. A playroom. A pony. Please, a pony? I don't need a room, just that!

Daisy – My own space. Seriously. MINE. Please. Yellow. A deck to tan.

Mikie – Blue. An arcade. (he's rich enough, right?) A boat.

Ollie – Bunk bed. A pinball machine. A skateboard ramp.

Ray – A video game room. A bed shaped like a pirate ship.

Eric – A room made of LEGO.

Tears well within my eyes and spill out before I can blink them back. They distort the ink on the page, making the words blur and run together. At the very end of the list, its author made sure to denote—*I will attend to my own personal requirements in time.*

He could do this for me, while having the confidence to claim that nothing I could offer him would ever be enough to make him bend where it really matters. His psyche. His security. *His* peace.

That wall will always remain between us—literally. Only in some dark room, deep in the night, can he ever face the trauma shaping him. And he will always choose to face it alone.

"Are you alright, Miss?" Tomas wonders from the driver's seat. Alarm deepens his tone as he reaches for his pocket, presumably for a cell phone. "Did you change your mind about the house? If you are not satisfied, I'm sure Mr. Koslov will—"

"No," I croak, waving him off. "I'm fine. It's just…"

I look down, surprised to find my fingers interlaced, the nails digging in. I'd been pinching myself without realizing it. I've already broken the skin—a bead of blood bubbles from the tiny wound, and my eyes fixate on the color.

Red. That fucking hue dominates my life now, a reminder of the violence that comes with Maxim Koslov. The insanity. The death. The rage.

If I ever did marry him, there is no way in hell I could ever wear white. Just this goddamn color that's come to drench our lives.

Red.

"Ms. Marconi?" Tomas inquires, sounding more alarmed.

"I want you to take me somewhere," I say, wiping at my eyes with the sleeve of my coat. "I don't want you to ask for Maxim's permission either. I don't want him to know where I am. If you don't know the address, Lucius will—"

"Do you understand what you are asking?" Tomas wonders, his voice soft.

I'm asking for him to risk pissing off an employer who isn't like any other. But I'm learning that it takes more than desperation to win a game. It requires a reckless willingness to gamble.

Everything.

"Please," I insist. "I need to do this alone."

"Miss…" I can visibly see him wrestle with the dilemma of informing Maxim or deferring to me. The second directive, must outweigh the first. At least in this instance.

"As you wish," he concedes with a sigh. "Though if you are in any danger, I will be forced to inform Mr. Koslov immediately. And I will only be able to maintain silence for a few hours, at the most. You understand."

"I won't be in any danger," I admit. "Though I'm afraid that you'll probably be incredibly bored."

NOT FOR THE FIRST TIME, I face my reflection and barely recognize the woman staring back. Yards of silken fabric spill from her slender body, conveying a cruel, twisted imitation of the perfect, beautiful creation most girls spend their entire lives envisioning.

In my case, the concept is more abstract than that of a beautiful gown fit for a princess, or a symbolic representation of what should be the best day of my life.

This dress is a promise, conveyed in glaring, contrasting shades of white and bloody red.

This is the life I'm willing to sign up for. The trade, I'm finally able to make—a harmony of violence and security. Death and life. Blood and the purity left behind once it's all washed away.

Looking at myself now, I realize that this is the only gown befitting of someone insane enough to marry Maxim Koslov.

"I must admit the overall effect is stunning," the designer exclaims as she races around me, pinning various pieces of fabric in place. "I do adore the original, more traditional concept. But traditions were made to be…adapted." She adjusts the scarlet bodice that hugs my torso before flaring out into a wide, billowing skirt. The base is every bit the beautiful dress Maxim first envisioned. But as the viewer's eye rises, swaths of scarlet intermingle with the ivory, consuming the gown entirely by the level of my chest.

I don't look wide-eyed and innocent in this design. I look like I'm bleeding from my heart, drenched in the color I've come to dread. In some ways, it's beautiful. In others, it's fucking terrifying.

But I'm tired of hiding from it.

"I can finish the alterations in a few days," the designer says while continuing to make more adjustments. "I think the color is lovely, but if you wanted to add a deeper red here—" She breaks off, gasping as a monstrous thud resonates from the entrance of the boutique—the door slamming hard enough to rattle the fragile glass.

His expression like thunder, the culprit storms in, his dark eyes flashing as they find me. "I've been looking everywhere for you," he growls, brandishing a clenched fist at Tomas, who stands alert beside a rack of clothing. "You order *my* men to hide you from me? I had to have fucking Lucius—" He breaks off as he finally takes in my appearance. "I…"

His mouth opens and closes wordlessly. Then he blinks and rakes a trembling hand through his hair. In the end, all he seems capable of doing is staring. His gaze traces the contours of my dress, tracking the blend of color and the bold shape. It's impossible to tell what he's thinking from here.

Rather than dwell on it, I face him with my head held high, my shoulders back. "How is this for a trade?"

He swallows hard, his throat rasping until he finally manages to spit out a handful of words. "I…I'll be in the car."

He turns and leaves the boutique, decidedly quieter than the way he entered.

It's nearly an hour before the seamstress manages to carefully dissect the gown, preserving the construction.

When I finally join Maxim out front, he's in the driver's seat and doesn't say a word as I claim the space beside him. He doesn't even look at me, turning his full attention to the road. Rather than the penthouse, I'm surprised when we arrive before Club XXX minutes later, just as night is beginning to fall.

Maxim climbs out and marches inside almost too quickly for me to keep up. Before I can fall behind, he grabs my wrist, dragging me down the hall to his secluded room in the back.

After stumbling over the threshold, he shoves me against the wall. The cold surface braces me as his bulk crushes me from the front.

"Fuck," he breathes, as his fingers bunch up my skirt and find the wetness already slicking my inner thighs underneath. He wastes no time, testing me with the width of his thumb.

When he flicks his wrist, nothing is preventing him from going deeper on the second explorative touch. Further than he meant to, judging from his raspy grunt. His free hand crawls up my spine, cinching my neck, forcing me to meet his gaze.

"Say it," he growls, grinding his pelvis against my hips. "You'll marry me?"

I suck in air through my teeth and release it in a single word. "Yes…"

"In that dress." He lowers his mouth to my throat, inhaling me. "You will wear my ring?"

My eyelids flutter at the intensity of his voice. "Y-Yes."

"And you'll take my name, even if it means nothing?"

"Yes."

He groans, cursing under his breath. "You truly were made for me." A crime in his book—and my punishment comes swiftly—his lips dominating mine, nipping teeth giving way for a tongue that batters me open and overtakes any resistance I may have felt. With the club full, someone might be able to hear us, even from here.

And when he finally wrenches up the skirt of my dress and plunges inside of me, anyone within a goddamn ten-mile radius probably hears me.

Hears him. His guttural roars echo every mewling cry to spill from my throat. Together, the sounds meld into a blistering crescendo—the only thing I can hear as my world comes apart.

I come clinging to him with all I have, my limbs shaking and ghosted with sweat. "Holy…fuck," I breath out against his skin.

"I'm going to fuck you in that dress," he swears as his hands cup my ass, lifting me into his arms. With staggering steps, he brings me to the bed and climbs onto the mattress, pinning me beneath him. "Mark you in it," he adds, describing more of his X-rated wedding day. "Take pieces of the silk. Make a whip. I'll use it on your pretty skin until all of you is painted red…" His voice shakes with need, and he hardens against my thigh, rousing an answering twitch in my belly. "And the ring," he adds, sliding his hand down my trembling stomach to the space between my legs. I'm forced to buck my hips into him further, relishing the sinful contact. "The things I will do to you with that ring." He swipes the pad of a finger over my entrance, swirling the moisture already there. "But that is nothing compared to your name." He chuckles deeply, and my breathing hitches at the foreboding sound. "I'll train your sweet ass to react to it," he tells me, nuzzling his open mouth against my shoulder. Without warning, he bites down. Once. Twice. I'm too tired to scream. I just moan, weakly clutching his arms. "I'll make you come every time I fucking say it. *Francesca…*"

He bites off the rest and groans again, sounding pained. Starving. Mad. "I will be the only man who can call you his." His hand sinks into my hair, and he uses a chunk of it as a leash to draw me into him, letting our mouths meet. He isn't content with claiming just my lips. His mouth travels across my jaw and finds my ear as he shifts his hips against mine, drawing his erection between my legs. "And how I will own you."

"Own?" I counter, finding my voice again. "I thought this was a trade?"

"Trade… Yes." He nuzzles my throat as if addicted to the taste of me. I doubt he's actually processed what I've said. He finds my nipple and captures it between his teeth through my dress, making my back arch off the mattress.

"A t-trade," I insist, sinking my fingers through his hair. I stroke through the damp strands until he finally faces me again. "Do you accept my terms?"

Rather than annoyed, his eyes glow, heavy-lidded with lust. A low hum revs in his throat, deepening the more I touch him. Could this be victory?

"My kitten," he grates, sounding pained. "She drives a hard bargain. Regardless, I accept the terms, but can you accept *mine*?"

He gives me a taste, entering me again. I'm sore and breathless from the first time—but my body gives me no say. It yields to him, dragging him deep. So deep that I forget what it feels like to ever go without him.

In the aftermath, he holds me tight, crushing my body to his chest. His hands stroke through my hair as if memorizing every strand.

"I want you in my dress," he admits. "My ring. You've made a tempting offer. So I'll take it. And in return…you get to play your dangerous little game."

"Dima?" I say, dread thickening my voice.

"Is that what you truly want?" His skeptical tone resonates cold in the wake of his lust—but his fingers absently stroke my hips, countering any real anger.

"I want to help you," I reply. "I wasn't lying when I asked you for a partnership." I press myself against him, sensing how his body relents to me as if in defiance of his stubborn frown. "I want your trust."

He grunts and parts his lips over my shoulder as if a mouthful of my flesh is the only thing worthy of silencing him. A jolt runs through me as he bites down, conveying his agreement.

He'll let me talk to Dima.

But as he rolls over and drags me to his side, I can't resist wondering who got the better bargain out of this trade.

CHAPTER EIGHTEEN

After we dress, Maxim makes a single phone call. To Milton, I presume. Their conversation passes quickly, surprisingly devoid of a shouted argument.

"It will happen here," Maxim announces once he hangs up. "Soon. Before I come to my senses and change my fucking mind. Come." He takes my hand, and we return to the main club, finding it empty.

In our absence, someone rearranged the furniture, leaving a single table in the center of the room, set with two chairs.

"He has an hour," Maxim warns as he leads me to one of the chairs and holds it out for me. "One fucking hour. He can't touch you. And I have my men watching…" He hesitates, as if he wants to say more. Demand I reconsider, maybe? In the end, he retreats, presumably returning to his private room. "I won't be far," he calls back to me. "Him, I do not trust. But you? I trust that you can handle him. And I trust that if you feel that you cannot, you will call for me…"

I shiver beneath the weight of his newfound confidence. Do I deserve it? I won't know for sure until the time comes when I'll have to pull the trigger in this ultimate game of roulette.

It isn't long before I sense the entire atmosphere in the building shift with the arrival of my opponent. Dima. For him to arrive so quickly…I can't escape the feeling that he knew well in advance this moment would come. Maybe not the exact time or day—but with enough certainty to stick around closely, awaiting Maxim's summons.

Oozing confidence, he strolls into the club dressed in a gray sweatshirt, with a red beanie crushing his curls to his skull. When he spots me, he flashes a grin, wiggling his fingers.

"I'm impressed," he exclaims, taking the chair across from me. "Very impressed. I'd assumed it would be at least a few months before Maxim would break down enough to humor my little request."

I fight to keep control of my expression. Do I smile and aim for politeness? Or do I copy Maxim's inherent hostility?

I mull over both options only to settle on neither. Something warns me Dima would see through the act either way.

So all I do is ask, "You were willing to wait that long just to talk to me?"

He smiles. "Oh, no. By then, Anatoli would have already beaten his favorite boy back into submission. I would be speaking to you through the iron bars of your cage after the old man tired of you and Maxim had already moved on to another pretty fool."

A shiver runs through me, constricting my throat. So much for uncertainty as to how to treat him—I'm starting to agree with Maxim. This is pointless, humoring a psychopath whose main goal only seems to be sowing chaos.

But I'm the idiot who decided to play the game. All I can do is see this round through to the end.

"So, what do you want?" I ask, making my tone as neutral as I can.

"Let's not waste time discussing such boring matters!" He snaps his fingers, beckoning a waitress who appears from nowhere with a bottle of wine. Her hand shakes as she sets two glasses onto the table and fills them to the brim. I try to meet her gaze, but she avoids me and scurries back down the hall the second Dima dismisses her. I watch her go—she isn't heading toward where I assume the kitchen to be.

Will she report to Maxim that I'm unscathed so far?

"Ah, dear Maxim has supplied us with the absolute best," Dima exclaims, drawing my attention back to him. He lifts a glass and hands it to me.

"Thank you," I say while setting it aside without taking a sip. "So why did you want to talk to me?"

"This is a marvelous establishment," Dima admits, eyeing our surroundings with an approving nod. "Such a unique atmosphere."

One he obviously doesn't feel comfortable within. It's warm enough inside that I feel fine, even in my short-sleeved dress. He, on the other hand, seems to sink into his sweatshirt, and a slight tremor in his jaw draws my notice. He's shivering.

"Are you okay?"

"I'm fine. Just cold," he says offhandedly. "Nothing abnormal. I am always cold. My therapist tells me that it's partly psychosomatic. All in my head," he explains, tapping his skull with his finger. "Mostly, it is due to medical reasons. Alas, you could stick me in the middle of a raging inferno, and it would never be warm enough. Anyway, as for why I am here?" He shrugs and shifts to face me directly. "I must admit you fascinate me."

"Why?" I counter, unnerved by the way his eyes flicker across my face as if missing nothing. Not my unease. Not a single fucking pimple.

He chuckles, eyeing his own glass. "You think you're special to him, don't you? You think you're the only woman to tempt him. The only woman to soften him. The only one…" He lifts his gaze to mine. "And you would be right. He's been through women the way most men change out socks. Rarely the same one twice. None of them have lived with him. None of them have desired to. But have you stopped to ask yourself why?"

"No," I lie. "But why does it matter to you?"

"Why?" His eyes widen in disbelief. "Maybe it's because Maxim doesn't love. He's incapable of it, as am I. We are similar in this, you see—and I came to that realization years ago. Living within that family has damaged us both. Even Milton, to an extent. While *they* may have forgotten that, alas, it can't be helped." He shakes his head, sending his curls bouncing beneath the rim of his beanie. His smile doesn't disguise the glimmer of darkness lurking beneath the cheerful expression. He's angry. *They have forgotten…*

"Perhaps I seek to warn you?" he adds.

I hate how confident he sounds. Smug. As if I'm an idiot he's decided to take pity on and inform that the sky is indeed *blue*.

"Warn me?" I say, forcing myself to stay focused. "About what?"

"Or maybe I seek to test him?" His lip quirks, transforming his expression from concerned to playful. He peeks toward the hall, where Maxim presumably is, and lets loose a wistful sigh. "He's stewing now, you do realize? Wondering what lies I'm telling you. What secrets I'll let slip about him. He's always been a jealous boy, too possessive for his own good. That is why he could never father children, you see. He would only ever see them as competition—"

"Just get to the point," I snap, losing my neutral tone.

His words sneak into my brain long after he's gone silent, sowing seeds of doubt that blossom into full-on panic. Could there come a day when I'll have to choose between my family and Maxim...

No. I shake my head, picturing the way he acted at the beach house. He's already proven the steps he'll go to in order to avoid that very situation—I can't deny that the effort pushed him to the breaking point.

"The point?" Dima sits back and sips from his wine glass. "Maybe Maxim and his love life are the least of my concern? My motives may be more selfish in nature."

"You just want to taunt him, then?" I deduce, pushing back from the table. Irritation prickles my skin. I'm such a fucking idiot, falling for his trap. "You just want to play with him for entertainment like Milton said."

"Yes." He nods thoughtfully. "Or closure. According to my therapist, I will never be truly happy unless I close old doors, so to speak. He's a bit of an old fuddy, duddy. He claims that I must discover what's been bothering poor Dima since he was a wee, little lad and finally slay that monster."

I stiffen in horror, still perched on the edge of my seat. "You want to kill him?"

"Maxim?" He frowns. "No. Where would the fun in that be? I *want* something from him, though. I want… acknowledgment. I want him to admit that he is as weak and as human as the rest of us. That he is a violent, broken, damaged fool, as am I. To pretend otherwise is simply unproductive. Having him say as much might do wonders for my psyche. His too."

"By toying with him?" I croak. Dima is still smiling, but the vitriol in his words stings deeper than it should. Perhaps because Maxim all but confessed the same thing? "Why do you feel like he can't change?"

"Because I cannot," he says simply. "I've tried. It's no fun. No family for poor Dima. No woman to ply with some ring. I've chosen against pretending it's even a possibility."

His lips part in a beautiful, chilling smile. "Therefore, I've decided my dear brother should realize the same before he hurts you in more ways than by using a whip."

I cringe, but he beams in triumph. "It isn't my place to kink shame," he adds. "Maxim's been known to dabble in masochism for a long while. Though who am I to judge? I have my own…quirks."

He waits as if daring me to ask him more. When I don't, his smile widens, baring all of his white, perfectly straight teeth.

"I don't prefer to tie up my women, but I do enjoy the odd mind game or two. Convincing some poor, desperate bachelorette that I may be the answer to her financial dreams—only to watch her run in disgust the more I put her desperation to the test. Love is relative, you see. A little humiliation here. Some deception there. You find out quickly what price some might put on their so-called happy ending."

I can't disguise my disgust this time. "That sounds insane—"

"Insane, yes." He forms a steeple with his fingers and perches his chin on top of it. "Because I am. *Clinically,* though I assume you were being a tad dramatic in your assumption. The old man had us both rigorously tested, you see. And I was tested yet again when I was separated from my brother and sold to…let's call it a 'boarding school.'"

I nearly choke. Maxim put it a different way. *The loser would go to Sevastyn,* he said. *Sevastyn,* the pedophile who gained influence through corruption. The same man Milton despised for equally murky reasons.

"So he *has* told you something," Dima suspects with a knowing grin. "Maxim is a very smart man. In fact, he possesses above-average intelligence, though he goes out of his way to disguise the full extent. Milton, now he is just a tad smarter. But me?" He waggles his eyebrows. "My intelligence was deemed immeasurable *twice.* My sanity, equally confounding. Depending on who you ask, I am afflicted by a long list of ailments and disorders.

Asperger's. Dissociative identity disorder. Antisocial personality disorder. Generalized anxiety. Paranoia. Post-traumatic stress. Attachment disorder. It goes on and on…"

He gestures with a bored flick of his wrist, and I nearly contemplate surrender. My fingers grip the sides of my chair, rooting me in place. Fear of Maxim's potential reaction is the only reason why I don't lurch to my feet and head straight down the hall.

Yet.

"So yes, I am insane," Dima continues, oblivious to my discomfort. "Though I wouldn't take it as an insult. In fact, I'm grateful for my many quirks. They've kept me humble, you see. In touch with my feelings." He extends his slender arms and hugs himself. "But as I work through my many…hang-ups, I was forced to confront the reality that there are some things in my past I must address. Even if the other parties involved may not be inclined to revisit such memories. I need to bury them once and for all."

The violent phrasing draws my interest enough for me to question, "Like?"

"*Like,* did Maxim tell you about the day he tried to kill me?" He tugs at the collar of his sweatshirt, revealing his scar. For the shock value of it, I realize. He wants me to jump in disgust at the raised, ropey strip of flesh.

But I don't.

"Yes." Does that surprise him? I can't tell. His amused grin doesn't reveal an answer either way.

"Let me guess. He told you some sob story about how I ruined his perfect, innocent childhood via our father's ruthless need to assert his authority? He told you that I was a weak, worthless rodent always scurrying underfoot? And I'm sure he boasted about taking a knife to my throat as well. So typical."

I school my expression to match his—hopefully unreadable.

"He did." Unconvinced, Dima leans forward, his eyes sparkling. "Do you want to hear the truth? The *truth* is that, one day, a stranger barged into the bordello where my mother worked and lived—she was a prostitute, you see—and he dragged me out by my hair. I'd never seen him before in my life, mind you. Still, he took me to a strange house, full of strangers who looked at me like I was nothing. Then he said I was his son." He wiggles his fingers, his eyes comically wide. "Quite the surprise, you see. But my newfound brother, didn't take the news too well. Not long after our meeting, he attacked me. Punched me in front of our father, who egged him on in approval. Always the showoff, he made a spectacle of it, dear Maxim. He knocked me down. Fractured my cheek —" he points to his left eye. "He spit on me. Told me I was a rat, unworthy of living. *Blah, blah, blah.* Given my previous life circumstances, those words were nothing new to me. But…"

He frowns, eyeing his hands, and a rare real emotion slips

through his façade. Confusion. His slim fingers grasp at the air as if trying to capture the memory and dissect it properly.

"You know what was new? Later that night, I realized that he had slipped something into my pockets without me realizing it. Do you want to know what I found? It was the oddest, strangest thing…"

My brain shies from the dare. What kind of object could make him look so conflicted? Nothing good, and I'm not afraid to admit it. "No—"

"Socks," he says simply before I can fully voice a refusal. "A single, scarlet pair. Hand-knitted by his mother, I suspect—she was the crafty sort. They were worn enough that I knew they had to be his. Possibly his favorites. He'd noticed that I had none of my own, you see—" He points to his ankles. "There was also a piece of candy hidden inside one—extravagant chocolate he must have stolen from our father's private collection. The bastard was quite the glutton…" He chuckles only to trail off, his lips pursed. "But do you want to know a secret? That was the first time anyone had ever given me anything. I couldn't wrap my mind around the concept. A present? Such a mythical thing! When I saw him again, Maxim, I looked for any hint of that kindness, but alas, I found nothing. He continued to beat me. Berate me. I thought, perhaps I'd imagined it? But no." He frowns more deeply, stroking his chin. "I continued to find small, tiny things shoved into my clothing. Combs. Toys. Food…"

His gaze turns distant, and for the first time, I see a hint of similarity between the two brothers. They both express confusion in the same terrifying way. Via anger at whatever dared challenge their understanding.

"It went on until we both were sent directly to Anatoli. I won't get into the details of that time." He waves a hand as if dismissing the horror away. "Eventually the day came when the old man demanded we fight to the death with the gusto of some ancient Roman emperor. Maxim agreed with no hesitation, of course. No fear. But I was bored of that life." He shrugs. "I was tired. I didn't care. That time was so…unstimulating. I was ready to die. I made it so easy for him—and death, you see, is one aspect of life the Koslovs fear more than anything. It's for the animals, in their view. Animals are slaughtered, not men. How to kill is one of the first things you learn in that fucking family. Maxim had already done it before, of course. It should have been nothing. But…" He frowns and picks up the bottle of wine. "More? Oh, you've not taken a sip." Laughing, he takes my glass in addition to his and alternates sipping from both. "Where was I? Oh yes. Killing me should have been nothing. If anything, it would have been too easy. Anatoli demanded it, and the first, most important rule of being a Koslov, is to never disobey. And Maxim, like a good boy, dug his knife into my throat. But…he failed to do it."

Failed. That's not the word I would use to describe the scar snaking down the column of his neck. "He still hurt you," I point out hoarsely.

Dima laughs. "Hurt me? Even a child knows which direction you cut a throat in." He drags his fingers across his own, perpendicular to his scar. "Maxim didn't spare my life by some fluke or pathetic mistake. He went *out of his way* to. I just want to know why. Is that so wrong?" With mock sadness, he bows his head and sighs. "I want to know why my brother spared me, and yet shuns me. Why he despises me enough to ignore my very existence for twenty years, and at the same time, never once, *ever*, attacks me directly. Even when I get bored enough to play with his little toys or disrupt his supply lines. He can use Milton as an excuse all he wants, but the man isn't stupid —" He extends his hand to me as if demanding the answer. "I want to know why he's decided to challenge his nature, especially now. Perhaps the first thing isn't all a mystery, though? To acknowledge me is to acknowledge that he was never really a Koslov. He failed the first test, after all. But I admit that lately, my curiosity has been piqued—because although he refuses to acknowledge any hint of kindness extended toward me, he seems more than eager to claim some young, average prostitute as his wife. No offense."

I stiffen. Am I even insulted? I don't know.

Laughing, Dima continues, "And I know one must be patient when it comes to these things. Milton—I mean, my therapist—" He winks. "He claims that '*you cannot rush him, Dima. He is not like you. You push him too far and...poof!*'" He mimes his head exploding with wiggling fingers. "'*Be patient. One day he will reach out to you. Give it time, time, time!*'" He rolls his eyes while mimicking

Milton's accent. "The man babies him to an extent. Though I suppose it can't be helped. He's kept the promise he made to me, at least. For twenty years, he's kept that promise…"

Rather than ask what he means, I take my time putting the pieces of his verbal puzzle together. Then, it comes to me. "You asked him to be Maxim's friend?"

It sounds so strange when said out loud. Grown men with a twisted web intertwining them, all of it cemented in friendship.

"Maxim is a delicate soul, pretty girl," Dima says with a tired sigh. "He would have been eaten alive without Milton's…let's call it independence. I had hoped the man would convince him to finally break from Anatoli. But it seems that nothing can cut that bond. Even you." He flicks his gaze in my direction just in time to catch my reaction.

Rather than take the bait, I sigh. "That doesn't hurt me."

"Perhaps. But that's why you're here, isn't it? You want me to help Maxi defeat the big bad wolf once and for all."

Is that why I'm here? My motives feel less relevant the longer this twisted conversation goes on. Despite all this time, I still don't know what *he* wants.

"How do I know you can even help him?"

"How?" Dima cackles, sloshing wine from his glass. He swipes at the drops with the sleeve of his sweatshirt, clearing them away. "You are very amusing! I'm beginning to see the appeal. Pretty girl, Anatoli will do anything to get his precious Maxi under his thumb once more. Why? He is his legacy. His good, loyal boy. Without Maxim, he has nothing but a loosely connected family tree of sycophants and grifters. Maxim is his crown. And the crown belongs to the king—no one else."

"But you can defeat him?"

He laughs again as if knowing some wonderful joke that I'll never even learn the punchline to. "Do you want to know the secret? Come close. Closer…" He beckons me with a wave of his hand. He waits until I finally sit forward before saying, "The only way for Maxim to ever defeat Anatoli is…to break the throne. Give up the name. Walk away. Anatoli will never touch him directly. In some ways, Maxim knows this. The old man certainly does."

"What do you mean?"

"Milton is a powerful man, pretty girl." He raises an eyebrow. "But the third member of his so-called club has even more influence. He is a *very* powerful, very rich man. The bastard has a lot of stock in pharmaceuticals, you see. He controls more money, property, and people than Anatoli can even dream of amassing. Maxim is his only firewall against total insignificance—and he needs his golden boy now more than ever. Even a Koslov can't live forever."

"How do you even know who the third member is if Maxim doesn't?"

He winks. "Let's say, I know a little about him. He's incredibly handsome. Highly intelligent. Very charming, though some might say…unassuming. And of the three, he has the most impeccable fashion sense—"

"You?" I blurt out.

"Little me?" Dima blinks innocently and places his hand over his heart. "As a child, I learned my place in this violent, dangerous game of money, and men. It's better not to play at all. That's the only way to win."

I exhale in frustration. Keeping up with him is damn near impossible, and I know now that it's futile to even try. "So all you want is Maxim to what? Accept you?"

"I *did*," he admits, his eyes downcast. "I wanted my tortured brother to take my hand and boldly step out into the light of freedom. Call it childish if you want. I call it progress—but I've changed my mind."

He props his hand beneath his chin and observes me more intently than ever. "I *like* you, Francesca. So now I want to help you. I want to help you learn the answer to the question you're too terrified to ask."

Alarm prickles through my nerves, warning me to back away. But I can't without conceding defeat—and his fucking grin proves that he knows it.

"And what is that?" I ask tiredly.

"Does he truly love you, Maxim? You love him, or will you deny it?" He smirks as if he'd like nothing more than for me to challenge him.

So I don't.

And the man practically bounces in his seat. "It's a good question, you agree? Not only that, but you want to know if he is even capable of love. If the day will ever come when he loses control again. When he kills you finally, or takes a knife to little Ainsley and hacks her to pieces on a sheet of plastic tarp—"

"S-Stop!" I brace my hands on the table, and it takes everything I have not to lurch to my feet. The memories of that night still haunt me, threatening to descend. Gritting my teeth and closing my eyes is the only way to keep them at bay. "How did you—"

"Milton doesn't spill Maxi's little secrets," Dima says. "But I have ways of learning what he knows. The messes he helps his friend clean up. The women he examines for him. The blood he has to wipe off his hands when Maxim makes yet another mistake…"

When I open my eyes again, he isn't smiling. "How can you even help me prove that?"

"Oh, I can. And I always pay my debts, pretty girl. But in this case, I will want something from you in exchange for such a favor."

"I don't want anything from you—"

"But you do," he insists. "You truly do. I know my brother far better than you. I have years of research to draw from, and I will tell you now that he is stubbornly resistant to change. Some might say incapable of it."

"Research," I echo, picking up on that particular word. "Like you were *researching* when you let Maxim's driver be killed in front of me?"

"Oh, Jacob?" He raises an eyebrow as if he'd completely forgotten about the incident already. "Jacob Marsten had a wife named Ilia, and a daughter named Mariah. And he had spent the better part of ten years, terrorizing the hell out of them. It was fun to him, you see. And with his skill set, he was incredibly good at finding their new home or apartment, no matter where they went. He liked to send Ilia love notes, detailing the many ways he would eventually reunite with her. Chilling stuff." He makes a show of shuddering. "So pardon me if I don't shed too many tears for the man."

I watch him warily. Is he telling the truth? I can't tell.

"Maxim didn't know any of this, of course," he adds, before the suspicion could even sneak into my thoughts. "He is very thorough in his hiring process, but my methods are a tad more unorthodox. So believe me when I say that I can get you the answer you want—and relatively soon. But as in Jacob's case, it may not lead to a pretty ending. Nonetheless, I will still insist upon my favor by the end, no matter the outcome."

"What favor?"

He stands abruptly and bows at his waist. "This was a marvelous, *marvelous* conversation. Better than I could have ever hoped. So much, so much better!" He claps gleefully. "But I must bid you *adieu*. Oh, and before I go, remember! You cannot repeat a word of what we discussed to dear Maxim, remember? That's the rule."

He scampers away, passing Tomas and another guard on his way out.

"Goodbye, Francesca!" he calls back from the end of the hall. "For now…"

CHAPTER NINETEEN

The second Dima leaves, Maxim appears by my side. "Come," he demands from behind me. By the time I stand and face his direction, he's already lumbering toward his private room, his steps slow and deliberate. As I cross the threshold in his wake, he keeps going until he's forced to brace his hands against the far wall, his back still to me.

"I know he told you lies," he hisses before I can say anything. "I know he fed you twisted ideas. But if I let his claims go unchallenged, I only have myself to blame. So here—" He points to the bed. On it is a silver folder, and the sight of it unnerves me almost as much as his rasping tone does. "Open it."

I approach the bed cautiously and stoop for the file. It's surprisingly heavy, and my heart skips as I peruse the documents within. I have no fucking clue what it might contain. Another contract? The deed to the house? Or something far more puzzling…

A frown tugs on my mouth as I scan the printed documents. They're phrased in legal terms, and considering I have yet to finish one semester of college, I can barely make sense of them. Some kind of declaration? It isn't until I read the last few lines that I finally register one crucial detail that makes my knees buckle in alarm.

His name.

It's printed wrong. A single X denotes his last name on every single page instead of Koslov, and I rub at my eyes, refusing to believe it.

Maxim X.

"I don't understand," I start to say. But then it clicks, and a wave of shock knocks me off balance. I sway, grasping at the mattress, my throat unbearably tight. My head swivels toward him so quickly my neck throbs in response. "You... You changed your name."

I struggle to say it. Given his feelings on being a Koslov, I can't believe it, either. Not until I see him. Still hunched against the wall, he stands with his spine bowed, exposed to any reaction I might have.

"You gave up your name for me?" I whisper.

"You were right." His accent sounds so heavy, as if each word is being ripped from the pit of his chest. "That name isn't fitting for a family. Admittedly, this one is just temporary. But I am willing to take on any one you want to claim what I am owed."

Me.

"W-Why?" I ask hoarsely. "I thought—"

"Do you refuse it?"

"No!" I lurch to my feet and stagger toward him. My fingers claw at his forearm until he pivots. Our eyes meet, and the emotion in his takes my breath away. They're wide, so dark they're fucking fathomless. I greedily hunt down whatever emotions they might reveal, but he turns away, averting his gaze.

"Don't..." I'm begging. I'm too desperate to care. "Look at me. Please."

Sighing, he stiffens, and I take his jaw between my fingers, making him face me.

"Dima said the name Koslov was a creed," he admits, fisting his fingers through my hair, holding me captive in return. "And he was right. If I gave you that name, you would never be safe—and not from Anatoli or his fucking bastard pawns. But from me. You would never be safe from *me*. If I lost control, I could always blame it on that fucking creed. I have already, haven't I?"

He stares down at his hands in remembrance of the damage they can inflict on a whim.

"By hiding behind that name, I could lie to you and claim that it was all I knew." The line of his jaw tightens as he captures my waist, dragging me against him. Near my ear, he confesses, "Even before I saw you in that dress... I knew what needed to be done. What I needed to sacrifice to keep you. I've done it."

"But what about your grandfather?" I ask as my brain restarts, running through every potential danger his name change might enhance. *Anatoli. Dima. The future.* There are so fucking many. "What about—"

"I can't think about him." He grips my chin, guiding me to look up at him. Dark and hollow, his eyes bore into mine, going deeper than ever before. In some ways, it feels like he's ripping me open more intimately than he could with a whip or during sex.

"And I don't need Dima to come to my rescue either," he snaps. "Whatever happens, I will face it... But I will need you to do one last thing for me."

"Anything." My brain is still struggling to process the gravity of what he's done. I'm numb with shock, barely aware of what I'm saying. "I'll do anything."

His nostrils flare at the intensity of the promise. I've never seen him so fucking charged. Raw power emanates from him, putting any previous authority he commanded to shame.

"Anything?" I tremble in anticipation at the hunger thickening his tone. He'll put that word to the test later, I'm sure. But now? He smooths his fingers along my jaw, tracing every divot and curve in my skin. "I need you to play in one last game for me."

"What?"

"I want you to pick another dress." He runs his fingers along my spine, and cups my lower back, snatching me to his chest. I grasp his shoulders, forced to stand on tiptoe. The added height brings my forehead near his mouth, and his lips find my temple. "Not as yourself, or even for me —but as the kitten who dug her claws into me. Wearing it, I want you to stand by my side, no matter the outcome. Can you do that?"

I don't have to ask him for clarification this time. An ominous thrill shoots through my entire body as I grip him tighter in agreement.

We both know the final round that awaits at the end of this game.

The one in which he'll finally declare checkmate.

Or submit to utter defeat.

WE SPEND the night in the club, sharing the bed that feels more broken-in than those in any of his other dwellings. In some moments, a sliver of space separates us. Other times, I regain consciousness in his arms, cocooned by his scent. By the time morning comes, I stir to find Maxim already dressed, pacing at the foot of the bed, a cell phone held to his ear.

"I'm ready," he murmurs into the receiver. "With or without him… Only way. Be ready when I call."

He hangs up and spots me from over his shoulder, his expression obscured by shadow. "Tomas will take you to the suite," he tells me. "I'll meet you there. There is one thing I have to do first."

He doesn't say what. In silence, he picks up my discarded dress instead and helps me into it. When he leads me through the club, it's empty, bathed in darkness. Tomas is already waiting at the entrance, a car parked in the driveway behind him.

Before I leave, Maxim takes my hand, drawing me close. His lips find my temple, lingering for a second before he pulls away.

I watch him reenter the club alone, curious as to what task might be on his mind now.

A part of me warns that I'll soon find out.

For better or for worse.

CHAPTER TWENTY

The first time I came to this place in Maxim's shadow, I wore the clothing of a doll—the twin to the black velvet ensemble he originally intended for me to wear to this meeting. The simple dress had obscured my shape, its primary purpose being to convey the ownership of the man beside me.

Nothing less, nothing more.

Now, a swath of red silk boldly displays the shape of my body while leaving little to the imagination. Cut dangerously short, it's something the old Francesca might have pined over from the window of a boutique she could only dream of shopping in. The kind of outfit I would have assumed was far too good for me back then. Too classy. Too bold.

Maxim wanted me to choose a dress fit for his kitten. For whatever reason, *this* ensemble fits that bill.

In approval, Maxim's fingers trace my lower back,

exploring every contour exposed by the tight fabric. Even he looks different as we exit the car, flanked by his security. Instead of a suit, he wears a loose-fitting white shirt and black slacks that enhance his bulk more than a jacket and tie ever could. It's a stark contrast to the professional attire of his guards as they draw up behind him.

To my surprise, he waves them off. "Stay here."

Tomas and his partner share a questioning look but remain near the car rather than follow. "As you wish, sir. His guards weren't expecting us," Tomas adds, glancing at a security booth guarding the entrance to the property. "If you wanted to come unannounced, I would assume you have a minute or two before they alert him. They knew better than to deny you entrance outright, at least."

"Be ready," Maxim warns as he cranes his neck, observing our destination. Before us looms a sprawling mansion in Black Briar Hills—a part of the city reserved for politicians, or those with enough money to buy them. It towers above, casting a shadow that diminishes even the sun fighting through a layer of morning cloud cover.

And I can't lie and pretend that I'm not fucking trembling inside, fighting back the memories of my first visit. This is the place where I experienced the cruelty of Maxim's family firsthand—and my first introduction to his uncle Sevastyn.

"Are *you* ready?" Maxim wonders as if reading my mind. He captures my hand, lacing our fingers together.

Am I? Something won't let me answer. Instead, I feed off the strength in his touch and shift my focus to him. The more I take in the rigid set of his jaw, the more I suspect the question wasn't directed at me. Is *he* ready?

The determined tilt of his head gives me a clue. So does the cold, hard intensity of his gaze. Gone is that unnerving distance.

He's more than ready.

"Come." He pulls me forward, and this time, we don't wait for a timid maid to open the door. He barges inside and heads to the heart of the house, every step bold and assured. It's as dark within as I remember, adorned with a chilling décor devoid of any warmth.

But Anatoli isn't in his study today.

Instead—as if smelling him out like a predator—Maxim drags me past that room and into another, wider space. A long dining table dominates the center of it. At its head sits an older man with white-blond hair. In one hand, he brandishes a knife while a maid sets a plate of steaming food before him.

Spotting Maxim, the woman jumps spilling food onto the table's polished surface. "M-Mr. Koslov—"

"Leave," Maxim tells her as he advances. To his grandfather, he inclines his head. "You've summoned me, so here I am."

"Maximov?" Red spots appear over Anatoli's cheeks as he snaps his fingers. At the silent command, his maid struggles to scrape up the fallen bits of egg and bacon with her bare hands. She fails, and after another pointed look from Maxim, she scurries from the room, leaving the mess behind.

Anatoli scowls, barely noticing her absence. "You dare come here unannounced—"

"I'm not here on your behalf," Maxim says over him. To my shock, he bows his head in reverence, and the air sticks in my lungs. I back up instinctively, ripping my hand from his. *It was a trap all along,* Dima's disembodied voice taunts me. *Did you really believe he would choose you?*

But as Maxim draws himself back to his full height, his gaze is honed, radiating the intensity of a creature who is anything but a pawn. Snippets of his past still strangle his expression like shackles, but I can sense the effort it takes for him to resist their pull.

And he does.

"I am here for your blessing," he says. "As well as to offer my condolences on the loss of Sevastyn."

"Loss?" His grandfather echoes, his black eyes emotionless. Watching him, I realize that he has no clue as to the fate of his son. "Explain."

"I apologize for not making myself clearer to you before," Maxim adds. "But now, there can be no mistake..." He reaches into his pocket and tosses a small, metal object onto the table. It bounces over the polished wood, nearly landing onto Anatoli's plate.

Frowning, the older man snatches it in his fist, holding it to the light. Slowly, recognition dawns over his features, and shock rapidly displaces the disgust.

"It is Sevastyn's, yes," Maxim confirms, and I finally recognize the object for what it is. A ring. Silver and ornate, he must have taken it from his uncle's body. If I squint, I swear I can see remnants of scarlet dried over the gleaming surface. "I return it to you, along with a warning. I am no longer yours to command."

"And if I don't grant you such a foolish request?" Anatoli counters.

Something cold and cruel slips into Maxim's gaze. My breathing stalls. Thoughts sputter into incoherence. There is nothing more beautiful than anger on him. And nothing more fucking terrifying.

"I do not think you want a war, Grandfather," he warns.

"War?" Anatoli scoffs and leans back into his chair. "You sound like *him*. The failed mutt. Is he the one who put this idea in your head?" He bares his teeth, but a muscle in his jaw trembles. He sputters, and a series of heaving coughs render him gasping, gripping the arms of his seat for balance. "Did you come to mock me too?" he wonders breathlessly. "I'm sure he's told you already. I don't know how the little bastard learned of it—" Another cough rips from his chest that he struggles to smother into the sleeve of his tailored jacket. "He made sure to send his condolences. But Maximov, I never took you as one to gloat."

Eyes narrowed, Maxim examines his grandfather, from the worn lines around his mouth, to his pale, papery skin, and the ragged sound of his breathing, audible from here. His upper lip quirks the more he assesses the man who tormented him for years, now barely able to sit upright unassisted.

"You're dying," he says finally. Awe colors his tone, mingled with disbelief. "Is that why you've been so desperate to bring me to heel? You truly have no one else—"

"And you would walk away?" Anatoli spits back. "No. I know you, *boy*. I saw it from the first fucking day you came to me, sniveling and weak. You crave the safety of power. You were always desperate for it. That is what set you apart from the rotten chaff. Am I to believe you'll just walk away?" He chuckles, eyeing Maxim from head to toe with raw, open malice. "No. You were never that foolish. And if you did forsake your name, it would never be for the sake of some whore. The fact that you brought her proves my point." He scoffs and waves his hand dismissively. "Leave. When I send for you, you come. Alone—"

"Did you not hear me?" Maxim interjects, but his tone is softer. Something in his expression changes the longer he eyes the man across from him. The anger fades, and resignation sets in, hardening the set of his jaw. "I'm no longer yours to command. Keep your bounty if you want. None of your pawns have been able to claim it anyway—"

"And yet you bring her here," Anatoli points out, his grin smug, his accent thick. "Why else if not to prove where your real loyalties lie? I could always call in another one of my men to deal with her, as Sevastyn did—"

"Why is she here?" Maxim echoes. He extends his hand toward me. I don't hesitate to take it, moving to stand by his side. "Because I don't fear you. Dima was right. You've lost your power. You're merely afraid of losing more. The Koslov name was only ever a leash to you—and you no longer have a grip on it."

His words eerily echo what Dima let slip during our supposedly private conversation. Had Maxim been listening in? Standing here now, I have no trouble deciding on an answer. Of course, he did—though I doubt he heard everything, or he'd be raising hell about Dima's revelation as the third X. No, like a true predator, he'd eavesdropped only long enough to glean what he felt like he needed to win.

Leverage.

"Is it money you want?" Anatoli chuckles. "You want to broaden your holdings? Fine. End this game, and you can have it."

"No." Maxim turns for the door, pulling me with him. "Send your peons after me again, and Dima's little games will be nothing in comparison to the hell I will bring down on you. Oh, and I'll ensure you receive your invitation to my wedding."

He barrels into the hall, tightening his grip on me. As I cross the threshold, I look back to find Anatoli still watching him, his expression unreadable.

"You will come back," he says. "A dog like you can't survive off of his leash for very long…"

Maxim stiffens, his steps faltering. His fingers clamp down over mine, nearly crushing them. Right as the pain builds, he relaxes his grip. More than that—it's like something drains from him all at once. Something dark and twisted that festered within him for so long. He sways, registering the loss of it, only to right his balance within the space of a heartbeat.

Slowly, his chin juts into the air as his posture straightens, stronger than ever. "Goodbye, Anatoli." He strolls down the hall without looking back.

"You'll come back," Anatoli insists. "You will…"

As we exit the house, his laughter chases us, interspersed with hacking coughs.

I watch Maxim as he hustles me into the car, scanning his features for any reaction. Surprisingly he looks…calm. Too calm.

"Is it done?" he asks Tomas, closing the door behind us.

The other man nods. "Mr. Hood is already on the line. He's managed to track down Danil's associates, as well as the bank containing Anatoli's American assets. All that's left is for you to say the word."

Maxim's lip quirks in a lethal smile. "Do it."

The car takes off down the driveway as Tomas speaks into the receiver of a cell phone withdrawn from his pocket.

"What's going on?" I ask, glancing between the two men. "What are you doing?"

"I'm breaking Anatoli's leash for good." Maxim takes my hand, tightening his grip so that I couldn't pull away even if I wanted to. "This visit was merely a formality," he explains, bringing my knuckles to his mouth. He swipes his lips reverently across them, raising goosebumps over the flesh. "I could declare open war, but with this method, I can diminish his influence with little bloodshed. He won't have the strength to attack me directly. Not now."

"How?" I ask.

"As we speak, Anatoli's remaining pawns are being dealt with, piece by piece. He'll have no choice but to leave the States. And in the process, he'll be leaving the city to *me*."

"It's done, sir," Tomas pitches in from the front seat. "Mr. Hood claims that everything is in place. It's only a matter of time."

"Good," Maxim says, inclining his head. "Now, we wait."

But it's not that simple. After being around him for this long, I'm able to suspect the truth in what he doesn't say.

He may succeed in driving his grandfather from the country now, but in the process, he completely forsakes any ties to his family.

Does he regret that?

No, his expression warns. Not one fucking bit.

CHAPTER TWENTY-ONE

"They're on their way," Maxim murmurs against my forehead. Sunshine spills in through the wide bay windows beside us, enhancing every nuance of his face. Two days after his meeting with his grandfather, and I can't tell if he's bothered by what happened. Or if he's finally at peace with the possibility that Anatoli might be gone from his empire—for now. I want to assume it's the latter. The gleam lurking in his gaze reinforces that hope, anyway.

"Lucius called and estimated they'll arrive within ten minutes," he adds. "Though, I believe everything is already sufficient."

I frown, skeptical of that. Within a little under a week, I've realized the power that money can buy. In some ways, it's like magic. Back in my old house, buying something like a new couch or mattress was an ordeal that required scouring the stores for a cheap deal, finding nothing, and eventually having to fish out whatever we needed from the dump.

In Maxim's world, a house can be fully furnished in a matter of hours, complete with a fresh coat of paint. Jonathan's recommended designer certainly knew her shit. A few minor touches and modest furniture work to transform the "rustic" waterfront home into a world befitting the aloof style of Maxim—combined with enough nuances to make six kids feel comfortable dwelling in the same space.

Muted, soft grays and pops of navy create a cozy interior. The kids' rooms each contain their various preferences—though Ainsley's pony will have to wait, according to Maxim. A stable was one thing that he couldn't guarantee within a week.

I hadn't had the sense of mind to decide if he was serious or not. Getting every detail perfected consumed my focus. Why?

I have no fucking clue. Nothing in our old house inspired the same obsessive need in me before. I never went from room to room, hunting for a single piece of dust that might be out of place.

I never felt invested.

"They will love it," Maxim insists for the umpteenth time. His hands snake around my waist, drawing me against him. "I will still maintain a property in the city for business reasons, but this..." He exhales raggedly, and I think I sense a hint of something that could be... contentment? "I am impressed with this."

My heart swells up as I scan our surroundings, attempting to see whatever he is. A house untainted by blood or death. A view of the water with the city in the distance. A home, untouched by the Koslov name.

"Thank you," I whisper, finding his hands with my own. "Thank you—"

"You thank me for a house?" he wonders incredulously. "I will thank *you* for this."

He tugs aside the collar of his shirt, revealing his chest. It takes me a second to understand what he wants me to see —but when I do, I gasp. There, scrawled amid the scarred flesh is a series of inked lines spelling out a single name —*kotyonok*. Inflamed skin around the edges of the tattoo betray just how fresh it is. A day? Hours?

As I gape, he takes my hand and slips something cool and round onto my finger. I look down, unsurprised by the sight of his ring.

His lips brush my shoulder, imparting more than words could ever say. Slowly, his fingers creep along my collar, slipping beneath the thin fabric of my dress.

"Sir?"

We break apart and turn to find Tomas in the doorway. "They are arriving now, sir."

Nerves flutter to life in my stomach as I follow Maxim to the front door. Two black cars advance toward us slowly, and the second they come to a stop, the kids stream out, craning their necks to take in the house.

"Holy shit," Mikie exclaims, using his hand as a visor. "We could actually have a fucking boat!"

"Watch your mouth," I scold, though my voice must lack the authority it used to.

"Holy shit!" The twins share manic grins and then take off, tearing into the house.

"Wait for me!" Eric calls, racing to keep up.

A hand tugs on my skirt, and I look down to find Ainsley staring up at me, wide-eyed.

"There is no pony," Maxim says coldly.

She blinks in shock, her bottom lip trembling. Before a single tear can fall, he extends his hand.

"But would you like to see where he will live when it's completed? Come with me."

"Really?" She practically squeals as he leads her on a path across the expansive acreage surrounding the house itself. There, near the back with a view of the water, a team of builders have already erected the base of a stable and cordoned off the footprint with caution tape.

Ainsley peers over every inch with Maxim in tow, her eyes bug-wide. "Is my pony really going to live here?" she asks him repeatedly.

"Yes. One pony, or two. Perhaps more…" He meets my gaze from across the structure. "Whatever your sister allows, of course. Do you want to see where you'll be able to ride him?" He points to a section of land a few yards away.

"Okay!" Ainsley merrily skips off while Maxim returns to my side.

"This is one small feature I attended to," he says while tucking a loose curl behind my ear, "I hope you aren't too offended."

Am I? I can't tell. The sun is shining, painting the property in shades of emerald with a pop of silvery blue marked by the water. It truly is a beautiful place. A private stable may not have been in my original list of requirements, but I can't muster the energy to truly care.

"She doesn't even know how to ride, though," I admit. "She just wants a pony because every girl her age is genetically programmed to want one."

"Even you?" he wonders, his voice uncharacteristically soft. When I nod, a rare smile creeps into the corner of his mouth. "Then I will have to ensure the stable is big enough for more than one pony. As for the riding, I can teach her. I would like to teach her." He frowns as if that simple phrasing surprises him—namely the intensity with which he says it. The man with a tortured past, forced to ignore his humanity, wants to teach a little girl how to ride a horse. He wants to live in a house overlooking the water. More importantly, he wants to shed his name and finally become someone different.

Himself.

"It's getting late," Maxim murmurs. As he speaks, he entwines our fingers. "I'm eager to see what surprises *my* room might contain."

I shiver at the innuendo. It's the one room in the entire house that we've yet to tour. My cheeks burn as I look back at the field. "Ainsley?"

"She probably already ran to tell the others news of her impending pony," Maxim says. "You go. I'll look around just in case she went further up the path."

When I reenter the house, I find the others on the deck in the back, observing the view of the water.

"This place is perfect," Daisy murmurs as I draw up beside her. "As perfect as you can get outside of a private island, but…perfect."

"You always gotta quantify shit," Mikie taunts. "It's amazing, Frankie."

"Yeah, amazing," the twins chirp in unison before scurrying off.

I can't ignore my smile anymore. It strains the corners of my mouth, making them ache. I'm not used to the expression—painful happiness.

"Maybe this Maxim guy isn't all that bad," Mikie adds. "Eh, Daisy?"

She stiffens, her eyes darting to me and away again. "Yeah," she says softly. "Maybe. Frankie…" She faces me, her eyes downcast, her bottom lip skewered between her teeth. "I'm sorry for what I said. I didn't mean—"

"It's okay." In some ways, can I even blame her for being suspicious? After everything we've been through, I can't.

She smiles, her posture relaxing. It's only when I register the lack of a distinctive, girlish bit of laughter that I remember my task. "Where's Ainsley?"

Daisy frowns. "I don't know. Last I saw her, she was with you."

"She's probably upstairs screaming inside her new room," Mikie suggests.

But when I enter the house, I don't find her in any room. Not near the waterfront either. Or outside. When I head back out by the stable, Maxim is walking to meet me, but Ainsley isn't with him either. Something in my expression makes him stop short.

"She wasn't at the house?"

"No!" My throat thickens as I race past him. "Ainsley? Ainsley?"

"I'm sure she hasn't gotten far," Maxim insists. "She's probably just playing—" He breaks off, frowning. His hand dips into his pocket, withdrawing his cell phone. Whatever number he finds on the screen makes his eyes narrow.

"I'm going to look for her near the shore," I say, starting for the dock. "God, I just hope she didn't go near the—"

"Francesca…"

I look back to find Maxim watching me with the cell phone pressed against his ear. Slowly, he offers it to me, his expression stone.

"What's wrong? Is it Lucius?" I take the phone warily. "Does he know where—"

"Did you give her the phone?" a man wonders, his accent distinct. "Ah, you did! I can tell from her breathing. Hello, Francesca!"

"D-Dima?"

"Yes, yes!" He chuckles playfully. "I'm afraid little Ainsley won't be coming home anytime soon. Though do not fear, Maxim alone knows what must be done to ensure her return—if he cares to, that is. In the meantime…I will show her every courtesy my brother ever showed me. Every last one. And just to give you a taste—" He breaks off just as a loud, high-pitched scream resonates through the receiver. "*Adieu!*"

I don't even know what I do next. What I say. My only coherent recollection is just…screaming. And someone holding me so tightly it hurts, his voice a persistent, echoing bellow.

"We'll find her."

Somehow Maxim gets me inside without the other kids noticing me. I'm vaguely aware of Lucius ushering them to another part of the house as Maxim calls in his guards, questioning them one by one.

Though he shouts, his voice eventually fades to an unintelligible murmur that serves as background noise to my own panicked psyche.

How could I be so stupid, stupid, stupid?

So reckless?

Of all the coherent thoughts to cross my mind again, the first is that I was right—this house was designed to amplify Maxim's voice until the rafters shake with it.

"How the hell did he get past the security?" he bellows at Lucius. He stands in the center of the living room now, bathed in the glow of a hanging lamp. It's already dark out, revealing the passage of hours. Hours while Ainsley suffers God only knows what…

"How?" Maxim snarls. "I demand answers—"

"As do I, sir," Lucius insists. "Heads will roll, I can assure you. As for his current location, we are tracking a vehicle most likely to be—"

"What if he hurts her?" I barely recognize the sound of my own voice. I can't stop rocking back and forth as a million twisted images run through my brain, each new one more horrible than the last.

I will show her every courtesy my brother ever showed me.

I should be out there, hunting for her. Kicking down whatever door I can to find her. But the fact that Maxim *isn't* betrays a truth even he has enough tact not to say out loud—*we would never find her.*

"God, what if he hurts her?"

"I've never known Dima to act this way," someone says from the back of the room. I look up, finding Milton standing apart from the other two. I didn't even notice him come in. He isn't wearing a suit, but a black shirt and a pair of slacks, his gaze distant. He stands near the window overlooking the bay, blending into the darkness of the sky behind him. "But I do know he would *never* be capable of harming a child."

"Then you don't know him as well as you thought," Maxim growls. He crosses to me, brushing my cheek with the flat of his palm. I'm too numb to react to the touch. I can barely look at him at all. "Leave. I should have never asked you to come—"

"Possibly," Milton says, fingering his collar. For the first time, doubt clouds his features. Then they harden with resolve. "I'm here. Whatever you need, I'll get it done."

"Start with where he might be," Maxim demands. "You know his haunts. His hiding places."

"I have my men on it already," Milton admits. "But Dima isn't stupid. He knows that you'd come to me, and he knows where I'd look for him."

"So your insight is worthless, then," Maxim snaps, starting to pace. "You can't think of *anything*—"

"It's my fault," I croak. "I talked to him. I fell into his trap."

And he was right. I put an innocent girl in danger. For what?

A sick game, a part of me wails. *One you knew you could never win.*

"Enough," Maxim commands, cutting through the hopeless thoughts. "You pitied him, but that does not make you weak. Whatever he's done…we can face it. Don't give him what he wants by doubting yourself now."

"He's been…different, lately," Milton admits, frowning. "You don't speak to him regularly, Maxim, so you wouldn't have noticed, but he's been gone for a while.

Over a year, I believe. It's not unusual for him to go off on his own for long periods, as I do, but..." His brows furrow. "It isn't like him to stay away that long. He kept his usual accounts though, always supplying regular contributions to the club. He only resurfaced in person a month ago, but we haven't discussed where he was."

"Contributions?" Maxim inquires. His eyes widen and narrow in quick succession as if a sudden realization came to him. "No. You don't mean—"

"That's something we can discuss another time," Milton says gently. Dima's secret as the third member of their partnership is apparently out in the open now. "When he returned, he seemed more interested than usual in your relationships. Mainly with Francesca."

Even in my daze, I marvel at the fact that he says my name for the first time. Not *woman*. Or *her*.

"And my relationship with Heidi—" the name of the "blond woman," Maxim mentioned, I assume. "Although my personal life has no relevance to this situation, Dima seemed more disturbed than I'm used to. He's not erratic. But, whatever is behind this, I suspect it's to prove an elaborate point."

"So, you still defend him?" Maxim demands. "Even now?"

"Defend him?" Milton says softly. "I *know* him. Just as I know you, and who did I come to first when I learned of this? I'm not in my office waiting for a call from Dima, I can tell you that."

"You're right." Something dampens Maxim's expression, and he sighs, raking his fingers through his hair. "We won't find him," he confesses, even as Lucius continues to make phone calls rapidly in the corner.

"You are sure that he gave no clue as to his motives?" Milton wonders. "None at all?"

"He said Maxim would know what to do," I whisper. I still hear him taunting me. I still hear Ainsley screaming…

"Is that true?" Milton turns to Maxim, an eyebrow raised. "Do you know what he could want?"

"No!" Maxim curls his hands into fists, and his gaze is so hopeless, that I know he's not lying. "I don't know what he could fucking want. I would give it to him if—" Suddenly he breaks off and sways. "That son of a bitch…"

I scan his face, desperate to follow his train of thought. Our gazes meet, and something in the set of his jaw has me lurching to my feet. He meets me halfway, clasping my wrist, dragging me against him.

My throat aches as I rush to speak, "He wants you to—"

"I know." He nods, his eyes glinting with fury. "Lucius!"

"Yes, sir?" Lucius appears by his side in an instant.

Still holding my gaze, Maxim says, "Empty all of my accounts into the club accounts. All of them. Every last one. I don't care what favors you have to call in. Get it done now."

"Right away, sir." Lucius races off while Milton advances from his corner, an eyebrow raised.

"You think that is what he wants?"

"What else?" Maxim snarls. "He wants everything I have. But as for the money…" He flicks his gaze to mine, his voice resonating with authority. "He can fucking take it."

It's past midnight when Tomas enters the room, his expression tense. With an apologetic nod in my direction, he crosses to Maxim and murmurs something near his ear.

Suddenly, Maxim lurches to his feet and races for the front door. I catch up to him, just in time to witness a ruby red car appearing in the driveway. Flashy and bold, it's something Maxim or his men wouldn't usually drive.

Frowning, I place my hand on his shoulder, straining my eyes to see through the tinted windshield. "Who…"

I barely finish forming the thought before the driver's side door opens, and a lanky figure climbs out, his hands raised.

"I wouldn't do anything rash," he warns with a smile as Maxim tenses, poised to lunge for him. "I may not be armed, but I am not alone—"

"Where's Ainsley?" I croak. "Where is she?"

"Ah, yes…" Dima flicks his gaze toward Maxim again, lingering over his face. "That would depend on a few small variables…"

"What?" Maxim demands. "Just name your fucking price."

"Fine." Dima sighs and inspects his spindly fingers. He almost looks bored, irritated to have his fun cut short. "I want you to beg. On your knees, of course. Beg for this child's life. Though, I will warn you that what has already been done to her has alas…already been done."

My heart sinks. Tears sting at my eyes, but I blink them back, swallowing down any cries. A resolve unlike anything I've ever felt strengthens my limbs, keeping me standing. No matter what happens, I refuse to give him the satisfaction of watching me suffer.

"Dima," Milton says, appearing at Maxim's shoulder. "What the hell are you doing—"

"Enough." Maxim lurches forward, his fists clenched. Then he sinks down to his knees, his hands at his sides, his body rippling with tension. "Is this what you want?" he demands. "Well, you have it. Give her back."

"Hmm." Dima frowns, and for the first time, a hint of alarm crosses his smug expression. Confusion. He eyes Maxim in utter silence, tapping his chin with the tip of his finger. Then he reaches into the pocket of his black sweatshirt and withdraws a knife.

A gasp rips from me as I step forward, but Maxim raises his hand, still crouched. "Don't."

Dima intently eyes the edge of his blade. He takes his time, inspecting every inch of its gleaming surface. "I said beg," he remarks coldly. "Not pretend as though you're ordering dinner. *Beg* for her life—"

"I'm begging." Maxim's voice resonates like thunder, guttural, and deep. "Give her back."

"Are you *really*, though?" Dima throws his knife into the air and catches it deftly by the handle. "I don't know if I believe you—"

"You want to kill me, is that it?" Maxim demands with a harsh, callous laugh. "Do it. If tormenting a child is how you bring me to my knees. So be it. But don't beat around the fucking bush. Do it!"

"Fine." Dima shifts in a graceful movement of muscle and slashes at Maxim's throat with the tip of his blade.

"No!" I tear down the path, uncaring. All I see is Maxim, his body still upright. It isn't until I'm nearly even with him that I realize the amount of blood trickling down his collar doesn't match what would stream from a lethal wound. My eyes trace the base of his throat, noting only a small, delicate scratch.

Dima eyes the streak of scarlet painting his blade. Then he sighs and pivots on his heel to open the back door of the car.

A small figure bounds out, her light hair flying out behind her. "Frankie!"

The sight of her distracts me even from Maxim's injury. "Ainsley!"

I run forward and grab her mid-step, wrenching her into my arms. I bury my face into her hair, holding her so tight she squirms in discomfort.

"What's wrong? Why are you crying? I had so much fun!" she exclaims, her voice high-pitched with excitement. "I love Uncle Dima! We saw real ponies, and then we ate candy, and we played screaming games, and—"

"Hush, baby." I tug at her arms, scanning her tiny limbs for any injuries. Any hint of blood. Her clothes are intact, devoid of so much as a fucking stain. The only change I notice makes me grit my teeth—her usual pink socks have been replaced by a scarlet, woolen pair.

Apart from them, I can't escape one glaring fact.

"You didn't hurt her." Confusion thickens my voice as I meet Dima's gaze.

"Her teeth, perhaps," he admits, with a wink. "I did not regulate her sugar intake—"

"You son of a bitch." Maxim is still laughing, his head turned skyward. A smile shapes his mouth, but there's nothing joyful about it. "You son of a fucking bitch..."

"Hurt me?" Ainsley questions, frowning. "I want to hang out with him again! Can I? Next time, can Eric come so we can—"

"Get her inside," Maxim warns, rising to his feet, his fingers balling into fists.

"Come with me, Ms. Ainsley." Lucius steps forward to ease her from my arms. "I believe it's time for bed."

"Ah," she whines, her voice fading as Lucius carries her inside. "I wanted to say goodbye to Uncle Dima—"

The moment she's gone, Maxim barrels down the front path, and there's no stopping him. He's toe to toe with Dima within a heartbeat. His fist slams into the other man's cheek, sending him sprawling against the hood of the car.

"Enough," Milton warns, stepping forward. "You've made your point. *Both* of you."

Laughing, Dima cradles his jaw and staggers to find his balance. Blood adds a ghoulish flourish to his haggard appearance. In tiny rivulets, it dribbles down his chin unchecked. "You can have your money back, little Maxi. Every dime. All of it, I promise..."

"Why?" I demand. "Why did you do this?"

He frowns. "Perhaps old Dima grew bored of waiting for Maxi to be receptive? If I wanted answers from him, I would have to take them. And I did." He meets my gaze, and whether intentionally or not, he doesn't try to disguise the raw confusion contrasting with his gleeful mask. Beneath the façade, turmoil rages underneath, making me recoil. Maxim has his demons, but nothing like this...

"If he and Milton can form their little families and play their little games... If they believe they can change, then why can't I? Perhaps it's time I take my own family. Play my own game?" He eyes his trembling fingers and forms a fist as if capturing something within it. "I believe it is what I am owed... And in all honesty, if Maxim can attract a woman and children to him, any man can."

"That's it?"

"Francesca!" Maxim's hand swipes at my shoulder, but even he can't stop me from pushing past him, approaching Dima head-on.

Towering over me, the man meets my gaze, unfazed— even when I raise my arm. I lash out, tracking the amusement flickering through his dark eyes as my palm lands across his cheek.

"I deserved that, I suppose," he murmurs, brushing his fingers along his reddening flesh—but his smile is too feral to be contrite. I doubt he even feels the pain at all. *You got what you wanted, didn't you?* His smug grin tells me. *You got your answer.*

And I got mine.

"Anyway, this was fun! I agree with dear Ainsley, we must do this again." Beaming, he turns on his heel and enters his car. As Maxim glowers, he issues a lazy wave and kisses the tips of his fingers.

"*Adieu!* And no hard feelings, Maxi? I hear from a little birdie that you've sent Anatoli running back to Russia—" He laughs, the sound booming. "He won't stay there for long… But for now, all is well, yes? You and Milton are the best of friends again, and poor Dima will take his leave. Though…" He chuckles before closing the door after him. As the window lowers, he adds. "I will be expecting my invitation to the weddings."

He drives off as Maxim glowers, his body rigid. A ferocity radiates from him like fire—fiercer than any rage I've ever sensed in him before. But I've come to know him enough to suspect that it doesn't stem from hurt pride or shame. No, this fury extends deeper than that. Into his core.

And it's expressed solely in the way he reaches back for me, yanking me against him. His touch conveys possession as he finds my hip, cupping it with his palm. Whatever he did just now—his capitulation to Vadim— was worth more than a thousand rings.

More than if he had slayed a million Anatolis.

More than any promise he could ever make through words alone.

CHAPTER TWENTY-THREE

The bedroom is the one space in the house that didn't get as much attention as the rest. Maybe because I subconsciously knew that he deserved to have say in it. That he would insist upon it.

Dark and unreadable, his eyes take in the plain white walls and modest furniture mainly consisting of the massive, wooden-framed bed we're seated on now. He's perched on the mattress' edge while I'm on my knees behind him, dabbing at the blood still flowing from his neck.

A wave of emotion constricts my throat, preventing me from speaking—in fact I don't think I've said a word since Dima and Milton left. All I can do is clean him off, conveying in gentle caresses with my cloth just how much I appreciate what he did.

Defended his family.

With the worst of the bleeding finally staunched, I set the

cloth aside and use my opposite hand to trace a path down his arm, seeking out his white-knuckled fingers. He's furious. I suspect the irritating pain is what keeps him from hunting down Dima—that and an emotion that swelters between us the longer my touch lingers over him.

Overwhelmed, I sink against his massive frame, pressing my lips to the crook of his shoulder. He stiffens, then gradually relaxes. This kind of intimacy is new for us both, as foreign as vanilla ice cream was to him just a few days ago.

As the seconds pass, my throat loosens, enough for me to croak out a single, tired question. "When do you want the wedding to be?"

He lifts his hand, bringing mine with it, displaying the ring on my finger. His free hand comes to trace the delicate circlet of marble, lingering over his name.

"When you are ready," he says, and that statement carries with it so many connotations. My thoughts swim at the prospect of deciphering them all. But, as always, he can never leave me with a solid choice—it always comes in the form of a game. The premise of this one, he proposes as a dare. "After we make this room suit us both."

Love to binge read? Grab Vadim's trilogy all in one box set!

Lana Sky is a reclusive writer in the United States who spends most of her time daydreaming about complex male characters and parenting her Cockapoo Joey. She writes dark, twisted romance across several genres. Her titles include everything from mafia romance to vampires.

facebook.com/AuthorLanaSky

twitter.com/lanasky101

amazon.com/author/lanasky

pinterest.com/lanasky101

goodreads.com/lanasky

instagram.com/lanasky101

bookbub.com/authors/lana-sky

For more titles by Lana Sky, please visit:

https://www.lanaskybooks.com